A Treasury of World War II Stories

ABOUT THE EDITORS

BILL PRONZINI is one of America's finest mystery, suspense, and espionage writers, as well as a leading critic in the field. He has published more than 40 novels, written hundreds of stories, and edited numerous anthologies in a wide variety of categories.

MARTIN H. GREENBERG has more than 300 anthologies to his credit. He is professor of regional analysis and political science at the University of Wisconsin–Green Bay.

A Treasury of World War II Stories

Edited by

Bill Pronzini
and
Martin H. Greenberg

BONANZA BOOKS
NEW YORK

This 1991 reprint of the 1985 edition is published by
Bonanza Books, distributed by Outlet Book Company,
Inc., a Random House Company, 225 Park Avenue South,
New York, New York 10003, by arrangement
with the authors.

Printed and bound in the United States of America

Library of Congress Cataloging-in-Publication Data

A Treasury of World War II stories / edited by Bill Pronzini and
Martin H. Greenberg.
p. cm.
ISBN 0-517-06014-0
1. World War, 1939-1945—Fiction. 2. American fiction—20th
century. 3. War stories, American. I. Pronzini, Bill.
II. Greenberg, Martin Harry. III. Title: Treasury of World War 2
stories. IV. Title: Treasury of World War Two stories.
PS648.W65T74 1991 90-24001
813'.0108358—dc20 CIP

8 7 6 5 4 3 2 1

Grateful acknowledgment for permission to reprint material is hereby given to the following:

"The Way It Is" excerpted from the book *The Ice-Cream Headache and Other Stories* by James Jones. Copyright © 1968 by James Jones. Reprinted by permission of Delacorte Press and Gloria Jones.

"The Commandos Go In" from *Radar Commandos* by Bernard Glemser. Copyright 1953 by Bernard Glemser. Reprinted by permission of Holt, Rinehart and Winston, Publishers.

"The Trap," Copyright 1943 by the Curtis Publishing Company; renewed by the Harold Matson Company, Inc. Reprinted by permission of the author. Originally published in 1943 in the *Saturday Evening Post* as "A Lot to Learn."

"The Paper House," Copyright 1952 by Norman Mailer; copyright renewed. Reprinted by permission of the author and his agents, the Scott Meredith Literary Agency, Inc., 845 Third Avenue, New York, New York 10022.

"Hide-Out for a Hero," Copyright © 1955 by the Crowell-Collier Publishing Company. Reprinted by permission of John Schaffner Associates, Inc.

"To the Castle" from *Humble Powers* by Paul Horgan. Copyright 1951 by Curtis Publishing Company. Copyright 1954 by Paul Horgan. Originally published in the *Saturday Evening Post* as "The Soldier Who Had No Gun." Reprinted by permission of Farrar, Straus and Giroux, Inc.

"Camps," Copyright © 1979 by Jack Dann. First published in *The Magazine of Fantasy and Science Fiction* and reprinted by permission of the author.

"Chicken Charley," Copyright © 1971 by Exclusive Man. Reprinted by permission of Larry Sternig.

"Operation Wild Ass," Copyright © 1967 by Popular Publications. Reprinted by permission of Larry Sternig.

"I'd Know You Anywhere," Copyright © 1963 by Davis Publications, Inc. Reprinted by permission of the author. First published in *Ellery Queen's Mystery Magazine*.

"Black Night, White Night," Copyright © by William Sambrot. Reprinted by permission of the author and his agents, Curtis Brown, Ltd. Originally published in *Adam* magazine.

"Act of Faith" excerpted from the book *Short Stories: Five Decades* by Irwin Shaw. Copyright 1946 by F. R. Pub. Corp. Copyright renewed © 1973 by Irwin Shaw. Reprinted by permission of Delacorte Press.

"The Enemy," Copyright 1942 by Pearl S. Buck. Copyright renewed © 1969 by Pearl S. Buck. Reprinted by permission of Harold Ober Associates Incorporated.

"Day of Terror" Copyright © 1956 by the Curtis Publishing Company, Inc. Reprinted by permission of the agents for the author's estate, the Scott Meredith Literary Agency, Inc., 845 Third Avenue, New York, New York 10022.

"The Women on the Wall" by Wallace Stegner. Copyright 1940 by Wallace Stegner. Copyright renewed © 1968 by Wallace Stegner. Reprinted by Brandt & Brandt Literary Agents, Inc.

"Sherman Was Right," Copyright © 1957 by Popular Publications, Inc. Reprinted by permission of the author.

"Layover in El Paso" from *The Wolf That Fed Us* by Robert Lowry. Copyright 1945, 1946, 1947, 1948, 1949 by Robert Lowry. Reprinted by permission of Doubleday & Company, Inc., and the author.

CONTENTS

Introduction • ix

ON LAND

The Way It Is • *3*
James Jones

The Commandos Go In • *19*
Bernard Glemser

The Trap • *37*
Hal G. Evarts

The Paper House • *51*
Norman Mailer

Hide-Out for a Hero • *67*
Celso Al. Carunungan

To the Castle • *83*
Paul Horgan

Camps • *119*
Jack Dann

Chicken Charley • *147*
Jack Ritchie

Operation Wild Ass • *161*
Leo R. Ellis

I'd Know You Anywhere • *175*
Edward D. Hoch

Black Night, White Night *or* The Battle of Dingle on the Dangle • *187*
William Sambrot

Act of Faith • *205*
Irwin Shaw

The Enemy • *223*
Pearl S. Buck

Day of Terror • *243*
James Warner Bellah

The Women on the Wall • *257*
Wallace Stegner

Sherman Was Right • *277*
Robert G. Fuller

Layover in El Paso • *311*
Robert Lowry

The Man Who Hated • *331*
William Sambrot

A Walk in the Sun • *349*
Harry Brown

A Judgment in the Mountains • *469*
Stephen Vincent Benét

AT SEA

Coral Sea • *489*
James A. Michener

The Kid in Command • *503*
Jacland Marmur

The Living Torpedo • *519*
Tom Yates

The Crew of the *Foraker* • *539*
Steve Frazee

The Exile • *553*
Robert Edmond Alter

Act of Honor • *569*
George P. Morrill

IN THE AIR

The Destroyer • *585*
William E. Barrett

East from Botwood • *623*
Leland Jameison

Bataan Landing • *641*
Arch Whitehouse

Bombardier • *659*
Paul Gallico

Hawk of the Sudan • *675*
David Goodis

Final Mission • *701*
J. L. Bouma

Hot Air Pilot • *715*
Jack Ritchie

Savoias Out of Sapporo • *725*
Arch Whitehouse

Introduction

WORLD WAR II was the most destructive war in world history and the central event of the generation of the men and women who fought in it. It disrupted lives, broke up families, and left physical and psychological scars on individuals—scars that would never heal.

It was a war started by madmen and militarists but fought by huge armies of mobilized men from all walks of life. In terms of military technology it saw the first widespread use of bombing by aircraft, the first really massive use of tanks and other armored vehicles, the first use of reasonably accurate guided missiles, and, of course, the first use of nuclear weapons. This war was also unique because of the damage done to civilians through direct attack and the use of gas chambers and concentration camps.

Because of its destructiveness, World War II produced all types of fiction—not just the glory-oriented, romantic works that are typically produced by the winning side after a war. Too many brave soldiers and civilians had died, too many of "the best years of our lives" had been lost.

This book is the largest and most comprehensive collection of World War II stories ever published. Its material has been drawn from a variety of original sources—the "pulp" magazines of the 1940s, whose yellowing pages still yield hidden and underrated writers and stories; the "slicks" like the *Saturday Evening Post* and *Collier's*, whose then-high rates of pay attracted some of America's finest writers; literary magazines of various types; and the so-called "men's magazines," a group that includes such diverse publications as *Argosy* and *Adam*.

The authors represented here include the world famous and the relatively unknown; writers who also produced famous novels about World War II like Harry Brown, whose notable novella *A Walk in the Sun* is reprinted here in its entirety. This is in several ways the seminal novel on the Italian campaign and on the theme of leadership. Also featured are the Nobel Prize–winning Pearl S. Buck, author of numerous stories set in China and Burma during the war, and Paul Gallico, whose novel *The Snow Goose* is still one of the best books of any kind on the evacuation from Dunkirk.

And then there are the "big four"—writers whose names are legendary among millions of readers. We have James Jones, perhaps our greatest commentator on military life, whose novels *From Here to Eternity, The Pistol, The Thin Red Line*, and *Whistle* have moved veterans and nonveterans alike. Indeed, the film version of *From Here to Eternity* (which starred Montgomery Clift, Frank Sinatra, and Burt Lancaster) is now as much a classic as the novel on which it is based. There is also a terrific story by Norman Mailer, whose *The Naked and the Dead* was one of the earliest postwar novels to achieve great fame. It was difficult to choose only one story by the late Irwin Shaw, whose *The Young Lions* ranks with the best works of the genre. And, of course, no book of this type would be complete without a story by James A. Michener, whose *Tales of the South Pacific* remain essential reading for anyone wishing to know what the war in the Pacific was really like.

But it is also a pleasure to reprint (in many cases for the first time) excellent stories by lesser-known writers of great talent like Jacland Marmur, Robert G. Fuller, Steve Frazee, Robert Edmond Alter, Arch Whitehouse, George P. Morrill, and William Sambrot.

These stories are set in most of the major theaters of the war—the Pacific islands, the North Atlantic, the struggle in Europe, North Africa, and the war in the air. But you will also find stories about the homefront, about boot camp, and about the Holocaust, because combat was only one part of this titanic struggle.

Return with us then, to those deadly, tragic, and glorious years of World War II, when great armies battled to determine the fate of the world.

BILL PRONZINI
MARTIN H. GREENBERG

ON LAND

JAMES JONES

The Way It Is

I SAW THE CAR coming down the grade and got up from the culvert. I had to push hard with my legs to keep the wind from sitting me back down. I stepped out into the road to stop him, turning my back to the wind, still holding the mess kit I had been scouring. Some of the slop of sand and grease dripped out of it onto my leg.

Then I saw Mazzioli was on the running board and had his pistol out and aimed at the driver's head. I tossed the mess kit, still full, over against the culvert and got my own pistol out.

I couldn't see the driver. It was hard to see the car in the red air of the dusk against the black of the cliff and with the cold wind pouring against my eyes. It was a foreign make, a runabout with strange lines and the steering wheel on the right-hand side. When it stopped Mazzioli jumped off the running board and motioned with his pistol.

"All right," he said in that thick voice. "Get out of there, you."

I knew the man when he climbed out. He used the road every day. He could have passed for a typical Prussian with his scraped jowls and cropped bullet-head. He wore a fine tweed jacket and plus-fours, and his stockings were of ribbed wool and very fine. I looked down at my leggin and kicked off the gob of sand and grease. It didn't help much. I hadn't even had my field jacket off for three weeks, since the bombing.

"What's up, Greek?" I said, peering through the deepening dusk. I had to yell to make it heard above the wind.

"I hopped a ride down the hill with this guy," he said woodenly. "All the way down he was asting me questions about the position. How many men? How many guns? Was there a demolition? What was the road-guard for? I mean to find out what's the story." He looked offended.

I walked over to him so I could hear above the wind. He was a little Wop but very meaty. His father ran a grocery store in Brooklyn.

"What do you figure on doing?" I asked. I thought I had seen the Junker before someplace, and I tried hard to make my mind work.

Mazzioli waved his pistol at the standing man. "Git over there, you, and put your back to the cliff," he said ominously. The beefy Junker walked to it slowly, his steps jerky from rage, his arms dangling impotently. He stood against the black, porous cliff and Mazzioli followed him. "Where's the men?" Mazzioli shouted to me above the wind. "I want a man to stand guard over this guy. You git a man and have him. . . ."

"There's nobody here but me," I called back. "I let them go up to the top of the hill. Two of them didn't get any chow tonight. They went up to number one hole to listen to the guitar awhile." I walked over to him.

I could see him stiffen. "Goddam you. You know there's always supposed to be three men and one noncom here all the time. That's the orders. You're supposed to be second in command. How do you expect to handle these men when you don't follow the orders?"

I stared at him, feeling my jaws tighten. "All right," I shrugged. "I let them go. So what?"

"I'm turning this in to Lieutenant Allison. The orders are the orders. If you want to be on this road-guard to do your duty, okay. If you want to be on this road-guard to stop Coca-Cola trucks you can go back upstairs to the position. This road-guard is vital, and as long as I'm in charge of it everybody does like the orders say."

I didn't say anything.

"You're a rotten soldier, Slade," Mazzioli said. "Now look what's happened. I wanted you to help me search this guy's car. Now there's nobody here to guard this guy."

"Okay," I said. "So I'm a rotten soldier. My trouble is I got too many brains." He was making me mad and that always got him. Ever since I went six months to the University downtown in Honolulu.

"Don't start giving me that stuff," he snarled.

The Junker against the cliff stepped forward. "See here," he said. "I demand you stop this bickering and release me. You're being an idiot. I am . . . ."

"Shut up, you," Mazzioli snarled. "Shut up! I warned you, now shut up!" He stepped to meet him and jabbed the muzzle of his pistol into the Junker's big belly. The man recoiled and stood back against the cliff, his beefy face choleric.

I stood with my hands in the pockets of my field jacket, my shoulders hunched down against the rawness of the wind and watched the scene. I had put my pistol away.

"All right," Mazzioli said to me. "The question is what're we gonna do now? If there's nobody here but you and me?"

"You're in command," I said.

"I know it. Keep quiet. I'm thinking."

"Well," I said. "You could have the guy drive you up the hill to the lieutenant. You could keep him covered till you turned him over to the lieutenant. Then you would be absolved," I said. Big words always got him.

"No," he said dubiously. "He might try something."

"Or," I said, "you could search the car and have me watch the guy."

"Yeh," he admitted. "I could do that . . . Yet . . . No, I don't want to do that. We may need more men."

It was dark now, as black as the cliff face, and I grinned. "Okay," I said, telling him what I had in my mind all along, "then I could call Alcorn down from up on the cliff and he could watch the guy."

"Yes. That's it. Why didn't I think of that before?"

"I don't know. Maybe you're tired."

"You call Alcorn down," he commanded me.

I walked toward the cliff wall that reared its set black face up and up in the darkness several hundred feet. The wind beat on me with both fists in the blackness.

"Wait a minute," Mazzioli called. "Maybe we shouldn't call Alcorn down. There's supposed to be a man up there all the time."

"Look," I said. "I'll tell you what I think. Before you go ahead, you better get the lieutenant's permission to do anything with this guy. You better find out who this guy is."

"I'm in charge of this road-guard," he yelled into the wind, "and I can handle it. Without running to no lieutenant. And I don't want back-talk. When I give you an order, you do it. Call Alcorn down here like I said."

"Okay," I said. I leaned on the culvert and called loudly, my face turned up to the cliff. There was no answer. I flashed my light covered with blue paper. Still no answer.

For a second I couldn't help wondering if something had got him. The Japanese invasion of Hawaii had been expected every day since Pearl was bombed. It was expected here at Kaneohe Bay on the windward side where the reef was low and there was good beach. Nobody doubted they would get ashore.

"What's the matter?" asked Mazzioli sharply from the darkness. "Is Alcorn asleep?"

"No," I said. "It's the wind; it carries off the sound. The light will get him." I picked up a handful of pebbles and threw them up the cliff with all my strength, trying to make no noise the Greek could hear.

Sixty feet up was a natural niche and the BAR man was stationed there twenty-four hours a day. It was a hidden spot that covered the road and the road-guard. In case of surprise it would prove invaluable. That was Lieutenant Allison's own idea. The road-guard was Hawaiian Department's idea.

Alcorn had stayed up there alone for the first four days after the bombing. In the four days he had one meal before somebody remembered him. Now he and the other man pulled twelve hours apiece.

The road-guard was part of the whole defense plan. It was figured out in November when the beach positions were constructed. The defense was to mine the Pali Road and Kamehameha Highway where it ran up over this cliff at Makapuu Point. It was planned to blow both roads and bottle them up in Kaneohe Valley and force them north, away from Honolulu. They were great demolitions and it was all top secret. Of course, in December they found maps of the whole thing in the captured planes. Still, it was very vital and very top secret.

A rock the size of my fist thumped into the sand at my feet. I grinned. "You missed me," I called up the cliff. "Come down from there, you lazy bastard." I barely caught a faraway, wind-tossed phrase that sounded like "truck, too." Then silence, and the wind.

The machine-gun apertures in the pillboxes up the hill all faced out to sea. Whoever planned the position had forgot about the road, and all that faced the road was the tunnels into the pillboxes. To cover the road the MG's would have to be carried up into the open, and it was a shame because there was a perfect enfilade where the road curved up the cliff. But they couldn't rebuild the pillboxes we had cut into solid rock, so instead they created the road-guard.

The road guard was to be five men and a BAR from up above. That was us. We were to protect the demolition when the Jap landed. It was not expected to keep him from getting ashore. We were to hold him off, with our BAR, till the demolition could be blown behind us. After that we were on our own. It was excellent strategy, for a makeshift, with the invasion expected truly every day. And the road-guard was vital, it was the key.

Every man at Makapuu volunteered for the road-guard. The five of us were lucky to get it. The job was to stop and search all vehicles for anything that might be used to blow the demolition. The Coca-Cola trucks and banana trucks and grocery trucks and fruit trucks used this road every day to go to market. We stopped them all, especially the Coca-Cola trucks.

In a couple of minutes I heard a scrambling and scraping and a bouncing fall of pebbles and Alcorn came slouching along the sand at the road edge, blowing on his hands.

"The Greek wants you, Fatso," I said.

He laughed, low and rich and sloppy. "I think I'm deef from this wind, by god," he said and scratched inside his field jacket. "What's he want now?"

"Come over here," Mazzioli ordered. We walked over through the blackness and the wind and I felt I was swimming under water against a strong current. The Greek swung his blue light from the Junker onto us. Alcorn's clothes hung from him like rags and on the back of his head was a fatigue hat with the brim turned up that defied the wind. He must have sewed an elastic band on it. Beside him I looked like I was all bucked up for a short-timer parade.

"Where's your helmet?" Mazzioli said. "You're supposed to wear your helmet at all times. That's the orders."

"Aw now, sarge," Alcorn whined. "You know the steel band of them things gives a man a headache. I cain't wear one."

I grinned and gave the brim of my own inverted soup-plate helmet a tug. Alcorn was a character.

"When are you men going to learn to obey orders?" the Greek said. "An army runs by discipline. If you men don't start acting like soldiers, I'll turn you in."

"Off with his head," I said.

"What did you say?"

"I said, coffee and bed. That's what we need. There's not a man on this position who's had three good hours sleep since this bloody war started. Putting up barbed wire all day and pulling guard all night. And then putting up the same wire next day because the tide washed it out."

Alcorn snickered and Mazzioli said nothing. The Greek had had charge of a wire detail that worked one whole night to put up three hundred yards of double apron wire on the sand beach below the road. In the morning it was gone. Not a single picket left.

"Alcorn," Mazzioli ordered, "get a rifle and keep a bayonet against this guy's belly till I tell you not to."

"I don't know where the rifles are down here," Alcorn said.

"I'll get it," I said.

I walked to the culvert and climbed down around it. The wall made a protection from the wind and I felt I had dropped into a world without breath. The absence of the wind made me dizzy and I leaned my face against the concrete. I felt the way you feel when you look out the window at a blowing rainstorm. All our blankets and stuff were down here. Against the wall of the culvert lay four rifles with bayonets on them, wrapped in a shelter-half. I pulled one out and made myself climb up into the wind again.

Alcorn took the rifle and kept the bayonet against the Junker's paunch. Every time the Junker moved or tried to speak Alcorn jabbed him playfully in the belly. The Junker was getting madder and madder, but Alcorn was having a fine time.

I knew the lewd nakedness of that scraped face someplace before. I went over in my mind all the people I had seen at the University.

The Greek was doing a bang-up job of searching the car, he even looked under the hood. I sat on the culvert and got my mess kit and put a handful of fresh sand in it from beside the road and rubbed it around and around. The dishwater that got out to us from the CP at Hanauma Bay gave us all the dysentery until we started using the sand.

I tried to think where I'd seen him. It wasn't the face of a teacher, it had too much power. I dumped the greasy mess from the mess kit and poured in a little water from my canteen. I sloshed it around to rinse the sand out, listening vacantly to the Greek cursing and fidgeting with the car.

Just three days ago a two-man sub ran aground off Kaneohe and the second officer swam ashore, preferring capture. It was expected the sub was scouting the invasion that was coming truly any day.

They said he was the first prisoner of the war. I got to see him when they brought him in. He was a husky little guy and grinning humbly. His name was Kazuo Sakamaki. I knew a girl at the University named Tsuneko Ogure. I almost married her.

It seemed like the wind had blown my mind empty of all past. It had sucked out everything but Makapuu and the black rocks and blue lights and the sand-choked grass. The University with its clear, airy look from the street, its crisp greenness all hidden away in a wind-free little valley at the foot of rocky wooded Tantalus, it was from another life, a life protected from the wind, a life where there were white clouds in the sun but no wind, just gently moving air.

I wiped the mess kit with the GI face towel I kept in it and clamped it together and stuck it back in my pack that lay by the culvert, wanting to go down behind the culvert and light a cigarette.

Maybe the Junker was one of the big boys on the University board. The big boys always sent their kids to Harvard or some school on the Mainland, but they were the board. The only white faces you saw were the instructors and the *haoles* who didn't have the dough to send their kids to the Mainland—and an occasional soldier in civvies, looking out of place. Only these and the board. And the tourists.

Then I remembered the scraped face, coming out of the main building on a hot still August day, wiping the sweat from the face with a big silk handkerchief.

"Couldn't find a thing," Mazzioli said, coming up from the car. "I don't know what to do. This guy looks like a German. He even talks like a German."

"Listen," I said. "No German who looks like a German and talks like a German is going to be a spy. Use your head. This guy is some kind of big shot. I seen him at the University."

"To hell with you and your University."

"No," I said. "Listen."

"Why would he ask me questions about the number of men and guns and pillboxes?"

"Hell, I don't know. Maybe he wanted to write an editorial for the *Advertiser*."

"I can't let him go," he said.

"All right. Send Alcorn up for the lieutenant and let him handle it. You worry too much, Greek."

"Yeh, I could do that." But he was dubious. He walked back to the car for a moment and then went over to Alcorn. "Alcorn, you go up and get the lieutenant down here. Tell him we got a suspicious character down here." He turned to me. "Slade, you watch this guy and don't take any chances with him. I'm going over this car again."

Alcorn handed me the rifle and started off up the road. Through the darkness Mazzioli hollered after him. "Double time and jerk the lead," he shouted. The wind carried it away. The wind carried everything away.

To me Mazzioli said, "If he tries anything, shoot the bastard."

"Okay," I said. I set the rifle butt on the ground and leaned on it. "Take it easy, mister," I said. "Remember there's a war on. The lieutenant's coming down, and you'll be on your way home in a little bit."

"I am not accustomed to such treatment," he said, staring at me with flat eyes, "and I intend to see somebody pays for this indignity."

"We're only doing our duty," I said. "We got orders to stop all suspicious persons. This is important to the defense plan."

"I am not a suspicious person," he said, "and you men. . . ."

I interrupted; it was probably the only chance I'd ever get to interrupt a big shot. "Well," I said, "you were asking suspicious questions about our position."

"... and you men should have something better to do than hold up citizens."

Mazzioli, looking harassed, came over from the car. "What's that?" he snarled. "What's your name?"

The Junker stared at him. "My name is Knight," he said, and waited for it to sink in. When Mazzioli's face was blank he added, "Of Knight & Crosby, Limited." His voice was cold with rage and hate.

Above the wind we heard the voices of Lieutenant Allison and Alcorn on the road.

I looked at the Greek but he showed nothing. Nobody could live in Hawaii without knowing Knight & Crosby, Ltd. The Big Five were as well known as Diamond Head.

Lieutenant Allison put one hand on Mazzioli's shoulder and the other on mine. "Now," he said paternally. "What's the trouble?"

Mazzioli told him the whole tale. I went back to the culvert and listened to the wind playing background music to the double tale of woe. After both stories were told, Lieutenant Allison escorted Mr. Knight to his runabout with extreme courtesy.

"You can appreciate, Mr. Knight, our position." Lieutenant Allison put his foot on the running board and rested his hands on the door. "You can understand my sergeant was only doing his duty, a duty conceived to protect you, Mr. Knight."

Mr. Knight did not speak. He sat with his hands gripping the wheel, staring straight ahead.

"I'm sorry you feel that way, Mr. Knight," Lieutenant Allison said. "These men were carrying out orders we have received from Hawaiian Department Headquarters."

Mr. Knight made no sign he had heard. He gave the impression he was suffering this association under duress and was fretting to have done and be gone.

"A soldier's duty is to follow out his orders," Lieutenant Allison said.

"All right," the lieutenant said. He took his foot off the running board and dropped his hands. "You may go, Mr. Knight. You can rest assured such a thing won't happen again, now that my men know who you are."

"It certainly won't," Mr. Knight said. "Bah!" He started his runabout with a roar and he did not look back.

I watched from the culvert and grinned contentedly. "Now there'll be hell to pay," I told Mazzioli.

After Knight was gone, Mazzioli called the lieutenant over to the other side of the road and spoke earnestly. I watched the excited movement of his blue light and grinned more widely.

Lieutenant Allison came over to me with the Greek following close behind. ''Alcorn,'' he called. Alcorn shuffled over from the base of the cliff.

''I've been having bad reports about you two men,'' Lieutenant Allison began. ''Where's your helmet, Alcorn?''

Alcorn shuffled his feet. ''It's up the cliff. I cain't wear one of them things more'n a half hour, Lootenant,'' he said. ''I get a turrible headache if I do. When Corporal Slade called me down, I clean forgot all about it.''

''You're all through down here,'' Lieutenant Allison said. ''Get back up there and get that helmet on. I'll be coming around inspecting and I don't want to catch you without a helmet. If I do there'll be some damned heavy details around here, and if that don't stop your headache, by god, maybe a court martial will.

''You're no different than anybody else. If I can wear a helmet all the time, then you can do it. I don't like it any better than you do.

''Now get the hell back up there.''

Alcorn saluted and started for the base of the cliff.

''Alcorn!'' Lieutenant Allison called after him in the darkness.

''Yessir?''

''You don't ever go to sleep up there, do you?''

''Oh, no sir.''

''You'd better watch it. I'll be inspecting tonight.''

I could hear the scrambling and falling of pebbles and I thought it was a very lonely sound.

''Come over here, Slade,'' Lieutenant Allison said. He walked away from Mazzioli and I followed him, pleased the calling-down would be in private instead of in front of the Greek. It was a luxury.

''I'm going back up the hill,'' Lieutenant Allison said. ''You walk part way with me. I want to talk to you.'' The two of us started up the road. ''I'm going to send those men back down here when I get to the top,'' Lieutenant Allison said. ''You won't need to go up.''

''Thank you, Sir,'' I said.

''Why did you let those men go up the hill tonight, Slade?''

''They didn't get any chow tonight, Sir,'' I said. ''I felt sorry for them.''

''You're not supposed to feel sorry for anybody. You're a soldier. You enlisted in the army, didn't you?''

''Yes, Sir,'' I said. ''But it was because I couldn't get a job.''

''A soldier's job is to feel sorry for nobody.''

''I can't help it, Sir,'' I said. ''Maybe my environment was wrong. Or maybe I haven't had the proper indoctrinization. I always put myself in the other guy's place. I even felt sorry for Mr. Knight. And he sure didn't need it.''

''What happened with Mr. Knight was the proper action to take. It turned out badly, but he could have been a saboteur with a carload of TNT to blow the demolition.''

''What will happen about Knight, Sir?'' I said.

''Mr. Knight is a big man in Hawaii. The Big Five run the whole territory. There may be some bad effects. I may even get an ass-eating. Nevertheless, Mazzioli acted correctly. In the long run, it will all turn out all right because we did what was right. The army will take that into account.''

''You believe that?'' I said.

''Yes,'' he said. ''I believe it. You don't realize how important that road-guard is to the whole war. What if the enemy had made a landing at Kaneohe tonight? They'd have had a patrol on you before you knew it. The very thing you did out of kindness might be what lost the war for us. It's not far-fetched; if they took this road and cliff, they'd have this island in a month. From there it'd be the west coast. And we'd be fighting the war in the Rocky Mountains.''

''All for the want of a horseshoe nail,'' I said.

''That's it,'' he said. ''That's why every tiniest thing is so important. You're one of the smartest men in the Company, Slade. There's no reason for me to explain these things to you. There's no reason why you shouldn't make OCS, except for your attitude. I've told you that before. What would you have done? Alone there with the men up on the hill?''

''I knew who he was,'' I said.

Lieutenant Allison turned on me. ''Why in the name of Christ didn't you tell Mazzioli!'' He was mad.

''I did,'' I said. ''But he didn't listen. Orders is orders,'' I said.

Lieutenant Allison stopped. We were halfway up the hill. He looked out over the parapet and down at the sea, vaguely white where it broke on the rocks.

''What's the matter with you, Slade? You don't want to be cynical about this war.''

''I'm not cynical about this war,'' I said. ''I may die in this war.

I'm cynical about the army. It's a helluva lot easier to be an idealist if you're an officer. The higher the officer, the higher the ideals." To hell with it, I thought, to hell with all of it.

"Slade," he said, "I'd like for you to buckle down. I wasn't kidding when I said you could make OCS. I'd like to see you go to OCS because you're smart. You could do it if you'd only buckle down."

"I've been an EM too long," I said. "I'm too cynical."

"You know, you could be shot for talking like this in the German Army."

"I know it," I said. "That's why I don't like the German Army, or the Japanese Army, or the British Army, or the Russian Army. I could get ten years in the American Army if you wanted to turn me in."

Lieutenant Allison was leaning on the parapet. "If I didn't like you, by god I would."

"Trouble with me," I said, "I'm too honest. They didn't have indoctrinization courses yet when I enlisted," I said.

"It's not a question of briefing," he said. "It's a question of belief."

"Yes," I said. "And also of who manufactures it."

"We have to be cruel now so we can be kind later, after the war."

"That's the theory of the Communist Internationale," I said. "I hear their indoctrinization courses are wonderful."

"They're our allies," he said. "When the enemy is defeated, why, it will all be set."

"I could never be an officer," I said. "I've not been indoctrinated well enough."

He laughed, "Okay, Slade. But you think over what I said, and if you want me to, I'll recommend you. You know, an intelligent man who refuses to use his intelligence to help win the war is a bottleneck. He's really a menace. In Germany he would be shot if he didn't use his intelligence to help win."

"Japan too," I said. "And in Italy and in Russia," I said. "Our country we only lock them up as conchies, as yet."

"Do you think I like being an officer?"

"Yes," I said. "I would like it. At least you get a bath and hot chow."

He laughed again. "Okay. But you think it over."

"I'll think about it," I said. "I'll think about all of it. But I never find an answer. Sometimes I wonder if there is an answer. The Greek is the man you ought to recommend."

"Are you kidding?" he grinned. "Mazzioli is a good sergeant."

"He believes the end justifies the means," I said. "He's been properly indoctrinated. I couldn't turn a man in if I had to."

Lieutenant Allison stood up from the parapet. "Think it over, Slade," he said.

"All right, Sir," I said. "But I can tell you one thing. It's damn fine I can talk to you. But I always remember you're not all officers and I'm not all the EM," I said.

"Thanks, Slade," he said.

I walked on back down the road. I stopped every now and then to listen to the sea's attack against the cliff. It would be nice to be an officer. The sea and the wind were like two radio stations on the same dial mark. You could even have a bed-roll and a dog-robber. The old Revolutionists in Russia, I thought, they really had it all figured out; they really had the world saved this time. I kicked a pebble ahead of me down the road.

I must have gone very slow because the three men from the top were on my heels when I reached the bottom.

"Hey, Slade," one of them said. He came up. "I'm sorry we got you in trouble tonight. Nobody guessed this would happen."

"Forget it," I said. "All I got was a ass-eating."

Mazzioli was sitting on the culvert. "I'm going to roll up," he said belligerently.

"Okay, Greek," I said. I sat on the culvert awhile, facing the wind. I liked to sit there at night alone, defying the wind. But a man could only do it so long. After a while a man got stupid from its eternal pummeling. A man got punch-drunk from it. Once before it made me so dizzy I fell down on my knees when I got up.

It was a wild place, the roaring sea, the ceaseless wind, the restless sand, the omniscient cliff.

I said good-night to the men on post and rolled up myself. When I went under the wall it took my breath again. I lay in my blankets and listened to it howl just over my head.

It was three o'clock when the messenger from up on the hill woke me.

"What?" I said. "What is it? What?"

"Where's the Greek?" he said.

"He's here."

"You gotta wake him up."

"What's up?"

''You're moving back up the hill. Lieutenant's orders.''

''Whose orders?'' I said. ''What about the demolition? What about the road-guard?''

''Lieutenant's orders. The road-guard is being disbanded. Altogether.''

''What's the story?'' I asked.

''I dunno. We got a call from the Company CP; the Cap'n was maddern hell. He just got a call from Department HQ; they was maddern hell. Told the Cap'n to disband the road-guard immediately. The orders'll be down in a couple days.''

I laughed. ''Orders is orders,'' I said.

''What?''

''Nothing,'' I said. ''Is the lieutenant still up?''

''Yeh. He's in hole number one, with the telephone. Why?''

''I got to see him about something,'' I said.

''I'm going back,'' he said. ''This wind is freezin' me. You sure you're awake?''

''Yes,'' I said. ''You take off.'' I got up and woke the rest of the detail. ''Get your stuff together, you guys. We're moving out. One of you call Alcorn down.''

The Greek sat up, rubbing his eyes. ''What is it? what's up? what's wrong?''

''We're moving out,'' I said. ''Back up the hill. The road-guard is disbanded.'' When I stood up the wind hit me hard. I got my pack and kicked my blankets up into a pile. I slung my rifle and pack and picked up the blankets.

''You mean the *road-guard?*'' Mazzioli's voice asked through the darkness and the wind. ''For *good?*''

I climbed up around the wall and the wind caught at my blankets and I almost lost them.

''That's the way it is,'' I said.

BERNARD GLEMSER

The Commandos Go In

THE DATE WAS the twenty-seventh of February, 1942. The time was late evening. The place was the briefing room of an airfield in the south of England. The commandos stood around quietly, calm and relaxed. Nobody could have guessed that in a few hours they would be storming through enemy-occupied territory like fiends.

Paul, standing among them with Gaston at his side, looked at them with admiration. In the past few days he had lived with them very closely; he knew them all by their first names, and they had accepted him as one of themselves. He had taken part in the many rehearsals for the raid; he had gone out on exercises, led by Major Cowles, who was to be in command of the raiding parties; he had eaten with these men, slept in a hut with them, and listened to their talk. They did not act or talk like supermen, he discovered. They seemed, in fact, to be extraordinarily mild and easygoing. But under that mildness was tremendous alertness; under that easygoing manner was great confidence in themselves and their comrades. They knew the strength of their combined striking power.

By now both Paul and Gaston had recovered from the effects of those eight nightmarish days of training. As the sergeant had warned, they were not commandos now; by comparison with the men in this room they were still rather like children. Even so, their bodies had hardened; they had learned that in an emergency they could call on hidden reserves of endurance. They felt alive and full of energy, as if they had just returned from a long vacation, instead of from one of the most rugged training camps in the world. They both felt that this night was going to be the greatest experience of their lives.

There was a rustle of interest as Major Cowles entered the room, followed by Professor Cheswick and Air Commodore Simpson. The major, a tall, broad-shouldered man, began to speak without any introduction. His voice was quiet, and he stood with one hand comfortably in his pocket.

"All of you know your jobs tonight," he began. "I'm only going to run over the operation briefly in case there are any last-minute questions."

He faced the huge aerial photographs of Bruneval and the scale models of the farm, the house on the cliffs, and the Fire Bowl. Then he pointed to the Fire Bowl, which housed the radar installation.

"First, let me state again what it's all about. The Nazis have developed this device, known as radar, which is a definite menace to all our future plans. We could destroy it, but that wouldn't help us very much. We want to capture various parts of it intact, so that our scientific experts can examine it in detail. This is your primary objective. We also need to capture a few of the Nazi technicians who operate this radar, since they might give us some useful information; that's your secondary objective.

"Furthermore, this is an historic occasion. It's the first invasion, in force, of France since the Germans drove us back at Dunkirk in 1940. And we want to make it good. We are going to strike panic into the hearts of the Nazis and encourage our good allies the French. From now on the Nazis are going to realize that they are not safe anywhere.

"Now, as to details. You will fly in Whitley bombers and be dropped over the target area at midnight. The assembly point, which you will all try to reach immediately, is the ditch you see on the photograph here. Our young friend Paul Martin has described it to you very exactly. It's in the cover of a row of trees on the edge of the woods.

"You will be in three groups, each under its own leader. The first group will storm the house on the cliffs and deal with any Nazi troops found there. The second group is the technical group. These men will capture the radar post and dismantle it. The third group will clear the way to the beach, opening up the way for our return.

"When the beach path is open, all three groups will assemble on the beach and give the signal to be taken off. Landing craft will come in for this purpose. These will be covered by other landing craft that will guard your withdrawal. Covering these, in turn, will be motor gunboats and two destroyers, so that you will be well protected on the return journey. These naval forces, incidentally, are already on their way to Bruneval and have reported that they are making good progress. Are there any questions?"

There were none.

Air Commmodore Simpson stepped forward, and said in his brisk manner, "I want to say a word about the flight arrangements. It's a perfect flying night—not much wind, a bright moon with a little cloud. Visibility should be good, and your pilots shouldn't have much difficulty finding the dropping area. You can expect some flak as you cross the French coast, but it will be light, I hope, and shouldn't give you any real trouble. We are also sending some planes to make a raid on a nearby area, which will draw off the enemy fighter planes located around Bruneval. I trust, therefore, that you'll have a comfortable trip."

Finally, Professor Cheswick stepped forward. He said with a chuckle, "I think this is the first time that science has had the help of a group of experts like yourselves. This is a piece of research that will go down in scientific textbooks as well as history books. That's all I have to say, and God bless every one of you."

"Thank you, Professor," Major Cowles said. He looked at his watch. "Zero hour for take-off is in fourteen and a half minutes. You'd better get ready, men."

The professor came hurrying toward Paul, and said, "How do you feel, my boy?"

Paul smiled at him cheerfully. "Fine, sir. I'm very happy that I shall be in France again soon, even if it's only for a short while."

"Take care of yourself," the professor said. "Remember, I have great plans for you when you come back." He turned to Gaston. "I'm relying on you to look after this lad, Sergeant. See that he doesn't get into any real trouble."

"Yes, sir," Gaston answered solemnly. "I'll keep an eye on him."

"Sir," Paul asked, "will the Resistance take any part in this raid tonight?"

"No," Professor Cheswick replied. "Not this time. We've warned them to stay in hiding, because there's too much danger of reprisals. But the day is fast coming when they'll take a full part in our raids. Don't worry about this now, Paul. Just be sure to come back safely."

The commandos were rubbing burnt cork on their faces and hands, leaving a thick black grime that would stay on for hours. They wore paratroopers' crash helmets, and they all carried heavy commando knives and hand grenades. Many of them had Sten guns—short, light Tommy guns that could pour out a terrifying hail of fire; some had automatic pistols. They were in very high spirits, laughing and joking as if they were going on an easy night exercise, not on a highly dangerous mission against the enemy.

They rocked with laughter as they saw Paul and Gaston cautiously applying the burnt cork, and they crowded around the two Frenchmen giving advice. At last Gaston said, grinning at Paul, "Eh, my little general! Even your own mother wouldn't recognize you now."

Paul grinned back. "And you, Sergeant, all you need is a banjo to make your fortune in a circus."

They were both armed with commando knives, but Paul had no gun. Gaston had both a Sten gun and a revolver.

The order came to assemble outside the briefing room, and the commandos trooped out and formed into squads in the darkness. Nearby, Paul could hear the sputter and whine of aircraft engines, bursting into shattering roars as they warmed up. As he stood at attention his hands were tightly clenched, and he could feel his heart beating rapidly. He was cold, but not with fear. It was like the line-up before a soccer game, when his body always tightened with expectation. He began to relax in a few moments, and he smiled to himself at the excitement of this adventure. He could never have imagined it in his wildest dreams; yet here he was, one of a company of commandos setting off for France. . . .

Then the darkness was split by a noise like the screeching of a thousand cats in agony. His blood froze; but at his side Gaston exclaimed, "Bagpipes!" Before Paul could get over his astonishment at the unearthly sound, his squad was marching toward the waiting planes.

The pipers led the way, stepping out at a steady pace, their pipes skirling Scottish songs that Paul had never heard before; but in some mysterious way the shrill sounds seemed to creep into his veins and make him tingle. It was the music of savage warriors, a noise that heartened men going into battle and terrified the enemy.

With the precision of guardsmen on a parade ground, the commandos marched around the perimeter of the airfield, and as each squad reached its plane it wheeled smartly. The pipes were still playing as the men entered the Whitleys. Paul found himself sitting on a narrow bench that ran along the side of the fuselage; with him was an almost unrecognizable Gaston and a horde of black-faced, grinning commandos. It seemed completely unreal. Then he heard the twin motors of the Whitley speed up, and felt the plane lurch as it began its slow waddle to the runway.

"Hold tight," Gaston said in his ear, and gripped his arm. The noise of the motors grew louder and louder, the plane seemed to be moving at incredible speed, and then all sensation ceased. He might have been sitting in an armchair in his own home. There was a cheer from the men, and Gaston's hold loosened.

As an officer came over to Paul and looked down at him with a smile, "How are you feeling, laddie?"

"Fine, sir. Just fine."

"Try to get a little sleep. We shan't reach the French coast until shortly before midnight."

Some of the commandos were singing . Some were playing cards. Gaston brought two sleeping bags from a pile in the rear of the plane and handed one to Paul. "Curl up in this, my general. Make yourself comfortable."

"Thank you," Paul said. He lay curled up warmly, suspended in space, lulled by the steady purring of the motors, thinking of Bruneval, which he was about to visit in this strange way. How exciting everything is, he thought vaguely, and his mind wandered off into a pleasant fog.

The next thing he knew, Gaston was shaking him. "Put on your parachute," Gaston said. "We're nearly there."

Paul scrambled out of his sleeping bag, tightened his helmet, and fastened his parachute. Gaston checked it, pulling at the various straps to make certain they were secure, and Paul did the same for him.

"Twenty minutes more," Gaston said, "and we shall be flying over our own country."

All the men were standing now, lined up at action stations. There was no tension, no sense that they were going into danger. They were simply waiting to descend from the plane to do an important job. The Whitley lurched suddenly and somebody said in a steady voice, "Hold on, boys. Flak." It lurched again and seemed to tip over slightly. The calm voice said again, "The Nazis have some flak ships down there. We're taking evasive action."

"Paul," Gaston said urgently, "stay close to me all the time. Remember. Stay close!"

A red light came on. The pilot of the Whitley was turning into the target. The hole in the floor of the fuselage through which the commandos would drop was open. The first men were already in position, waiting for the green light which was the signal to jump. Paul had practiced the routine many times already; he knew exactly what was going to happen, but he was surprised at the speed with which it was happening now, in actual combat conditions.

There it was! The green light! The first men had dropped . . . the line was moving forward . . . Gaston was behind him holding on to his shoulder, and for some reason Paul could hear the shrill wailing of the bagpipes in his ears again. Suddenly he himself was sitting over the drop hole looking down into darkness—an R.A.F. sergeant had hooked up his static line—there was a whispered *go* and he was through the hole and his legs were blowing sideways as he was caught in the Whitley's slip stream. There was a jerk at his shoulder as the static cord pulled his parachute open, and he saw it billow out and rise over his head, blotting out the sky. Then he was floating in a black silent world, without any sensation of falling, until the earth rose up slowly to meet him. He landed on it—in the midst of a soft white coldness—with a thump, and found himself being dragged forward. He grabbed the shrouds of the parachute, fumbled with the catch to release it, and tumbled on his chest into a foot of snow, gasping but uninjured.

Bruneval! But was this Bruneval? He stood up cautiously and looked around him. Yes. The woods were over to his left, the farmhouse and the house on the cliffs and the Fire Bowl were ahead of him, hidden in the darkness. He could see the gray shapes of the commandos against the snow, crouching as they ran to the assembly point in the ditch, and then he heard Gaston's voice calling quietly, "Paul! Paul!"

He called back, "Gaston."

"A moi!" Gaston exclaimed. *"A moi!"* The traditional French cry of comrades in battle : "To me! To me!"

Paul found him quickly, only a few yards away. "Are you all right?" Gaston asked anxiously, and Paul answered, "Yes."

"Let's get to the assembly point then. Hurry!"

They began to run. The snow blanketed all noise; the world seemed asleep. Even the throb of the Whitley bombers had dwindled. There was only this uncanny movement of silent men, all running swiftly toward the ditch under the trees. Scattered over the snow were cylindrical containers holding additional equipment for the raid—guns, dynamite, signaling apparatus. These the commandos scooped up as they ran.

"France!" Gaston laughed. "My beautiful France!" He snatched up a handful of snow in his stride, and held it until it melted, as if it were something infinitely precious. Paul knew how he felt. Even in these tense moments he was overjoyed at being back in his own land; every tree, every stone in his path was familiar. He had walked with his father and mother here, played at boys' games with his friends, and the recollection that the Nazis occupied it made him burn with anger.

"Here's the ditch," he panted to Gaston. For one awful moment he thought that it was empty, that some mistake had been made and the commandos had gone somewhere else. But then he saw the black-faced men crouching on their haunches, waiting motionless for the order that would send them into action, and he slipped quietly down among them.

"Here's Paul," somebody whispered, and he heard his name going down the line. "Paul . . . Paul . . . Paul." Then the whispering came back to him. The commando at his side touched his arm and muttered in his ear, "Squeeze past me, son. Report to Major Cowles."

This was no time for questions. He obeyed the order immediately, edging past the men until he reached the major.

"Paul Martin reporting, sir," he whispered.

"Paul!" the major said. "Thak God you're safe. Now listen. We go into action in three minutes. But all our men aren't here yet. I've just had a report that two of the Whitleys were driven off course by the flak and dropped their squads somewhere to the southwest, behind the woods. These were the men who had the job of clearing the way to the beach. They were expected to wipe out the machine-gun posts on the cliffs. Without them we may be cut off. Do you understand?"

"Yes, sir."

"It's possible that they're lost in the woods. This is what I want you to do, Paul. Stay here while we go forward. If these troops haven't arrived by the time you hear firing, go into the woods and find them. It's vitally important that they find their way to the cliffs. If those defenses aren't knocked out we'll never get down to the beach."

Paul's heart began to beat fast. He had known it all along. He had known that he could be of help to the commandos on this mission, and here was his chance.

"One minute to go," the major said, almost under his breath. He was staring at the sweep second hand of his illuminated watch. "Fifty-five . . . fifty . . . forty-five . . . "

There was not a sound from the crouching commandos. Paul held his breath.

"Thirty . . . twenty-five . . . twenty. . . . "

Paul's hands were clenched behind his back. In his mind's eye he could see the machine guns bristling out of the emplacements that guarded the Fire Bowl, he could see the Nazis waiting in their dugouts, peering into the darkness for any sign of danger, never expecting that danger was so near.

"Ten seconds . . . five. . . . "

The major blew his whistle, a muted rattle like the choked, angry sound of a hawk about to pounce. That was all. Without any other order, the major crept out of the ditch and went running toward the house on the cliffs. Ranged on either side of him were the hunched, threatening figures of the commandos. And still there was no sound—no sound of clattering footsteps, no sound of clinking guns.

Then all the figures disappeared into the night. Paul, left alone, felt as if he had dreamed the attack had begun. The commandos seemed to have vanished utterly, like ghosts.

These first few minutes were critical. If the attack were discovered too soon the machine guns would open fire, mowing down and perhaps halting the commandos. But there was still only silence. Total silence.

The Nazis guarding Bruneval felt at peace with themselves. Most of them were in the farmhouse, sound asleep. Those others who were on duty were snug in their dugouts, and a little bored. There wasn't much to do, guarding this radar installation. After all, Germany was the undisputed master of Europe now, and there was nothing to fear from the Allies. True, a few bombers had flown overhead about ten minutes before, probably on their way to bomb some luckless town in Germany; but these bombing raids were ineffectual, and the Nazi night fighters would deal with the interlopers. Had not Adolph Hitler himself declared that Europe was a fortress the enemy would never penetrate? Why didn't the stupid Allies realize they had lost the war? Why didn't they stop making foolish speeches about returning here? They sat in the machine-gun posts bored, half-asleep, waiting for their spell of duty to end so that they could go back to bed in the farmhouse and snore comfortably for a few hours.

The major had reached the house on the cliffs. Silently, his men surrounded it. The second group of commandos had reached the Fire Bowl. This, too, was surrounded without a sound.

An instant later came the signal for attack—a fierce blast on the major's whistle. Now there was no time to waste, no further need to move in silence. He dashed up to the door of the house, found it open, and rushed through. His men poured after him, guns and grenades ready to deal with any Nazi troops they found there. There were none in the rooms downstairs. The major went flying upstairs, shouting in a tremendous voice, "Surrender! Come out with your hands up!" A German soldier came out onto the landing, a rifle nervously in his hands, bewildered by this unexpected noise. Before he could fire, a bullet tore through his heart. He was the only occupant of the house, the major discovered. The Nazis had been so sure of themselves that they had not taken the trouble to put more than one man in it to guard it through the night.

Swiftly the major detailed a dozen commandos to hold the house. Since it stood between the farmhouse, where the main force of the Nazis slept, and the Fire Bowl, it could act as a barrier in case the Nazis attempted to fight. From the Fire Bowl itself came the dull explosions of grenades, and the major went speeding through the snow to discover what was happening there. Six Nazis had made a hopeless effort to defend the installation; grenades had killed five of them and the sixth had been captured after making an attempt to escape. The squad of technicians was already dismantling the apparatus, while a number of commandos stood alert outside. Pieces of the precious equipment, so vital to the Nazis and the Allies alike, were being carried out swiftly.

But at the road that led to the beach only a handful of commandos lay concealed in the darkness, waiting to destroy the six or seven machine-gun posts that barred the way down. There were not enough men to take the post. They waited, hoping desperately that the remainder of their section would arrive so that they could launch their attack. Otherwise, those machine guns could hold up the entire raiding party long enough for the Nazi troops in the farmhouse to come into action. Suddenly they heard the first staccato clatter from the farmhouse—two machine guns firing erratically into the night, unsure who or where the attackers were, just firing blindly out of windows.

The way to the beach *had* to be cleared. Beyond the beach, a quarter of a mile out to sea, were the landing craft and the motor gunboats and the destroyers, watching anxiously for the signal to come in close to take the commandos off. Enemy destroyers and E-boats had passed them on patrol, and had miraculously missed them. But that, truly, was a miracle, and the small fleet was in deadly danger every moment it was stationary. If the commandos did not reach the beach soon, the Nazis would have sent out a general alert that would bring scores of their warships to this area. That would bring, too, land reinforcements which would seal off the beach forever.

At the first sound of firing Paul slipped out of the ditch and went toward the woods. His only weapon was his heavy knife, and he loosened it in its sheath so that it would be ready for immediate use if necessary. His mind was working very clearly. After he had gone a little way he stopped and stood with his head cocked forward, holding his breath. If the missing commandos had reached the woods he would hear some sound—the slight scrape of a boot against tall grass, the crackle of a branch underfoot.

He heard nothing. There was only the gentle sighing of the trees, laden down by snow.

He crept forward another hundred yards and listened again. Behind him he heard muffled shots; ahead, still nothing.

He reached the outskirts of the woods and began to work his way along them, toward the village where he had been born and had lived all his life. Then, in a low crouching rush, he went scurrying up a chalky bank, which gave him enough height to look over the nearby fields, and stood straining ears and eyes to catch some sign of the missing men. It was a dangerous place. A roving Nazi patrol might easily have spotted him here. But his personal danger no longer mattered; all that mattered was getting those commandos in action against the beach defenses.

He waited for several minutes. The cold air was beginning to numb his body. Suddenly he thought he heard a tiny sound over to his left, and he stiffened. The sound was not repeated.

Now he realized he was in double danger. The sound might have been made by a Nazi trailing after him, or by a commando tracking him down in the belief that he was a Nazi guard. He knew only too well how the commandos worked—creeping through the snow like cats, pouncing out of nowhere, killing with a single knife-thrust. They couldn't be expected to know that Major Cowles had sent him out to find them.

Was the sound made by a Nazi or a commando? There was only one way to find out. He took a whistle from his pocket and blew it very gently, his hands cupped over it, making a noise that might be a bird or a small night-prowling animal.

He waited for a reply. None came.

He blew the whistle again in the same way, repeating it in desperation. This time, clearly and decisively, a whistle answered. As soon as he heard it he went running down the bank, wildly calling out, "This way! This way!"

A voice snarled out of the darkness, "Who goes there?"

"Paul," he answered. "Paul," and stopped abruptly, realizing that the commandos would take no chances, that by now a dozen guns were leveled at him, ready to blast him into eternity if he made one false move.

A shadow wavered across the snow, followed by other shadows. "Paul *who*?" the voice demanded. It came from another direction now.

"Paul Martin."

"What are you doing here?"

"Major Cowles sent me to lead you to the machine guns overlooking the beach. We heard that you were lost."

The voice laughed. Paul recognized it as belonging to a Scottish sergeant. "Och, Paul, and thank the Lord it's you, laddie. But you took an awful risk standing in yon place. I nearly put a bullet through your handsome head."

"There's no time to lose, Sergeant," Paul cried. "They've begun to attack the Fire Bowl."

The shadows had reached him, had materialized as men in familiar uniform. "Aye, Paul, we heard the firing," the sergeant said. "We were making our way toward it, through yonder gap in the trees—"

"No," Paul interrupted. "I can show you a short cut through the woods. We go this way."

The sergeant blew a short blast on his whistle. "On the double!" he shouted. There was no need now for silence. The commandos were going through, no matter who tried to stop them.

"Lead on," he said grimly to Paul. "They'll be needing us. Let's get there fast."

The machine-gun fire from the farmhouse was growing fiercer. Bewildered by the unexpected attack, unable to guess how the raiders had reached Bruneval, the Nazis were making a confused effort to defend themselves. The major and his men calmly returned the fire, lying flat in the snow. They were grouped around the Fire Bowl, protecting it, trying to give the technicians every second they needed to complete their job. Equipment had already begun to move toward the cliffs. Everything was going as planned, except the final and most urgent task of clearing the way down to the beach. The major wondered whether Paul had been successful in finding the missing commandos, what was happening in the woods. . . .

In the distance, traveling along a road that led to the farm, Paul saw the dimmed lights of three cars. They must be bringing up reinforcements, he realized, and there might be more Nazis following. It couldn't be helped. His first duty was to protect the men who were dismantling and carrying off the all-important apparatus. He and his commandos would stay to the bitter end, if it came to that, and fight a delaying battle to allow the apparatus to be taken aboard the landing craft. This was the purpose of the raid. It was his duty to see that it was fulfilled.

But the technicians had worked fast and efficiently. A corporal, wriggling flat on his stomach, reached the major and reported cheerfully, "The last load is on its way to the cliffs, sir."

"Have you set the demolition charges to destroy everything that's left?"

"Yes, sir. They'll go off in about three minutes."

"Good."

The major's whistle blew for retreat. Still facing the farmhouse, the commandos began to move back steadily, blazing away from a dozen different directions, confusing the Nazis, who must have felt by now that an entire Allied army had suddenly descended upon them. Their confusion was increased by the violent explosions under the Fire Bowl.

All that remained now was to get down to the beach and signal the waiting ships. But was the way clear? The major decided to find out for himself. He sprinted ahead, past the piles of equipment, and reached the gap between steep cliffs that led down to safety. It was dark here, and he could not see what the position was. The machine-gun posts, concealed in shadow, were silent.

Were their crews dead? Had the guns been knocked out?

He could not tell. His men were running toward him, and he blew a short warning blast on his whistle to halt them. Before anybody made another move, he had to find out for certain what had happened.

The commandos halted warily at his command. Then, from the beach, a gruff voice called, "Come on down. The boats are here. It's all right."

"Come on, men," the major cried. "Hurry!"

They began to move, but as they did so a voice called from the other side of the gap, "Major! Get back! The beach isn't taken yet! Get back!" At once machine guns opened fire. Two of the commandos fell.

"Flat on your faces!" the major bawled. "It's a trap!"

The machine guns had opened fire a second too early. The commandos snaked back, their bodies pressed to the ground, taking with them their two wounded comrades.

Coldly, the major considered the situation. After all this, after achieving full success in dismantling the Fire Bowl and bringing the equipment as far as the cliff top, they might be completely halted by the machine guns defending the beach path. It was bitter.

He shouted across the gap, "How many men do you have over there?"

"Major, only half my section. Not enough to attack all the emplacements."

The major bit his lip. He needed every man he had on this side to fight off the Nazis from the farmhouse and their reinforcements. And yet these machine guns had to be wiped out.

"Sergeant!" he snapped.

"He's been wounded, sir," a commando replied from the shadows.

"Corporal!"

"Sir!"

"Take nine men to reinforce the section across the gap. You will destroy the machine guns that fired on us."

"Yes, sir."

The major heard his men creep off and wondered what would happen now. You gave an order, destroy the guns, and you could trust your men to try to carry out that order. But it might not work out. Forty men could do it in a swift maneuver, attacking from different directions; twenty might be massacred. That would make the situation even more desperate. If only Paul had managed to bring the missing men here in time!

In a couple of minutes the action would start. He waited tensely.

The Germans in the farmhouse had not yet made any move. They still seemed to be dazed, uncertain what had hit them, and a group of commandos was still keeping them occupied with accurate fire, preventing them from showing their heads. But that could only last a little while longer. . . .

Then the major heard a shout, a wild sound that must have struck terror into the Nazis' hearts, *"Caber Feigh!"* "The Antlers of the Deer!" The war cry of the Scottish Highlanders. The shout came nearer, and he laughed aloud, knowing what it meant.

"Here are your men," he called vehemently across the gap. "Wait for them! Wait for them!"

In the growing clamor another voice rang out. It was Gaston. "Paul!" he cried. *"A moi! A moi!"*

The battle for the machine guns was short. A horde of ferocious commandos went swarming over the cliff, Tommy guns blazing, hurling their grenades into the sandbagged emplacements where the Nazis cowered under this paralyzing attack, wiping the crews out before they had a chance to fire. In a great savage rush, the black-faced men poured down to the beach, the Scots yelling their war cry, *"Caber Feigh! Caber Feigh!"* guns and grenades and the screams of the dying shattering the night.

Then, abruptly, it was over. A powerful voice called exultantly, "The way is clear, Major," and then quietly, efficiently, the secrets of the Fire Bowl were carried down, and the commandos took their places under the shelter of the cliffs. From the beach, bright with moonlight, a signal flashed out to the waiting ships to come immediately.

Gaston was hugging Paul with joy. "I thought you were lost in those woods forever, my little general," he said. "I kept wondering what I should tell the professor when I returned."

"This is my own country," Paul said. "I couldn't get lost in it."

The major came over, still tense and yet pleased. "You did a wonderful job, Paul," he said. "We shouldn't be here now if those missing troops hadn't arrived in time."

"Did we get all the apparatus from the Fire Bowl, sir?" Paul asked earnestly.

"Everything we need, my lad."

"What about casualties, sir?"

"We lost one man. Two were wounded. But I've just made a quick check, and there are still seven missing. They belonged to the sections that were dropped away from the target area."

"Sir!" Paul cried. "Let me go back and find them."

The major said heavily, "No, Paul. I can't let you take another chance like that. You've already done your part."

There was a cry, "Sir! The boats are coming in!"

Grinding into the shallow water came the monstrous shapes of the landing craft, carrying fresh troops who could cover the commandos' withdrawal. A cheer went up as the ramps were lowered.

"Paul," the major ordered. "Get on board. Go with him, Sergeant."

Neither Paul nor Gaston dared to disobey the order. They waded into the icy water and clambered up the ramp of the nearest boat. Following them came three disheveled Nazi prisoners, and commandos carrying the secrets of the Fire Bowl. Too late, some guns opened up from the cliff top, but the guns mounted on the landing craft answered with a torrent of fire that silenced them.

There was no further opposition. A minute later the landing craft backed away and trundled out to sea, to the waiting warships. The raid was over. Triumphantly, the flotilla made for England.

In the warmth of a cabin, wrapped in blankets and still faithfully guarded by Gaston, Paul fell asleep.

He dreamed of Bruneval, which he was now leaving again for the second time. He dreamed of Bruneval, peaceful, quiet, free of the Nazis. In his dream he saw green grass and wild flowers growing where the Fire Bowl had been. Not only Bruneval, but the whole of France was free; the people could laugh and talk as they pleased; the invader had been defeated and driven out. And in this dream somebody was talking to him.

It was the commando major saying, "You did your part," and Paul smiled in his sleep.

HAL G. EVARTS

The Trap

THEY HAD FACED DEATH before, so that they were stoic rather than calm, and quite unafraid. A somber quiet lay over the jungle, stifling already under the morning sun, and they forced their passage quickly, but without panic. The pilot, a captain, took the lead, and behind him, at a distance to avoid swinging branches, walked the colonel, and last, the sergeant gunner.

Their plane had been shot down on a routine flight not more than ten miles inside enemy lines. In the colonel's view it was ironic that this should happen to him at this particular time; to fall short by such a margin somehow typified his entire career. And although he realized, if the others did not, that their chances were negative, he would not admit as much to himself.

"You all right, sir?"

The colonel was a tall, spare man with worn features and wind-chapped face, and the deference the two Americans accorded his rank and age gave him grim amusement. "I'm all right, captain," he said a little stiffly. "Carry on."

Panels of sunlight slanted through the leaves, checkering the ground and sucking up steam vapors, and their soles alternately thudded in beds of fern and crackled on twigs and sticks, while from surrounding thickets birds kept up a chatter of alarm. They had no side arms, not so much as a pocket knife, and against the undergrowth their khaki was conspicuous. Altogether they were equipped about as badly as possible. On the other hand, the Japanese were expert at this sort of thing and knew the terrain.

Still, the colonel thought stubbornly, he would get back. More or less, he had to get back.

His watch crystal had been smashed, but when he judged they had been on the move a quarter of an hour he called a halt. The bush was astir with buzzing insects and furtive rustlings underfoot, and momentarily he relaxed, surprised to find that he was panting. The air was close with the odor of decay, and the ground was soggy, carpeted in patches with moss, and visibility was limited between the trunks of gum and teak and clumps of bamboo.

The captain eyed his pocket compass. "Why don't we hole up till dark?" he suggested.

The colonel was a British infantry observer and had no authority whatsoever over these men, yet he wanted to be fair and, at the same time, practical. "That occurred to me," he said.

"I did a lot of hunting in the States, sir," the captain went on seriously. "In rough country too. We're far enough now so they can't find us, not even with dogs."

The colonel repressed a smile. "I doubt if they'll use dogs." He was a specialist in guerrilla and infiltration tactics, and had been decorated for his work in the Malay and Burma campaigns; if there was any military field in which he qualified it was this. "What," he addressed the sergeant, "do you think?"

"Me?" The sergeant was dark, almost swarthy, with high cheekbones and black eyes and straight black hair. "Me?"

"This is an individual matter," the colonel said. "It's likely to be every man for himself."

The sergeant folded his arms. "I'd keep going."

The colonel took out a map and smoothed it on a log. The plane had crashed in a wide valley that paralleled the Burma-Assam frontier and by his reckoning an Allied outpost lay atop the next ridge. To reach that point they would have to bypass a Naga village and its network of trails. "My plan," he said, "is to strike due west across the valley toward our lines. I don't need to tell you how sticky daytime travel is. But we can't wait for night."

The sergeant shrugged. "You mean for us to split up?"

"Well——" the colonel began. It was his impulse to point out that three men alone might slip through where three together might not, but a sense of responsibility restrained him. On their own, neither of the others would last long, he imagined. "I rather think not."

"Very good, sir." The captain's tone was faintly injured.

The colonel sighed as they moved off again. When he returned he would be a brigadier; the recommendation had gone forward. He did not intend to be cheated of it, but he realized that years of service and the struggle for promotion had encrusted on him so that he could never easily unbend.

He wanted to say: "See here. We're in a mess, a proper mess, but we're soldiers, you know, not schoolboys." He wanted to say something like that very much, but he could not.

Watching the captain's awkward footwork, he tried to place himself in the Japanese position. By now they would have located the wreckage and would be spreading out to intercept. The fact that this was a forward zone would intensify their search, so under the circumstances his only hope was speed. Keeping to heavy cover, he might average one mile an hour, certainly no more. With the best of luck, say, ten hours. Ten hours of hard and labored going. That was too slow, yet the colonel saw no alternative.

There were ways of covering your trail, various tricks of bushcraft which he could not afford now. He plunged on, disregarding their noise. Creepers hung nooselike from overhanging limbs, forcing him to stoop, and mats of thorn ripped at his tunic. The first weariness settled in his thighs, sharpening into pain, and angrily he closed his mind to it. Then, abruptly, he blundered onto the log where they had rested before.

The captain stared at his compass card. He shook the needle once and looked up slowly to meet the colonel's eyes.

"Let me see, captain." The colonel wiped a sleeve across his face. Turning the instrument in his palm, he checked it point by point. "It's off," he said after a pause. "Way off."

The captain bit his lip. "But how can it be?"

"We're going in circles," the sergeant declared.

"There's just one explanation," the colonel said. "We must be near an iron deposit. It won't true."

He looked from one to the other, pitying them in a way. In the air they were brave, trained for swift and violent death, but the jungle required a special kind of courage. A man needed patience and a certain resilient quality, and the captain, at least, lacked both. "I'll take over for a while," he said.

It was not unlike sea navigation on a cloudy day. The sky was obscured by a canopy of trees, and the light below was a deceptive green, brooding and almost submarine in texture, and he could get no bearings; he felt at home, yet everything seemed shadowy and unreal. Also they had lost time. Not a great deal, but their lead was reduced.

In spite of everything, the colonel thought, he would make it. He recognized his ambition and pride for what they were, but he had worked hard, and nothing was going to stop him now. He would make it if he had to crawl in on his hands and knees.

The strip ahead was such that he expected anything from entrenched positions to foxholes and snipers, and the closer he approached the front the thicker they would get, while, behind, a patrol worked out his track. That they would track him, someway, he never doubted. Escape, so far, had been too easy, too good to be true.

The pain in his legs had become a steady ache before he stopped again. A narrow stream, muddy and sluggish, cut a slot through the forest. Where it twisted back upon itself the water had overflowed, creating a swamp in miniature, choked with reeds and tules and lilies. Farther down, both banks were worn slick where a trail led into a ford.

To continue in a westerly direction they would have to cross somewhere. The colonel studied the wall opposite. Flowers were bowing in a breeze and swarms of gnats hovered low. Above, the sky was clear and peaceful. He was about to slide in when a shot broke the midday hush. A bullet chipped bark beside him.

The colonel flattened in the grass with something like relief, the Americans dropping to his right. The suspense, the dread of the past few hours was gone, for here at least was a tangible threat. The report died away. There was no movement or further sound. Gradually his nerves tightened once more.

He lay rigid, his eyes squinted against the glare. Flies settled on the back of his neck and the heat grew almost unbearable. He tried to pick out the shape of a man or the glint of a gun barrel. Each second's delay pared down his slender advantage, but until he spotted the marksman he dared not move, not even raise his head.

He decided it must be a lone Jap guard; no body of men could be so well camouflaged. But if the report had carried, others would come to investigate. Perhaps the soldier, seeing himself outnumbered, had slipped away for help. If so, he was a fool for lying on his belly with precious time ticking away.

This was jungle fighting, he thought, the waiting and uncertainty, trying to outguess the other fellow and read his mind—the one type of modern war in which individuals counted. Any officer worth his braid knew that.

"Shall we rush, sir?"

"Wait a bit."

The Jap would be ready, his sights trained. If he was any kind of shot he would pick them off, all of them, before they got started. The colonel's muscles began to cramp. How long had he been here? Five minutes? Ten? He couldn't tell. He had a choice: he could make a break for it, as the captain wished, or he could wait. Sooner or later the sniper was bound to stir, show himself.

The captain squirmed. "You game, Charlie?"

"That guy's still over there," the sergeant whispered.

"You see him?"

"Not yet, I don't. But he's there."

The captain snorted. "I thought you're the one who wanted to keep going!"

With that he lunged to his feet and in a single bound cleared the bank. The colonel was too startled even to swear. The captain struck with a furious splash, hurling up spray, and dived on the first shot. A spout lifted just beyond where he had been. Ripples subsided over the surface and a bubble floated to the top.

In midstream he bobbed up for air. Before he could submerge, a second instantaneous shot spun him half around. He gasped and rolled over, the water darkening in his wake. He floundered another few strokes and then, mercifully, sank. Silence closed over the river.

The colonel swallowed. "Tough."

He shot the sergeant a curious look; the man's face was devoid of emotion. The captain's sacrifice had been stupid, and worse, futile, but it left the colonel shaken and almost ill, "Don't lose *your* head, sergeant," he snapped.

The sergeant grunted. "I see him now."

"You sure?"

The sergeant jerked his head. The colonel followed his gaze, searching the area foot by foot. His eyes shifted over a bulge at the base of a pauk bole some hundred yards downstream and swung back. The outline, indistinguishable against a massive, tangled background, had altered slightly.

The colonel frowned. He might possibly retreat and try a crossing somewhere else. But that meant more time and, besides, the sniper, if not eliminated, would alert the whole valley.

You want me to get him?"

The sergeant sounded so matter-of-fact the colonel looked around. "No," he said slowly. "No, I'll tend to him."

"You'll need help."

The colonel shook his head. "If I'm not back in half an hour you'd better clear out."

Cautiously he began his withdrawal. Pressed to the ground, he hitched back gently, a few inches at a time. When he gained the nearest screen of brush he was trembling with fatigue. For a moment he leaned against a tree, shading his eyes as he fixed the position in his mind. Then he circled through the jungle as fast as he could drive his legs.

This was not bravura, he told himself. He had an obligation, a duty to return safely, and this was the best way of doing the job. It would give him personal pleasure to dispose of this particular Jap.

Up to a point the stalk proved less difficult than he anticipated. Some distance below the ford he emerged around a bend and removed his shoes. Keeping afloat by easy paddles, only his face exposed, he drifted with the current to the other side. Stealthily then he crept forward, working out his route with such absorption that he was within a few yards before he saw the sniper.

The Jap lay motionless, in drab dungarees and jerkin and a cap draped with net, his attention focused upriver. To approach from the rear the colonel had to traverse an open glade. Irresolutely he measured the distance, calculating risks. However he attacked, the sniper must hear in time to wheel and fire at point blank range.

The Jap eased the rifle to his shoulder. Puzzled, the colonel froze in a crouch. He could see where he had left the sergeant. A piece of metal flashed in the grass, vanished and flashed again. The sniper fired. There was the ping of a hit and the metal leaped and fell back, then resumed its forward progress. With deliberation the Jap fired once more, then emptied his magazine in a final nervous burst.

The colonel reached him at a dead run. The Jap whirled, incredulity on his face, tried to fire, and then clubbed the gun. The colonel took a glancing blow on the shoulder, not troubling to swerve, and knocked it aside and pinned him down. He rammed a knee into his back, clamped a hand under the chin and yanked. The sniper writhed and went limp.

A minute later the sergeant rejoined him. He eyed the body without interest and hitched up his trousers. His belt was missing. "Thanks," the colonel said. "That was a neat stunt."

He did not add that he had been wrong, the sergeant right; that without the diversion his attempt would have been as fatal as the captain's—a blunder. He said, "What was it—exactly?"

"Buckle," the sergeant said. "Tied my belt to a vine and pulled it along to draw his fire."

"I see." He had new respect for this sergeant, yet the man's competence troubled him in an obscure and indefinable way. The sergeant's manner held no rebuke, but the colonel felt somehow defensive, as though he were in the ridiculous position of standing trial.

"Somebody's coming."

The colonel straightened. "I don't hear anything."

"Coming just the same."

It was the colonel's instinct to put distance between himself and the river. He hesitated. He had been wrong before. The sergeant had keener ears, the perceptions of a twenty-year-old. "Into the pool," he decided. "We may throw them off."

Together they carried the sniper to the bank. Thoughtfully the colonel unfastened the knife. The blade was of fine steel, honed to a razor edge, and the handle was inlaid with ivory design. It was, he recognized, some sort of ceremonial dagger. He had never killed a Japanese with his own hands before, probably never would again; that was not a general's work. But he had an urge to keep some souvenir.

"We better weight him," the sergeant said.

The colonel looked around for rocks and his eye fell on the rifle and ammunition belt. One .25-caliber would be useless in a showdown; deception was important now. He rolled the body over, hooked on the sling and belt and let it slide from sight. The knife he tucked self-consciously under his belt.

With the sergeant then he shoved back into the depths of the swamp and ducked down. The tepid water gurgled around his neck. He parted some reeds and peered out. A fish jumped and he started, then braced his feet. Mosquitoes set up a monotonous, insistent drone.

"Natives maybe."

The sergeant hissed.

A drop of sweat rolled into the colonel's eye and he blinked. A squat, brown form in loincloth seemed to detach itself from the woods. The tracker sniffed, and stood quivering, poised like an animal. Slipping soundlessly on from tree to tree he came direct to the grass plot where they had lain before, and bent over.

Half a dozen Japanese, armed with automatics, filtered out of the bush. They were so near, the colonel could hear their shrill, excited voices. The tracker gestured as though in dispute and pointed to the shallows. A soldier gave him a shove. He waded in gingerly and swam across, skirting the pool, and stopped on its fringe.

The colonel took a deep breath and held it. A rancid native smell blew in his nostrils. The tracker growled and turned away at the bark of a voice. Between the tules the colonel caught a glimpse of a flat, ugly skull, and then the tracker had crawled out and was meeting the Japanese. There was a brief parley and they pushed on along the trail behind him single file and were gone.

The colonel wiped the slime from his face and looked at the

sergeant. The sergeant's expression was impassive. When he had stood the tension as long as he could the colonel said, ''Regular bloodhound.''

''He's good,'' the sergeant agreed.

''Naga. They're head hunters.''

''Yeah?'' The sergeant spat. ''He's good, but those Japs aren't much.''

They dragged themselves out on shore and squatted there, listening. The colonel's shoulder throbbed with every heartbeat. He felt hollow, exhausted. He had been lucky, more so than he deserved, and such luck couldn't last forever. ''They'll be back,'' he said.

The sergeant knelt beside the trail, examining the Japanese boot prints. Shakily the colonel climbed to his feet. He and the sergeant had traveled roughly half the distance, which left another five miles to go. Five miles, he kept thinking; it threaded through his mind like a mocking refrain.

''Still got that knife?''

Resignedly the colonel handed it over. The sergeant tested the blade on his thumb and eased up the trail after the patrol. Boughs and creepers interlaced overhead in a tunnel and the gloom was crepuscular. The colonel compressed his lips and followed to where the sergeant was inspecting a stand of half-grown bamboo.

''Booby trap?''

The sergeant grunted. Choosing a length of liana, he cut and doubled it, and on his second cast looped the tip of a limber pole that tapered from a three-inch butt. The colonel watched in growing wonder.

The sergeant took a purchase around a root and began heaving. Bit by bit the tree flexed until it was bent double in the shape of an inverted U, the top barely clearing the ground. He hitched it down tight and stripped the crown. The green, hard wood he whittled to a point and sharpened. A second piece of liana he stretched across the trail ankle-high. One end he bound just behind the tip, the other he pegged down by driving a bamboo stake and securing it in a notch. Carefully he slackened off his hitch until the trip mechanism strained taut, concealing the barb among the trailside foliage.

Quickly he obliterated all traces of his work. Then he backed down the trail a few paces and flipped the knife up into a tree trunk where the white inlaid handle stuck out in plain view.

''Sure you know what you're doing, sergeant?''

"I figure we can shake the Japs."

The colonel rubbed his chin. The Yankees he had known were friendly, easygoing chaps; the sergeant had a different quality—a kind of stolid reserve—beyond the colonel's experience. He said, "Where did you learn that?"

"Back home," the sergeant said. "Used to trap some. Gators mostly."

The colonel nodded. He did not understand, but it was no time for questions. The subdued twitter of birds had sprung up, mingling with the rattle of dry fronds and the mournful creak of branches. The air was sultry and oppressive. He was aware of a paralyzing dread he would fail, after all, and then the sergeant beckoned and they squeezed aside into the bush and sprawled out.

The colonel set his teeth. It seemed to him that he had spent most of his life waiting, so he could be patient a little longer. He knew, too, that his best had never been quite good enough and that whatever future he had, depended on his wisdom and self-control now, and then as the patrol came around a turn he forgot himself entirely.

The tracker loped in front, and the Japanese were pressing to keep up. They had lost the spoor and were intent on the trail, and they did not notice the knife handle until almost too late. The leader shouted. The Naga recoiled and threw up his head. He shuffled uneasily, straining, ready to bolt.

The Japanese bunched up behind. The leader raised his hand. He scowled at the knife and darted a suspicious glance into the jungle. Then he prodded the Naga with his muzzle. The Naga drew back and the Japanese hit him.

From where he lay, the colonel could not see the tracker's feet, only his upraised eyes, fixed on the trunk. Sullenly he edged forward. With a sudden, vicious twang the release cord slipped its catch and the Naga screamed. Like a steel spring the tip slashed up and out in a hissing arc, lifting his body high and flinging it to one side. He fell with a dull impact and lay still.

For a stunned second the Japanese stood in the middle of the trail, held as in a trance by the tree's subsiding tremor. A strange look came over the leader's blank features and then he whirled and ran. With a howl the five others stampeded for the river.

The awful, urgent terror of their flight left the colonel dazed. He lifted himself on one elbow while he could still hear crashing somewhere off to the east, and stared at the tracker. The torso was mangled beyond recognition, but the face wore a snarl of defiant hate. It had an effect of barbarity, an utter primitiveness, that touched memory and confused him alike.

"I reckon they won't be back for a while," the sergeant said with indifference.

No, the colonel thought, not for some while. The patrol had lost considerable face. Perhaps they were plagued with devils; perhaps they would go off and commit seppuku. He hoped so, fervently. But by the time another tracker was recruited he and the sergeant would be out of reach.

The sergeant had retrieved the knife and was on his knees beside the body. He made an incision across the forehead and above the ears and held up a portion of skin and hair. The colonel opened his mouth to demur, but closed it.

"Something to show folks I been in this war," the sergeant said. "Got me a souvenir, too." He grinned broadly and wiped off the blade. "Here's your knife, colonel."

The following afternoon the colonel was seated in the operations room of an American air unit a few miles inside British lines. He had enjoyed a night's sleep, a bath and shave, and save for a slight stiffness he had no physical reminders of his ordeal. The pattern of army routine revolved about him unchanged and with such familiarity that he found it hard to be thankful for his return, hard even to believe that he had been gone.

The youngish American across the desk, a major, was solicitous, polite, and properly respectful. "I don't mind telling you we were worried, sir," the major was saying.

The colonel puffed absently at his cigar. A telegram, a confirmation of rank, rested in his pocket. He was a brigadier—a general, with three stars and crown. The thought warmed him, filled him with a solid sense of achievement that was the nearest thing to happiness he could know, yet it did not leave him completely satisfied.

"You must have had a close shave, sir," the major went on.

"M'm'm," the colonel said.

"They're nasty business, those Nagas," the major said. "You may be interested to know that they collect heads to hang in their lodges. Like our own American redskins collected scalps."

"Proper savages, eh?"

The major paused, somewhat at a loss and awed by classic English restraint. "Why," he said, "I was just reading Sergeant Kokochee's report, and although he doesn't tell much——"

"Sergeant Kokochee?"

"The gunner, sir. Charlie Kokochee. A Florida boy."

The colonel regarded the fine, gray ash on his cigar. "Florida?" he said thoughtfully. "Haven't I heard of a place called the Everglades? All jungle, swamp, not dissimilar to North Burma?"

The major, a native of Nebraska, was a little vague on his geography. "Possibly, sir," he said. "The sergeant, you know, is Indian himself. A full-blooded Seminole. Quite a coincidence, isn't it?"

"Quite," the colonel said dryly.

The interview was closed. The major pushed back his chair in relief. He could now complete the report: "One fighter shot down; pilot lost; observer and gunner returned to base." He thrust out his hand. "I understand congratulations are in order, sir. May I wish you success in your new command?"

"Thank you," the colonel said. And then he made a remark that struck the major as odd if not downright pompous. "Thank you," the colonel said. "We all have a lot to learn."

NORMAN MAILER

The Paper House

FRIENDSHIP IN THE ARMY is so often an accident. If Hayes and I were friends, it was due above all else to the fact that we were cooks on the same shift, and so saw more of one another than of anyone else. I suppose if I really consider it seriously, I did not even like him, but for months we went along on the tacit assumption that we were buddies, and we did a great many things together. We got drunk together, we visited the local geisha house together, and we even told each other some of our troubles.

It was not a bad time. The war was over, and we were stationed with an under strength company of men in a small Japanese city. We were the only American troops for perhaps fifty miles around, and therefore discipline was easy, and everyone could do pretty much what he wished. The kitchen was staffed by four cooks and a mess sergeant, and we had as many Japanese KPs to assist us. The work was seldom heavy, and duty hours passed quickly. I never liked the Army so much as I did during those months.

Hayes saw to it that we had our recreation. He was more aggressive than me, older and stronger, much more certain of his ideas. I had no illusions that I was anything other than the tail to his kite. He was one of those big gregarious men who need company and an uncritical ear, and I could furnish both. It also pleased him that I had finished two years of college before I entered the army, and yet he knew so much more than me, at least so far as the army was concerned. He would ride me often about that. "You're the one who's cracked the books," he would say as he slammed a pot around, "but it seems none of those books ever taught you how to boil water. What a cook!" His humor was heavy, small doubt about it. "Nicholson," he would yell at me, "I hear there's a correspondence course in short-arm inspections. Why don't you advance yourself? You too can earn seventy-eight bucks a month."

He was often in a savage mood. He had troubles at home, and he was bitter about them. It seems his wife had begun to live with another man a few months after he entered the army. He had now divorced her, but there were money settlements still to be arranged, and his vanity hurt him. He professed to hate women. "They're tramps, every one of them," he would announce. "They're tramps and I can tell you it's a goddam tramp's world, and don't forget that, sonny." He would shift a boiler from one stove to another with a quick jerk-and-lift of his powerful shoulders, and would call back to me, "The only honest ones are the honest-to-God pros."

I would argue with him, or at least attempt to. I used to write a letter every day to a girl I liked in my home town, and the more time went by and the more letters I wrote, the more I liked her. He used to scoff at me. "That's the kind I really go for," he would jeer. "The literary ones. How they love to keep a guy on the string by writing letters. That's the kind that always has ten men right in her own back yard."

"I know she dates other fellows," I would say, "but what is she supposed to do? And look at us, we're over at the geisha house almost every night."

"Yeah, that's a fine comparison. We're spending our money at this end, and she's coining it at the other. Is that what you're trying to say?"

I would swear at him, and he would laugh. At such moments I disliked him intensely.

There was, however, quite another side to him. Many evenings after finishing work he would spend an hour washing and dressing, trimming his black mustache, and inspecting critically the press in his best uniform. We would have have a drink or two, and then walk along the narrow muddy streets to the geisha house. He would usually be in a fine mood. As we turned in the lane which led to the house, and sat in the vestibule taking off our boots, or more exactly, waiting luxuriously while a geisha or a maid removed them for us, he would begin to hum. The moment we entered the clean pretty little room where the geishas greeted the soldiers, his good mood would begin to flood him. I heard him be even poetic once as he looked at the girls in their dress kimonos, all pretty, all petite, all chirping beneath the soft lights, all treading in dress slippers upon the bright woven straw mats. "I tell you Nicholson," he said, "it looks like a goddam Christmas tree." He loved to sing at the geisha house, and since he had a pleasant baritone voice, the geishas would crowd about him, and clap their hands. Once or twice he would attempt to sing a Japanese song, and the errors he made in pitch and in language would be so amusing that the geishas would giggle with delight. He made, altogether, an attractive picture at such times, his blue eyes and healthy red face contrasting vigorously with his black mustache and his well-set body in its clean uniform. He seemed full of strength and merriment. He would clap two geishas to him, and call across the room with loud good cheer to another soldier. "Hey, Brown," he would shout, "ain't this a rug-cutter?" And to the answer, "You never had it so good," he would chuckle. "Say that again, Jack," he might roar. He was always charming the geishas. He spoke a burlesque Japanese to their great amusement, he fondled them, his admiration for them seemed to twinkle in his eyes. He was always hearty. Like many men who hate women, he knew how to give the impression that he adored them.

After several months he settled upon a particular girl. Her name was Yuriko, and she was easily the best of the geishas in that house. She was quite appealing with her tiny cat-face, and she carried herself with considerable charm, discernible even among the collective charm all geishas seemed to possess. She was clever, she was witty, and by the use of a few English words and the dramatic facility to express complex thoughts in pantomime, she was quite capable of carrying on extended conversations. It was hardly surprising that the other girls deferred to her, and she acted as their leader.

Since I always seemed to follow in Hayes's shadow, I also had a steady girl, and I suspect that Mimiko, whom I chose, had actually been selected for me by the artifice of Yuriko. Mimiko was Yuriko's best friend, and since Hayes and I were always together, it made things cosy. Those alternate Sundays when we were not on duty in the kitchen, we would pay for the girls' time, and Hayes would use his influence, established by the judicious bribes of cans of food and pounds of butter to the motor pool sergeant, to borrow a jeep. We would take the girls out into the country, drive our jeep through back roads or mountain trails, and then descend to the sea where we would wander along the beach. The terrain was beautiful. Everything seemed to be manicured, and we would pass from a small pine forest into a tiny valley, go through little villages or little fishing towns nestled on the rocks, would picnic, would talk, and then toward evening would return the girls to the house. It was very pleasant.

They had other clients beside us, but they refused to spend the night with any other soldier if they knew we were coming, and the moment we entered the place, word was sent to Yuriko or Mimiko if they were occupied. Without a long wait, they would come to join us. Mimiko would slip her hand into mine and smile politely and sweetly, and Yuriko would throw her arms about Hayes and kiss him upon the mouth in the American style of greeting. We would all go together to one of the upper rooms and talk for an hour or two while saki was drunk. Then we would separate for the night, Yuriko with Hayes, and Mimiko with me.

Mimiko was not particularly attractive, and she had the placid disposition of a draft animal. I liked her mildly, but I would hardly have continued with her if it had not been for Yuriko. I really liked Yuriko. She seemed more bright and charming with every day, and I envied Hayes for his possession of her.

I used to love to listen to her speak. Yuriko would tell long stories about her chldhood and her parents, and although the subject was hardly calculated to interest Hayes, he would listen to her with his mouth open, and hug her when she was done. ''This baby ought to be on the stage,'' he would say to me. Once, I remember, I asked her how she had become a geisha, and she told about it in detail. ''Papa-san, sick sick,'' she began, and with her hands, created her father for us, and old Japanese peasant whose back was bent and whose labor was long. ''Mama-san sad.'' Her mother wept for us, wept prettily, like a Japanese geisha girl, with hands together in prayer and her nose touching the tip of her fingers. There was money owed on the land, the crops were bad, and papa-san and mama-san had talked together, and cried, and had known that they must sell Yuriko, now fourteen, as geisha. So she had been sold and so she had been trained, and in a few moments by the aid of a montage which came instinctively to her, she showed us herself in transition from a crude fourteen-year-old peasant, to a charming geisha of sixteen trained in the tea ceremony, her diction improved, her limbs taught to dance, her voice to sing. ''I, first-class geisha,'' she told us, and went on to convey the prestige of being a geisha of the first class. She had entertained only the wealthy men of the town, she had had no lovers unless she had felt the flutterings of weakness in her heart, her hands busy fluttering at her breast, her arms going out to an imaginary lover, her eyes darting from one of us to the other to see if we comprehended. In ten years she would have saved money enough to buy her freedom and to make an impressive marriage.

But, boom-boom, the war had ended, the Americans had come, and only they had money enough for geisha girls. And they did not want geisha girls. They wanted a *joro,* a common whore. And so first-class geishas became second-class geishas and third-class geishas, and here was Yuriko, a third-class geisha, humiliated and unhappy, or at least she would be if she did not love Hayes-san and he did not love her.

She was moody when she finished. "Hayes-san love Yuriko?" she asked, her legs folded beneath her, her small firm buttocks perched upon the straw mat while she handed him a saki cup, and extended her hand to the charcoal brazier.

"Sure, I love you, baby," Hayes said.

"I, first-class geisha," she repeated a little fiercely.

"Don't I know it," Hayes boomed.

Early the next morning as we walked back to the dormitory where the company was installed, Hayes was talking about it. "She jabbered at me all night," he said. "I got a hangover. That Jap saki."

"The story Yuriko told was sad," I murmured.

He stopped in the middle of the street, and put his hands on his hips. "Listen, Nicholson, wise up," he said angrily. "It's crap, it's all crap. They'd have you bleed your eyes out for them with those stories. Poor papa-san. They're all whores, you understand? A whore's a whore, and they're whores cause they want to be whores and don't know nothing better."

"It's not true," I protested. I felt sorry for the geishas. They seemed so unlike the few prostitutes I had known in the United States. There was one girl at the house who had been sold when she was thirteen, and had entered service a virgin. After her first night of work, she had wept for three days, and even now many of the soldiers selected her shame-facedly. "What about Susiko?" I said.

"I don't believe it, it's a gag," Hayes shouted. He gripped me by the shoulder and made a speech. "I'll wise you up. I don't say I'm Superman, but I know the score. Do you understand that? I know the score. I don't say I'm any better than anybody else, but I don't kid myself that I am. And it drives me nuts when people want to make me swallow bull." He released my shoulder as suddenly as he had gripped it. His red face was very red, and I sensed what rage he had felt.

"All right," I muttered.

"All right."

In time he came to treat Yuriko the way he treated anyone with whom he was familiar. He indulged his moods. If he were surly, he did not bother to hide it; if he were aggressive, he would swear at her; if he were happy, he would sing for her or become roisteringly drunk or kiss her many times before Mimiko and myself, telling her that he loved her in a loud voice which often seemed close to choler. Once he abused her drunkenly, and I had to pull him away. The next day he brought Yuriko a present, a model of a wooden shrine which he had purchased from a Japanese cabinet maker. All the while it was evident to me that Yuriko was in love with him.

I used to think of the rooms upstairs as paper rooms. They were made of straw and light wood and parchment glued to wooden frames, and when one lay on the pallet in the center of the floor, it seemed as if all the sounds in all the adjoining rooms flowed without hindrance through the sliding doors. Mimiko and I could often hear them talking in the next cubicle, and long after Mimiko would be asleep, I would lie beside her and listen to Yuriko's voice as it floated, breathlike and soft, through the frail partitions. She would be telling him about her day and the events which had passed in the house. She had had a fight with Mama-san, the wrinkled old lady who was her madame, and Tasawa had heard from her brother whose wife had just given him a child. There was a new girl coming in two days, and Katai who had left the day before had proven to be sick. Mama-san was limiting the charcoal for the braziers, she was stingy without a doubt. So it went, a pageant of domesticity. She had re-sewn the buttons on his battle jacket, he looked good, he was gaining weight, she would have to buy a new kimono for the number two kimono had become shabby, and the number three was hopeless. She was worried about Henderson-san who had become drunk two nights in a row and had struck Kukoma. What should she do about him?

And Hayes listened to her, his head in her lap no doubt, and mumbled gentle answers, relaxed and tender as she caressed the bitterness from his face, drawing it out with her fingertips while her childlike laugh echoed softly through the rooms. There were other sounds: of men snoring, girls giggling, two soldiers in a quarrel, and the soft muted whisper of a geisha crying somewhere in some one of the rooms. So it washed over me in this little house with its thirty paper cells in the middle of a small Japanese city while the Japanese night cast an artist's moon over the rice paddies and the pine forests where the trees grew in aisles. I envied Hayes, envied him with the touch of Mimiko's inert body against mine, envied him Yuriko's tenderness which she gave him so warmly.

He told her one night that he loved her. He loved her so much that he would re-enlist and remain in this Japanese city for at least another year. I overheard him through the parchment walls, and I would have asked him about it next morning if he had not mentioned it himself. "I told her that, and I was lying," he said.

"Well, why did you tell her?"

"You lie to a dame. That's my advice to you. You get them in closer and closer, you feed them whatever you want, and the only trick is never to believe it yourself. Do you understand, Nicholson?"

"No, I don't."

"It's the only way to handle them. I've got Yuriko around my finger." And he insisted on giving me a detailed account of how they made love until by the sheer energy of his account, I realized what he wished to destroy. He had been sincere when he spoke to Yuriko. With her hands on his face, and the night drifting in fog against the windows, he had wanted to re-enlist for another year, had wanted to suspend her fingers upon his face, and freeze time so it could be retained. It must have all seemed possible the night before, he must have believed it and wanted it, seen himself signing the papers in the morning. Instead, he had seen me, had seen the olive-drab color of my uniform, and had known it was not possible, was not at all possible within the gamut of his nature.

He was drunk the following night when he went to see her, moody and silent, and Yuriko was without diversion to him. I think she sensed that something was wrong. She sighed frequently, she chatted in Japanese with Mimiko, and threw quick looks at him to see whether his mood was changing. Then—it must have meant so much to her—she inquired timidly. "You re-enlist one year?"

He stared back at her, was about to nod, and then laughed shortly. "I'm going home, Yuriko. I'm due to go home in one month."

"You repeat, please?"

"I'm getting out of here. In one month. I'm not re-enlisting."

She turned away and looked at the wall. When she turned around, it was to pinch his arm.

"Hayes-san, you marry me, yes?" she said in a voice sharp with its hurt.

He shoved her away. "I don't marry you. Get away. You skibby with too many men."

She drew in her breath, and her eyes were bright for a moment. "Yes. You marry skibby-girl." Yuriko threw her arms about his neck. "American soldier marry skibby-girl."

This time he pushed her away forcefully enough to hurt her. "You just go blow," he shouted at her.

She was quite angry. "American soldier marry skibby-girl," she taunted.

I had never seen him quite as furious. What frightened me was that he contained it all and did not raise his voice. "Marry you?" he asked. I have an idea what enraged him was that the thought had already occurred to him, and it seemed outrageous to hear it repeated in what was, after all, the mouth of a prostitute. Hayes picked up his bottle and drank from it. "You and me are going to skibby, that's what," he said to Yuriko.

She held her ground. "No skibby tonight."

"What do you mean, 'no skibby tonight?' You'll skibby tonight. You're nothing but a *joro*."

Yuriko turned her back. Her little head was bent forward. "I, first-class geisha," she whispered in so low a voice we almost did not hear her.

He struck her. I tried to intervene, and with a blow he knocked me away. Yuriko fled the room. Like a bull, Hayes was after her. He caught her once, just long enough to rip away half her kimono, caught her again to rip away most of what was left. The poor girl was finally trapped, screaming, and more naked than not, in the room where the geishas met the soldiers. There must have been a dozen girls and at least as many soldiers for an audience. Hayes gripped her hairdress, he ripped it down, he threw her up in the air, he dropped her on the floor, he laughed drunkenly, and among the screams of the girls and the startled laughter of the soldiers, I got him out to the street. I could hear Yuriko wailing hysterically behind us.

I guided him home to his cot, and he dropped into a drunken sleep. In the morning, he was contrite. Through the dull headache of awakening, he certainly did not love her, and so he regretted his brutality. "She's a good girl, Nicholson," he said to me, "she's a good girl, and I shouldn't have treated her that way."

"You ripped her kimono," I told him.

"Yeah, I got to buy her another."

It turned out to be a bad day. At breakfast, everybody who passed on the chow line seemed to have heard what had happened, and Hayes was kidded endlessly. It developed that Yuriko had been put to bed with fever after we left, and all the girls were shocked. Almost everything had halted for the night at the geisha house.

"You dishonored her in public," said one of Hayes's buddies with a grin. "Man, how they carried on."

Hayes turned to me. "I'm going to buy her a good kimono." He spent the morning selecting articles of food to sell on the black market. He had to make enough to amass the price of a good kimono, and it worried him that the supplies might be too depleted. The afternoon was taken up with selling his goods, and at dinner we were two weary cooks.

Hayes changed in a hurry. "Come on, let's get over there." He hustled me along, did not even stop to buy a bottle. We were the first clients of the evening to appear at the geisha house. "Mama-san," he roared at the old madame, "where's Yuriko?"

Mama-san pointed upstairs. Her expression was wary. Hayes, however, did not bother to study it. He bounded up the stairs, knocked on Yuriko's door, and entered.

Yuriko was sweet and demure. She accepted his present with a deep bow, touching her forehead to the floor. She was friendly, she was polite, and she was quite distant. She poured us saki with even more ceremony than was her custom. Mimiko entered after a few minutes, and her face was troubled. Yet it was she who talked to us. Yuriko was quiet for a long time. It was only when Mimiko lapsed into silence that Yuriko began to speak.

She informed us in her mixture of English, Japanese, and pantomime that in two weeks she was going to take a trip. She was very formal about it.

"A trip?" Hayes asked.

It was to be a long trip, Yuriko smiled sadly.

Hanes fingered his hat. She was leaving the geisha house?

Yes, she was leaving it forever.

She was going perhaps to get married?

No, she was not getting married. She was dishonored and no one would have her.

Hayes began to twist the hat. She had a *musume?* She was going away with a *musume?*

No, there was no *musume*. Hayes was the only *musume* in her life.

Well, where was she going?

Yuriko sighed. She could not tell him. She hoped, however, since she would be leaving before Hayes, that he would come to see her often in the next few weeks.

''God dammit, where are you going?'' Hayes shouted.

At this point, Mimiko began to weep. She wept loudly, her hand upon her face, her head averted. Yuriko leaped up to comfort her. Yuriko patted her head, and sighed in unison with Mimiko.

''Where are you going?'' Hayes asked her again.

Yuriko shrugged her shoulders.

It continued like this for an hour. Hayes badgered her, and Yuriko smiled. Hayes pleaded and Yuriko looked sad. Finally, as we were about to leave, Yuriko told us. In two weeks, at two o'clock on Sunday afternoon, she was going to her little room, and there she would commit hara-kiri. She was dishonored, and there was nothing else to be done about it. Hayes-san was very kind to apologize, and the jewels of her tears were the only fit present for his kindness, but apologies could never erase dishonor and so she would be obliged to commit hara-kiri

Mimiko began to weep again.

''You mean in two weeks you're going to kill yourself?'' Hayes blurted.

''Yes, Hayes-san.''

He threw up his arms. ''It's crap, it's all crap, you understand.''

''Yes. Crap-crap,'' Yuriko said.

''You're throwing the bull, Yuriko.''

''Yes, Hayes-san. Crap-crap.''

''Let's get out of here, Nicholson.'' He turned in the doorway and laughed. ''You almost had me for a minute, Yuriko.''

She bowed her head.

Hayes went to see her three times in the week which followed. Yuriko remained the same. She was quiet, she was friendly, she was quite removed. And Mimiko wept every night on my pallet. Hayes forbore as long as was possible, and then at the end of the week, he spoke about it again. ''You were kidding me, weren't you, Yuriko?''

Yuriko begged Hayes-san not to speak of it again. It was rude on her part. She did not wish to cause him unnecessary pain. If she had spoken, it was only because the dearer sentiments of her heart were in liege to him, and she wished to see him often in the week which remained.

He snorted with frustration. ''Now, look, you . . . cut . . . this . . . out. Do you understand?''

''Yes, Hayes-san. No more talk-talk.'' She would not mention it again, she told us. She realized how it offended him. Death was an unpleasant topic of conversation in a geisha house. She would attempt to be entertaining, and she begged us to forgive her if the knowledge of her own fate might cause her to be sad at certain moments.

That morning, on the walk back to the schoolhouse, Hayes was quiet. He worked all day with great rapidity, and bawled me out several times for not following his cooking directions more accurately. That night we slept in our barrack, and in the early hours of the morning, he woke me up.

"Look Nicholson, I can't sleep. Do you think that crazy honey is really serious?"

I was wide awake. I had not been sleeping well myself. "I don't know," I said. "I don't think she means it."

"I know she doesn't mean it," he swore.

"Yeah." I started to light a cigarette, and then I put it out. "Hayes, I was just thinking though. You know the Oriental mind is different."

"The Oriental mind! God damn it. Nicholson, a whore is a whore. They're all the same I tell you. She's kidding."

"If you say so."

"I'm not even going to mention it to her."

All through the second week, Hayes kept his promise. More than once, he would be about to ask her again, and would force himself into silence. It was very difficult. As the days passed, Mimiko wept more and more openly, and Yuriko's eyes would fill with tears as she looked at Hayes. She would kiss him tenderly, sigh, and then by an effort of will, or so it seemed, would force herself to be gay. Once she surprised us with some flowers she had found, and wove them in our hair. The week passed day by day. I kept waiting for the other men in the company to hear the news, but Hayes said not a word and the geishas did not either. Still, one could sense that the atmosphere in the house was different. The geishas were extremely respectful to Yuriko, and quite frequently would touch her garments as she passed.

By Saturday Hayes could stand it no longer. He insisted that we leave the geisha house for the night, and he made Yuriko accompany us to the boot vestibule. While she was lacing our shoes, he raised her head, and said to her, "I work tomorrow. I'll see you, Monday."

She smiled vaguely, and continued tying the laces.

"Yuriko, I said I'd see you, Monday."

"No, Hayes-san. Better tomorrow. No here, Monday. Gone, by-by. You come tomorrow before two o'clock."

"Yuriko, I'm on duty tomorrow. I said I'll see you Monday."

"Say good-by now. Never see me again." She kissed us on the

cheek. ''Good-by, Nick-san. Good-by, Hayes-san.'' A single tear rolled down each cheek. She fingered Hayes's jacket and fled upstairs.

That night Hayes and I did not sleep at all. He came over to my cot, and sat there in silence. ''What do you think?'' he asked after a long while.

''I don't know.''

''I don't know either.'' He began to swear. He kept drinking from a bottle, but it had no effect. He was quite sober. ''I'm damned if I'm going over there tomorrow,'' he said.

''Do what you think is best.''

He swore loudly.

The morning went on and on. Hayes worked rapidly and was left with nothing to do. The meal was ready fifteen minutes early. He called chow at eleven-thirty. By one o'clock the KPs were almost finished with the pots.

''Hey, Koto,'' Hayes asked one of the KPs, a middle-aged man who had been an exporter and spoke English, ''Hey, Koto, what do you know about hara-kiri?''

Koto grinned. He was always very polite and very colorless. ''Oh, hara-kiri. Japanese national custom,'' he said.

''Come on,'' Hayes said to me, ''we've got till three o'clock before we put supper on.'' He was changing into his dress clothes by the time I followed him to the dormitory. He had neglected to hang them up the night before, and for once they were bedraggled. ''What time is it?'' he asked me.

''A quarter past one.''

''Come on, hurry up.''

He ran almost all the way to the geisha house, and I ran with him. As we approached, the house seemed quiet. There was nobody in the vestibule, and there was nobody in the receiving room. Hayes and I stood there in empty silence.

''YURIKO!'' he bawled.

We heard her feet patter on the stairs. She was dressed in a white kimono, without ornament, and without make-up. ''You do come,'' she whispered. She kissed him. ''By-by, Hayes-san. I go upstairs now.''

He caught her arm. ''Yuriko, you can't do it.''

She attempted to free herself, and he held her with frenzy, ''I won't let you go,'' he shouted. ''Yuriko, you got to stop this. It's crap.''

"Crap-crap," she said, and suddenly she began to giggle.

"Crap-crap," we heard all around. "Crap-crap, crap-crap, crap-crap."

Squealing with laughter, every geisha in the house entered the room. They encircled us, their voices going "crap-crap" like a flock of geese.

Yuriko was laughing at us, Mimiko was laughing at us, they were all laughing. Hayes shouldered his way to the door. "Let's get out of here." We pushed on to the street, but the geishas followed. As we retreated across the town, they flowed out from the geisha house, and marched behind us, their kimonos brilliant with color, their black hair shining in the sunlight. While the townspeople looked and giggled, we walked home, and the geishas followed us, shouting insults in English, Japanese, and pantomime. Beneath their individual voices, with the regularity of marching feet, I could hear their cadence, "Crap-crap, crap-crap."

After a week, Hayes and I went back to the house for a last visit before we sailed for home. We were received politely, but neither Yuriko nor Mimiko would sleep with us. They suggested that we hire Susiko, the thirteen-year-old ex-virgin.

CELSO AL. CARUNUNGAN

Hide-Out for a Hero

DURING THE LAST WAR, when the enemy bombed the town of Santa Cruz in Luzon, Philippines, Uncle Ciano and Aunt Clara moved to our town, for their house was destroyed, and their son, Manuel, was killed in action on Bataan. Uncle Ciano was a good carpenter and he missed his shop, and when they lived at our house, he would carve little boats for me at night, using the sharpened kitchen knife.

There was very little to do around the house during those days, for there were many of us living together and the chores were few. After we children helped Father and Uncle Ciano build the air-raid shelter under the house, there was almost nothing for us to do. Uncle Ciano hated staying around doing nothing all day, so he went out every morning, going from one farm to another looking for odd jobs to do, and returned at night before dinner.

Each night he brought something home with him. Sometimes he brought things to eat, like melons and Batangas oranges and cassava cakes, which some village women cooked along the roads. This was during the hard last years of the war, and food in any form was uppermost in our minds. We liked Uncle Ciano very much.

But one night Uncle Ciano came home late, around twelve o'clock, and the whole household was already asleep. Mother had thought that he was not coming home that night; there were times when darkness overtook him on the way from town and he would seek shelter in some friend's house—for there were many enemy sentries along the way with fixed bayonets, and they asked many questions.

It was I who awoke first. I heard Uncle Ciano talking in whispers to someone with him—and in English! It had been many years since I had heard him speak English, and it was odd hearing him speak it at such a strange hour and in whispers.

I got up, rubbing my eyes and hearing my father snore his loud, rhythmic snore. I heard their footsteps soft on the bamboo floor going toward the kitchen. Uncle Ciano lighted the coconut-oil lamp, and as I raised the mosquito netting under which I slept, I saw the man with him. For a moment I did not know whether to go to the kitchen and meet him or crawl back under my netting, but I decided to go to the kitchen.

Uncle Ciano smiled when he saw me. His face was dirty and his hair was white with dust. The man stood up from his bench and he was dirty too, his clothes full of oily spots. And he smiled.

''Juancho,'' Uncle Ciano said in English. ''This is our new friend, Michael Cooper. He's an American.''

During those years, seeing an American in our town was like seeing a man from another planet. You had to rub your eyes hard to see if you were dreaming or not. And if you weren't, it was still hard to believe.

''How do you do, Mr. American,'' I said in my best English.

''Hi,'' he said, extending his hand to me as if I was a real grown man. He made me feel warm all over and I did not rub my eyes any more to see if I was dreaming.

''I found him on my way home,'' Uncle Ciano said simply, as he turned toward the stove and started a fire.

I saw Uncle Ciano's sack on the table. It was empty. It seemed that he had brought nothing home that night but an American whose face was dirty and whose clothes were oily and who smiled and made me warm all over.

As Uncle Ciano placed some fire sticks on the stove, I looked closely at Michael Cooper and saw him wiping his face with the sleeves of his shirt, and perspiration shone on his face and neck in the dimming coconut-oil light. I forgot all the things to eat that Uncle Ciano did not bring that night; I went to the cabinet under the cupboard where our towels were kept and gave a white one to the American.

''Thank you,'' he said, and I saw that he was missing one lower tooth. I also saw that there was a small scar on his forehead—thin like a line—but he was a nice-looking man.

After a while Uncle Ciano turned to us beside the table, and he asked me to get some cups and we would have some *salabat* to drink.

''The *salabat* is our favorite drink,'' Uncle Ciano said as he poured some into our cups. ''It is made by boiling small pieces of ginger and adding cane sugar to taste.''

The American lifted his cup and carefully tasted the *salabat*. I did not drink because I was watching him eagerly. Somehow it was interesting to see an American drink *salabat*. After sipping he exhaled and lights shone in his eyes, and I knew he liked it. "Hey!" he said. "That's good."

"I'm glad you like it," Uncle Ciano said. "That's all we can afford to drink nowadays."

Then Uncle Ciano turned to me and placed his hands on my shoulders and walked me toward my mosquito netting. "Juancho," he said, "I wonder if you can let him sleep under your netting tonight. You can sleep beside me, and I'll tell you how I found him."

Uncle Ciano knew my fondness for stories. "All right," I said. "I'll sleep beside you."

I watched the American slip under the netting. He could not stretch his legs, for my netting was short and my mat was not too long either. But I know he was satisfied, for in a few moments he was snoring—not as loud as my father, but it was a peaceful and soft snoring that was like the passing of the wind through the thorny bamboo groves. I felt sleepy too, and I yawned.

After Uncle Ciano had blown out the light, I waited breathlessly for his story, but after he stretched his arms and legs he fell asleep at once. I felt cheated, but I knew that he was tired and that I would hear his story the next morning; for he loved to tell stories, and only exhaustion and hunger could keep him from telling them.

The following morning we were awakened by my mother's scream. Uncle Ciano and I hurried out of our netting, for we both knew why she had shouted. We knew, although we had forgotten, that each morning Mother woke me up so that I could go downstairs to get some firewood and to feed the chickens. This morning Mother must have lifted up my netting only to find someone else sleeping there.

Father was there quicker than we, and so were Aunt Clara and my younger brothers and sisters. They were all looking at the American, who was now sitting inside the mosquito netting and staring at the people outside. The children were twittering and Mother was pale and nervous, and Aunt Clara had her hand covering her mouth and her hair was unkempt, for she'd just waked up. It was a funny sight and I laughed.

Michael got out of the netting when Uncle and I came. Uncle stood beside the American and all of us lined up in front of them, and it was like the time when my teacher introduced our new principal in school. "I want you all to meet our new friend, Michael Cooper," Uncle Ciano said. "He's an American."

Father shook Michael's hand and smiled, while Pedro—my

youngest brother, only seven years old—asked Uncle if he did not bring home any fruits or cakes to eat. "No," Uncle Ciano said. "But I brought home the American." He said it proudly.

"It would have been better if you'd brought home something to eat," Aunt Clara said, her voice bitter.

"Don't mind her," Uncle Ciano said, turning to Michael. "She cannot forget our son, Manuel, who died on Bataan. Every time she sees a soldier she gets like that."

The American said nothing. But Mother went up beside him and looked at him from head to foot. "You need a bath, Miguel," Mother said in Tagalog.

I told Michael what it meant, for he looked at me bewildered-like. When I told him he winced a little, but he looked down at himself and then he turned to Mother. "Yes, ma'am," he said. "I certainly do."

We all laughed, because we thought he was funny when he bent to look at his dirty clothes, and the sound of his voice was warm and he was smiling. He turned to me and I saw his light blue eyes shining and I knew he was more or less feeling at home. . . .

That night Uncle and Father told us that Michael was going to be with us for a while. "It's our duty to protect our friends," Uncle Ciano said.

"He's not our friend," Aunt Clara said. "If it were not for the Americans, we wouldn't have been involved in this war. And Manuel—"

"Clara," Uncle Ciano said sharply. "Can't you forget your son for even a minute?"

"Look at him," Aunt Clara said. "He says 'your son,' when God knows he was 'our son.'"

"All right, all right," Father said. "This is no time to quarrel."

"He's a nice man," Mother said. "His eyes are clear-blue, and he talks nicely."

"He can sleep in the air-raid shelter downstairs," Uncle Ciano said. "It's comfortable enough, and it's safer there."

"Yes," Father said. "That's a fine place for him to stay."

"I still don't—" Aunt Clara said. But she stopped abruptly when she saw Michael coming up the steps from the garden.

He looked nice and fresh and his smile was good to see. "Good evening," he said softly.

"Good evening," Uncle Ciano said.

"*Buenas noches*," Mother said. She did not know how to speak English.

Then we all ate our dinner, and Uncle Ciano told us how he found Michael near the Malamig River, sitting near the falls like a dazed man and not knowing what to do.

"My plane was shot down a week ago when we raided the airfield near Manila," Michael told us after Uncle Ciano finished his story. "I bailed out and dropped near some mountains, and I walked for several days. I ate fruit from the trees along the way, and the other day I caught and ate a wild chicken."

Mother looked at Michael as he talked. She did not understand what he was saying, but she liked to hear him, and her face was soft and glowing in the coconut-oil light.

"I avoided the provincial roads because of the sentries and the patrols. I walked in the wilderness, hoping I would find some wonderful people like you to help me out. I prayed very hard."

"Ask him if he's a Catholic," Mother said, nudging Father. We were all Catholics, and Mother went to church every day and made devotions to St. Anthony.

Father asked Michael, and he said, "No, I'm a Protestant."

"He also believes in God," Father told Mother. "He's also our brother."

Mother smiled. It was sweet, like the taste of ripe summer mangoes. "He's nice,' she said.

But Aunt Clara got up from the table and went to her room, and she stayed there sulking all evening. She did not finish her meal, and since the gizzard was untouched on her plate, I reached out my hand and took it—for that's the part of the chicken I like the most.

Michael laughed at me, and I felt superior to all my brothers and sisters, for I was the first one to meet him and last night he had slept on my mat.

After dinner I went down with Michael to the air-raid shelter, and he told me about America and the tall buildings and the long, long bridges; and I asked him about the Lone Ranger, for I've read many comic books about him. We talked till midnight and he said that I should call him Mike next time, because that was what his friends called him in America. When Mother called me upstairs so that Mike could rest and I could go to sleep, we shook hands as if I were really grown-up.

That night I dreamed that I was in a big, big boat that had music coming from nowhere; it was like a floating city, and it was passing under huge bridges that were so high up the boat passed under them with many feet to spare. And then I saw the Lone Ranger, and his horse bowed to me, and I was laughing like a boy going crazy with joy.

The following morning Uncle Ciano told me that I was snoring louder than my father, and I knew it was because of the dream. I told Mike about the dream and he said, "You must love America too. As soon as I get back, I'll try to see if I can get you to come and visit us."

I could not speak. There was a stone in my throat and my heart was so overflowing with gladness that the words would not come out. But later that night I told Father about Mike's promise, and he only smiled—a kind of amused smile, as if someone had told a nice joke.

I believed Mike, though. I believed, too, that someday I would meet the Lone Ranger and see the long bridges and the tall buildings of America.

"America is ten thousand miles away," Father said. "You have not even been to Manila."

I said nothing. Father had never been to Manila either. In our family, only Uncle Ciano had been there. He had been to many places.

One night Uncle Ciano came in with Nicolás, who used to be our neighbor and was now with the mountain guerrillas. He had a big bolo hanging from his waist, and he spoke fast but softly. I sat quietly near the door to Aunt Clara's room, because Father would drive us children away if we interfered with important talks like this.

"Ciano told me about the American," Nicolás said, his voice low.

"We must help him," Father said. "He's downstairs in our air-raid shelter. Would you like to meet him?"

"Yes."

I stood up quickly. "I'll call him," I volunteered.

"All right, boy," Father said. I rushed downstairs and saw Mike reading some old comic books. He had already read my books from school and all of the books in our house; it's a shame we did not have books that were for men like him. Father never read much and Uncle was more interested in carpentry, so all the reading matter in our house was either my books from school or the comic books I got in exchange for the tomatoes I raised.

When I told him about Nicolás, Mike stood up and almost hit the ceiling, for he was tall and he did not stoop. He walked fast and climbed the steps two at a time and I was left behind. When I got upstairs, he was already talking with Nicolás.

"We receive communications by short wave in our camp at the

Makiling Mountains. We send messages from there too,'' Nicolás said.

''I must get back to my outfit very soon,'' Mike said. ''I don't want to impose too much on these kind people. If the enemy finds me here, it will be terrible for these friends of mine.''

''Yes, I know,'' Nicolás said. ''They were searching every house around the Makiling Mountains last week. They have heard of your bailing out in that area.''

''If you'll write down your name and outfit,'' Uncle Ciano said, ''Nicolás will try to contact the U.S. Army in Australia for you. Maybe they can get you on the next U.S. submarine that stops near Batangas Bay. That is about a hundred kilometers from here.''

''All right,'' Mike said, and he wrote on a piece of paper and gave it to Nicolás. After Nicolás had left, we all went to the air-raid shelter, and there Mike told us again how thankful he was for our hospitality.

''You're very nice,'' Mother said in Tagalog. ''We like you.''

Mike knew it was a kind remark because Mother's voice was tender and her face was soft and sweet. ''Thank you,'' he said.

Then Aunt Clara came down. Her eyes were red and she was nervous and her face was flushed. She had been crying again. In her hand she held the picture of my cousin Manuel.

She went to where Mike was sitting and stared at him for a moment, and then, holding the picture close to Mike's face, she said, ''This is my son. See—he was handsome and good. Now he's gone and he's the only one we had. He's gone and dead and it's because of—''

Uncle Ciano rushed forward and held Aunt Clara. ''You're going mad, Clara,'' Uncle Ciano said. ''Don't you see that Michael is suffering enough already? He's also in the war—and he's fighting for us too.''

''But he's—he's alive,'' Aunt Clara said, sobbing. ''And my son—my only son is dead.''

Uncle Ciano walked her toward the door and up the bamboo steps to her room. From upstairs I could hear the voice of Uncle Ciano like a raspy whisper and Aunt Clara's sobbing, muffled as if she had her face on her pillow.

''I'm sorry for her,'' Mike said to me when they had all left.

Then, suddenly, we heard the sound of boots overhead, and we knew it was not a good sound. Enemy boots! They always sounded hollow, for they were too big for the men that wore them. In a minute we heard a knock upstairs.

"*Kempeitai!*" a growling voice said. "Military Police. Open the door."

Someone opened the door and I prayed fervently, closing my eyes, that it was not Aunt Clara. I breathed easier when I heard Father's voice, although I was still nervous as I thought about what Aunt Clara would say if she was asked.

"Ah, Señor Yamamoto," Father said. "Good to see you."

Yamamoto was the owner of the candy factory in the town of San Pablo, and he used to buy coconuts from my father before the war. "No longer Señor Yamamoto, Tomás," the man said. "*Captain* Yamamoto now."

"Excuse me, Captain Yamamoto," Father said. "What can I do for you?"

"An American bailed out some time ago. We're searching every house for him." Yamamoto's voice had changed since the last time we saw him before the war. It was no longer pleasant.

"Nobody's here but my family and my relatives," Father said. "With the price of living nowadays, I can't afford to feed another soul."

"I am no longer an economist, Tomás," Yamamoto said. "I am a loyal servant of the Emperor, and I wish to die serving him well."

"But what I mean," Father said, "is that there are no other persons in this house outside of my family and relatives. You know me, Captain Yamamoto—I never cheated you."

"I know," Yamamoto said. "You count your coconuts well. But—oh, well, I guess you're all right."

Then he went out, and soon I heard the hollow sound of the boots marching away. I rushed upstairs. Mother was pale, and my sisters were all hunched behind the chair in the dining room. I wondered what had happened to Aunt Clara, so I went to their room. I saw Uncle Ciano on the bed, his hands clamping Aunt Clara's mouth. She was very red in the face, and perspiration beads were shining on her face and neck, and her blouse was torn, for she was struggling to free herself.

When Uncle Ciano saw me he let Aunt Clara loose. She stood up immediately, brushing her skirt and pulling at her torn blouse. "*Diablo!*" she said, glaring at Uncle Ciano. "I was not going to do anything. Why did you do that to me?"

"I have never trusted angry women," Uncle Ciano said. Then he turned to me. "Has Yamamoto gone?"

"Yes, Uncle," I said. We both walked out, and as I turned near the door I saw Aunt Clara holding her rosary; she was praying before the statue of St. Anthony, who is the patron saint of people who lose things.

A few evenings later when Uncle Ciano came home for dinner, he told us that the U.S. submarine was arriving the following night—at a point on the shore of Batangas Bay, which empties into the stormy China Sea.

Mike was informed after dinner. Since the night that Yamamoto had come so unexpectedly, he never had dinner with us upstairs. I always took food down to him.

"We have to leave very early tomorrow morning," Uncle Ciano said. "We have to be down at the river before daybreak. A banca will be waiting for us near the stone bridge, and Nicolás will be there. We hope to be near the shore of Batangas Bay before eleven tomorrow night. The submarine will be up at eleven."

Mike hardly said anything. When Uncle Ciano left him, I sat beside him on his bunk. The silence bothered me, but I did not want to speak either. Something terrible was inside me, and I did not know what it was. I wanted to shout or scream like Aunt Clara when she learned Manuel had died, or like my sister Maria when her dog Rajah was run over by a truck. I was quiet, but inside me it was terrible.

"Don't worry, Juancho," Mike said finally. "As soon as I get back, I'll send for you, and you'll study there as I've promised you before. You'll meet my family. They live in Brooklyn near a baseball park."

I said nothing. I was thinking of the nights when he had told me stories of the Lone Ranger, and when we had just sat there doing nothing but fingering the comic books that we both had read hundreds of times.

"In fact," Mike said, "as soon as I get to Australia I'll write to my folks about you and tell them how nice you are and how your family saved my life."

"But now—now, you're going away," I said at last. "And I'll miss you."

"Isn't this what we've both been waiting for, Juancho?" Mike asked. "A good chance for me to get away?"

"Yes," I said sadly.

Then I stood up and saw the comic books lying on the air-raid-shelter floor, and one of them was torn. I kicked it and the pages flew out, and Mike looked at me and his face was sad although he was smiling. "I'll keep my promise to you, Juancho," he said. "Don't worry."

But I was not thinking of his promise any more. "Good-by," I said, hiding my face with my arms, for now I was crying.

"So long, pal," Mike said.

Then I ran upstairs and laid my mat on the floor and my pillow became damp with my crying. . . .

When I woke up the following morning, Mike and Uncle Ciano were already gone and Mother was in the kitchen washing the dishes that they had used.

It was a beautiful day. The sun was up early and the fields had a yellow shine because of the golden rice stalks, and birds were fluttering overhead. I used to throw stones at them and sometimes I used a slingshot, but now I just watched them; and when Father followed me to the fields we both just looked at the birds silently.

Uncle Ciano came back the following evening. His clothes were dirty and there was a bloodstain on his left shoulder. Aunt Clara cried when she saw the stain. She ran to him and sobbed on his chest.

Father came from the well, and when he saw the stain, his eyes opened wide. "What happened, Ciano?" he said after a while.

"The enemy tried to shoot our banca near the town of Bauan," Uncle Ciano said, "but we paddled faster. I was hit, but it's nothing."

"And Miguel?" Mother asked.

Aunt Clara looked bitterly at my mother. "I can't understand you," she said sternly. "You think of nothing but that—that American. You're not even worried about Ciano. Look—the bloodstain on his shoulder."

"He looks all right," Mother said.

"I am all right," Uncle Ciano said.

"And what happened to Michael?" Father asked. "Did he—"

"He's safe now. We saw him board the submarine. He's all right."

"Thank God," Mother said.

Then Uncle Ciano went to the sink and Mother helped Aunt Clara wash the wound on his shoulder, which was really nothing but a scratch. Aunt Clara cried again as she bandaged the wound.

That night it rained very hard, and although the rain seeped in through the roof, nobody stirred; we all slept well.

A few months later, in February, the Americans came and liberated our town. We all rushed to see the first American GIs, hoping that Mike would be among them. He wasn't. No one in that company knew him.

One day Mother made some rice cakes and we all went to see Major

Jones, the army commander in our town. We asked him if he knew or had heard of Michael Cooper. He looked over many papers and opened many boxes, and finally he said that Mike's name was not there.

"However," Major Jones said, "if his name turns up in any of our files, I'll let you know right away. Leave your name and address with us and we'll see what we can do."

"Miguel is a wonderful man," Mother said. "We all loved him." Mother spoke in Tagalog, and the major smiled because he did not understand her. Mother smiled too.

That night when we arrived home, Aunt Clara was in the kitchen, already starting to cook. "Did you receive any news about your friend?" she asked.

"No," Mother said. "Nothing."

"I knew it all along," Aunt Clara said, smiling. For months, this was the first time I had seen her smile. "They do that all the time. You help them now—they forget you later."

"Miguel is a fine man," Mother said firmly.

"He'll never forget us," I said. "He promised me."

"I don't believe a word he said," Aunt Clara said. "Now that he's safe, nothing else matters."

Uncle Ciano came into the house with some canned goods. He was now working at the army camp; he never brought home fruits any more. Sometimes he brought American apples or grapes, but that was very seldom.

When he entered the kitchen, Aunt Clara turned to him. "These people are still hoping your friend will remember them," she said, gesturing with her hand. "If he was *really* your friend, he would have at least written you by this time. I bet you my new slippers that he'll never show up any more."

"I know it's been a long time," I said glumly.

"He's probably busy," Father said. "You know how it is during a war."

"He's forgotten you, that's all," Aunt Clara said, her voice loud and strong.

We ate dinner quietly, and as soon as we were through, Father and Uncle Ciano again went downstairs to the chicken coop. The air-raid shelter was gone now. We had already filled it up with earth and put more chicken coops on top of it.

One night, several weeks after our visit to Major Jones, I dreamed that Mike came, and he was like a tall, handsome knight with a shining uniform and a great big sword. When he smiled, his missing tooth was back and we couldn't help but smile back at him, and Aunt Clara was so impressed that she embraced him. We were all laughing and he patted and mussed my hair and told me to get ready, for we were both leaving for America that night. I shouted and tears were in my eyes and I told Aunt Clara, "You see—you see!" And she said nothing. She went to the kitchen and cooked for us all and it was a wonderful dinner. Aunt Clara was very happy and she sang as she cooked, and Mike said that it was the most delicious dinner he had ever tasted in his life.

Then I woke up and it was dark in the house, for the windows were closed. The brightness of the dream made the house seem even darker. But suddenly I heard the voice of my sister Maria from the garden, and when I opened the window I saw that the sun was high, and there was an American who was not a soldier standing at the foot of the steps.

He was a middle-aged man and he wore a Panama hat, and he carried a cane under one arm and a brown box under the other. He looked like a politician.

My father opened the door of our house after commanding me to fold my mat quickly. "Come up," Father said to the man.

"It took me a long time to find you," the man said when he reached the living room. "I'm an officer at the American Embassy in Manila."

"What can I do for you, *señor?*" Father asked, after taking the man's hat and hanging it on the nail behind the door.

"Well, Major Jones gave me your address," the man said. He sat down and laid the brown box on the floor and his cane on the table. "He told me that some time ago you came to him inquiring about a Michael Cooper."

"Yes, yes," Mother said when she heard Miguel's name. "Yes," was the only English word she knew.

"Well, I've got some news for you," the man said. "I received a letter from his parents in Brooklyn, New York, asking me to help locate a boy name Juancho Cruz and a man named Ciano."

"Yes, yes," Mother said.

"I am Juancho," I said.

Uncle Ciano came out of their room. "I'm Ciano," he said.

"That's fine," the man said, taking a letter from his coat pocket. "I have a letter here with instructions from the Cooper family."

Aunt Clara came in from the kitchen and she saw the man who looked like a politician.

"It's about Miguel," Mother said to her proudly.

"He's coming?" Aunt Clara asked.

"Wait," Mother said. "Let's listen to the man."

The man bent down to open the brown box on the floor, and then he read the letter. "The carpentry tools are for Ciano; the dress materials are for Tomás's wife and children; the jacket is for Tomás; and the light blue nylon blouse is for Clara," he said.

"I'm Clara," my aunt said.

My heart beat very fast because I thought Michael had forgotten me, but the man spoke again after taking another envelope from his pocket. "And here's a paid-for ticket to America for the boy, Juancho," he said, and my head whirled and I thought I was suspended from a tall coconut tree, head down.

It was like the Christmas the priest came to our house, giving us presents of different medals, and the times when our grandfather was alive and would bring us many toys because he came from Manila.

"But how's Mike?" I asked.

"He wrote to his parents when he was in Australia. He asked them to send you these gifts," the man said.

"And where is he now?" Uncle Ciano asked.

"Michael Cooper was with the American bombing group that cleared the way for the return of MacArthur's forces to Leyte last November," the man said.

"And what happened?" Uncle Ciano asked, moving close to the man.

"Well," the man said, "he—his plane was shot down, unfortunately . . ."

"You mean—" Father began.

"Yes, *señor*," the man said softly. "He's dead."

Mother put her hands on her mouth and her eyes closed for a second. Then she started to sob. I held onto Uncle Ciano's arm and I felt him tremble and he could not talk.

"I was instructed to help Juancho with all the arrangements . . ." The man went on talking, but no one was listening to him any more.

My heart was beating so loud that the whole house was full of its beating. I wanted to cry, and finally I screamed and ran out of the house and I went down to where the air-raid shelter had been. For a moment, I thought that the shelter was still there—but suddenly, I heard the chickens flapping their wings and I realized that I was lost for a moment and I was terribly embarrassed.

I returned to the living room and saw that the man was now talking with Uncle Ciano and Father. I saw Aunt Clara go to her room and I followed her. I wanted to say something mean to her, for she had been cruel to Mike, but I saw her take the rosary from the table and start to pray. When she saw me, she stopped praying and embraced me.

"He was a hero like my son Manuel," she said, her eyes welling. "God bless him."

I knelt down and started to pray with her, and soon my mother and father and Uncle Ciano came into the room and we all prayed. I could hear my mother sigh as she prayed, and Uncle Ciano was murmuring words I could not understand. But Aunt Clara's voice was the loudest of all, for she led in the praying.

"Forgive us our trespasses,' she said, "as we forgive those who trespass against us . . ."

We all bowed our heads for a moment, and when I raised my eyes I saw that Aunt Clara's face was shining and her eyes were sparkling with tears.

PAUL HORGAN

To the Castle

HOW COLD IT WAS in Italy. You would never expect it. We were near Gaeta in May of 1944, in a ditch, early in the morning, with about forty-five minutes left. Behind us was the bulk of the coastal army. Ahead of us lay the ragged hazards of the German retreat. Within us broke and drifted uncertainties like the broken and drifting clouds of the cold dusty sky. We did not want to look at one another, any of us, in the platoon, and yet now and then our eyes would meet.

As the heavy minutes passed, the soldiers waited for me, the lieutenant, to revoke what they knew could not be revoked. I looked at myself. I was no more afraid with my body than most other people. I felt that when I was brought to die it would not be from cut, wound, or break; I am one of those who will die of morality rather than of anything firstly physical. This, of course, would be small comfort to my men, if they knew it. Was there anything inherent in me for them to respect if by my actions I failed them now? There was nothing. Of what importance to them was my past as a teacher in the university, with its dry honors, its hard-won gray pages in authoritative quarterlies, its passions of kinship with all mankind through the printed humanities? None. And of what importance were these things to me, now, when they, the soldiers, my living burdens, wanted of me what nobody could give?

I thought of them one by one, almost as if in farewell, not as before a battle, but as at the end of a betrayal, for my unit was fallen apart in as many pieces as my thoughts. It was not enough that I knew it. They all knew it. If you licked your lips you could taste the fine, filtering dust of the wartime skies of Italy that kept falling, falling, tinily and divisively in the pallid light. You would shiver. But it was colder inside, at the heart, and there you would shake and shake before the human claims that you could not meet, and must.

Radley was a brave child. His heavy helmet looked too big for him.

It shadowed his big eyes. They shone on me and, when he saw me looking, some stir of sympathy made him smile dustily like a little boy covered with cake crumbs.

Sommersgill liked me at first, then didn't, then did again. In this moment he hated me. His mouth and nostrils flared in a grin of contempt. He had an athlete's face, square, bluntly carved, never a window, but only medium of refraction. In his doubled fist he carried every solution until the fist might be blown away. For this he hated me and all.

Shawcross was as thin as a naked chicken. His head bobbled on his poor neck. He seldom spoke. He was an embodied sigh. What others did, he could do, but barely. And so he never shirked. Now he sat feeling his pulse and I thought that he was estimating how many beats remained to him, and that it would be I who would fix the figure.

Martinsen was droll and wicked. Whenever there was a chance, he made pictures in his talk of what love did to a fellow, and everybody would listen, some sick, some sorry, some enlivened, some nearly crazy under his hot-breathed words. He found a sort of vast innocence in doing and saying before other men that which tempted and exasperated them in private. He was a wild and wonderful soldier, besides. Now his lascivious smile convicted me of his death, and forgave me comically.

Bauer was a solemn, nervous man who had to swallow deeply every time he wanted to say anything important. There was a sorrowful smile on his face most of the time, appealing for forgiveness for something he had never done, and promising behavior more acceptable in the future. He was barely literate, but some faint understanding of art dwelt far within him, and in our progress up the coast from Salerno he marveled at some of the fine architecture we saw, and he would swallow at his associates and speak of palaces as though he had been disinherited from them. He pulled his weight silently and full of qualms.

Pazzetti lay with his pale eyes shut, but he did not sleep. His fingers were interlaced on his breast and he kept them flexing. His mouth was open on his bad black teeth. How a young man could be so awkward and so old I never knew. Men groaned if they drew him on a detail. But his heart beat, and his eyes saw, and his body felt, and his soul strove. He was a man in danger, and his poor shape merely by existing implored of me its restoration.

Gates was fat. His eyes were like folds in a round loaf of cornbread, and his face had the texture of coarse meal. I thought he had to be so fat to contain all the uninformed ill nature that he carried. He wooed his comforts by inflicting, or at least threatening, physical pain. He knew something, in a creative sense, about hurting unto death. He did not want to die, either. He had hidden messages for me in his thick, shiny, creased fingers.

There were a few other faces for me to travel, but before I could search them a jeep came out of the dusty perspective and rolled to a stop before us. There was a man alone in it, an officer, a major, I saw, at the wheel. I arose to speak to him.

''Yes, sir,'' I said.

''Yes, lieutenant,'' he replied, in a soft voice, with precision, and smiling. He turned his neck like a craning youngster and showed me the insigne on the other side of his collar. It was the silver cross of a chaplain.

''Oh, yes. Yes, chaplain,'' I said.

He set his hands akimbo on his thighs.

''What goes, here?''

He looked up and down our ditch full of soldiers. He was small, wiry under the bunched-up field clothes he wore. His face was brown from weather, and some ancestry that gave him also very black, shining eyes. He had a white smile almost too big for his thin little face.

''We've just come off patrol, and are resting here a while.''

Behind me someone made a sarcastic sound. The chaplain raised his eyebrows at the noise and asked of me, ''How's everybody?''

When I did not answer, he looked at me sharply, with a kind of professional expertness and penetration that made me look down. He hunched over to the near side of his jeep and hung his puny legs over the side and swung his boots gently.

''Yes,'' he said with his head tilted a little, ''I see. There is much to see. Perhaps much to do. Tell me,'' he added, pulling me closer with rapid little lifts of his chin, ''what was all that last night, then, the patrol? Where'd you go? Wha'd you do? They never tell me, back there; say it isn't my business. I swiped me a jeep this morning and got loose on this road. Oh, my. I'll catch the devil if my colonel ever finds out. Come on,'' he coaxed, smiling and winking both eyes, longing to partake of what we had done, giving excitement and splendor to what nobody would tell him, until the soldiers in the dusty ditch looked at one another, and leaned a trifling bit toward the chaplain and me.

''Lieutenant?'' he begged, with lifts of his chin.

This gesture made his helmet rock ridiculously on his small head, and he lifted it off with both hands. His hair was clipped short and was sparkling black. His brow was pale above his sunburned cheeks. He looked like a ragged brat with his impish, wheedling exterior.

''Why, yes,'' I said, ''chaplain, this is what it's all about.''

He settled himself forward, folding his arm bones on his thigh bones, hunched and attentive.

''We're four miles more or less from the little town of Vitri,'' I continued, ''on Highway 7. Inland, on Highway 6, the main body of the Fifth Army is fighting up the Liri Valley. There's a lateral road connecting Highways 6 and 7, and the junction is just at the edge of Vitri going into town from here. Army wants to get the forces on the two highways joined up so the Allied front will be solid from the sea inland.''

''Good! Good!''

''Yes, but after the junction the highway goes on through the village and just as the country opens out again, there is a big swoop of high rock on the left, and on top of the rock is a castle, an ancient castle with towers, and clifflike walls, and little portholes just as good today as they used to be for arrows and small brass cannon. The castle was put there to command the road centuries ago, and it still commands the road now. Behind it is the sea. If we are going to Rome——''

''Rome!'' exclaimed the chaplain with indescribable joy, but hastily, not to hold me up.

''——to Rome, all these divisions of ours along the coast here, we have to go by that road, and whoever holds the castle holds the road too. So we were sent out on reconnaissance to see what we could see. We got to the village safely by sticking to the hills. The village is empty and destroyed. But the castle—we came on a little crest and lay for hours watching. And we saw.''

''You saw the enemy?''

''Machine gun and probably mortar. A dozen Germans could hold up an army on the highway. The castle has stone parapets and platforms, and we could see now and then some of the German soldiers moving about on them. Our intelligence says that the main body of Germans has fallen back to a defense line farther north, and that they left behind just this pocket of resistance in the castle and a few patrols. We stayed till nightfall. Just before dark we had a treat. The Germans tested their armament by firing several rounds from each piece. We knew what we had to know then. We came back. It took us all night."

"Any trouble keeping together?"

The soldiers looked at one another. Who was he? How could he see their experience so familiarly?

"Yes, even though the moon rose. I lost one man and went back for him."

"While the others waited?"

"They waited, and once we were pinned down by a few mortar bursts across a gully. Nobody hurt."

"Thank God. Well. Let's see what we have here. This handful of men went forward and returned with vital information. What's next?"

Who didn't feel the thing get tense between us all?

"We reported to headquarters by radio. Then they gave it to us. We got orders to move out again, this time to attack the castle."

"Alone?" His eyes sparkled with wonder and challenge.

"No; there's an armored infantry detachment coming along the lateral road connecting us with Highway 6. They will meet us at the junction of the roads. We're supposed to hit the castle from two sides."

He looked at the men.

"Had any sleep?"

"No."

"Eaten?"

"Some field rations."

"Yes. Yes, I think I see. I suppose they understand why, in all probability, those orders came?"

"I think so. After all, we know the situation first hand where other troops wouldn't."

"Exactly." He indicated the platoon with a flick of his eyes and asked me in a quiet voice that they could not hear, "How do they feel about it?"

"How do you think? They know we've got an army corps behind us, and yet nobody to spell us for a bit."

He looked past me to the faces of the detail in the ditch. He read all their exhaustion and resentment. Between faces he would steal a glance at me, and in me he saw as much failure.

The chaplain spoke even more quietly than before, and asked, "What time are you supposed to move out?"

"At 0930 hours."

Then with soft, terrible realism, he asked, "Will they go?"

It was the question I had been trying to bury in myself. Now a weight fell in me, and I went heavy as I stood.

"I don't know."

"Don't know! But you're their leader!"

"Yes. I still don't know."

So he discovered our condition. He found us as casualties, really, wounded in our wills. He put his hand on me and looked at me without judging me, as a doctor might, yet with a brisk travel of thought behind his eyes. He seemed to find that there was work to do, mercy to make, health to find for others. He brought his thoughts back to tactics.

"Will there be barrage to cover you?"

"No, sir. They don't want to shell or bomb the castle because they might break up the road. We need the road for the main body of vehicles."

"Yes. I see."

"If we fail, they will send planes and order artillery to concentrate on the castle. But only as a last resort."

"And that," he said, "would wreck our advance on Rome, for a little while, at least."

"Yes."

"M-m-m," he mused, looking beyond me to the soldiers.

Then he seemed to awaken from an abstraction of presence, and he yawned and stretched, making a hoot and howl, and ended up laughing with tears in his eyes. Then he jumped out of the jeep and knelt on the ground before the scattered platoon. I thought he was going to pray and I feared for his dignity before them. But he settled back until he sat on his boots, with his palms down on his thighs, like an Indian.

Gates was near him. Gates made a fat man's elegant inclination of the body, and said with a sneer, "Well, Reverend, go on, give us the Word."

The chaplain put out a finger at Gates to tie his attention for a moment while he looked at someone else.

"You," he said, lifting his chin at Radley, "where're you from?"

"Arizona," said Radley.

"No; this is wonderful. I am from New Mexico."

"No kiddin'?"

"No kiddin'. From Bernalillo, on the Rio Grande. *Habla usted español*?"

"*Sí, poquito.*"

"*Qué maravilloso*."

Everyone turned and stared at Radley. They saw a rare and splendid thing. They saw an individual. They envied him. Out of the mechanical mass of men sent to war, they now met someone who was allowed to be himself all over again, in just that trifling exchange with the chaplain.

I now saw that the chaplain was a New Mexico Mexican, a priest, probably a Franciscan. His black eyes and hair, his white smile, his brown face, his humble little thin person.

He turned back to Gates, who was waiting in contempt to be answered.

"Now let's see," he said, and as he talked, he leaned forward, scraping dry grass and winter weeds together in the ditch and piling on little twigs and bits of refuse which made a cone for a fire and striking a light with his lighter, "what's your name?"

"Gates."

"Want the Word, eh, Gates?"—in excellent humor, blowing on the tiny fire, and toasting his hands with satisfaction so complete that it made the other fellows feel warm to watch him in the cold early morning.

"Not if you ask me, personally," replied Gates with a nasty parody of respectfulness; "I've had all the morale lectures I can stomach, thank you."

"Oh. So then you were just being unpleasant. Then we can forget you, for the moment."

The chaplain turned to the others.

"But I do have a word. I don't know enough about it. I always talk about it if anybody will answer. My word is one you all know, and you all must know more than I about it." He made a little monkeylike cringe of humorous humility, his brown paws twisting each other. "You must not think me foolish to bring it up, but in every crowd there is one man at least who can teach me something," and he turned and beamed on the offensive Gates with wicked drollery.

Everybody laughed. The laugh was like the discharge of a new energy into the dead taste of the dusty air.

"Who can tell me?" he asked. "My word is 'television,' and I am crazy to know how practical it is, and what we will be doing with it someday. No. First, how does it work? I cannot understand. I cannot believe."

They were set back for a moment by this. This was nothing like what they'd expected.

Gates rallied first, and said, ''Why, Reverend, I thought you knew all the answers.''

''Oh-ho, no, Corporal Gates, not all the answers. Only the big ones.'' He did not wait for that to take effect on anyone else, but turned and asked, ''They speak of a certain kind of tube. Is it a tube? How? No. I cannot.''

Pazzetti lunged an inch or two taller.

''I suppose,'' he said with gloomy expertness that turned to pride as he spoke the beloved jargon of his other life, ''the major has reference to the camera tube, which operates by the use of lenses, a signal plate of mica covered with a mosaic of photo-sensitive material, and a couple of deflection coils. We call this the iconoscope.''

''We, we!'' cried the chaplain. ''You belong to the men who make the future. Listen to him! I knew someone could tell me! But I don't know any more than I did. Who? Explain it.''

Martinsen raised his hand and the chaplain nodded to him.

''I worked in a radio shop once. We worked on a TV set. That camera tube has a lot of little teeny reflectors that hold the light and then they make a discharge of electrons and the tube sights the picture to be shown and the electrons turn into waves and that's how it goes out.''

''You mean something you see becomes something you can't see that goes through the air?''

''Yes,'' said Pazzetti, regaining his dear subject, ''you could put it that way, to simplify it.''

Martinsen chose to take exception to this. ''Waddaya mean, simplify? There's nothing wrong to simplify it, that's what the padre asked for.''

''Okay, okay,'' said Pazzetti. ''But there's a lot more to it than that.''

''So there's a lot more. The picture goes in here and comes out there, that's all he wants to know.''

The fellows stirred. They were becoming partisans. Some had faith in Pazzetti's morbid exactness. Others were willing to skip the details and recognize the results, with Martinsen.

Radley said, ''I saw it at the World's Fair in New York. My family took me. I was just a kid, but I remember it.''

''Yes, you do. You certainly do,'' said the chaplain, with his hands opened out in the gesture of saying ''The Lord be with you.'' He saw enough of Radley as a little boy, and let Radley see it, too, and a young life rose up and was lived again.

What he did for Radley, then, he did for the others, if they did not know it.

''And these waves, then?'' he asked of Pazzetti, to keep the privileges evenly divided, ''what of them? Where? What happens to them? Just waves? Where's the picture all this time? There is a picture, I know, because I saw it once, too, like the lad from Arizona, there, but—I'm hopeless. Tell me; do tell me.''

Pazzetti stood up. On his ghost-gray unshaved face there was a lumbering smile of self-depreciation that measured nicely just how fully he was restored out of a battlefield ditch and was again a prosperous authority on electronics, at which he made his living.

''You see, father,'' he said, and everyone now knew this was a priest as the chaplain let the title stand, ''the waves are released on a certain frequency, and if they are received on the same one, they can be converted back into images by the use of a super-heterodyne mixer section, an oscillator, a synchronizing amplifier, both horizontal and vertical synchronizing pulse separators, a video amplifier, sweep circuits both vertical and horizontal, and of course, the light tubes, loud speakers, and picture tube.''

''And a box to keep it in,'' added the chaplain with a groggy smile, overwhelmed with information. For relief, ''What did the picture show, that you saw?'' he asked Radley.

''A lady. She was singing.''

''The one I saw,'' said the chaplain, ''had two jugglers and a trained dog. He was a marvelous dog. Walked on two legs and wore a pair of eyeglasses, read a newspaper and smoked a pipe. He had a hat like Sherlock Holmes. They forgot one thing, though, because the newspaper was upside down.''

A small laugh.

''Though how should I know,'' he added; ''maybe dogs can read better that way. Sometimes some of the things I read, I think I would do better with them upside down. Yes?''

He nodded to a fellow in the back who'd raised his hand, The group had quietly, without any formal organization, turned into a class, a senate, a body with a presiding officer, in the most natural way in the world. Many of them felt like talking now. Many of them were delivered from their anonymous doom. Many of them felt again that they might live.

''Tell me that dogs don't think,'' said the young man in back. ''I've got a dog at home, we live in an apartment on the second floor, out by Anacostia, in Washington, and we take an evening paper, only it's a different one, and my dog will go down and get ours, and never touch theirs.''

He bridled and looked about for disbelief or challenge. Anyone who doubted that would doubt the picture of home in his heart, and if that were doubted, then all existence was threatened.

Sommersgill turned to him with a pursed sweet tough smile on his handsome heavy face. ''Kind of dog is it?'' he asked, with his attitude still veiled.

''A wire-haired fox terrier.''

''Oh.'' Sommersgill nodded, as if that made everything all right, and barely averted a dangerous necessity if it had turned out to be any other breed. He turned to look at the chaplain with an eternally adolescent charm and received a wink in return which allowed him to be who he was, with admiration.

For that was what the chaplain was doing for everyone. He gave each of them a chance to be what he was, good or bad, bright or stupid, but individually. His topics and questions were innocent toys for the mind to play with; but they made it play, in each of his listeners, instead of sink. What war never used he made them use, however primitively. Their identities were restored.

I saw them turning into men before my eyes, and I was stung by the humble means of their restoration, and as I saw their power, their love for what they loved showing free in all their little associations of argument and memory, I was astonished over them, and I knew in a new kind of starvation the degree of my failure with them earlier.

The mechanism of dispute stirred Corporal Gates in his own way, bringing him the same life-giving satisfaction which came to the others.

''Okay, Reverend,'' he said, ''what's the low-down?''

''Low-down?''

''Ya-a. What are you doing way up here?''

''Wasting your time, corporal.''

Even those who liked Gates laughed then.

Gates' face turned red with anger.

''All you Holy Joes belong back at the rear echelon with all the other chickenfits. What I call the other ninety percent. Only ten percent of an army ever does any fighting. I read that and I know it is true. So give, Reverend. Did you lose your way, or make a wrong turn in your nice little jeep there? I don't see why every foot soldier can't have a nice little jeep to drive. I'd as soon have my corns on my butt as on my feet. How about it?''

Several voices rose in protest over Gates. The other men felt outraged. Something precious had come to them in the last half hour. It had reached to their hidden hearts. It had dissipated the heavy anger that hung within them. It had made men of them again, and soldiers, by permitting them to be anything else. Calling out, they made Gates shut up. The ones nearest to him closed against him physically. There was a fight about to happen.

"Let him go," called the chaplain, scratching himself at the neck like a merry little monkey. "Let's see what he will do"—making an object of civilized curiosity out of Gates, whose mouth dried up with fury. And then the chaplain turned back the much too long cuff of his field jacket to see his wrist watch. He showed it to me.

"Did you say O-nine-thirty?" he asked.

"Yes. I've been watching. It is about time."

"Yes. Are you ready?"

I looked at the soldiers. The chaplain stood beside me.

"All right, men," I said, "it's time to move out. On your feet. Let's go."

That curious sense—the instant divided, with two destinies waiting for one to be chosen. Nobody moved. Then the chaplain turned away from them, and began to whistle a vague tune, slowly toeing idle lines in the dirt. In silence, he plainly said to them that he must not look upon them, if they chose ill.

The instant healed its halves together. The soldiers began to get up. If there was no refusal, there was no eagerness, either, but something far more moving, and that was a sense of modest pity reaching from man to man, who by a strength greater than his body's, told his legs to stand, his arms to clutch his rifle like a beloved child who will save him, his feet to take him forward until by every chance he might walk or crawl straight into pain and death. Every soldier accomplishing that prospect under his heavy helmet achieved a masterpiece of will.

I fell them in by the roadside and was about to take my place at the head of the file and give the command to walk, when someone, Radley, I think, called out, "How about it, father, give it to us, a blessing before we go?"

The chaplain walked over to his jeep by the roadside and leaned in and took out the ignition key. Turning round toward us again, he said, "Sure thing."

The Catholic soldiers knelt down and some of the others, including myself, while he opened his hands to the sky, then brought them together before him, saying, "*Benedicat vos omnipotens*," then making the sign of the cross with slow, wide, ample gestures taking in zenith and nadir, east and west, "*Pater et Filius et Spiritus Sanctus, Amen.*" And then he added, smiling cleverly, "I'd better keep my car key, if I want to find it when I get back. Some joe might come along and just drive it away. The way I did, back there."

"What do you mean," somebody called, "are you going with us?"

"I'm gone," he said humorously.

"But you don't even have a gun, father!"

"No; my business forbids me to have one."

"Nuts, you can't go this way!"

"Nuts to you," he said inoffensively. "I've got to see how all our arguments come out."

So, promising them continuity, future, completion, he walked beside me when I gave the soldiers the word to go. They now owned him. He was a sort of divine mascot. He was man, like them, and he was part of the overreaching power of providence. What other small unit had its very own Holy Joe? Their spirits rose. What a joe!

As he went he considered me, sidelong. "You do not mind, lieutenant?"

"No, of course not, chaplain. I don't know what we'd have done without you."

"Well, maybe you're right. Especially if you had much more time to think about it." So he knew that. "But so long as I don't intrude," he said. "I am unarmed, and I have no office of command, and of course I am under your orders, lieutenant, so long as we are in the field."

"Yes, sir."

"The minute I prove to be a nuisance you must send me back."

"Very well."

"But I'd love to go all the way to Rome with you."

"Rome? We won't make Rome on this trip."

"No, I know, but a week, two weeks, maybe. I cannot wait to be there again."

"You've been there?"

"Oh, yes. I was a student at St. Anthony's in Rome—the Franciscan college. Many years ago. I always promised that I would go back. I used to say that when I died I would go to Rome. A joke, of course."

The landscape was harsh as we went. In the file that followed me, a few fellows were whistling in strongly accented beats, no two doing the same tune, but each lost and satisfied in his own melody.

"Why must I return to Rome so badly? Oh, well, I do know. She is the mother of the world, and because of my faith and my life, you know, her heart is at St. Peter's. The very walls of that church are like limestone cliffs in certain places of the river where I come from. Back home, sometimes, I would find my way to those cliffs, in a canyon, and put my hand on the rock, warm from sunlight, and with my eyes shut pretend that I was in Rome. And then, when I was a seminarian, studying in Rome, I would sometimes go to St. Peter's and put my hand on the warm travertine blocks of the wall and shut my eyes and be home again on the Rio Grande, and I would say a prayer. At such times I was sure of becoming a great saint, a bishop, not through ambition, you understand, but through goodness." He laughed cheerfully. "I have to go back and see if my prayers are still there in the wall. I don't want very much here on earth. But one thing I would like. I would like something of me to be in Rome forever."

He smiled over his own sentiment, but without in any way diminishing it. "But probably," he added, with a glance at me sidewise, "the most enduring of all things is an act of the spirit. Perhaps you cannot believe that."

"Oh, yes; oh, yes, I can believe that," I answered, but hardly, and perhaps for a little while I almost hated him because he came to save what I would surely have lost.

I left his side and let the column march past me as though I were checking on their condition. In a few minutes I was feeling better, and returned to the head of the file.

"Remember," he said gently, not looking at me, "you must send me back any time you think you should."

At this I could not forebear laughter, because he was so sharp in reading my feelings.

"No, no, chaplain. We are all in this together now."

"Yes. Yes. Very good. You know something? You will probably be in Rome before me."

"You never know."

"True. We do have some enemy guns left between us and the Tiber."

And it was not long until past Gaeta we came to the hills that rose on our left and undulated parallel to the Tyrrhenian Sea. All about us was the litter of earlier battles, destruction made by the retreating German guns as well as our own. I halted the column and reminded every man of his part in our duty; reissued warnings as to mines, booby traps, and cover. Once again we checked all equipment—mortars, wire cutters, rifles, carbines, ammunition, grenades, field rations. And then I gave the order to follow me and we began to ascend the near slope carefully.

There is an official report of the action that followed. It appeared in a publication of the War Department Historical Division called "Reconnaissance and Patrol Action, Ground Forces," and was published in 1946. It is accurate as to the material facts, and was based on interviews and written reports undertaken shortly after the whole episode. I saw most of what it reports. I may have felt what my soldiers felt. But I do not trust my feeling, for no matter how respectfully I shared the experience of those men, I cannot presume to live it again for them and imagine their heartbeats and the chills of their flesh. I can speak only for myself—and I must do so. For the rest, I quote from the official report, making comments wherever the further truth might be put to its liberating purpose.

The report:

Lieutenant English's detachment of two squads returned to the ridges southwest of Vitri on schedule. The terrain rose in terraces formerly farmed under irrigation. Vegetation was sparse and torn by earlier artillery fire. The first objective of the patrol was to reach a commanding position above the junction of the roads at the southern outskirts of Vitri, there to await in concealment the arrival of the 504th Armored Infantry from the battle areas to the northeast along Highway 6. The second objective of the patrol was to proceed by the ridges as the 504th advanced by the road in the valley until the two forces should face the Castle of Vitri from front and rear, from which positions they were to destroy enemy positions in the castle and clear a small but important obstacle from the path of the Fifth Army coastal movement upon Rome.

The estimated time of meeting at the junction was 1120 hours.

Ascending the spine of the ridges, Lieutenant English halted his detachment just below the crest of the first hill and, taking two men, S/Sgt. Sommersgill and Pfc. Pazzetti, cautiously advanced to the crest while the remainder of the men covered him with small arms. The crest proved to be clear, and on the return of Pfc. Pazzetti with the proper order, the rest of the party moved up and the advance con-

tinued. This procedure was followed on each of the ensuing eminences.

At 1025 the detachment heard bombardment from the north. German artillery was laying a concentration upon the lateral road between Highways 6 and 7. This was the road upon which the 504th Armored Infantry was to proceed to the southwest. The wind was from the north and the sound of the cannonading carried distinctly.

We all heard it. First we would hear the shells when they went wild and passed over us instead of over the road where our own forces were coming. The shells, which we could not see, sounded near to us, and made an airy whistle, like the wings of ducks cutting fast through the air—wha-wha-wha—soft and exciting and mysterious. Then the shells would land a good distance away behind us, and depending on the wind, rumble in our ears or sound like spray.

Radley was next to me at one point when the first shells went over, and he prayed. I heard him. "Holy Mary, Mother of——"

Whamp!

Poomb!

"——God, pray for us sinners, now——"

Qui-i-ish!

"——and at the hour of our death——"

And he would bend his head and hold his breath, and his prayer, as those funny-paper noises broke and shook the earth under us.

"—Amen."

Radley raised his face from the dirt and smiled like a child in relief, and unashamed.

And then, as the shells landed and exploded far away, the wind brought the slamming of doors, great doors, in a vast room, full of gray cold sky and nothing else.

The report continues:

Realizing that impassable conditions due to enemy artillery fire along the connecting road might require a change of plan, Lieutenant English attempted to contact his headquarters by radio, but could hear only an echo of his own voice. He then gave the order to advance, reminding the men that the terrain was familiar to them. Cpl. Gates stated that it was his belief that they were not retracing their steps of the night before, but were taking a different course. Other members of the same squad disagreed with him, and pointed out what had become, to them, landmarks. Cpl. Gates remarked that he did not remember a low mound at the edge of a terrace that lay ahead. Sgt. Shawcross declared that he remembered it, and that it simply looked different by daylight. He said he knew what was on the other side. Without permission from Lieutenant English, he then proceeded to cross the terrace at a run and disappeared over the small mound. There was an immediate explosion, followed by silence. Lieutenant English and T/Sgt. Martinsen carefully advanced to check on what happened.

They found Sgt. Shawcross and two German soldiers, all dead of a grenade. Evidently the Germans were about to launch the grenade when Sgt. Shawcross unexpectedly landed upon them. The German position was well dug-in, equipped with mortar and grenades, and presented the likelihood of other similar installations which the night patrol, having proceeded with silence and caution, had not alerted and betrayed into action.

Shawcross we moved from his bloody brotherhood with the enemy. The chaplain came to him and prayed for him. I took his tags and pocket treasures. He went out like a little rocket, one flare of motion, a dashing track of movement, and his only, last burst of color, fire and sound. It may have been the death of a feeble man, but it saved how many of our lives I could not guess.

The report continues:

The party moved forward again cautiously along the narrow trail of the next ridge and encountered no obstacles as the last crest and its long rocky approach came into view.

The time was now 1055. Twenty-five minutes remained until the estimated time of meeting with the other forces coming from Highway 6. The approach to the last crest was a long sharp ridge rising to a maximum height at its terminus of approximately five hundred feet. It was for the most part bare of vegetation, and was sharp enough for parties only a few feet below on either slope to be concealed from one another. Lieutenant English instructed S/Sgt. Sommersgill to take all but one man and lead them up the west side of the ridge, keeping as near the top as possible without showing themselves, while he himself, taking Pfc. Radley, would go up the other side to watch for enemy movements below, in the vicinity of Highway 7 leading to Vitri. The detachment would assemble at the crest from which they could judge their next problem.

* * *

"Yes, sir," in every inch of him, was what Sommersgill proclaimed to me. He was now my ardent follower, worthy of the trust I had given him, valiant because I made him so, and ever the same youth with the heroically carved face that for so long looked down in marble upon Greek games and Roman forums. I had taught him by the dozens for years. What lumbering struggle to evoke from those bulky varsity sweaters and those brows pale from leather helmets, one instant's genuine awareness of anything whatever out of the past or implicit in the future. The instant of the breath, the gaze, the touch, the want, the wish, was all that was real to them, and it was real in a contentment so profound that any other human cognition whatsoever always appeared by contrast to be perverse, malicious, or just all made up. Now Sommersgill had his series of instants to realize, and he was admirably ready.

The chaplain went with me and Radley, which made Radley very happy. Boy. Was this protection! Bless me, father, for I have sinned.

S/Sgt. Sommersgill moved out, leading his detail, while Lieutenant English and Pfc. Radley crawled forward and upward on the opposite side of the ridge. The artillery barrage had continued and now it suddenly ceased. Lieutenant English halted to listen, not at first realizing what had caused him to do so. Far away to the north could be seen lingering smoke above the concealed German gun positions. Bombs from Allied planes soon fell and exploded upon the enemy emplacements.

Oh, but there was a curious feeling about our part in what was going on. We knew heavy battles were alight not far inland, and many more would have to be fought before Rome, and after. Yet to ourselves we seemed to be the only ones moving at all in that wasteland. We knew that if we were not doing the job we were doing, someone else would be sent to do it. But the important fact there was that it was we, not someone else, who crawled like mantises up the rocky slope making the movements of life—our lives—amid the enormous mapped activity about which we knew, and some of which we could see. Way behind us, endless columns of troop-transport trucks, and foot soldiers, ammunition and supply trains, hospitals and chaplains' gear and printed booklets and movie film and radio stars and graves-registration people were coming up Highway 7 and were going to go by here toward Rome because we would make it possible—we on our rocky spine.

Inland, deeply parallel to us, on Highway 6, the tanks were meat-grinding their way up the Liri Valley and little outfits like ours were jabbing in and out of the mountains between distance and death. Above us and ahead went our planes, knowing nothing about us each, but something about us all, and doing what they alone could do to keep the connection. Up the coast at Anzio our beachhead was spreading slowly like spilled ink on a map toward the other stain which we from the south were inching forward in our capillary nature.

Lieutenant English and Pfc. Radley were able to move faster than S/Sgt. Sommersgill and his large detail. The crawling was rough over the rocky incline. They paused to rest several times. Lieutenant English saw Pfc. Radley lift his head and listen, as though he heard something across the ridge, and then heard him say, 'How are you guys doing, sergeant?' thinking that the other detail was exactly opposite on the other slope of the ridge. Even as he waved Pfc. Radley to be quiet, a grenade came over the ridge and exploded ten feet away from Pfc. Radley, a fragment striking him in the belly. Lieutenant English rolled himself upward, on the bare ridge, readying a grenade as he did so, and as soon as he had visibility, lobbed his grenade at three German soldiers crouching near the crest. The grenade killed one, and wounded another. The third, covered from the explosion by his comrades, rose to run down the slope. Lieutenant English fired at him with his carbine, but missed. But in a moment shots came from elsewhere and the German fell.

Lieutenant English saw S/Sgt. Sommersgill's detachment farther down the enemy side of the ridge. Cpl. Gates fired the shots that brought down the third German. This marked the last resistance encountered by the detachment in reaching their first objective, the crest overlooking the junction of the roads, the village and castle of Vitri, and the sickle-shaped piece of high ground, flat on top, that swept around the rear of the village and faced the castle. This piece of high ground was called the Subway Station, for its resemblance to a platform, dropping away to the depression where tracks might run. In effect it was a large natural moat, no doubt taken into account when the castle was built.

Oh, yes; protection for Radley, in the way he really must have meant, after all, for the chaplain knelt by him and gave him the rites for the dying. The chaplain was hunched up over his praying hands, his head on one side, leaning over the young soldier, smiling at him, making the sign of the cross over his face, all but touching him, and yet touching him like the rays of the sky throughout his being, with enormous, entire responsibility of one man for another, and showing the pure immeasurable empowerment of love. Radley was conscious and beyond pain from shock, and he rested happy in the echoes of the noises of impact and destruction until under the thin, little, brown, hardly contained love of God in the chaplain, he died. Not everybody has a chance to see the love of God. I saw it. It made me look away because my need for it myself was only general, not particular and final. Mine was the harder need, I think.

Once on the crest, the detachment had a little time to rest, for they reached it at 1105. They identified now the second, and final, objective of their mission, the castle of Vitri. The crest fell away on a long incline, smoother and even barer than the uphill approach just traversed. Lieutenant English kept his men out of sight just below the last ridge. He used his field glasses to study the double situation before him.

He saw that the castle was manned on two levels. Openings in the battlements revealed machine guns and enemy soldiers on a first platform facing east about eighty feet above the highway, and similar armament on a second platform, set back at a higher level, facing south. The main tower rose above to a height of about sixty feet. There was no evidence that this topmost pinnacle was manned. Tall, narrow slits in the old masonry of the tower showed daylight beyond, indicating the far wall of the tower was largely a gaping ruin. The main normal access to the castle was to the west. A moat ran about the base of the castle. The whole structure was a ruin, but with well-preserved features, such as the walls above the town, the platforms with their battlemented edges, and the profile of the tower. Various courtyards, interior rooms, and levels could be assumed from the general conformation presented to observation from Lieutenant English's hill crest, but not with accuracy. Lieutenant English estimated that from one squad to a platoon of German soldiers occupied the castle, for he could clearly see men moving about on the two armed platforms.

To his right, he could see the lateral road as it approached the village and the junction with Highway 7. According to plan, he expected to see the forward elements of the Allied armored force coming along that road within a little while. At 1120 the meeting was to take place. Lieutenant English detailed Cpl. Gates and Pfc. Pazzetti to be in readiness to descend the inland slope of the ridge to make contact with the armored column and to return with instructions bearing on a co-ordinated attack upon the castle. However, from where he was, it looked to Lieutenant English as if the meeting might be delayed if not canceled, for he saw smoke rising in the distance above what seemed to be the course of the connecting road, and assumed that the enemy artillery concentration had been leveled on the advancing armored column headed for the junction at Vitri.

Once again he tried his radio to report on what he saw and to ask for any information concerning a possible change of plan. This time he thought he was about to make contact with the main body to the rear on Highway 7, but what sounded at first like response was another echo of his own voice.

He now, after the loss of two men, had a total of fourteen men in his two squads. One of these was injured as a result of a fall during the advance. Lieutenant English ordered him to find cover and remain there in case the unit moved out again.

The German artillery now resumed its action, and there was no doubt that it was leveled against the connecting road, for the party on the crest could plainly see the shell bursts all along the route of the Allied armored-infantry column.

The castle. It belonged in a Book of Hours, or a tapestry. It was not a large fortress. But in its time it had no need to be, for its perch on its high-cliffed rock was worth a thousand men at arms. The land rose from the level of the town, and swooped up three times as high as any roof at its base. The castle walls continued the rise of the cliff at its very edge. The rock was black. The walls were like volcanic waste. The sky was heavy with sandy light. The sea beyond was a band of pale iron. Far away were the slow drifts of smoke from artillery fire, and bombed places. In the cold morning the German soldiers had made a little bonfire on the parapet in the shelter of the battlements. Its striving flame made the only bit of bright color in all of Italy.

There it sat under its eighth century of sky, the castle, alive once more with defenders, blindly restored to its first purpose, and rising across my path with its requirement of duty, beautiful, impossible, and brutally appealing. An anger as cruel as the castle's founding purpose rose in me as I faced it.

There seemed a brutality about that rotting old masonry which directly menaced me.

When I spoke into my walkie-talkie, who answered me? The voice of one who could tell me nothing. What was the fact about television? If you release something on a certain frequency, and there is a receiving apparatus adjusted to the same frequency, you will receive what is sent. I spoke, and none heard me. I sent, and I was not received. At 1120 hours I must speak once more. I must send what nobody with me wanted to hear. My power to make images was gone.

I raised my glasses and looked out at the road that came to a junction at the base of my hill. The shells were bursting in fading depths of gray, cold distance. My heart jumped. If the enemy stopped the armored-infantry column which was to come to meet us here, then I would be alone and powerless. It would be folly to launch an attack against the castle with only my meager forces. My spirits rose and I knew myself well as I betrayed with hidden relief those other men, the armored column even at that instant suffering destruction from enemy shellfire. Many a pearly, sumptuous burst I could see far away along the connecting road meant a steel blow against a jaw like this one, or a shower of earth burying a body like mine, or a sightless fling of metal into a soft belly such as here made a qualm of guilt, or a crash of thigh bone against a steel car and a papery crumble of a man's stance to an inert heap of flesh like me, or a single ray of mind ending in darkness forever such as I could mimic in self-hatred by shutting my eyes against my own gladness.

For I knew they were not coming. They could never survive and pass through that shellfire. Dead, maimed, scattered, the men would fall. Ringing and echoing to bursts, the armored vehicles would lurch to a halt, like great beetles dried to dust inside their housings. And if they did not come, I need do nothing but return to Gaeta.

My watch moved to 1116, 1117, 1118 hours. There was no sign on the road below.

"They seem to be a little late," said a light, cadenced voice next to my ear. It was the chaplain, showing me his watch.

"Yes."

"Well, it is hard to make direct connections in things of this sort. I suppose you will wait for them a while, anyway?"

If I thought I was free of him, then I was wrong. He looked at me and I believed he saw the pictures traveling behind my eyes. He received.

"Yes, we'll wait a while, of course. But they'll never come through that. Look at it."

I handed him my glasses. He screwed up his narrow little face and pawed the glasses like the cleverest of primates and read in the distant air the rearing idea of those bursts. He nodded and gave the glasses back.

"They will never come," he said. "May God be with them. It was a fine idea, but it didn't work. And then?"

"And then?"

"Yes. Have you thought it all out?"

"Thought what out? There is nothing to think out. Our plan has failed, that is all."

"Yes, it has failed, but there is always another."

"Another?"

"That is, if the original purpose which was so important still seems so important."

"Oh?"

"The main body on Highway 7. Won't they still be coming up? I suppose they still plan to go to Rome."

"Surely."

"How miserable, lieutenant, for anyone who does not have Rome to go to. Or some equivalent for Rome, in his life."

He knew the depth of my betrayal then.

Why could not this moment have been the morality of which I must die?

I looked at him, and his small brilliant black eyes pierced me with their darts of light that passed through me as easily as through air. They gave me pain. Some sweetness for the world shone in his eyes, that embraced man as he was, weak or strong, loyal or false, good or evil.

"Isn't it odd," he said almost in a whisper, "this is one of those occasions when military necessity and the real meaning of sacrifice come together as one and the same thing?"

He pointed back toward Highway 7 at the south, and then nodded to the castle's garrisoned obstacle to northward progress, and Rome—Rome.

I put my head down and shut my eyes. In my own darkness I could see. There I saw what I must do.

When I looked up again, the chaplain was still gazing at me, and as I raised my head, he raised his, watching, synchronized with my movements, alive and alert to me in every way.

"Good, good," he said excitedly in his little whisper when he saw my face. "Tell me what to do. It is going to be bad, very tough; we may even flub it, but I bet we don't. Tell me!"

I said nothing. Like a little chipmunk he peered over the stony crest at the castle.

"The one to capture, the real castle, is not over there," he said, gesturing toward the old stained walls; "it is a much tougher fort, with much cleverer defenses"—gesturing toward his breast, the secret cave of personality. "Get this one, and that one"—lifting his chin a trifle like a Mexican to indicate the real castle again—"will fall easy, or if it does not fall, it will not matter."

I did not answer him. I backed up on my belly like a crab until I was among the soldiers and I told them to retire with me a little distance down the slope hidden from the castle.

The report continues:

Lieutenant English considered it probable that the armored-infantry column would never be able to keep its rendezvous at the Vitri junction. Enemy shellfire was too consistent, sustained, and concentrated to permit any progress in that direction. He therefore estimated the situation as to the castle's vulnerability, and weighed it against the importance of the mission assigned to his detachment, viz., the silencing of the enemy fire that commanded the Vitri road along which our main body expected to pass early in the afternoon.

Retiring with his men a short distance, Lieutenant English explained the situation to them. It was now 1135 with no sign of the armored column from the east. He told the detachment that if there was no sign of its arrival by 1200, they would prepare to carry out their mission unaided.

In reply to questions, some of them in the nature of protests, Lieutenant English posed the alternatives. He could wait for forward elements to come along on Highway 7 and with tank-mounted artillery knock out the battery in the castle. But this would be an observed operation, permitting the enemy to radio the position of the main body to rear German artillery which would then lower heavy fire on our forces. On the other hand, an attempt on the castle by a small force would avoid this danger and through surprise might succeed. The last alternative was to withdraw to report, but inherent in this course was the same danger as in the first alternative above.

Lieutenant English then outlined his improvised plan for proceeding with his mission. He divided his available force of thirteen men into three parties. The first was to consist of himself and two men; the second of four men, armed with 60mm. mortars in two teams, commanded by T/Sgt. Martinsen; and the third of six men, armed with rifles and grenades, including the rifle-grenade, commanded by S/ Sgt. Sommersgill. At 1200 hours, unless by then the armored column on the connecting road had begun to make its appearance, these would carry out their assigned duties, which were as follows:

Lieutenant English and his two men were to enter the castle by the Subway Station approach, going down into the dry moat and up again through the main gate at the rear. To facilitate their entry through surprise these three men, regardless of the danger attendant upon it, were to be dressed in the uniforms of the Germans who had been killed or wounded on the ridge in the path of S/Sgt. Sommersgill's party. T/Sgt. Martinsen's party was to infiltrate the village, keeping cover and taking up a position from which to launch mortar fire onto the lower platform of the castle as soon as they could hear the sound of grenades and small-arms fire at the upper platform. S/Sgt. Sommersgill's detachment was to make an approach to the Subway Station and rush the main gate as reinforcements when they heard the sounds of action at both front and rear of the castle. Lieutenant English, in order to give T/Sgt. Martinsen time to reach and take up his position below in the town, would not begin his action at the castle until 1315 hours, when the detonations of his attack would be the signal for the action of the co-ordinated support. The principles employed in the movement were those of dispersion, co-ordination, and surprise.

Pfc. Pazzetti was sent back with another man to strip the Germans of their uniforms and arms. Returning, they reported that the German who had been wounded was now dead. One of the uniforms was extremely bloody from grenade explosion at close quarters. Lieutenant English put this on, and his two other men also changed clothes. They had a good supply now of captured grenades in addition to their own. A captured German burp gun was now also available. In their German helmets, and wearing used and soiled German uniforms, these men were at a few paces not distinguishable from Germans.

It was agreed that as soon as the fight was joined at the castle, they would remove their upper clothing as a safety measure so as to be recognized by their own troops and not fired upon. After a few more questions and answers of a routine nature Lieutenant English returned to the crest of the hill and waited 1200 hours and the possible relief along the connecting road, which, however, did not materialize.

Therefore, at 1205, the movements began according to plan, Lieutenant English and his two masquerade Germans, followed at a discreet distance by the reinforcing party of S/Sgt. Sommersgill, proceeding under cover down the offside slope until it fell away into the open approach which afforded no concealment; and T/Sgt. Martinsen's detail following a gully down to the highway along whose edge they would proceed as skirmishers into the cover of the empty town.

The blood was cold and moist and soft on my belly inside the dead German's tunic. His blood was upon me, not only metaphorically but physically. I used his blood to dupe his friends. We went forward down the slope hidden from the castle. We went fast now. Everything appeared to go fast. Before long we were at the end of our cover, where the ridge flattened out and turned its two opposite slopes into a single long wide hillside facing the sky. The chaplain was beside me when I halted and waited for Sommersgill's men to catch up with us, there to await our time to act.

"I must stay here," said the chaplain, sweeping his brilliant little hand down across his American uniform. "I would ruin you if I came along now, they would see my outfit, and wonder why I was with three Germans. Unless you could capture me and take me with you?" he added in delight. "Push me ahead with a rifle muzzle, and my hands up, and my mouth opening and closing, scared, you know, and wabbling on my knees, like that, do you think?"

"No, chaplain. You'd just get hurt and you couldn't help."

"Yes, sure, I knew you'd have to do it someday and send me back when I got to be a nuisance." He sighed without vanity. "Still," he added, "when these other fellows take out after you, I can come with them. Okay?"

"Okay, chaplain."

He shut one eye in a sportive wink, snikked a bit of wordless slang with his back teeth and tongue through one side of his mouth, and thumb-and-fingered a circle of confirmation and glee.

The report:

In their bloodied German uniforms Lieutenant English and his two men, Pfc. Pazzetti and Pvt. Bauer, set out, the latter two supporting the former as though he were badly wounded. It was 1310 hours. They had about two hundred yards to go. Proceeding rapidly, to give the effect of a charge for cover, they came to the flattened level area which was called the Subway Station, and seeing that its edge dropped gently into the deep moat which was lined with grass and winter weeds, they went down into it and skirted the base of the walls. A graveled path led up to the main gate of the castle from the moat. The raiding party climbed this and came to the gate.

Lieutenant English held a grenade in his right hand inside his tunic. Pfc. Pazzetti and Pvt. Bauer carried rifles in their free hands. Large stones fallen from the masonry of the entrance arch partly blocked the entrance, beyond which could be seen a courtyard open to the sky and paved with large blocks between which grass grew. In the opposite wall of the courtyard was an entrance to a long corridor, or tunnel, at the distant end of which our men saw an arched patch of daylight and a wide space. On that far wide space German soldiers were visible moving idly back and forth. Lieutenant English saw that that distant open space was the upper one of the platforms on which guns were mounted.

Hoping Martinsen was in position below in the town to go into action on hearing sounds of fighting at the castle, Lieutenant English, impersonating the attitude of a wounded man, now moved forward into the courtyard with his two helpers. He was ready to haul out his grenade, pull its pin with his teeth and let it fly. As the party passed through the deep archway of the main gate they made a certain amount of noise. A young German soldier, then another, came from out of sight in the courtyard beyond to see what approached, and then observing what they believed were wounded comrades, showed concern and came forward to help.

They came like inquiring young cats with the diffuse light in the pale fur of their heads.

They were sentries on duty, but at ease, not expecting so unlikely an attempt as a hand-to-hand attack upon the castle. Their helmets were off, their tunics unbuttoned, and they laid down their rifles as they approached. In another moment they would recognize their enemies, so Lieutenant English suddenly shoved his supporters aside, giving them a chance to bring their rifles to the ready, while he covered the sentries with his captured machine pistol. In their astonishment the sentries were speechless, and under warning, made no sound as they were bound with their own belts and gagged by the two enlisted men. They were then dragged out of sight behind some stone rubble in a corner of the courtyard. The first defense of the castle had been breached.

The next objective was the distant platform to be approached through the long dark corridor. The raiders resumed their masquerade of limping wounded and entered the tunnel. As they neared its far exit they readied grenades and pulled the pins eight steps before reaching the tunnel's end. Coming out into daylight again they saw that seven Germans were ranged along the southern parapet by two machine guns, while two others were squatting by a heavy mortar that faced out toward the east over the lower platform and the road below. One of the Germans noticed the intruders and exclaimed, and as they all began in irregular movement to rise up to help the wounded, Lieutenant English and the two other soldiers lifted their grenades, two to the south parapet, one to the east, and fell flat to the paving as the detonations went off.

That was the signal to T/Sgt. Martinsen below. Lieutenant English counted up to eleven and then heard the sound of a 60mm. mortar from below, and he knew that T/Sgt. Martinsen was in action. A second later a mortar shell exploded out of sight on the lower platform to the east, and was almost immediately answered by machine-gun fire from that position, invisible to those on the upper platform.

The grenade bursts killed two Germans, badly wounded two others, and disorganized the remaining five, one of whom, however, reached for his rifle. Lieutenant English shot him with his machine pistol. The others saw that they were covered at close range, and upon being told by Lieutenant English to surrender, complied with their hands in the air. Pfc. Pazzetti gathered up the emplaced German weapons and pitched them over the parapet into the moat far below, while Pvt. Bauer disarmed the Germans of body weapons and herded them into a corner of the platform and mounted guard over them. Lieutenant English then went to look over the east battlement to see the lower platform. He could see one of the gun emplacements and its squads.

T/Sgt. Martinsen's mortar fire from the village below had done damage and was keeping it up. One German gun was knocked out and its survivors were making for shelter out of sight below. The second machine gun was protected from the view of the upper platform by a jutting canopy of stone which later proved to be part of an ancient forge used in the castle armory. Under this protection the second machine gun kept up a fierce fire upon the town where T/Sgt. Martinsen's mortars betrayed their position with smoke. As he watched, Lieutenant English saw one of the mortars knocked out. T/Sgt. Martinsen had found good positions in heaps of rubble in the village.

There was now silence while he moved to a new position with his remaining mortar. Lieutenant English rolled a grenade off the stone canopy below, and it fell clear and exploded, but did not silence the machine gun below, which seemed to be shielded by a wall that supported the roof.

He then turned back to his own men and gave the order to throw off their German tunics. They threw the coats over the side. Instructing Pvt. Bauer to remain on guard with the prisoners and taking Pfc. Pazzetti with him, Lieutenant English then started for the tunnel to find a way down to the lower platform in order to silence the remaining machine gun which T/Sgt. Martinsen's mortars had not been able to reach. But before they had taken a step or two, they were fired upon from within the tunnel, and immediately threw themselves against the wall through which the tunnel opened. Lieutenant English was grazed by a bullet which bloodied his left shoulder.

He could not believe that S/Sgt. Sommersgill had already reached the castle with his reinforcements, and in any case it had been prearranged that he was not to fire upon German soldiers with half their uniforms off. It seemed therefore likely that survivors of the knocked-out machine gun on the lower platform had come to engage the invading party on the upper level.

Lieutenant English crawled close to the edge of the tunnel archway and called, "Sommersgill! Are you in there?" There was no reply. All firing ceased for a minute.

The silence was as sweet as cold water in the desert. I listened. Tiny secret sounds came from the dark tunnel. The breathing of human beings. It made me want to laugh. I could figure the glare of cunning and caution in the animal eyes within the corridor; the illusion of safety in secrecy such as those men long ago rehearsed in play, and as I had seen at home my own young children seek.

Reluctant to risk tossing a grenade into the tunnel if by any misunderstanding his own men should be there, Lieutenant English tried again. "Sergeant Sommersgill! This is English! Answer me!" The answer was a grenade tossed out onto the platform. But in order not to hurt those within the tunnel it had to be tossed too far to hurt those on the grass-lined pavement, provided they flung themselves on their faces, which they did. At almost the same moment, the machine gun below began to fire again, and Lieutenant English was glad to hear

T/Sgt. Martinsen's 60mm. reply. The two-man mortar teams could carry only a limited supply of ammunition, and he feared that T/Sgt. Martinsen's detail might already have run out of shells.

There was then another sound far back in the tunnel. Driven before it, five Germans ran out of the tunnel, firing back into the darkness. In close pursuit was S/Sgt. Sommersgill, followed by his reinforcing party. The Germans were trapped and without being ordered to do so, dropped their weapons and folded their hands on top of their heads. Lieutenant English checked the number of the rescuing group, which should have numbered six. One was missing. S/Sgt. Sommersgill reported, "Cpl. Gates was hit by machine-gun fire as we came down the slope. We had to leave him there."

And there was another. The report nowhere mentions the chaplain. He was not supposed to be with us, he had no combat duty to perform, and his regular assignment in no way would account for his activities of that day. Therefore officially he was not present, and the report ignored him.

"Sommersgill, where is the padre?" I asked.

"I don't know," he replied. "He was tailing us, but we lost him somewhere."

The report then says that I said:

" 'Sommersgill, there must be a way down to that lower platform. The Germans in the tunnel must have come from down below, inside, somewhere. Take some men and go to see. We can't shut them up from here.' To which S/Sgt. Sommersgill replied, 'Yes, sir.' "

He licked his left thumb with a fast little jab like a man going into a football play, and took three men into the tunnel.

I went to the parapet and looked over the long hill that flowed like a sigh down toward the castle. There, lying along halfway down the slope, was a figure. It was Gates, in agony. His bulky body rolled and rocked in cradled pain. I imagined a call coming from those coarse-grained lips and a milky look in his terrified eyes.

As I watched, the earth about him sprang up in small fountains and drifted as dust on the moving air. The machine gun was again shooting at him from the platform below.

Next I saw emerge from the sheer shelter of the castle under me the little scrambling person of the chaplain, running in a dodging zigzag.

He ran to Gates. He made a picture of supreme gaiety, if you looked at it abstractly. His dancing flight, his arms hugged to his side in their pumping motions, his twinkling legs, his bare head shining without its too-heavy helmet, was a hilarious defiance of the intelligence behind the machine gun on the platform below. Where the bullets made earthen spray, he was absent. Where he ran a second ago, he no longer was. The bullets spun a waving line that crossed his path always a trifle too late, for with a jump, he was either on a new course, or after a feint, safe on his old one.

I held my breath as I watched. Other soldiers joined me, to see. It was as plain as spoken thought that the chaplain could not bear to see a wounded man mercilessly fired upon without protection.

"To Gates!" said someone, and we all remembered his treatment of the chaplain hours ago up the road.

The little flying figure got there. He threw himself down against Gates and began to haul out a first-aid kit. The bullets swept now closer and closer and in a narrower arc with every sweep. The world was in a staring silence as we watched the dusty little fountains spring up closer and closer to the two huddled men. The chaplain felt something on his bare neck. It was flying dirt. He turned and made a quick glance. There was much to see, but he turned back, and making himself into as big a man as he could, he spread his arms over Gates, he laid his body along Gates' side, and gave himself as a shield for life in whatever way you interpret the word.

The hot spatter found him and packed him with death. The sweeps caressed him again and again, quite without necessity.

"Sommersgill," I thought, begging him to hurry.

The work out on the bland, dusty, cold-lighted slope was over in very little time, however long it seemed as we watched.

There came a burst of fire somewhere else, it came from below, and the machine gun ceased. We heard another spurt of rifle fire, and then that, too, stopped. There was a yell. I went to the other side of the parapet and looked over. Sommersgill was down there, yelling with happiness and shaking his arms at the sky. The exultation of having made a scoring play was upon him and he gave it to the others. Suddenly one of them pointed to Sommersgill's right leg. It was streaming with blood. He looked down at himself and his carved mouth went half open. His steps faltered.

Comrades went to hold him up, relieving him of his weapons. They started to walk him toward rest and comfort out of my sight. He walked as though in a dream of walking. He was borne along slowly by succor, and the echoes of dying cheers seemed to sting shrilly like locust swarms about his bent head. In his triumph the athlete was hurt and taken from the arena.

The report then concludes:

Lieutenant English went down to the lower platform, finding his way through an entrance that gave off the first courtyard and down stone stairs in bad repair. Another tunnel like the one above led to the open air of the lower platform. There he found more prisoners—the crew of the machine gun in the armory. Pfc. Pazzetti was dead, having been shot in the forehead. S/Sgt. Sommersgill was wounded. The platform was cleared, and all prisoners were then assembled from all parts of the castle in the first courtyard and a guard posted. The castle was carefully searched for hidden pockets of resistance, but none further was discovered. Lieutenant English sent two men to find T/Sgt. Martinsen to report, and to bring him in with his men. With two other men, Lieutenant English went to the long hill approach to see what could be done for Cpl. Gates. The castle was taken, and the mission of this small reconnaissance patrol was accomplished without the massive reinforcements originally planned for the operation.

Gates was living. He was a huge heavy baby who cried and cried, in great sluicing sobs, for the goodness in the world that was his to know, and feel, through the life that had been given to him by the death of another man.

The chaplain lay beside him barely in a whole body. His face was just collected enough to hold an expression. His eyes were shut from the lower lids up, like a little bird's. A wry smile was on his mouth. A painful frown was on his brow. There had not in the first place been much of him to protect anybody with, and there was less now, but so long as there is enough, it must surely never matter how much; and there was enough here.

My men helped Gates to go with them. I sat on my heels by the chaplain and thought of what I should think of. In my great victory was my great shame. I grieved for him as the sacrifice that had to be illustrated before it could be believed.

In our triumph over a ruin on the Appian Way to Rome, we had on that day made certain progress. He had said to me that morning that I would be in Rome before him. But his joke came back, too, about going to Rome when he died. It was only polite to smile now with agreement, and to say, yes, he was there, then, already, and ahead of us after all. Even alone with his death I was a little embarrassed when I did what I did; but I did it. I leaned down and took from his field-jacket collar the gold leaf and the silver cross of his rank and service and put them into my pocket, knowing what somehow I would manage to do with them when I could.

Then I put his poor hands together in crimson prayer on his templed chest where the little arched bones were in ruins, making him as respectable as possible under the circumstances; and returned to the castle.

We tried our radio. This time we got through. I reported that the way through Vitri was clear. Our men gathered around as I talked into the mike. They pulled at my eyes with theirs to get what was thought of our report.

Once again I was able to send, and be received. The power to make images was restored to me. The soldiers would now go with me to anything; and that was well, for there was yet more to do in the world that held us.

At 1540 hours we saw the first sign of the coastal main body coming up from the south, from the sleeping names that were awakened out of antiquity by the news of the year 1944—up from Messina, up from Paestum, Salerno, Naples, Santa Maria, Capua, the Volturno, the Garigliano, Minturno, Gaeta. Tanks led the column.

At the junction nobody met them but my detachment. They went winding by in their engined grandeur, through the village of Vitri, past the silent and deserted castle where men at arms had once more fallen on that day, and out on Highway 7 toward the next German defense position on the way to Rome. The corps went by. Nobody in it really knew what had made it possible for them to pass at this particular point. My soldiers watched for a while. Tankers in their turrets might wave indifferently as they went by us. One dogface to another might grin in cordial mockery. The corps ground its way by and late in the afternoon absorbed us once again, as we were given places to ride, in a truck.

"You?" I could imagine the chaplain saying with his shining black-currant eyes and his enormous grin. "To be appreciated, thanked, praised? This is what you are waiting for?"

And then his image gestured toward the men going past who were alive and unhurt.

We rode our truck in the column. It was colder. We thought of our dead awaiting the graves-registration squad, and our wounded, safe in a tent hospital to the rear, and we shivered, not only with the cold but with the mystery of our survival, the good heaviness of our bones and flesh riding the bumps of the road, and the flight of chance all about us in our battle.

The road curves to the right leaving Vitri. An evening wind was rising off the Tyrrhenian Sea. As we looked back at the castle, the sky was torn open and the clouds raged near above us. Shafts of light made a triumph in the scene, and the whole blaze of the place made heroes of us as we rumbled on our way toward night and our next billet.

By deep twilight we were at the edge of the Pontine Marshes. Our truck was halted near one of the first of the reclaimed fields of Benito Mussolini's technology. A few new stucco houses badly damaged by retreating Germans stood off in the irrigated meadow. The nearest one showed lamplight. We made our billet for the night by the roadside, heated our rations, and then got to talking. The day passed by us again. Everyone should have fallen asleep bolt upright like the volcanic mummies of Herculaneum, but the excitement and accomplishments of the day were too great to die away so soon. They would be forgotten, frowned over, and vainly called for soon enough.

Martinsen was the first to raise to the spoken level of the mind the desire for completion, the punctuation of the long sentence written in action that day. He made two or three long, deep, quivering breaths and said, Did they know what? He had seen a woman near the house across the field.

My platoon was not employed in forward action any more in the battle for Rome. Early in June we entered the city by the Porta di San Sebastiano. The late-afternoon air was dense with dust, and dusty rose-colored parallels of light shafted over the rosy stones of Rome. Our column moved slowly but without any freeing halts. I could see the dome of St. Peter's like a soft cloud in the filtering dust above the city. It looked immense from a distance and seemed to retain its size without increasing as we neared it, though all other buildings about it grew with diminished distance. Something moved in me when I saw the whole face of St. Peter's as we crossed the Via della Conciliazione on our way out of the city. It was in warm gray shadow. Vast, sumptuous, implacably majestic, it yet seemed alive with the dancing heart of the small nimble man I had left on the hillside of Vitri.

A few days later I had my chance to return to Rome with a courier bag for an Allied military mission that was at work there. I went as on a pilgrimage.

The vast basilica was not off limits. I went in early afternoon to St. Peter's. My purpose was not to sight-see, but for a while I acted as if it were. I had with me the chaplain's insignia.

I dissembled my purpose, but for over an hour that afternoon I searched the walls of St. Peter's for a little crevice, a broken bit of time itself, a tiny tomb where I could put something as in a shrine. The impulse was as old as man and probably disreputable among my colleagues of that other life, and I was willing to keep it secret. But it was stronger than the rational amenities and lost in the spell of my debt to him. I searched until I found, in the gray ocherous travertine walls of the exterior, the little crumbled break in the body of the stones where I could put something of him as a part of the might and splendor where his light and modest spirit knew its home. I took the gold leaf and the silver cross and, making sure that I was not watched, I reached up on the wall and tapped them into a narrow deep crack between blocks of stone. With the clip of my .45 I was able to tap them home deep and out of sight.

The centuries now enclosed something of him with the saints who were buried within the cathedral, on the spot where the Emperor Constantine ordered the first basilica of St. Peter's to be built. I hoped nobody would ever find and dislodge those little bits of U.S. Army metal.

I hoped so. Perhaps I prayed so. I prayed without knowing how. Perhaps a man could think he had to know too much before he could get himself to do anything.

There were other human faculties to trust and to train as well as the chambered intellect. I was due back that night. I didn't linger in Rome. I crossed the Tiber in my car. I shall always see the rosy clay of the Rio Grande and the vista of the buildings of Rome as the same color.

We moved north into Umbria during June, and one day after we reached Narni there were orders for a number of officers and men to report to a formation to be held in front of the municipal palace. The little city was lost in a dream of earlier ruins than those of the current war. Summer was over the country now, and the sun shone through golden dust. The land was fair and all things of its mindless nature seemed disposed with justice and goodness.

But when I went to the town square to report in formation I was endangered by the cheap crime of cynicism, because in the way of victories, with forty-three other soldiers, I was decorated that day by the Commanding General of the Fifth Army for, in my case, the assault upon and capture of the Castle of Vitri.

JACK DANN

Camps

AS STEPHEN LIES in bed, he can think only of pain.

He imagines it as sharp and blue. After receiving an injection of Demerol, he enters pain's cold regions as an explorer, an objective visitor. It is a country of ice and glass, monochromatic plains and valleys filled with wash-blue shards of ice, crystal pyramids and pinnacles, squares, oblongs, and all manner of polyhedrons—block upon block of painted blue pain.

Although it is midafternoon, Stephen pretends it is dark. His eyes are tightly closed, but the daylight pouring into the room from two large windows intrudes as a dull red field extending infinitely behind his eyelids.

"Josie," he asks through cottonmouth, "aren't I due for another shot?" Josie is crisp and fresh and large in her starched white uniform. Her peaked nurse's cap is pinned to her mouse-brown hair.

"I've just given you an injection; it will take effect soon." Josie strokes his hand, and he dreams of ice.

"Bring me some ice," he whispers.

"If I bring you a bowl of ice, you'll only spill it again."

"Bring me some ice. . . ." By touching the ice cubes, by turning them in his hand like a gambler favoring his dice, he can transport himself into the beautiful blue country. Later, the ice will melt; and he will spill the bowl. The shock of cold and pain will awaken him.

Stephen believes that he is dying, and he has resolved to die properly. Each visit to the cold country brings him closer to death; and death, he has learned, is only a slow walk through ice fields. He has come to appreciate the complete lack of warmth and the beautifully etched face of his magical country.

But he is connected to the bright, flat world of the hospital by plastic tubes—one breathes cold oxygen into his left nostril, another passes into his right nostril and down his throat to his stomach; one feeds him intravenously, another draws his urine.

"Here's your ice," Josie says. "But mind you, don't spill it." She places the small bowl on his tray table and wheels the table close to him. She has a musky odor of perspiration and perfume; Stephen is reminded of old women and college girls.

"Sleep now, sweet boy."

Without opening his eyes, Stephen reaches out and places his hand on the ice.

"Come, now, Stephen, wake up. Dr. Volk is here to see you."

Stephen feels the cool touch of Josie's hand, and he opens his eyes to see the doctor standing beside him. The doctor has a gaunt, long face and thinning brown hair; he is dressed in a wrinkled green suit.

"Now we'll check the dressing, Stephen," he says as he tears away a gauze bandage on Stephen's abdomen.

Stephen feels the pain, but he is removed from it. His only wish is to return to the blue dreamlands. He watches the doctor peel off the neat crosshatching of gauze. A terrible stink fills the room.

Josie stands well away from the bed.

"Now we'll check your drains." The doctor pulls a long drainage tube out of Stephen's abdomen, irrigates and disinfects the wound, inserts a new drain, and repeats the process by pulling out another tube just below the rib cage.

Stephen imagines that he is swimming out of the room. He tries to cross the hazy border into cooler regions, but it is difficult to concentrate. He has only a half hour at most before the Demerol will wear off. Already, the pain is coming closer, and he will not be due for another injection until the night nurse comes on duty. But the night nurse will not give him an injection without an argument. She will tell him to fight the pain.

But he cannot fight without a shot.

"Tomorrow we'll take that oxygen tube out of your nose," the doctor says, but his voice seems far away and Stephen wonders what he is talking about.

He reaches for the bowl of ice, but cannot find it.

"Josie, you've taken my ice."

"I took the ice away when the doctor came. Why don't you try to watch a bit of television with me; Soupy Sales is on."

"Just bring me some ice," Stephen says. "I want to rest a bit." He can feel the sharp edges of pain breaking through the gauzy wraps of Demerol.

"I love you, Josie," he says sleepily as she places a fresh bowl of ice on his tray.

* * *

As Stephen wanders through his ice-blue dreamworld, he sees a rectangle of blinding white light. It looks like a doorway into an adjoining world of brightness. He has glimpsed it before, on previous Demerol highs. A coal-dark doorway stands beside the bright one.

He walks toward the portals, passes through white-blue conefields.

Time is growing short. The drug cannot stretch it much longer. Stephen knows that he has to choose either the bright doorway or the dark, one or the other. He does not even consider turning around, for he has dreamed that the ice and glass and cold blue gemstones have melted behind him.

It makes no difference to Stephen which doorway he chooses. On impulse he steps into blazing, searing whiteness.

Suddenly he is in a cramped world of people and sound.

The boxcar's doors were flung open. Stephen was being pushed out of the cramped boxcar, which stank of sweat, feces, and urine. Several people had died in the car and added their stink of death to the already fetid air.

"Carla, stay close to me," shouted a man beside Stephen. He had been separated from his wife by a young woman who pushed between them as she tried to return to the dark safety of the boxcar.

SS men in black, dirty uniforms were everywhere. They kicked and pommeled everyone within reach. Alsatian guard dogs snapped and barked. Stephen was bitten by one of the snarling dogs. A woman beside him was being kicked by the soldiers. And they were all being methodically herded past a high barbed-wire fence. Beside the fence was a wall.

Stephen looked around for an escape route, but he was surrounded by other prisoners, who were pressing against him. Soldiers were shooting indiscriminately into the crowd, shooting women and children alike.

The man who had shouted to his wife was shot.

"Sholom, help me, help me," screamed a scrawny young woman whose skin was as yellow and pimpled as chicken flesh.

And Stephen understood that *he* was Sholom. He was a Jew in this burning, stinking world, and this woman, somehow, meant something to him. He felt the yellow star sewn on the breast of his filthy jacket. He grimaced uncontrollably. The strangest thoughts were passing through his mind, remembrances of another childhood: morning prayers with his father and rich uncle, large breakfasts on Saturdays, the sounds of his mother and father quietly making love in the next room, *yortseit* candles burning in the living room, his brother reciting the "four questions" at the Passover table.

He touched the star again and remembered the Nazis' facetious euphemism for it: *Pour le Sémite*.

He wanted to strike out, to kill the Nazis, to fight and die. But he found himself marching with the others, as if he had no will of his own. He felt that he was cut in half. He had two selves now; one watched the other. One self wanted to fight. The other was numbed; it cared only for itself. It was determined to survive.

Stephen looked around for the woman who had called out to him. She was nowhere to be seen.

Behind him were railroad tracks, electrified wire, and the conical tower and main gate of the camp. Ahead was a pitted road littered with corpses and their belongings. Rifles were being fired, and a heavy, sickly sweet odor was everywhere. Stephen gagged, others vomited. It was the overwhelming stench of death, of rotting and burning flesh. Black clouds hung over the camp, and flames spurted from the tall chimneys of ugly buildings, as if from infernal machines.

Stephen walked onward: he was numb, unable to fight or even talk. Everything that happened around him was impossible, the stuff of dreams.

The prisoners were ordered to halt, and the soldiers began to separate those who would be burned from those who would be worked to death. Old men and women and young children were pulled out of the crowd. Some were beaten and killed immediately, while the others looked on in disbelief. Stephen looked on, as if it was of no concern to him. Everything was unreal, dreamlike. He did not belong here.

The new prisoners looked like Musselmanner, the walking dead. Those who became ill, or were beaten or starved before they could "wake up" to the reality of the camps, became Musselmanner. Musselmanner could not think or feel. They shuffled around, already dead in spirit, until a guard or disease or cold or starvation killed them.

"Keep marching," shouted a guard as Stephen stopped before an emaciated old man crawling on the ground. "You'll look like him soon enough."

Suddenly, as if waking from one dream and finding himself in another, Stephen remembered that the chicken-skinned girl was his wife. He remembered their life together, their children and crowded flat. He remembered the birthmark on her leg, her scent, her hungry lovemaking. He had once fought another boy over her.

His glands opened up with fear and shame; he had ignored her screams for help.

He stopped and turned, faced the other group. "Fruma," he shouted, then started to run.

A guard struck him in the chest with the butt of his rifle, and Stephen fell into darkness.

He spills the ice water again and awakens with a scream.

"It's my fault," Josie says as she peels back the sheets. "I should have taken the bowl away from you. But you fight me."

Stephen lives with the pain again. He imagines that a tiny fire is burning in his abdomen, slowly consuming him. He stares at the television high on the wall and watches Soupy Sales.

As Josie changes the plastic sac containing his intravenous saline solution, an orderly pushes a cart into the room and asks Stephen if he wants a print for his wall.

"Would you like me to choose something for you?" Josie asks.

Stephen shakes his head and asks the orderly to show him all the prints. Most of them are familiar still lifes and pastorals, but one catches his attention. It is a painting of a wheat field. Although the sky looks ominously dark, the wheat is brightly rendered in great, broad strokes. A path cuts through the field and crows fly overhead.

"That one," Stephen says. "Put that one up."

After the orderly hangs the print and leaves, Josie asks Stephen why he chose that particular painting.

"I like Van Gogh," he says dreamily as he tries to detect a rhythm in the surges of abdominal pain. But he is not nauseated, just gaseous.

"Any particular reason why you like Van Gogh?" asks Josie. "He's my favorite artist too."

"I didn't say he was my favorite," Stephen says, and Josie pouts, an expression that does not fit her prematurely lined face. Stephen closes his eyes, glimpses the cold country, and says, "I like the painting because it's so bright that it's almost frightening. And the road going through the field"—he opens his eyes—"doesn't go anywhere. It just ends in the field. And the crows are flying around like vultures."

"Most people see it as just a pretty picture," Josie says.

"What's it called?"

"Wheat Field with Blackbirds."

"Sensible. My stomach hurts, Josie. Help me turn over on my side." Josie helps him onto his left side, plumps up his pillows, and inserts a short tube into his rectum to relieve the gas. "I also like the painting with the large stars that all look out of focus," Stephen says. "What's it called?"

"*Starry Night.*"

"That's scary too," Stephen says. Josie takes his blood pressure, makes a notation on his chart, then sits down beside him and holds his hand. "I remember something," he says. "Something just—" He jumps as he remembers, and pain shoots through his distended stomach. Josie shushes him, checks the intravenous needle, and asks him what he remembers.

But the memory of the dream recedes as the pain grows sharper. "I hurt all the fucking time, Josie," he says, changing position. Josie removes the rectal tube before he is on his back.

"Don't use such language, I don't like to hear it. I know you have a lot of pain," she says, her voice softening.

"Time for a shot."

"No, honey, not for some time. You'll just have to bear it."

Stephen remembers his dream again. He is afraid of it. His breath is short and his heart feels as if it is beating in his throat, but he recounts the entire dream to Josie.

He does not notice that her face has lost its color.

"It's only a dream, Stephen. Probably something you studied in history."

"But it was so real, not like a dream at all."

"That's enough!" Josie says.

"I'm sorry I upset you. Don't be angry."

"I'm *not* angry."

"I'm sorry," he says, fighting the pain, squeezing Josie's hand tightly. "Didn't you tell me that you were in the Second World War?"

Josie is composed once again. "Yes, I did, but I'm surprised you remembered. You were very sick. I was a nurse overseas, spent most of the war in England. But I was one of the first women to go into any of the concentration camps."

Stephen drifts with the pain; he appears to be asleep.

"You must have studied very hard," Josie whispers to him. Her hand is shaking just a bit.

It is twelve o'clock and his room is death-quiet. The sharp shadows seem to be the hardest objects in the room. The fluorescents burn steadily in the hall outside.

Stephen looks out into the hallway, but he can see only the far white wall. He waits for his night nurse to appear: it is time for his injection. A young nurse passes by his doorway. Stephen imagines that she is a cardboard ship sailing through the corridors.

He presses his buzzer, which is attached by a clip to his pillow. The night nurse will take her time, he tells himself. He remembers arguing with her. Angrily, he presses the buzzer again.

Across the hall, a man begins to scream, and there is a shuffle of nurses into his room. The screaming turns into begging and whining. Although Stephen has never seen the man in the opposite room, he has come to hate him. Like Stephen, he has something wrong with his stomach; but he cannot suffer well. He can only beg and cry, try to make deals with the nurses, doctors, God, and angels. Stephen cannot muster any pity for this man.

The night nurse finally comes into the room, says, "You have to try to get along without this," and gives him an injection of Demerol.

"Why does the man across the hall scream so?" Stephen asks, but the nurse is already edging out of the room.

"Because he's in pain."

"So am I," Stephen says in a loud voice. "But I can keep it to myself."

"Then, stop buzzing me constantly for an injection. That man across the hall has had half of his stomach removed. He's got something to scream about."

So have I, Stephen thinks; but the nurse disappears before he can tell her. He tries to imagine what the man across the hall looks like. He thinks of him as being bald and small, an ancient baby. Stephen tries to feel sorry for the man, but his incessant whining disgusts him.

The drug takes effect; the screams recede as he hurtles through the dark corridors of a dream. The cold country is dark, for Stephen cannot persuade his night nurse to bring him some ice. Once again, he sees two entrances. As the world melts behind him, he steps into the coal-black doorway.

In the darkness he hears an alarm, a bone-jarring clangor.

He could smell the combined stink of men pressed closely together. They were all lying upon two badly constructed wooden shelves. The floor was dirt; the smell of urine never left the barrack.

"Wake up," said a man Stephen knew as Viktor. "If the guard finds you in bed, you'll be beaten again."

Stephen moaned, still wrapped in dreams. "Wake up, wake up," he mumbled to himself. He would have a few more minutes before the guard arrived with the dogs. At the very thought of dogs, Stephen felt revulsion. He had once been bitten in the face by a large dog.

He opened his eyes, yet he was still half asleep, exhausted. You are in a death camp, he said to himself. You must wake up. You must fight by waking up. Or you will die in your sleep. Shaking uncontrollably, he said, "Do you want to end up in the oven, perhaps you will be lucky today and live."

As he lowered his legs to the floor, he felt the sores open on the soles of his feet. He wondered who would die today and shrugged. It was his third week in the camp. Impossibly, against all odds, he had survived. Most of those he had known in the train had either died or become Musselmanner. If it were not for Viktor, he, too, would have become a Musselmann. He had a breakdown and wanted to die. He babbled in English. But Viktor talked him out of death, shared his portion of food with him, and taught him the new rules of life.

"Like everyone else who survives, I count myself first, second, and third—then I try to do what I can for someone else," Viktor had said.

"I will survive," Stephen repeated to himself as the guards opened the door, stepped into the room, and began to shout. Their dogs growled and snapped, but heeled beside them. The guards looked sleepy; one did not wear a cap, and his red hair was tousled.

Perhaps he spent the night with one of the whores, Stephen thought. Perhaps today would not be so bad. . . .

And so begins the morning ritual: Josie enters Stephen's room at a quarter to eight, fusses with the chart attached to the footboard of his bed, pads about aimlessly, and finally goes to the bathroom. She returns, her stiff uniform making swishing sounds. Stephen can feel her standing over the bed and staring at him. But he does not open his eyes. He waits a beat.

She turns away, then drops the bedpan. Yesterday it was the metal ashtray; day before that, she bumped into the bedstand.

"Good morning, darling, it's a beautiful day," she says, then walks across the room to the windows. She parts the faded orange drapes and opens the blinds. "How do you feel today?"

"Okay, I guess."

Josie takes his pulse and asks, "Did Mr. Gregory stop in to say hello last night?"

"Yes," Stephen says. "He's teaching me how to play gin rummy. What's wrong with him?"

"He's very sick."

"I can see that; has he got cancer?"

"I don't know," says Josie as she tidies up his night table.

"You're lying again," Stephen says, but she ignores him. After a time, he says, "His girlfriend was in to see me last night, I bet his wife will be in today."

"Shut your mouth about that," Josie says. "Let's get you out of that bed, so I can change the sheets."

Stephen sits in the chair all morning. He is getting well but is still very weak. Just before lunchtime, the orderly wheels his cart into the room and asks Stephen if he would like to replace the print hanging on the wall.

"I've seen them all," Stephen says. "I'll keep the one I have." Stephen does not grow tired of the Van Gogh painting; sometimes, the crows seem to have changed position.

"Maybe you'll like this one," the orderly says as he pulls out a cardboard print of Van Gogh's *Starry Night*. It is a study of a village nestled in the hills, dressed in shadows. But everything seems to be boiling and writhing as in a fever dream. A cypress tree in the foreground looks like a black flame, and the vertiginous sky is filled with great, blurry stars. It is a drunkard's dream. The orderly smiles.

"So you did have it," Stephen says.

"No, I traded some other pictures for it. They had a copy in the West Wing."

Stephen watches him hang it, thanks him, and waits for him to leave. Then he gets up and examines the painting carefully. He touches the raised facsimile brushstrokes, and turns toward Josie, feeling an odd sensation in his groin. He looks at her, as if seeing her for the first time. She has an overly full mouth, which curves downward at the corners when she smiles. She is not a pretty woman—too fat, he thinks.

"Dance with me," he says, as he waves his arms and takes a step forward, conscious of the pain in his stomach.

"You're too sick to be dancing just yet," but she laughs at him and bends her knees in a mock plié.

She has small breasts for such a large woman, Stephen thinks. Feeling suddenly dizzy, he takes a step toward the bed. He feels himself slip to the floor, feels Josie's hair brushing against his face, dreams that he's all wet from her tongue, feels her arms around him, squeezing, then feels the weight of her body pressing down on him, crushing him. . . .

He wakes up in a bed, catheterized. He has an intravenous needle in his left wrist, and it is difficult to swallow, for he has a tube down his throat.

He groans, tries to move.

"Quiet, Stephen," Josie says, stroking his hand.

"What happened?" he mumbles. He can only remember being dizzy.

"You've had a slight setback, so just rest. The doctor had to collapse your lung; you must lie very still."

"Josie, I love you," he whispers, but he is too far away to be heard. He wonders how many hours or days have passed. He looks toward the window. It is dark, and there is no one in the room.

He presses the buzzer attached to his pillow and remembers a dream. . . .

"You must fight," Viktor said.

It was dark, all the other men were alseep, and the barrack was filled with snoring and snorting. Stephen wished they could all die, choke on their own breath. It would be an act of mercy.

"Why fight?" Stephen asked, and he pointed toward the greasy window, beyond which were the ovens that smoked day and night. He made a fluttering gesture with his hand—smoke rising.

"You must fight, you must live; living is everything. It is the only thing that makes sense here."

"We're all going to die, anyway," Stephen whispered. "Just like your sister . . . and my wife."

"No, Sholom, we're going to live. The others may die, but we're going to live. You must believe that."

Stephen understood that Viktor was desperately trying to convince himself to live. He felt sorry for Viktor; there could be no sensible rationale for living in a place like this. Everything must die here.

Stephen grinned, tasted blood from the corner of his mouth, and said, "So we'll live through the night, maybe."

And maybe tomorrow, he thought. He would play the game of survival a little longer.

He wondered if Viktor would be alive tomorrow. He smiled and thought, If Viktor dies, then I will have to take his place and convince others to live. For an instant, he hoped Viktor would die so that he could take his place.

The alarm sounded. It was three o'clock in the morning, time to begin the day.

This morning, Stephen was on his feet before the guards could unlock the door.

"Wake up," Josie says, gently tapping his arm. "Come on now, wake up."

Stephen hears her voice as an echo. He imagines that he has been flung into a long tunnel; he hears air whistling in his ears but cannot see anything.

"Whassimatter?" he asks. His mouth feels as if it is stuffed with cotton; his lips are dry and cracked. He is suddenly angry at Josie and the plastic tubes that hold him in his bed as if he were a latter-day Gulliver. He wants to pull out the tubes, smash the bags filled with saline, tear away his bandages.

"You were speaking German," Josie says. "Did you know that?"

"Can I have some ice?"

"No," Josie says impatiently. "You spilled again, you're all wet."

". . . for my mouth, dry. . . ."

"Do you remember speaking German, honey, I have to know."

"Don't remember, bring ice, I'll try to think about it."

As Josie leaves to get him some ice, he tries to remember his dream.

"Here now, just suck on the ice." She gives him a little hill of crushed ice on the end of a spoon.

"Why did you wake me up, Josie?" The layers of dream are beginning to slough off. As the Demerol works out of his system, he has to concentrate on fighting the burning ache in his stomach.

"You were speaking German, Where did you learn to speak like that?"

Stephen tries to remember what he said. He cannot speak any German, only a bit of classroom French. He looks down at his legs (he has thrown off his sheet) and notices, for the first time, that his legs are as thin as his arms. "My God, Josie, how could I have lost so much weight?"

"You lost about forty pounds, but don't worry, you'll gain it all back. You're on the road to recovery now. Please, try to remember your dream."

"I can't, Josie! I just can't seem to get a hold of it."

"Try."

"Why is it so important to you?"

"You weren't speaking college German, darling, you were speaking slang. You spoke in a patois that I haven't heard since the forties."

Stephen feels a chill slowly creep up his spine. "What did I say?"

Josie waits a beat, then says, "You talked about dying."

"Josie?"

"Yes," she says, pulling at her fingernail.

"When is the pain going to stop?"

"It will be over soon." She gives him another spoonful of ice. "You kept repeating the name Viktor in your sleep. Can you remember anything about him?"

Viktor, Viktor, deep-set blue eyes, balding head and broken nose, called himself a Galitzianer. Saved my life. "I remember," Stephen says. "His name is Viktor Shmone. He is in all my dreams now."

Josie exhales sharply.

"Does that mean anything to you?" Stephen asks anxiously.

"I once knew a man from one of the camps." She speaks very slowly and precisely. "His name was Viktor Shmone. I took care of him. He was one of the few people left alive in the camp after the Germans fled." She reaches for her purse, which she keeps on Stephen's night table, and fumbles an old, torn photograph out of a plastic slipcase.

As Stephen examines the photograph, he begins to sob. A thinner and much younger Josie is standing beside Viktor and two other emaciated-looking men. "Then, I'm not dreaming," he says, "and I'm going to die. That's what it means." He begins to shake, just as he did in his dream, and, without thinking, he makes the gesture of rising smoke to Josie. He begins to laugh.

"Stop that," Josie says, raising her hand to slap him. Then she embraces him and says, "Don't cry, darling, it's only a dream. Somehow, you're dreaming the past."

"Why?" Stephen asks, still shaking.

"Maybe you're dreaming because of me, because we're so close. In some ways, I think you know me better than anyone else, better than any man, no doubt. You might be dreaming for a reason; maybe I can help you."

"I'm afraid, Josie."

She comforts him and says, "Now tell me everything you can remember about the dreams."

He is exhausted. As he recounts his dreams to her, he sees the bright doorway again. He feels himself being sucked into it. "Josie," he says, "I must stay awake, don't want to sleep, dream. . . ."

Josie's face is pulled tight as a mask; she is crying.

Stephen reaches out to her, slips into the bright doorway, into another dream.

It was a cold, cloudless morning. Hundreds of prisoners were working in the quarries; each work gang came from a different barrack. Most of the gangs were made up of Musselmanner, the faceless majority of the camp. They moved like automatons, lifting and carrying the great stones to the numbered carts, which would have to be pushed down the tracks.

Stephen was drenched with sweat. He had a fever and was afraid that he had contracted typhus. An epidemic had broken out in the camp last week. Every morning, several doctors arrived with the guards. Those who were too sick to stand up were taken away to be gassed or experimented upon in the hospital.

Although Stephen could barely stand, he forced himself to keep moving. He tried to focus all his attention on what he was doing. He made a ritual of bending over, choosing a stone of a certain size, lifting it, carrying it to the nearest cart, and then taking the same number of steps back to his dig.

A Musselmann fell to the ground, but Stephen made no effort to help him. When he could help someone in a little way, he would, but he would not stick his neck out for a Musselmann. Yet something niggled at Stephen. He remembered a photograph in which Viktor and this Musselmann were standing with a man and a woman he did not recognize. But Stephen could not remember where he had ever seen such a photograph.

"Hey, you," shouted the guard. "Take the one on the ground to the cart."

Stephen nodded to the guard and began to drag the Musselmann away.

"Who's the new patient down the hall?" Stephen asks as he eats a bit of cereal from the breakfast tray Josie has placed before him. He is feeling much better now; his fever is down and the tubes, catheter, and intravenous needle have been removed. He can even walk around a bit.

"How did you find out about that?" Josie asks.

"You were talking to Mr. Gregory's nurse. Do you think I'm dead already? I can still hear."

Josie laughs and takes a sip of Stephen's tea. "You're far from dead! In fact, today is a red-letter day, you're going to take your first shower. What do you think about that?"

"I'm not well enough yet," he says, worried that he will have to leave the hospital before he is ready.

"Well, Dr. Volk thinks differently, and his word is law."

"Tell me about the new patient."

"They brought in a man last night who drank two quarts of motor oil; he's on the dialysis machine."

"Will he make it?"

"No, I don't think so; there's too much poison in his system."

We should all die, Stephen thinks. It would be an act of mercy. He glimpses the camp.

"Stephen!"

He jumps, then awakens.

"You've had a good night's sleep, you don't need to nap. Let's get you into that shower and have it done with." Josie pushes the tray table away from the bed. "Come on, I have your bathrobe right here."

Stephen puts on his bathrobe, and they walk down the hall to the showers. There are three empty shower stalls, a bench, and a whirlpool bath. As Stephen takes off his bathrobe, Josie adjusts the water pressure and temperature in the corner stall.

"What's the matter?" Stephen asks after stepping into the shower. Josie stands in front of the shower stall and holds his towel, but she will not look at him. "Come on," he says, "you've seen me naked before."

"That was different."

"How?" He touches a hard, ugly scab that has formed over one of the wounds on his abdomen.

"When you were very sick, I washed you in bed as if you were a baby. Now it's different." She looks down at the wet tile floor as if she is lost in thought.

''Well, I think it's silly,'' he says. ''Come on, it's hard to talk to someone who's looking the other way. I could break my neck in here and you'd be staring down at the fucking floor.''

''I've asked you not to use that word,'' she says in a very low voice.

''Do my eyes still look yellowish?''

She looks directly at his face and says, ''No, they look fine.''

Stephen suddenly feels faint, then nauseated; he has been standing too long. As he leans against the cold shower wall, he remembers his last dream. He is back in the quarry. He can smell the perspiration of the men around him, feel the sun baking him, draining his strength. It is so bright. . . .

He finds himself sitting on the bench and staring at the light on the opposite wall. I've got typhus, he thinks, then realizes that he is in the hospital. Josie is beside him.

''I'm sorry,'' he says.

''I shouldn't have let you stand so long; it was my fault.''

''I remembered another dream.'' He begins to shake, and Josie puts her arms around him.

''It's all right now; tell Josie about your dream.''

She's an old, fat woman, Stephen thinks. As he describes the dream, his shaking subsides.

''Do you know the man's name?'' Josie asks. ''The one the guard ordered you to drag away.''

''No,'' Stephen says. ''He was a Musselmann, yet I thought there was something familiar about him. In my dream I remembered the photograph you showed me. He was in it.''

''What will happen to him?''

''The guards will give him to the doctors for experimentation. If they don't want him, he'll be gassed.''

''You must not let that happen,'' Josie says, holding him tightly.

''Why?'' asks Stephen, afraid that he will fall into the dreams again.

''If he was one of the men you saw in the photograph, you must not let him die. Your dreams must fit the past.''

''I'm afraid.''

''It will be all right, baby,'' Josie says, clinging to him. She is shaking and breathing heavily.

Stephen feels himself getting an erection. He calms her, presses his face against hers, and touches her breasts. She tells him to stop but does not push him away.

"I love you," he says as he slips his hand under her starched skirt. He feels awkward and foolish and warm.

"This is wrong," she whispers.

As Stephen kisses her and feels her thick tongue in his mouth, he begins to dream. . . .

Stephen stopped to rest for a few seconds. The Musselmann was dead weight. I cannot go on, Stephen thought, but he bent down, grabbed the Musselmann by his coat, and dragged him toward the cart. He glimpsed the cart, which was filled with the sick and dead and exhausted; it looked no different than a carload of corpses marked for a mass grave.

A long, gray cloud covered the sun, then passed, drawing shadows across gutted hills.

On impulse, Stephen dragged the Musselmann into a gully behind several chalky rocks. Why am I doing this? he asked himself. If I'm caught, I'll be ash in the ovens too. He remembered what Viktor had told him: "You must think of yourself all the time or you'll be no help to anyone else."

The Musselmann groaned, then raised his arm. His face was gray with dust and his eyes were glazed.

"You must lie still," Stephen whispered. "Do not make a sound. I've hidden you from the guards, but if they hear you, we'll all be punished. One sound from you and you're dead. You must fight to live; you're in a death camp; you must fight so you can tell of this later."

"I have no family, they're all—"

Stephen clapped his hand over the man's mouth and whispered, "Fight, don't talk. Wake up; you cannot survive the death camp by sleeping."

The man nodded, and Stephen climbed out of the gully. He helped two men carry a large stone to a nearby cart.

"What are you doing?" shouted a guard.

"I left my place to help these men with this stone; now I'll go back where I was."

"What the hell are you trying to do?" Viktor asked.

Stephen felt as if he was burning up with fever. He wiped the sweat from his eyes, but everything was still blurry.

"You're sick, too, You'll be lucky if you last the day."

"I'll last," Stephen said, "but I want you to help me get him back to the camp."

"I won't risk it, not for a Musselmann. He's already dead; leave him."

"Like you left me?"

Before the guards could take notice, they began to work. Although Viktor was older than Stephen, he was stronger. He worked hard every day and never caught the diseases that daily reduced the barrack's numbers. Stephen had a touch of death, as Viktor called it, and was often sick.

They worked until dusk, when the sun's oblique rays caught the dust from the quarries and turned it into veils and scrims. Even the guards sensed that this was a quiet time, for they would congregate together and talk in hushed voices.

"Come, now, help me," Stephen whispered to Viktor.

"I've been doing that all day," Viktor said. "I'll have enough trouble getting you back to the camp, much less carry this Musselmann."

"We can't leave him."

"Why are you so preoccupied with this Musselmann? Even if we can get him back to the camp, his chances are nothing. I know—I've seen enough—I know who has a chance to survive."

"You're wrong this time," Stephen said. He was dizzy and it was difficult to stand. The odds are I won't last the night, and Viktor knows it, he told himself. "I had a dream that if this man dies, I'll die too, I just feel it."

"Here we learn to trust our dreams," Viktor said. "They make as much sense as this. . . ." He made the gesture of rising smoke and gazed toward the ovens, which were spewing fire and black ash.

The western portion of the sky was yellow, but over the ovens it was red and purple and dark blue. Although it horrified Stephen to consider it, there was a macabre beauty here. If he survived, he would never forget these sense impressions, which were stronger than anything he had ever experienced before. Being so close to death, he was, perhaps for the first time, really living. In the camp, one did not even consider suicide. One grasped for every moment, sucked at life like an infant, lived as if there were no future.

The guards shouted at the prisoners to form a column; it was time to march back to the barracks.

While the others milled about, Stephen and Viktor lifted the Musselmann out of the gully. Everyone nearby tried to distract the guards. When the march began, Stephen and Viktor held the Musselmann between them, for he could barely stand.

"Come on, dead one, carry your weight," Viktor said. "Are you so dead that you cannot hear me? Are you as dead as the rest of your family?" The Musselmann groaned and dragged his legs. Victor kicked him. "You'll walk or we'll leave you here for the guards to find."

"Let him be," Stephen said.

"Are you dead or do you have a name?" Viktor continued.

"Berek," croaked the Musselmann. "I am not dead."

"Then, we have a fine bunk for you," Viktor said. "You can smell the stink of the sick for another night before the guards make a selection." Viktor made the gesture of smoke rising.

Stephen stared at the barracks ahead. They seemed to waver as the heat rose from the ground. He counted every step. He would drop soon; he could not go on, could not carry the Musselmann.

He began to mumble in English.

"So you're speaking American again," Viktor said.

Stephen shook himself awake, placed one foot before the other.

"Dreaming of an American lover?"

"I don't know English and I have no American lover."

"Then, who is this Josie you keep talking about in your sleep . . . ?"

"Why were you screaming?" Josie asks as she washes his face with a cold washcloth.

"I don't remember screaming," Stephen says. He discovers a fever blister on his lip. Expecting to find an intravenous needle in his wrist, he raises his arm.

"You don't need an I.V.," Josie says. "You just have a bit of a fever. Dr. Volk has prescribed some new medication for it."

"What time is it?" Stephen stares at the whorls in the ceiling.

"Almost three P.M. I'll be going off soon."

"Then I've slept most of the day away," Stephen says, feeling something crawling inside him. He worries that his dreams still have a hold on him. "Am I having another relapse?"

"You'll do fine," Josie says.

"I should be fine now; I don't want to dream anymore."

"Did you dream again, do you remember anything?"

"I dreamed that I saved the Musselmann," Stephen says.

"What was his name?" asks Josie.

"Berek, I think. Is that the man you knew?"

Josie nods and Stephen smiles at her. "Maybe that's the end of the dreams," he says; but she does not respond. He asks to see the photograph again.

"Not just now," Josie says.

"But I have to see it. I want to see if I can recognize myself. . . ."

Stephen dreamed he was dead, but it was only the fever. Viktor sat beside him on the floor and watched the others. The sick were moaning and crying; they slept on the cramped platform, as if proximity to one another could ensure them a few more hours of life. Wan moonlight seemed to fill the barrack.

Stephen awakened, feverish. "I'm burning up," he whispered to Viktor.

"Well," Viktor said, "you've got your Musselmann. If he lives, you live. That's what you said, isn't it?"

"I don't remember; I just knew that I couldn't let him die."

"You'd better go back to sleep; you'll need your strength. Or we may have to carry *you*, tomorrow."

Stephen tried to sleep, but the fever was making lights and spots before his eyes. When he finally fell asleep, he dreamed of a dark country filled with gemstones and great quarries of ice and glass.

"What?" Stephen asked, as he sat up suddenly, awakened from damp black dreams. He looked around and saw that everyone was watching Berek, who was sitting under the window at the far end of the room.

Berek was singing the Kol Nidre very softly. It was the Yom Kippur prayer, sung on the most holy of days. He repeated the prayer three times, and then once again in a louder voice. The others responded, intoned the prayer as a recitative. Viktor was crying quietly, and Stephen imagined that the holy spirit animated Berek. Surely, he told himself, that face and those pale, unseeing eyes were those of a dead man. He remembered the story of the golem, shuddered, found himself singing and pulsing with fever.

When the prayer was over, Berek fell back into his fever trance. The others became silent, then slept. But there was something new in the barrack with them tonight, a palpable exultation. Stephen looked around at the sleepers and thought, We're surviving, more dead than alive, but surviving. . . .

"You were right about that Musselmann," Viktor whispered. "It's good that we saved him."

"Perhaps we should sit with him," Stephen said. "He's alone."

But Viktor was already asleep; and Stephen was suddenly afraid that if he sat beside Berek, he would be consumed by his holy fire.

As Stephen fell through sleep and dreams, his face burned with fever.

Again he wakes up screaming.

"Josie," he says, "I can remember the dream, but there's something else, something I can't see, something terrible. . . ."

"Not to worry," Josie says, "it's the fever." But she looks worried, and Stephen is sure that she knows something he does not.

"Tell me what happened to Viktor and Berek," Stephen says. He presses his hands together to stop them from shaking.

"They lived, just as you are going to live and have a good life."

Stephen calms down and tells her his dream.

"So you see," she says, "you're even dreaming about surviving."

"I'm burning up."

"Dr. Volk says you're doing very well." Josie sits beside him, and he watches the fever patterns shift behind his closed eyelids.

"Tell me what happens next, Josie."

"You're going to get well."

"There's something else. . . ."

"Shush, now, there's nothing else." She pauses, then says, "Mr. Gregory is supposed to visit you tonight. He's getting around a bit, he's been back and forth all day in his wheelchair. He tells me that you two have made some sort of a deal about dividing up all the nurses."

Stephen smiles, opens his eyes, and says, "It was Gregory's idea. Tell me what's wrong with him."

"All right, he has cancer, but he doesn't know it and you must keep it a secret. They cut the nerve in his leg because the pain was so bad. He's quite comfortable now, but remember, you can't repeat what I've told you."

"Is he going to live?" Stephen asks. "He's told me about all the new projects he's planning, so I guess he's expecting to get out of here."

"He's not going to live very long, and the doctor didn't want to break his spirit."

"I think he should be told."

"That's not your decision to make, nor mine."

"Am I going to die, Josie?"

"No!" she says, touching his arm to reassure him.

"How do I know that's the truth?"

"Because I say so, and I couldn't look you straight in the eye and tell you if it wasn't true. I should have known it would be a mistake to tell you about Mr. Gregory."

"You did right," Stephen says. "I won't mention it again. Now that I know, I feel better." He feels drowsy again.

"Do you think you're up to seeing him tonight?"

Stephen nods, although he is bone tired. As he falls asleep, the fever patterns begin to dissolve, leaving a bright field. With a start, he opens his eyes: he has touched the edge of another dream.

"What happened to the man across the hall, the one who was always screaming?"

"He's left the ward," Josie says. "Mr. Gregory had better hurry if he wants to play cards with you before dinner. They're going to bring the trays up soon."

"You mean he died, don't you."

"Yes, if you must know, he died. But *you're* going to live."

There is a crashing noise in the hallway. Someone shouts, and Josie runs to the door.

Stephen tries to stay awake, but he is being pulled back into the cold country.

"Mr. Gregory fell trying to get into his wheelchair by himself," Josie says. "He should have waited for his nurse, but she was out of the room and he wanted to visit you."

But Stephen does not hear a word she says.

There were rumors that the camp was going to be liberated. It was late, but no one was asleep. The shadows in the barrack seemed larger tonight.

"It's better for us if the Allies don't come," Viktor said to Stephen.

"Why do you say that?"

"Haven't you noticed that the ovens are going day and night? The Nazis are in a hurry."

"I'm going to try to sleep," Stephen said.

"Look around you; even the Musselmanner are agitated," Viktor said. "Animals become nervous before the slaughter. I've worked with animals. People are not so different."

"Shut up and let me sleep," Stephen said, and he dreamed that he could hear the crackling of distant gunfire.

* * *

"Attention," shouted the guards as they stepped into the barrack. There were more guards than usual, and each one had two Alsatian dogs. "Come on, form a line. Hurry."

"They're going to kill us," Viktor said; "then they'll evacuate the camp and save themselves."

The guards marched the prisoners toward the northern section of the camp. Although it was still dark, it was hot and humid, without a trace of the usual morning chill. The ovens belched fire and turned the sky aglow. Everyone was quiet, for there was nothing to be done. The guards were nervous and would cut down anyone who uttered a sound, as an example for the rest.

The booming of big guns could be heard in the distance.

If I'm going to die, Stephen thought, I might as well go now, and take a Nazi with me. Suddenly, all of his buried fear, aggression, and revulsion surfaced; his face became hot and his heart felt as if it were pumping in his throat. But Stephen argued with himself. There was always a chance. He had once heard of some women who were waiting in line for the ovens; for no apparent reason, the guards sent them back to their barracks. Anything could happen. There was always a chance. But to attack a guard would mean certain death.

The guns became louder. Stephen could not be sure, but he thought the noise was coming from the west. The thought passed through his mind that everyone would be better off dead. That would stop all the guns and screaming voices, the clenched fists and wildly beating hearts. The Nazis should kill everyone, and then themselves, as a favor to humanity.

The guards stopped the prisoners in an open field surrounded on three sides by forestland. Sunrise was moments away; purple-black clouds drifted across the sky touched by gray in the east. It promised to be a hot, gritty day.

Half-step Walter, a Judenrat sympathizer who worked for the guards, handed out shovel heads to everyone.

"He's worse than the Nazis," Viktor said to Stephen.

"The Judenrat thinks he will live," said Berek, "but he will die like a Jew with the rest of us."

"Now, when it's too late, the Musselmann regains consciousness," Viktor said.

"Hurry," shouted the guards, "or you'll die now. As long as you dig, you'll live."

Stephen hunkered down on his knees and began to dig with the shovel head.

"Do you think we might escape?" Berek whined.

"Shut up and dig," Stephen said. "There is no escape, just stay alive as long as you can. Stop whining, are you becoming a Musselmann again?" Stephen noticed that other prisoners were gathering up twigs and branches. So the Nazis plan to cover us up, he thought.

"That's enough," shouted a guard. "Put your shovels down in front of you and stand in a line."

The prisoners stood shoulder to shoulder along the edge of the mass grave. Stephen stood between Viktor and Berek. Someone screamed and ran and was shot immediately.

I don't want to see trees or guards or my friends, Stephen thought as he stared into the sun. I only want to see the sun, let it burn out my eyes, fill up my head with light. He was shaking uncontrollably, quaking with fear.

Guns were booming in the background.

Maybe the guards won't kill us, Stephen thought, even as he heard the crackcrack of their rifles. Men were screaming and begging for life. Stephen turned his head, only to see someone's face blown away.

Screaming, tasting vomit in his mouth, Stephen fell backward, pulling Viktor and Berek into the grave with him.

Darkness, Stephen thought. His eyes were open, yet it was dark. I must be dead, this must be death. . . .

He could barely move. Corpses can't move, he thought. Something brushed against his face, he stuck out his tongue, felt something spongy. It tasted bitter. Lifting first one arm and then the other, Stephen moved some branches away. Above, he could see a few dim stars; the clouds were lit like lanterns by a quarter moon.

He touched the body beside him; it moved. That must be Viktor, he thought. "Viktor, are you alive, say something if you're alive." Stephen whispered, as if in fear of disturbing the dead.

Viktor groaned and said, "Yes, I'm alive, and so is Berek."

"And the others?"

"All dead. Can't you smell the stink? You, at least, were unconscious all day."

"They can't *all* be dead," Stephen said; then he began to cry.

"Shut up," Viktor said, touching Stephen's face to comfort him. "We're alive, that's something. They could have fired a volley into the pit."

"I thought I was dead," Berek said. He was a shadow among shadows.

"Why are we still here?" Stephen asked.

"We stayed in here because it is safe," Viktor said.

"But they're all dead," Stephen whispered, amazed that there could be speech and reason inside a grave.

"Do you think it's safe to leave now?" Berek asked Viktor.

"Perhaps. I think the killing has stopped. By now the Americans or English or whoever they are have taken over the camp. I heard gunfire and screaming; I think it's best to wait a while longer."

"Here?" asked Stephen. "Among the dead?"

"It's best to be safe."

It was late afternoon when they climbed out of the grave. The air was thick with flies. Stephen could see bodies sprawled in awkward positions beneath the covering of twigs and branches. "How can I live when all the others are dead?" he asked himself aloud.

"You live, that's all," answered Viktor.

They kept close to the forest and worked their way back toward the camp.

"Look there," Viktor said, motioning Stephen and Berek to take cover. Stephen could see trucks moving toward the camp compound.

"Americans," whispered Berek.

"No need to whisper now," Stephen said. "We're safe."

"Guards could be hiding anywhere," Viktor said. "I haven't slept in the grave to be shot now."

They walked into the camp through a large break in the barbed-wire fence, which had been hit by an artillery shell. When they reached the compound, they found nurses, doctors, and army personnel bustling about.

"You speak English," Viktor said to Stephen as they walked past several quonsets. "Maybe you can speak for us."

"I told you, I can't speak English."

"But I've heard you!"

"Wait," shouted an American army nurse. "You fellows are going the wrong way." She was stocky and spoke perfect German. "You must check in at the hospital; it's back that way."

"No," said Berek, shaking his head. "I won't go in there."

"There's no need to be afraid now," she said. "You're free. Come along, I'll take you to the hospital."

Something familiar about her, Stephen thought. He felt dizzy and everything turned gray.

"Josie," he murmured as he fell to the ground.

* * *

''What is it?'' Josie asks. ''Everything is all right, Josie is here.''

''Josie,'' Stephen mumbles.

''You're all right.''

''How can I live when they're all dead?'' he asks.

''It was a dream,'' she says as she wipes the sweat from his forehead. ''You see, your fever has broken, you're getting well.''

''Did you know about the grave?''

''It's all over now, forget the dream.''

''Did you know?''

''Yes,'' Josie says. ''Viktor told me how he survived the grave, but that was so long ago, before you were even born. Dr. Volk tells me you'll be going home soon.''

''I don't want to leave, I want to stay with you.''

''Stop that talk, you've got a whole life ahead of you. Soon you'll forget all about this, and you'll forget me, too.''

''Josie,'' Stephen asks, ''let me see that old photograph again. Just one last time.''

''Remember, this is the last time,'' she says as she hands him the faded photograph.

He recognizes Viktor and Berek, but the young man standing between them is not Stephen. ''That's not me,'' he says, certain that he will never return to the camp.

Yet the shots still echo in his mind.

JACK RITCHIE

Chicken Charley

SECOND LIEUTENANT JORDAN came to my company in January 1944.

I had been waiting at the orderly room window when the jeep drew up and stopped. The lieutenant appeared to be in no hurry to get out. He sat there sipping his Coke and talking to the driver, Pfc. Oliver. Oliver had a Coke too.

I went back into my office and waited.

After a while I took off my glasses and wiped the green mould off the silver temple pieces. Probably something to do with body chemistry and the Hawaiian humidity, I thought.

Lieutenant Jordan came in eight minutes later.

He saluted casually. "Lieutenant William Jordan reporting for duty, sir." He put a large brown envelope on my desk.

Jordan was a big man, probably over six foot two and from what I'd heard he had been a fullback in the Big Ten.

I folded my hands. "Lieutenant Jordan, at nine thirty-five I received a phone call from Headquarters informing me that you had been assigned to this company. I dispatched a vehicle to pick you up immediately. The distance between here and Headquarters can be covered easily in eleven minutes. The same applies for the return trip. You should have been here at approximately ten o'clock. However, Lieutenant, it is now eleven-thirty. Where were you?"

He grinned. "I thought I'd let Oliver show me around the post a little."

I stared at him for a few seconds. "The next time you find yourself impelled to look over the post," I said, "do it in your own time and on foot. Where did you get the Cokes?"

He blinked and then said, "I dropped in at the Bachelor Officers' Quarters and hit the machine."

"One for you and one for Pfc. Oliver?"

"Yes, sir."

"Don't do it again," I said. "And take those empties back to where you got them. There have been complaints about bottles missing."

The grin came back. "Yes, sir."

I glanced at my watch. "The company will be back in about twenty minutes. Wait in the orderly room and I'll introduce you to Harrison, your platoon sergeant."

I spent the time going through Lieutenant Jordan's file. He had been in the army fifteen months, an officer for six, and overseas two weeks—including ten days on the slow convoy from San Francisco.

At five to twelve, the company returned from the grenade range and the NCOs began trooping into the orderly room to check the bulletin board.

I recognized Staff Sergeant Harrison's voice.

"Damn it," he said. "Chicken Charley's got me assigned to the garbage pail gestapo again."

I walked to the doorway. "Sergeant Harrison," I said. "Once around."

Color came to his face. "Yes, sir." He left the orderly room.

At the window, I watched him break into a trot.

T/5 Riley, the company clerk, felt the need to tell Lieutenant Jordan what was happening. "When the captain gets mad about something he makes you double time around the area. If you don't do it in less than six minutes, he tells you to do it again."

Sergeant Harrison returned to the orderly room in five minutes twenty seconds and I introduced him to Lieutenant Jordan.

At twelve-thirty I walked down C street to the consolidated mess hall.

Ahead of me I saw Colonel Mobley leave the building and get into his command car. It pulled away.

Inside, I went through the line with my tray and took it to one of the officers' tables.

As I ate, I watched Sergeant Harrison at his station near the exit. His arms were folded and he seemed very little interested in what the men were dumping into the garbage pails in front of him as they passed on the way out.

I rose and went over.

"Sergeant Harrison," I said. "The purpose of your assignment here is to see that the men do not dump perfectly good food into the garbage pails. If you see them about to do so, it is your job to send them back to the tables and have them finish their trays."

He closed his eyes for a second. "Yes, sir."

''The army does not mind how much a man puts on his tray,'' I said. ''But it does insist that he eats it.''

''Yes, sir, Captain,'' he said. ''I already got the message.''

I went back to my table. I did not feel very hungry, but I finished my tray.

Five minutes after I got back to the orderly room, Colonel Mobley phoned.

''Captain,'' he said. ''This morning I saw one of your men and a strange officer joy riding around and drinking Cokes.''

''Yes, sir,'' I said. ''The officer was assigned to the company this morning.''

''That's no excuse. We can't have officers guzzling Cokes with enlisted men. I expect you to see to it that your officer remembers that.''

''Yes, sir.''

''And another thing, that was one of your sergeants at the garbage pails, wasn't it?''

''Yes, sir.''

''I saw a lot of perfectly good food wasted.''

''Yes, sir,'' I said. ''I'll do something about the sergeant too.''

When the colonel hung up, I decided I would confine both Sergeant Harrison and Lieutenant Jordan to the post for the weekend.

In the evening after chow, I went back to the BOQ and reread my mother's letter.

> I don't know if you remember Grace Harlow or not. She was that little blonde girl who lived down the street next to the Dawsons? Well, anyway, she's in the Nurses' Corps now and I met her mother while I was trying to get some decent meat from the butcher. It turns out her daughter's in the Hawaiian Island too and at Schofield.
>
> If you're anywhere near there, why don't you look her up? I'm sure she's lonely in that big army, and would like to see a familiar face for a change.

I refolded the letter and put it back into my locker. Yes, I remember Grace Harlow. During my senior year at Jefferson High I had asked her out one night.

I showered and shaved and began dressing.

Captain Tracey, C Company, had the other bunk in our room. He lay on the cot with his hands behind his head. ''Don't tell me you're going out on a date, Charley?''

He grinned. ''With what?''

"That's it."

"A nurse."

He sat up. "How the hell did you manage that? There aren't enough of those to go around and even a doll like me has to suffer."

I took off my glasses and wiped them. "Still waters run deep."

I left my name at the Nurses Quarters and waited about a half an hour before Grace Harlow came out of the building.

She looked me over and clicked her tongue. "Well, Charley, so they made you a captain. And in the infantry. I would have figured you for Quartermaster or something." She looked around. "Is that your jeep over there?"

"No," I said, "I walked."

"Don't tell me you couldn't swing a jeep?"

"It isn't that," I said. "I didn't think that I ought . . ." I paused. "I thought it might be a nice night for a walk."

She sighed. "Why not? But let's head in the direction of the Officers' Club. I could stand a drink."

We began walking.

"I guess I haven't seen you since high school graduation," I said.

She watched a tall lieutenant pass. "You went on to college and became a lawyer or something?"

"Yes," I said.

She smiled to herself. "Who did you finally get to go with you to the Senior Prom?"

"Helen Lawrence."

"Wasn't she the valedictorian?"

"Salutatorian," I said. "I was the valedictorian."

"That's right," she said. "You were kind of a grind. Didn't you play the clarinet in the band?"

"No. A violin in the orchestra."

At the Officers' Club the bar was crowded but I managed to get two drinks and bring them back to a table.

"How have things been going with you, Grace?" I asked.

She shrugged. "I got married after high school, but it didn't work out." Suddenly she smiled and I was aware that it was not at me. I turned and looked up. It was Lieutenant Jordan.

He grinned. "Hi, Captain, and all."

Grace still smiled. "Who's the big man, Charley?"

"One of my officers," I said.

"Why don't you invite the lieutenant to sit down, Charley?"

Grace said, "Any friend of yours is a friend of mine."

I introduced them to each other and Jordan took a chair.

"I'm new around here," he said. "So I still need somebody to show me around."

Grace showed even white teeth. "Then I suppose you haven't seen Honolulu yet?"

"No," Jordan said. "But maybe this weekend I could wangle a jeep and . . ." He stopped and grinned. "We'd better make that next weekend, Grace. The captain has me confined to the post for drinking Coke with an enlisted man."

The jukebox began a new number and he turned to her. "How about a dance?"

I watched them on the floor. They danced to four records and then went to the bar. They stayed there.

After about twenty minutes I finished my drink and went back to BOQ.

I sat down to finish writing the letter I'd begun earlier in the day.

> I looked up Grace Harlow. We had a few drinks and talked over old times. She seems to be looking quite well.

In the morning the company marched to the parade ground. After drill, we dispersed into platoon groups for gas mask instruction.

I heard laughter from Jordan's platoon and walked over there.

He had his gas mask in one hand. "If you smell gas, all you got to do is slap this thing over your face and keep it there until somebody sounds the all clear. That's the simple way to do it. But then we all know the army isn't happy unless you do this damn thing by the numbers. So bear with me and don't go to sleep. At the count of one . . ."

I stepped forward. "Excuse me, Lieutenant." I faced his platoon. "There are undoubtedly quicker ways of putting on a gas mask than by the numbers. However you are taught the drill so that, by practice, the action becomes automatic. In the event of an actual gas attack, there is always the possibility of panic. You might fumble with your mask, possibly drop it and that delay could prove disastrous. But if you have gone through the procedure by numbers over and over again, you will have worn a groove in your brain, so to speak. You will react automatically, whether you are frightened or not." I turned to Jordan. "You may continue, Lieutenant."

"Gee, thanks, Captain," he said.

The men laughed.

Jordan grinned. "Now let's all be good boys and get to work on that groove in your brains. Let's do this thing by the numbers and make the captain happy."

The men thought that was funny too.

"All right," I said. "Once around the parade ground."

Sergeant Harrison got the men on their feet and into formation. They doubled off.

Lieutenant Jordan still stood beside me. He lit a cigarette.

"Lieutenant Jordan," I said. "You part of the platoon. Once around."

He looked me over for a few seconds and then threw down the cigarette. He began moving away.

"Lieutenant Jordan," I said. "You dropped something."

He came back slowly and picked up the cigarette. "I left it here because I thought you might be dying for a smoke."

"Lieutenant Jordan," I said. "Twice around the parade ground. Just you. Not the platoon."

Two weeks later we got orders to pack up and get ready to board the troop transports. The colonel gave permission for company beer parties.

I was outside the orderly room when the 2½-ton truck pulled up in front of Barracks C. Lieutenant Jordan helped the men unload the cases of beer.

I walked over. "Lieutenant Jordan, is that your platoon's ration of beer?"

He put the last case on the stack. "That's right, Captain."

"I have been counting cases," I said. "It seems to me that you have exactly twice your quota."

He grinned. "The Pfc who made the issue at the warehouse must be new. He didn't know that these were double cases strapped together. So we got twice as much."

"Take half of the beer back," I said.

He regarded me evenly. "That's not exactly going to make my men happy, Captain."

"Perhaps not," I said. "But I believe the Pfc will appreciate it just the same."

The beer party began at three. At four I left my office and walked through Barracks A, and then B, and then entered C.

It was the same as the others—the smell of beer and smoke and the sound of men talking and laughing.

Sergeant Harrison and Lieutenant Jordan were seated together on a bunk near the GI can filled with ice and bottles.

"How are things going, men?" I asked. "Any complaints?"

"No complaints, Captain," Harrison said. He reached into the ice and water and brought out a bottle of beer. He opened it, grinned, and turned to Jordan.

"Care for another beer, Lieutenant?"

"Don't mind if I do, Sergeant," Jordan said.

I waited for perhaps thirty seconds and then said, "Well, have a good time."

The orderly room was empty except for Sergeant Yancy, CQ for the day. His feet were on the company clerk's desk and he smiled slightly. "How many beers did you get, Captain?"

"Take your damn feet off the desk," I said. I went into my office and read a newspaper.

We had been on the troop transport for six days when I went looking for Lieutenant Jordan. He lay on a deck chair in shorts and he was developing a nice sun tan.

"Lieutenant Jordan," I said. "Are you positive your platoon is aboard this ship?"

He took off his sunglasses. "Why, Captain?"

"Because I haven't seen you leave officers' country since you boarded this ship," I said. "I thought the reason might be that you left your men back at Schofield."

He flushed. "They're here and they're doing all right."

"Lieutenant," I said. "Down in the center of this ship there are men doing KP. The grind is fourteen hours a day, the temperature is one twenty, and the humidity approaches rain."

"Sure, it is rough," Jordan said. "But somebody has to do it."

"I agree, Lieutenant. The KP quota for your platoon is one man per day. But not the same man. I have just discovered that Private Robinson has been on KP for six consecutive days."

"All right, Captain," Jordan said. "So I'll send somebody else down there."

"But not for another stretch of six days," I said. "I expect to see a different face every twenty-four hours."

It had turned to February when our transport eased through one of the atoll's channels and anchored in its position in the lagoon.

The big ships were already here and probably had been for days. We clustered at the railings and watched the giant wagons shell the island.

There were two and a half square miles of land ahead of us, but it was a ribbon of an island and the widest part was less than six hundred yards across. When we'd studied the air photos, it had been thick with palms. Now very few of them were still standing.

Lieutenant Jordan stood beside me, his eyes fixed in a stare.

The island had become a haze of gray dust, streaked here and there by the black smoke of half a hundred fires. Planes from the carriers made another low pass over, dropping their bombs into the boiling mess.

"Nobody could live through that," Jordan said. "Nobody."

"The marines probably thought the same thing at Tarawa," I said.

Jordan shook his head fiercely. "No, I tell you. Nobody could live through that. They'll all be dead before we land."

I looked at him. His hands were tight on the railing, and a trickle of sweat moved down his left cheek.

"We all get a little nervous at a time like this," I said. "All of us."

Jordan didn't say anything.

The landings at the biggest end of the island were made the next morning, but it was another twenty-four hours before our turn came to go down the nets.

The men from the second platoon were going over the side when I went to look for Jordan.

I found him sitting on his bunk in full combat gear.

"Time to shove off, Jordan," I said.

"Yeah," he said. "Yeah." He rubbed absently at the stubble of his beard. "How are we doing? It's not over, is it?"

"No," I said. "We got about a third of the island. From now on it's just a matter of pushing them up the shoestring."

I waited a few more seconds. "Let's go, Jordan."

He got up slowly. "Sure. Sure."

Long before we landed we could smell what a couple of days in the hot sun does to a few thousand bodies.

The landing area was jammed with men, supplies, and vehicles, and more were coming in all the time.

Colonel Mobley got the company commanders together. "It's going so damn good that everybody's worried," he said. "Unless the Japs are hiding it, they don't have any heavy stuff left. Just small arms and mortars."

He put some rocks on the edges of the map to keep the wind from blowing it away and we gathered around. "The front is right here and moving up all the time," Mobley said. "The people who are supposed to know think that the Navy did such a terrific job this time that not more than five hundred or a thousand Japs could still be living." He wiped his face with a handkerchief and grinned at me. "Nothing like Attu, is it, Charley? Not much chance for frostbite."

''No sir,'' I said.

It wasn't until four-thirty in the afternoon that we got the order to move up. I noticed the men throwing away their gas masks and stopped the column. ''Pick up those masks,'' I ordered.

Sergeant Harrison spit some coral dust out of his mouth. ''Have a heart, Captain. They're just something extra to carry. The Japs don't use no gas.''

''There's always a first time,'' I said. ''Pick up the masks and make it snappy.'' I looked over Harrison's platoon. ''Where's Lieutenant Jordan?''

''I don't know,'' Harrison said. ''I guess he went up ahead.'' He grinned. ''Now there's one soldier who don't have to wait for orders to get into a fight.''

I got the company moving again and waited until it passed me. Then I walked back to the area we'd left.

I decided to give myself ten minutes. No more.

They were almost gone when I found him.

Lieutenant Jordan lay at the bottom of one of the concrete pits the Japs used for air raid shelters. I didn't know how long he had been dead, but the blood around the black-rimmed hole in the side of his head was dry.

I eased myself down beside him and picked up the .45 automatic next to his right hand. I removed the clip and replaced it with another from his cartridge belt. Then I slipped the automatic back into his holster and snapped the tab shut.

Graves Registration would think the enemy had killed him.

On my way back to the company I threw away the clip with the one bullet missing.

It all ended at low tide on the third day when the last twenty-five Japs tried to scramble over the half-submerged coral reef to the next dry land. None of them made it.

My company lost eleven men dead, thirty-seven wounded.

It was one of the easier islands. Later they came bigger and not so easy.

I don't go to the conventions, but this year the convention came to my city and Harrison looked me up.

On the way to the nearest bar, I learned that he was now a police sergeant in Philadelphia.

Inside Gordon's Tap, Harrison said, ''You'll buy me a drink, won't you, Charley?''

''Of course,'' I said. ''I'd be glad to.''

He showed his teeth. ''You don't mind if I call you Charley?''

I smiled. ''We're all civilians now.''

''That's right,'' Harrison said. ''All civilians and one just as good as the other. Isn't that right, Charley?'

''Right,'' I said.

He asked for whiskey and soda and I decided to take the same.

Harrison leaned toward me and I was aware that he had been drinking before he picked me up. ''Did any of the other boys ever look you up?''

''No,'' I said. ''But I'd be happy to see any of them.''

He laughed. ''At least half the company swore they'd see you again. They sure did.''

We got our drinks and Harrison downed his immediately. ''How about another one for an old enlisted man, Charley?''

''Certainly,'' I said. I put a bill on the bar.

Harrison lit a cigar and blew some of the smoke my way. ''Did you know that Jordan's home town named a post after him. William Jordan Post No. 2186.'' He grinned. ''You don't think anybody will ever name a post after you, do you, Charley?''

''No,'' I said. ''I guess not.''

Harrison tried the cigar again. ''Now there was a man's man. A soldier's soldier. You could talk to him. None of that GI crap.''

He swallowed his second drink and flicked the glass back toward the bartender. ''He told us all about you, Charley. How he stole your girl at Schofield, and you never forgot it.''

I sipped my drink.

''Is that why you sent him to the front?'' Harrison asked.

I looked up.

Harrison wasn't smiling now. ''I been thinking it over, Charley, and it come to me that a platoon commander don't leave his platoon unless he's ordered to. Is that what you did, Charley? Ordered him up alone hoping that he'd get himself killed?''

''No,'' I said.

Harrison put his cigar on the ash tray. ''Do you know why I really looked you up, Charley?''

I said nothing.

His face was dark and showed the drink. ''I promised myself that some day I'd smash your teeth down your throat.''

Harrison had big hands and the right one was clenched in a fist. He glared at me for a almost a minute.

Then he slowly exhaled and the hand opened. He shook his head. "Maybe ten years ago, but not now. I got too much to lose. I'd get kicked off the force."

He walked out.

When I got back home, my two boys were on the living room floor watching the parade downtown on television.

My oldest son turned on one elbow. "You got to be a major, didn't you, Dad?"

"Yes," I said.

"I'll bet your men would have followed you to hell."

"That's right," I said. "Just to be absolutely positive that I really got there."

My wife, Helen, looked at me and so I didn't say anything more.

After the kids were asleep, I got drunk.

LEO R. ELLIS

Operation Wild Ass

SERGEANT CREADY WAS so tired, and so bone-numbed close to freezing, he was scared to lie down for fear rigor mortis would set in before he could get up again. It wasn't just the cold that had him punchy, either. It was a combination of a lot of things, such as: Private Jason Pody; the way they were running World War Two; the fact that he had foot-slogged it most of the way across France without even one pass to Paris. Private Jason Pody, and now, this lousy German castle. It was this lousy castle, he figured, that would finally flip Sergeant Cready for a section eight. Cready could take castles or leave them. But this one was different because it *had* to be taken. Headquarters had ordered C Company to occupy the valley beyond, and this castle stood in the way, guarding the only pass into the valley. Lieutenant Spicer felt differently about castles. He loved them. But Spicer had been some kind of history professor and should have been put into logistics, or the commissary, instead of the infantry.

So far, the castle had been tough. Damned tough, for C. Company had lost a lot of men just storming the front gate towers, and once inside, Sergeant Cready found that they hadn't gained much. There was still a wide cobblestone courtyard between them and the castle, where the Jerries were holed up behind thick walls and zeroed in on the open area with two machine guns. Now, it was pretty much of a frozen Mexican standoff, with nobody willing to start anything.

A short burst from the gun in the castle made Cready look up. He cursed as he saw pockmarks being stitched against a low stone wall to his right. He knew who was behind the wall; it was Private Jason Pody and Corporal Bailey, and he sure as hell didn't want to lost Bailey. Vaulting the wall, he wormed his way to where the two men were lying on their bellies.

"Get that goon out of here," Bailey said, even before Cready got there. "He's going to get us both killed."

"What the hell you done now, Pody?"

The long, gangling figure propped itself up on its elbows. With his head bobbing in the round helmet, and the huge, bony nose under it. Private Pody looked like a comic-strip turtle.

"Gosh, Sarge. I didn't mean nothing. Honest, I didn't!"

"He sits up," Bailey complained. "That gooseneck makes his head show and it draws their fire."

"I got to," Pody said. "Different parts of me get cold."

"Well, don't stand on your head," Cready snapped. "You'll get shot in the end where you brains are."

Private Pody grinned. "Gosh, Sarge, that's pretty good."

"He crawls around here with the safety off on that carbine, too."

"Check that safety, stupid."

"He won't remember," Bailey said. "Can't you make him surrender, Sarge? We could run up a white flag and maybe trade him for a pack of tobacco or something like that."

"It's against regulations—I think."

"What I don't understand," Bailey said, "is why they try to protect us against the Germans and not against Pody."

"That's the Army, Bailey." Sergeant Cready crooked a finger. "Come on with me, yardbird. I'll have to find somewhere else for you." Cready turned on his hands and knees, starting to crawl back.

"Sure, Sarge. I'm right behind you."

Cready turned. "Check that safety," he growled.

Sergeant Cready took Private Pody to the gate towers and pointed down to the woods. "You get down there and guard that road, stupid. You stay there until you're relieved. You got that?"

"Sure, Sarge, I got that fine." Pody grinned. "But what'll I do if I see any Germans?"

Sergeant Cready clenched his fists. "I heard they were scraping the bottom of the barrel back in the states," he groaned, miserably, "but what they went and sent me was the bunghole."

Lieutenant Spicer had taken a small building as a CP, and Cready found him in there, crouched beside the windowless opening, studying the castle.

"I would of knocked," Sergeant Cready said, "only there ain't any door." He stomped his feet on the dirt floor. "Cripes, it's colder in here than it is outside."

Lieutenant Spicer crawled away from the opening and stood up. He was about Cready's age—twenty-eight—but he was thin and wore heavy, rimmed glasses. ''It's in better condition that I imagined,'' he said, as though completing a thought.

''It's these stone walls,'' Cready said. ''They draw in the frost and hold it.''

''It's criminal the way they've allowed some of these old castles to go to ruin.''

''I feel like a side of beef hanging in a refrigerator,'' Cready said.

Lieutenant Spicer was tapping his cheek. ''The keep itself is in good condition, except for the corbels. And the barbican, where we came in, is solid. So are the curtain walls, except for those crumbling bastion towers.''

Sergeant Cready fumbled a cigarette to his lips and looked up. ''Huh?''

''The bastions,'' Spicer said, shaken out of his trance. ''They are in bad shape.''

Cready was searching for a match. ''Oh,'' he said vaguely. ''You'll have to put in a requisition then.''

Spicer flipped his thumb across the wheel of his lighter and held the flame to Cready's cigarette. ''A bastion, Sergeant,'' he explained patiently, ''is a projecting part of a fortification. A form of irregular pentagon, having its base in a main line, or at an angle to the fortification itself.''

''Yeah,'' Cready said. ''I don't know whether supply's got any of those or not. I'll check when we get back.''

Spicer was peering at him suspiciously when they heard the shots in the distance.

''That was a full clip,'' Cready said.

''You'd better alert the men,'' Lieutenant Spicer said nervously. ''Have them set up a——''

''Simmer down,'' Sergeant Cready said. ''That's Private Pody. He's gone and forgot the safety again.''

''Private Pody?'' Lieutenant Spicer pondered. ''Isn't he the replacement who had the whole company volunteering for firing-squad duty, in case you could talk me into having him court-martialed?''

''Yeah. I'd go down and see what happened, only I don't think I could stand it if he hasn't shot himself.'' Sergeant Cready beat his hands together. ''Forget him,'' he said, ''we've got to figure out how to root those guys from that castle.''

Sergeant Cready still hadn't worked anything out when Private Pody came flying into the room, his arms flapping wildly as he tried to regain his balance. Standing behind him in the doorway was a short, squat man holding a forty-five automatic. He had his hip-length jacket zippered up tight, like a fat woman in a corset.

"Why, it's Major Coodle!" Spicer gasped.

"Who's in charge here?" Major Coodle asked.

"Me—Lieutenant Spicer, sir."

"Then put that man under arrest!" The major was jabbing the automatic at Pody.

"Yes, sir. On what charges, sir?"

"Attempted murder. Cold-blooded attempted murder."

Private Pody ambled back across the room. "Aw, no, General, sir—"

"You shut up!" Major Coodle whirled on Spicer. "And have him sign a statement of charges for my wrecked jeep. Now I can't get out of here."

"Yes, sir."

Private Pody came up to Cready, his eyes pleading. "I didn't mean to do nothing wrong, Sarge, honest. I was standing guard like you told me, when I heard this noise coming down the road. I thought it was a German tank—"

"Preposterous!" Major Coodle roared.

"Not with Private Pody, it ain't, sir," Cready insisted. "One time he shot down a raven for a Messerschmidt."

"The man's a menace."

"We know that, sir. But we can't spare anybody to guard him."

The major glared from Cready to Pody, then back again. "You'll do, Sergeant," he said. "From now on, I'm holding you personally responsible for his every action."

"Hell's bells, Major—" Sergeant Cready stopped and closed his eyes. "Yes, sir."

Shoving Pody over against the wall, Sergeant Cready made a fist and ground it up against Pody's chin as a warning.

Major Coodle jammed his automatic back into the holster and faced Lieutenant Spicer. "I had to come clear up here personally to find out what is holding things up," he said accusingly. "This company is four hours late on the timetable already. Four hours"—he glared down at his watch and then back up again—"and twenty minutes. What's holding things up around here? Why isn't there some action?"

"We ran into some resistance, sir," Cready said.

Major Coodle turned on him. "How big a force?"

"We figure about twelve men," Cready said uneasily. "But—"

The major disposed of the force with a contemptuous snort as he waddled over to the window. He stood there for a few seconds, framed in the opening, glaring at the castle. A stacatto roar outside sent him flying backward in a hail of stone splinters, and he landed on his fat round behind in the middle of the room.

"But they have two machine guns," Sergeant Cready said.

Major Coodle pushed his helmet back and struggled to his feet. "You might have told me, Sergeant," he said shakily.

"It must have slipped my mind, sir."

"Well, there's no doubt that we have a problem here," the major said, rubbing his hands together. "Maybe you had better give me the layout."

Lieutenant Spicer took off his glasses, held them out and peered through them. "This is a feudal castle," he said replacing the glasses, "that was built, I should judge, around the twelfth century. It was placed in this strategic position for one purpose: namely, to repel any invading army that wished to enter the valley. I might add, sir, that it has done an extremely effective job of accomplishing just that."

"You talk like you were reading a book," the major grumbled. "I don't intend to put on a suit of armor and joust with the thing. We're equipped with something besides bows and arrows, you know."

"It has stood there for centuries," Lieutenant Spicer said primly.

"What the thunder kind of ice does that cut?" Major Coodle demanded. "This is the twentieth century, man! The United States Army is mechanized. Capable of fighting a modern war. Even you ought to have enough sense, Lieutenant, to know that modern weapons have revolutionized warfare since the middle ages."

"It still stands," Lieutenant Spicer said dramatically. "Impregnable!"

"Poppycock!" the major yelled, losing his temper. "You just let me get a few modern planes up here. Let them drop a few modern bombs—and you'll find out how impregnable that precious castle of yours is!"

Sergeant Cready saw Spicer wince as if he had been hit in the belly. He figured the lieutenant had taken a low blow from the major and broke in. "The weather is socked-in, sir. The fly boys ain't been off the ground in days."

Lieutenant Spicer smiled his appreciation at Cready. "That's right, Major."

"Maybe so," Major Coodle sputtered, "but if I had some artillery,

I'd show you. Even if I had tanks . . ." He stopped, his face getting redder. Then he exploded. "Dammit!" he yelled, "that's the trouble with a modern mechanized army. It's never around when you need it!"

"My contention exactly, sir."

Major Coodle took a furious turn around the room, drawing up before Lieutenant Spicer. "You're supposed to be an authority on these things, Lieutenant," he said, his voice somewhat under control now. "How would a medieval army attack this blamed castle?"

Lieutenant Spicer pondered. "They might build towers against the blind walls and storm it from above, sir."

"Building towers is for the engineers, Lieutenant," the major said sarcastically. "We happen to be the infantry."

"Yes, sir. Well, the most common method was to lay siege—"

"Siege?" Major Coodle turned purple. "This piddling castle is keeping us out of the valley, so the advance is held up. It may throw the whole war out of kilter—and you're suggesting we wait for twelve Germans to starve to death. Is that what you're suggesting, Lieutenant?"

"No, sir."

Major Coodle rolled his eyes up. "Doesn't anyone around here have one sensible suggestion?"

"I do, General."

Sergeant Cready froze as Private Pody sauntered to the center of the room. It was too late to stop him now. Major Coodle had turned.

"If the general would lead an attack on that castle personally, I'll bet—"

Major Coodle let out a roar. "Get that man out of here!" He was clawing at his holster as Spicer jumped in front of him.

Sergeant Cready grabbed Private Pody's throat and clapped his other hand over the man's mouth, all the time trying desperately to keep out of the line of fire.

"You're responsible, Sergeant!" Major Coodle yelled, shaking a trembling finger at Cready. "I'm holding you responsible."

"Yes, sir," Sergeant Cready said, booting Private Pody toward the doorway with his knee. "He's leaving right now, sir."

Outside, Sergeant Cready was too shaken to turn loose on Private Pody. Things had piled up until he was too close to the breaking point to risk it. He felt that if he let himself blow up now, it would be the end; he would never come down again. He would be prime fodder for the psycho ward. "Look, knucklehead," he said, his voice trembling. "Even a knucklehead should know better than to say something like that. Even a knucklehead should . . . You knucklehead!"

"Gosh, I'm sorry, Sarge, honest. But the general told it to you all wrong. I didn't come near him when I was shooting. I can't hit nothing with a carbine. You know that."

"You wrecked his jeep," Cready said miserably. "He's stuck here now."

Private Pody spit on the ground. "Naw, he just run it into a tree a little when I put a hole in his front tire."

Sergeant Cready was clutching at straws now. It was all that was left to him; but if Major Coodle *did* have his jeep, he was pretty sure that Major Coodle would be glad to get the hell out of here. The major would probably be happy to hitail it back and send up reinforcements. When he was back where it was safe, Cready was counting on the major to forget everything—especially Sergeant Cready.

"Get down there and fix that jeep tire," he ordered. "Hup—and on the double."

Cready knew he should have gone with Pody, but he couldn't. Since the major hadn't busted him on the spot, he was still a sergeant, and a sergeant's first duty was to his men. So, for the next twenty minutes, Sergeant Cready had to forget his own troubles while he dodged sniper bullets on an inspection tour.

The castle had been a permanent billet for the Germans, so the men had been able to scrounge firewood. They had found a well and were reasonably comfortable, with a couple of crap games going. Fianlly satisfied, Cready headed for the woods.

He found the jeep, just as Private Pody had said, but there was no Private Pody around. The front tire was off and lying on the ground. Sergeant Cready picked up part of it and went numb. It was the inner tube, cut in two and a big section gone. He rushed around to the back. There was no spare. Pody had ruined his last chance.

Major Coodle's possessions had been dumped on the floor of the jeep, and while going through the maps, papers, and chocolate bars, he found part of a highly polished paratrooper boot and a bottle of officer-issue whiskey. The bourbon was almost all there, but the top of the boot had been sliced off, and Cready remembered the hunting knife Private Pody always carried. Sergeant Cready dropped the ruined boot and took a long pull on the bottle. Then he leaned against the jeep and tried to concentrate on a plan of action.

Nudged by the bourbon fumes, an idea began to form. He would desert. Somehow, he would get over to the eastern front and join the Russian army. Right now, that seemed the only place in the world where Major Coodle coldn't get at him. He took another long drink. He wanted to remember the hearty taste of bourbon, because he would be drinking vodka from now on.

There was one thing he had to do before he left, though. That was to find Private Pody and exterminate him. It wasn't only because of what Private Pody had done to him; he wanted his men to remember Sergeant Cready as having done one noble deed before he left.

Cready wandered around the woods, and when he couldn't find Pody, he returned to the jeep. He unscrewed the cap from the bottle and threw it into the bushes. He slumped to the frozen ground and finished the bottle.

A great inspiration came to Sergeant Cready through his efforts. He wasn't going to desert. He would meet this like a soldier. He would go back, face Major Coodle and take his place in history. A martyr, sacrificed to appease military injustice. Songs would be sung about Sergeant Cready's brave defiance against tyranny. He pulled himself to his feet and stood wobbling, while tears flooded his eyes. He could see Sergeant Cready now, bravely standing against the wall, spurning the blindfold while he took a last drag from his cigarette before baring his chest.

In this new role, there was no room for petty hates, and a great compassion overcame him. He wanted to forgive everybody—and that included Private Pody.

As Cready staggered toward the castle, he began to realize that he had never really understood the real Private Jason Pody. He hadn't tried to understand the poor fellow who had been sent to him for help and guidance. He had wronged Private Jason Pody deeply, and now the most important thing in the world was to find Pody and make him understand and forgive before it was too late.

At the gate tower, Pody loomed through Cready's alcoholic haze. "Hey, Sarge," he said. "I've been looking for you."

Sergeant Cready threw himself on Pody. "Buddy Pody," he mumbled.

Private Pody tried to pull away. "I wanted to show you what I made," he said. He shoved an object at Cready.

Cready ran his hand over a five-foot fork, cut from a tree. Two long strips of inner tubing hung from the tip ends and were joined together at the bottom with a leather pouch.

Sergeant Cready fondled the leather. "Major Coodle's boot?" He giggled.

Pody nodded. "I hope he won't be sore when he finds out what I'm going to do with it," he said.

"To hell with Major Coodle! What is it?"

"A slingshot," Pody said. "I ain't so good with the weapons the army gave me, but back home, I'm a whiz with a slingshot. I can plink a squirrel's eye out at thirty yards."

"I believe it, ol' buddy."

Private Pody looked worried and uneasy. "I made it to square things with you and the general, Sarge."

"To hell with the general."

"Don't talk like that, Sarge. It ain't right." Pody was trying to get out of Cready's grasp. "I figured if I take that castle, the general won't be sore at you no more."

"You're going to take that castle just for *me*?" Sergeant Cready was holding onto Pody for support.

"I guess maybe it was some my fault to begin with," Pody said.

"You're the best damned ol' buddy a guy ever had. You know what? I'll go with you and we'll whip the whole lousy German army singlehanded together."

Private Pody led Cready to a high-sided cart he had found beside one of the buildings. It had two large wooden wheels and a small, swiveled wheel in back. It had been used to haul wood and was still filled with logs. Pody climbed up on the load with the slingshot and jammed the handle down between the logs and the side of the cart. When it was solid, he jumped down and surveyed his work.

The forks of the slingshot stuck up above the load, with the rubber strips hanging down on the outside. Pody picked up a musette bag—the one that had held Major Coodle's possessions—hefted it and hung it on the side of the cart.

Sergeant Cready had been draped over the wooden wheel watching him. Now Pody turned and looked at him dubiously. "If you still want to go, Sarge, she's ready."

With Sergeant Cready pushing on the wheel, and Pody behind him, pulling on the rear corner of the cart, the clumsy vehicle moved out into the open courtyard.

All the guns in the castle opened up at once and all of them raked the cart. When C Company saw what was going on, they returned the fire to furnish cover.

Private Pody was using his weight against the side to steer and managed to maneuver the cart close to the castle, in front of one of the towers housing a machine gun.

Sergeant Cready had been pushing up on the wheel, not knowing what was heppening, but now that they had stopped, he tried to straighten up. He found he was stiff, gasping for air, and he could feel sweat running down inside his shirt. Dimly, he saw Private Pody take a grenade from the musette bag, fit it into the leather pouch and then back away from the cart.

It was the noise that finally penetrated Sergeant Cready's befogged brain, and the din in the hollow courtyard swelled until he thought his head was going to burst. Then he realized his position: stranded out here in an open space, behind a little barricade and directly under the German guns with no way to get back.

He was cold sober when he saw Pody crouched out there in the open under a hail of lead. "Get back in here, you idiot!"

Private Pody looked up and grinned, then went carefully about lining himself up between the uprights, the grenade hugged to his chest and the rubber bands stretched to the snapping point.

"I'll come out there and break every bone in your by damn body!" Cready yelled at Pody.

Private Pody was calm as he ducked his head and pulled the pin with his teeth. He held the grenade against his chest while he squinted up at the castle—and then let go.

Cready saw the bands snap and felt Pody's body hit the cart beside him. He held his breath until he heard the muffled boom, then stuck his head up over the load. A cloud of smoke was boiling out of the window where the gun had been.

Private Pody looked over and gulped. "Bull's-eye," he said.

Sergeant Cready nodded weakly, his mouth too dry to say anything.

It was the cheer that went up from C Company that made him really believe it. This harebrained, clabber-headed scheme was working. One of the machine guns had been knocked out.

"Come on," he said. "Let's move over to the other one."

When they were lined up again, Sergeant Cready reached over and slapped Pody on the back. "You're great!" he shouted. "Put this one in their hip pocket."

Private Pody seemed shaken, and his motions were fumbling as he fitted a grenade into the pouch. He stood out at the end of the rubber bands, almost stricken as he held the grenade to his body.

The guy's jittery, Cready thought. "Take it easy," he called. "You can do it."

It didn't help. Pody was wild-eyed and stumbling. He let go, but his aim was far off and the grenade hit the wall, dropped, and then rolled back. When it exploded, the concussion blew under the cart and nearly knocked Cready's legs out from under him.

"What are you trying to do?" he roared, "Kill me, you idiot?"

Private Pody's head came up. "That's it, Sarge," he said, his eyes blinking. "You talking soft-like ruint my confidence."

"Oh, it did, did it!" Sergeant Cready yelled. He swelled up, shoved his reddened face up into Pody's and let the whole thing go in one long blast. "Get out there, you knucklehead, and do that right, or I'll stomp that by damn Adam's apple down that skinny neck of yours!"

"I'm sorry, Sarge. Honest, I'll do better."

It was a different Private Pody now. He grabbed two grenades, backed out into the flying lead, and without pausing, shot one straight through the window. Then, with a flourish, he lobbed another one in after it.

With the machine guns knocked out, C Company rushed in and mopped up. The castle had been taken.

In the CP, Major Coodle was pacing the room, his hands scarcely reaching behind his back. "I have always maintained that it is the individual initiative of the American soldier that makes ours the greatest army in the world," he was saying. "It was a great victory, and we could drink a toast to it"—he stopped and glared at Cready—"if I had any liquor left."

Sergeant Cready grunted and looked out the window. He could see Private Pody outside, still holding the slingshot and being back-slapped by the other men of C Company.

Lieutenant Spicer turned. "I was just wondering what that that old castle must think," he said, his eye misty. "Here, after all these centuries, it has again been stormed and taken by a medieval weapon."

Sergeant Cready's mouth tasted as if he had been chewing on a baby blanket. He wished he'd had enough sense to stash away a couple of drinks in that bottle. He scarcely heard what Lieutenant Spicer was saying.

''No doubt it has had the petraria used against it,'' Lieutenant Spicer continued. ''Also, probably the trebuchet, the mangonal and the ballista.''

''Huh?'' Major Coodle said.

''Medieval war machines, Major. They were all devised to hurl missiles.'' Spicer stopped and stroked his chin. ''However, in principle, I would say that Private Pody's machine was more like an onager. This machine was named after its action, which some people likened to the kick of an onager. An onager,'' Lieutenant Spicer said, as though explaining things to a rather stupid class, ''is a wild ass.''

Sergeant Cready turned from watching Private Pody. ''Yeah, Lieutenant''—and he sighed wearily—''I guess you're right. This whole thing has been pretty much strictly Operation Onager.''

EDWARD D. HOCH

I'd Know You Anywhere

16 November 1942

FROM THE TOP of the dune there was nothing to be seen in any direction—nothing but the unchanging, everchanging sameness of the African desert. Contrell wiped the sweat-caked sand from his face and signaled the others to advance. The tank, a sick sad monster wanting only to be left to die, ground slowly into life, throwing twin fountains of sand from the path of its tracks.

"See anything?" Grove asked, coming up behind him.

"Nothing. No Germans, no Italians, not even any Arabs."

Willy Grove unslung the carbine from his shoulder. "They should be here. Our planes spotted them heading this way."

Contrell grunted. "With old Bertha in the shape she is, we'd be better off not running into them. Six men and a battered old tank against the pride of Rommel's Afrika Korps."

"But they're retreating and we're not, remember. They just might be all set to surrender."

"Sure they might," Contrell agreed uncertainly. He'd known Willy Grove—his full name was an impossible Willoughby McSwing Grove—for only a month, since they'd been thrown together shortly before the North African invasion. His first impression had been of a man like himself, drafted in his early twenties into an impossible war that threatened to envelop them all in blood and flame. But as the weeks passed, another Willy Grove had gradually become evident, one that stood next to him now, peering down into the empty, sand-swept valley before them.

"Damn! Where are they, anyway?"

"You sound like you're ready for a battle. Hell, if I saw them coming I think I'd run the other way." Contrell took out the remains of a battered and almost empty pack of cigarettes. "A sand dune on the Tunisia border is no place for a couple of corporals."

Grove squatted down on his haunches, resting the carbine lightly against his knee. "You're right there—about the corporal part, anyway. You know, I been thinking the last few weeks—if I get back to the states in one piece I'm going to go to OCS and become an officer."

"You found yourself a home."

"Go on, laugh. There's worse things a guy could do for a living."

"Sure. He could rob banks. What in hell do army officers do when there's no war around?"

Willy Grove thought about that. "Don't you worry. There's goin' to be a war around for a good long time, maybe the rest of our lives."

"Think Hitler will last that long?"

"Hitler, Stalin, the Japs. It'll be somebody, don't you worry."

Contrell took another drag on his cigarette, then suddenly came to sharp attention. There was something moving at the top of one of the dunes, something . . . "Look!"

Grove brought up his binoculars. "Damn! It's them, all right. The whole stinkin' German army."

Contrell dropped his cigarette and went sliding down the dune to tell the others. The officer in charge was a paste-colored captain who rode the dying tank as if it were his grave. He looked down as Contrell spoke and then spoke a sharp order. "We'll take Bertha up the dune and let them see us. They might think we've got lots more and call it quits."

"Sure. Sir." And then again, Contrell thought, they just might blast the hell out of you.

By the time the wounded steel monster had been moved into position, the first of the three German tanks was within firing range. Contrell watched the big guns coming to bear on each other—two useless giants able only to destroy. He wondered what the world would be like if guns had the power to rebuild too. But he had little time to think about that or anything else before the German gun recoiled in a flash of power, followed an instant later by the thud of the sound wave reaching them. A blossom of sand and smoke filled the air to their left as the shell went wide of its mark.

"Hit the ground!" Grove yelled. "They've got us zeroed in!"

Old Bertha returned the fire, scoring a lucky near-miss on the nearest tank, but the odds and the firepower were all against her. The German's second shell hit the left tread, the third slammed into the turret, and Bertha was as good as dead. Someone screamed—Contrell thought it might have been the captain.

Grove was stretched out on the sand a dozen feet away. "Damn things are iron coffins," he said, gasping at the odor of burning flesh.

Contrell started to get up. "Did any of them get out?"

"Not a one. Stay down! They're coming this way."

"God!" It was a prayer on Contrell's lips. "What'll we do?"

"Just don't move. I'll get us out of this somehow."

Two of the enemy tanks remained in the distance, while the third one—basking in its kill—moved closer. Two German soldiers were riding on its rear, and they hopped down to run ahead. One carried a rifle, the other what looked like a machine pistol to Contrell. He tensed his body for the expected shots, his face nearly buried in the sand.

The German tank commander appeared in the turret and shouted something. The soldier with the machine pistol turned—and suddenly Willy Grove was on his feet. His carbine chattered like a machine gun, cutting down the German from behind. With his left hand he hurled a grenade in the direction of the tank, then threw himself at the second German before the man could bring up his rifle.

The grenade exploded near enough to knock the officer out of action, and Contrell moved. He ran in a crouch to the German vehicle, aware that Grove was right behind him. "I got 'em both," Willy shouted. "Stay down!" He pulled the dying officer from the top of the tank and fired a burst with his carbine into the interior. He clambered up, swinging the 50-caliber machine gun around.

"Hold it!" Contrell shouted. "They're surrendering!"

They were indeed. The crews of the other two tanks were leaving their vehicles, coming forward across the sand, arms held high.

"Guess they had enough war," Grove said, training the machine gun on them.

"Haven't we all?"

Grove waited until the eight men were within a hundred feet, then his finger tightened on the trigger and a burst of sudden bullets sprayed the area. The Germans looked startled, tried to turn and run, and died like that, on their feet.

"What the hell did you do that for?" Contrell shouted, climbing up to Grove's side. "They were surrendering!"

"Maybe. Maybe not. They might have had grenades hidden under their arms or something. Can't take chances."

"Are you nuts or something, Grove?"

"I'm alive, that's the important thing." Grove jumped down, hitting the sand with an easy, sure movement. "We tell the right kind of story, boy, and we'll both end up with medals."

"You killed them!"

"That's what you do in war," Grove said sadly. "You kill them and collect the medals."

30 November 1950

KOREA WAS A LAND of hills and ridges, a country poor for farming and impossible for fighting. Captain Contrell had viewed it for the first time with a mixture of resignation and despair, picturing in his mind only the ease with which an entire company of his men could be obliterated without a chance by an army more familiar with the land.

Now, as November ended with the easy victories of autumn turning to the bitter ashes of winter, he had reason to remember those first impressions. The Chinese had entered the war, and every hour fresh reports came from all around the valley of the Chongchon, indicating that their numbers could be counted not in the thousands but in the hundreds of thousands. The word on everyone's mind, but on no one's lips, was "retreat."

"They'll drive us into the sea, Captain," one of his sergeants told Contrell.

"Enough of that talk. Get the men together in case we have to pull out fast. Check Hill 314."

The hills were so numerous and anonymous that they'd been numbered according to their height. They were only places to die, and one looked much like another to the men at the guns.

Some tanks, muddy and caked with frost, rolled through the morning mists, heading back. Contrell stepped in front of the leading vehicle and waved it down. He saw now that it was actually a Boffers twin 40-mm. self-propelled mount, an antiaircraft weapon that was being effectively used as infantry support. From a distance in the mist it had looked like a tank, and for all practical purposes it was one.

"What the hell's wrong, Captain?" a voice shouted down at him.

"Can you carry some men back with you?"

The officer jumped down, and something in the movement brought back to Contrell a sudden memory of a desert scene eight years earlier. "Willy Grove! I'll be damned!"

Grove blinked quickly, seeming to focus his eyes, and Contrell saw from the collar insignia that he was now a major. "Well. Contrell, wasn't it? Good to see you again."

"It's a long way from Africa, Willy."

"Damn sight colder, I know that. Thought you were getting out after the war."

"I was out for three weeks and couldn't stand it. I guess this army life gets to you after a while. How are things up ahead?"

Grove twisted his face into a grimace. "If they were any damned good, you think we'd be heading this way?"

"You're going back through the Pass?"

"It's the only route left. I hear the Chinese have got it just about cut off too."

"Can we ride on top your vehicles?"

Grove gave a short chuckle. "Sure. You can catch the grenades and toss them back." He patted the .45 at his side as if it were his wallet. "Climb aboard."

Contrell issued a sharp order to his sergeant and waited until most of his few scattered forces had found handholds on the vehicles. Then he climbed aboard Major Grove's "tank" himself. Already in the morning's distance they could hear the insane bugle calls that usually meant another Chinese advance. "The trap is closing," he said.

Grove nodded. "It's like I told you once before. The fighting never stops. Never figured back then that we'd be fighting the Chinese, though."

"You don't like fighting Chinese?"

The major shrugged. "Makes no difference. They die just like anyone else. Easier, when they're high on that stuff they smoke."

The column rolled into the Pass, the only route that remained open to the south. But almost at once they realized that the hills and wooded stretches on either side of the roads were filled with the waiting enemy. Contrell looked back and saw his sergeant topple over to the ground, cut through the middle by a burst from a hidden machine gun. Ahead of them, a truckload of troops was stalled across the road, afire. Grove lifted himself up for a better view.

"Can we get around them?" Contrell asked, breathing hard.

"Around them or through them."

"They're South Koreans."

Those still alive and able to run were scrambling off the burning truck, running toward Grove's vehicle. "Get off!" Grove shouted. "Keep back!" He reached down and shoved one of the South Koreans over backward, into the roadside dust. When another clambered aboard in his place, Grove carefully took out his .45 pistol and put a bullet through the man's head.

Contrell watched it all as if he were seeing an old movie unwinding after years of forgotten decay. I've been here before, he thought, thinking in the same breath of the medals they'd shared after the North African episode. Men like Grove never changed—at least, not for the better.

"They were South Koreans, Willy," he said quietly, his mouth close to the major's ear.

"What the hell do I care? They think I'm running a damned bus service?"

Nothing more was said about it until they'd rumbled south into the midst of the retreating American army. Contrell wondered where it would all stop, the retreat. At the sea, or Tokyo—or California?

They took time for a smoke, and Contrell said, "You didn't have to kill that Gook, Willy."

"No? What was I supposed to do, let them all climb aboard and get us all killed? Go on, report it if you want to. I know my military law and I know my moral law. It's like the overcrowded lifeboat."

"I think you just like to kill."

"What soldier doesn't?"

"Me."

"Hell! Then what'd you re-up for? Fun and games?"

"I thought I might do something to keep the world at peace."

"Only way to keep the world at peace is to kill all the troublemakers."

"That Gook back there was a troublemaker?"

"To me he was. Just then."

"But you enjoyed it. I could almost see it in your face. It was like North Africa all over again."

Major Grove turned away, averting his face. "I got a medal for North Africa, buddy. It helped me become a major."

Contrell nodded sadly. "They do give medals for killing. And I guess sometimes they don't ask for too many details."

Someone called an order and Grove stubbed out the cigarette. "Come on, boy. Don't brood over it. We're moving on."

Contrell nodded and followed him. Once, just once, he looked back the way they'd come . . .

24 August 1961

MAJOR CONTRELL HAD BEEN in Berlin only three hours when he heard Willy Grove's name mentioned in a barside conversation at the Officers' Club. The speaker was a slightly drunk captain who liked to sound as if he'd been defending Berlin from the Russians single-handed since the war.

"Grove," he said with a little bit of awe in his voice. "Colonel Willoughby McSwing Grove. That's his name! They say he'll make general before the year is out. If you coulda seen the way he stood up to those Russians last week, if you coulda seen it!''

''I'd heard he was in Berlin,'' Contrell said noncommittally. ''I know him from the old days.''

''Korea?''

Contrell nodded. ''And North Africa nearly twenty years ago. When we were all a lot younger.''

''I didn't know he fought in World War II.''

''That was before we were officers.''

The captain snorted. ''It's hard to imagine old Grove before he was an officer. You shoulda seen him last week—he stood there, watching them put up that damned wall, and pretty soon he walked right up to the line. This Russian officer was there too, and they stood like that, only inches apart, just like they were daring each other to make a move. Pretty soon the Russian turned his back and walked away, and damned if old Grove didn't take out his .45! We all thought for a minute he was going to blast that Commie down in his track, and I think we'd all have been with him if he did. You know, you go through this business long enough—this building up and relaxing of tensions—and after a while you just wish somebody like Colonel Grove would pull a trigger or push a button and get us down to the business once and for all.''

''The business of killing?''

''What else is there, for a soldier?''

Contrell downed his drink without answering. Instead, he asked, ''Where is Grove staying? Is he married now?''

''If he is, there's no sign of a wife. He lives in the BOQ over at the air base.''

''Thanks.'' Contrell laid a wrinkled bill on the bar. ''The drinks were on me. I enjoyed our conversation.''

He found Colonel Grove after another hour's searching, not at his quarters but at the office overlooking the main thoroughfare of West Berlin. His hair was a bit whiter, his manner a bit more brisk, but it was still the same Willy Grove. A man in his forties. A soldier.

''Contrell! Welcome to Berlin! I heard you were being assigned here.''

They shook hands like old friends, and Contrell said, ''I understand you've got the situation pretty well in hand over here.''

''I did have until they started building that damned wall last week. I almost shot a Russian officer.''

''I heard. Why didn't you?''

Colonel Grove smiled. "You know me better than to expect lies, Major. We've been through some things together. You're the one who always said I had a weakness for killing."

"Weakness isn't exactly the word for it."

"Well, whatever. Anyway, you probably know better than anyone else my feelings at that moment. But I kept them under control. There's talk of making me a general, boy, and I'm keeping my nose clean these days. No controversy."

"And I'm still a major. Guess I don't live right."

"You don't have the killer instinct, Contrell. Never did have it."

Major Contrell lit a cigarette, very carefully. "I don't think a soldier needs to have a killer instinct these days, Willy. But then, we've been debating this same question for nearly twenty years now, off and on."

"Haven't we, though." Willy Grove smiled. "I'm sorry I don't have somebody I can kill for you this time."

"What would you have ever done in civilian life, Willy?"

"I don't know. Never thought about it much."

"A hundred years ago you'd have been a Western gunman probably. Or forty years ago, a Chicago bootlegger with a tommy gun. Now there's just the army left to you."

Grove's smile hardened, but he didn't lose it. Instead, he rose from behind the desk and walked over to the window. Looking down at the busy street, he said, "Maybe you're right, I really don't know. I do know that I've killed fifty-two men so far in my lifetime, which is a pretty good average. Most of them I looked right in the eye before I shot them. A few others got it in the back, like that Russian nearly did last week."

"You could have started a war."

"Yes. And some day perhaps I will. If I had the power to . . ." He let the sentence go unfinished.

"They're not all like you," Contrell said. "Thank God."

"But I have enough of them on my side. Enough of them who know that army means war and war means death. You can't escape it, no matter how hard you try."

He looked at the white-haired colonel and remembered the captain he'd spoken with in the bar earlier that afternoon. Perhaps they were right. Perhaps he was the one who was wrong. Had he wasted away his whole life pursuing an impossible dream of an army without war or killing?

"I'll still do it my way," he said.

"Good luck, Major."

A week later Contrell heard that a Russian guard had been killed at the wall in an exchange of gunfire with West Berlin police. One story had it that an American officer had fired the fatal shot personally, but Contrell was unable to verify this rumor.

5 April 1969

IT WAS THE DAY before Easter in Washington, a city expectant under a warm spring sun. The corridors of the Pentagon were more deserted than usual for a Saturday, and only in one office on the west side was there any activity. General Willoughby McSwing Grove, newly appointed Chairman of the Joint Chiefs of Staff, was moving into his suite of offices.

Colonel Contrell found him bent over a desk drawer, distributing the contents of a bulging brief case to their proper places. He looked up, a bit surprised, at his Saturday visitor. "Well . . . Contrell, isn't it? Haven't seen you in years, Colonel? You're coming along."

"Not as fast as you, General."

Grove smiled a bit, accepting the comment as a sort of congratulation. "I'm at the top now. Good place to be for a man of my age. The hair's all white, but I feel good. Do I look the same, Colonel?"

"I'd know you anywhere, General."

"There's a lot to be done, a damned lot. I've waited and worked all my life for this spot, and now I've got it. Our new President has promised me free reins in dealing with the international situation."

"I thought he would," Contrell said quietly. "Do you have any plans yet?"

"I've had plans all my life." He wheeled around in his swivel chair and stared hard out the window at the distant city. "I'm going to show them what an army is for."

Colonel Contrell cleared his throat. "You know, Willy, it took the better part of a lifetime, but you finally convinced me that killing can be necessary at times."

"Well, I'm pleased to know that you've come around to . . ." General Grove started to turn back in his chair and Contrell shot him once in the left temple.

For a time after he'd done it, Contrell stood staring at the body, hardly aware that the weight of the gun had slipped from his fingers. There was only one thought that crowded all the others from his mind. How would he ever explain it all at the court-martial?

WILLIAM SAMBROT

Black Night, White Night or *The Battle of Dingle on the Dangle*

IT WAS JUST a few weeks ago, while I was in London, that I first heard of the battle of—I'll call it "Dingle on the Dangle," which is ludicrous, I know, but as far from the true name of that lovely little hamlet as one can get, English place names being what they are.

As you doubtless know, throughout that fair green land so beloved of poets, certain villages and even towns are named in such a manner. Morton on Lugg, for example. Morton being the town, Lugg the river meandering through it. So with Dingle, a tiny village on the river Dangle.

I ran into ffyfe-Smithe in Covent Garden, in the course of a rather unfruitful visit to my overseas agent who lurks there in lieu of some habitat more suitable—under a toadstool, say. In any event—(and why are so many of these stouthearted English afflicted with these lower-case hyphenated names?) Smitty, as we called him back during the war, was strolling along with the most extraordinarily beautiful girl I've ever seen in London—a town noted for its lovely women.

I accosted him, and after a bit of that glacial affront most English assume when they're hailed by a total stranger, Smitty recognized me. Following the mutual outcries common to such encounters, Smitty introduced me to the girl—his daughter-in-law. Her name was Miriam. She was stunning, tall, with dark creamy complexion, black hair, and extremely blue eyes—but undeniably, to my experienced American eye, Miriam was more that somewhat touched with the tar-brush, to use a bad colloquialism.

Low husky voice, gorgeous teeth and smile—she was a smashing beauty, is all I can say, and when she left us, I was quick to tell Smitty so over a scotch in the nearest pub.

"You're son's a lucky fellow, Smitty," I said. "And God! Are we really that old?"

He nodded. "She's"—he hesitated a fraction "—half American, you know."

"Yes," I said noncommittally. "I rather thought so." I sipped the scotch.

"Her father—" Again he hesitated. "He was a Yank, you know. Killed during the war. Battle of Dingle on the Dangle." He gave me a cool ironic stare.

I nodded. "Pilot?"

"No," Smitty said slowly, "matter of fact, he was a sergeant—in the U.S. Army Engineer corps."

"Engineer Corps?" I stared at him. "But—you say he was killed in the battle of—Dingle on the Dangle?"

He nodded, looking down at his drink. "Ah—bayoneted, you might say."

"*Bayoneted*. In a battle—in England?" He nodded. "You're putting me on, Smitty."

"Putting you on?"

"Pulling my leg."

"I assure you—no such thing. I was there and saw it all." He gave me a penetrating look. "Mean to say you never heard—?"

"Absolutely not, Smitty," I said.

He nodded thoughtfully. "No, I suppose not. It was pretty well hushed up." Abruptly he made up his mind. "Well, it was a long time ago. Can't see the harm in telling you now—not that things have improved since then—I mean to say, have you got time?"

"Bags of it."

Smitty had been liaison officer between certain British Air Force commands and certain manufacturers in America. This was in early '41, prior to America's entry into the war. but lend-lease was in full force. Bombers shuttled from Canada to England in great droves—which, incidentally, was how I'd first met Smitty: as a civilian pilot I flew American-built bombers from Canada to England, I'd flown Smitty literally dozens of times back and forth. But after December 7th, '41 I switched to the B-17s and joined the real war. Smitty and I lost contact.

All that aside, part of the lend-lease meant the construction of a great many air strips throughout the length and breadth of England.

One such field, designed primarily as an emergency landing strip, was constructed in the midst of the lush greenery outside the little town of Dingle, on the Dangle River. It had a small contingent of technical personnel and this one group of Army Engineers, leftovers from the early construction days.

They were the 15th Sanitary Engineers, to be exact. A group of swinging cats, all—Negroes, of course, since sanitary engineers were ditch-diggers, sewer-layers, and the like. They'd been there since early '41—before America was even at war, as part of the lend-lease, presumably. In plain words, these black troops were the first Yanks this particular segment of England had ever encountered.

The town was jumping with women; this area was an important farming center and here were grouped many of the British Land Army—the tough-spirited strong-armed girls who volunteered to do their fighting for England in the fields, wielding rakes, hoes, and scythes. It was a lonely life—and a hard one.

Remember—this was rural England of early 1941. Very few colored had ever been in rural England. In fact, Dingle had slept alongside the meandering River Dangle for centuries, hardly disturbed by the waves of history which Britannia, ruler of the seas, constantly engendered. A sleepy backwash.

Oh, they knew there was a war on—after all, there were the Land Army girls. Also, every lad from fourteen up was gone—had been gone for years now. They knew all about Hitler—Churchill made sure of that. But other than the wireless, life slipped along monotonously—until the 15th Sanitary Engineers made the scene.

The tall velvety-skinned Negroes came as a piquant shock to the girls of Dingle. So carefree; they danced and sang divinely. And their laughter! Unreservedly wholehearted, encompassing their whole bodies, hands-clapping, slapping thighs, showing their magnificent teeth (to the unfailing awe and envy of the chalk-toothed English), moving rhythmically with easy grace.

To start the ball rolling, one of the 15th's wits, more to put the chicks on than anything else, had casually mentioned they were "night-fighters," given injections to turn themselves black. Just waiting for the outbreak of hostilities between America and Germany to start their true roles of deadly combatants. Meanwhile, they were just digging these here ditches and laying sewers more for exercise than anything.

Some of the soldiers let it be known they were American Indians—and why not? Some of them were about one-twentieth Cherokee or Seminole or what-have-you.

In the end, none of these claims meant a thing to the girls, or were even remembered. True, they were black—but they were men. Generous to a fault. Outgoing, gentle. Above all—gentle.

And how they could make love!

Dingle was an ancient town going back well over eight hundred years. But never, in all that time, had it known the warmth, the gaiety, the sheer happiness the 15th field unit brought.

There was the swing band; these men blew real jazz—not that the girls of Dingle knew it—or even cared as to its purity—but they knew rhythm, and what that swinging band did to their pulses was good enough for them.

There was the dancing: they took to jitterbugging as if they'd rested all day and tomorrow would never come.

There were the field rations. In a country long at war, accustomed to rigid austerity, the garrison-type food and goodies that poured from the 15th's cornucopia was overwhelming. And appreciated. And given without strings. These were kind men.

It was pure delight (assuming, Smitty said reminiscently, such a shock at such an early hour could be borne) to hear reveille blown throughout the 15th's small encampment nestled in the deep green fields outside Dingle.

The bugler came on smooth and sweet—but oddly muted as though taking pity on those forced to sleep, cold and alone, in those little tin huts known as quonsets. Then the horn gathered force, rising harder, hotter, jazzy but mocking, somehow. Riffing wildly, suddenly the time-worn tune became something right out of Basin Street, sliding imperceptibly into the ''King Porter Stomp,'' or whatever, swinging like mad, until the bugler, abruptly aware he was knocking his own brains out, broke up, laughing. It was the same every morning.

Roll call, with this outfit, was brief—out of the full complement of one hundred and ten men (a company) less than a quarter showed up. The rest? They were in their real homes, in town, with their wives, steadies, or in the case of those few restless souls who preferred variety to the tried and true, with one-night stands. But there were few of these.

The women of Dingle were not triflers; they loved as hard as they worked. And, like women everywhere, they had a tendency to want to solidify their relationships. There were many marriages with the men of the 15th, prior to America's entry into the war. Snug harmony prevailed along the banks of the Dangle.

This idyll (Smitty said) continued for well over two years. Oddly enough, America's entry into the war didn't change things much. The few Air Corps personnel, a branch of the Army then, pretty well understood that Dingle was private property, so to speak, and there was little attempt to muscle in on the 15th's private domain.

And then, into this miniature garden of Eden, came the 32nd Heavy

Construction Company, a company of engineers. Real engineers. Bridge builders and the like—trained combat troops. All white. All from South Carolina.

These men were billeted in the fields—a staging area not too far from Dingle. They came in late one night, grinding along with their big prime-movers loaded with bulldozers, parts of Bailey bridges, and other impedimenta of their trade. These men had been trained to a fine edge in the states. They'd had a tough crossing, and now they were in the mood to celebrate once they were granted leave. Which wasn't long in coming.

They hit Dingle like a *tsunami*—that earthquake shock wave that flows through water with unbelievable speed and smashes the shore with devastating force. Big men, sunburned, hard-muscled. Thirsty for whiskey and women. It was early afternoon of a fine spring day.

They found the one main pub, the Coach and Four, crowded with the black troops from the 15th. It was a quiet scene: a mild game of darts going on, a few of the 15th with their wives or girlfriends—but very few; most of the girls were hard at work in the field. Within two minutes the first fight started.

"Git!" One huge red-faced Pfc, battlescarred, busted-beaked, yanked a black to his feet, and with a ferocious heave threw him toward the door. The black staggered, righted himself, came at the man, swinging wildly. He never made it. The huge white, feet solidly planted, a smile of pure satisfaction on his face, swung a fist like a sledgehammer square in the black's mouth. He went back against the bar. Another white kicked him in the groin. Another grabbed him and whirled him toward the door where he was passed expertly along, from one man to the other until finally he was hurled out onto the cobbled street.

"Gentlemen! Gentlemen!" The barmaid shrieked shrilly.

"Out!" The tough Pfc, Earl Lathrop, gestured toward the other blacks who stood silently, unmoving.

"Give it to him, George, the big bully," one of the girls, Margaret MacAdams, told her husband, a black giant nearly seven feet tall, with great sloping shoulders and immense arms bulging his olive drab. But he stood motionless, staring at the whites grouped near the door.

George nodded. "All right," he said quietly. "We're going."

"George MacAdams—you're not taking that—George!" Margaret shook his arm, staring up at him, unbelieving.

But the blacks walked out without a word. As George MacAdams passed him, Lathrop, the big white Pfc said curtly, ''Hold it—George.''

George paused, regarding him impassively.

''Y'all a New Yawk nigger, George?'' the voice was soft, but full of naked menace.

George said nothing, but a veil came down over his eyes.

The private gestured toward Margaret who now stood, hands pressed to her mouth, bewildered.

''Ya like that white meat, don't you black boy? Ya know what we do in C'lina we catch a black boy messin' with white girls?''

He reached in his pocket and suddenly there was a *click!* and a long blade flashed in the dark pub.

George stood there, arms dangling, while behind him, his wife gasped, then made a sudden determined move, pausing only when George held out a hand, palm toward her, stopping her.

''It's all right, Margaret,'' he said. Then looking calmly at Lathrop, his deep voice rumbling in the quiet pub, George said, ''This ain't Carolina. This ain't even the U.S.A. This is another country, man. They do things different here.''

''An' ah'm heah to tell ya, black boy, things are just the same as back home.'' Lathrop gestured with his knife. ''Y'all spread the word—this is white folks town—from now on. You heah me, nigger?''

George stiffened slightly, but his big arms still dangled, relaxed, his shoulders hunched slightly.

''Don't call me nigger, private.'' He turned a shoulder slightly toward Lathrop so that his three stripes were evident. ''See those stripes?''

''Stick them stripes in youah black ass, nigger.''

George hit him. So swift, so powerful was the blow that the terrible crunch of his fist came only split seconds before the sound of crashing glass that followed as the big Pfc went over a table and through a leaded window, still clutching his switchblade knife. He hung half out, face pale, completely unconscious, blood streaming from his shattered mouth.

''Oh! good show, Georgie!'' Margaret cried, shining-eyed.

George turned. His eyes glittered as he stared at the silent whites. None made a move.

''This is a different country,'' he said. ''I told him.'' He stepped toward the door, walking slowly past the whites who stood back out of his way. He turned and opened the door.

"George—look out!" Margaret screamed suddenly.

George whirled, and caught the thrown bottle full in the face. He sagged, and the whites were on him slugging, grabbing, tearing. He went down, and while two of them held back the struggling, screaming Margaret, the rest began on George (said Smitty) that peculiarly American ritual known as "stomping."

This scene was repeated with slight variations in the other smaller pub, in the little town square, and along the gently meandering Dangle, where quite a few of the blacks were wont to take their ladies punting, drifting quietly under the ancient trees, with the gaggles of geese, the occasional proud swan for company. The thud of boots on ribs and the meaty smack of fists in faces, the struggling grunting men on the mossy banks seemed strangely horrifying in such a peaceful setting.

That night there were fewer demonstrations—if only because both pubs were shut tightly, and the men of the 15th stayed in their respective cottages scattered about the community. But the night was horrid with the raucous bellowings of the outraged whites who stumbled up and down the village streets demanding drink and women and vengeance on the blacks—not necessarily in that order.

The townfolks, of course, were scandalized by the behavior of the whites, more than ever convinced that their own "boys," the blacks, were the true representatives of the Americans. Not a few, in fact, were vociferous in their insistence these red-necked interlopers were little better than the enemy just across the channel: "Not gentlemen," which is, in that part of England, about as bad a put-down as is possible.

When the 32nd's company commander, Major Leroy Martin (a bulky shouldered regular-army type, up from the depression-day ranks—a man who knew a pick from a shovel) learned of the situation in Dingle, he instantly called his opposite number, the company commander of the 15th Sanitary Engineers. A meeting was arranged forthwith.

The casualties of that first invasion were fairly light—mostly cracked heads, jaws and ribs. Dental problems (the Pfc, Earl Lathrop, specifically). Ordinarily, the 32nd's hard-cased commander wouldn't have turned a hair—boys will be boys; back in the states every weekend's pass produced the same sort of casualty list—but then, that had been whites fighting whites. This was something calling for strong medicine.

The 15th Sanitary Engineer's company commander was a sagging-shouldered round-bellied old-timer, Major Anderson. A bottle-a-day sergeant in the regular army, a white man. Shunted from pillar-to-post by a dismayed Army, he'd found his niche in the 15th, along with a handful of other white officers, sad-sacks, all. They left the company's control in the capable hands of Sergeant MacAdams and devoted themselves to serious drinking.

When Martin's jeep rolled through the 15th's area, he was impressed in spite of himself. True, some of the quonsets were pretty wild, painted in varous shades, but there were neat lawns in front of each, small gardens, whitewashed bricks outlining each area. Streets swept and spotless. There were even curtains on the few windows on the huts. The vehicles in the motor pool gleamed. The smells drifting from the mess hut were distinctly un-army in their appetizing aroma.

But the place was silent. An air of tense waiting prevailed.

Martin took one look at Anderson and he knew he was home free. Watery-eyed, blinking, his little red button nose blue-veined like a road map, Anderson did all the listening while Martin did the talking. Anderson did, however, protest the 15th's right of prior entry, so to speak.

"Gah-dammit, Majah, ah'm *tellin'* you—ah ain't askin' you," Martin bellowed. "Theah's no such thing as 'priah rights' in this heah ahmy. Ah don't give a damn how long youah troops been sittin' heah—theah'll be trouble—ah mean cuttin' and worse if the sit'ation ain't remedied, and raht now. Theah's only one solution, as ah see it—." Martin leaned a thick arm over Anderson's desk and held up two fingers. "One night youah men go in—next night mah men go."

Anderson cleared his throat nervously. "Be pretty tough enforcing that, major. My boys—"

Martin thumped the desk, cutting Anderson off. "Gah-dammit, Majah—this is the *ahmy!* What you mean—enforce it? You pull those black bastids back in this camp wheah they belong—you heah? They got no call livin' in that town lak civilians. Gah-dammit, man, we'ah at wah! This heah is wheah they billeted, and this is wheah they stay."

He hitched closer, and his voice dropped an octave, became hoarsely chummy. "We both know what'd happen if'n ah had to go to a higher echelon, majah. This whole set-up is a scandal. *White girls* with blacks. Wha—if word of this gets around—''

Anderson stiffened. A look of vague alarm on his face. ''It's different here, ah, Martin,'' he said. ''They don't have a color line, like we do back—''

''It ain't different, far as the U.S. Ahmy is concerned,'' Martin said. ''*We* got a color bar, and you damn well know it. Ah say we get started enforcing it, and raht now.''

Anderson sat a little straighter. ''Now hold on, Martin. My boys work hard—they got a right to have passes and go into town. I'm not about to restrict them to the area—and that's what enforcing a color bar amounts to.''

''Not necessarily,'' Martin said. ''You just give mah men free play—like ah say—theih own night in town without any colored around. Thing's work out.'' He smiled grimly.

Anderson nodded slowly, a worried crease on hs forehead. ''Okay—we'll give it a try.'' When Martin sat back with a satisfied grunt, Anderson brightened. ''What say to a little snort?'' Without waiting for an affirmative, he dove for the jug in the bottom drawer of his desk.

''Don't mind if ah do,'' Martin said indifferently. He smiled ironically, watching Anderson's shaky hand pouring out the whiskey.

The way it worked was simplicity itself: One day the men of the 15th were granted passes, good until reveille the next morning. All troops must stand roll call. On that day, all men of the 32nd were restricted to the general area of their billets.

On the next day, the situation was reversed: All 15th were restricted to the area while the 32nd were given passes good until 0540, on the next morning. Reveille must be stood; all troops show up for roll call without fail.

These orders were made known to both embattled encampments. They were instantly designated ''White Night'' and ''Black Night.''

Further, to enforce these regulations, on Black Night a certain number of whites were designated Military Police and told to patrol the town, making certain there were no whites infiltrating the area. And of course, on White Nights, a similar number of blacks were made MPs and given similar responsibilities.

Satisfaction reigned supreme in the 32nd Heavy Construction Company. There was no question in their minds but once they impressed upon the lovely English lasses their duties and responsibilities to their own race, that the girls would see the light, and a normal state of affairs rapidly ensue—white with white.

The first passes following the command decision fell to the blacks. They made their way into the town, somewhat more subdued than usual. However, things quickly warmed up, and before the fall of soft spring night, the town was swinging. Music flowed from the Coach and Four. Laughter, the clink of bottles, dancing. There was punting on the Dangle, strolling couples and later, recumbent forms dappled the cool mossy banks.

Throughout this, rigid faced, the MP contingent from the 32nd stamped the town from end to end, glaring at the happy couples—especially at those pushing perambulators.

Next morning, every man of the 15th Sanitary Engineers stood roll call for the first time within memory. They seemed happy and relaxed, unconcerned about the day's restriction that lay ahead.

Those from the 32nd that got passes made for town promptly at noon. By four P.M. (1600 Zulu) all the booze was gone and the pubs closed. By dark, they were wandering the streets in loud profane groups—alone. There were no girls strolling the winding paths alongside the Dangle. No fair companions to punt the quiet river. The pubs stayed closed. The town was flat. Dead. The few black MPs stayed discreetly away. The 32nd had Dingle all to itself—but who wanted it?

This sad state of affairs was discussed bitterly and at length the next day with Major Martin. Big Earl Lathrop (the Pfc who'd had the fight with George MacAdams, the Negro sergeant) his front teeth missing, jaw swollen, was the mouthpiece for the furious whites.

Martin listened coldly, then told them flatly, "If y'all cain't handle this little matter youahself, that's tough titty. Ah don't want to heah anothah word out of you." He stalked off and left the men looking excitedly at one another.

The next night, Black Night, the town was jumping again. A repetition of the previous Black Night. All the girls were there, and as if to impress upon the surly white MPs their true feelings, everyone wore bright fresh frocks—none wore the coveralls or work clothes of their trade. It seemed, if such a thing were possible, that there were more women than men. The pubs' supply of beer and whiskey apparently was inexhaustible. The band at the Coach and Four swung like crazy.

Word of this, via the MPs, quickly spread through the 32nd, naturally. The men gathered in tight little knots, discussing this final outrage. Here they stood, totally unfulfilled, while back there in town those black mothers were balling it up. It was too much. Lathrop decided the issue.

Even with his jaw in a sling, the big Pfc was tough. They'd bust up the town in a hit and run raid—and they'd go prepared—no firearms, but each man with a weapon of his own choosing. Hell, Lathrop aruged, Major Martin wouldn't press charges—he had practically laid it in their laps. He was on their side.

And anyway, said Lathrop, there'd be no comebacks because—one final cunning touch—they'd go in blackface.

There was a moment of stunned silence at this stroke of genius on Lathrop's part. Then as one of the men burst into spontaneous whoops of glee, pounding Lathrop's sore ribs. After discussing tactics, they dispersed to collect their weapons and blacken their faces and arms.

They drifted into town in small groups, every man packing an iron pry-bar, or big lug wrench, jack-handles, and the like. They met in the square near the Coach and Four. A blast of jazz poured out, music and laughter. A white MP came by, glaring at the men, then hesitated, puzzled. Blacks—one with red hair? And that one—a black face and blazing white neck? Before he could ponder this longer they burst into the Coach and Four and the riot was on.

They bashed skulls, battered ribs, broke arms right and left, swinging their semi-lethal weapons with might and main. They tore girls' dresses. One kicked in the bass drum and hurled the snare and cymbals through a window. Others parried with the musicians, iron bars against saxes and horns, denting and finally twisting and breaking the instruments. Bottles crashed. Chairs flew. Blacks dropped right and left while their girls screamed and scratched and fought as best they could.

The battle flowed outside and up and down the single main street. When they were through, the town was strewn with dazed and seriously injured blacks. The bell in the old church began tolling, and Lathrop dashed around, gathering up his men, ignoring the shrieking women. They headed for the fields, and one by one, made their way back into camp.

It had been more fun, even, than if they'd had a night on the town with a woman all agreed.

There were, as a result of that night's raid, thirty-seven black soldiers in the hospital. Two were near death with depressed skull fractures.

In response to Major Anderson's complaints, Martin hauled over his contingent of that night's MPs. To a man they swore there wasn't one white face in Dingle. The pub-keeper, a badly shaken woman, also testified tearfully that she hadn't seen any whites in the brawl. It had all been so awfully fast—so unexpected.

"Looks like y'all got a little problem heah among youah own men, Anderson," Martin drawled, and his eyes were snapping with pride. "I keep mine in line—y'all better do lakwise."

Anderson stared at him for a long time, then he nodded slowly. "Funny," he said, "never had a thing like this before." He turned to the barmaid. "We'll pay for the damages, of course, Elsie. Just send us the charges."

There were a few violent dissenters, however. Margaret MacAdams, George's wife in point of fact. A tall, hard-handed girl, she brought along her dress as exhibit A.

"Look at this, Major," she said hotly, "this is shoe-blacking. And it came from one of those men's arms when he tried to—to embrace me. He even smelled of it."

"Ah—er—Major Martin," Anderson said apologetically. "This is Margaret MacAdams." He coughed delicately. "She's—ah—married to one of my men. Sergeant MacAdams. A fine man. Fine man."

Martin gave her a basilisk stare. "What are you getting at?"

"They were your men," she said passionately. "We weren't fooled even a little bit, major. They blacked their faces. They're cowards—they can't even fight like decent soldiers. We know all about how it is in your country. But we're not like that here, you see. We asked to be let alone. George MacAdams is my husband, and I have my right to be with him, just as he has his right to be with me, free from molestation."

Martin stood up. "Ah'm satisfied this here's none of mah responsibility, *Mrs. MacAdams,*" he gave her a hard stare, "or any of mah men's either." He walked stiffly out. Anderson took her dress and sniffed it. He shook his head, sadly.

There were a lot of dirty faces in the 32nd that day—shoe polish was hard to get off.

That night—White Night, very few men from the 32nd went into town. Those that did, however, were astounded to discover there were actually a few women about. Also, the Coach and Four was serving scotch—limited amounts, to be sure—but genuine scotch. The few black MPs walked somberly along, their pistol-belts, bayonet scabbards, and holsters gleaming white. No one bothered the MPs. Even the girls paid scant attention to them. The girls left early: "Have to get up early, Yank," they said. But before they left, they dropped the electrifying word—a promise of a big affair on the next White Night—"To meet your white chums," they said. It was, to put it mildly, sensationally good news.

What was even better news came the next evening, Black Night, from the white MPs on duty. The town was dead. Very few blacks about. Hardly any girls. The tables had been turned. Whoops and hurrahs in the 32nd billets when the word was passed along to them.

"Told you," Lathrop bellowed gleefully. "They knew damn well they been doin' wrong. Just took a little skull-knockin' to bring them around."

They turned out en masse that next White Night. At least half a hundred men of the 32nd, shaved, shinolaed, shampooed—some had even washed their feet. They milled around in the square outside the Coach and Four, where a couple of dozen girls were on hand. The Coach and Four, oddly enough, was closed and dark.

"They'll open at eight sharp, boys," one of the girls assured the goatish men. "The rest of the girls will be along by then." There was talk, rumbling laughter, much spitting and hitching up of trousers.

On the outskirts of the crowd, somber-faced, marched the few black MPs. Outstanding among them was Sergeant George MacAdams, walking stiffly because of bandaged ribs, the bayonet on his hip looking like a small dagger against his great bulk.

At the stroke of eight the lights came on in the Coach and Four. The door was thrown open. At that instant, on the outskirts of the crowd a girl's piercing scream rang out.

"Help! Rape! Rape!"

And from inside the Coach and Four erupted a horde of tough young farm girls—with Margaret MacAdams in the lead, brandishing a sharpened hayfork. The rest carried sickles, small spades, hoes, axe-handles, pitchforks—a variety of semi-lethal farm implements—implements they'd used from sun-up to sun-down for some years. And now, full of righteous fury, they wielded them with effective skill.

They waded into the packed men, slashing clothing, walloping heads, jabbing groins, cracking shins, cutting a devastating swath through the panicked men who fell back on all sides.

But Margaret MacAdams was apart from it. Holding her pitchfork at quarter-arms, she scanned the crowd, searching for one person. He wasn't hard to find. Pfc Lathrop stood head and shoulders above the others, bellowing mightily, fending off women, and trying to rally his battered troops.

Unhesitatingly, Margaret MacAdams headed straight for him. Her glittering pitchfork came up, her bared teeth gleaming in the dim light.

"No—Margaret! No!"

George MacAdams plunged through he milling mob, throwing men right and left like so much chaff, heading straight for Lathrop. It was like a ballet in slow motion—Lathrop staring, pop-eyed, at the gleaming pitchfork raised high as Margaret MacAdams came for him, bringing the pitchfork down in a swift fatal plunge, all the strength of her strong arms propelling it straight for his chest. And behind, bulling through the mob, George.

He grabbed Lathrop and pulled him down—only to get the six sharp tines squarely in the hollow where his thick throat met the bulging brown curve of his chest. He fell without a sound, the dark blood spurting high.

In an instant, the mob scene fell apart. Margaret, screaming wildly, fell on George, keening, cradling his body. He died in her arms.

"There was a serious flap, of course," Smitty told me moodily. "It had repercussions right up to Supreme Allied Headquarters. Among other things, Dingle was declared forever off-limits for all troops."

He sighed. "You understand—the married girls had staged the whole thing, attempted rape and all that, so as to have self-defense as their excuse for administering a good beating to the white boys—nothing else was intended. Unfortunately—they hadn't realized how deadly serious Mrs. MacAdams had been. It all turned out badly."

"Yes—especially for George MacAdams—and his wife," I murmured. "How did it all end?"

He toyed with his drink. "Mrs. MacAdams was pregnant—carrying Miriam—you know. Hysterical for a long time after that. No charges were brought against her." He paused. "It was declared death by misadventure."

"Eminently just, I'd say," I said. "How about the others—the 32nd?"

He shrugged. "I'm told they distinguished themselves at the Normandy landings—but then, why not? They were, after all, excellent soldiers." He smiled wryly. "They did their part."

"And the 15th Sanitary Engineers?"

"They were transferred immediately, of course. To the States. A camp in Louisiana, I believe." He lifted his drink. "Dingle was poorer without them."

IRWIN SHAW

Act of Faith

''PRESENT IT IN a pitiful light,'' Olson was saying, as they picked their way through the mud toward the orderly room tent. ''Three combat-scarred veterans, who fought their way from Omaha Beach to—what was the name of the town we fought our way to?''

''Konigstein,'' Seeger said.

''Konigstein.'' Olson lifted his right foot heavily out of a puddle and stared admiringly at the three pounds of mud clinging to his overshoe. ''The backbone of the army. The noncommissioned officer. We deserve better of our country. Mention our decorations in passing.''

''What decorations should I mention?'' Seeger asked. ''The marksman's medal?''

''Never quite made it,'' Olson said. ''I had a cross-eyed scorer at the butts. Mention the bronze star, the silver star, the Croix de Guerre, with palms, the unit citation, the Congressional Medal of Honor.''

''I'll mention them all.'' Seeger grinned. 'You don't think the CO'll notice that we haven't won most of them, do you?''

''Gad, sir,'' Olson said with dignity, ''do you think that one Southern military gentleman will dare doubt the word of another Southern military gentleman in the hour of victory?''

''I come from Ohio,'' Seeger said.

''Welch comes from Kansas,'' Olson said, coolly staring down a second lieutenant who was passing. The lieutenant made a nervous little jerk with his hand as though he expected a salute, then kept it rigid, as a slight superior smile of scorn twisted at the corner of Olson's mouth. The lieutenant dropped his eyes and splashed on through the mud. ''You've heard of Kansas,'' Olson said. ''Magnolia-scented Kansas.''

''Of course,'' said Seeger. ''I'm no fool.''

''Do your duty by your men, Sergeant.'' Olson stopped to wipe the rain off his face and lectured him. "Highest ranking noncom present took the initiative and saved his comrades, at great personal risk, above and beyond the call of you-know-what, in the best traditions of the American army."

"I will throw myself in the breach," Seeger said.

"Welch and I can't ask more," said Olson, approvingly.

They walked heavily through the mud on the streets between the rows of tents. The camp stretched drearily over the Rheims plain, with the rain beating on the sagging tents. The division had been there over three weeks by now, waiting to be shipped home, and all the meager diversions of the neighborhood had been sampled and exhausted, and there was an air of watchful suspicion and impatience with the military life hanging over the camp now, and there was even reputed to be a staff sergeant in C Company who was laying odds they would not get back to America before July Fourth.

"I'm redeployable," Olson sang. "It's so enjoyable . . ." It was a jingle he had composed to no recognizable melody in the early days after the victory in Europe, when he had added up his points and found they only came to 63. "Tokyo, wait for me . . ."

They were going to be discharged as soon as they got back to the States, but Olson persisted in singing the song, occasionally adding a mournful stanza about dengue fever and brown girls with venereal disease. He was a short, round boy who had been flunked out of air cadets' school and transferred to the infantry, but whose spirits had not been damaged in the process. He had a high, childish voice, and a pretty baby face. He was very good-natured, and had a girl waiting for him at the University of California, where he intended to finish his course at government expense when he got out of the army, and he was just the type who is killed off early and predictably and sadly in motion pictures about the war, but he had gone through four campaigns and six major battles without a scratch.

Seeger was a large, lanky boy, with a big nose, who had been wounded at Saint Lô, but had come back to his outfit in the Siegfried Lane, quite unchanged. He was cheerful and dependable and he knew his business and had broken in five or six second lieutenants who had been killed or wounded and the CO had tried to get him commissioned in the field, but the war had ended while the paperwork was being fumbled over at headquarters.

They reached the door of the orderly tent and stopped. "Be brave, Sergeant," Olson said. "Welch and I are depending on you."

''Okay,'' Seeger said, and went in.

The tent had the dank, army-canvas smell that had been so much a part of Seeger's life in the past three years. The company clerk was reading a July 1945 issue of the *Buffalo Courier-Express*, which had just reached him, and Captain Taney, the company CO, was seated at a sawbuck table he used as a desk, writing a letter to his wife, his lips pursed with effort. He was a small, fussy man, with sandy hair that was falling out. While the fighting had been going on, he had been lean and tense and his small voice had been cold and full of authority. But now he had relaxed, and a little pot belly was creeping up under his belt and he kept the top button of his trousers open when he could do it without too public loss of dignity. During the war Seeger had thought of him as a natural soldier, tireless, fanatic about detail, aggressive, severely anxious to kill Germans. But in the past few months Seeger had seen him relapsing gradually and pleasantly into a small-town wholesale hardware merchant, which he had been before the war, sedentary and a little shy, and, as he had once told Seeger, worried, here in the bleak champagne fields of France, about his daughter, who had just turned twelve and had a tendency to go after the boys and had been caught by her mother kissing a fifteen-year-old neighbor in the hammock after school.

''Hello, Seeger,'' he said, returning the salute in a mild, off-hand gesture. ''What's on your mind?''

''Am I disturbing you, sir?''

''Oh, no. Just writing a letter to my wife. You married, Seeger?'' He peered at the tall boy standing before him.

''No, sir.''

''It's very difficult,'' Taney sighed, pushing dissatisfiedly at the letter before him. ''My wife complains I don't tell her I love her often enough. Been married fifteen years. You'd think she'd know by now.'' He smiled at Seeger. ''I thought you were going to Paris,'' he said. ''I signed the passes yesterday.''

''That's what I came to see you about, sir.''

''I suppose something's wrong with the passes.'' Taney spoke resignedly, like a man who has never quite got the hang of army regulations and has had requisitions, furloughs, requests for courts-martial returned for correction in a baffling flood.

''No, sir,'' Seeger said. ''The passes're fine. They start tomorrow. Well, it's just . . .'' He looked around at the company clerk, who was on the sports page.

"This confidential?" Taney asked.

"If you don't mind, sir."

"Johnny," Taney said to the clerk, "go stand in the rain someplace."

"Yes, sir," the clerk said, and slowly got up and walked out.

Taney looked shrewdly at Seeger, spoke in a secret whisper. "You pick up anything?" he asked.

Seeger grinned. "No sir, haven't had my hands on a girl since Strasbourg."

"Ah, that's good." Taney leaned back, relieved, happy he didn't have to cope with the disapproval of the Medical Corps.

"It's—well," said Seeger, embarrassed, "it's hard to say—but it's money."

Taney shook his head sadly. "I know."

"We haven't been paid for three months, sir, and . . ."

"Damn it!" Taney stood up and shouted furiously. "I would like to take every bloody chair-warming old lady in the Finance Department and wring their necks."

The clerk stuck his head into the tent. "Anything wrong? You call for me, sir?"

"No," Taney shouted. "Get out of here."

The clerk ducked out.

Taney sat down again. "I suppose," he said, in a more normal voice, "they have their problems. Outfits being broken up, being moved all over the place. But it is rugged."

"It wouldn't be so bad," Seeger said. "But we're going to Paris tomorrow. Olson, Welch, and myself. And you need money in Paris."

"Don't I know it." Taney wagged his head. "Do you know what I paid for a bottle of champagne on the Place Pigalle in September . . . ?" He paused significantly. "I won't tell you. You won't have any respect for me the rest of your life."

Seeger laughed. "Hanging," he said, "is too good for the guy who thought up the rate of exchange."

"I don't care if I never see another franc as long as I live." Taney waved his letter in the air, although it had been dry for a long time.

There was silence in the tent and Seeger swallowed a little embarrassedly, watching the CO wave the flimsy sheet of paper in regular sweeping movements. "Sir," he said, "the truth is, I've come to borrow some money for Welch, Olson, and myself. We'll pay it back out of the first pay we get, and that can't be too long from now. If you don't want to give it to us, just tell me and I'll understand and get the hell out of here. We don't like to ask, but you might just as well be dead as be in Paris broke."

Taney stopped waving his letter and put it down thoughtfully. He peered at it, wrinkling his brow, looking like an aged bookkeeper in the single gloomy light that hung in the middle of the tent.

"Just say the word, Captain," Seeger said, "and I'll blow . . ."

"Stay where you are, son," said Taney. He dug in his shirt pocket and took out a worn, sweat-stained wallet. He looked at it for a moment. "Alligator," he said, with automatic, absent pride. "My wife sent it to me when we were in England. Pounds don't fit in it. However . . ." He opened it and took out all the contents. There was a small pile of francs on the table in front of him. He counted them. "Four hundred francs," he said. "Eight bucks."

"Excuse me," Seeger said humbly. "I shouldn't have asked."

"Delighted," Taney said vigorously. "Absolutely delighted." He started dividing the francs into two piles. "Truth is, Seeger, most of my money goes home in allotments. And the truth is, I lost eleven hundred francs in a poker game three nights ago, and I ought to be ashamed of myself. Here . . ." he shoved one pile toward Seeger. "Two hundred francs."

Seeger looked down at the frayed, meretricious paper, which always seemed to him like stage money, anyway. "No, sir," he said, "I can't take it."

"Take it," Taney said. "That's a direct order."

Seeger slowly picked up the money, not looking at Taney. "Some time, sir," he said, "after we get out, you have to come over to my house and you and my father and my brother and I'll go on a real drunk."

"I regard that," Taney said, gravely, "as a solemn commitment."

They smiled at each other and Seeger started out.

"Have a drink for me," said Taney, "at the Café de la Paix. A small drink." He was sitting down to write his wife he loved her when Seeger went out of the tent.

Olson fell into step with Seeger and they walked silently through the mud between the tents.

"Well, *mon vieux?*" Olson said finally.

"Two hundred francs," said Seeger.

Olson groaned. "Two hundred francs! We won't be able to pinch a whore's behind on the Boulevard des Capucines for two hundred francs. That miserable, penny-loving Yankee!''

''He only had four hundred,'' Seeger said.

''I revise my opinion,'' said Olson.

They walked disconsolately and heavily back toward their tent.

Olson spoke only once before they got there. ''These raincoats,'' he said, patting his. ''Most ingenious invention of the war. Highest saturation point of any modern fabric. Collect more water per square inch, and hold it, than any material known to man. All hail the quartermaster!''

Welch was waiting at the entrance of their tent. He was standing there peering excitedly and short-sightedly out at the rain through his glasses, looking angry and tough, like a big-city hack driver, individual and incorruptible even in the ten-million colored uniform. Every time Seeger came upon Welch unexpectedly, he couldn't help smiling at the belligerent stance, the harsh stare through the steel-rimmed GI glasses, which had nothing at all to do with the way Welch really was. ''It's a family inheritance,'' Welch had once explained. ''My whole family stands as though we were getting ready to rap a drunk with a beer glass. Even my old lady.'' Welch had six brothers, all devout, according to Welch, and Seeger from time to time idly pictured them standing in a row, on Sunday mornings in church, seemingly on the verge of general violence, amid the hushed Latin and Sabbath millinery.

''How much?'' Welch asked loudly.

''Don't make us laugh,'' Olson said, pushing past him into the tent.

''What do you think I could get from the French for my combat jacket?'' Seeger said. He went into the tent and lay down on his cot.

Welch followed them in and stood between the two of them, a superior smile on his face. ''Boys,'' he said, ''on a man's errand.''

''I can just see us now,'' Olson murmured, lying on his cot with his hands clasped behind his head, ''painting Montmartre red. Please bring on the naked dancing girls. Four bucks worth.''

''I am not worried,'' Welch announced.

''Get out of here.'' Olson turned over on his stomach.

''I know where we can put our hands on sixty-five bucks.'' Welch looked triumphantly first at Olson, then at Seeger.

Olson turned over slowly and sat up. ''I'll kill you,'' he said, ''if you're kidding.''

''While you guys are wasting your time,'' Welch said, ''fooling around with the infantry, I used my head. I went into Reems and used my head.''

``Rance,'' Olson said automatically. He had had two years of French in college and he felt, now that the war was over, that he had to introduce his friends to some of his culture.

``I got to talking to a captain in the air force,'' Welch said eagerly. ``A little fat old paddle-footed captain that never got higher off the ground than the second floor of Com Z headquarters, and he told me that what he would admire to do more than anything else is take home a nice shiny German Luger pistol with him to show to the boys back in Pacific Grove, California.''

Silence fell on the tent and Welch and Olson looked tentatively at Seeger.

``Sixty-five bucks for a Luger, these days,'' Olson said, ``is a very good figure.''

``They've been sellin' for as low as thirty-five,'' said Welch hesitantly. ``I'll bet,'' he said to Seeger, ``you could sell yours now and buy another one back when you got some dough, and make a clear twenty-five on the deal.''

Seeger didn't say anything. He had killed the owner of the Luger, an enormous SS major, in Coblenz, behind some paper bales in a warehouse, and the major had fired at Seeger three times with it, once nicking his helmet, before Seeger hit him in the face at twenty feet. Seeger had kept the Luger, a long, heavy, well-balanced gun, very carefully since then, lugging it with him, hiding it at the bottom of his bedroll, oiling it three times a week, avoiding all opportunities of selling it, although he had been offered as much as a hundred dollars for it and several times eighty and ninety, while the war was still on, before German weapons became a glut on the market.

``Well,'' said Welch, ``there's no hurry. I told the captain I'd see him tonight around eight o'clock in front of the Lion D'Or Hotel. You got five hours to make up your mind. Plenty of time.''

``Me,'' said Olson, after a pause. ``I won't say anything.''

Seeger looked reflectively at his feet and the other two men avoided looking at him. Welch dug in his pocket. ``I forgot,'' he said. ``I picked up a letter for you.'' He handed it to Seeger.

``Thanks,'' Seeger said. He opened it absently, thinking about the Luger.

``Me,'' said Olson, ``I won't say a bloody word. I'm just going to lie here and think about that nice fat air force captain.''

Seeger grinned a little at him and went to the tent opening to read the letter in the light. The letter was from his father, and even from one glance at the handwriting, scrawly and hurried and spotted, so different from his father's usual steady, handsome, professional script, he knew that something was wrong.

"Dear Norman," it read, "sometime in the future, you must forgive me for writing this letter. But I have been holding this in so long, and there is no one here I can talk to, and because of your brother's condition I must pretend to be cheerful and optimistic all the time at home, both with him and your mother, who has never been the same since Leonard was killed. You're the oldest now, and although I know we've never talked very seriously about anything before, you have been through a great deal by now, and I imagine you must have matured considerably, and you've seen so many different places and people . . . Norman, I need help. While the war was on and you were fighting, I kept this to myself. It wouldn't have been fair to burden you with this. But now the war is over, and I no longer feel I can stand up under this alone. And you will have to face it some time when you get home, if you haven't faced it already, and perhaps we can help each other by facing it together . . ."

"I'm redeployable," Olson was singing softly, on his cot. "It's so enjoyable, In the Pelilu mud, "With the tropical crud . . ." He fell silent after his burst of song.

Seeger blinked his eyes, at the entrance to the tent, in the wan rainy light, and went on reading his father's letter, on the stiff white stationery with the University letterhead in polite engraving at the top of each page.

"I've been feeling this coming on for a long time," the letter continued, "but it wasn't until last Sunday morning that something happened to make me feel it in its full force. I don't know how much you've guessed about the reason for Jacob's discharge from the army. It's true he was pretty badly wounded in the leg at Metz, but I've asked around, and I know that men with worse wounds were returned to duty after hospitalization. Jacob got a medical discharge, but I don't think it was for the shrapnel wound in his thigh. He is suffering now from what I suppose you call combat fatigue, and he is subject to fits of depression and hallucinations. Your mother and I thought that as time went by and the war and the army receded, he would grow better. Instead, he is growing worse. Last Sunday morning when I came down into the living room from upstairs he was crouched in his old uniform, next to the window, peering out . . ."

"What the hell," Olson was saying, "if we don't get the sixty-five bucks we can always go to the Louvre. I understand the Mona Lisa is back."

"I asked Jacob what he was doing," the letter went on. "He didn't turn around. 'I'm observing,' he said. 'V-1's and V-2's. Buzz-bombs and rockets. They're coming in by the hundreds.' I tried to reason with him and he told me to crouch and save myself from flying glass. To humor him I got down on the floor beside him and tried to tell him the war was over, that we were in Ohio, 4,000 miles away from the nearest spot where bombs had fallen, that America had never been touched. He wouldn't listen. 'These're the new rocket bombs,' he said, 'for the Jews.'"

"Did you ever hear of the Pantheon?" Olson asked loudly.

"No," said Welch.

"It's free."

"I'll go," said Welch.

Seeger shook his head a little and blinked his eyes before he went back to the letter.

"After that," his father went on, "Jacob seemed to forget about the bombs from time to time, but he kept saying that the mobs were coming up the street armed with bazookas and Browning Automatic rifles. He mumbled incoherently a good deal of the time and kept walking back and forth saying, 'What's the situation? Do you know what the situation is?' And he told me he wasn't worried about himself, he was a soldier and he expected to be killed, but he was worried about Mother and myself and Leonard and you. He seemed to forget that Leonard was dead. I tried to calm him and get him back to bed before your mother came down, but he refused and wanted to set out immediately to rejoin his division. It was all terribly disjointed and at one time he took the ribbon he got for winning the Bronze star and threw it in the fireplace, then he got down on his hands and knees and picked it out of the ashes and made me pin it on him again, and he kept repeating, 'This is when they are coming for the Jews.'"

"The next war I'm in," said Olson, "they don't get me under the rank of colonel."

It had stopped raining by now and Seeger folded the unfinished letter and went outside. He walked slowly down to the end of the company street, and facing out across the empty, soaked French fields, scarred and neglected by various armies, he stopped and opened the letter again.

"I don't know what Jacob went through in the army," his father wrote, "that has done this to him. He never talks to me about the war and he refuses to go to a psychoanalyst, and from time to time he is his own bouncing, cheerful self, playing in tennis tournaments and going around with a large group of girls. But he has devoured all the concentration camp reports, and I have found him weeping when the newspapers reported that a hundred Jews were killed in Tripoli some time ago.

"The terrible thing is, Norman, that I find myself coming to believe that it is not neurotic for a Jew to behave like this today. Perhaps Jacob is the normal one, and I, going about my business, teaching economics in a quiet classroom, pretending to understand that the world is comprehensible and orderly, am really the mad one. I ask you once more to forgive me for writing you a letter like this, so different from any letter or any conversation I've ever had with you. But it is crowding me, too. I do not see rockets and bombs, but I see other things.

"Wherever you go these days—restaurants, hotels, clubs, trains, you seem to hear talk about the Jews, mean, hateful murderous talk. Whatever page you turn to in the newspapers you seem to find an article about Jews being killed somewhere on the face of the globe. And there are large, influential newspapers and well-known columnists who each day are growing more and more outspoken and more popular. The day that Roosevelt died I heard a drunken man yelling outside a bar, 'Finally, they got the Jew out of the White House.' And some of the people who heard him merely laughed and nobody stopped him. And on V-E Day, in celebration, hoodlums in Los Angeles savegely beat a Jewish writer. It's difficult to know what to do, whom to fight, where to look for allies.

"Three months ago, for example, I stopped my Thursday night poker game, after playing with the same men for over ten years. John Reilly happened to say that the Jews were getting rich out of this war, and when I demanded an apology, he refused, and when I looked around at the faces of the men who had been my friends for so long, I could see they were not with me. And when I left the house no one said good night to me. I know the poison was spreading from Germany before the war and during it, but I had not realized it had come so close.

"And in my economics class, I find myself idiotically hedging in my lectures. I discover that I am loath to praise any liberal writer or any liberal act and find myself somehow annoyed and frightened to see an article of criticism of existing abuses signed by a Jewish name. And I hate to see Jewish names on important committees, and hate to read of Jews fighting for the poor, the oppressed, the cheated and hungry. Somehow, even in a country where my family has lived a hundred years, the enemy has won this subtle victory over me—he has made me disfranchise myself from honest causes by calling them foreign, Communist, using Jewish names connected with them as ammunition against them.

"And, most hateful of all, I find myself looking for Jewish names in the casualty lists and secretly being glad when I discover them there, to prove that there at least, among the dead and wounded, we belong. Three times, thanks to you and your brothers, I have found our name there, and, may God forgive me, at the expense of your blood and your brother's life, through my tears, I have felt that same twitch of satisfaction . . .

"When I read the newspapers and see another story that Jews are still being killed in Poland, or Jews are requesting that they be given back their homes in France, or that they be allowed to enter some country where they will not be murdered, I am annoyed with them, I feel they are boring the rest of the world with their problems, they are making demands upon the rest of the world by being killed, they are disturbing everyone by being hungry and asking for the return of their property. If we could all fall through the crust of the earth and vanish in one hour, with our heroes and poets and prophets and martyrs, perhaps we would be doing the memory of the Jewish race a service. . . .

"This is how I feel today, son. I need some help. You've been to the war, you've fought and killed men, you've seen the people of other countries. Maybe you understand things that I don't understand. Maybe you see some hope somewhere. Help me. Your loving father."

Seeger folded the letter slowly, not seeing what he was doing because the tears were burning his eyes. He walked slowly and aimlessly across the dead autumn grass of the empty field, away from the camp.

He tried to wipe away his tears, because with his eyes full and dark, he kept seeing his father and brother crouched in the old-fashioned living room in Ohio and hearing his brother, dressed in the old, discarded uniform, saying, "These're the new rocket bombs. For the Jews."

He sighed, looking out over the bleak, wasted land. Now, he thought, now I have to think about it. He felt a slight, unreasonable twinge of anger at his father for presenting him with the necessity of thinking about it. The Army was good about serious problems. While you were fighting, you were too busy and frightened and weary to think about anything, and at other times you were relaxing, putting your brain on a shelf, postponing everything to that impossible time of clarity and beauty after the war. Well, now, here was the impossible, clear, beautiful time, and here was his father, demanding that he think. There are all sorts of Jews, he thought, there are the sort whose every waking moment is ridden by the knowledge of Jewishness, who see signs against the Jew in every smile on a streetcar, every whisper, who see pogroms in every newspaper article, threats in every change of the weather, scorn in every handshake, death behind each closed door. He had not been like that. He was young, he was big and healthy and easy-going and people of all kinds had seemed to like him all his life, in the army and out. In America, especially, what was going on in Europe had seemed remote, unreal, unrelated to him. The chanting, bearded old men burning in the Nazi furnaces, and the dark-eyed women screaming prayers in Polish and Russian and German as they were pushed naked into the gas chambers had seemed as shadowy and almost as unrelated to him as he trotted out onto the stadium field for a football game, as they must have been to the men named O'Dwyer and Wickersham and Poole who played in the line beside him.

They had seemed more related in Europe. Again and again in the towns that had been taken back from the Germans, gaunt, gray-faced men had stopped him humbly, looking searchingly at him, and had asked, peering at his long, lined, grimy face, under the anonymous helmet, "Are you a Jew?" Sometimes they asked it in English, sometimes French, or Yiddish. He didn't know French or Yiddish, but he learned to recognize the phrase. He had never understood exactly why they had asked the question, since they never demanded anything from him, rarely even could speak to him, until, one day in Strasbourg, a little bent old man and a small, shapeless woman had stopped him, and asked, in English, if he was Jewish.

"Yes," he said, smiling at them.

The two old people had smiled widely, like children. "Look," the old man had said to his wife. "A young American soldier. A Jew. And so large and strong." He had touched Seeger's arm reverently with the tips of his fingers, then had touched the Garand he was carrying. "And such a beautiful rifle . . ."

And there, for a moment, although he was not particularly sensitive, Seeger got an inkling of why he had been stopped and questioned by so many before. Here, to these bent, exhausted old people, ravaged of their families, familiar with flight and death for so many years, was a symbol of continuing life. A large young man in the uniform of the liberator, blood, as they thought, of their blood, but not in hiding, not quivering in fear and helplessness, but striding secure and victorious down the street, armed and capable of inflicting terrible destruction on his enemies.

Seeger had kissed the old lady on the cheek and she had wept and the old man had scolded her for it, while shaking Seeger's hand fervently and thankfully before saying good-by.

And, thinking back on it, it was silly to pretend that, even before his father's letter, he had been like any other American soldier going through the war. When he had stood over the huge dead SS major with the face blown in by his bullets in the warehouse in Coblenz, and taken the pistol from the dead hand, he had tasted a strange little extra flavor of triumph. How many Jews, he'd thought, has this man killed, how fitting it is that I've killed him. Neither Olson nor Welch, who were like his brothers, would have felt that in picking up the Luger, its barrel still hot from the last shots its owner had fired before dying. And he had resolved that he was going to make sure to take this gun back with him to America, and plug it and keep it on his desk at home, as a kind of vague, half-understood sign to himself that justice had once been done and he had been its instrument.

Maybe, he thought, maybe I'd better take it back with me, but not as a memento. Not plugged, but loaded. America by now was a strange country for him. He had been away a long time and he wasn't sure what was waiting for him when he got home. If the mobs were coming down the street toward his house, he was not going to die singing and praying.

When he was taking basic training he'd heard a scrawny, clerklike-looking soldier from Boston talking at the other end of the PX bar, over the watered beer. "The boys at the office," the scratchy voice was saying, "gave me a party before I left. And they told me one thing. 'Charlie,' they said, 'hold onto your bayonet. We're going to be able to use it when you get back. On the Yids.' "

He hadn't said anything then, because he'd felt it was neither possible nor desirable to fight against every random overheard voice raised against the Jews from one end of the world to another. But again and again, at odd moments, lying on a barracks cot, or stretched out trying to sleep on the floor of a ruined French farmhouse, he had heard that voice, harsh, satisfied, heavy with hate and ignorance, saying above the beery grumble of apprentice soldiers at the bar, "Hold onto your bayonet. . . ."

And the the other stories—Jews collected stories of hatred and injustice and inklings of doom like a special, lunatic kind of miser. The story of the naval officer, commander of a small vessel off the Aleutians, who, in the officers' wardroom, had complained that he hated the Jews because it was the Jews who had demanded that the Germans be beaten first and the forces in the Pacific had been starved in consequence. And when one of his junior officers, who had just come aboard, had objected and told the commander that he was a Jew, the commander had risen from the table and said, "Mister, the Constitution of the United States says I have to serve in the same navy with Jews, but it doesn't say I have to eat at the same table with them." In the fogs and the cold, swelling Arctic seas off the Aleutians, in a small boat, subject to sudden, mortal attack at any moment . . .

And the two young combat engineers in an attached company on D-Day, when they were lying off the coast right before climbing down into the landing barges. "There's France," one of them had said.

"What's it like?" the second one had asked, peering out across the miles of water toward the smoking coast.

"Like every place else," the first one had answered. "The Jews've made all the dough during the war."

"Shut up!" Seeger had said, helplessly thinking of the dead, destroyed, wandering, starving Jews of France. The engineers had shut up, and they'd climbed down together into the heaving boat, and gone into the beach together.

And the million other stories. Jews, even the most normal, and best adjusted of them, became living treasuries of them, scraps of malice and bloodthirstiness, clever and confusing and cunningly twisted so that every act by every Jew became suspect and blameworthy and hateful. Seeger had heard the stories, and had made an almost conscious effort to forget them. Now, holding his father's letter in his hand, he remembered them all.

He stared unseeingly out in front of him. Maybe, he thought, maybe it would've been better to have been killed in the war, like Leonard. Simpler. Leonard would never have to face a crowd coming for his mother and father. Leonard would not have to listen and collect these hideous, fascinating little stories that made of every Jew a stranger in any town, on any field, on the face of the earth. He had come so close to being killed, so many times, it would have been so easy, so neat and final.

Seeger shook his head. It was ridiculous to feel like that, and he was ashamed of himself for the weak moment. At the age of twenty-one, death was not an answer.

"Seeger!" It was Olson's voice. He and Welch had sloshed silently up behind Seeger, standing in the open field. "Seeger, *mon vieux*, what're you doing—grazing?"

Seeger turned slowly to them. "I wanted to read my letter," he said.

Olson looked closely at him. They had been together so long, through so many things, that flickers and hints of expression on each other's faces were recognized and acted upon. "Anything wrong?" Olson asked.

"No," said Seeger. "Nothing much."

"Norman," Welch said, his voice young and solemn. "Norman, we've been talking, Olson and me. We decided—you're pretty attached to that Luger, and maybe—if you—well . . ."

"What he's trying to say," said Olson, "is we withdraw the request. If you want to sell it, okay. If you don't, don't do it for our sake. Honest."

Seeger looked at them, standing there, disreputable and tough and familiar. "I haven't made up my mind yet," he said.

"Anything you decide," Welch said oratorically, "is perfectly all right with us. Perfectly."

They walked aimlessly and silently across the field, away from camp. As they walked, their shoes making a wet, sliding sound in the damp, dead grass, Seeger thought of the time Olson had covered him in the little town outside Cherbourg, when Seeger had been caught going down the side of a street by four Germans with a machine gun on the second story of a house on the corner and Olson had had to stand out in the middle of the street with no cover at all for more than a minute, firing continuously, so that Seeger could get away alive. And he thought of the time outside Saint Lô when he had been wounded and had lain in a minefield for three hours and Welch and Captain Taney had come looking for him in the darkness and had found him and picked him up and run for it, all of them expecting to get blown up any second.

And he thought of all the drinks they'd had together and the long marches and the cold winter together, and all the girls they'd gone out with together, and he thought of his father and brother crouching behind the window in Ohio waiting for the rockets and the crowds armed with Browning Automatic rifles.

"Say," he stopped and stood facing them. "Say, what do you guys think of the Jews?"

Welch and Olson looked at each other, and Olson glanced down at the letter in Seeger's hand.

"Jews?" Olson said finally. "What're they? Welch, you ever hear of the Jews?"

Welch looked thoughtfully at the gray sky. "No," he said. "But remember, I'm an uneducated fellow."

"Sorry, Bud," Olson said, turning to Seeger. "We can't help you. Ask us another question. Maybe we'll do better."

Seeger peered at the faces of his friends. He would have to rely upon them, later on, out of uniform, on their native streets, more than he had ever relied on them on the bullet-swept street and in the dark minefield in France. Welch and Olson stared back at him, troubled, their faces candid and tough and dependable.

"What time," Seeger asked, "did you tell that captain you'd meet him?"

"Eight o'clock," Welch said. "But we don't have to go. If you have any feeling about that gun . . ."

"We'll meet him," Seeger said. "We can use that sixty-five bucks."

"Listen," Olson said, "I know how much you like that gun and I'll feel like a heel if you sell it."

"Forget it," Seeger said, starting to walk again. "What could I use it for in America?"

PEARL S. BUCK

The Enemy

DR. SADAO HOKI'S HOUSE was built on a spot of the Japanese coast where as a little boy he had often played. The low square stone house was set upon rocks well above a narrow beach that was outlined with bent pines. As a boy Sadao had climbed the pines, supporting himself on his bare feet, as he had seen men do in the South Seas when they climbed for coconuts. His father had taken him often to the islands of those seas, and never had he failed to say to the grave little boy at his side, "Those islands yonder, they are the steppingstones to the future for Japan."

"Where shall we step from them?" Sadao had asked seriously.

"Who knows?" his father had answered. "Who can limit our future? It depends on what we make it."

Sadao had taken this into his mind, as he did everything his father said, his father who never joked or played with him, but who spent infinite pains upon him who was his only son. Sadao knew that his education was his father's chief concern. For this reason he had been sent at twenty-two to America to learn all that could be learned of surgery and medicine. He had come back at thirty, and before his father died he had seen Sadao become famous not only as a surgeon but as a scientist. Because he was now perfecting a discovery which would render wounds entirely clean, he had not been sent abroad with the troops. Also, he knew, there was some slight danger that the old General might need an operation for a condition for which he was now being treated medically, and for this possibility Sadao was being kept in Japan.

Clouds were rising from the ocean now. The unexpected warmth of the past few days had at night drawn heavy fog from the cold waves. Sadao watched mists hide outlines of a little island near the shore and then come creeping up the beach below the house, wreathing around the pines. In a few minutes fog would be wrapped about the house too.

Then he would go into the room where Hana, his wife, would be waiting for him with the two children.

But at this moment the door opened and she looked out, a dark blue woolen haori over her kimono. She came to him affectionately and put her arm through his as he stood, smiled, and said nothing. He had met Hana in America, but he had waited to fall in love with her until he was sure she was Japanese. His father would never have received her unless she had been pure in her race. He wondered often whom he would have married if he had not met Hana, and by what luck he had found her in the most casual way, by chance literally, at an American professor's house. The professor and his wife had been kind people, anxious to do something for their few foreign students, and the students, though bored, had accepted this kindness. Sadao had often told Hana how nearly he had not gone to Professor Harley's house that night—the rooms were so small, the food so bad, the professor's wife so voluble. But he had gone and there he had found Hana, a new student, and had felt he would love her if it were at all possible.

Now he felt her hand on his arm and was aware of the pleasure it gave him, even though they had been married years enough to have the two children. For they had not married heedlessly in America. They had finished their work at school and had come home to Japan, and when his father had seen her the marriage had been arranged in the old Japanese way, although Sadao and Hana had talked everything over beforehand. They were perfectly happy. She laid her cheek against his arm.

It was at this moment that both of them saw something black come out of the mists. It was a man. He was flung up out of the ocean—flung, it seemed, to his feet by a breaker. He staggered a few steps, his body outlined against the mist, his arms above his head. Then the curled mists hid him again.

"Who is that?" Hana cried. She dropped Sadao's arm and they both leaned over the railing of the veranda. Now they saw him again. The man was on his hands and knees crawling. Then they saw him fall on his face and lie there.

"A fisherman perhaps," Sadao said, "washed from his boat." He ran quickly down the steps, and behind him Hana came, her wide sleeves flying. A mile or two away on either side there were fishing villages, but here was only the bare and lonely coast, dangerous with rocks. The surf beyond the beach was spiked with rocks. Somehow the man had managed to come through them—he must be badly torn.

They saw when they came toward him that indeed it was so. The sand on one side of him had already a stain of red soaking through.

"He is wounded," Sadao exclaimed. He made haste to the man, who lay motionless, his face in the sand. An old cap stuck to his head, soaked with sea water. He was in wet rags of garments. Sadao stooped, Hana at his side, and turned the man's head. They saw the face.

"A white man!" Hana whispered.

Yes, it was a white man. The wet cap fell away and there was his wet yellow hair, long, as though for many weeks it had not been cut, and upon his young and tortured face was a rough yellow beard. He was unconscious and knew nothing that they did to him.

Now Sadao remembered the wound, and with his expert fingers he began to search for it. Blood flowed freshly at his touch. On the right side of his lower back Sadao saw that a gun wound had been reopened. The flesh was blackened with powder. Sometime, not many days ago, the man had been shot and had not been tended. It was bad chance that the rock had struck the wound.

"Oh, how he is bleeding!" Hana whispered again in a solemn voice. The mists screened them now completely, and at this time of day no one came by. The fishermen had gone home, and even the chance beachcombers would have considered the day at an end.

"What shall we do with this man?" Sadao muttered. But his trained hands seemed of their own will to be doing what they could to stanch the fearful bleeding. He packed the wound with the sea moss that strewed the beach. The man moaned with pain in his stupor, but he did not awaken.

"The best thing that we could do would be to put him back in the sea," Sadao said, answering himself.

Now that the bleeding was stopped for the moment he stood up and dusted the sand from his hands.

"Yes, undoubtedly, that would be best," Hana said steadily. But she continued to stare down at the motionless man.

"If we sheltered a white man in our house we should be arrested, and if we turned him over as a prisoner, he would certainly die," Sadao said.

"The kindest thing would be to put him back into the sea," Hana said. But neither of them moved. They were staring with a curious repulsion upon the inert figure.

"What is he?" Hana whispered.

"There is something about him that looks American," Sadao said. He took up the battered cap. Yes, there, almost gone, was the faint lettering. "A sailor," he said, "from an American warship." He spelled it out: "U.S. Navy." The man was a prisoner of war!

"He has escaped," Hana cried softly, "and that is why he is wounded."

"In the back," Sadao agreed.

They hesitated, looking at each other. Then Hana said with resolution, "Come, are we able to put him back into the sea?"

"If I am able, are you?" Sadao asked.

"No," Hana said. "But if you can do it alone. . . ."

Sadao hesitated again. "The strange thing is," he said, "that if the man were whole I could turn him over to the police without difficulty. I care nothing for him. He is my enemy. All Americans are my enemy. And he is only a common fellow. You see how foolish his face is. But since he is wounded. . . ."

"You also cannot throw him back to the sea," Hana said. "Then there is only one thing to do. We must carry him into the house."

"But the servants?" Sadao inquired.

"We must simply tell them that we intend to give him to the police—as indeed we must, Sadao. We must think of the children and your position. It would endanger all of us if we did not give this man over as a prisoner of war."

"Certainly," Sadao agreed. "I would not think of doing anything else."

Thus agreed, together they lifted the man. He was very light, like a fowl that has been half-starved for a long time until it is only feathers and skeleton. So, his arms hanging, they carried him up the steps and into the side door of the house. This door opened into a passage, and down the passage they carried the man toward an empty bedroom. It had been the bedroom of Sadao's father and since his death it had not been used. They laid the man on the deeply matted floor. Everything here had been Japanese to please the old man, who would never in his own home sit on a chair or sleep in a foreign bed. Hana went to the wall cupboards and slid back a door and took out a soft quilt. She hesitated. The quilt was covered with flowered silk and the lining was pure white silk.

"He is so dirty," she murmured in distress.

"Yes, he had better be washed," Sadao agreed. "If you will fetch hot water I will wash him."

"I cannot bear to have you touch him," she said. "We shall have to tell the servants he is here. I will tell Yumi now. She can leave the children for a few minutes and she can wash him."

Sadao considered a moment. "Let it be so," he agreed. "You tell Yumi and I will tell the others."

But the utter pallor of the man's unconscious face moved him first to stoop and feel his pulse. It was faint, but it was there. He put his hand against the man's cold breast. The heart too was yet alive.

"He will die unless he is operated on," Sadao said, considering. "The question is whether he will not die anyway."

Hana cried out in fear. "Don't try to save him! What if he should live?"

"What if he should die?" Sadao replied. He stood gazing down on the motionless man. This man must have extraordinary vitality or he would have been dead by now. But then he was very young—perhaps not yet twenty-five.

"You mean die from the operation?" Hana asked.

"Yes," Sadao said.

Hana considered this doubtfully, and when she did not answer Sadao turned away. "At any rate something must be done with him," he said, "and first he must be washed." He went quickly out of the room and Hana came behind him. She did not wish to be left alone with the white man. He was the first she had seen since she left America, and now he seemed to have nothing to do with with those whom she had known there. Here he was her enemy, a menace, living or dead.

She turned to the nursery and called, "Yumi!"

But the children heard her voice and she had to go in for a moment and smile at them and play with the baby boy, now nearly three months old.

Over the baby's soft black hair she motioned with her mouth, "Yumi—come with me!"

"I will put the baby to bed," Yumi replied. "He is ready."

She went with Yumi into the bedroom next to the nursery and stood with the boy in her arms while Yumi spread the sleeping quilts on the floor and laid the baby between them.

Then Hana led the way quickly and softly to the kitchen. The two servants were frightened at what their master had just told them. The old gardener, who was also a house servant, pulled the few hairs on his upper lip.

"The master ought not to heal the wound of this white man," he said bluntly to Hana. "The white man ought to die. First he was shot. Then the sea caught him and wounded him with her rocks. If the master heals what the gun did and what the sea did they will take revenge on us."

"I will tell him what you say," Hana replied courteously. But she herself was also frightened, although she was not superstitious as the old man was. Could it ever be well to help an enemy? Nevertheless, she told Yumi to fetch the hot water and bring it to the room where the white man was.

She went ahead and slid back the partitions. Sadao was not yet there. Yumi, following, put down her wooden bucket. Then she went over to the white man. When she saw him her thick lips folded themselves into stubborness. "I have never washed a white man," she said, "and I will not wash so dirty a one now."

Hana cried at her severely, "You will do what your master commands you!"

"My master ought not to command me to wash the enemy," Yumi said stubbornly.

There was so fierce a look of resistance upon Yumi's round dull face that Hana felt unreasonably afraid. After all, if the servants should report something that was not as it happened?

"Very well," she said with dignity. "You understand we only want to bring him to his senses so that we can turn him over as a prisoner?"

"I will have nothing to do with it," Yumi said. "I am a poor person and it is not my business."

"Then please," Hana said gently, "return to your own work."

At once Yumi left the room. But this left Hana with the white man alone. She might have been too afraid to stay had not her anger at Yumi's stubbornness now sustained her.

"Stupid Yumi," she muttered fiercely. "Is this anything but a man? And a wounded, helpless man!"

In the conviction of her own superiority she bent impulsively and untied the knotted rags that kept the white man covered. When she had his breast bare she dipped the small clean towel that Yumi had brought into the steaming hot water and washed his face carefully. The man's skin, though rough with exposure, was of a fine texture and must have been very blond when he was a child.

While she was thinking these thoughts, though not really liking the man better now that he was no longer a child, she kept on washing him until his upper body was quite clean. But she dared not turn him over. Where was Sadao? Now her anger was ebbing and she was anxious again, and she rose, wiping her hands on the wrung towel. Then lest the man be chilled she put the quilt over him.

"Sadao!" she called softly.

He had been about to come in when she called. His hand had been on the door and now he opened it. She saw that he had brought his surgeon's emergency bag and that he wore his surgeon's coat.

"You have decided to operate!" she cried.

"Yes," he said shortly. He turned his back to her and unfolded a sterilized towel upon the floor of the *takonoma* alcove, and put his instruments out upon it.

"Fetch towels," he said.

She went obediently but how anxious now, to the linen shelves and took out the towels. There ought also to be old pieces of matting so that the blood would not ruin the fine floor covering. She went out to the back veranda where the gardener kept strips of matting with which to protect delicate shrubs on cold nights and took an armful of them.

But when she went back into the room she saw this was useless. The blood had already soaked through the packing in the man's wound and had ruined the mat under him.

"Oh, the mat!" she cried.

"Yes, it is ruined," Sadao replied, as though he did not care. "Help me to turn him," he commanded her.

She obeyed him without a word, and he began to wash the man's back carefully.

"Yumi would not wash him," she said.

"Did you wash him, then?" Sadao asked, not stopping for a moment his swift concise movements.

"Yes," she said.

He did not seem to hear her. But she was used to his absorption when he was at work. She wondered for a moment if it mattered to him what was the body upon which he worked, so long as it was for the work he did so excellently.

"You will have to give the anesthetic if he needs it," he said.

"I?" she repeated blankly. "But never have I!"

"It is easy enough," he said impatiently.

He was taking out the packing now and the blood began to flow more quickly. He peered into the wound with the bright surgeon's light fastened on his forehead. ''The bullet is still there,'' he said with cool interest. ''Now I wonder how deep this rock wound is. If it is not too deep it may be that I can get the bullet. But the bleeding is not superficial. He has lost much blood.''

At this moment Hana choked. He looked up and saw her face the color of sulphur.

''Don't faint,'' he said sharply. He did not put down his exploring instrument. ''If I stop now the man will surely die.'' She clapped her hands to her mouth and leaped up and ran out of the room. Outside in the garden he heard her retching. But he went on with his work.

It will be better for her to empty her stomach, he thought. He had forgotten that of course she had never seen an operation. But her distress and his inability to go to her at once made him impatient and irritable with this man who lay like dead under his knife.

This man, he thought, there is no reason under heaven why he should live.

Unconsciously this thought made him ruthless and he proceeded swiftly. In his dream the man moaned, but Sadao paid no heed except to mutter at him.

''Groan,'' he muttered, ''groan if you like. I am not doing this for my own pleasure. In fact, I do not know why I am doing it.''

The door opened and there was Hana again. She had not stopped even to smooth back her hair.

''Where is the anesthetic?'' she asked in a clear voice.

Sadao motioned with his chin. ''It is as well that you came back,'' he said. ''This fellow is beginning to stir.''

She had the bottle and some cotton in her hand.

''But how shall I do it?'' she asked.

''Simply saturate the cotton and hold it near his nostrils,'' Sadao replied without delaying for one moment the intricate detail of his work. ''When he breathes badly, move it away a little.''

She crouched close to the sleeping face of the young American. It was a piteously thin face, she thought, and the lips were twisted. The man was suffering whether he knew it or not. Watching him, she wondered if the stories they heard sometimes of the sufferings of prisoners were true. They came like flickers of rumor, told by word of mouth and always contradicted. In the newspapers the reports were always that wherever the Japanese armies went the people received them gladly, with cries of joy at their liberation. But sometimes she remembered such men as General Takima, who at home beat his wife cruelly, though no one mentioned it now that he had fought so victorious a battle in Manchuria. If a man like that could be so cruel to a woman in his power, would he not be cruel to one like this for instance?

She hoped anxiously that this young man had not been tortured. It was at this moment that she observed deep red scars on his neck, just under the ear. "Those scars," she murmured, lifting her eyes to Sadao.

But he did not answer. At this moment he felt the tip of his instrument strike against something hard, dangerously near the kidney. All thought left him. He felt only the purest pleasure. He probed with his fingers, delicately, familiar with every atom of this human body. His old American professor of anatomy had seen to that knowledge. "Ignorance of the human body is the surgeon's cardinal sin, sirs!" he had thundered at his classes year after year. "To operate without as complete knowledge of the body as if you had made it—anything less than that is murder."

"It is not quite at the kidney, my friend," Sadao murmured. It was his habit to murmur to the patient when he forgot himself in an operation. "My friend," he always called his patients and so now he did, forgetting that this was his enemy.

Then quickly, with the cleanest and most precise of incisions, the bullet was out. The man quivered, but he was still unconscious. Nevertheless, he muttered a few English words.

"Guts," he muttered, choking. "They got . . . my guts. . . ."

"Sadao!" Hana cried sharply.

"Hush," Sadao said.

The man sank again into silence so profound that Sadao took up his wrist, hating the touch of it. Yes, there was still a pulse so faint, so feeble, but enough, if he wanted the man to live, to give hope.

But certainly I do not want this man to live, he thought with bitterness.

"No more anesthetic," he told Hana.

He turned as swiftly as though he had never paused, and from his medicines he chose a small vial and from it filled a hypodermic and thrust it into the patient's left arm. Then, putting down the needle, he took the man's wrist again. The pulse under his fingers fluttered once or twice and then grew stronger.

"This man will live in spite of all," he said to Hana, and sighed.

The young man woke, so weak, his blue eyes so terrified when he perceived where he was, that Hana felt compelled to apology. She served him herself, for none of the servants would enter the room.

When she came in the first time she saw him summon his small strength to be prepared for some fearful thing.

"Don't be afraid," she begged him softly.

"How come . . . you speak English?" he gasped.

"I was a long time in America," she replied.

She saw that he wanted to reply to that, but he could not, and so she knelt and fed him gently from the porcelain spoon. He ate unwillingly, but still he ate.

"Now you will soon be strong," she said, not liking him and yet moved to comfort him.

He did not answer.

When Sadao came in the third day after the operation he found the young man sitting up, his face bloodless with the effort.

"Lie down," Sadao cried. "Do you want to die?"

He forced the man down gently and strongly and examined the wound. "You may kill yourself if you do this sort of thing," he scolded.

"What are you going to do with me?" the boy muttered. He looked just now barely seventeen. "Are you going to hand me over?"

For a moment Sadao did not answer. He finished his examination and then pulled the silk quilt over the man. "I do not know myself what I shall do with you," he said. "I ought, of course, to give you to the police. You are a prisoner of war—no, do not tell me anything." He put up his hand as he saw the young man about to speak. "Do not even tell me your name unless I ask it."

They looked at each other for a moment, and then the young man closed his eyes and turned his face to the wall. "Okay," he whispered, his mouth a bitter line.

Outside the door Hana was waiting for Sadao. He saw at once that she was in trouble.

"Sadao, Yumi tells me the servants feel they cannot stay if we hide this man here anymore," she said. "She tells me that they are saying that you and I were so long in America that we have forgotten to think of our own country first. They think we like Americans."

"It is not true," Sadao said harshly. "Americans are our enemies. But I have been trained not to let a man die if I can help it."

"The servants cannot understand that," she said.

"No," he agreed.

Neither seemed able to say more, and somehow the household dragged on. The servants grew daily more watchful. Their courtesy was as careful as ever, but their eyes were cold upon the pair by whom they were hired.

"It is clear what our master ought to do," the old gardener said one morning. He had worked with flowers all his life, and had been a specialist too in moss. For Sadao's father he had made one of the finest moss gardens in Japan, sweeping the bright green carpet constantly so that not a leaf or a pine needle marred the velvet of its surface. "My old master's son knows very well what he ought to do," he now said, pinching a bud from a bush as he spoke. "When the man was so near death why did he not let him bleed?"

"That young master is so proud of his skill to save life that he saves any life," the cook said contemptuously. She split a fowl's neck skillfully and held the fluttering bird and let its blood flow into the roots of a wistaria vine. Blood is the best of fertilizers, and the old gardener would not let her waste a drop of it.

"It is the children of whom we must think," Yumi said sadly. "What will be their fate if their father is condemned as a traitor?"

They did not try to hide what they said from the ears of Hana as she stood arranging the day's flowers in the veranda near by, and she knew they spoke on purpose that she might hear. That they were right she knew too in most of her being. But there was another part of her, which she herself could not understand. It was not sentimental liking of the prisoner. She had not liked him even yesterday when he had said in his impulsive way, "Anyway, let me tell you that my name is Tom." She had only bowed her little distant bow. She saw hurt in his eyes, but she did not wish to assuage it. Indeed, he was a great trouble in this house.

As for Sadao, every day he examined the wound carefully. The last stitches had been pulled out this morning, and the young man would in a fortnight be nearly as well as ever. Sadao went back to his office and carefully typed a letter to the chief of police reporting the whole matter. "On the twenty-first day of February an escaped prisoner was washed up on the shore in front of my house." So far he typed, and then he opened a secret drawer of his desk and put the unfinished report into it.

On the seventh day after that two things happened. In the morning the servants left together, their belongings tied in large square cotton kerchiefs. When Hana got up in the morning nothing was done, the house not cleaned and the food not prepared, and she knew what it meant. She was dismayed and even terrified, but her pride as a mistress would not allow her to show it. Instead she inclined her head gracefully when they appeared before her in the kitchen, and she paid them off and thanked them for all that they had done for her. They were crying, but she did not cry. The cook and the gardener had served Sadao since he was a little boy in his father's house, and Yumi cried because of the children. She was so grieving that after she had gone she ran back to Hana.

"If the baby misses me too much tonight, send for me. I am going to my own house and you know where it is."

"Thank you," Hana said, smiling. But she told herself she would not send for Yumi however the baby cried.

She made the breakfast and Sadao helped with the children. Neither of them spoke of the servants beyond the fact that they were gone. But after Hana had taken morning food to the prisoner she came back to Sadao.

"Why is it we cannot see clearly what we ought to do?" she asked him. "Even the servants see more clearly than we do. Why are we different from other Japanese?"

Sadao did not answer. But a little later he went into the room where the prisoner was and said brusquely, "Today you may get up on your feet. I want you to stay up only five minutes at a time. Tomorrow you may try it twice as long. It would be well that you get back your strength as quickly as possible."

He saw the flicker of terror on the young face that was still very pale.

"Okay," the boy murmured. Evidently he was determined to say more. "I feel I ought to thank you, Doctor, for having saved my life."

"Don't thank me too early," Sadao said coldly. He saw the flicker of terror again in the boy's eyes—terror as unmistakable as an animal's. The scars on his neck were crimson for a moment. Those scars! What were they? Sadao did not ask.

In the afternoon the second thing happened. Hana, working hard at unaccustomed labor, saw a messenger come to the door in official uniform. Her hands went weak and she could not draw her breath. The servants must have told already. She ran to Sadao, gasping, unable to utter a word. But by then the messenger had simply followed her through the garden and there he stood. She pointed at him helplessly.

Sadao looked up from his book. He was in his office, the outer partition of which was thrown open to the garden for the southern sunshine.

"What is it?" he asked the messenger, and then he rose, seeing the man's uniform.

"You are to come to the palace," the man said. "The old General is in pain again."

"Oh," Hana breathed, "is that all?"

"All!" the messenger exclaimed. "Is it not enough?"

"Indeed it is," she replied. "I am very sorry."

When Sadao came to say good-bye she was in the kitchen, but doing nothing. The children were asleep and she sat merely resting for a moment, more exhausted from her fright than from work.

"I thought they had come to arrest you," she said.

He gazed down into her anxious eyes. "I must get rid of this man for your sake," he said in distress. "Somehow I must get rid of him."

"Of course," the General said weakly, "I understand fully. But that is because I once took a degree in Princeton. So few Japanese have."

"I care nothing for the man, Excellency," Sadao said, "but having operated on him with such success. . . ."

"Yes, yes," the General said. "It only makes me feel you more indispensable to me. Evidently you can save anyone—you are so skilled. You say you think I can stand one more such attack as I have had today?"

"Not more than one," Sadao said.

"Then certainly I can allow nothing to happen to you," the General said with anxiety. His long, pale, Japanese face became expressionless, which meant that he was in deep thought. "You cannot be arrested," the General said, closing his eyes. "Suppose you were condemned to death and the next day I had to have my operation?"

"There are other surgeons, Excellency," Sadao suggested.

"None I trust," the General replied. "The best ones have been trained by Germans and would consider the operation successful even if I died. I do not care for their point of view." He sighed. "It seems a pity that we cannot better combine the German ruthlessness with the American sentimentality. Then you could turn your prisoner over to execution and yet I could be sure you would not murder me while I was unconscious." The General laughed. He had an unusual sense of humor. "As a Japanese, could you not combine these two foreign elements?" he asked.

Sadao smiled. "I am not quite sure," he said, "but for your sake I would be willing to try, Excellency."

The General shook his head. "I had rather not be the test case," he said. He felt suddenly weak and overwhelmed with the cares of his life as an official in times such as these, when repeated victory brought great responsibilities all over the south Pacific. "It is very unfortunate that this man should have washed up on your doorstep," he said irritably.

"I feel it so myself," Sadao said gently.

"It would be best if he could be quietly killed," the General said. "Not by you, but by someone who does not know him. I have my own private assassins. Suppose I send two of them to your house tonight—or better, any night. You need know nothing about it. It is now warm—what would be more natural than that you should leave the outer partition of the white man's room open to the garden while he sleeps?"

"Certainly it would be very natural," Sadao agreed. "In fact, it is so left open every night."

"Good," the General said, yawning. "They are very capable assassins—they make no noise and they know the trick of inward bleeding. If you like I can even have them remove the body."

Sadao considered. "That perhaps would be best, Excellency," he agreed, thinking of Hana.

He left the General's presence then and went home, thinking over the plan. In this way the whole thing would be taken out of his hands. He would tell Hana nothing, since she would be timid at the idea of assassins in the house, and yet certainly such persons were essential in an absolute state such as Japan was. How else could rulers deal with those who opposed them?

He refused to allow anything but reason to be the atmosphere of his mind as he went into the room where the American was in bed. But as he opened the door, to his surprise he found the young man out of bed, and preparing to go into the garden.

"What is this!" he exclaimed. "Who gave you permission to leave your room?"

"I'm not used to waiting for permission," Tom said gaily. "Gosh, I feel pretty good again! But will the muscles on this side always feel stiff?"

"Is it so?" Sadao inquired, surprised. He forgot all else. "Now I thought I had provided against that," he murmured. He lifted the edge of the man's shirt and gazed at the healing scar. "Massage may do it," he said, "if exercise does not."

"It won't bother me much," the young man said. His young face was gaunt under the stubbly blond beard. "Say, Doctor, I've got something I want to say to you. If I hadn't met a Jap like you—well, I wouldn't be alive today. I know that."

Sadao bowed but he could not speak.

"Sure, I know that," Tom went on warmly. His big thin hands, gripping a chair, were white at the knuckles. "I guess if all the Japs were like you there wouldn't have been a war."

"Perhaps," Sadao said with difficulty. "And now I think you had better go back to bed."

Sadao slept badly that night. Time and time again he woke, thinking he heard the rustling of footsteps, the sound of a twig broken or a stone displaced in the garden—a noise such as men might make who carried a burden.

The next morning he made the excuse to go first into the guest room. If the American were gone, he then could simply tell Hana that so the General had directed. But when he opened the door he saw at once that it was not last night. There on the pillow was the shaggy blond head. He could hear the peaceful breathing of sleep, and he closed the door again quietly.

"He is asleep," he told Hana. "He is almost well to sleep like that."

"What shall we do with him?" Hana whispered her old refrain.

Sadao shook his head. "I must decide in a day or two," he promised.

But certainly, he thought, the second night must be the night. There rose a wind that night, and he listened to the sounds of bending boughs and whistling partitions.

Hana woke too. "Ought we not to go and close the sick man's partition?" she asked.

"No," Sadao said. "He is able now to do it for himself."

But the next morning the American was still there.

Then the third night of course must be the night. The wind changed to quiet rain and the garden was full of the sound of dripping eaves and running springs. Sadao slept a little better, but he woke at the sound of a crash and leaped to his feet.

"What was that?" Hana cried. The baby woke at her voice and began to wail. "I must go and see."

But he held her and would not let her move.

"Sadao," she cried, "what is the matter with you?"

"Don't go," he muttered, "don't go!"

His terror infected her and she stood breathless, waiting. There was only silence. Together they crept back into the bed, the baby between them.

Yet when he opened the door of the guest room in the morning, there was the young man. He was very gay and had already washed and was now on his feet. He had asked for a razor yesterday and had shaved himself, and there was faint color in his cheeks. "I am well," he said joyously.

Sadao drew his kimono around his weary body. He could not, he decided, go through another night. It was not that he cared for this young man's life. No, simply it was not worth the strain.

"You are well," Sadao agreed. He lowered his voice. "You are so well that I think if I put my boat on the shore tonight, with food and extra clothing in it, you might be able to row to that little island not far from the coast. It is so near the coast that it has not been worth fortifying. Nobody lives on it because in storm it is submerged. But this is not the season of storm. You could live there until you saw a Korean fishing boat pass by. They pass quite near the island because the water is many fathoms deep there."

The young man stared at him, slowly comprehending. "Do I have to?" he asked.

"I think so," Sadao said gently. "You understand—it is not hidden that you are here."

The young man nodded in perfect comprehension. "Okay," he said simply.

Sadao did not see him again until evening. As soon as it was dark he had dragged the stout boat down to the shore, and in it he put food and bottled water that he had bought secretly during the day, as well as two quilts he had bought at a pawnshop. The boat he tied to a post in the water, for the tide was high. There was no moon and he worked without a flashlight.

When he came to the house he entered as though he were just back from his work, and so Hana knew nothing. "Yumi was here today," she said as she served his supper. Though she was so modern, still she did not eat with him. "Yumi cried over the baby," she went on with a sigh. "She misses him so."

"The servants will come back as soon as the foreigner is gone," Sadao said.

He went into the guest room that night before he went to bed and himself checked carefully the Americn's temperature, the state of the wound, and his heart and pulse. The pulse was irregular, but that was perhaps because of excitement. The young man's pale lips were pressed together and his eyes burned. Only the scars on his neck were red.

"I realize you are saving my life again," he told Sadao.

"Not at all," Sadao said. "It is only inconvenient to have you here any longer."

He had hesitated a good deal about giving the man a flashlight. But he had decided to give it to him after all. It was a small one, his own, which he used at night when he was called.

"If your food runs out before you catch a boat," he said, "signal me two flashes at the same instant the sun drops over the horizon. Do not signal in darkness, for it will be seen. If you are all right, but still there, signal me once. You will find fish easy to catch, but you must eat them raw. A fire would be seen.'

"Okay," the young man breathed.

He was dressed now in the Japanese clothes that Sadao had given him, and at the last moment Sadao wrapped a black cloth about his blond head.

"Now," Sadao said.

The young American without a word shook Sadao's hand warmly and then walked quite well across the floor and down the step into the darkness of the garden. Once—twice—Sadao saw his light flash to find his way. But that would not be suspected. He waited until from the shore there was one more flash. Then he closed the partition. That night he slept.

"You say the man escaped?" the General asked faintly. He had been operated upon a week before, an emergency operation to which Sadao had been called in the night. For twelve hours Sadao had not been sure the General would live. The gall bladder was much involved. Then the old man had begun to breathe deeply again and to demand food. Sadao had not been able to ask about the assassins. So far as he knew they had never come. The servants had returned, and Yumi had cleaned the guest room thoroughly and had burned sulphur in it to get the white man's smell out of it. Nobody said anything. Only the gardener was cross, because he had got behind with his chrysanthemums.

But after a week Sadao felt the General was well enough to be spoken to about the prisoner.

"Yes, Excellency, he escaped," Sadao now said. He coughed, signifying that he had not said all he might have said but was unwilling to disturb the General further. But the old man opened his eyes suddenly.

"That prisoner," he said with some energy, "did I not promise you I would kill him for you?"

''You did, Excellency,'' Sadao said.

''Well, well!'' the old man said in a tone of amazement. ''So I did! But you see, I was suffering a good deal. The truth, I thought of nothing but myself. In short, I forgot my promise to you.''

''I wondered, Your Excellency,'' Sadao murmured.

''It was certainly very careless of me,'' the General said. ''But you understand it was not lack of patriotism or dereliction of duty.'' He looked anxiously at his doctor. ''If the matter should come out, you would understand that, wouldn't you?''

''Certainly, Your Excellency,'' Sadao said. He suddenly comprehended that the General was in the palm of his hand and that as a consequence he himself was perfectly safe. ''I can swear to your loyalty, Excellency,'' he said to the old General, ''and to your zeal against the enemy.''

''You are a good man,'' the General murmured, and closed his eyes. ''You will be rewarded.''

But Sadao, searching the spot of black in the twilighted sea that night, had his reward. There was no prick of light in the dusk. No one was on the island. His prisoner was gone—safe, doubtless, for he had warned him to wait only for a Korean fishing boat.

He stood for a moment on the veranda, gazing out to the sea from whence the young man had come that other night. And into his mind, although without reason, there came other white faces he had known—the professor at whose house he had met Hana, a dull man, and his wife had been a silly, talkative woman, in spite of her wish to be kind. He remembered his old teacher of anatomy, who had been so insistent on mercy with the knife, and then he remembered the face of his fat and slatternly landlady. He had had great difficulty in finding a place to live in America, because he was a Japanese. The Americans were full of prejudice and it had been bitter to live in it, knowing himself their superior. How he had despised the ignorant and dirty old woman who had at last consented to house him in her miserable home! He had once tried to be grateful to her because she had in his last year nursed him through influenza, but it was difficult, for she was no less repulsive to him in her kindness. But then, white people were repulsive, of course. It was a relief to be openly at war with them at last. Now he remembered the youthful, haggard face of his prisoner—white and repulsive.

Strange, he thought, I wonder why I could not kill him?

JAMES WARNER BELLAH

Day of Terror

WHEN PEOPLE HEARD the ambulance that Sunday afternoon, they assumed it was a car crash—golfers on the Oahu course, people in other cars. It came out Nuuanu Avenue from Honolulu, with a police car barreling well ahead. It climbed up fast behind Pali and the siren echoed off across Koolau Range.

Braven and Sally Powell's house is up behind Pali. Their gateposts, in carved stone, carry the old Powell house flag from the wind-and-water days; a white tern on a crimson burgee—known from the Farallones to Java Head. That is where the ambulance turned in, between those gateposts.

That Sunday they had Cab Duryea and one of his network contract writers, Sam Roth. Braven knew Cab well from the years gone, and they had always kept a sound friendship, as two men in entirely opposite pursuits of livelihood sometimes will. It caught Braven in the pit of the stomach every time he saw the Cab Duryea Show, or Cab in a motion picture. And it warmed Cab in his inner bone structure to realize that Braven actually knew Eisenhower, F.D.R., and Marshall—because he had been called in several times to work for them.

Sam Roth was a homeless man, a sensitive man, an ugly man until he smiled. When he smiled, all that he was opened up briefly, and his decency, his innate kindness reached out like a soft hand to touch you, and you were the better for that smile.

The Powells' lanai spreads like an open fan across the back of the house, running out to a lawn that crescents the lip of the spur of hill the place is built on. Just below, and to the right of the mound, on the hillside, is the old Buddhist shrine.

Admiral ''Flank-Speed'' Oesterreich had brought a smoothly chromium-plated young woman called Clarissa Sunbury. Flared white sport skirt, wide belt, insistent legs, and a sweatered neck full of tinkling stuff that matched one wristful. From Winston-Salem.

Quiet old Leander McCullogh was there. And big, fat, wonderful Josephine Liholiho Cunningham, almost seventy years old now.

Just before the telephone rang, Sam Roth said, "Forgive me for a gawping remark, Mrs. Powell, but this house of yours is an amazing house—a wonderful house," and he nodded to the living room through the open glass doors. "That is, of course, a royal Hawaiian feather cloak?" Sam asked. "Behind the glass panel inside? I mean a real one? I have been through the Bishop Museum."

"It is," Sally said. "And we have got to let them take it. It's ridiculous to keep it here at home. Yes. It's real."

"And," Sam went on, "it is all one with the clipper ship log books in the library? The old telescopes and quarter-deck speaking trumpets on the racks in the hall? Your jade and lacquer in the cabinets? I mean it is not a collection? It doesn't feel like a collection."

Sally smiled. With quiet intensity, he was trying to establish permanence that some of it might be his for an hour. "Not a collection as you mean it," she said. "My husband's family were New England and San Francisco shipping people. Mine were too, with a sideline in opium. This that we have is the residual pack rat loot of years of Pacific trade."

In Sam Roth's eyes she saw the defensive veil flicker. It had hurt him that she had seemed to throw it all away lightly with the opium remark. So she said, "That cloak was a present to some young Powell years ago. I think in one of Captain Vancouver's ships. He did something extremely praiseworthy here in the Islands in the first Kamahameha's time."

Very solemnly, Sam nodded. "Thank you, Mrs. Powell," and they were friends from that moment, and because they were friends he indicated the two portraits within. "Your children, when they were young? Lovely, eager boy faces."

Braven Powell had moved behind his wife to the giant coffee maker. When they came close that way there always seemed to be a kinesthetic consciousness between them. Without looking, those two people always seemed to feel each other near, and a quick shadow of a secret smile sometimes flashed between them, which is a splendid thing to see after thirty years of marriage.

"Yes," Sally said. "Our two oldest boys—when they were young," and then the telephone rang. Braven had the coffee for Josephine L.C. Sally stepped inside to answer the phone.

Leander McCullogh's old blue eyes looked into Sam Roth's; then he stooped and put the lighted end of his cigarette into a white porcelain ash tray and pressed hard. "I did the portraits some years back, Mr. Roth. Don't walk into it again, but don't feel badly. Those two splendid boys—did not live."

Clarissa Sunbury had waited a pointed moment after Josephine Cunningham sat down next to her. Then she laughed sharply at something Cab Duryea said over the way, and she got up and crossed deliberately to Cab. Braven Powell brought the coffee to Josephine.

"Flank-Speed," who had been leaning over Josephine's enormous right shoulder, laughing with her, left her with Braven and stepped at once across to the Sunbury girl, took her arm, turned her to the lanai edge and, in his quiet voice, said, "Remember, Winston-Salem, that I picked you up two days ago in a hotel lobby. That you are a *guest* here. Josephine's skin is dark, but she is the whitest woman I have ever known. Royal as any Hapsburg—if you want your nose rubbed in it. You are among gentle people. I will call a cab for you or bring you a drink now. Which?"

Clarissa looked at him for a moment with utter fury in her eyes; then she said, "You may bring me a drink . . . dad."

Well behind them, Braven turned his sleek, planed, graying head toward the open doors where Sally held the telephone covered with her left hand.

"It's Mike Takezawa," she told him. "Could he bring a Baron Saito—who has no English?"

"Why not?" Braven smiled. "'Flank-Speed' was a language officer in Tokyo before the war. I'll struggle through the amenities. Cab here will give with the USO 'Dozo' and 'Ha.' Of course, tell Mike to bring him. By all means."

Cab Duryea winked at Sam Roth. "I told you, boy. All real—and now yet a Baron. And you wanted to stay at the hotel and read the Sunday papers?"

Sam Roth said, "With a comedian, why mention André Gide? So I said 'Sunday papers.' Do you get a sense of the whole vast Pacific maelstrom drawn into focus on this hilltop? Culturally—which is a lousy word—spiritually—which is little better? In its quintessence of understanding—which is the best way I can put it. From San Francisco to the Sunda Strait? Wonsan to the Auckland Islands?"

"As a boy in Rochester," Cab grinned, "I really wanted to be a concert violinist. I compromised. Relax and don't prod me with your troubled soul. You make good money selling it. Compromise."

"The long-legged broad, then." Sam shrugged, and he walked over to Clarissa Sunbury at the lanai edge, toying now with the drink the admiral had brought her, but still angry at herself, which is the worst kind of anger.

When you time and space it, at least an hour must have gone by from the time Mike Takezawa called until he drove in. If you know the Japanese you must know that they are no more an integrated race than Americans are. There are recognizable strains of Indian, Mongol, Ainu, Chinese, Polynesian, and Malayan in them, but at times in their islands they breed a bloodline of body structure and head and face that produces men who do not fit the general concept of a Japanese at all—nor even Asian.

Mike Takezawa was of that type. So was the Baron; both pleasant-faced men, slender-bodied and well tailored. Braven Powell went out to meet them when the car drove up. Through the open doors and the great room beyond with the two portraits of Chance and Norwood at twelve and thirteen and the crimson-and-yellow cloak of King Kamehameha behind its glass protection, you could see Mike shake hands with Braven and make the introductions. You could see the Baron place his hands upon the fronts of his thighs above the knees and bow several times. Braven returned the bows exactly as they were given, stiltedly speaking the ceremonial words of welcome. He was not at the moment an American in the awkward travesty of a foreign mannerism—a buffoon attempting to kiss the hand of a grandame. The Oriental flavor of his manner went well back into Braven's boyhood, when his father first took him around the company's Asiatic trade routes—to know at first hand the "Powell ports," as occasional older men still call them in San Francisco.

As they came through to the lanai, "Flank-Speed" Oesterreich leaned toward Leander McCullogh. "Am I wrong, Lee, or is this the same Saito who was Minister for Naval Air in '41? The one the Japs imprisoned themselves, after Pearl Harbor?"

Leander said, "The thought was in my mind for a second when Sally spoke the name, but I think *that* Saito died. They were of the old order, those Saitos. His sons were killed in action, as I remember, and his wife committed *jigai.*" Leander's long fingers brushed his throat. "The throat piercing of the Japanese women of station. I think afterward that Saito just died."

Then the Admiral stepped over to Braven, Mike, and the Baron, and opened the secondary batteries of his language-school Japanese, and it was suddenly plain that that Baron was old, for the smile of gratitude for his own tongue, fairly competently handled, was an old man's timid smile.

Mike Takezawa is the traveling Air-Nippon Diplomatic boy—the friend maker, the pourer-on of the oil. Yale, half a dozen years back; Savile Row clothing, and with his Stork Club patter beautifully handled. They went around the company counter to each other, "Flank-Speed" introducing the Baron, slowly, of necessity, to translate; Mike Takezawa offering himself with the words here and the smiles there that are the tools of his Vishnu-Siva trade. Which is by way of saying somewhat two-faced.

Sam Roth watched it with the gutted feeling that he couldn't ever write it better. That no producer would dream of casting it as it was, if he did. Himself, out of the Russian pogroms two generations back, through the ghettos of Westphalia to New York's East Side, and Harvard. Standing beside Clarissa Sunbury, born probably to Carolinian sharecroppers, once removed, but smoothed by fashion magazines into an acceptable hotel woman. Craggy, white-haired Leander McCullogh, as fine a painter as Grant Wood—better, possibly because Leander paints air you can breathe. Cab Duryea—close friend to Bob Hope, Jackie Gleason, and Braven Powell. Braven Powell with his roots deep in the bucko days of the Pacific, overlaid with the smooth, pleasant, hard patina of San Francisco—and not yet run back to shirt sleeves—and not going back in his time, for his fine mind was still there for two Presidents and a chief of staff to use as a by-product of the Trans-Pacific Steam Navigation Company, which he still runs under the white-tern house flag of almost two centuries' standing. Sally, Braven's good lady wife. Josephine Liholiho Cunningham—three hundred pounds of Hawaiian royalty and a most graceful dancer still, at seventy, for her soul was born gay. Admiral "Flank-Speed" Oesterreich from an Ohio farm, through Annapolis, to an almost Nelsonian legend in destroyers.

Within this circle, the quiet old Baron Saito—samurai if you care for a misunderstood word. Bowing to each, mouthing his own courtesies in his own language for "Flank-Speed's" and Braven's elided translations. With Mike Takezawa shaking hands the other way round, quipping easily, smiling, tossing the blithe word.

It was Sam Roth who first felt it go sour—felt the breath of fear in his nostrils. It came to Sam down the ten thousand years of his race memory, and the rising hackles chilled his upper spine.

"I hope," Mike Takezawa said to Sally, "that you will overlook the way I have had to do this. With no warning, I mean?"

"Don't be silly, Mike. On Sunday this house is flung wide. A movable feast. Which is the way Braven and I like it."

"I mean, you see," Mike said, "that there was pressure . . ." And Sam Roth knew that what Mike was really doing was throwing old Saito into somebody else's lap, to keep his own lap clean for his job with the airline.

"Stop apologizing, Mike," Sally laughed. "It doesn't sit you well. You are quite welcome. So is your friend."

Sam Roth thought, *Good; you've got the old Japanese right back in your own lap.*

Then it was that "Flank-Speed" abruptly stopped speaking. He was at the lanai edge with the Baron. He had just made the introduction to Clarissa and to Sam. Clarissa, still holding her drink with her right hand, offered her left. Braven Powell stood slightly behind them, and "Flank-Speed" turned a quick glance toward him as the Baron spoke briefly and then stepped off onto the lawn, his back to the whole company, and stood looking down at the Buddhist shrine on the slope below, his hands clasped before him in an attitude of humility.

"Did you understand what he said, Braven?" the Admiral asked quietly.

"I'm afraid I didn't. I don't have much grasp of idiom. Only words."

The Admiral looked quickly across at Sally. Her back was turned. She was talking to Josephine and Leander. He looked at Mike. He said softly to Braven again, "I don't think you want any part of this, Braven. I think I'll wring Mike Takezawa's fine-shirted neck for him . . . *Mike!*"

Mike smiled and came up to Admiral Oesterreich. "What the hell is this, Mike?"

Mike spread his hands. "It's really rather sad, Admiral, if you take the broad view. He is an old man—of the older thinking. He merely wants to see the place."

"Then why be Asiatic about it? Why the indirection? You're an American. Why not tell Sally and Braven what you *really* wanted? And why pick today, with a lot of people here?"

"Does it do any real harm?" Mike asked pleasantly enough. "It's the first time I ever knew about it myself, and I've been here a dozen times. I've seen the shrine a dozen times. You could have knocked me down with a feather when they told us at Headquarters what was under the mound beside it. Shall we leave, then, Braven? Perhaps that would be best?''

Braven Powell studied Mike Takezawa's face for a moment. His expression did not change from open friendship, except in the eyes. His eyes shadowed slightly. ''No, of course, you will not leave—until the Baron has made his prayer—or whatever.''

Then Mike pressed his luck through the silence that hung at the lanai edge, because he was vaguely embarrassed, disturbed. ''He was imprisoned for years,'' Mike said softly in his bid for justification. ''But he is an honored man now in Japan, for the new people now in power know that he was right about Pearl Harbor. That it should not have happened. He is old. His wife and two sons are gone. He makes his peace. The grave of his oldest son he has visited already in Burma. Now he comes for the one here. He travels under courtesy diplomatic passport. When he came here, our Tokyo foreign office, under Foreign office request, put him in my charge. At Headquarters here—through Washington—he was given the information to find the other grave. Believe me, Braven—''

''Shut up,'' ''Flank-Speed'' growled.

For a moment Braven Powell stood quite still—a tall, beautifully built figure of an aging man going on into the years with his courage intact.

Then he said, ''Sally, why don't you take Miss Sunbury and Josephine, Cab, and Leander through to the sun room and show them the miniature cryptomeria trees?''

Sally Powell turned sharply about, as if she were reacting to a strange noise in the night. She saw her husband's face, felt the impelling timbre of his voice.

She smiled and said, ''From Nikko. You won't believe it, but they are older than the oldest California redwood, and not over eighteen inches high . . .'' And in a moment the lanai was empty, except for Sam Roth in the shadowed peacock chair, and the four men on the lanai edge. Sam could not move, for he knew if he did he would be violently sick on the yellow tiles.

At the lanai edge, the Baron Saito stood down on the lawn, still facing the shrine, and took a few steps toward the mound. Admiral

Oesterreich stood behind him to the left, Braven Powell behind and to the right. Mike Takezawa, behind all of them, closed the diamond they formed. It was ridiculously like a lodge drill-team stance for a moment; or a travesty of a military figure. A reviewing officer, perhaps, and his aides.

"Make it plain to him," Braven said, "that the shrine was here long before the house was built. That I did not put it up to mark the incident."

The Admiral said it in Japanese, and Saito bowed understanding without turning from his contemplation.

"It is Buddha Amitabha," Braven went on, "with a Bodhisattva on either side. The smaller figurines, those are."

The Admiral nodded. "He has told me that himself. He is a devout man. Instructed."

"Professor Gustafson," Braven said, "places it as a seventh century copy. Done here perhaps a century ago, when the first Japanese came to Hawaii. Why it was put up no one knows, but the Islanders always distrusted it. It has been *kapu* as long as Hawaiian memory. Taboo." Braven's voice, as he said these things, had lost all inflection. Except for the controlled thread of emotion woven through it, his voice might have been a transcription. When he stopped, the old Baron Saito began to speak softly with the intense, quiet sound of a man at prayer.

"He is reading from the inscription," the Admiral said. "The First Truth is the Truth of Pain. The Second is that the fact of Pain leads to all cravings—that one may escape. The Third is that the controlled cessation of craving brings about the cessation of Pain. The Fourth Truth is that the Path to that goal must inevitably lead to right views, right intention, right action, and all the rest of rightness."

"I am an Episcopalian," Braven said. "We are not in fundamental conflict. If he would like to go down to the mound, you may tell him he may. Make it plain, however, that we had nothing to do with it. The authorities took complete charge. It was their decision. It was almost an hour after the attack began on Pearl Harbor. The plane must have been hit by automatic fire from Schofield. It was obviously crippled." Braven stepped down and raised an arm toward the roof of his house. "It came in at a steep angle, with all guns firing, and plowed in right beside the shrine. Went deep into the soft hillside and burned. If his son was the pilot, what is left is still there, as well as the gunner's body. The whole crash was merely mounded over after Intelligence was finished."

* * *

Now, a strong man at the portal of his weak years must learn to live with the deterioration of his body, for if he does not, it will betray him. There was just the faintest quaver in Braven Powell's voice as he spoke the last sentence. He closed his lips tightly upon it.

"Flank-Speed" stepped to him and gripped his upper arm. "And that's all? You won't tell him the rest?"

"He's my guest," Braven said, "and a sad old man. What good would it do fourteen years afterward?"—and Braven freed his arm. "I will go in and find Sally now," he said.

There was a final awful moment for Sam Roth. He had not moved, for he still could not. His whole slender, dark body had gone cold.

His heart froze when Mike Takezawa said, "Tell him *what* rest, Admiral?"

"Flank-Speed" spun around and faced Mike Takezawa "you *stupid* bastard!" Then he leveled his long finger. "Those two boys inside, Chance and Norwood. The portraits on the wall. Twelve and thirteen years old. Have you any idea what that Sunday morning was or how far we really are from the States out here? When Braven left to do what he could as a reservist, they got their .22 rifles. When that plane came over, they stood to it as boys will. No! I'm a liar—as *men* will! Real men—firing into its useless, murderous, futile, dying fire." "Flank-Speed" brought both open hands up under Mike Takezawa's face, palms up, the fingers pronged rigidly. Then he dropped them. "They were both killed."

In Sam Roth's throat, the bile surged in fiery bitterness. He covered his mouth and swallowed desperately.

Mike Takezawa put both his hands to his face. "I *swear* I didn't know, Admiral. I never heard—the story."

"You have now," Oesterreich said. Then they both turned. The Baron Saito had made his prayer to his dead son's grave, come back from the mounded grassy slope; stood, a man apart now in his soul, as if waiting.

Mike drew in a deep breath. "Now you will tell the Baron too?"

"He'd tell me, you can bet! Why should I let *him* off? I'm old too. So is Braven Powell. The Baron seeks the Path. Maybe I can give it to him through the older law of an eye and a tooth—for an eye and a tooth." He turned slowly to the Baron Saito, and he told him curtly, the way he would pass an order on his bridge.

The old Japanese listened carefully. Then, for a moment he stood quite still, looking at Admiral Oesterreich. Then he put his old worn hands to the tops of his thighs above his knees and bowed in his fashion.

Mike let him go on ahead to leave, following slowly after him. Saito crossed the lanai, passed Sam Roth in the peacock chair without seeing him, and went into the broad, quiet living room. Sam Roth was the only one who had the old Japanese in his line of sight now, but Sam still couldn't move. Saito stopped before Norwood's eager young face and bowed solemnly to the boy. He then turned to the portrait of Chance Powell, and in one deft and rhythmic motion bowed deeply and, with the jerk of old muscles, went to his knees and haunches, his forehead on the floor. He looked up at Chance's fine young face. Then he took the emperor knife from wherever it was that he carried it, plunged it into the left side of his abdomen, drew it sharply across to the right and cut upward, just as Mike got to the doorway and shouted—just as Sam screamed, "No!"

The three of them were beside the old man, trying stupidly to straighten him from his body-clench of final pain.

"Flank-Speed" snarled: "Get an ambulance, Mike!"

As they remembered afterward, the increasing staccato of Tony Powell's hot rod had been chattering up the drive toward the house for several seconds before. It fired into the car oval now with a final machine-gun burst and broke off. Before Mike could ring the operator, young Tony pulled open the front door and bear-cubbed to a full stop.

"What the *hell*?"

"Flank-Speed" said, "Tony, they are in the sun room. Your mother and some people. Keep them there. Send your father—"

"Sure, Uncle Frank. How'd it happen?" Then it came over his surface youthful mind, like smashing glass, that it was no accident. "For God's sake—hara-kiri? Who is he?"

"Tony!" the Admiral said. "Move!" for the youngster stood there, stiff, the planes of his fine-boned face gone tight, his long legs planted rigidly, the wild anger flaming in his eyes. "Who let him do it? In this room, of all places?" His arm flashed up as his father's had when he pointed to the house roof outside. "With my two brothers' pictures!" Then, as youth will in its eternal frantic frustration, "Get him out of here! I won't have my mother and father face this lousy mess!" Then he saw his father in the lanai doorway and he drew in his breath sharply.

Braven Powell said, "steady, Tony," and he said to "Flank-Speed," "Is there still a pulse?" and the Admiral said, "Fluttering out."

* * *

Mike Takezawa said, "The ambulance is on its way. I don't get it. To have had the knife on him, he must have planned it all along. Planned to do it at his son's graveside, not knowing it was so near a private house."

"Near a private house!" Tony snorted. "How near can you *get?*"

"Steady, Tony," Braven said. "You told him, didn't you, 'Flank'?"

And the Admiral said, "Of course I told him. You don't think I'd ever let any Jap off, do you?"

In his blind anger, Tony sputtered again.

"Stop it, Tony," Braven shook his head. "In his own way of living, he has done this house the greatest honor in his power. He has turned his back to his own, and paid tribute to ours. He has apologized as handsomely as any man can, by a very ancient code. The least we can do is to be gracious enough to accept it." Braven's eyes flashed briefly to each of the eager young faces on the wall, and there seemed to be a book in his mind that was closing at last—that had left him all these years with a tragic sense of incompleteness, but that now was bringing to him the full knowledge that Someone else writes the stories and that no man born of woman has the right of final criticism.

When the ambulance was gone and they were all gone—Miss Sunbury and "Flank-Speed," Josephine and Leander McCullogh, Cab Duryea and Sam Roth—Braven Powell poured a stiff brandy for Sally and he said, "I've never analyzed the fact of love because it has never seemed necessary to me, my dear. It was always enough that I always knew I loved you."

He smiled, "But if I hadn't, I would have admired you and trusted you and looked up to you in a completeness of friendship that I have never been able to give to any man. I hope that means something to you, for it is the nearest I have ever come to understanding a fundamental fact."

"Will you please stop, Braven?" she cried. "I don't want to cry in front of Tony."

Big Tony surged across to her and stood with his hands thrust deep into his pockets, his lips pressed tight, shaking his head slowly.

Then he said, "Gee, mom, you are quite a guy. Quite a character. The way you handled it!"

"When you have a job, Tony, you do it."

"That's why I came back up." He turned to his father. "A man gets crazy at times, sir. I guess it's natural to want to tear free and go on your own. I guess with me there was more of a push than there usually is, because—because it somehow seemed, until now, that I was just the third-string man. Please don't get me wrong. You fellows never made me feel it.'' He tapped his chest. ''I just felt it myself deep inside—that either Chance or Norwood would have been your boy. Well''—his young chin went up—''even before it happened, I came back after this morning's family hassle at breakfast, Dad, to tell Cab Duryea to stuff the network job. *I'm* your boy. When do we start on the run-around, sir?'' and he grinned. ''Through the Powell ports? When do I start working for the line?''

''About that cloak of Kamehameha's,'' Sally said. ''Let's let the museum wait a while longer. Shall we, Braven?''

Going out through the gateposts, Cab said, ''That's the old Powell house flag, Sam—a white tern on a crimson burgee.''

''But you don't know what it means,'' Sam said. ''You don't read André Gide. When you see the petrel at sea in sail, you're a hundred miles offshore. But when you see the white tern at dawn, you'll make your landfall that day.''

WALLACE STEGNER

The Women on the Wall

THE CORNER WINDOW of the study overlooked a lawn, and beyond that a sunken lane between high pines, and beyond the lane a point of land with the old beach club buildings at one end and a stone wall around its tip. Beyond the point, through the cypresses and eucalyptuses, Mr. Palmer could see the Pacific, misty blue, belted between shore and horizon with a band of brown kelp.

Writing every morning in his study, making his old notebooks into a coherent account of his years on the Galapagos, Mr. Palmer could glance up from his careful longhand and catch occasional glimpses, as a traveler might glance out of the window of a moving train. And in spite of the rather special atmosphere of the point, caused by the fact that until the past year it had been a club, there was something homey and neighborly and pleasant about the place that Mr. Palmer liked. There were children, for one thing, and dogs drifting up and down, and the occasional skirr of an automobile starting in the quiet, the diminishing sound of tires on asphalt, the distant racket of a boy being a machine-gun with his mouth.

Mr. Palmer had been away from the States a long time; he found the noises on the point familiar and nostalgic and reassuring in this time of war, and felt as if he had come home. Though California differed considerably from his old home in Ohio, he fell naturally and gratefully into its procession of morning and afternoon, its neighborhood routines, the pleasant breathing of its tides. When anything outside broke in upon his writing, it was generally a commonplace and familiar thing; Mr. Palmer looked up and took pleasure in the interruption.

One thing he could be sure of seeing, every morning but Sunday. The section was outside the city limits, and mail was delivered to a battery of mail boxes where the sunken lane joined the street. The mail arrived at about eleven; about ten-thirty the women from the beach club apartments began to gather on the stone wall. Below the wall was the beach, where the tides leaned in all the way from Iwo and Okinawa. Above it was the row of boxes where as regularly as the tide the mail carrier came in a gray car and deposited postmarked flotsam from half a world away.

Sometimes Mr. Palmer used to pause in his writing and speculate on what these women thought of when they looked out across the gumdrop blue water and the brown kelp and remembered that across this uninterrupted ocean their husbands fought and perhaps bled and possibly died, that in those far islands it was already tomorrow, that the green water breaking against the white foot of the beach might hold in suspension minute quantities of the blood shed into it thousands of miles away, that the Japan current, swinging in a great circle up under the Aleutians and back down the American coast, might as easily bear the mingled blood or the floating relics of a loved one lost as it could bear the glass balls of Japanese netfloats that it sometimes washed ashore.

Watching the women, with their dogs and children, waiting patiently on the stone wall for that most urgent of all gods, that Mercury in the gray uniform, Mr. Palmer thought a good deal about Penelope on the rocky isle of Ithaca above the wine-dark sea. He got a little sentimental about these women. Sometimes he was almost frightened by the air of patient, withdrawn seriousness they wore as they waited, and the unsmiling alacrity with which they rose and crowded around the mailman when he came. And when the mail was late, and one or two of them sat out on the wall until eleven-thirty, twelve, sometimes twelve-thirty, Mr. Palmer could hardly bear it at all.

Waiting, Mr. Palmer reflected, must cause a person to remove to a separate and private world. Like sleep or insanity, waiting must have the faculty of making the real unreal and remote. It seemed to Mr. Palmer pathetic and somehow thrilling that these women should have followed their men to the very brink of the west, and should remain here now with their eyes still westward, patiently and faithfully suspending their own normal lives until the return of their husbands. Without knowing any of the women, Mr. Palmer respected and admired them. They did not invite his pity. Penelope was as competent for her waiting as Ulysses was for his wars and wiles.

Mr. Palmer had been working in his new house hardly a week before he found himself putting on his jacket about eleven and going out to join the women.

He knew them all by sight, just from looking out the window. The red-haired woman with the little boy was sitting on the wall nearest him. Next was the thin girl who always wore a bathing suit and went barefooted. Next was the dark-haired one, five or six months pregnant. And next to her was the florid, quick, wrenlike woman with the little girl about five. Their faces all turned as Mr. Palmer came up.

"Good morning," he said.

The red-haired woman's plain, serious, freckled face acknowledged him, and she murmured good morning. The girl in the bathing suit had turned to look off over the ocean, and Mr. Palmer felt that she had not made any reply. The pregnant girl and the woman with the little girl both nodded.

The old man put his hands on his knees, rounded his mouth and eyes, and bent to look at the little boy hanging to the red-haired woman's hand. "Well!" he said. "Hi, young fella!"

The child stared at him, crowding against his mother's legs. The mother said nothing, and rather than push first acquaintance too far, Mr. Palmer walked on along the wall.

As he glanced at the thin girl, he met her eyes, so full of cold hostility that for a moment he was shocked. He had intended to sit down in the middle of the wall, but her look sent him on further, to sit between the pregnant girl and the wrenlike woman.

"These beautiful mornings!" Mr. Palmer said, sitting down with a sigh.

The wrenlike woman nodded, the pregnant one regarded him with quiet ox-eyes.

"This is quite a ritual, waiting for the mail," Mr. Palmer said. He pointed to the gable of his house across the lane. "I see you from my window over there, congregating on the wall here every morning."

The wrenlike woman looked at him rather oddly, then leaped to prevent her daughter from putting out the eyes of the long-suffering setter she was mauling. The pregnant girl smiled a slow, soft smile. Over her shoulder Mr. Palmer saw the thin girl hitch herself up and sit on her hands. The expression on her face said that she knew very well why Mr. Palmer had come down and butted in, and why he watched from his window.

"The sun's so warm out here," the pregnant girl said. "It's a way of killing part of the morning, sitting out here."

"A very good way," Mr. Palmer said. He smoothed the creases in his trousers, finding speech a little difficult. From the shelter of his mother's legs the two-year-old boy down the wall stared at him solemnly. Then the wrenlike woman hopped off the wall and dusted her skirt.

"Here he is!" she said.

They all started across the mouth of the lane, and for some reason, as they waited for the mailman to sort and deliver, Mr. Palmer felt that his first introduction hadn't taken him very far. In a way, as he thought it over, he respected the women for that, too. They were living without their husbands, and had to be careful. After all, Penelope had many suitors. But he could not quite get over wanting to spank the thin girl on her almost exposed backside, and he couldn't shake the sensation of having wandered by mistake into the ladies' room.

After that, without feeling that he knew them at all, he respected them and respected their right to privacy. Waiting, after all, put you in an exclusive club. No outsider had any more right on that wall than he had in the company of a bomber crew. But Mr. Palmer felt that he could at least watch from his window; and at the mailboxes he could, almost by osmosis, pick up a little more information.

The red-haired woman's name was Kendall. Her husband was an army captain, a doctor. The thin girl, Mrs. Fisher, got regular letters bearing a Marine Corps return. The husband of Mrs. Corson, the wrenlike woman, commanded a flotilla of mine-sweepers in the western Pacific. Of the pregnant girl, Mrs. Vaughn, Mr. Palmer learned little. She got few letters, and none with any postmarks that told anything.

From his study window Mr. Palmer went on observing them benignly and making additions to his notes on the profession of waiting. Though the women differed sharply one from another, they seemed to Mr. Palmer to have one thing in common: they were all quiet, peaceful, faithful to the times and seasons of their vigil, almost like convalescents in a hospital. They made no protests or outcries; they merely lived at a reduced tempo, as if pulse rate and respiration rate and metabolic rate and blood pressure were all tuned down. Mr. Palmer had a notion how it might be. Sometimes when he awoke very quietly in the night he could feel how quietly and slowly and regularly his heart was pumping, how slow and regular his breathing was, how he lay there mute and cool and inert with everything turned down to idling speed, his old body taking care of itself. And when he woke that way he had a curious feeling that he was waiting for something.

Every morning at ten-thirty, as regular as sun and tide, Mrs. Kendall came out of the beach club apartments and walked across the point, leading her little boy by the hand. She had the child tuned down, too, apparently. He never, to Mr. Palmer's knowledge, ran or yelled or cried or made a fuss, but walked quietly beside his mother, and sat with her on the big stump until five minutes to eleven, and then walked with her across to the end of the stone wall. About that time the other women began to gather, until all four of them were there in a quiet, uncommunicative row.

Only once in all that drowsy spring was there any breaking of the pattern. That was one Monday after Mr. Palmer had been away for the weekend. When he strolled out at mail time he found the women not sitting on the wall, but standing in a nervous conversational group. They opened to let him in, for once accepting him silently among them, and he found that the thin girl had moved out suddenly the day before: the Saturday mail had brought word that her husband had gone down in flames over the Marianas.

The news depressed Mr. Palmer in curious ways. It depressed him to see the women shaken from their phlegmatic routine, because the moment they were so shaken they revealed the raw fear under their quiet. And it depressed him that the thin girl's husband had been killed. That tragedy should come to a woman he personally felt to be a snob, a fool, a vain and inconsequent chit, seemed to him sad and incongruous and even exasperating. As long as she was one of the company of Penelopes, Mr. Palmer had refused to dislike her. The moment she made demands upon his pity he disliked her very much.

After that sudden blow, as if a hawk had struck among the quiet birds on the wall, Mr. Palmer found it less pleasant to watch the slow, heavy-bodied walking of Mrs. Kendall, her child always tight by the hand, from apartment to stump to wall. Unless spoken to, she never spoke. She wore gingham dresses that were utterly out of place in the white sun above the white beach. She was plain, unattractive, patient, the most remote, the most tuned-down, the quietest and saddest and most patient and most exasperating of the Penelopes. She too began to make wry demands on Mr. Palmer's pity, and he found himself almost disliking her. He was guilty of a little prayer that Mrs. Kendall's husband would be spared, so that his pity would not have to go any further than it did.

Then one morning Mr. Palmer became aware of another kind of interruption on the point. Somebody there had apparently bought a new dog. Whoever had acquired it must have fed it, though Mr. Palmer never saw anyone do so, and must have exercised it, though he never saw that either. All he saw was that the dog, a half-grown cocker, was tied to the end of a rose trellis in the clubhouse yard. And all he heard, for two solid days, was the uproar the dog made.

It did not like being tied up. It barked, and after a while its voice would break into a kind of hysterical howling mixed with shuddering diminuendo groans. Nobody ever came and told it to be still, or took care of it, or let it loose. It stayed there and yanked on the rope and chewed at the trellis post and barked and howled and groaned until Mr. Palmer's teeth were on edge and he was tempted to call the Humane Society.

Actually he didn't, because on the third morning the noise had stopped and as he came into his study to begin working he saw that the dog was gone. Mrs. Corson was sitting in a lawn chair under one of the cypresses, and her daughter was digging in the sandpile. There was no sign either of Mrs. Kendall or Mrs. Vaughn. The owner of the house was raking leaves on the lawn above the seawall.

Mr. Palmer looked at his watch. It was nine-thirty. On an impulse he slipped on a jacket and went down and out across the lawn and down across the lane and up the other side past the trellis. Where the dog had lain the ground was strewn with chewed green splinters.

Mrs. Corson looked up from her chair. Her cheeks were painted with a patchwork of tiny ruddy veins, and her eyes looked as if she hadn't slept. They had a stary blankness like blind eyes, and Mr. Palmer noticed that the pupils were dilated, even in the bright light. She took a towel and a pack of cigarettes and a bar of cocoa-butter off the chair next to her.

"Good morning," she said in her husky voice. "Sit down."

"Thank you," Mr. Palmer said. He let himself down into the steeply slanting wooden chair and adjusted the knees of his slacks. "It *is* a good morning," he said slyly. "So quiet."

Mrs. Corson's thin neck jerked upward and backward in a curious gesture. Her throaty laughter was loud and unrestrained, and the eyes she turned on Mr. Palmer were red with mirth.

"That damned dog," she said. "Wasn't that something?"

"I thought I'd go crazy," Mr. Palmer said. "Whose dog was it, anyway?"

Mrs. Corson's rather withered, red-nailed hand, with a big diamond and a wedding ring on the fourth finger, reached down and picked up the cigarettes. The hand trembled as it held the pack out.

"No thank you," he said.

Mrs. Corson took one. "It was Mrs. Kendall's dog," she said. "She took it back."

"Thank God!" said Mr. Palmer.

Her hands nervous with the matchbox in her lap, Mrs. Corson sat and smoked. Mr. Palmer saw that her lips, under the lipstick, were chapped, and that there was a dried, almost leathery look to her tanned and freckled skin.

He slid deeper into the chair and looked out over the water, calm as a lake, the long light swells breaking below him with a quiet, lulling swish. Up the coast heavier surf was breaking farther out. Its noise came like a pulsating tremble on the air, hardly a sound at all. Everything tuned down, Mr. Palmer was thinking. Even the lowest frequency of waves on the beach. Even the ocean waited.

"I should think you'd bless your stars, having a place like this to wait in," he said.

One of Mrs. Corson's eyebrows bent. She shot him a sideward look.

"Think of the women who are waiting in boardinghouse rooms," Mr. Palmer said, a little irritated at her manner. "Think of the ones who are working and leaving their children in nurseries."

"Oh, sure," Mrs. Corson said. "It's fine for Anne, with the beach and yard."

Mr. Palmer leaned on the arm of the chair and looked at her quizzically. He wished any of these women would ever put away their reticence and talk about their waiting, because that was where their life lay, that was where they had authority. "How long has your husband been gone?" he asked.

"Little over two years."

"That's a long time," Mr. Palmer said, thinking of Penelope and her wait. Ten years while the war went on at Troy, ten more years while Ulysses wandered through every peril in the Mediterranean, past Scylla and Charybdis and Circe and the Cyclops and the iron terrors of Hades and the soft temptations of Nausicaa. But that was poetry. Twenty years was too much. Two, in all conscience, was enough.

"I shouldn't kick," the woman said. "Mrs. Kendall's husband has been gone for over three."

"I've noticed her," Mr. Palmer said. "She seems rather sad and repressed."

For a moment Mrs. Corson's eyes, slightly bloodshot, the pupils dilated darkly, were fixed questioningly on Mr. Palmer's. Then the woman shook herself almost as a dog does. "I guess," she said. She rose with a nervous snap and glanced at her watch. From the sandpile the little girl called, "Is it time, Mommy?"

"I guess so," Mrs. Corson said. She laid the back of her hand across her eyes and made a face.

"I'll be getting along," Mr. Palmer said.

"I was just taking Anne down for her pony ride. Why don't you ride down with us?"

"Well . . ."

"Come on," Mrs. Corson said. "We'll be back in less than an hour."

The child ran ahead of them and opened the car doors, down in the widened part of the lane. As Mr. Palmer helped Mrs. Corson in she turned her face a little, and he smelled the stale alcohol on her breath. Obviously Mrs. Corson had been drinking the night before, and obviously she was a little hung over.

But my Lord, why not? he said to himself. Two years of waiting, nothing to do but sit and watch and do nothing and be patient. He didn't like Mrs. Corson any less for occasional drinking. She was higher-strung than either Mrs. Vaughn or Mrs. Kendall. You could almost lift up the cover board and pluck her nerves like the strings of a piano. Even so, she played the game well. He liked her.

At the pony track Anne raced down the fenced runway at a pink fluttering gallop, and Mr. Palmer and Mrs. Corson, following more slowly, found her debating between a black and a pinto pony.

"Okay," the man in charge said. "Which'll it be today, young lady?"

"I don't know," the girl said. Her forehead wrinkled. "Mommy, which do you think?"

"I don't care, hon," her mother said. "Either one is nice."

Pretty, her blonde braids hanging in front and framing her odd pre-Raphaelite face, Anne stood indecisive. She turned her eyes up to Mr. Palmer speculatively. "The black one's nice," she said, "but so's the . . ."

"Oh, Anne," her mother said. "For heaven's sake make up your mind."

"Well . . . the black one, then," Anne said. She reached out a hand and touched the pony's nose, pulling her fingers back sharply and looking up at her mother with a smile that Mr. Palmer found himself almost yearning over. She was a pretty, dainty little child, no mistake.

"You're a nitwit," her mother said. "Hop on, so we can get back for the mailman."

The attendant swung her up, but with one leg over the saddle Anne kicked and screamed to get down. "I've changed my mind," she said. "Not this one, the pinto one."

The attendant put her up on the pinto and Mrs. Corson, her chapped lips trembling, said, "Another outburst like that and you won't get on any, you little . . . !"

The pony started, led by the attendant who rocked on one thick-soled shoe. For a moment Mrs. Corson and Mr. Palmer stood in the sun under the sign that said "Pony Rides, 10 Cents, 12 for $1.00." They were, Mr. Palmer noticed, in the Mexican part of town. Small houses, some of them almost shacks, with geraniums climbing all over them, strung out along the street. Down on the corner beyond the car was a tavern with a dusty tin sign. Mrs. Corson unsnapped her purse and fished out a wadded bill and held it vaguely in her hand, looking off up the street past the track and the pinto pony and the pink little huddle on its back and the attendant rocking along ahead on his one thick shoe.

"I wonder," she said. "Would you do me a favor?"

"Anything."

"Would you stay here five minutes while I go to the store? Just keep an eye on her?"

"Of course," he said. "I'd be glad to go to the store for you, if you'd like."

"No," she said. "No, I'd better get it." She put the crumpled bill into his hand. "Let her have all the rides she wants. I'll be back in a few minutes."

Mr. Palmer settled himself on a chair against the stable wall and waited. When Anne and the attendant got back he waved the bill at them. "Want another ride?"

"Yes!" Anne said. Her hands were clenched tightly in the pony's mane, and her eyes danced and her mouth was a little open. The attendant turned and started down the track again. "Run!" Anne cried to him. "Make him run!"

The crippled hostler broke into a clumsy hop-skip-and-jump for a few yards, pulling the pony into a trot. The girl screamed with delight. Mr. Palmer yawned, tapped his mouth, smiled a little as he smelled the powder-and-perfume smell on the dollar bill, yawned again. Say what you would, it was decent of the woman to come out with a hangover and take her child to the pony track. She must feel pretty rocky, if her eyes were any criterion.

He waited for some time. Anne finished a second ride, took a third, finished that and had a fourth. The attendant was sweating a little. From the fence along the sidewalk two Negro children and a handful of little Mexicans watched. "How about it?" Mr. Palmer said. "Want another?"

She nodded, shaken with giggles and sudden shyness when she looked around and found her mother gone.

"Sure you're not getting sore?" Mr. Palmer patted his haunch suggestively.

She shook her head.

"Okay," the hostler said. "Here we go again, then."

At the end of the fifth ride Anne let herself be lifted off. The hostler went inside and sat down, the pony joined his companion at the rail, cocked its hip and tipped his right hoof and closed its eyes. Anne climbed up into Mr. Palmer's lap.

"Where's Mommy?"

"She went to buy something."

"Darn her," Anne said. "She does that all the time. She better hurry up, it's getting mail time."

"Don't you like to miss the mail?"

"Sometimes there's packages and things from Daddy," Anne said. "I got a grass skirt once."

Mr. Palmer rounded his mouth and eyes. "You must like your daddy."

'I do. Mommy doesn't, though."

"What?"

"Mommy gets mad," Anne said. "She thinks Daddy could have had shore duty a long time ago, he's had so much combat, but she says he likes the navy better than home. He's a commander."

"Yes, I know," Mr. Palmer said. He looked up the street, beginning to be fretful. The fact that the woman spent her whole life waiting shouldn't make her quite so callous to how long she kept other people waiting. "We are going to miss the mailman if your mommy doesn't hurry," he said.

Anne jumped off his lap and puckered her lips like her mother. "And today's a package!"

Mr. Palmer raised his eyebrows. "How do you know?"

"The fortune teller told Mommy."

"I see," the old man said. "Does your mother go to fortune tellers often?"

"Every Saturday," Anne said. "I went with her once. You know what she said? And it came true, too."

Mr. Palmer saw the girl's mother coming down the sidewalk, and stood up. "Here comes Mommy," he said. "We'd better meet her at the car."

"She said we'd get good news, and right away Daddy was promoted,'' Anne said. ''And she said we'd get a package, and that week we got *three!*''

Mrs. Corson was out of breath. In the bright sun her eyes burned with a curious sightless brilliance. The smell of alcohol on her was fresher and stronger.

''I'm sorry,'' she said as she got in. ''I met a friend, and it was so hot we stopped for a beer.''

On the open highway, going back home, she stepped down hard on the throttle, and her fingers kept clasping and unclasping the wheel. Her body seemed possessed of electric energy. She radiated something, she gave off sparks. Her eyes, with the immense dark pupils and suffused whites, were almost scary.

When they pulled up in front of Mr. Palmer's gate, opposite the mail boxes, the little red flags on some of the boxes were still up. On the stone wall sat Mrs. Kendall, her son Tommy, and the pregnant girl, Mrs. Vaughn. ''Late again,'' Mrs. Corson said. ''Damn that man.''

''Can I play, Mommy?'' Anne said.

''Okay.'' As the child climbed out, the mother said, ''Don't get into any fixes with Tommy. Remember what I told you.''

''I will,'' Anne said. Her setter came up and she stopped to pull its ears.

Her mother's face went pinched and mean. ''And stop abusing that dog!'' she said.

Mr. Palmer hesitated. He was beginning to feel uncomfortable, and he thought of the pages he might have filled that morning, and the hour that still remained before noon. But Mrs. Corson was leaning back with the back of her hand across her eyes. Through the windshield Mr. Palmer could see the two women and the child on the wall, like a multiple Patience on a monument. When he looked back at Mrs. Corson he saw that she too was watching them between her fingers. Quite suddenly she began to laugh.

She laughed for a good minute, not loudly but with curious violence, her whole body shaking. She dabbed her eyes and caught her breath and shook her head and tried to speak. Mr. Palmer attended uneasily, wanting to be gone.

''Lord,'' Mrs. Corson said finally. ''Look at 'em. Vultures on a limb. Me too. Three mama vultures and one baby vulture.''

''You're a little hard on yourself,'' Mr. Palmer said, smiling. ''And Anne, I'd hardly call her a vulture.''

''I didn't include her,'' Mrs. Corson said. She turned her hot red eyes on him. ''She's got sense enough to run and play, and I hope I've got sense enough to let her.''

''Well, but little Tommy . . .''

''Hasn't had his hand out of Mama's since they came here,'' Mrs. Corson said. ''Did you ever see him play with anybody?''

Mr. Palmer confessed that he hadn't, now that he thought of it.

''Because if you ever do,'' Mrs. Corson said, ''call out all the preachers. It'll be Christ come the second time. Honest to God, sometimes that woman . . .''

Bending forward, Mr. Palmer could see Mrs. Kendall smoothing the blue sweater around her son's waist. ''I've wondered about her,'' he said, and stopped. Mrs. Corson had started to laugh again.

When she had finished her spasm of tight, violent mirth, she said, ''It isn't her child, you know.''

''No?'' he said, surprised. ''She takes such care of it.''

''You're not kidding,'' Mrs. Corson said. ''She won't let him play with Anne. Anne's too dirty. She digs in the ground and stuff. Seven months we've lived in the same house, and those kids haven't played together once. Can you imagine that?''

''No,'' Mr. Palmer confessed. ''I can't.''

''She adopted it when it was six months old,'' Mrs. Corson said. ''She tells us all it's a love-child.'' Her laugh began again, a continuous, hiccoughy chuckle. ''Never lets go its hand,'' she said. ''Won't let him play with anybody. Wipes him off like an heirloom. And brags around he's a love-child. My God!''

With her thin, freckled arm along the door and her lips puckered, she fell silent. ''Love-child!'' she said at last. ''Did you ever look at her flat face? It's the last place love would ever settle on.''

''Perhaps that explains,'' Mr. Palmer said uncomfortably. ''She's childless, she's unattractive. She pours all that frustrated affection out on this child.''

Mrs. Corson twisted to look almost incredulously into his face. ''Of course,'' she said. Her alcoholic breath puffed at him. ''Of course. But why toot it up as a love-child?'' she said harshly. ''What does she think my child is, for God's sake? How does she think babies are made?''

''Well, but there's an old superstition,'' Mr. Palmer said. He moved his hand sideward. ''Children born of passion, you know—they're supposed to be more beautiful . . .''

''And doesn't that tell you anything about her?'' Mrs. Corson said. ''Doesn't that show you that she never thought of passion in the same world with her husband? She has to go outside herself for any passion, there's none in her.''

''Yes,'' Mr. Palmer said. ''Well, of course one can speculate, but one hardly knows . . .''

''And that damned dog,'' Mrs. Corson said. ''Tommy can't play with other kids. They're too dirty. So she gets a dog. Dogs are cleaner than Anne, see? So she buys her child this nice germless dog, and then ties him up and won't let him loose. So the dog howls his head off, and we all go nuts. Finally we told her we couldn't stand it, why didn't she let it loose and let it run. But she said it might run away, and Tommy loved it so she didn't want to take a chance on losing the pup. So I finally called the Society for the Preservation of Cruelty to Animals, and they told her either to give it regular running and exercise or take it back. She took it back last night, and now she hates me.''

As she talked, saliva had gathered in the corner of her mouth. She sucked it in and turned her head away, looking out on the street. ''Lord God,'' she said. ''So it goes, so it goes.''

Through the windshield Mr. Palmer watched the quiet women on the wall, the quiet, well-behaved child. Anne was romping with the setter around the big stump, twenty feet beyond, and the little boy was watching her. It was a peaceful and windless morning steeped in sun. The mingled smell of pines and low tide drifted across the street, and was replaced by the pervading faint fragrance of Ceanothus, blooming in shades of blue and white along Mr. Palmer's walk.

''I'm amazed,'' he said. ''She seems so quiet and relaxed and plain.''

''That's another thing,'' Mrs. Corson said. ''She's a cover-yourself-up girl, too, Remember Margy Fisher, whose husband was killed a few weeks ago? You know why she never wore anything but a bathing suit? Because this old biddy was always after her about showing herself.''

''Well, it's certainly a revelation,'' Mr. Palmer said. ''I see you all from my window, you know, and it seems like a kind of symphony of waiting, all quiet and harmonious. The pregnant girl, too—going on with the slow inevitable business of life while her husband's gone, the rhythm of the generations unchanged. I've enjoyed the whole thing, like a pageant, you know.''

''Your window isn't a very good peekhole,'' Mrs. Corson said dryly.

''Mm?''

''Hope's husband was killed at Dieppe,'' said Mrs. Corson.

For a moment Mr. Palmer did not catch on. At first he felt only a flash of pity as he remembered the girl's big steady brown eyes, her still, rather sad face, her air of pliant gentleness. Then the words Mrs. Corson had spoken began to take effect. Dieppe—almost three years ago. And the girl six months pregnant.

He wished Mrs. Corson would quit drumming her red nails on the car door. She was really in a state this morning, nervous as a cat. But that poor girl, sitting over there with all that bottled up inside of her, the fear and uncertainty growing as fast as the child in her womb grew . . .

''Some naval lieutenant,'' Mrs. Corson said. ''He's right in the middle of the fighting, gunnery officer on a destroyer. You ought to hear Hope when she gets scared he'll never come back and make a decent woman of her.''

''I'd not like to,'' Mr. Palmer said, and shook his head. Across the lane the placid scene had not changed, except that Mrs. Kendall had let Tommy toddle fifteen feet out from the wall, where he was picking up clusters of dry pine needles and throwing them into the air.

The figures were very clean, sharp-edged in the clear air against the blue backdrop of sea. An Attic grace informed all of them: the girl stooping above the long-eared red setter, the child with his hands in the air, tossing brown needles in a shower, the curving seated forms of the women on the wall. To Mr. Palmer's momentarily tranced eyes they seemed to freeze in attitudes of flowing motion like figures on a vase, cameo-clear in the clear air under the noble trees, with the quiet ocean of their watchfulness stretching blue to the misty edge. Like figures on a Grecian urn they curved in high relief against the white molding of the wall, and a drift of indescribable melancholy washed across the point and pricked goosepimples on Mr. Palmer's arms. ''It's sad,'' he said, opening the door and stepping down. ''The whole thing is very sad.''

With the intention of leaving he put his hand on the door and pushed it shut, thinking that he did not want to stay longer and hear Mrs. Corson's bitter tongue and watch the women on the wall. Their waiting now, with the momentary trance broken and the momentary lovely frozen group dispersed in motion, seemed to him a monstrous aberration, their patience a deathly apathy, their hope an obscene self-delusion.

He was filled with a sense of the loveliness of the white paper and the cleanly sharpened pencils, the notebooks and the quiet and the sense of purpose that waited in his study. Most of all the sense of purpose, the thing to be done that would have an ending and a result.

"It's been very pleasant," he said automatically. At that moment there came a yowl from the point.

He turned. Apparently Anne, romping with the dog, had bumped Tommy and knocked him down. He sat among the pine needles in his blue play suit and squalled, and Mrs. Kendall came swiftly out from the wall and took Anne by the arm, shaking her.

"You careless child!" she said. "Watch what you're doing."

Instantly Mrs. Corson was out of the car. Mr. Palmer saw her start for the point, her lips puckered, and was reminded of some mechanical toy tightly wound and tearing erratically around a room giving off sparks of ratchety noise. When she was twenty feet from Mrs. Kendall she shouted hoarsely. "Let go of that child!"

Mrs. Kendall's heavy gingham body turned. Her plain face, the mouth stiff with anger, confronted Mrs. Corson. Her hand still held Anne's arm. "It's possible to train children . . ." she said.

"Yes, and it's possible to mistreat them," Mrs. Corson said. "Let go of her."

For a moment neither moved. Then Mrs. Corson's hands darted down, caught Mrs. Kendall's wrist, and tore her hold from Anne's arm. Even across the lane, fifty feet away, Mr. Palmer could see the white fury in their faces as they confronted each other.

"If I had the bringing up of that child . . . !" Mrs. Kendall said. "I'd . . ."

"You'd tie her to your apron strings like you've tied your own," Mrs. Corson said. "Like you tie up a dog and expect it to get used to three feet of space. My God, a child's a little animal. He's got to run!"

"And knock other children down, I suppose."

"O my God!" Mrs. Corson said, and turned her thin face skyward as if to ask God to witness. She was shaking all over. Mr. Palmer could see the trembling of her dress. "Listen!" she said, "I don't know what's the matter with you, and why you can't stand nakedness, and why you think a bastard child is something holier than a legitimate one, and why you hang on to that child as if he was worth his weight in diamonds. But you keep your claws off mine, and if your little bastard can't get out of the way, you can just . . ."

Mrs. Kendall's face was convulsed. She raised both hands above her head, stuttering for words. From the side the pregnant girl slipped in quietly, and Mr. Palmer, rooted uneasily across the lane, heard her quiet voice. "You're beginning to draw a crowd," she said. "For the love of mike, turn it down."

Mrs. Corson swung on her. Her trembling had become an ecstasy. When she spoke she chewed loudly on her words, mangling them almost beyond recognition. "You keep out of this, you pregnant bitch," she said. "Any time I want advice on how to raise love-children, I'll come to you too, but right now I haven't got any love-children, and I'm raising what I've got my own way."

A window had gone up in the house next to Mr. Palmer's, and three boys were drifting curiously down the street, their pants sagging with the weight of armament they carried. Without hesitating more than a moment, Mr. Palmer crossed the street and cut them off. "I think you'd better beat it," he said, and pushed his hands in the air as if shooing chickens. The boys stopped and eyed him suspiciously, then began edging around the side. It was clear that in any contest of speed, agility, endurance, or anything else Mr. Palmer was no match for them. He put his hand in his pocket and pulled out some change. The boys stopped. Behind him Mr. Palmer heard the saw-edged voice of Mrs. Corson. "I'm not the kind of person that'll stand it, by God! If you want to . . ."

"Here," Mr. Palmer said. "Here's a quarter apiece if you light out and forget anything you saw."

"Okay!" they said, and stepped up one by one and got their quarters and retreated, their heads together and their armed hips clanking together and their faces turning once, together, to stare back at the arguing women on the point. Up the street Mr. Palmer saw a woman and three small children standing in the road craning. Mrs. Corson's voice carried for half a mile.

In the hope that his own presence would bring her to reason, Mr. Palmer walked across the lane. Mrs. Corson's puckered, furious face was thrust into Mrs. Kendall's, and she was saying, "Just tell me to my face I don't raise my child right! Go on, tell me so. Tell me what you told Margy, that Anne's too dirty for your bastard to play with. Tell me, I dare you, and I'll tear your tongue out!"

Mr. Palmer found himself standing next to Mrs. Vaughn. He glanced at her once and shook his head and cleared his throat. Mrs. Corson continued to glare into the pale flat face before her. When Mrs. Kendall turned heavily and walked toward the wall, the wrenlike woman skipped nimbly around her and confronted her from the other side. "You've got a lot of things to criticize in me!" she said. Her voice, suddenly, was so hoarse it was hardly more than a whisper. "Let's hear you say them to my face. I've heard them behind my back too long. Let's hear you say them!"

"Couldn't we get her into the house?" Mr. Palmer said to the pregnant girl. "She'll raise the whole neighborhood."

"Let her disgrace herself," Mrs. Vaughn said, and shrugged.

"But you don't understand," Mr. Palmer said. "She had a beer or so downtown, and I think that, that and the heat . . ."

The girl looked at him with wide brown eyes in which doubt and contempt and something like mirth moved like shadows on water. "I guess *you* don't understand," she said. "She isn't drunk. She's hopped."

"Hopped?"

"I thought you went downtown with her."

"I did."

"Did she leave you at the pony track?"

"Yes, for a few minutes."

"She goes to a joint down there," Mrs. Vaughn said. "Fortune telling in the front, goofballs and reefers in the rear. She's a sucker for all three."

"Goofballs?" Mr. Palmer said. "Reefers?"

"Phenobarb," Mrs. Vaughn said. "Marijuana. Anything. She doesn't care, long as she gets high. She's high as a kite now. Didn't you notice her eyes?"

Mrs. Kendall had got her boy by the hand. She was heavily ignoring Mrs. Corson. Now she lifted the child in her arms and turned sideways, like a cow ducking to the side to slip around a herder, and headed for the stone wall. Mrs. Corson whipped around her flanks, first on one side, then on the other, her hoarse whisper a continuing horror in Mr. Palmer's ears.

"What I ought to do," Mrs. Corson said, "is forbid Anne to even speak to that bastard of yours."

Mrs. Kendall bent and put the child on the ground and stood up. "Don't you call him that!" she shouted. "Oh, you vulgar, vicious, drunken, depraved woman! Leave me alone! Leave me alone, can't you?"

She burst into passionate tears. For a moment Mr. Palmer was terrified that they would come to blows and have to be pulled apart. He started forward, intending to take Mrs. Corson by the arm and lead her, forcefully if necessary, to the house. This disgraceful exhibition had gone on long enough. But the pregnant girl was ahead of him.

Mr. Palmer caught his cue. He put out his hand to Anne, and walked her down across the mouth of the lane. He did not look back, but his ears were sharp for a renewal of the cat fight. None came. By the time the man in gray had distributed the papers and magazines to all the battery of boxes, and was unstrapping the pack of letters, Mr. Palmer was aware without turning that both Mrs. Corson and Mrs. Kendall were in the background by the gray car, waiting quietly.

ROBERT G. FULLER

Sherman Was Right

WHEN MAJOR HAROLD BARROW reported to General Vogel's command headquarters in Noumea it caused a sensation. Clerks, runners, paymasters, quartermasters, cooks, and bakers—all the officers and men who weren't on guard—flocked to the giant Quonset for a glimpse of Major Barrow. They had already nicknamed him "Killer." This brave Marine was to take over the command of the First Parachute Battalion.

"He's got eyes of ice," a captain whispered to a lieutenant.

"He looks like a Captain Bligh," a first sergeant told a sergeant-major.

"He's a fat old slob," one private told another.

"Still, he must be the toughest officer in the Corps," a regimental runner said to the privates.

"Yeah," one of the privates agreed. "Washington sure must have a lot of respect for him."

"Or he's number one on their nasty list," the other private suggested.

"Anyway," the runner spoke what they all knew to be a truth, "they'll make him a colonel if he tames those beasts up at Tontuta."

Major Harold Barrow certainly did not look like a lion tamer. He was fat and fifty and his hips were much wider than his shoulders. His hair was thin and he wore thick glasses. Compared to the physical specimens he was to command, he would look more like an aged student reporting to the gym master for reconditioning than a two-fisted commanding officer.

General Vogel wasn't impressed by Major Barrow because he had just finished reading the Major's service record. He knew that Barrow had not been given command of the 1st Parachute Battalion because he was a tough or respected Marine. He got the command because all the colonels to whom such a command should have gone had enough seniority or political connections to refuse the proposition when approached with it. And although Major Barrow was anxious to get overseas and into action, he took the job under protest. He had heard of the paratroopers. But he hadn't married a female relative of the commandant and he didn't have any friends in Congress. He was stuck with the detail.

"Major Barrow," General Vogel said, "we know how you drew this assignment, but that's not important now. It's tough duty, but I expect you to do your best."

"Yes, sir. I will."

"According to your folder, you graduated at the bottom of your class and the rest of your career has been just about as distinguished as your academic record." The general leaned back in his canvas chair. "Word from Washington has it that you were slated for Stateside duty throughout this war. You aren't held in very high regard by the brass, and you shouldn't construe this assignment as a promotion."

Major Barrow, not being able to say "yes, sir," or "no, sir" to such statements, vaguely nodded his head.

"But you can make this the turning point of your career," General Vogel continued. "You can make them take notice of you in Washington and qualify yourself for excellent field commands."

"How, General?" the major asked eagerly.

"By getting the paratroopers back into line," Vogel replied. "They are fine men but they're a little bomb-whacky and hard to handle. If you're smart enough, or lucky enough, to snap that outfit into the combat team it once was, you'll be made. But we've sent some fine officers up there and they didn't make out."

"What happened to them, sir?"

"One had a nervous breakdown. Two are waiting for their courts-martial. The MPs are still looking for the one who went over the hill."

"Oh."

"You are a regular, not a nation saver, Barrow," the general went on, softening his voice, "and you have eighteen years in this lash-up. You never were a pusher and as a result you got a lot of colorless jobs which have added up to a very unspectacular career for a Marine officer. However, if you handle this assignment to my satisfaction, I'll give you a fitness report that will mean a promotion, and you'll be the golden boy of D.C."

"Well," the major replied, "thank you for your interest in me, sir."

"Interest in you, my neck!" the general roared. "I want that battalion on the next push. I need them. They're fighting fools but they're falling apart. I'm interested only in salvaging a fighting machine, and if you're the guy who can do it, you're my man."

The general arose, dismissing Barrow. "If you muff this detail, the rest of your time will be spent in a quartermaster's shack on the forgotten list. You had better make a name for yourself because if you don't make out, you're a washout. You got the word. Good luck."

On the long jeep ride to Tontuta, on the far end of the island of New Caledonia, Harold Barrow tried to plan his strategy. An old regular who really loved the Corps but who had missed all the boats, he now had a chance to make the grade. But he must be careful. He couldn't let the hellions at Tontuta ruin the opportunity he had grudgingly accepted. He determined to be a success. He would be tough and snap the men into line. Or he would be kind and understanding and bring the men around through affection. He would give them a speech and lay it on the line as soon as he got there. Or he would say nothing and keep them guessing.

Finally, he decided to wait and see just what the situation was before making his plans. "I won't do a thing today except look around. Tomorrow I'll swing into action," he promised himself.

"My name is Major Harold Barrow," the new commanding officer introduced himself to the captain who had the duty as officer of the day for the parachute battalion.

"This outfit is positively going to the dogs," the captain shouted at Major Barrow by way of rejoinder.

"You mean because I have been given this command?" the major flushed angrily.

"No, sir." If the major was angry, the captain was furious. "Do you know what they did?" he demanded of Barrow. "Do you?"

"No." The major didn't even know who "they" were.

"Well," the captain complained, advancing toward the major with his fists clenched, "while the chaplain was giving the men a lecture on the evils of drink, a couple of nuts in this outfit set off a satch charge against the Quonset storehouse and blew part of the side of it off. Then they stole all the officers' whiskey. They even looted the chaplain's sacramental wine. How about that?"

"Why didn't you post a guard on the Quonset?" the major shouted back.

"I did. Naturally, I did," the captain protested. "The corporal of the guard was sitting no more than three tents away from the Quonset playing poker when the TNT went off."

"Did he see anyone near the hut?"

"No, sir. He says he didn't even hear the blast."

"How closely did you question him?" the major wanted to know.

"Well, not too closely," the captain admitted. "He's been drunk ever since. Hard to understand him."

"How come he was playing poker while he was corporal of the guard?" The major thought that was a reasonable question.

The captain thought the question over for a moment. "Well, he's a good poker player. I guess he *likes* to play poker. When he's winning, he's generally good for a five-dollar touch." The captain sat down in the only chair in the tent.

The major felt he hadn't been following the captain's line of reasoning and decided to change the subject.

"Tell me something about the outfit, Captain."

"Adams, sir. Ronald Adams," the captain volunteered. "I've been with this lash-up since it was formed. Tell you anything you want to know."

"How come it has such a bum rep?" Barrows queried.

The captain leaped to his feet. "What do you mean, bum rep? I'll stack this outfit up against any other unit in the Corps and spot you ten Congressional Medals. Why, on Gavutu—"

"That isn't what I mean, Captain," the major said. "I mean why do they have such a disciplinary problem here? I heard about this battalion back in San Diego."

Adams eased himself back into his chair.

"Well, Major, I reckon they were kept too long in action. They're all battle-whacky. They called it shell shock in World War One."

"That bad?" the major prodded.

"Actually, they were more than a little goofy before they went into action, judging by their service records," the captain admitted. "But in action they were superb."

"Really?"

"The First Parachute Battalion, First Marine Division, held more medals and combat promotions than any other unit," the captain proclaimed most proudly as he left his chair and came to attention. "They had a record for courts-martial, too," he added.

''Where did you hit?''

''We landed on Gavutu on August seventh,'' Adams said, ''and with the exception of the Raiders on Tulagi, we were the only ones to see any real action in the early days of the campaign. We got pretty well shot up, and by the time we left Bloody Ridge, over on Guadalcanal, we didn't have enough men to form a good combat team.''

''So they pulled you out and sent you here to New Caledonia?'' Barrow asked.

''Not exactly, sir. In those days, no one was being pulled out unless he had bones sticking through his skin.'' Captain Adams answered. ''But one day General Vandergrift visited our area and when he saw that all the men had placed white crosses over the heads of their foxholes, he was impressed. Later, when he saw the paratroopers out on Henderson Field trying to catch Japanese bombs in bushel baskets, he figured we had had it and sent us here for retraining and recreation. Imagine that! Recreation on this rock. He must have hated our guts.''

''The retraining?''

''They put us to work on the waterfront at Noumea as longshoremen. Men with open wounds,'' the captain protested. ''But that didn't last long. Too much valuable cargo turned up missing. Stuff the troopers were supposed to have handled,'' Adams said with a smile. ''One day the skipper of the USS *President Hayes* complained that the ship's refrigerator had been stolen. Imagine that!''

'Impossible,'' Barrow agreed.

''Fact. Weighed tons. No one believed him. Anyway, when the merchants from this outfit began to sell ice cream to the Tonk storekeepers in Noumea, wholesale, they figured that the skipper might have a case and they yanked us off the waterfront.''

''And then the battalion was sent here?'' Barrow surmised.

''Yes, sir. On direct orders from General Vogel.'' Adams nodded. ''And we haven't been bothered by anyone since. The general and his staff pulled a surprise inspection one day but they didn't stay very long. As far as I know, the general never discussed what he saw, so it must have been his junior officers who started all those crazy rumors about cannibalism and white slavery. The general was heard to compare us with the surviving mutineers of the *Bounty*, but we never had a ship in our task force by that name. I guess it was a gag.''

''Tell me one thing,'' said Barrow. ''How come the officers of this battalion haven't kept up morale and discipline?''

''The morale is very high. The discipline is a matter of interpretation. These men have been in action and it's hard to make them knuckle down to the old chicken routine. And the officers have been through it, too, so they just pretend not to see too much. Besides, if we threw all the men into the brig, who would act as guards over the prisoners?''

That made sense to Major Barrow. ''Thanks for the info, Adams. Now I'd like to be introduced to my executive officer.''

''I'm sorry, Major, but that's Captain Blasingame and he and I are not speaking. I'll introduce you to the first sergeant and he'll introduce you to the bum.''

Major Barrow shrugged and let himself be led across the street to the first sergeant's tent.

''First Sergeant LeClair, this is Major Barrow, our new commanding officer,'' Adams said to the top kick sitting at a desk going over papers.

''Another one,'' the sergeant said without looking up. ''Welcome, Major. Hope you stay awhile.''

''Thanks.''

Adams left and was on his way back to the duty tent.

''What's the matter between Captain Adams and Captain Blasingame, the exec?'' Barrow asked the sergeant.

''It was all Blasingame's fault,'' the top kick said with some heat. ''He should be shot.''

''What happened?''

''Adams was making out but good with the loveliest girl in Noumea,'' the sergeant explained, ''and you know how scarce girls are on this island. They were engaged. Anyway, Adams was wining and dining her at the Hotel Metropole when the exec joined them. During the evening, Adams went to the head and when he came back, both the girl and Blasingame were gone. Blasingame has been going with her ever since. When Captain Adams saw the girl the next day, she wouldn't speak to him except to use vile and abusive language. You know what Blasingame did?''

''Can't imagine.''

''He told the girl that Adams was a nice guy but that he was a rake and a philanderer. Said that Adams had a wife in Jessup, Georgia, and another one in Los Angeles. And Adams ain't got no wife in L.A. Now, what do you think of a guy like that? And Adams had been buying the drinks.''

"I guess Adams has a case."

"You bet. Still," the sergeant mused, "I'm not so sure but what maybe Adams does have a wife in Los Angeles."

First Sergeant LeClair handed Major Barrow a letter that had just come over his desk. "You might as well start on your new job now as ever."

Major Barrow read the communication.

"This is from the motor pool. They request the use of a few jeeps and a recon truck. This doesn't make sense."

"It would if you knew the men of this outfit," the top kick told him. "This is the only battalion in the world where every private has his own jeep and a lot of them have recon trucks. Out in the woods behind the camp they have at least three ten-tonners, too."

"Where did they get them?"

"That's a silly question."

"Yes. I guess so," the major admitted. "What do they use them for?"

"They go courting and hell-raising in the jeeps and they use the heavy jobs for bootlegging and smuggling," the Top replied. "Noumea is tracking down a rumor that they're running guns to the Japs."

The major laughed. "That's a good one."

"I don't disbelieve it."

Two burly Marine MPs entered the tent with a scrawny-looking man held between them.

"We've caught Private Williams," they proudly announced.

"Where did you find him?"

"He was the first sergeant over in the Casual and Replacement Depot," the MPs said.

"How did you work that, Williams?" The first sergeant was only mildly interested.

"I heard they were shorthanded for high-ranking enlisted men," the private explained, "so I packed my sea bag and reported there with top-kick stripes on my arm. I told them I was a first sergeant and that my service record book would be forwarded later. They believed me and made me first sergeant of C Company."

Major Barrow was very interested. "How did you get through the duties?"

"Easy. I appointed some men sergeants and put them in charge of all working parties. They were made permanent before I left. Then I had two liberty passes made out for each man. One was always in my desk so that every man was always logged in, and the men carried the other one with them so that they were always on authorized liberty. See, that way a guy can never be over the hill. I ran off a hundred per cent more beer chits than there were men so we couldn't have a beer shortage. One can for each man, and I got a can for each man.''

One of the MPs spoke up. ''The commanding officer wants to know if you'll transfer Williams back to him after he's done his brig time. He says Williams did a fine job and he wants to make him his permanent first sergeant.''

''I'll be darned,'' breathed the major as Williams was led out.

''That's nothing. Wait until they catch up with Corporal Mihalek over in Magenta,'' the top said sadly.

''One of our men?''

''Yes, sir. He's been over the hill two months. He set himself up a tent and found himself a pair of colonel's insignia. He made himself commanding officer of the area. I heard that he even had a chicken colonel thrown into his brig, and he's been promoting and busting men left and right. And General Vogel gave him the Efficiency Award last month for running the best command on the island. He better get out of the Pacific Theater when they catch him.''

''If you know where he is, why don't you have him brought in?'' The major thought that was a logical question.

''Ain't I got enough troubles without getting that guy back?''

One of the MPs ducked back into the tent. ''Private Williams said to give these to you and to thank you for the loan of them.'' He threw several sets of first-sergeant stripes on the desk.

''Tell the thief he's welcome.''

Major Barrow leaned back in his chair and closed his eyes and tried to imagine what kind of outfit he had joined. He had never heard of such fantastic gall, even among Marines. If he had never been an outstanding success as a Marine officer, he was none the less sincere and conscientious. He had many years behind him in the Corps and had loved every minute of it. He truly believed that the Marines were an important part of the defense of the United States in time of war and peace and he could see absolutely no humor in the disintegration of one of its best fighting arms. The day of judgment shall surely hit this outfit come reveille tomorrow morning, he vowed.

The telephone rang and the major reached over and answered it for First Sergeant LeClair. He listened, dazed, to the voice on the other end of the line and then gently put the phone back on its cradle.

"Who was it?" asked the top.

"General Vogel."

"What does he want?"

"It's about Private First Class Checkoway. I'm not sure I got it all straight."

"You probably did. What has Checkoway done?"

"It seems he stole a plane over on the Magenta strip and flew it, without a compass, all the way to Henderson Field on Guadalcanal. When he got to Guadal he gave them some fast talk and they tanked him up. Then he flew the F4U up to Rabaul and bombed the place and made three passes over the emplacements, strafing. The plane was rigged with a camera. Gee, Top, we've never been able to get anything within a thousand miles of that place. It's the strongest Jap position south of the Home Islands." The major was out of breath just from thinking about that trip.

"Checkoway okay?"

"Believe it or not, yes. The general said that if the kid has a good service record, he's going to write him up for a Congressional Medal of Honor. Otherwise, he goes to Portsmouth Naval Prison. What kind of record does he have?"

"Probably the best one in this battalion," LeClair said, "but that's not good enough. He'll go to Portsmouth. It must be nice in New Hampshire at this time of year, the lucky bum."

"That's a hell of an attitude for a first sergeant." Barrow arose angrily from his chair.

The top had seen officers come and go in this battalion and he knew the signs. "Why don't you go over to officers' country, Major? It's nice and peaceful over there."

"I wasn't sent up here to find peace in officers' country, LeClair," the major told him. "I was sent here to command a problem outfit and I'm going to do just that. Now, suppose you get up and take me on a cruise of this area."

"I advise against it, sir. But if you insist . . ."

"I do."

They stepped out into the immaculate company streets lined on both sides by pyramidal tents which had signs over their front entrances announcing that they were the "Hotel Ritz," "Pink House," (named after a notorious institution outside Noumea where men who weren't particular as to companionship were entertained) and such slogans as, "The Fastest Men in the World Pass Through These Portals." The major winced as he read some of the legends.

The sides of the tents were rolled up and Barrow noticed a large group of men sitting in the one which bore a sign reading, "With the Help of God and A Few Marines, MacArthur Returns to the Philippines."

"Crap game?" he asked the top.

"Nope. Those are all P.A.L.s—prisoners-at-large. That guy in the center is the first sergeant of B Company giving the boys a series of lectures on how to beat a court-martial. They all got courts coming up. He charges a buck a lecture, money back if the boys don't beat the raps. I guess it's okay. They're all entitled to counsel. In the afternoon they have a class in Japanese. Most of the men sit in on it."

"Why?"

"You know. Just in case we lose."

The first sergeant led the major into one of the tents. Ten men, including the officer of the day, were seated on the bunks, sipping a concoction of alcohol and grapefruit juice which they called "stump juice." When the two visitors entered, one of the men, the host, got up and mixed them drinks in canteen cups.

"Where did this come from?" the major asked.

"What?" asked the host.

"This alcohol."

"What alcohol?" the host parried.

"Never mind."

At that time four men stepped into the tent and opened a foot locker and took out MP arm brassards and white helmets. The company clerk, one of the guests, handed them official-looking passes. Grabbing sub-machine guns, the four men went out of the tent and took their places on two large trucks parked at the end of the company streets. Then the major knew where the alcohol had come from. These shrewdies were impersonating MPs and were driving stolen trucks down to the waterfront to have them loaded with five-gallon tins of ninety-proof as they came off the ships.

The host reached under the blanket which hung over the cot and to the floor and brought out a box of cigars which he passed around. Major Barrow noticed the neat rows of five-gallon tins and boxes of cigars and candy which were piled under the cot. It was the same with every tent in the area. Why, there must be thousands of dollars worth of loot in this camp, he thought idly as he sipped his stump-juice cocktail.

It was awfully strong stuff, he was thinking, because every once in awhile it seemed to him that the sea bag in the next tent moved. He shook his head but the image persisted. Finally, he could stand it no longer and excused himself and went into the next tent. It was the domicile of the chaplain's assistant.

''Anything in that bag, soldier?'' he naively asked.

''Dirty clothes, sir.''

''Open it.''

The chaplain's assistant opened the sea bag and an obviously scared little Javanese woman stepped out. She was naked.

''Now, how do you suppose she got in there?'' The chaplain's assistant was very shocked. ''If I find the guy who did this I'll kill him. I'll send a wire to the Secretary of the Navy.''

''One of your altar boys, Holy Joe?'' Barrow sneered. ''Get her out of here.'' The girl was bundled out.

The top and the men in the adjoining tent had not seen the incident —to all outward appearances—and were busy writing new verses to the Marine's Hymn when Major Barrow rejoined them.

The officer of the day, who should have been on duty, was adjudged the best lyricist when he came up with a new and original verse which one of the men promptly copied down to send to the ''Leatherneck,'' the Corps publication.

The OD sang, to the delight of the men:

''If you have a buddy, good and true,
Clobber him before he clobbers you.''

They thought that was splendid. They applauded. Sentimentalists.

''Geranis,'' the OD told one of the men, ''Go down to the river and spell Slovachka and Michalski.''

The major casually watched the men walk down to the river. Then he stared. It was true. The prisoners were holding submachine guns while the chasers had a swim.

Barrow couldn't restrain himself. ''What kind of an OD are you?'' he demanded. ''Letting those prisoners hold machine guns while the guards go swimming.''

The OD gave him a blank stare. ''What prisoners?''

''Never mind,'' he said resignedly. Then, to the first sergeant, ''Let's get out of here.'' He paused in the entrance of the tent and thanked the host for the drink. ''It was very good,'' he said truthfully.

Back in the first sergeant's tent, they picked up two new complaints that had been lodged against the battalion. The army command registered a formal charge that every time an MP left his jeep to make an arrest or to break up a crap game, men in paratrooper's boots stole his jeep. It was no joke to the MPs. They were having to walk their beats.

The other gripe was submitted by the Naval Medical Headquarters. Every single sheet had been stolen from Mobile Hospitals Five and Seven except those for the nurses' quarters. The navy strongly alleged that the men of the 1st Para Bn had swiped them.

The major stoutly defended his men but promised to have an investigation made. He posted an order on the company bulletin board pointing out the loss of the sheets and requested any person having knowledge of their whereabouts to inform him.

But after a few minutes hesitation, he declined to go into the armorer's tent, in front of which stood the bulletin board, where several men were carefully measuring large pieces of white cloth which were being cut to the size of flags. Two of the men were tacking down the seams and another was stenciling a red circle in the middle of each piece. Tonight these would be sold to the sailors from the fleet anchored in Noumea Bay as authentic Japanese battle flags. They should bring around fifty dollars apiece.

When Major Barrow rejoined the first sergeant, a Frenchman was standing near the front of the tent.

"Is Colonel Crocker in, sirs?" he asked the two Marines.

The major didn't know who they were talking about, but the top was intrigued. There was one Crocker in the command but he was a buck private.

"I'll inquire," LeClair told the Frenchman. "Whom shall I say is calling?"

"Jacques Pierre Valencourt. Please tell him that I have come for the consignment of anisette."

LeClair motioned for Major Barrow to accompany him as he went to find "Colonel" Crocker. "This Valencourt is the richest trader on the island and a real political influence. How do you suppose Crocker could have gotten tied up with him?"

"Colonel" Crocker was sitting with the group of men who were drinking stump juice out of canteen cups.

"Colonel," the top advised him, "Jacques Valencourt is here to see about a consignment of anisette. Will you see him, sir?"

"Sure, Top. Tell him I'll be out as soon as I get dressed."

A few minutes later the private entered the tent with full colonel chickens on his shoulders. The major knew by now that if he inquired about them, they would turn invisible, so he refrained.

Not a bit abashed, Private Crocker and the French trader began a parlay that rocked the major and the first sergeant down to their toes. It developed that Crocker was employing Javanese and Tonkinese by the score to distill aniseed for him and he was selling the booze, wholesale, to the Frenchman who, in turn, was supplying the American officers' mess and the French government forces with the stuff. It was big business.

The top and the major tried not to listen nor to stare at the insignia on the private's shoulders. They felt like junior leaguers.

As the Frenchman was leaving, he turned to the "colonel" and said that the truck was in just as good working order as the colonel had promised and that he was having very good luck with it.

The colonel-private said that he was glad. The Frenchman's truck, which was parked near the first sergeant's tent, was a five-ton GI and under its coat of new paint could be read the legend that made one suppose that it had recently been the property of Headquarters Company, Seventh Marines.

"Did you sell the Frenchman that truck?" Barrow stupidly demanded.

"What truck?"

"Never mind."

The major decided he wouldn't wait until the next day to lower the boom on the battalion of renegades, and had begun plotting his discipline when Pfc. Reedtz came into the tent and asked for his back pay.

"Reedtz," LeClair shouted, and he jumped out of his chair and began shaking the man's hand. "Where have you been? We ain't seen you for months. We thought you stole a sailor suit and went back to the States. You're listed as a deserter."

"I been to Auckland, New Zealand. Went down for the first day of the summer meet and kind of liked it so I stayed awhile. I got married while I was there." Reedtz was sitting on the edge of the first sergeant's desk as he spoke.

The major, fascinated by the reception LeClair had accorded the deserter, wished to know how the prodigal son had gotten to New Zealand and back to New Caledonia.

Reedtz was an honest man. "A clerk down in command, in Noumea, gave me a copy of rest and recreation furlough papers. Naugle, the company clerk in C Company, typed me out a set and I wrote in the three endorsements. I signed General Vogel's name—but only on one copy which I destroyed in Auckland. Then I got aboard the MS *Cape Flattery* and gave the mate a copy of my papers and took passage on her to Auckland. To get back, I told the Navy disbursing officer in New Zealand that I was on furlough and had lost all my papers. He got me a seat on the Pan American Clipper. Very cold, flying back here."

"You better lock him up, First Sergeant."

"Yeah, Major, I guess so," the Top agreed. "But you'll have to help me write up the specifications for his court-martial. I wouldn't know where to begin."

"This girl I married," Reedtz offered helpfully, "her old man is a member of the New Zealand House of Parliament."

If Barrow had learned only one thing in his eighteen years as a regular in the Marine Corps, he had learned not to fight the problem. So he lost interest in the escapades of Pfc. Reedtz. But he did want to know one thing after hearing about the AWOL who was commanding officer at Magenta and of the AWOL who had bombed Rabaul in a stolen plane and of the AWOL who had gone to New Zealand and married the politician's daughter.

"What's the strength of this command, First Sergeant?"

"We started with four hundred and eighty men, sir," the first sergeant hedged.

"How many do we have now?"

"All told, about two hundred on the books."

"Where's the rest?"

"Mostly battle casualties and a few transfers."

"Of the two hundred, how many are present or can be accounted for?"

"Sometimes as many as a hundred and twenty-five."

"Oh, no! This outfit can't be that bad. No outfit can be that bad." The major felt the bottom drop out of the surge of hope that he had felt for a re-start of his career when he left General Vogel's office. "To hell with this war. I quit. First Sergeant, I want to be enrolled in that course in Japanese."

Major Barrow left the tent and stood on the boardwalk that ran the length of the street and tried to think of something sensible to do to start his disciplinary ball rolling. He filled his lungs with air and bellowed across the area.

''Now hear this. Every officer in this battalion is confined to quarters and every enlisted man is under arrest and designated a prisoner-at-large.''

That will hold them until I get my thoughts organized, Barrow assured himself.

The major retired to his tent, took two aspirins, and did not leave his quarters until the next day. Then, with First Sergeant LeClair accompanying him, he gave the men and the area a detailed inspection. He made the men destroy all their filthy pin-up pictures, take the obscene signs from their tent doors, confiscated all the alcohol they hadn't been able to hide, and arraigned twenty men for courts-martial. Five sergeants were busted to corporal and all the corporals were busted to privates. Weapons were taken away from all the prisoners and each member of the command was made to dress in the uniform of the day. Every man who wasn't on guard was put on working parties, and all hands fell out for troop and drill two hours each day with a sunset march in review.

At the end of a week, he had obtained a kind of surly obedience to his commands, but the men showed no enthusiasm for him or his reform program. They thought he was foolish and asked each other, ''Don't he know there's a war on?''

In ten days it was apparent that he had not really established any bona fide discipline. He had succeeded only in destroying the morale of his men. Actually, the battalion was worse off than when he had joined it and he knew that he was a failure.

''I told you these men had been in action,'' Captain Adams said one day. ''You can't give them a diet of that old Stateside chicken stuff. They can't digest it. They know what life is all about. Every one of them has come within a hair's-breadth of being killed and they have burried a lot of their buddies. Why don't you treat them like men insted of recruits?''

''Shut up and speak when you're spoken to, Captain.''

The captain shut up, as did all the officers and men when Major Barrow was around. They didn't give him the satisfaction of hating him. They merely came to despise him. After his first day with the battalion, they never again offered him a canteen cup of stump juice, their official emblem of welcome and comradeship.

Major Barrow had backed himself into a corner. He knew he had done it all wrong and he was sorry. He felt bad because he was a personal failure and because he believed that he had injured his country's war effort by weakening a combat group. He felt bad because he had developed a sincere affection for his high-spirited hellions, whom he really admired for their brash attitude and war record. He decided that his only honorable course would be to make out such a report to General Vogel telling him that regrettably he would not now have this battalion ready for the next push. He resigned himself to life in a quartermaster's shack on the forgotten list.

But before he could send the memo to Noumea, General Vogel sent him an official communiqué which launched the affair of Marylyn Lamour which, in turn, ended in an explosion that rocked, not only the island of New Caledonia, but Broadway, Hollywood, and Washington, D.C.

Major Barrow was so furious that he was actually frothing at the mouth after he read the mimeographed bulletin handed him by the general's runner. It was addressed to all commands and read in part:

"Marilyn Lamour will entertain the troops stationed on this island tomorrow evening in the Pieta area. All officers and enlisted men are invited to attend the entertainment with the exception of the men of the First Parachute Battalion, First Mar-Div."

"Now what in hell could have inspired a message like that?" he demanded of the first sergeant as he tacked the memo on the bulletin board in front of the armorer's tent.

"Well," the top tried to explain, "at the last couple of USO shows the men didn't appreciate some of the acts or the music and they stopped the show."

"How?"

"I guess you'd call it a kind of a riot."

"That's no excuse for embarrassing me and this organization in such a way," Barrow shouted, his eyes blazing.

"You got a case," the sergeant agreed. "Don't blame me."

A few of the men came up to read the message on the board and the word spread like a prairie fire in the wind. Marylyn Lamour was dearly loved by the troopers, as she was dearly loved by all red-blooded men, and there were more than a hundred pictures of the lady, in various poses, in the tents of the paratroopers.

The men and officers gathered around the bulletin board and Major Barrow, who had not moved since posting the horrible document.

"Well," Barrow shouted at the crowd, "what are you going to do about that?"

"Any suggestion, Major?" LeClair asked in behalf of the men.

The major's eyes swept the angry group of men around him. "I admit that you people have better imaginations that I, so I have no suggestions. But something is going to be done. Something had better be done. Or I'll lead this battalion on Pieta and wreck the joint."

A cheer went up from the men, and, with surprise, Major Barrow realized that the ovation was partly for him. Mostly, of course, it was in anticipation of seeing Miss Lamour.

"Well, let's think of something."

The men returned to their tents and talked in excited whispers. Plan after plan was discussed and discarded, and candles burned until long into the night. No one turned out for troop and drill in the morning and the parleys went on. The problem was finally resolved.

Late in the afternoon the USS *America* pulled into the dock in the harbor of Noumea. In addition to carrying replacements for the army units on New Caledonia, the *America* had as her star passenger the lovely Marylyn Lamour, rage of the barracks and the thing voted most worth fighting for by the combined forces. Accompanying her was a ten-piece orchestra and lesser attractions, including comedians and dancers. There was a large delegation to greet her and a holiday mood prevailed over the otherwise gloomy Port of the Rock.

When Miss Lamour stepped down the gangway, posing briefly for the service photographers, the "Ohs" and "Ahs" that went up were genuine and spontaneous. Marylyn was beautiful beyond description, from the top of her golden hair down to her provocative ankles. To withhold this from the paratroopers was cruel and unusual, gave aid and comfort to the enemy, left no meaning to the war, and courted disaster.

An immaculate lieutenant stepped out of the crowd gathering around Miss Lamour and introduced himself as the recreation officer and representative of General Vogel. He offered the lovely girl his arm and escorted her to the jeep he had standing by to take her to the general's quarters for cocktails. The Lieutenant was very proud of his responsibility but was crestfallen when another jeep roared up alongside his with the red and gold flag and the two stars of a major general flying from the fender. A major was sitting in the driver's seat.

The major exchanged salutes with the lieutenant and handed him a message written on General Vogel's letterhead.

"I'm Major Fogleman from Intelligence, Lieutenant," the major explained. "The general has decided it would be too dangerous to permit Miss Lamour to perform in Pieta after the bulletin went out and the show is to be held in Dumbea. I'm to escort Miss Lamour to the general and you're to arrange transportation for the band and other entertainers. Sorry, old man."

The jeep carrying Miss Lamour and the major sped around the corner, passed the Banque d'Indo-Chine, and proceeded on the road to Dumbea. It passed the Dumbea area but didn't even slow down. It finally pulled up at the area designated as Tontuta, land of the paratroopers, who had rigged a giant sign over the main street which read in letters two feet tall: "Welcome, Marylyn Lamour. We Love You."

"She's here. She's here." The shout went up from all the lusty-lunged paratroopers who had been waiting, biting their fingernails, in anticipation of America's new sweetheart.

"Wow!" Captain Adams finally spoke to Captain Blasingame.

"Yeah," Blasingame agreed.

The noisy welcome accorded Marylyn aroused Major Barrow who was napping in his tent. He hurried out to the battalion streets to see what the commotion was all about and recognized Marylyn Lamour immediately from the many pictures he had seen in the tents of his men.

The major who had driven the jeep hurried Miss Lamour over to him, and before Barrow could speak a word of greeting, the driver said, "Miss Lamour, I would like to introduce you to General Vogel." He nodded toward Major Barrow.

"What are you talking about, Crocker?" Barrow whispered to the driver.

"I'm so happy to meet you, General Vogel," the actress said, offering Major Barrow her hand.

"Of course," Barrow stammered. "Well, let's all have a drink."

Several of the men dashed for their tents and the major could hear the rumble of five-gallon tins. Soon the Marines were back with buckets of stump juice, a canteen cup of which was handed to Miss Lamour.

"It's delicious, General," Marylyn exclaimed. "You must give me the recipe."

"Sure, doll," a private spoke up. "Five gallons of medical alcohol and two quarts of grapefruit juice. Serve in a well-chilled canteen cup. It's got to have that flavor of aluminum to be any good."

"Give her a mess kit and we'll have some chow," the cook bellowed. "Spam à la Lamour."

* * *

Miss Lamour and the officers and men all ate in the enlisted men's mess hall, standing at the boards that surrounded the tent. They had no chairs and tables. The Spam and dehydrated cabbage tasted so good, with Miss Lamour as guest, that the cook escaped being promised a beating for the first time in three months.

"It's delicious," Miss Lamour exclaimed.

"Aw, really, Marylyn." The cook blushed. "It stinks, but it's all we got."

"If she says it's delicious, it's delicious, you baker with his brains baked out," the men began to shout.

Sensing catastrophe, Major Barrow, whom Miss Lamour persisted in calling General Vogel, suggested that they adjourn from the crowded mess hall and commence the entertainment in the broad company streets.

"But my music isn't here," Miss Lamour protested.

"Think nothing of it, dearie," First Sergeant LeClair consoled her. "I'm the best harmonica player this side of Borah Minevitch."

A good sport, Miss Lamour hummed some of her numbers with the top kick, and when they put on the show, it went off surprisingly well.

"You're terrific, Sergeant." Miss Lamour beamed on him. "But I can't help wondering what happened to the band."

"That's the history of this rock, doll," she was told. "Always a foul up somewhere."

"But you didn't foul up on Guadalcanal, did you General?" Marylyn asked the Major.

He blushed modestly and then whispered to Captain Adams, "Let me borrow a few of your campaign bars, will you?"

And then the cry came down from the lookouts who were watching the road to Noumea. The dread cry: "Here they come. Here they come. Hide the merchandise."

The major insignia came off Crocker's shoulders and were tucked into his back pocket. The sign of greeting that hung over the company street was torn down and hidden in the tub of dehydrated cabbage. The general's flag was ripped off the fender of the jeep and stuffed into the gas tank. The stump juice was whipped into one of the tents of the bartender.

"What are we going to do with her?" the major screamed in panic.

Holy Joe, the chaplain's assistant, ran up the major. "Put her in a sea bag. Put her in a sea bag."

''Shut up.''

''We'll wrap her in sheets and bury her and give her a straw to breathe through,'' the armorer offered.

''I could put her in one of my pots,'' the cook volunteered, ''but I couldn't get her in one piece.''

''Hey,'' Crocker exclaimed, ''the cook's got a good idea. Come on.'' He grabbed one of his buddies and ran into the woods behind the tent area. He was back in seconds with the largest pot the major had ever seen. A small vat.

''What's that?''

''I use it for distilling aniseed. The Navy Construction Battalion made it for me.''

Miss Lamour was becoming alarmed. The conversations she had heard and the agitated conduct of the men unnerved her.

''What's the matter, General?'' she pleaded. ''What happened?''

''Hill bandits,'' Major Barrow answered. ''They're going to attack the camp. Terrible people. We've got to hide you.''

''Give me a rifle,'' she suggested. ''I'll defend myself.''

''Couldn't think of it. Against our code of honor.''

Unceremoniously, America's sweetheart was dumped into the vat used for making bootleg anisette and dragged behind the galley where the cook sat on the lid protecting her from the hill bandits.

Marylyn Lamour was no more than hidden when the jeep carrying General Vogel roared into the area. With him was General Belanger, commander of the French Forces in the Pacific. Before the vehicle had stopped, Vogel leaped out and charged up to Major Barrow.

''Where is she?'' Vogel screamed, his face nearly purple with rage. ''Where? Where? Where?'' He paused and glanced around the area at the faces viewing him with feigned surprise.

''I'll send you to Portsmouth for this, Barrow. I'll have you executed. Where is she?'' The famed Vogel voice was booming full blast.

''Who?'' the major asked in wide-eyed innocence.

''Marylyn Lamour, that's who.'' The general was nearly out of his head.

''We wouldn't know, General,'' Major Barrow answered stiffly. ''We weren't invited to her performance.''

''Please, Major!'' The general deflated and began to plead. ''If you know where she is, just tell me, and we'll forget the whole thing.''

''Don't know nothing,'' the major said smugly.

"I'll see that you get a promotion," the general said.

"Sorry, I can't help you." Barrow knew the general would skin him alive once he got the actress.

"*Mon Dieu*," the French general at Vogel's side shouted in alarm. "They're armed. They're all carrying weapons."

"Who?" the major was startled and looked toward the hills.

General Belanger spun on General Vogel. "You told me this area was set aside as a concentration camp for your penal battalion. How is it you allow them to be armed?"

General Vogel was embarrassed and then alarmed when he saw the hostile look in the eyes of the paratroopers. Now the battalion knew why they never had any French visitors—especially the female French who visited other camps.

Seeing the general's predicament—caught in the trap he had devised for the benefit of the French, embarrassed before the paratroopers, and desperate to find the lost actress—Major Barrow decided to strike a blow for his men.

"I meant to ask you, General, if you would consent to having this battalion transferred to the States for retraining. They went through a lot in the Solomons and—"

But the general was not that desperate. "Are you out of your mind, Barrow? Send this pack of Indians back to the States? As a group? Have you lost all love for your native land?"

"And has anyone advanced one good reason why they should have been sent here?" the French general wished to know. "After all, the French are your allies."

"Haven't I got enough troubles without you nagging me?" Vogel yelled at Belanger.

"I shall write to the Secretary of the Navy," the Frenchman threatened.

"And if you do, I'll tell Madame Belanger about a certain Red Cross worker in Noumea with whom you are consorting, General," Vogel lashed back.

"Please forget I spoke." The French general returned to the jeep and, in silence, waited for the penal battalion to strike down General Vogel.

The Marine general returned to Major Barrow. "This is serious, Major," he said. "If anything happens to that girl, they'll hang me in front of the White House."

''What happened?'' Barrow smirked.

''Some devil in paratrooper's boots, masquerading as a major from my intelligence section, kidnaped her.''

''It couldn't have been one of my men, General.''

''Oh, no?'' the general bleated. ''Well, where are the major's insignia you're supposed to be wearing?''

The major's hands jumped to his shoulders, feeling for his gold leaves. They were gone, stolen by Crocker while he slept.

''I don't go around pulling my rank on my men all the time like some officers,'' he said weakly.

An approving cheer from the troopers drowned out the general's reply.

''Maybe you and your pack of con men and thieves didn't kidnap Miss Lamour, Barrow. Personally, I think you did,'' Vogel said through clenched teeth. ''But I can't take a chance on staying around here to find out. Heaven help you and these men, though, if I find out that you know anything about this.'' He strode toward his jeep and told the driver to head for Noumea.

''Well, he's gone.'' The first sergeant aroused the major, who had relapsed into a state of semi-shock. ''What do we do now?''

''We've got to get her out of this area somehow,'' Barrow answered vaguely. ''Bring her out here.''

''Let's not. She'll only disrupt our thinking.'' The top was a wise and practical man.

''It's a good thing you didn't break her out,'' the sometimes Colonel-once-Major Private Crocker observed. ''Look.''

A squad of MPs from the guard company were swarming over the area, going through the tents, opening locker boxes, and emptying sea bags.

''I knew that general was a double-crosser,'' LeClair said. ''He tried to catch us off guard, the cheat.''

''I got her!'' one of the MPs shouted with joy. Major Barrow felt his knees buckle.

''That ain't her,'' he heard another MP answer. They had a small naked Javanese woman between them who had tumbled out of a sea bag in the chaplain's assistant's tent. The other MPs gathered around to view the discovery and then lost interest in their search.

''Take off,'' they were ordered, and left to comb another camp.

Miss Lamour was let out of the vat and brought back to the first sergeant's tent. "How did the battle go?" she asked, rubbing her back.

"We repulsed them," the major assured her.

"I didn't hear a shot fired," she said.

"Hand to hand. Bayonet work, miss. That's how we always fight them. They don't have rifles." The major was surprised at his own glibness.

"General, you're so gallant."

"We can't thank you enough for the marvelous entertainment, Miss Lamour," Barrow told her. "It was wonderful and I'm sure there are other units waiting to hear you sing. I'll have you driven back to Noumea in a closed recon truck. Just in case there are any snipers around."

"That will be exciting." Miss Lamour was enjoying her candid look at the way of life of these Marines. "And I've never enjoyed giving a performance as much as I have this one."

"You might have time for an encore, doll," said Sergeant Michaud, in charge of the lookouts.

Barrow looked up. "What now?" he asked with a sigh.

"They've set up a road block half a mile from here. No traffic getting by without a shakedown."

"Who?" Marylyn asked. "The hill bandits?"

"Of course," the first sergeant told her.

"We've got to get this young lady to Noumea." There was a note of desperation and pleading in Major Barrow's voice as he addressed this remark to the paratroopers who were grouped in front of the tent.

"How?" the company clerk wanted to know. "There's only one road out of here."

"We'll go around the road, then," the major thought that was a good idea.

"Not with her, you won't," he was informed. "There's hundreds of feet of cliff on one side of the road and thick woods on the other. I don't think a rugged man could make it, let alone a sweet, adorable, luscious dream like Marylyn."

"We'll build a raft and float her out on the Dumbea River," the armorer said.

"Smuggle her out in a sea bag," suggested Holy Joe.

"That river ain't more than two inches deep in some places and there are Army camps and hospitals all along it. They'd open the sea bag."

''We'd better lay low for awhile until the heat's off.'' The first sergeant was a tactician. ''Let's sleep on the problem.''

''Hey, the first sergeant's making jokes.''

But the men agreed. Marylyn Lamour was given the major's tent, and Barrow moved in with Captains Adams and Blasingame.

The candles burned late into the night and plans were exchanged from tent to tent, but in the morning the eyes of the troopers were not bright with schemes; they were haggard from lack of sleep and lack of a plan. The MPs had cut them off more successfully than the Japanese Imperial Army had been able to.

For three days and three nights the paratroopers paced the floors of their tents, bit their fingernails, and pulled their hair, but found no way of circumventing the road block. They began to lose confidence in themselves, an experience they didn't believe possible.

And, as they listened to the radio, they began to know fear. What had started as a revengeful joke had turned into an international situation of utmost gravity. The newscasts were ominous and frightful.

HOLLYWOOD: ''The motion picture industry has lost its most promising young star, Marylyn Lamour, who has been reported missing in the Pacific area. Her studio has announced plans to do the story of her life in technicolor, the gallant story of the first of filmdom to fall on the field of battle.''

NEW YORK: ''The Theater Group today announced plans to build a memorial in remembrance of the loveliest casualty of the war. A dignified shaft of white marble will stand near Forty-Second and Broadway, a silent reminder of the girl who loved life so much *[the announcer's voice broke]* that she was willing to die in what she considered to be the good cause.''

COMMENTATOR: ''Why haven't the details of Marylyn Lamour's disappearance been disclosed to the American public? Who's covering up for whom? How about it, Pentagon? How about it, White House?

WHITE HOUSE: ''We are doing all we can to uncover the details of the supposed death of Miss Lamour. In the meantime, we look upon her demise as we do that of any of our young people who have made the supreme sacrifice. She died in battle.''

Marylyn wept softly as she heard the sentimental bulletins. At other times she was overawed and overjoyed at the publicity she was getting and, when she was sure that she was still alive, her face glowed with vanity and happiness over the concern expressed by the world for her.

"Boy, am I a celebrity!" she squealed with delight. "Me, in technicolor. Gee!"

It was Reedtz who made the oninous announcement. "When we finally do get the girl out of here, she's going to spill the whole story. So, actually, what are we doing but postponing the executions?"

That did it. With a dull thud, the whole glorious bottom fell out.

And, on top of that Crocker had finally come up with the solution. "Hey, did anyone remember? We're parachutists."

"So what?"

"Well, what are parachutes for?" It was as simple as that.

But the first sergeant, always a realist, stuck a pin in that bubble. "We ain't got no planes and the girl ain't no 'chute jumper."

"Oh, yeah?" Crocker said in triumph. "It isn't a half mile to the strip and there's planes over there."

"You going to fly them?"

"You forgot our hero, Checkoway, who sits in yon brig, pining away. He hasn't stolen a plane in weeks."

Even if the idea didn't come off, Major Barrow knew he would promote Crocker.

"And Michaud was an instructor at Lakehurst. He can teach her a simple tumble so that she wouldn't break her sweet, adorable, lovely neck when she lands."

The enthusiasm was mounting to the boiling point when Reedtz again threw in the monkey wrench. "Better kill her and bury her. She'll expose us when she gets out of here. What's she going to tell people? Hill bandits!"

"Reedtz is right," the Major said. "There's only one thing to do. Runner, get Miss Lamour out here."

The men sat in a semicircle on the company street and quizzically watched their commanding officer as he stood before them with the actress by his side.

"Miss Lamour," he began, "there are no hill bandits. We kidnaped you."

"You did? Why?" She didn't know if the situation was funny or serious. She was perplexed.

"Read this." Major Barrow handed her a copy of the bulletin sent out from the general's office, prohibiting the paratroopers from sitting in on her show.

''Well, I don't blame you,'' she said sympathetically. ''It isn't democratic.''

''Right now, the important thing is getting you back. After this hoax, you can imagine what will happen to us. The President himself will shoot us.'' The men thought the major was doing a good job, although somewhat dramatic.

''Oh, no!'' A realization struck Marylyn which had escaped the Marines. ''I'll be ruined. All that publicity. Killed in action. They'll think it was all a gag and I'll be the laughingstock of Hollywood.''

''That puts us all in this thing together,'' the first sergeant said, getting up from the ground. ''But if you'll go along with us, Marylyn, everything will be all right.''

''You won't expose me?''

''Not if you don't expose us,'' the top kick promised.

''But what will I tell people?''

''Leave that to us.''

''Anything you say, fellows.''

''How would you like to make a parachute jump, Miss Lamour?'' Barrow asked.

''I'd love to. That would be exciting.''

As the men came to attention before their gallant lady, Major Barrow pinned a set of paratroopers wings on her blouse. ''You are hereby made an honorary member of of the First Parachute Battalion,'' he said with great feeling, ''And your name shall be inscribed on the rolls of this organization forever.''

The men applauded.

It was easy for Sergeant Michaud to teach Marylyn the rudiments of tumbling, and the work was made especially easy because the beautiful actress and the wild men had come, in their time and circumstances together, to love one another.

In the evenings, the men directed her in the role she would play on her return to Noumea.

Checkoway sneaked over to Magenta strip, which he knew quite well, having stolen an F4U there not so long ago.

He came back with bad news. ''The only plane over there is a DC6.''

''What's wrong with that?''

''It's a transport. We could put a company in it.''

"Okay," Major Barrow said expansively, "we'll put a company in it."

Reedtz again. "Can you fly the thing, Checkoway?"

"I don't know. I never saw the controls of a plane before I stole the F4U."

"Saddle up," the major commanded.

"We've got to chance it. Take some kind of a cable and rig it for static lines. We've got to land together."

One company of men advanced ahead of the jumping party, clearing a path with machetes, and the actress and the major and the company to make the jump followed.

"Everybody got plenty of ammunition?" the top asked.

"Yes."

"Don't forget to hide the 'chutes as soon as you land."

"Right."

Crocker had peered into the window of the pilot's hangout and reported that the aviators were eating, napping, or reading comic books.

"Let's get the show on the road," Marylyn suggested.

After an agonizingly slow start, Checkoway managed to get the big ship off the ground. A few minutes later Adams, acting as jumpmaster, gave the command: "Coming on the range." A few seconds later: "Stand by." The men and the movie queen snapped the hooks on the end of their static lines onto the cable. "Jump."

When the major hesitated in the doorway of the plane, Marylyn gave him a boot on his majority and followed him into space. The troopers were right behind her. The plane was circling back toward Magenta when they hit the ground.

They hid the parachutes and then began to blaze away at the nearby water's edge with rifles, Johnson light machine guns and Browning automatic rifles. The noise of the firing could be heard well beyond Noumea where one detachment of Marines rushed to surround the nickel mines to protect them from saboteurs and the regiments were broken out on a dead run toward the beaches to repulse a landing party.

Marylyn, putting on an Academy Award performance, tore her clothes, rolled in the soft dirt and mussed up her pretty hair. She lay sobbing at the feet of the paratroopers when General Vogel drove up.

"Miss Lamour," he shounted in elation, yet with concern. "Are you all right?"

''Yes,'' she cried. ''they came just in time. They saved me. It was horrible.''

''Who saved you?''

She pointed at the paratroopers, who stood holding their weapons.

''From whom, Miss Lamour?''

''From them.'' She pointed to the sea.

''What's going on here, Major Barrow?'' the general asked, dubious, concerned.

''We've been combing this island for days, looking for Miss Lamour, General,'' Major Barrow said to his superior with a strong tone of anger in his voice. ''If no one else could find the lady, we believed we could. And we had to if we wanted to get one look at her after that stinking bulletin you sent us.''

''I'll send a written apology to your battalion the first thing in the morning.'' He turned to Marylyn. ''Come, dear. We'll get you straightened out and you can tell Naval Intelligence what happened.''

After Crocker drove them home safely in the recon truck he ''borrowed'' in Noumea, the major asked for Checkoway. He was in the mess hall, drinking coffee.

''You landed okay?'' the major asked.

''Pancaked. Couldn't find the controls for the landing gear.''

''Got away from Magenta all right?''

''Easy. Some of our men showed up in MP gear and arrested me.''

''At Magenta they fell for that old gag?''

''Didn't you know?'' Checkoway quizzed the major. ''Colonel Mihalek, the commanding officer over there, is one of our corporals from C Company.''

The men gathered around the radios the next morning waiting for the first news broadcast. It was wonderful. ''Captured by the last gang of Vichy French on the island, Miss Lamour was held captive for five horror-filled days. On the eve of her execution, demanded by the Nazis because she refused to give any information concerning ship movement or troop stations, the group was attacked and routed by the fearless men of the First Parachute Battalion who drove them into the sea. Miss Lamour said that the troopers killed and wounded several of the Vichyites but that they were dragged into their escape boat by their colleagues. The boat has not been found and the entire gang is believed to have drowned. Miss Lamour couldn't give much information on the questions put to her because her captors spoke no English and she speaks no French.''

Hollywood and Broadway were elated, it seemed, and her studio awarded Miss Lamour the biggest contract in its history. The President sent congratulations to General Vogel and a citation to the First Parachute Battalion. Marylyn sent the men a wire expressing the wish that they could be beside her on her tickertape parade down Broadway.

"It ain't going to be the same around here without that girl." Whoever said that, spoke for the battalion.

But General Vogel wasn't quite taken in. He visited the paratroopers a few days later.

"You men think you're smart," he said.

"Yes, sir."

"Well, so do I." He smiled expansively. "Damn smart."

The men exchanged nods.

"Now, about that trip to the states," Vogel began.

The faces of the men lit up.

"It's out," the general went on. "Stand by and pack up. You're going to be the first men to hit the beach on the next push. Ha-ha-ha."

"What a creep." Unanimous.

The men and the major had forgotten their feud since Marylyn had visited them, and the men terminated hostilities when they sent a company clerk to his tent with the message: "The men of C Company cordially invite you to take stump juice with them this afternoon at two." It was the nicest message that he had ever received.

But that afternoon the major was saddened by the official announcement he received telling him to alert his command for embarkation. He knew the rumors were true that the push was going to be staged on Cape Gloucester. It would be a tough campaign. Each morning he expected to see the company streets deserted, the men gone, hiding in the hills of New Caledonia.

And he was not prepared for the roll call that was held on the morning that the men filed aboard the USS *Heywood*, their troop ship. That was the day he got a whole new philosophy of life.

Sergeant Schmidt turned up in civilian clothes. He had just flown in from Brisbane, Australia. Four men reported in from Auckland and Wellington, New Zealand. Pfc. Cannizzaro hopped ships down from the Russells where he had been with the Third Raider Battalion, conquering the islands. Corporal Mihalek left his berth as commanding officer of Magenta and took his place in the ranks alongside Private Williams, late of Casual and Replacements. Vogel compromised and gave Checkoway a Silver Star and let him go along. Two nuts sent wires that they could be picked up on Guadalcanal and one crackpot showed up in a sailor's suit. He had conned his way aboard the *Big Mo* and had set up an ice-cream stand. Admiral Bull Halsey raised hell and wanted him back. The best one of all, though, was Corporal Zanghetti who came all the way back from San Francisco where he had established a thriving taxi business.

It was a perfect roll call. Two hundred and nine men were accounted for; six more than were on the books.

Not yet unpacked, the major set down his cup of stump juice when the bosun's mate of the *Heywood* entered his quarters.

"Compliments of the captain," the bosun began.

"Yes?"

"He wanted me to tell you–" The bosun hesitated.

"Well?"

"The Marines have locked the crew out of their fresh-water showers."

"So?"

"Both the crews' and the officers' mess have been burglarized and all the whiskey stolen."

"Do tell."

"And a full chest of .45s has turned up missing."

"Go on."

"The crap games on the boat deck are so big that the crew can't even get through for a sweep-down."

"Uh-huh."

"And someone has set up a still in the forward head and is distilling raisins."

"Proceed."

"Just before the ship left Noumea, someone stole the entire supply of ship's sugar."

"Imagine that."

"And someone sold the captain's gig to a Kanaka longshoreman."

"Fantastic."

"The ship's clock is missing."

"Horrible."

"All the alcohol has been drained out of the torpedoes we carry."

"Tsk-tsk."

"And a naked Javanese girl was found in the sea bag of the chaplain's assistant and he requests permission to send a wire to the Secretary of the Navy."

"Permission granted."

"And . . . "

"Enough. Such a poorly run ship. I'd better go see the captain and find out if he's accusing my men of such conduct."

"Can't be done, sir," the bosun advised him. "The captain has locked himself in his cabin and won't see anyone except the navigation officer."

The navigation officer, an Annapolis man, overextended himself with the major one night as they sailed north.

"I have never seen such a rat-trap outfit as yours," he observed to Major Barrow.

"You never saw a better one, you trade school deck ape," the major loyally shouted as the canteen cup of stump juice shook in his hand.

"Well, we'll see," the officer said as he backed out of the room. He was a little leery of this belligerent, alcohol-drinking Marine major.

A week later the naval officer, who had access to the communications coming in over the decoder, did see, and he was amazed. Casualties were high in the early actions and each communiqué made some mention of the paratroopers. It seemed incredible to him that such a small outfit could win so many Congressional Medals and Navy Crosses.

The major came aboard the *Heywood* one night and directed the naval officer to send a message to Command for him. The navy man was glad to. The message read:

"The object of all military training is to win battles. How'm I doing, General Vogel? *(Signed)* Major Harold Barrow, Commanding Officer, First Parachute Battalion."

"Are you going to send a message like that to the general?"

"No. *You* are."

"Okay. Okay."

The navigation officer was surprised and happy when he read the general's reply to the major's pompous message.

"Major Barrow: The Secretary of the Navy joins me in sending congratulations on your fine job. Congratulations also on your promotion to colonel."

But it was quite some time before the naval officer could have the good news delivered to the major. There was no ship-to-shore contact.

Over on the beach, the Coast Guard radioman was furious when he found that his radio set was missing and he couldn't communicate with the fleet for naval artillery support for the troops or for badly needed supplies, while upon the lines, a group of alcohol-drinking Marines sat around their major and gleefully made comments as they listened to Tokyo Rose play jazz music which was coming in wonderfully well over their new high-frequency radio.

ROBERT LOWRY

Layover in El Paso

THE COACHES ARE crammed and jammed, and by the time that Los Angeles–Chicago train gets to Douglas, Arizona, there's no more room anywhere, and a whole pack of eager disappointed soldiers are left behind, waiting with their little furlough-bags at the station. Inside the train everybody has gone mad with the fury of the war. Who cares! says the soldier going back to his tent from a furlough. Who cares! says the girl whose boy friend is far away. Who cares! says the lonely wife returning from visiting her husband for the last time before overseas duty. She holds hands with two soldiers she never saw before, and she has starry eyes and a short skirt, and helps kill a pint on the platform.

The train moves slowly through the desert—everyone is bored looking out the window at the thirsty, burnt-out flatland. The people go in upon themselves to pass the time. A fat lady with two kids dozes off to sleep, her head rocking back and her mouth opening with a soprano snore. A girl named Edna with mascaraed green eyes looks hard at a soldier passing; on his next trip through the cars he sits down and talks with her and wonders what he'll get around to when the coach is dark tonight. A thin effeminate fellow about thirty-five in a snappy blue suit explains to two soldiers sitting across from him that he's traveling for the government on very important business; otherwise he'd be in uniform too. He'd like nothing better, of course! The two soldiers just listen to him for a while, then get up and leave. Loud shouts and laughter come from the men's washroom—thirty GIs who couldn't find seats have gotten around to telling all the dirty jokes they can think of.

Red couldn't keep his eyes open. He was coming from Indio, California, and he'd already been on the train one rocky, cold night. In Indio he was on kitchen detail to an air force unit; he washed their trays for them. But nobody looking at him would have suspected this;

he wore a uniform like anybody else and might have been a pilot for all some girls knew. It was the one good thing about being a soldier: everybody dressed pretty much alike.

Across from him sat an old lady with faded blue eyes, wearing a dilapidated straw hat held on with a stickpin. She carried all her stuff in a shopping bag and a paper box tied up with soiled Christmas-package ribbon. She was very eager to talk and chose Red as the one to listen. It was all about her son who'd been killed in the last war. The kind of pie he'd liked, and some of his sayings as a child. She leaned forward eagerly as she spoke, looking like a bird that hears a worm in the ground, and every time Red started dozing off she talked still louder and higher, and put her hand on his arm. Finally, he remembered someplace he had to go up the car a ways, and mumbled something in apology and beat it.

Out on the platform a sailor offered him a drink. He took a long one and coughed. "Thanks, pal," he said.

The sailor was a short stocky fellow, with button eyes set wide apart under thick eyebrows. "Hey, there's a couple quail I been talking to up in the next car," the sailor said. "You wanta try out on one of them?"

"Sure," Red said.

So they shoved into the next car—went right on through, with Red looking anxiously at every face to see what kind of babe it would be.

The two of them were sitting in the last seats. "Jesus," Red said, "they're kinda old, ain't they?"

"This is Red," the sailor was saying. "I don't know either of yer names but I guess you know em yerself so it's all right."

So the two babes laughed, and since the seats opposite were empty Red and the sailor sat down.

Both the babes wore pants and both of them, judging by the little lines around their eyes, were thirty-five years old anyhow. The one had a tilted-up nose and large eyes, but when she smiled the whole coach was filled up with big teeth. The other kept looking at Red. She was smaller, had shrewd bright eyes and short black hair with just a few strands of gray in it. She wore a blue pants suit with an orange polka-dot kerchief around her neck. Her sandaled feet she kept tucked up under her. Red just looked at her. He'd spent nine months out on the California desert and he couldn't help it.

"Where you coming from, Red?" she asked in a voice that reminded him of somebody like Katharine Hepburn.

"Oh, I'm comin from Indio," he said.

"Furlough?" she asked.

"Yeah," Red said. He found he was holding on pretty hard to the arm of the seat. She was smiling at him all the time; there were little crinkles around her sharp eyes and her manicured hand played with the kerchief. She's kind of tight, Red thought.

"Your first furlough?" she asked.

"Yeah," Red said. "I waited a heck of a time for it. Ten months. Seemed like a heck of a time, anyhow."

"Where you going?"

"I'm goin home—back to Elder, Tennessee."

"Wife and kids?"

Red blushed and looked down at this hands. "Ah, I haven't got any wife and kids," he said. "Just mom and pop and a couple brothers and sisters."

"Well, you *might* have a wife and kids," she said, looking at him sidewise. "I mean, you're *capable* of it, aren't you?"

"Yeah, I guess I'm capable of it," Red said. The blush still hadn't faded.

"Come on, let's go out on the platform and have a drink," the sailor said.

Before long they all had their arms around one another and were singing "What a Friend We Have in Jesus." It didn't feel to Red like she had anything on under that costume. The whiskey and her made him feel faint. She kept laughing and saying clever things. Her name was Kay, and the bigtoothed woman she called Boots. They had a standing joke between them about somebody named Harry, but Red couldn't figure out exactly who he was. Kay was always saying, "Oh, *Harry* doesn't know the half of it!" And then a little later Boots would say, "If Harry could see you now!" And Kay would say, "But sweet, he's such a *bore*. I can't *bear* boring people. I'm out for a good *time,*" and pull Red's head down to her and bite his ear. Once she put her tongue in his ear, which sobered him for a minute—it was such a surprise.

About seven o'clock they got hungry and went and stood in the chow line.

"This is one of the reasons I just *hate* the war," Kay said. "You've got to *wait* and *wait* and *wait.*" She looked mad for a second, but then she began to laugh. She took Red's cap off and put it on her own head; it sure made her look funny. Then they were all giggling and laughing and Boots said, ''Did you ever hear about the lady moron who went to bed naked with a fellow and nine months later she woke up with a little more on?'' and Kay pinched her fat rear and said, *''That's* what you get for telling *that.''* Red saw other soldiers in line looking at him and he knew they were wondering. He felt pretty swell. He'd thought for ten months about something like this happening when he went home on the train.

It was sort of funny in the diner, though. There were just two dinners advertised on the menu because of the food rationing, and she got in a big argument with the colored waiter about a shrimp cocktail. She *must* have a shrimp cocktail. ''Just what's on the menu, ma'am,'' he said. ''You could at least find out if they *have* a shrimp cocktail,'' she said. ''Yes, ma'am,'' he said. He went away and came back and said, ''They got some shrimp back there, but it ain't for servin in no cocktail.''

''Why, I never *heard* of such a thing,'' she said, looking from the waiter to Red and then back to the waiter. ''Go get me the steward.''

''Yes'm,'' the tall Negro said.

In a minute the steward come, a frowning fellow in a navy-blue suit with menus in his hand. She explained the whole situation to him very slowly, as if to a child, and he didn't say anything till she was all finished. Then he just said, ''No,'' and walked away.

It took about fifteen minutes more to get the waiter back and meanwhile Red was trying to pick out his choices on the two meals. He wanted to choose the same things she chose, but everything he said he liked she disagreed with. ''Are you *really* going to order milk?'' she asked. ''I simply can't *stand* milk.'' So he ordered coffee.

The sailor and Boots had had to take a table at the other end of the car, but the four of them finished about the same time and went out on the platform for another drink. Kay kept her arms around Red's neck most of the time; she was about a foot shorter than him and he had to stay bent over so she could reach him. He kissed her a lot, and she took to that all right. He got in some good feels too. Only once did she object and then she said, ''Oh *don't,* darling,'' and kissed him again. Red didn't know what to make of her.

They all went back to their seats and there were only two available so the women sat on the men's laps. They made so much noise everybody looked at them, and Red felt kind of embarrassed. He tried to pass it off by winking at one pimply faced Pfc across the aisle, but the Pfc just stared through his tortoise-shell glasses for a minute, then turned around and went on reading *A Critique of Pure Reason*.

The women weren't embarrassed at all, though; they kept shouting and laughing at each other, and Boots reached over and pulled Red's ear and said, "Hey, Red, I bet you never heard about the little moron who thought a mushroom was someplace to pitch woo in," then filled up the car with those teeth again. Kay's arm was around Red's head, and her hair was up under his chin. She kept buttoning and unbuttoning one of his shirt buttons. "*Oh* but I'm tired—simply *dead*. I think I'll just go to sleep right here. *Red* doesn't mind if I sleep on top of him tonight, do you, Red?"

Red didn't know what to say to that; he looked over at the kid reading the book and then back at the sailor. "Naw," he said.

He could feel himself blushing but it was okay too, only he'd never met any woman like Kay before, except maybe in the movies. These women really live fast, he thought.

Red halfway dozed off, and woke up to see the big creased face of the conductor over hem.

"Better get your luggage together," the conductor was saying to Kay. "Next stop is El Paso."

"Oh, my *God,*" Kay was saying, "my luggage is all over the *train.*" So Red had to help her go round it up; it was pretty swell stuff, all yellow leather and heavy as hell.

The four of them were still half asleep when they got off the train. Red carried luggage under his arms and in both hands, and sweated as bad as he did back in Indio.

When they arrived in the station, Kay suddenly stopped and turned around to him, the way some movie actress like Bette Davis would, and said "Darling, are you taking *another* train out right away or spending the night in El Paso?"

The question hit Red like a ton of bricks, and he glanced over the the sailor and Boots for an answer, but the sailor was whispering in Boots's ear and they were laughing to beat the band. Then he looked back at Kay—her shrewd eyes with the little crinkles around them were regarding him in a kind of funny way. What the devil did she mean?

"I hadn't thought about it," Red said.

"We-ell, you'll have a *horrible* time if you try to find a place to stay in *this* ole town." She studied a ring on her right hand for a minute, then looked up at him. "But I was thinking: Boots and I have an apartment and you can sleep over there if you *want* to."

Red still just stared at her. His blood pressure was up about twenty points and a big lump had settled in his throat. She'd taken off her jacket and he noticed all of a sudden how her two little breasts pushed through the thin white blouse.

". . . if you'll promise to be real *good,*" she was saying, and she laughed at him again.

Jesus, Red thought, I'll never get back to Elder now, and I told Mom, and they're all going to be there looking for that train.

But there didn't seem to be anything else to do, what with her looking at him that way, like a challenge or something, so he just mumbled, "I guess I'll stay here tonight," and Kay laughed at him, and went on gazing into his eyes for almost a minute. Then she ran over to Boots and said, "Red wants to get some sleep in El Paso tonight and I told him he could stay over at our place," and Boots looked at Red and then back to Kay. "Why, that's swell," she said, "Georgie's going to stay too." Red and Georgie caught each other's eye for a second—they were in complete understanding. They went back together for their bags, but neither said anything.

With themselves and all the luggage bundled into a taxi, they drove out through town a long ways before they finally stopped on some dark street. The others waited for Red while he paid the driver, and then there was the business of opening the front door.

The apartment was on the second floor and it was a pretty swell place with real low, plain furniture like nothing Red had ever seen before. He was almost afraid to move, it was all so nice, and he only sat down after Kay had told him to a couple times.

"Wait, I'll go out and fix us all a drink," Kay said, and Red saw how small and nicely built she was from the rear.

Red and Georgie sat on the couch and the two babes sat in separate chairs. They drank the whiskey-and-sodas and Kay talked about how *horrible* trains were, and how she always *swore* she'd never take another trip, but then when the time came she always *did* anyhow. She had a scratch on her suntanned leg and while leaning over to examine it, she explained how she'd got it when she'd slipped on the train step in Los Angeles. Red felt like getting down and examining it too.

But as she was talking, Red suddenly had a funny feeling: he thought of those little five- or six-line notes his mom always wrote him and that last one was plain as day right there in front of him: *Well son were sure glad all about youre furlo*. . . . Twenty one-dollar bills had been enclosed—he'd already spent four of them on the dinner and a couple more on the cab. He thought of his old man too, a tall skinny fellow who never said much, just worked hard all day in the field. He remembered that funny look, as if he were going to cry, on his old man's face the day he'd left, ten months go. Now look at me, Red thought.

Kay was standing up, pushing her arms above her head and yawning—a position that sure made her figure stand out. ''I'm *dead,*'' she was saying, ''simply *dead.* I think I'll get in the tub and just *soak* for a while—I've *never* felt so filthy before. . . . That couch opens up, darlings. You two can sleep there snug as bugs.''

Red just sat and looked at her. She looked down at him and smiled. ''And remember what I said to *you,* Mr. Red, about being *good.*'' She came over and kissed him on the cheek and smoothed his hair. ''Hmmmm?''

Red couldn't get up enough nerve to reach out and pull her down to him. He didn't know what to make of her. What kind of a woman was she, anyhow, and where'd she get all the dough to keep this big apartment? . . . He watched which of the two bedrooms she went into, though.

He and the sailor lay on the couch in the dark.

''I never did get home on a leave yet,'' the sailor said. ''I tried about three other times, but I never make it; I always get into something like this. It ain't bad though, they got a good set-up. Boots says she works in an office and yours lives off some rich guy she's divorced from. Ain't a bad set-up for us, is it?''

''Looks pretty good,'' Red said.

They lay there a while longer, then the sailor said, ''Well, I know what I'm gonna do,'' and jumped out of bed.

''Where you goin?'' Red asked, straining his eyes, but not able to make out anything.

''I ain't goin to play tiddly-winks, soldier,'' the sailor's voice came back from halfway across the room.

Red heard the door open and close, and Boots's voice saying, ''Oh don't, Georgie—'' There was a little scuffle and then he heard her giggling.

Well, I'll be damn, Red thought. He didn't move for a minute, his heart was raising so much Cain.

Then he got out of bed and went in his bare feet across the room to Kay's door.

He listened for a while outside—couldn't hear a sound above the pounding of his heart, He reached out, turned the knob and pushed. The door opened!

He stood flatfooted. His heart was making twenty-foot leaps trying to get out of his throat.

Then he heard her stir. He took three steps into the room.

"Is that *you,* Red?" she asked.

He went on over to the bed.

"Yeah?"

He got into the bed and knelt above her.

"But *Red,* you promised you'd be *good,*" she said.

He couldn't think of anything to say, so he grabbed her and kissed her. For a minute she tried to push him away and talk with his mouth on hers, but then she gave up and put her arms around him. This is the part they always leave out of the movies, Red thought. It was such a damn thing to think, he felt like laughing right there.

When he woke up, nobody was in the bed with him and he lay for a moment trying to remember everything that had happened, and not feeling very good about anything. I ought to be on the train, he thought. I ought to be on the train going back home to Elder right this minute.

She came into the room without looking at him and began combing her hair in front of the mirror. It made his heart stop dead to see her like that, stark naked.

Pretty soon she turned around and for a minute gave him a blank early morning stare, like she didn't even know him. Then her face came all together and got that quick crinkle-eyed smile. "Sleep well?" she asked, coming over to the bed.

My God, she was beautiful and put together, Red thought. She was little, but she was sure put together. It made him want to cry almost, looking at a woman like her.

She was smiling down at him and kind of mysteriously and he realized all of a sudden, he hadn't answered her question. Did he sleep well? "I slept pretty good," he said.

"You *know* you're going to the bullfight with me this afternoon, don't you, darling?" She sat down on the bed. "Now don't muss my hair!"

So Red got dressed and they went out in the kitchen and she sure looked swell, sitting across the breakfast table from him in that flowered kimono, her little sharp face sort of turned to one side, smiling and talking to him. He couldn't take his eyes off her.

''You know . . . I like you a lot,'' Red said.

''Want some more toast, darling?'' she answered.

''I never thought I had a chance with you on the train.''

''I *told* you to be good last night,'' she said. ''And you just *wouldn't.*''

''I think you're really . . . really a swell girl.''

She didn't seem so old to him now. Everything he was saying just slipped out; he just listened to it and it didn't sound like him speaking at all.

''I guess you got lots of guys crazy about you,'' he said. ''But I could really go for you.''

''Oh, you'll go home to that little girl in Tennessee and forget *all* about me,'' she said. ''You won't even be able to remember the color of my *eyes,* darling.''

''They're blue,'' Red said automatically. He hadn't really noticed the color before and he felt a little ashamed.

Watching her over there at the sink rinsing the dishes, he couldn't help it—he went over and grabbed her clumsily and tried to kiss her. But the look that came over her face made him let go quick. ''Go *away,*'' she said, really mad. ''Can't you see I'm *busy?*''

''I'm sorry,'' Red said, and got the towel and began drying.

He was just finishing up when Georgie and Boots came out; they were both all dressed and feeling pretty good about something. While they ate, he sat in the front room and read the funnies, and Kay filed her nails and talked about how terribly *boring* she found Sundays. If it weren't for the bullfights, she didn't know *what* she'd do—she got *so* tired of movies. That was the reason she traveled so much, she said.

Red couldn't keep from stealing glances at her all the time; she looked so pretty, sitting over there. And he got that sick, lonely feeling inside and he didn't know what to do about it.

Walking along beside her in Juarez he felt very proud of himself, and kept looking at her out of the corner of his eye. He still couldn't believe a woman like her would really have a guy like him—she was sure something, prancing along down there in her oxfords and her green plaid suit. When he looked at the couple ahead he thought, Georgie got the short end of the bargain this time, all right, even if Boots does keep throwing her arms around his neck and laughing at him with her big teeth every other minute.

''There's the bull ring!'' Kay said, and Red looked and there it was: the dirty white curved front of the bull ring. He felt desperate.

''Let's not go to the bullfight, Kay,'' he said.

That crease was between her eyes when she looked up at him.

"Why, darling, whatever do you *mean?*" she asked.

For a couple steps he couldn't say anything; he felt all hot and there was a tightness in his head.

"It's just"—he swallowed—"it's just that I'm pretty crazy about you, that's all. I don't think you know how crazy I am about you, Kay." He was looking straight ahead with a blank scared expression; his mind was running wild and he didn't know what he was saying, but he was going to let it all come out anyhow—the way it all felt like coming out. "I wish we could ditch Georgie and Boots and go somewhere and be all alone together, even a restaurant, and just talk. God Almighty, Kay," he swallowed again, "I'm crazier about you than I ever—"

"Why, *Harry!*" Kay screamed.

It scared Red so he jumped and turned white. She was running wildly across the street toward a dapper middle-aged fellow in a pepper-and-salt suit. Red watched them embrace, then stand there holding hands while they talked and smiled.

In a minute she came rushing back across the street. Georgie and Boots had stopped: they were watching to see what was up.

"Do you mind *awfully,* Red?" Kay asked.

"Mind what?" Red said.

"But I haven't seen Harry in *such* a long time and he wants me to have a drink with him. Do you *mind?*"

"No," Red said.

"You go on to the fight with Georgie and Boots and we'll see you there."

"Okay," Red said.

He watched her run across the street away from him. He felt rotten all the way down to his shoe soles.

Georgie and Boots came on over.

"She's just that way, Red, don't pay any attention to her," Boots said.

"Yeah," Red said.

"Come on along, Red," Boots said, taking his arm.

He looked at her and suddenly he liked her. He hadn't liked her much before, but she didn't seem so ugly and loud now. He went along with them to wait in line and get the tickets. Afterward they stopped in a café and had a drink—it would be an hour till the bullfight started.

Boots tried to be gay, but pretty soon even she got quiet and the three of them just stared at the rest of the people. There was a little excitement over in the corner where a Mexican kid was trying to sell a banderilla—dried blood, hair, and all—to a drunken GI. The kid was giving his sales talk plenty of punch by using the table top for the bull's hump and pretending he was inserting the banderilla. After gazing dreamily at the performance for a while, the GI finally jerked off the tablecloth and started acting like a bullfighter and a bull both at once. He ran all around the room, making faces and waving the cloth and imitating the bull with snorts and stomps.

"You think we'll see Kay at the fight?" Red asked.

"Sure," Boots said. 'We'll look for her. You'll probably get to sit with her."

"Yeah," Red said. He finished off the tequila with one gulp, feeling at that moment like running out of the café and taking the first train east. But somehow he went on sitting there: he couldn't pull himself together. How could Kay be so swell to him one minute and then just turn around and leave him like that the next?

They went to the bullfight and Red kept looking all around, but he didn't see her. There were a lot of Americans at the fight and they were all pulling for the bull—everybody yelled and screamed when the bullfighter got scared and hid behind a kind of wooden backstop down there. Then when he tried to sneak up behind the bull and jab him with a knife, people went hog-wild, standing up and throwing stuff and booing. Red didn't want to look at the fight. He felt lousy. He wanted to get out of there.

The three of them ate supper together in an El Paso restaurant. Red couldn't eat all of his steak; he just sat looking out of the window. The little big-eyed waitress took a shine to him and acted hurt that he didn't eat, but he was feeling too rotten even to pay any attention to her. All he wanted to do was stare out the window at the sign across the street. It went off and on and off and on forever, saying: LOANS.

"I guess I oughta be movin on," he said, when they got back to the apartment and Kay wasn't there.

"Hell, you can't shove off without tellin Kay good-bye," Georgie said.

"I oughta be goin soon, though," Red said. "I let my folks know I was comin."

They sat in the living room. Georgie and Boots were over on the couch together; he was fooling around with two pieces of string, trying to show her how to tie the different kinds of knots. But when he'd get one made for her, she'd giggle and look at his face instead of at the knot.

Red got the idea and said, ''Think I'll go out and walk around a bit.''

He walked around the dark streets. A dog barked at him and he didn't even tell it to shut up. When he got back to the apartment, Georgie and Boots were gone.

He lay down on the couch and closed his eyes. He didn't know how long he'd been sleeping, when he woke up and there she was standing over him.

''Hello, darling,'' Kay said.

He sat up and rubbed his eyes like a little kid.

''But you've been *sleeping* and you've forgotten all *about* me, darling,'' she said. Her hair was mussed—he could see she was tight.

''Naw,'' he said.

She sat down on his knee and ran her fingers through his hair. ''You've forgotten all *about* little ole me.''

He started to say something, but she was kissing his mouth so he couldn't. He kissed her too. He tightened his hold on her. ''Oh, Red,'' she said, lying back in his arms and giggling up at him, ''you sure do things to me.''

He didn't know what to say. All of a sudden, looking down at her like that, he began to bawl. He tried to stop himself but couldn't.

''Now, now, Red baby,'' she said, smiling, and dug his handkerchief out of his pocket and dabbed at the tears. He felt ashamed of crying.

''I never did that before,'' he said when he got himself in gear again.

She grinned at him, making a *tck-tck* noise with her tongue and moved her head from side to side. ''Red baby,'' she said. ''*Tck-tck-tck.*''

''Your hands are cold,'' he said, ''Are you cold?''

She went on grinning, raising her eyebrows and narrowing her eyes. ''You're sweet . . . and you're a Red baby,'' she murmured, shoving her cold hand inside his shirt so that he jumped a little.

God, she was nice when she was like this. He'd never known a girl as nice as her. He forgave her for running off—forgave her for everything. There was just one thing: he wanted to ask her who Harry was, but he couldn't bring himself to. She's pretty pie-eyed, he thought. God, she's nice.

She jumped up. ''Oh come *on,* you old Red,'' she said, swaying a little. ''I thought you were a great big *strong* man. Come on, let's see you *catch* me!''

And she took off into the kitchen, with him after her. She ran first one way around the table, then the other, laughing shrilly when she knocked over a chair. He heard a lamp crash a minute after she'd dodged into the living room again, and he went bounding in there just in time to see the door to her room slam closed. He heard the key turn in the lock and he heard her giggling softly.

Breathing hard, feeling all excited, he stood up close to the door. "Let me in, Kay."

She didn't answer.

"Please let me in."

He couldn't hear her at all now. He waited maybe five minutes, then he knocked timidly. She didn't make any sound. He knocked louder. Still no answer.

He waited a long while outside her door. Gradually his heart calmed down and he went over and sat on the couch.

He sat there for half the night, just looking at the design in the rug. He didn't think of anything at all.

She woke him next morning.

"Is it late?" he asked.

She was wearing her flowered kimono. She gave him her smile. "Did you *sleep* well, darling?"

She even buttered his toast for him at the breakfast table. Why in hell was she so kind to him now, he wondered, after the funny way she'd acted last night? He kept looking at her, trying to find the answer in her face.

"I was a little high last night, wasn't I," she said. "I hope I didn't seem *too* silly."

"That was okay," he said. "I thought you were swell. I don't mind anything you do."

She was studying him, looking so nice and pert-like with that smile lingering around her mouth. "You don't?" she asked.

"Ah, Kay."

But even as his insides dissolved at the contact her hand made with his, it flashed across his mind that he was really supposed to be getting home about this time. He reached in his pants pocket and felt the thirty-thirty shell he was bringing for his brother Jack.

"What have you got there? Secrets?"

He brought out the shell. "I was just bringing it home for my brother; he wrote and said to."

"You have a *brother*?" she asked. "Redhead like you?"

"Yeah," he said. "He's only fifteen, crazy about guns and huntin. I used to hunt some too."

Her fingers slipped in against the palm of his hand; she leaned a little toward him. "What'd *you* hunt, baby?"

"Oh . . . like rabbits . . . squirrels . . ." But his voice trailed off—she was smiling at him in such a peculiar way and squeezing his hand.

"Love to see you shoot your gun sometime, honey," she murmured, and her fingers slipped in under his shirtcuff, pulled at the hairs on his wrist. Then suddenly she jumped up and made him get up too and put his arm around her. Like that she led him into the bedroom and closed the door.

"Undress me, baby," she whispered, standing close against him. "Do *everything* for me."

He didn't say a word. He did what she said.

In the afternoon they went to a movie that had Cary Grant, and Kay said she just *loved* Cary Grant. When they got back to the apartment, Georgie and Boots were leaving. Georgie looked pretty worn out, but Boots was still wearing her big toothy smile.

"I feel almost ashamed of myself going out for breakfast this time of day," she said to Kay, and Kay said, "Well, I'd *think* so."

Alone with him in the living room she said, "I've just *got* to leave you by yourself tonight, darling. You don't *mind*, do you?"

"No," Red said.

She gave his hand a squeeze, ran off to take a shower, and came out in a plain black dress with a high collar that made her look like a queen or something.

He read magazines all evening, looking up vacantly every now and then to wonder where she was. He felt angry, but at the same time he didn't know what to do about it. Once he went into her room and stood there in the darkness wishing she'd come back and be with him.

He'd never felt this way before. He felt helpless, like a dog that's been run over.

He read more magazines. Read the jokes in *Esquire* and finally got into an article about Errol Flynn's latest yachting trip with a girl who on the first page was fifteen but who grew to be nineteen farther back in the magazine.

Yet he was always finding himself staring off at the wall.

He heard himself saying, "I oughta go home. I really oughta go home. My old man would be mad as hell if he knew I was here like this."

He didn't have but $5.95 left.

I'll never get to Elder if I don't watch out, he thought. I got to start now, beat it out of here now or I'll never get there.

He stood up. For a single moment he was going.

Then he thought of Kay and sat back down again.

When he woke up it was morning. Georgie and Boots were eating breakfast in the kitchen, and Boots told him that Kay had gone out early. "She had to meet somebody," Boots said. "She didn't know exactly when she'd be back."

He drank some orange juice. Those two were all interested in themselves—he felt glad he didn't have to think of anything to contribute to the conversation.

He went into the living room and stared at the wall. If I started home now, he thought, I could still make it. I could stay for a couple days and still have time to get back.

He went out at noon. Went across the line and took in the row of bars down the main street. He got so drunk he wanted to fight, and in the Chicago Club he struck out wildly at a big soldier with two girls standing next to him. Without even being hit he flopped full length on the floor, and when he came to he was in the gutter out on the street and it was night. He got up and made his way to the International Bridge. The side of his face was covered with blood, but the MP at the soldiers' gate didn't say anything.

He had to ring the apartment bell for fifteen minutes before Georgie came and let him in. Georgie had on one of Boots's kimonos. It was dark in the room so Georgie didn't see what a hell of a shape Red was in. Georgie was mad at having had to get out of bed anyhow—he beat it back into the bedroom.

Red tried to wash the blood off. But finally he settled for just getting rid of his shirt and going to sleep on the couch.

When he woke up next morning his mouth was swollen big and he noticed he had one tooth missing. He stared at his face in the mirror for a while, before he realized what was different: it was all on one side. He couldn't even laugh at himself.

After a shower he felt better . . . till he reached in his pocket and found that he had no money at all. But there was his furlough-rate train ticket—and some woman's handkerchief, with lipstick on it. He tried to remember who'd given it to him but he couldn't remember anything.

I'm no good at all, he thought, looking straight ahead. I'm not worth anything. I don't even deserve to get home.

He was hungry, but there was nothing in the kitchen except some bread.

I hope to hell I never get home now, he thought. He went over and looked out the window. Nothing down there to look at.

When he went back into the living room, he noticed that Kay's door was a little ajar. He looked in—the bed hadn't been slept in.

So he got his grip and put on his cap and went out the door.

I don't deserve to get home, he thought again. I'm just about the lowest kind of heel that ever lived. They've got the kids up at the station every day, watching for me.

Out on the street, walking fast, he realized for the first time that he was free of that apartment, and he felt good. He hadn't realized how wonderful it would feel, being free of that apartment. He began to run, he felt so good, and after a ride on a bus he was at the railroad station.

By God, I'm going to make it, he thought. By God, I'll get home after all.

He ran up to the first train official he saw and asked: "Where's the New Orleans train?"

The paunchy official took out his watch and considered it a long time before he answered. "It's just now leaving. If you run maybe you can still make it. Got your ticket?"

Red ran out on the platform and saw the train all set to go. One door was still open so he leaped on and then the train started. I'm on the damn thing! he told himself. By God, I'm really on the damn thing!

He pushed up into the car, shoved his grip on the rack, and sat down puffing. Next to him was a man with a detective-story magazine. The man said something to Red, but Red didn't want to talk to anybody; all he wanted to do was sit here and let this old train take him home. He didn't want to meet anybody or look at anybody till he got there.

He dozed off finally. The conductor had to wake him to get his ticket.

The conductor looked at Red's ticket, then looked at Red. I must look funny, Red thought, with this swollen jaw.

"Where you going, soldier?" the conductor asked.

"I'm goin to Elder, Tennessee," Red said.

The conductor's smile was sarcastic; he glanced around at several other passengers to bring them in on the joke.

"Well, you're sure going a funny way to get to New Orleans," the conductor said. "This train is bound for Los Angeles."

Red just looked at the conductor. The conductor meanwhile was punching the detective-story fan's ticket.

"I can fix it for you to get off at the next stop and catch the train going the other way," the conductor said.

"When is the next train?"

The conductor looked at his watch. "Next train at . . . twelve-thirty-two A.M. tomorrow.

Red began to figure quickly. If this was the right train, he thought, I'd have one day at home. But this ain't the right train and I won't have any days at home so there's no sense going on.

"I'll just stay on this way," Red said.

The conductor punched his ticket, gave him part of it back, and went on up the aisle.

He sat for a long time looking out of the train window without seeing anything. He felt the thirty-thirty shell in his pocket. I can mail it to him, he thought.

After a while he went out on the platform. There was a bunch of other soldiers out there and they gave him a drink from their bottle.

"Just gettin back from a furlough?" one fat soldier with a great mop of black hair asked.

"Yeah," Red said. He turned his face away so they wouldn't see it.

WILLIAM SAMBROT

The Man Who Hated

IT WAS COLONEL Jack Dumphrey (retired) D.S.O., O.B.E., who told me the haunting story of the man who hated as we drove up the winding steep road that led to the famous Benedictine Abbey of Monte Cassino, in Italy.

I was in Naples, last summer, a guest of Dumphrey's, when the Abbey sent him an urgent request for some technical information concerning a magnificent Renaissance painting which hung in one of the Abbey's newly restored chapels.

Dumphrey had been a colonel, Military Intelligence, on duty with the 2nd New Zealand Corps during the battle for Cassino in World War Two. He was (and is) a renowned scholar of Renaissance Italy; thoroughly conversant with the language. Directly after the fall of Cassino, he was given a large part of the responsibility for tracking down the considerable number of antiquities, art treasures, and the like, which were stolen or missing from the shattered Abbey after the great siege of Monte Cassino.

He'd interviewed many of the refugees who'd survived the siege, as well as the abbot and four monks who remained in the Abbey prior to its destruction. He had an intimate knowledge of what had occurred during those fatal days preceding the destruction, and using that knowledge, he'd been of great service to the Benedictine Order in recovering their irreplaceable treasures.

So, when Dumphrey received the Abbey's urgent request for technical information concerning their painting, he decided to go there in person, inviting me to go along.

We drove up from Naples to Cassino, using Highway Six—the twenty-five-century-old road the Romans called the Via Casilina, and just as we approached the gleaming new city of Cassino, with the River Rapido beyond, Dumphrey slowed the car.

"Observe, if you please," he said, in ironic caricature of the Italian tour guide, "before you lies the City of Cassino, and beyond, the swift flowing River Rapido. It was here that a great battle was fought between the Germans and the Allies, in 1944. A very great battle, costing many lives. And they fought for—the possession of Monte Cassino."

He pointed, up to where a mountain, gray-blue, swathed in mist, looked above the valley. And atop that mountain, a great building stood, huge even at this distance, somber, remote, not a part of this world of smartly dressed tourists, of traffic zooming down the highway.

"The Monastery of the Benedictines—the Abbey of Monte Cassino," Dumphrey said, but his voice had lost its mocking tinge. "For fourteen centuries it has stood up there, resisting every effort of man to bring it down—not the least of which was our own, of February 1944."

I looked up at that great brooding building and a feeling of awe enveloped me. It reared upon that mountain, and the immense weight of history seemed to press down upon it.

"That monastery—it's uncanny," I said, "but it seems—well—alive. Invincible, somehow. I—I can't describe the effect it has upon me."

Dumphrey looked up at it for a long moment, and it was as if he were seeing things, hearing sounds from another time. "Yes," he finally said, "the monastery has always affected men. Profoundly. One man that I know of, in particular. He hated the Abbey—hated it so bitterly that he was willing to crawl through hell, literally; to risk certain maiming—death, even, in order to ensure it would be destroyed."

"Destroyed! Was this during the war?"

"Yes," Dumphrey said. "February 1944."

"Even so," I said slowly, "what makes a man hate like that?"

"He had a thousand six hundred and eighty-one reasons," Dumphrey said. "That was the number of casualties his division suffered trying to cross the Rapido. And he blamed them all on the Abbey."

We were approaching the circuitous road that wound up and around Monte Cassino. As we climbed past the points that were like a drumroll on the hearts of those who fought and bled there: Point 593; Hangman's Hill; Castle Hill—thickly wooded with second-growth now, but all points named in anguish, baptized in the blood of the armies that had tried to storm the reaches of Monte Cassino three times before succeeding on the fourth—steering the car past these landmarks of which he spoke so quietly, Dumphrey told me of the man who hated:

His name was Lt. Anthony Page (Dumphrey said). He was an American, an interpreter on detached duty with the 4th Indian Division, British Expeditionary Force. His own outfit, the American 36th Infantry Division, had been decimated in January, drowned like rats in the Rapido; cut to pieces by murderously accurate German mortar and machine-gun fire.

And now it was the British who suffered. Beneath the brooding shadow of the Abbey, they were dug in as best as they could in the hard rocky ground, unable to move without bringing down the deadly accurate German fire.

Nothing could move in the daytime. Troops up on the slopes of the mountains went without food, dug into the flinty ground, hanging on with the grim knowledge that they could go no higher—nor retreat. Ammo was brought up on men's backs—even the sturdy little mules couldn't handle the job.

Men suffered and died during the day, helpless to move. And over it all, the Abbey looked down with a thousand eyes, seeming to watch every movement, to transmit their presence to the watchful German mortars and machine guns.

The Germans claimed that they would not use the Abbey for observation posts; it was sanctified ground. The Vatican had been unable to verify the Germans' claim that they were not using the Abbey for observation. And yet—the precision of their fire made it seem all too certain that once again they lied and were using the Abbey.

The Allies were reluctant to bomb the fourteen-century-old monastery, with its many precious treasures; the citadel which had kept alight the lamp of knowledge through the dark ages. And so, when a young infantry officer, Lt. Anthony Page volunteered to attempt to penetrate the German defenses and slip into the Abbey of Monte Cassino, to determine once and for all if they were using it, he was sent directly to Military Intelligence, Colonel Jack Dumphrey.

Lt. Page stood before Dumphrey, a tall fierce-eyed young man, tense with hatred.

"We've got to bomb that place, sir; pulverize it; wipe it off the face of the earth once and for all." His eyes burned, a fiery dark blue. "I'm positive they're using it for observation. Look what they did to my own outfit—they murdered us. We didn't have a chance. And now they're chopping the 4th to pieces. Sitting up there in that monastery, safe, while they kill us bit by bit."

"I know it appears that way, Page," Dumphrey said, "but reconnaissance shows negative insofar as the Abbey is concerned. And of course any decision to bomb the Abbey would be strictly a top-level one."

"But they don't know for sure," Page burst out. "If they *knew*—I speak the language like a native. Dressed like a peasant, I can get in there."

"Are you aware that of all the patrols we've tried—only one got to within even a dozen yards of the monastery enclosure?"

Page leaned over the desk, jaw thrust out. "Look, sir, one man can go where ten couldn't. I've been over every inch of that ground with a spotting 'scope—that's all I do is stare at that damned place. I've got a route all picked out."

"Yes. Well—" Dumphrey looked out, to where the Abbey thrust up into the wispy rain clouds. So close. "What is your plan of action, Lieutenant?"

"The First Royal Sussex are planning an assault on Point 593," Page said eagerly. "Under cover of their action, I'll move across Snakeshead Hill, keep away from Point 593, and cut straight across to the monastery. It's about a thousand yards."

"And if the First Sussex assault fails?"

Page frowned. "I'll be pinned down out there. I'll just have to sweat it out, sir. I'll move only at night. If it takes me a week, crawling all the way, I'll get there."

"Granted that," Dumphrey said, "there's the additional problem of getting back—and with the information, assuming you've gotten it."

"I'm not worried about getting back," Page said. "I'll take along a flare pistol. The second I know the Germans are using the Abbey—I'll give a signal—a red flare."

"And if the Germans aren't using the Abbey?"

His lips curled in a cold smile. "Then—there's no problem, is there, sir?"

"On the contrary," Dumphrey gave him a hard stare. "It's quite as important to know if they're *not* using it."

Page looked thoughtful, then he nodded. "Yes, I see where it would be. Okay, I'll take along a green flare, too. If it's clear—and I'm not able to make it back—then green is for negative."

Dumphrey studied him closely for a long moment, then he shook his head. "I admire your spirit, Page, and I think I understand your motives—but—no, I can't sanction such an operation."

Page remained rigid, obviously fighting for control. Suddenly he said, "You can't sanction it—but do you expressly forbid it, sir?"

"I—no," Dumphrey said reluctantly. "But I very strongly urge you not to attempt it."

Triumph gleamed in Page's eyes. "All I ask, sir, is that you keep a close lookout for a red flare above the monastery during the next few nights after the Royal Sussex assault."

Dumphrey stood up, hand extended. "I'll be watching," he said. "Just remember—green is for negative."

A thousand yards is less than a mile. But this thousand yards was a churned-up death trap of deep ravines, bare exposed ridges, covered with thickets of spiny brush, entanglements of barbed wire dangling with booby-traps, trip-wires leading to anti-personnel mines, with the deadly schuhmines sewn thickly in every patch of dirt. And every inch of the thousand yards was exposed to German fire.

The assault failed.

In a terrific rainstorm, while the Royal Sussex streamed along, a hundred yards to his right, Page had squirmed off to the left, cutting directly across the miniature no-man's land that led up the slopes of Monastery Hill. Almost instantly he'd been hit. The suicidal frontal attack by the Royal Sussex on Point 593 was halted by a swift barrage of fire. The high explosive shells sent a storm of flint-edged rock fragments skittering about. One of these fragments pierced Page's left arm, grating deep to the bone, smashing it, knocking him unconscious.

When the chilly rain revived him it was already a watery dawn. He was less than three hundred yards away from the furthest point held by the 4th Division atop Snakeshead Ridge.

The day was cold and foggy but he lay, motionless, weak from loss of blood and no food. As night approached, he moved on—not back to his own lines, but—toward the Monastery. Squirming under barbed wire, moving painfully, instinctively, across rock-strewn, corpse-littered ground, he followed the course he'd set for himself.

Feverish, aware only of his terrible desire to see the Abbey leveled, he moved up, up into the perimeter of a fifty or so yards that circled the great monastery; declared neutral ground by the Germans.

He felt the rough terrain give way suddenly to the smoothness of a dirt road; the only road, he knew, that led directly to the great main door of the Abbey. He lurched along the road, feeling for the bulky flare-pistol against his chest.

He staggered, stumbled, fell to his knees, the warm blood oozing down his side. The left half of his body was soggy with blood.

Just ahead, the great wall, pierced by the door, loomed, its top lost in the darkness. He was weak, terribly weak. The silence was eerie, the night seemed to thicken and coagulate about his head, pressing down on his chest. He gasped for breath. He lay there, alongside the road, his head roaring, seeming to swell and diminish with each heartbeat.

Suddenly he froze. The great door creaked open; the hard ringing of boots thudding on terrazo inside the Abbey was clearly audible. Men were approaching. The door slammed shut behind them. He crouched as they came near; matches flared, dim in the foggy night, as cigarettes were lit. He sucked in his breath.

Germans. Jack-booted, field-gray greatcoats; guns slung; bayonets at waist, one, even, with grenades clipped to belt. Boots stamping arrogantly in the packed dirt, they passed within inches of him, arguing, talking in loud careless gutturals. One walked alone, an officer. In a moment they were past and below; a truck motor roared, gears shifted and it moved down the hill out of hearing.

Germans. Coming out of the Abbey. Here on what they claimed was sanctified ground. He'd been right. Hate, savage and hot, flooded through him. He fumbled under his torn saggy jacket, feeling for the flare pistol—the pistol he'd loaded with the red flare before he left his own lines.

It took all his feeble strength to lift the heavy pistol. His head was roaring. Flecks of flame seemed to dance before his eyes. He had an overwhelming impulse to lie down, to sleep, never to waken again. Moving like a man under water, he raised the pistol and concentrated on pulling the trigger. It seemed to him that the whole world was bathed in fiery red as he slumped over, unconscious.

He awoke in a room filled with quiet motionless bodies. A low-ceilinged room, damp, with stone floor and sweating walls. A dim candle gave scant light. A monk, in rough cowl and hood slipped silently from one to another of the bodies lying on the floor, making the sign of the cross over them, murmuring rapid Latin. An awful stench filled the room. An occasional low moan came from one or another of the motionless bodies.

Page tried to sit up and discovered that his left arm was bound tightly to his body—a professional job. He was wearing the rough robe of the Benedictine lay brother. His wristwatch and shoes were missing. Also, the flare pistol and remaining green flare. He was wearing plain open sandals; his feet were freezing.

He peered around, and with a chill of horror noticed a pile of crudely made coffins against one wall.

A small padded figure approached and bent over him, and suddenly long auburn hair slipped from under a kerchief; a pair of great luminous eyes in a thin pinched face glowed down at him. He saw that it was a young girl; a small thin girl grotesquely padded with layer upon layer of ragged clothing. Still, her brow was broad, there was a calm serenity in her eyes that Da Vinci captured so well in the Mona Lisa. She was twelve or thirteen.

She put a small hand on his forehead, then leaned closer, watching him gravely.

"You have no fever," she said, her voice curiously hoarse. "You are one of the lucky ones."

He struggled to rise and she helped him half sit up. He looked about the room filled with the terrible still forms.

"What is this? Where am I?"

"You are in the Abbey," she said matter-of-factly. "It is the fever. They are dead—or dying."

Her name, she told him, was Marina. Orphaned, she had come in earlier in the month, one of the two hundred or so refugees, driven from the caves of Monte Cassino by the saturation shelling of the Allies. They'd swarmed into the monastery, in which there were only six monks, including the aged Abbot, a secular priest, and a handful of sick refugee peasants—those who'd been too ill to flee when the Germans had ordered the place evacuated before the first great battle.

The water supply was tainted, apparently. There was too little food. The monks did what they could, but the inevitable occurred: Disease broke out. People died, falling in every nook and cranny of the vast labyrinthine corridors, adding to the pestilence.

It was a burial party, sneaking out of the gate in the predawn hours, before the shelling commenced, which had stumbled across him and brought him inside, at the insistence of Dom Agostino, the young monk now bent wearily over the sick and dying. The refugees had taken Page's shoes and most of his miserable clothing. It was Dom Agostino who'd covered his nakedness with the rough monk's habit.

"Why don't the Germans help?" Page said angrily.

She shook her head. "They did before—but now they aren't allowed near the Monastery."

He stared at her. She looked back, her large eyes innocent.

The silent monk, Dom Agostino, approached and leaned over him. He was young, Page saw, nearly his own age, and his face was drawn, his eyes bright, feverish-looking.

"He has no fever," Marina said softly to the monk. "The Englishman will live."

Page jerked upright, wincing at the sudden tearing pain that brought black spots swimming before his eyes.

"Why did you call me an Englishman?" he said harshly.

The monk pressed gently on his shoulders. "You talked much during your fever—in English. And your boots—no peasant has such boots. And the strange pistol."

"Where is it?" Page asked. "Don't let the Germans see it."

"It is in a safe place," Dom Agostino said. "There are no Germans here."

"But—I saw them, last night," Page said. "Four of them, coming out of here."

Dom Agostino shook his head. "You have been here three nights and two days already." He hesitated. "Ah—three nights ago. Oberlieutenant Kestler and some men were here. They are stationed below. Kestler came only to obtain the signature of the Abbot on some receipts for certain archives that were sent to Rome some weeks ago. He will not be back."

"There must be others," Page insisted. "The Germans must be using this place as an observatory. It wouldn't take many—one or two men with radios is enough. They could be hidden anywhere in a hundred places and you'd never even know it."

Dom Agostino looked at him wearily. "No, there is only one entrance. If any came through it, I would have known. Those that came, left. If there were any here now, I would tell you."

Beyond, a man cried out thickly and Dom Agostino turned, ran a shaking hand over his glistening face, then slowly moved off, threading his way through the bodies on the floor.

Page stared after the exhausted sick monk, then he looked around the dank immense stone room. From somewhere, far below, he heard the tolling of a bell, then the faint sound of voices, chanting an antiphonal hymn. Thunder rolled and crashed dimly and for the first time he realized that it must still be raining.

Three days he'd been here. And still the place was intact. Which meant they were waiting for the weather to clear.

He stood up, feeling again that nightmarish feeling he'd had when he lay alongside the road. He was sick; very sick, but it didn't matter. Nothing mattered but the *knowing*.

He beckoned to Marina, and said, "Help me. I've got to get outside. I want to search the whole monastery."

"But it is dangerous above," she said. "Shells fall there. And— you are sick."

He roared at her, a weak sound, but she shrank from him. Suddenly timid, she found him a piece of wood—a fragment left over from the building of the coffins, and leaning on her, using the wood as a cane, Page slowly ascended the damp marble stairs. Up, through echoing cold corridors, empty; and finally, he came up into the main central courtyard.

"The Bramante Cloister," Marina murmured.

He stopped, staring, staring. Even under lowering clouds, the impact of grandeur was overwhelming. Under the steady downpour the great courtyard gleamed softly, serene—and empty. In the very center, a graceful pillared arch rose above a cistern. Above, on three sides, were soaring arches: the Loggia Del Paradiso, the gallery that surrounded this courtyard. They rose up through the mist, breathtakingly lovely. And empty.

On the fourth side, an enormous stone staircase, rising to yet another of five cloisters, and beyond the great Cathedral, with its altar pieces made by Michelangelo, its fabulous Catarinozzi organ, the frescoed dome soaring above the altar beneath which was the tomb of St. Benedict, founder, at rest here since the year 543 A.D.

Empty. All, all empty. A few groups of ragged refugees scurried through the vast echoing corridors, or crouched over small fires built in odd corners, with smoke darkening ancient marble mosaics. A few corpses, laid out decently, awaiting opportunity to get outside the walls for hurried burial.

Only these.

In his robe, his shattered arm limp against his body under the tight bandages, leaning heavily on the frightened young girl, Page moved from cloister to cloister, his heart thudding at the sight of the silent somber statues of the Popes and Kings in the Cloister of the Benefactors. Only the rain fell. Only the occasional distant crash of gunfire. The ancient Abbey was desolate, but eerily magnificent, brooding solemnly with its memories of the ages.

But no Germans. None. No radio post. No observatories. The

Germans had respected the sanctity of the Abbey, as they said they would. And finding this, he was filled with terrible anguish. *He had been wrong*.

The hate drained from him beneath the immemorial dignity of the Abbey. Anguish took its place. He had been wrong. He had acted in too much haste, and because of him, this fourteen-century-old monument of man's eternal quest for God would be destroyed, brought down, reduced to rubble.

He staggered back, down the endless echoing corridors, his head filled with a tremendous roaring, as though already the planes were overhead. He hurried, dragging Marina along, not hearing her frightened pleas for him to slow down.

He made his way down to the great room, far below the main level, and stumbling over moaning dying fever victims, he found Dom Agostino. The monk was half-slumped over on a bench, face extremely pale.

Page clutched the monk's robe. "Listen. Listen." He thought he was screaming, but it came out a hoarse whisper. "They are going to bomb the Abbey—as soon as the weather clears. The signal has already been given. I gave it. I'm an American. I came here to find out if the Germans were using this place. I gave the signal that they were. Do you understand?"

Suddenly Dom Agostino seemed to dwindle, to recede and become fuzzy, infinitely small. His face then swelled, loomed over him, became gigantic.

"You should not have gone out," the monk murmured. "You are very sick. The fever."

Page made a terrific effort to rise. "The pistol," he said feebly. "It's still not too late. The pistol. Green flare. Green is for negative. Give me the pistol."

The monk gently pressed him down against the rough mat; he had a sudden image of Marina, eyes wide, scary, bringing a cloth. The cloth was pressed to his forehead, cool; wonderfully cool.

"You mustn't worry," the monk's voice came from a great distance. "The pistol is in a safe place. Rest with God."

When Page awoke, his head was very clear. He felt weak, terribly weak; his shoulder a quivering mass of agony. He had a sense of much time having past; of a dim recollection of figures moving about him, a good deal of rushing and crying out. And of Marina, coming and going, her face pinched and thin, her eyes grown larger. He had no other memory of Dom Agostino, other than the quiet voice telling him the flare pistol was in a safe place.

He sat up, wincing. The room was freezing, and still. A dim light filtered down from above. There were still some bodies in the room, but the coffins were all gone. Dom Agostino was gone. Page tried to rise, but failed. From below, clearly audible, he heard the thin chanting of a few voices, and the tolling of a bell. He listened, realizing that there was no thunder. The air seemed fresh, and clear.

He tried twice before he could get to his feet. The silence was uncanny. Other than the dim murmuring of the monks chanting somewhere below, there was no sound. No refugees were about. He moved out, supporting himself by holding onto the cold damp walls. A breeze moved down the corridor, fresh, bracing. He rounded a turn and saw in the distance a crude coffin, with a candle alongside; several figures were huddled near it.

He approached closer and saw that Marina was kneeling before the coffin, praying. In the coffin, waxy hands clasping a rosary, was the wasted body of Dom Agostino.

Marina saw him and she rose, making the sign of the cross quickly. She hurried to him and took his good arm. ''We are all leaving,'' she said, her voice shaky. ''The Allies are going to bomb us—look.'' She pressed a leaflet into his hand. ''An airplane dropped many of these.''

Dazed, he stared at it, unable to fully comprehend the meaning of it at first. It was written in Italian, addressed simply, ''Italian Friends'':

> We have until now been careful to avoid bombarding Monte Cassino. The Germans have taken advantage of this. The battle is now closing in more and more around the sacred precincts. Against our will we are now obliged to direct our weapons against the Monastery itself. We warn you so that you may save yourself. Leave the Monastery at once. This warning is urgent. It is given for your own good.
>
> THE FIFTH ARMY

''Oh my God! What have I done?'' He stared wildly at her. ''When did they drop this?''

''Yesterday,'' Marina said. ''And early this morning, a German officer came. He told the Abbot that one of the paths leading to Highway Six would be opened to us from midnight tonight until dawn, tomorrow. We are all leaving.''

''Midnight—tonight?'' He looked instinctively at his wrist, forgetting that his watch was gone. ''What time is it now?''

''It is about three hours since daylight,'' she said.

''The weather—is it still raining?''

"No, it is clear and beautiful, finally," she said.

The flare pistol. If he could find it, there still might be time, even in broad daylight, to launch that green flare; to hope that Colonel Dumphrey would see it and interpret it correctly.

But the flare pistol was in a safe place, and the only one who knew where that safe place was lay dead in his coffin, face still and at peace. And watching Dom Agostino's calm features, Page heard, in the distance, the first faint hum of approaching bombers.

Without haste, the mourners lifted the coffin and moved off, walking down the steep flight that led deeper into the recesses of the Monastery.

The hum above became a drone, a sound of approaching implacable power. The first great flight came over, rigid, drawn along in beautiful geometric patterns, silver against the blue sky. The drone became a roar, a drumming surf sound, hypnotizing Page and Marina who clung to each other, staring into one another's eyes.

Tiny specks came free from the rigid pattern above, fell toward the Monastery, growing in size, whistling, and then they struck, erupting into glaring blasts, bringing down the thousand-year-old architecture in ugly jagged chunks.

The bombs fell. Down crashed the serenely lovely Bramante Cloister. Down into rubble tumbled the Loggia Del Paradiso. The Cathedral dome sagged, then abruptly collapsed with a sound louder, even, than the crashing bombs. Shattered beneath it lay the fabulous Michelangelo altar piece. Battered to bits were the organ pipes. Smashed to shards were the carved altar rails, the pews, hewed out of wood by pious loving hands, turned to dust these many centuries past. Gone the graceful fluted columns, the arched domes that had echoed to solemn prayer, that had rebuffed nine hundred years of sun and rain.

Marble dust rose in choking white clouds, and still the bombs fell. The first great flight moved off, their sound grew faint, then was lost. New sounds arose: the sliding crashing tumbling sounds of marble, and beneath the rubble, groans and cries of the refugees—those who had sought sanctuary in the Cathedral and now lay crushed beneath it.

Yells, outcries, as refugees took advantage of the lull to flee the monastery, chancing the mine fields, the mortar and artillery that lay outside these yet-unbreached walls.

And below, the slow muted Gregorian chant arose, the ageless *Opus Dei*, the divine office in praise of God.

Page stood there, just below the zone of destruction, holding Marina, feeling the rapid uneven beat of her heart. They looked at one another, the soldier from America, the young girl from Italy. Her eyes were wide, her face pale with the shock, the sacrilege.

"Where is God?" she whispered. "Is God dead?"

The medium bombers came next, sweeping over low and fast, accurately placing their lighter bombs upon the rubble that the greater bombs had left. Once again the rolling thunder of explosions blasted without stop. Clouds of gritty powdered stone rose. There were more crashes, more falling statuary.

A deep wide fissure appeared in the west wall; the ten-foot-thick wall that had witnessed the storming of sandaled feet of the Lombards, had seen the fall of the Caesars, and heard the hail of the conquering Saracens. The stones dropped out, there was a peculiar grinding creaking sound, and then the entire west roof collapsed.

The roof came down, carrying with it several levels of the lower reaches. And just as the last of the bombers moved off, the ceiling above Page and Marina collapsed; a huge stone fell between them, shattering his right leg, wrenching her from his arms, rolling her to the precise spot where a tremendous cascade of limestone blocks fell seconds later, burying her, killing her instantly. . . .

"And when we found him in Colloquio, at the Red Cross station some time after the fall of Cassino," Dumphrey concluded, "Page was desperately ill, suffering from the after effects of shock. Among other things," he wheeled the little car around the final turn of the Monte Cassino road and the great door of the restored Abbey was before us, "Lt. Anthony Page had lost the use of his voice. He was mute."

Dumphrey parked the car and we got out, standing, silent, looking at the immense high wall, restored again, gleaming in the hot Italian sunshine. Three times, in all those centuries, these walls had been breached—but never the foundations. Patiently, stone by stone, they'd been rebuilt upon the everlasting foundations laid down by Benedict, in 523 A.D.

"Call it coincidence—call it miraculous," Dumphrey said, as we stood outside the great door, "but some very odd effects of the bombing were noted. For one thing, the original cell which St. Benedict himself had occupied fourteen centuries before was found intact. Also, at the foot of the tomb which holds the remains of the saint, an enormous artillery shell was found. It had landed there at some time during the shelling which followed the bombardment—but had never exploded."

We went through the impressive entrance door and into the central courtyard, cool, serenely majestic, and I said, "How very terrible that one man should have borne upon his conscience the destruction of such magnificent buildings."

"Actually," Dumphrey said, pausing, looking about, "I did all I could to convince Page that no flare had ever been seen on that night—or any subsequent night after his entry into the Abbey."

I looked at Dumphrey in surprise. "But—is that true, or were you merely trying to ease the suffering of a dying man?"

"The very question Page asked," Dumphrey said. "Of course it's true. And incidentally, Anthony Page didn't die. As for the decision to bomb the Abbey, that had already been made by General Freyberg, of the 2nd New Zealand Corps, and acceded to by his superior, General Mark Clark, of the Fifth Army.

"As I learned later, the decision to bomb had been made the very day Page volunteered to enter the Abbey. Actually, all that the Air Force was waiting for was a twenty-four-hour advance forecast of decent weather—which wasn't forthcoming for some days."

"Did you finally manage to convince Page?" I asked.

Dumphrey shook his head. "He was certain he'd fired that flare, even though he was crawling in a coma at the time, and that the firing had influenced the decision to bomb. There was only one way he could ever discover the truth: find the 'safe place' in which Dom Agostino had secreted the pistol. *He had to know*."

Dumphrey hesitated. "It was Marina's death," he said softly, "which weighed so heavily upon him—that and the answer to her last words—that tragic question: 'Is God Dead?' "

I looked around at the massive building that surrounded us. It stretched for hundreds of yards along the mountaintop. Then I pictured it as it must have been after the destruction—an enormous pile of rubble, extending far down beneath our feet.

"An impossible task," I said. "It could never be found."

"Impossible?" Dumphrey smiled. "You forget that Page once crawled through a thousand yards of hell with a shattered shoulder—and for a reason considerably less important to him. He took his discharge in Rome and then began to delve in the archives at the Vatican, looking for the original plans of the Abbey. He found them; became something of an expert on them, in fact. He volunteered his services here after the war, when rebuilding was started. Of course his object was to find Dom Agostino's 'safe place.' And he found it."

"The pistol—was it there?"

"Oh yes," Dumphrey looked off to where a monk approached us hurriedly. "Page found the flare pistol, and his wristwatch, and even the green flare—all in quite good condition."

He broke off as the monk, an assistant prior, a silent strong-jawed old man in plain robe, with cowl keeping his face in deep shadow, hurried up to us. He grasped Dumphrey's hand in an expression of sincere friendship. Dumphrey introduced me, and as we walked along yet another Cloister, the prior talked in swift Italian to Dumphrey, and in turn, Dumphrey translated.

"Here," he said, pointing to where a row of statues stood, intact, seemingly untouched, "these are seventeen statues of the Benefactors that had been almost totally destroyed. They were put back together with the original pieces that were found by sifting through mountains of rubble."

"An incredibly detailed job," I said. "You must indeed have dedicated men here."

Dumphrey translated and the old monk nodded. He pointed off to where a group of workers and lay brothers were fitting delicate bits of marble to form a frieze on the capital of an Ionic column. Among them, a monk, taller than the others, wearing plain rough robe and cowl, with feet thrust into rude sandals, held a blueprint of sorts tucked up under his left arm which seemed oddly bent inward, as though it had been broken and mended badly. With his right hand, he gestured upward.

"We have many dedicated men," Dumphrey translated the prior's words, "and they work solely for the love and greater glory of God. Men from all walks of life; some of them men of very great energy and talent—like Brother Anthony, there, who has a most extensive knowledge of the original architecture of the Abbey."

Dumphrey broke off interpreting and said something in Italian to our guide. The prior hesitated, then looked keenly at me. He finally smiled, nodded, and called to the tall monk he'd pointed out as Brother Anthony.

Brother Anthony turned and looked at us for a long moment. Then he began slowly to walk toward us and we saw that his right leg was cripped badly. He walked with a noticeable limp.

He approached and took Dumphrey's outstretched hand in a firm clasp. They looked at one another in silence. Brother Anthony's face, darkly tanned, was gaunt; his eyes, in the shadow of the cowl, were deeply blue, astonishingly brilliant.

The prior spoke briefly to him and Brother Anthony turned his gaze on me. The strength and calm of his face was striking. "I'm happy to meet a fellow countryman," he said. It seemed strange to hear an American accent coming from this strong person in humble Benedictine robes. He inclined his head courteously to us then limped back to where the group of workers were preparing a scaffold.

The old prior murmured something to Dumphrey and Dumphrey nodded, concealing a smile.

"The prior wants me to tell you that Brother Anthony is of American descent," Dumphrey said dryly. "But—I gather you've already guessed that—and who he is."

I flashed a quick look back at Brother Anthony. "Page?"

"Yes," Dumphrey said, "Brother Anthony is the man I've been telling you about—the former Lt. Anthony Page."

"But—you said he was mute."

"He was—until the moment he found the flare pistol, there in Dom Agostino's 'safe place.' He broke open the pistol—and inside was the red flare he'd inserted so many years before—and never had the strength to fire."

Dumphrey looked out through a high narrow window, piercing the stone wall, framing a view of the Liri valley far below Monastery Hill, with the River Rapido, a thin shining ribbon lost in the blue haze.

"He found his voice then—but he found something else, too," Dumphrey said. "He found peace, and the realization that he wanted to dedicate his life to the restoration of the Abbey as one answer to Marina's last question. And—he has."

HARRY BROWN

A Walk in the Sun

THE LIEUTENANT HAD been wounded while they were still on the water. He was a slight, dark man named Rand, rather silly, and if he hadn't been doing something silly at the time he might never have been wounded. He had taken out his glasses and was leaning against the side of the landing barge, trying to focus on some firing off to the left. It was the first of the firing. Evidently one of the shore batteries had decided something was wrong and they had sent over a couple of shells. One of the destroyers had replied, a cruiser had joined in, and some batteries farther along the coast had also opened up. No one was hitting anything, and the whole action was taking place about three miles away.

The gun flashes were spectacular, however, and Lieutenant Rand had taken out his field glasses to watch what was going on. Not that he could see anything. That was the silly part of it. He might have been able to pick up the silhouette of a destroyer for a second, but by the time he could have adjusted his glasses the destroyer would have zigzagged out of range. The destroyers weren't waiting around for the lieutenant. Nevertheless he stuck his head up in the air and tried to pick up one of the ships, or possibly one of the shore batteries. Of course, disregarding the fact that it was a pointless thing to do, there seemed to be no danger in it. The firing was some miles off, the barge was still about twenty-four hundred yards from shore, and the night, or rather early morning, was dark. There were no stars. And in a way it was a natural act on Lieutenant Rand's part. He was bored and he was nervous. He had been in the barge for some hours, and it was not the most comfortable place in the world. As the time of landing approached a growing tension was added to nervousness and discomfort. The men's mouths were dry. Sounds magnified themselves. The dark closed in like a smotherer's pillow.

Lieutenant Rand, a wry young man, had a dry natural curiosity, one that manifested itself in a love of facts. He had often expressed regret in mess that he was not in the artillery, because the computation of trajectory and like subjects fascinated him. Before the war he had been a C.P.A. in Hartford, Connecticut, and had he come a little later in the draft, or a little earlier, he might have found himself as a Finance officer in some quiet army backwater. As things turned out, however, he came just at the right time to be sent to the Infantry, and then to OCS, and then, much too hurriedly for his ordered mind, to the Mediterranean. He was new to the company, replacing Lieutenant Grimes, who had been picked off by a sniper while climbing a wall in a small town near Gela, in Sicily. The company had gone through the whole Sicilian campaign short an officer, until Lieutenant Rand had finally caught up with it in Messina. This landing operation was the first action he had ever seen, and the guns that were flashing over on the left were the first serious guns he had ever heard. Therefore, to his logical mind it was logical that he watch them.

One of the shore batteries evidently decided that there was a whole fleet behind the cruiser and the destroyer. Its fire moved aimlessly over the sea in the direction of the barges, as though the shells were feeling for something. No one paid a great deal of attention to either the shells or Lieutenant Rand. As far as the men were concerned the shells could take care of themselves, and so could the lieutenant. When one burst very near the barge the men took it without rancor. They knew that the shells were disinterested; they were not aimed for them. A man can always tell when a shell is looking for him. A shell that is seeking a man out doesn't whine. It snarls. So when the shell struck near the barge some of the men said 'Bastards,'' impersonally and quite without feeling, and let it go at that. And when the next shell, almost immediately afterwards, struck some three hundred yards to the right, they knew that there was no need to worry.

Lieutenant Rand had his glasses to his eyes when the shell struck, trying to adjust them with the thumb and middle finger of his left hand. He had pushed his helmet back on his head, because the steel rim kept getting in the way of the eyepieces, and it annoyed him. He was aware of a great mushrooming whiteness in front of him, and then someone pinched his left cheek very hard. Lieutenant Rand said ''Oh,'' and turned around to see who was pinching him. Then he slid slowly down to a sitting position.

Sergeant Porter, who had been standing behind the lieutenant, felt a steady pressure on the calf of one leg. When he looked to find out what it was he could dimly make out the lieutenant sitting on the floor of the barge, his hands hanging down at his sides. At first he thought that Rand had gone to sleep, and for a moment he felt annoyed that he should choose to sleep when it was almost time to pile out. Then he remembered that a moment before Lieutenant Rand had been standing up looking over the side. A shell had hit quite close, too. No one could go to sleep that quickly, unless he'd been without sleep for days. Sergeant Porter bent down by the lieutenant.

"Anything the matter, sir?" he asked.

"Oh," Lieutenant Rand said. "Oh. Oh." The words were more a surprised grunt than anything else. The lieutenant did not move his arms.

Cautiously Sergeant Porter ran his hands over Rand's chest. He felt nothing. Then he touched his face.

"Jesus," he said. "All gone."

He wiped his hand on his thigh. "Pete," he said. "Hey, Pete."

Staff Sergeant Halverson came over. "What's the matter?"

"Shell splinter got the lieutenant. Smashed his face all to hell."

Halverson bent down. "I can't see anything," he said.

"I can feel it," Sergeant Porter said. "Messy. I think it took his whole face away."

"Where's your flashlight?"

"You can't shine a light out here, Pete."

"Oh. Oh," Lieutenant Rand said. He caught his breath twice.

"I can shine a light if I have to shine a light. Where's the thing?"

Porter took his flashlight out of the hip pocket of his fatigues and passed it to Halverson. "Cover over him," Halverson said. "I'm just going to take a quick look."

They bent over Rand, their helmets almost touching. Halverson switched on the light. "I told you," Sergeant Porter said. Lieutenant Rand's left cheek and eye were covered with blood. It was impossible to make out whether or not the eye was still there. Even by the brief, dim glare of the flashlight the two sergeants could see that a good part of his cheek had been carried away. Jagged white bits of bone, splinters from a smashed zygoma, stuck out at several places. Blood dripped down on his shoulder. Lieutenant Rand's mouth kept opening and closing, like the gills of a fish out of water. His good eye was wide open.

"Douse that light," somebody hissed.

Staff Sergeant Halverson switched off the flashlight. "Go get that god-damned First Aid man. What's his name? McWilliams. He might as well start earning his money."

"Where is he?" Porter asked.

"Down in the stern," Halverson said. "I saw him down in the stern."

Porter picked his way among the men toward the stern. The night was so dark that men five yards away from the lieutenant did not know he had been wounded. There was a silent cluster of cramped figures in the stern. "Where's McWilliams?" Porter said. "Where's McWilliams, the First Aid man?"

"Who's that?" a man said.

"Sergeant Porter."

One of the figures rose to his feet and broke with the darkness. "Here I am, Sergeant," McWilliams said. "You want me?"

"The lieutenant's hurt up front," Porter said. "Sergeant Halverson said for you to go up."

"What's the matter with him, Sergeant?" McWilliams wanted to know. He spoke in a slow, dispassionate drawl.

"Get the hell up and see," Porter said. "You want me to bring him down here?"

"I was just asking," said McWilliams. He moved toward the front of the barge.

"What's the matter with the lieutenant, Sergeant?" a man asked. "Old rockin' chair get him?" Porter recognized the voice as that of Rivera, a machine gunner.

"God-damn shell got him," he said.

Rivera whistled. "No kidding?" a man said. "Honest to God?" said another. "That's the trouble with these tubs," Rivera said. "They only make the armor plate six inches thick. That wouldn't keep out a BB from a BB Daisy air gun. You meant that one that hit so close?"

Porter nodded his head wearily, then remembered that no one could see him nodding in the dark. "Yeah," he said.

"He dead?" Rivera asked.

"Not yet," Sergeant Porter said. 'He had his head over the side. He was looking through the binoculars."

"That's a Purple Heart, sure as hell," Rivera said. "How'd you like to have a Purple Heart, Jakie?"

"Depends where I got the Purple Heart," Private Friedman said. "In the leg, okay. In the guts, no."

"A Purple Heart means a nice quiet trip to Jersey City," Rivera said. "I would like a nice quiet trip to Jersey City."

"I'd like a nice quiet trip anywheres," said Private Judson. "I ain't had a quiet trip since this war started. Jersey City will do fine."

"It blew the hell out of the side of his head," Sergeant Porter said. He felt guilty, as though Lieutenant Rand's wound was a secret that he shouldn't be telling. He knew he should go back and see if there was anything he could do, but he did not want to go back. He did not want to help Halverson. If the lieutenant was going to die, he was going to die, and there was nothing Eddie Porter could do about it. Nothing in the world.

"In the head, no," Private Friedman said. "I don't want a Purple Heart in the head."

"Joey Sims got a Purple Heart in the head," Rivera said. "I bet to Christ he'll look better when they're through with him than you do now."

"It depends on the position," Private Friedman said. "Position is everything in life."

"Is Sergeant Halverson in command now, Sergeant?" Rivera asked.

"He knows what to do," Porter said. Halverson had been in command before, after they lost Lieutenant Grimes. Halverson had been in command almost from Gela all the way to Messina. Halverson had done all right. If the captain had liked him a little more, he probably would have been commissioned in the field. But the captain had preferred to hang on and wait for a replacement. The platoon had had very bad luck with lieutenants. First Grimes, and now Rand. If Halverson had got the breaks he might have been sitting very pretty right now.

Porter was just as glad that Halverson hadn't got the breaks, for Porter did not like Halverson. He was afraid of him. Halverson was cold and competent, and Porter distrusted coldness and competence. Even in a war, he felt, the human element should enter in. He did not, of course, think of it just in that way, nor could he have phrased it in such a fashion if he had been called upon to do so. There was enough coldness and competence in the machines, the tanks, and the planes. Nothing was colder than a battened-down tank moving over a field. It was cold, heartless, brainless, but it was alive. It could reason and it could kill. Sergeant Porter was afraid of tanks in the same way he was afraid of Sergeant Halverson. Sergeant Porter was not a good soldier, not because he was afraid, but because he was afraid of the wrong things. All soldiers, unless they have gone berserk, are afraid, but there are qualities and grades of fear. There is more to war than the rifle and the knife thrust in the dark.

The knot of men lapsed into silence in the darkness. They really had not wanted to talk, but they had forced themselves to say something. Talking was a form of bravado. If a man said something, no matter what it was, it seemed to him that he was saying: "Here I am, very calm, very collected. Nothing's going to happen to me. The rest of the company's going to be wiped out, but nothing's going to happen to me. See, I can talk. I can form sentences. Do you think I could make conversation if I knew I was going to die?" Yet every man, inwardly, had a hard core of doubt that rested in the pit of his stomach and threatened to disgorge itself at any moment. Their voices, when they talked, were strange, but none of them noticed the strangeness, because when each man spoke his own voice sounded odd, and so it all seemed correct somehow. If a phonograph record of the men's voices had been made then and played back to them later, not one of them would have recognized himself. They would have thought it was a joke—a very elaborate joke. And in a way it would have been.

Sergeant Porter worked his way back toward the bow of the barge. Once he stepped on a man's hand, and the man swore at him. Porter paid no attention.

Three or four of the platoon were gathered around Lieutenant Rand. Halverson was leaning against the side of the barge. In the darkness McWilliams was sprinkling sulfa on the wound. "How is he?" Porter asked. Halverson shrugged in the dark. "He's stopped his noise," he said. "I thought he was going to say something a while back. He tried to say something. Where were you?"

"Down there," Porter said.

"I wanted you."

"What for?"

"It doesn't matter now," Halverson said. "Stick around."

"You going to take over?" Sergeant Porter asked.

"I've got to see the captain," Halverson said. "As soon as we land I've got to see him. That is, if I can find him. I can't take over without seeing him."

Porter tried to make out Halverson's expression, but all he could see was shadows. He knew that Halverson was looking at him, and the thought made him frown, made him want to say something. He didn't like to have people looking at him. It made him nervous. It always had.

"Do you know what to do?" he asked.

"There's a house," Halverson said. "A farm. Three or four houses, as a matter of fact. That's where we're going."

"Pretty hard to find, isn't it?"

"That's the objective. It's on the map. There's a road from the beach leads right past it."

"How far?"

"A hell of a way. Six miles."

The frown deepened on Porter's face. "What the hell do they expect on a beach, a reception committee?" he said.

"That's the story," Halverson said. "That's all I know. How's it coming, Mac?"

"All right, I guess," McWilliams said. "We better get him to a doctor, though, or he ain't going to be pretty any more. He might not be alive any more either."

"Bad, hey?" Halverson said.

"I guess so," McWilliams said. "I guess he got a pretty bad shock, too. He's trying to talk all the time. Can't you hear him?"

The two sergeants listened. "I don't hear anything," Porter said.

"It ain't words," McWilliams said. "It's just talk."

"Where are his binoculars?" Halverson wanted to know.

"They must have fallen overboard," Porter said. "I didn't hear them fall."

Halverson bent down. "Is he comfortable, Mac?"

"He wouldn't know whether he was comfortable or not," McWilliams said. "No sense in moving him, though. He'll be all right where he is."

"That's good," Halverson said. He rose to his feet. "Hell of a thing."

"He don't mind," said McWilliams.

The whole barge knew that the lieutenant had been wounded, but no one seemed terribly interested. It was not that they didn't care. It was simply that most of them had seen a lot of death, and death, unless it was of a really special variety, was not something that a man got up and moved around to investigate. There was no sense in getting up and walking over just to see a wounded man, even if you knew him quite well. And besides, the lieutenant was new. He hadn't been with the company more than—how long was it?—oh, two weeks or so. Not really long enough to get acquainted, anyway. He hadn't really slugged it out in the field with them. He didn't know anything about the Kaserine or Bizerte or any of those places. He was, as a matter of fact, a visitor who had come to stay a little while and then had gone away. The company wouldn't ever see him again, in all probability, nor would his platoon, which probably knew him better than anyone else. After all, he was lucky. It was quick in and quick out for Lieutenant Rand.

"What did the lieutenant do before he got in the army?" Private Archimbeau asked. Not that he really cared. He just wanted to make conversation. He wanted to talk.

"He was a civilian," Private Trasker said. "A lousy civilian."

"You kill me," Private Archimbeau said.

"He was a business man," said Private Cousins. "He worked in an office."

"I worked in an office," Private Trasker said. "But I wasn't no business man."

"The whole god-damned army's made up of business men," said an unidentified voice.

"You kill me," said Private Archimbeau. "He'll be a business man in 1958, when we're fighting the Battle of Tibet. I got the facts down cold. They'll put him on a nice hospital ship and take him to a nice hospital and give him a couple of medals and take him home and give him his walking papers. Then he'll go back to business while we fight the Battle of Tibet. I got the facts."

"Maybe he'll die," Private Cousins said.

"Nobody dies," said Private Trasker.

The lieutenant's wound worried Corporal Tyne. Not that Rand was a good man or anything like that; not at all. Rand, as far as Corporal Tyne knew, wasn't a very good man at all. Competent, maybe—but not good. In the army the word "good" is a superlative. A good officer is the Merriwell type. He always gets where he wants to go, and he keeps his casualties down. He knows when to be hard and when to relax. He will bear down on his men in barracks, but when he's out in the field he will call them Joe and Charlie and swear at them and pat them on the back as though he were the coach of a football team. Lieutenant Rand had never called any of his men Joe or Charlie, nor had he sworn at them or patted them on the back. He had taken them as they came, rather like figures on an adding machine, and he had always seemed slightly surprised that they added up to human beings. Rand was a quiet, aloof man who had a habit of doing the wrong thing quietly and aloofly. He hadn't really been at home in the Infantry, even in the little time he had been in the company. You had to be calm, and Rand wasn't calm, even though he walked measuredly and never smiled and ate with a solemn, rather annoying preciseness. If Rand had been a calm man he would never have stuck his head over the side of the board and tried to make out the firing.

But he had, and there he was, sitting down and gasping, his cheek torn to shreds. That put it on Halverson again. Tyne absent-mindedly pushed his helmet, the straps of which hung loosely on either side of his face, down hard. It gave him a warm, comfortable feeling. Halverson would be all right. He knew his way around. He had done a nice job in Sicily, keeping his eyes open, doing the right thing, never getting out of line. Corporal Tyne admired Halverson; he didn't like him, but he admired him. For what he did, he was a good man.

"You should have seen his face." It was Sergeant Porter.

"I've seen faces before." Tyne said.

"Yeah, but the first time, before anything had happened. The guy may die, Bill."

Corporal Tyne said nothing. He studied Sergeant Porter's figure, looming before him. Porter was a good three inches taller than he was, and heavier. Fatter, too. His face, had Tyne been able to see it, would have been a cross between a thug's and a child's. Sergeant Porter's eyes always looked just a little frightened, but he had the heavy jaw of a preliminary boy. He was a beautiful drill sergeant, but he seemed to lack something in the field. Two hundred years ago, when battles had been parades, Eddie Porter would have done all right, but not now. He could not quite seem to connect the facts of battle in his mind, did not seem to realize that men no longer marched into machine guns, that they went in or, better, around them on their bellies, hugging every blade of grass or pebble that would give them a bit of cover. It was amazing how big a blade of grass could seem when the bullets were cutting over one's head. Sergeant Porter didn't understand that. Sergeant Porter, Tyne felt, did not comprehend war; it had passed him by and gone over his head, the way the bullets had. He did not comprehend it, and he was afraid of it.

"Halverson's taking over again," Sergeant Porter said.

"I thought so."

"I don't like it. We don't know where we're going. Halverson only has a vague idea of where we're going. Some farmhouse, that's all he knows. Some farmhouse six miles up a road. He doesn't know what's there or why. Probably the beach is mined."

"There shouldn't be any mines up here," Tyne said. "It should be like getting out of bed."

Porter felt in his pockets, searching for nothing. Through one pocket he scratched his thigh gently.

"He's got to see the captain," he said, "before he takes over. No one knows where the captain is. He might be in any god-damned barge on the ocean. They can't keep formation in the dark. I'm nervous, Bill."

"So am I. So's everybody. He'll find the captain, all right."

Corporal Tyne looked at the illuminated dial on his watch. "Nearly time," he said.

The lieutenant had stopped trying to talk, and his head had sunk down. "Stay with him, Mac," Staff Sergeant Halverson said. "You can pick us up later. when it gets light you'll see a road running from the beach. We'll be up that road."

"Can't we leave him here?" McWilliams asked. "I might get lost. I don't want to go walking around by myself up any damned road."

"Stay with him," said Halverson.

"I wish to God those guns would stop," McWilliams said.

Sergeant Halverson looked at his watch. Nearly time. He started to work his way toward the stern of the boat. "Hoist tail," he said, over and over again. "Hoist tail." The barge perceptibly slackened speed. The men began to get to their feet. A few of them attempted to stretch. "Porter," Halverson called softly. "Where the hell are you, Porter?" "Here I am," Porter said. He moved toward the sound of Halverson's voice. Tyne followed him. "Listen, Porter," Halverson said. "Take them a hundred yards up from the barge and hit the dirt. I'll go find the captain and then come back. That's all you have to do. Take them up a hundred yards and then hit dirt. It doesn't matter where you are. I don't care if it's in a pigpen."

"Okay, Hal," Porter said.

The platoon gathered around Halverson. "Most of you know that the lieutenant got wounded," he said, "and until I see the captain I'm taking over. You know what to do. Just go with Sergeant Porter and do what he tells you. Understand?"

There was a soft, almost inaudible murmuration of voices. Off to the left the naval guns and the shore batteries fell suddenly silent.

"Cold water," said Private Rivera. "Every time it's cold water. Son of a bitch."

"I'll take you in in a wheel chair," Private Friedman said. "You and your Purple Heart." He began to hum softly.

"My mama done tol' me,
When I was in knee pants,
My mama done tol' me,—
'Son ...'"

"Bing Crosby," said Private Rivera.

"That's what they call me," Friedman said.

"I wish to Christ I was home in bed," said Private Judson.

Corporal Tyne went over to the lieutenant, unstrapped his map case, and threw it over his own shoulder. It was funny that no one had thought to do that. There was always something, some little thing. Tyne didn't know what was in the map case, but there must be something.

He looked out over the bow of the barge at the approaching land. It seemed very flat, very level, but far in the distance he could see hills. Light was beginning to appear over the crest of the hills. When he had been a small boy, at summer camp, Corporal Tyne, along with two hundred and fifty other boys, had had to take a dip in cold water before breakfast.

2

THEY GOT OFF the barges into water that was waist deep but surprisingly warm. They kept to one side of the barge so that Lieutenant Rand wouldn't be disturbed. Halverson was the first out, and Porter followed him. As he hit the water Porter gasped, and then he realized that it wasn't as cold as he had thought it was going to be, and that the gasp had been purely automatic. All up and down the beach there was a clank of steel on steel and the scurrying of men.

"I'm going to find the captain now," Halverson said. "Get 'em up there, won't you, Porter?"

"Sure thing," Porter said.

Halverson disappeared in the darkness off to the left, the water gurgling around his waist.

Tyne jumped down beside Porter. ''Take up the rear, will you, Bill?'' Porter said. ''See they all get off. We'll take it in single file.'' He started wading toward shore. Archimbeau got off the barge and followed him, and one by one the men hit the water. Tyne, standing by the prow, counted them as they splashed down. Twenty-four. Twenty-five. ''Last one in's a bastard,'' Rivera said as he hopped off. Fifty-two, counted Tyne. One missing. McWilliams. That was all right. ''Watch him, Mac,'' he called into the barge, and then began wading toward shore himself.

The landing was going beautifully. Not a shot had been fired from the shore. Evidently the enemy had been caught cold; they thought it was a fleet moving up the coast. They *must* have thought that. But whatever they thought, they'd be sending the planes over pretty soon. Tyne hadn't heard a plane all night. As he walked up the beach away from the water, following Judson, the last man out, he listened to the sounds going on around him. Men were moving everywhere. He heard a sudden high-pitched laugh that was cut short almost as soon as it began. Somewhere two helmets struck each other.

The silence was bad, very bad. If there had been firing they would at least have known that men were around, but in the silence they could only guess and expect the worst. It might be an ambush, a trap. It might be anything. The enemy might be fifty miles away or they might be lying around the beachhead waiting, with grenades and artillery and flame-throwers and tanks and God only knew what else. If a machine gun should start up, a man would know what to do. But a man could not fight a vacuum.

The beach was pebbly and rough. Twice Sergeant Porter tripped on stones, and once he almost fell headlong. He was walking fast because he did not want to spend too much time on the beach, where anything might happen. He wanted to get a hundred yards up from the water and then hit the ground. He still believed that the beach was mined, and as he walked he clenched his teeth and held his hand very tightly around his carbine. He tripped on another stone. ''Jesus,'' he said.

An average pace was thirty inches. That made a hundred yards about a hundred and twenty paces. He had figured it out back on the barge. It was hard to concentrate on the mines and the distance and everything else all at the same time. The rocks on the beach grew larger and then suddenly broke off, at a slight rise, into high grass. Porter saw the dim outline of a tree. He counted off pace 103, and he stuck his hand out in front of him, on the chance that a tree might suddenly rear before his face. At pace 120 he stopped. "We'll hold here," he said aloud, to no one in particular. "Hit the dirt." Archimbeau hit the dirt. As the men came up they fanned out to right and left and sat down.

When Tyne came up to Sergeant Porter the sergeant was still standing, with Sergeant Hoskins, of B Squad, beside him. "All here," Tyne said. "Good," said Porter. "Let's take it easy." The two sergeants and the corporal sat down.

"Well, I just conquered Italy," Private Rivera said to Private Friedman.

"You can have it." Private Friedman said. "You can have the whole country. I don't want any part of it."

"I ain't going to give you any part of it," said Rivera. "I found the god-damned place, and it's mine."

"It's yours," said Private Friedman.

"Cold," Private Judson said.

"It can't be cold. It's sunny Italy," said Rivera.

"You read the wrong book," Friedman said.

"I read the Soldier's Handbook," said Rivera. "It said this was sunny Italy. You calling the Soldier's Handbook a liar?"

"What page?" Friedman wanted to know.

"I forget the god-damned page."

"You always forget the god-damned page," Friedman said. "I wouldn't trust you with a popgun."

"You got to trust me with a popgun," said Private Rivera. "I'm a machine gunner with a machine gun."

"You ain't safe to live with," said Private Friedman.

Tyne wished he could have a cigarette, but the very thought of a cigarette made his mouth feel dry. He took out his canteen and wet his lips. "How long do you think Hal will take?" Sergeant Porter asked.

"Shouldn't be long," Sergeant Hoskins said. Hoskins was a tall, quiet man from Nashville. He was Old Army, and in his day he had been broken more than a dozen times for drunkenness and kindred sins. He took it all in his stride. He had the Soldier's Medal, picked up in 1939 when he had saved a nurse from drowning in a Georgia pool.

He was a good soldier, and, had he been dependable, he would have been a good officer. Halverson liked him, but didn't trust him. In Sicily the platoon had been held up once for twenty minutes while Hoskins sampled the wares of a deserted wineshop.

"We'll never find that christly road," Porter said.

About a mile to the left a machine gun opened up.

"There it goes," Porter said.

"We know where we are now, all right," said Hoskins.

Tenseness came to Tyne's face with the quickness of a smile. He could feel all the muscles from his forehead to this chin grow taut and then as suddenly relax. It was as though he had received a somehow painless slap in the face. He opened his mouth and caught his breath between his teeth. The palms of his hands were sweaty.

"Bet they get her in ten minutes," Hoskins drawled.

For no reason at all, Tyne smiled. The war had resolved itself into one machine gun, firing off somewhere in the distance. That was the only enemy—one small machine gun. Once it was silenced, everything would be over. Everything. And they weren't even in on it. They had been given a spectator's role. They could sit off to one side and listen while the war was being fought and won. Life was as easy as that.

Tyne suddenly felt intensely hungry, hungry for anything—an apple, a slice of bread, a sour plum, butter. "Where's the gun?" he asked.

Hoskins listened. "Down by the beach. I can't see a damned thing."

Slowly it was getting light, brightening over the foothills to the east. The sun that had burned down on New Guinea was working its way over the Middle East toward the Apennines. It was becoming light enough to make out faces and expressions, and hands. When Tyne looked at his hands he saw that they were very dirty. He could not understand this phenomenon of war. A man's hands never seemed to be clean, whether he touched anything or not. Always moist grime seemed to settle in his palms and between his fingers. War was a dirty business; it had a special dirt that went with it, as old warehouses have a finely sifted dust that gathers in all their dark and hidden corners. Possibly a criminologist used to defining types of dirt and types of dust could take a sample from an infantryman's fingernail, put it under his microscope, and identify it as from a soldier. Soldier's faces, no matter where they are fighting, are always dirty, and the dirt is always the same color, no matter where it comes from. Perhaps the soldier's dirt is a natural camouflage, tending to make him blend with the landscape. Whatever it is, it is always with him.

"How long will it take Halverson?" Sergeant Porter asked. "It shouldn't take him more than a few minutes to find the captain. He must have been right around here somewhere."

"This is the army, boy," said Hoskins. "Nothing ever happens when it should in the army. You know that."

"There was no god-damned need for Rand to get hurt."

"He done it, anyway."

"What are you going to do if Halverson doesn't come back, Porter?" Tyne asked.

"How the hell do I know?" Porter said. "Halverson didn't really know himself. Maybe the lieutenant knew. If Halverson doesn't come back we might just as well stay here for all the good it will do us."

"They'll be sending planes over pretty soon," said Hoskins

"The hell with the planes," Porter said. "If they send the planes we'll move. If Halverson can't do something without running to the captain it doesn't mean that we've got to sit around here and get blown apart. If the planes come over we take a powder. The hell with Halverson."

"Take a powder where?" Tyne asked.

"Try and find that farmhouse," said Porter. He pulled a blade of grass from the ground and started to break the stem in sections about an inch long.

Tyne was lying on one elbow, his legs stretched out. Lieutenant Rand's map case was under him; his hip bone rested on it. For a moment he thought of telling Porter that he had it; then he changed his mind. There would be time enough for that. Halverson, with any luck at all, would show up in a few minutes.

Tyne was annoyed at Porter. The sergeant was always finding something that either surprised him very much or worried him very much, and this was one of Porter's worrying days. The thing was, events had a habit of going wrong on Porter's worrying days. It was almost as though, by sheer force of will, he badgered Fate into changing a predestined course and making his life miserable.

There was, however, no reason for Porter's worrying. If one excepted the lieutenant's wound, things had gone very well so far. The spot had been a good one for a landing, the enemy had obviously been surprised, and by the time he could rally a counterattack it would probably be too late. It was a very good landing, and if nothing happened for the next two hours or so, it would all be over but the shouting. In two hours they would be getting the tanks and the artillery off, and if the tanks were hot that day and if they worked fast they would have a bridgehead that was out of enemy artillery range by nightfall. Porter, as yet, had no real reason for worrying. No real reason at all.

It was very cold. It always is, just before dawn. And no matter if a man has been out all night, he is apt to begin to shiver when four o'clock in the morning comes around. Perhaps the heat of his body goes down. Whatever the reason, he feels cold the most severely at that time. His feet grow icy; he shivers; his teeth chatter. Nothing can warm him. A fire does no good. Eventually the cold passes, but even at nine o'clock in the morning, in the sun, he is still cold. The early morning is a little like death.

"Sergeant, I want a discharge," Private Archimbeau said. "I'm all fought out."

"Shut up," Porter said dispassionately. Archimbeau talked a lot, but he was a good man.

"In the last war," said Private Archimbeau, "they sent a guy to France. That was all there was to it, they just sent him to France. Then he went home. Simple. Real simple. That's a nice kind of war to have around. But what do they do this time? Do they send you to France? No, they do not send you to France. They send you to Tunisia, and then they send you to Sicily, and they send you to Italy. God knows where they'll send you after that. Maybe we'll be in France next year. Around Christmas time, maybe. Then we work our way east. Yugoslavia. Greece. Turkey. No, not Turkey. All I know is, in 1958 we're going to fight the Battle of Tibet. I got the facts."

"Kill that," Porter said.

Archimbeau stretched out on his back with his hands clasped behind his head. His rifle lay crosswise on his stomach. "So I want a discharge. A honorable discharge. I've done my share of it. The next guy can pick up where I left off."

"You tell 'em, Jack," said Private Trasker.

"It's taking them a hell of a long time to shut that gun up," Hoskins said. "I don't know what they're doing down there."

"Maybe they can't find it," Porter said.

"If it gets a few of them in the guts they'll find it," Hoskins said. "They'll find it then, boy."

"This is a lovely way to fight a war," Private Trasker said. "Just lie down and listen. And they're paying us, too."

The machine gun chattered away over on the left. It was firing in short bursts. Evidently they were trying to get around it, and the gunners were saving up until they saw someone move—until they saw a rifle or a face or a helmet in the grass. That was the way they did it. If the gunner kept his finger on her you knew he had either plenty to shoot at or that he was a very stupid gunner. Few of the Germans were stupid gunners. Sometimes the Italians kept firing just for the sake of the noise.

"That's a Jerry gun," Sergeant Hoskins said.

"You sure?" Porter asked. "I never could tell the damned things apart."

"Sure I'm sure. I bet I can even tell you the color of the guy's hair."

"I think I hear planes," Tyne said.

Everybody listened. It was growing brighter by the minute. Now the platoon could make out a grove of trees about two hundred yards ahead of them. They saw no movement anywhere. Between the bursts of the machine gun they listened.

"I guess I was wrong," Tyne said. "I thought I heard them."

"They'll probably be ours, anyway," Porter said.

"They'd better be," said Trasker. "We got enough guys in the air force. Hey, Jack, you know my brother's in the air force?"

"Where in the air force?" Archimbeau wanted to know.

"My kid brother, for Christ's sake," said Trasker. "He's in the States. Scott Field, Illinois. You ever hear of Scott Field, Illinois?"

"I never even heard of Illinois," Archimbeau said. "I don't get around much any more."

There were three muffled explosions, and the machine gun fell silent. "Told you," Hoskins said. "Eight minutes."

"It should of been you, Rivera," Friedman said. "Always it should of been you."

"It always is me," Rivera said.

As it grew lighter they discovered that they could see neither the beach nor the water. They were in a little hollow among a few scraggly trees, and there was a slight sandy rise between them and the ocean. Now that the machine gun had stopped there seemed to be no life around them. The area was alive with troops, but for all they knew it might have been a desert island. There was nothing to tell them that there was anyone around—no firing, no shouting, no sound of motors. Nothing. The destroyer and the cruiser had stopped firing long ago; so had the shore batteries. As day came, slowly and almost unwillingly, a soft wind drew in from the sea and stirred the trees over their heads. The wind carried with it the smell of rain.

Inland the wood waited for them. Porter thought he saw a piece of road along one side of it, but he couldn't be sure. It might, for all he knew, be a bare patch in the ground. Objects were deceptive; they never semed to be what they were. But the wood looked warm and safe. Porter wished he were there, that the whole platoon were there. The wood means safety from the planes, and the planes would be coming soon. The planes always came soon.

"I never saw anything like it," Hoskins said. "I never saw anything like it in my life. Everybody's gone away. They forgot us. They don't want us in the war. Halverson must be playing blackjack down in the barges."

He yawned.

"Archimbeau," Porter said. "Go take a look down there, Archimbeau."

Archimbeau rose leisurely and started back toward the beach.

"Go on your gut," Porter said. "And leave your gun here. Nobody's going to shoot you."

"Why the gut, then?" Archimbeau wanted to know.

"Because I said the gut," Porter said.

Archimbeau got down on his stomach as soon as he was out of the little hollow and out in the open. He had about fifty yards to go, and every ten feet or so he stopped and listened. The platoon watched him as he worked his tortuous way toward the top of the little ridge. Finally he disappeared in a slight dip.

"When do we eat, Porter?" Trasker asked. "I'm hungry as hell."

"You've got your rations," Porter said. "You can eat when you want to. They're your rations. Nobody's going to take them away from you."

"Every god-damned squad ought to have a god-damned cook go along with them," Private Lang said. "That's the only way to run a god-damned army."

"Do you think he'll find him?" Porter said to Tyne.

Tyne was pulling blades of grass from the ground and putting them in a little pile. "Find who?"

"Archimbeau. Halverson, for God's sake," Porter said. "Who did you think I was talking about?"

"Oh," Tyne said. He pulled out some more blades of grass. "I don't know.''"

"Nobody ever finds anybody," said Hoskins.

"What do you think, Tyne ?"

"About what?"

"The situation."

Tyne stopped pulling out blades of grass. "Just what is the situation, Eddie?"

"All I know is what Halverson told me. We've got to go up a road for six miles until we run into a farmhouse. Then we stop. That's all I know about it. That's all Halverson knows about it. For all I know, that's all the lieutenant knew about it. Six miles is a long way to go, especially to get to a farmhouse. We aren't a whole battalion, for Christ's sake. And its'a long way from the water."

"What's the house for?" Hoskins asked.

"It beats me," Sergeant Porter said. "Maybe it commands a road or something. If they want a bridgehead they're spreading it pretty thin. If Halverson can't find the captain we're in a hell of a hole."

"Take it easy, Eddie," Tyne said. "Nothing's gone wrong yet. We haven't been here very long. How about a cigarette?"

Porter looked at the brightening landscape around him. "Anyone who wants to smoke can smoke," he said.

Rivera punched Friedman in the ribs. "A butt," he said.

"What happened to the one I gave you last night?"

"I sent it home. They're cutting down on the butts at home. A butt."

Friedman gave him one.

"A match," Rivera said. "Thanks. It pays to have friends."

A figure was crawling along toward them from the direction of the beach, moving forward on his elbows, with a sidewise motion of the knees. Archimbeau.

He came back much faster than he had gone, his face serious, the front of his uniform dark and damp with dew. As he reached the hollow he rose to his feet, brushing at his chest.

"What's the dope?" Sergeant Porter said.

"Damned if I know," Archimbeau said. "I didn't see Halverson anywheres. They're bringing down some wounded now—"

"From where?" Porter asked.

"They ran into some trouble with that machine gun. Some Jerries just happened to be driving by with that machine gun, so they opened up. I was talking to a couple of guys down there."

"How about Halverson?"

"I told you I don't know anythng about Halverson or the captain or nobody. I saw Mac, though. He says the lieutenant's dying. Mac says if the lieutenant dies he'll go look for Halverson. The god-damned ocean's full of stuff now. I guess they're bringing in the rolling stock. The heavy stuff, they're bringing in. The damned place is crawling."

Tyne took a drag from his cigarette and blew it out slowly. "How does the beach look?" he asked.

"Empty. They're bringing in some wounded, though."

"Where was the machine gun?" Porter asked.

"They didn't tell me. Over there somewheres." Archimbeau gestured vaguely.

"Maybe there's a road over there," said Sergeant Porter.

It was strange to be so close to things and yet to be so far away. That was war. That was always war. It was confused and it was incoherent and it was unreasonable. Nothing ever happened quite on time, nothing ever happened exactly as was expected. War, itself a paradox, was full of paradoxes. A platoon of men, in on the first landing on an enemy coast, could be completely bypassed by events. They could sit in a hollow while all around them things went, or should be going, according to plan, and while the platoon, itself an integral part of the whole operation, seemed to be entirely forgotten. Yet, had the platoon been unnecessary, it might very well have found itself caught underneath shells and planes, with machine guns and mortars and tanks battering away at it from all directions. The men of the Quartermaster Corps, who appear to lead quiet lives, unscarred by battle, could tell stories of just such occasions. They happen all the time. They probably always have happened.

War, without virtue in itself, breeds virtue. It breeds patience in the impatient and heroism in the cowardly. But mostly it breeds patience. For war is a dull business, the dullest business on earth. War is a period of waiting. Each day of it is crammed with the little hesitations of men uncertain of themselves and awed by the ghastly responsibilities—responsibilities of life and death, the responsibilities of gods—that have been thrust into their hands. The soldier waits for food, for clothing, for a letter, for a battle to begin. And often the food never is served, the clothing is never issued, the letter never arrives, and the battle never begins. The soldier learns to wait meekly, hoping that something will happen. And when the period of waiting is at an end the something that does happen isn't what he expected. So in the end he learns to wait and expect nothing. That is patience, God's one great gift to the soldier.

But he refuses to confess his patience. He curses the fact that he has to wait. He howls at those who cause the waiting. He swears at himself for being such a fool as to wait. And that too is good, in a way. For the man who waits silently is not a good soldier. He is no more than a stone.

"They think I'm going to spend my life here, they're crazy," Private Judson said.

"Take the subway home," said Private Friedman. "Here's a nickel. It's the only nickel I got. It's my last tie with the States. Take it. It's yours. It's worth it to get rid of you."

"Take a tank for a franc," Rivera said.

"A poet," Friedman said. "A Shakespeare. The bard of Avenue A The card of Avenue A."

"You guys kill me," said Archimbeau.

"He's worked to death," Friedman said. "He's got those open period blues. He had to crawl down to Jones Beach for a little reconnoiter and he's worked to death. He wouldn't have kicked if it had been Coney Island."

"Do it yourself," Archimbeau said. "When I'm out of the army and you're sweating it off in Tibet you'll be laughing out of the other side of your face."

"For Christ's sake, Sergeant," Trasker said to Porter, "how long are we going to stay here? My tail's cold."

"We'll stay till it freezes to the ground," Porter said. "There's a lot there to spare."

"Got any ideas where to go, Trasker?" Sergeant Hospkins asked.

"Pike's Peak," Trasker said. "If I was there I'd run up backwards."

"I'd go up on my hands, pushing a peanut with my nose," Archimbeau said. "And then I'd take a train."

"The railroads are jammed these days," Rivera said.

"Oh, for Christ's sake," Porter said. He got to his feet. "Come on over here with me, Hoskins," he said. "You, too, Bill." He walked a few yards away and leaned against the bole of a tree.

Hoskins and Tyne followed him. Tyne left the map case behind him.

"Look," Porter said in a low voice, "something's wrong. I know something's wrong. Halverson shouldn't have taken so long to find the captain. I don't know what he did. Maybe he went looking for him over there. And if he did, God knows when he'll get back. Am I right?"

"It sounds right," Tyne said very precisely. Hoskins nodded solemnly.

"There's no sense in it," Porter went on. "There's no sense in it at all. Now, we know where to go, or at least we think we know where to go, and if we hang around here any longer we'll screw up the whole works."

"Planes will be over pretty soon," Hoskins said. His voice was almost sad.

"Sure as hell they will," Porter agreed. "And sure as hell they're going to send a few tanks along here pretty soon, while we're still up in the god-damned air. My idea is that we ought to leave someone here in case Halverson shows up, and go ahead ourselves while he's waiting. Six miles is a hell of a long way."

"A hell of a long way," Hoskins said.

"What do you think?"

"It's up to you, Eddie." Tyne said carefully. "You know what you're doing."

Hoskins nodded his head without saying anything.

"I've got to know," Porter said.

"Do it, then," Tyne said. "I've got something . . . " he started to say.

Porter held up his hand, palm outward, and Tyne broke off in the middle of his sentence. "Listen," Porter said.

The platoon, which had been talking among itself while watching the noncommissioned officers, was suddenly silent. Hoskins stood with his head cocked slightly to one side. He ran his tongue over his lips.

"Hear anything?" Porter asked.

From somewhere came a faint thunder. It was hard to ascertain the exact direction of the sound.

"God-damned guns," Hoskins said.

"Hey, Sergeant, it's guns," Rivera called.

"Where they coming from?" Porter asked. "They're coming from out to sea, aren't they?"

"I think so," Tyne said. The sea was the only logical place, unless another landing had been made somewhere along the coast and had run into trouble.

"Ack-ack," Hoskins said.

"You sure?" Porter wanted to know.

"Tolerable sure," said Hoskins.

Sergeant Porter moved away from the tree and threw his shoulders back as though his neck were sore.

"That's it, then."

"Must be ships shooting at planes," Hoskins said.

"That's the way it is," said Porter. "That's sure as hell the way it is. Come on."

He went back to the platoon. "All right, off and on," he said. "We're going over in the woods. Squad columns. Hop to it, for Christ's sake."

Archimbeau was doubtful. "How do we know those ain't our planes?"

"Because the ships are ours, dope," Trasker told him. "We got the only ships on the water. I wouldn't be a sailor for nothing."

The platoon got to its feet in a hurry. Hoskins whistled up his squad, and Sergeant Ward, who was quiet and kept out of things, who had sat quietly on the fringe of the gathering, picked up his carbine and spoke a quiet order.

"Who's going to stay here, Eddie?" Tyne asked.

"Stay here for what?" Porter asked. He wanted to get to the woods in a hurry.

"Halverson."

Porter's hand flickered impatiently. "I don't know," he said.

"I'll stay," Tyne said. "I've got nothing to do."

Porter smiled at him quickly. "Okay," he said. "Okay. You stay here. For Christ's sake, get moving, God damn it. We haven't got all day. Get those squads moving. Spread 'em out. You stay here, Bill We'll be over in the woods."

"Leave me your glasses, will you?"

"Sure." Porter lifted the strap over his head and passed Tyne his binoculars. "Help yourself. We'll be over in the woods. Let's go."

The platoon moved out of the hollow, fanning out as it went. It was clear going all the way to the woods. Tyne watched the backs of the men as they receded from him. Once Porter yelled something up the line, but he could not make out what it was. The words ran together as the wind increased in the trees. The platoon reached the line of woods, and one by one the men vanished into the foliage. It seemed very silent in the hollow. Where there had been whispering and the sound of voices there was nothing but a rustling of leaves, Far away, somewhere beyond the world of that moment, the guns continued to bark out at something in the sky. Tyne sighed, lit a cigarette, and lay down on his stomach. Then, as though he were doing a guilty act, he snuffed the cigarette out on the ground. He propped himself on his elbows, took off his helmet, and began focusing the binoculars on the sky beyond the ridge that hid the beach from his sight. He thought he could hear the motors of planes, but he wasn't sure.

Then he remembered that the map case, which he was planning to give Porter, was still with him—was, as a matter of fact, lying underneath his legs, with the strap caught on a tiny shrub. He looked at his watch. It was 0817. Precisely.

3

McWILLIAMS CAME WALKING over the ridge as though he were looking for daisies. He had a long, thin head that made his helmet appear much bigger and broader than it was. Had his helmet jogged up and down over his eyes as he walked it would have seemed perfectly in order. His fatigues were too small for him, and his skinny wrists jutted out from the curtailed sleeves like the obscene legs of a dressed chicken.

McWilliams paid no attention to the war. He took it as it came. He asked questions, but not because he was interested. It was merely because he wanted to be absolutely sure of everything that concerned him. The war as a whole was nothing to McWilliams; it was the little things that mattered. If McWilliams came walking over a ridge in a battle area instead of crawling on his belly, it means that he had turned the whole situation over in his mind and had decided that there was no danger involved if Ransom McWilliams walked upright over a ridge in a battle area. If he had decided that it was all right to walk into the arms of Satan himself, he would have done just that. He was slow and he was Southern and he was dependable. Once McWilliams was told to do a thing he did it. He was a good man to have round.

As he came into the hollow Tyne rose up to meet him. McWilliams looked around him curiously. "Where's everybody?" he asked.

"Gone into the woods," Tyne said. "Planes are headed this way."

"Yeah," McWilliams said. "I heard the guns."

He sat down beside Tyne.

"The lieutenant's dead," he said.

"Too bad," Tyne said.

McWilliams stared at Tyne solemnly. "I suppose so," he said. "Halverson's dead, too. Deader than hell and Jesus."

Tyne, for no particular reason, felt as though he had received a punch in the solar plexus. After a moment he said "Is he?"

"Uh-huh," McWilliams said. "Machine gun got him. He was looking for the captain, and they stitched him right across the middle."

"How do you know?" Tyne asked.

"Tolliver told me. You know Tolliver? B Company. He saw Halverson."

"What about the captain?"

"I don't know anything about the captain."

Tyne stared at the binoculars in his hand. That left it up to Porter, all the way around. The situation, which had seemed to be more or less in hand, was no longer good. The situation was deteriorating rapidly. "God damn it to hell," he said to himself, but aloud.

"What?"

"Nothing. What's going on down there?"

A package of cigarettes was in McWilliams's hand. "Mind if I smoke?" he said. "Is it okay? Okay. They're bringing in the big stuff. Transports and Christ knows what else down there. Everywhere you look. I heard those guns. Planes 're coming in, all right. Be here pretty soon."

"Pretty soon," Tyne said. He peered through the binoculars again. As he did so he thought of Lieutenant Rand, trying to see the guns flash through the night. It had been a very silly thing to do. Probably no more silly, though, than trying to see a plane when you couldn't even hear a plane.

"I'm glad I'm not down on the beach any more," McWilliams said. "That place is sure going to get hell strafed out of it. It sure is."

"We'd better be getting over in the woods," Tyne said. "The planes will be here in a minute."

There was a high whine that came into the air unexpectedly. It sounded quite near, as though a lot of planes were flying very high almost overhead.

"There they are," McWilliams said. "Put out that butt."

"Can't see a light in daylight."

"They can see smoke."

Anti-aircraft guns went off very near at hand, beyond the ridge that cut off the sea. The transports and their escort were going into action. The guns beat out a fast tattoo, in pairs, whumping their shells up into the air as fast as they could throw them into the breech and slam it shut. "Noisy," McWilliams said. "You know that god-damned lieutenant never moved his hands? Never moved them."

There were five deep explosions that reverberated over the ridge. One of the enemy planes, wherever it was, had dropped a stick among the transports. All the explosions, however, had sounded exactly like each other. The plane must have missed. The guns snapped on.

Another stick came down, and this time a deeper roar went with it. Over the ridge a black mushroom of smoke raced toward the reaches of the air. That was no miss, no miss at all. The air rolled back across the little hollow. A hot wind struck the trees.

"Hit something that time," McWilliams said.

"We'd better sit tight here," Tyne said. "There may be a few fighters around somewhere. I don't want any fighters to catch me in an open field."

"I don't want any fighters to catch me in an open field, neither," McWilliams said. "I wonder what the hell's happening down there now."

"Plenty," said Tyne. "Plenty of plenty."

This was it, the way it was expected to be. This was what might have happened during the landing itself. Tyne found himself thinking of the coast of France. He had never seen that coast, but he imagined that now it was just one long concrete wall, bristling with guns. They would set the water afire with oil, too. They would do everything they could. When that day came, Tyne wanted to be somewhere else, far, far away. This, in itself, was bad enough. And even this was mild. In this you knew where everything was. You were here and the bombs were there. It all fitted beautifully together. You were here and the bombs were there. Nothing could have been simpler. In the transports men were being killed, but they weren't you. You were where you were and the men who were being killed were where they were. It had even been worse in London. Then you knew where you were, but you never knew where the bombs were. Now you had a grandstand view. The only trouble was that you couldn't see anything. Very little is seen in war, anyway. Wars are fought by ear.

"I'd like to see that," McWilliams said. The black column of smoke soared higher. Over the roar of the guns there was a series of minor explosions that weren't bombs but very likely were exploding ammunition. There couldn't be many planes in the sky, though, because only two sticks had been dropped; not many planes, that is, unless they were taking their time and making several runs and putting them where they hurt. "Wonder where our planes are," McWilliams said.

"They'll be along."

"They're taking their time."

"They have a lot of it."

But there should have been air support. By rights there shouldn't be an enemy plane in the sky. Tyne couldn't understand it. The only solution seemed to be that this landing was a feint, a diversion. Perhaps the main landing had been made somewhere else, and all the planes had gone there. The planes did, after all, have a long distance to come. With the gas a fighter got it couldn't do much more than arrive, turn around, and go back. It must be that this landing had been a diversion. Yet the water was supposed to be jammed with ships. McWilliams had said so, and McWilliams had seen them. It didn't make sense. It couldn't be that the planes had missed the bus.

Another stick of bombs fell. The planes sounded lower.

"Can I go take a look, Corporal?"

"You stay the hell where you are. I want you here." The binoculers were absolutely useless. Tyne could see absolutely nothing in the sky. Puffs of ack-ack, that was all. But no planes. He was glad that the trees gave him some cover. You never could tell, though. Let the bombardier up there, whatever he was, be a fraction of an inch off, and they might not even find your dog tags. Unconsciously Tyne pressed his body into the earth as though he hoped the ground would gape open and swallow him.

Earth is a marvelous thing. A man does not appreciate earth, just ordinary dirt, until he has been under fire. Then, when he feels that three inches of dry sod scraped up in front of his eyes gives him adequate protection, dirt comes into its own. Foxholes can be dug in it; slit trenches can be dug in it. An hour's work can make enough protection to outlast the worst possible bombing attack. If the hole is deep enough a tank will pass over it, and all the man in the hole will have to do is duck his head a little. And even when there is no cover, absolutely none, a man can feel life surging through him if he just hugs the ground. And he will feel that if he stretched out his arms he could draw in the whole world and hold it to his chest.

Through the eyepieces of the binoculars Tyne at last saw the planes, six of them, in two Vs, flying very high, looking completely unwarlike, completely out of things. It did not seem possible that such minute instruments could do so much damage. They reminded him of stuffed swans that glide over a stage setting, or perhaps in a ballet. They were out of the picture. They held no meaning. They were too far away to hold any meaning at all; one could not connect them with the bombs. Tyne had found them by following the ack-ack puffs.

"I see the planes" he said. "Six of them."

"That all?" McWilliams asked. "Not many, is it? You'd think they'd have a couple of hundred around up there. It just goes to show you."

"It just goes to show you what?"

McWilliams looked at him owlishly. "It just goes to show you," he repeated."

"It's funny," Tyne said. "Maybe there 're more coming." He swerved the binoculars behind the ack-ack bursts, hoping to pick up more planes. There were none.

"I tell you what, Corporal," McWilliams said slowly. "I got an idea. What say I take the glasses and go over on the ridge there and take a look at the water. We ought to know what's going on, hadn't we? I think we ought to know what's going on."

"We know what's going on," Tyne said. "There's no point in it."

"You never can tell," McWilliams said.

"We've got to be getting along to the platoon," said Tyne.

"You wouldn't go through an open field with those planes up there, would you, Corporal? I wouldn't do that."

"No, I wouldn't either," Tyne admitted.

The anti-aircraft fire stopped without warning. Evidently the bombers were out of range. It was odd that they had passed on after only dropping two sticks; it increased Tyne's feeling that this landing had been a feint. The bombers had probably gone on after bigger game. There must be a more important landing taking place farther down the coast. A few odd pieces of shrapnel smashed down around them.

"They ought to know," McWilliams said.

"Who ought to know?"

"The guys," said McWilliams. "Suppose I went and took a look over the ridge. Maybe there's a new landing coming off. They'd want to know if there was, wouldn't they? It stands to reason."

"Go and take a look, McWilliams," Tyne said. "Go and take a look. Get it off your mind."

McWilliams grinned at him. "It's just for the record," he said. "I think it's a good idea."

"Don't hang around, though. Those bombers may be back." Tyne handed him the binoculars. "Take a good look."

Belly to the ground, McWilliams began worming his way toward the ridge. He was exercising caution, now that there were planes around. McWilliams might have ideas, but he was nobody's fool. Once he got an idea in his head it was hard to get it out. And McWilliams had an idea he wanted to see what was going on in the water; the easiest way was to let him see. Tyne watched him crawling, and he could imagine his face. McWilliams's jaw would be jutted out slightly and his mouth would be open about an inch. Tyne remembered McWilliams's face on a day when it had looked just like that. It had been in Sicily, and McWilliams, as a runner, had come crawling up to a slit trench where Tyne was sitting. His jaw had jutted out and his mouth had been open. It was his special expression that he saved for crawling. He made it look hard.

He was halfway across the open space to the ridge when the anti-aircraft guns opened up again, and when they did he hesitated for a moment and looked back. Tyne neither shouted nor made a gesture. He lay flat, trying to see the sky and McWilliams all at the same time. McWilliams continued his crawl.

By the time he reached the ridge the third stick of bombs had fallen. Tyne could not tell whether they had hit anything or not. McWilliams sprawled on the ridge, legs apart, focusing on the ships. Once he turned around and shook his head violently. The movement was meaningless to Tyne. It couldn't mean that nothing had been hit, because the smoke from some ship or other was still moving up the sky. Perhaps it was a signal that nothing was coming ashore at the time. A shake of the head could mean a thousand things. But Tyne could not think of one.

Silence came almost like a clap of thunder; the guns stopped as though a great hand had been placed over their mouths. A new note came into the air, high-pitched, fierce. Fighters.

"Come on back," Tyne yelled.

McWilliams turned, waved his hand, and pointed up in the air. He shook his head again. Far up in the sky the rattle of a machine gun could be heard. Immediately afterwards a comet of smoke appeared high over the water. It described a painfully slow parabola toward the ground and then disappeared behind the wide cloud of smoke that was rising from the wounded ship. The air cover had at last arrived. The ships were holding fire for fear they would hit one of their own planes. McWilliams followed the falling plane with the binoculars as it appeared on the other side of the smoke and plummeted into the sea. When it had passed out of sight he turned around and waved his hand in a small, violent circle. It was his accolade. More machine guns were sounding up in the sky.

Tyne began to feel very uncomfortable. He wished that McWilliams would come back, that he were in the woods with the platoon, that something would happen that would be right. The feeling was growing on him that nothing had been right so far. Everything was wrong. His position was wrong. McWilliams, with the binoculars to his eyes, was wrong. The whole landing had been wrong. He felt, rather foolishly, as though he had come to a summer resort for a vacation, a summer resort that he didn't like. The people were not the kind of people he had expected to find, and there was a director of athletics who made him indulge in games that held no interest for him. Even the swimming was bad. He noted that his hunger, which had cut him a little while ago, had completely vanished. Now, on the contrary, he felt slightly nauseated, as though he had eaten too much. It was hard for the body to keep up with things. The body was a backward instrument.

"Come back, McWilliams," he called.

McWilliams's voice came across to him clearly. "In a minute, Corporal."

The planes moved across the sky. It was impossible to tell their position by the sound of their motors, but they seemed to be going toward the north. Occasionally a machine gun would chatter, like a riveting machine far away. The sun was full up in the sky, glancing off the wet leaves, drying the dew. Tyne could feel that his knees, where he had been lying, were wet.

"Come on back, McWilliams," Tyne called again.

He could almost hear McWilliams sigh as he took the binoculars from his eyes, turned his body around, and began the tedious crawl back to the hollow.

Tyne saw the planes coming a long way off—three fighters, Messerchmitt 110s. They were coming along the coastline from the north, flying very fast, and very low. They couldn't have been more than a hundred feet off the ground. He watched them coming in the same way a bird must watch a snake. They seemed to be coming right at him, and he couldn't move. Their silhouettes swelled on the horizon, over the level earth. At what must have been the far end of the beach, perhaps a mile away, they started firing. They were strafing the barges.

There was no anti-aircraft fire. The planes were too low, they had come too suddenly, hedgehopping, and any shrapnel from the anti-aircraft might have caught the men on the beach. The Messerschmitts roared along, all guns chattering, unopposed. McWilliams saw them coming almost at the same time as Tyne did. He turned to look at them almost casually, as though they were annoying flies. Then, when they started to fire their guns, he leaped up and ran for the hollow. He had gone perhaps twenty feet when the planes were upon him. Tyne could see the earth fly as their bullets cut a swath through it. McWilliams suddenly faced the planes and flung his arms in front of him as though the gesture could ward them off. Then he went back a few paces and collapsed with his arms still outflung. He too had been stitched. Right up the middle.

After he had fallen Tyne cried out "McWilliams!" His voice was lost in the roar of the receding planes. "Son of a bitch!" he screamed after them. "Son of a bitch." He grabbed his rifle and fired three rapid shots after them. Foolish. The Messerschmitts went down the coast about three miles, went into an Immelmann, and came back along the beach. Tyne fired the rest of his magazine at them when they were still out of range and then threw himself down behind a tree. The machine guns opened up again. He watched the planes, fascinated. One track of bullets cut the ground perhaps three feet from McWilliams's body.

As the Messerschmitts passed to the north end of the beach one of them soared up, banked leisurely, and came back, this time behind Tyne. He scrambled around to watch it. The plane cut in very low over the woods where the platoon was hiding and opened up. Even from a distance of two hundred yards Tyne could see the tops of the trees quiver and shake as the bullets smashed into and through them. He felt completely lost. The Messerschmitt came back over the woods and started to rake it again, but this time the machine guns stopped almost as soon as they had begun. The plane had evidently run out of ammunition. It disappeared over some foothills to the northeast.

For a moment after the planes had gone Tyne sat stupefied. The attack had shocked him. Planes always did. They were an impossible, unimaginable force. He could understand men against men, and even men against tanks, but planes were something else again. He had once read a fantastic story about gigantic insects that turned against man; the planes were those insects. Tanks, which could be taken for gigantic beetles, were terrifying too in their way, but one always knew that inside the tanks were men, and men were vulnerable. But the planes moved too fast. It was impossible to conceive of any human being, any human element, hidden in their bowels and controlling them. They had a life of their own, vindictive, murderous. Even his own planes made Tyne feel uncomfortable.

For nearly three minutes he remained where he was, sitting up with his back against a tree. Over the ridge he could hear sounds from the beach. Men were shouting. Someone was screaming in a high-pitched voice. It sounded almost like a woman.

Deliberately Tyne rose to his feet and walked out into the open where McWilliams was lying. As soon as he saw the body he knew that there was nothing to be done. There is something about a dead man's face that cannot be explained. Something has gone from the features. It is as though life lent an aura, a glow, that, unseen, could yet be perceived through some unknown sense. The face of a dead man resembles what the dead man is—a lump of clay. The face somehow merges with the earth. Clothes hang awkwardly on the body and bunch up strangely; the clothes seem foreign to the body that is wearing them.

That was the way it was with McWilliams. Looking at his face, Tyne could not conceive that he had ever known him, that he had ever eaten and talked with him. He knew that there was no need to touch the body to see if life still existed. McWilliams's eyes were wide open. Blood seeped through the front of his fatigues. One of the bullets had gone through his neck; there was a lot of blood there. Tyne had seen much of death, but he had never reconciled himself to it. Death was indecent, obscene. There was something naked about a body, the nakedness of being unsouled, and there is no deeper nakedness than that.

There was no time for Tyne to muse on the incontrovertible fact of death, even had he wanted to. He stared down at McWilliams's body for a moment and then looked hesitatingly at the ridge. It might be a good idea to take a quick look at the beach. The wounded man was still screaming. He heard a deep voice call "Bring it up, bring it up!"

Instead of mounting the ridge, however, he walked over to where McWilliams had dropped his rifle. Tyne laid his own rifle down carefully and picked up McWilliams's. There was no explanation for his action; he just did it. Then he turned on his heel, walked back to the hollow, picked up the map case, and went out in the open field toward the wood.

As he walked he lit a cigarette. He was a very much frightened young man.

4

TRASKER WAS DEAD. Sergeant Hoskins had a bullet in the calf of his left leg, and Private Giorgio, of Sergeant Ward's squad, had a smashed shoulder. The platoon had got off easily. The pilot of the Messerschmitt had seen something gleam in the woods. No one knew what it was, but the pilot must have seen something; otherwise he wouldn't have taken the crack at them. If he hadn't run out of ammunition it might have been worse. As it was, the platoon never knew what hit them. They had not seen the plane come over. They had heard it machine-gunning the beaches, but when it went after the woods the trees had hid it from their sight until the bullets started to smash down among them. They had been very lucky.

Trasker had taken a slug in the mouth. He had been talking to Archimbeau—talking in a loud voice, because the planes were making a lot of noise—when they got him. He had started to say "For Christ's sake, Arch—" but he had never got any farther. It was an odd thing to say as one's last words, but that was just the way it was. Archimbeau felt very badly about it. When Trasker had fallen over he had reached out to grab him, and then he saw where the wound was, so he didn't bother. There was no point in it, once you saw the wound. They hadn't even been able to shoot at the plane; they hadn't seen it.

Hoskins knew it was a Messerschmitt that had put the hole in him, because Hoskins was an older soldier and he knew things like that. It was his business to know them. Some of the men in the platoon, Giorgio for instance, might never know who or what had shot them, because their minds didn't run in that direction. But Hoskins knew. He wasn't in any real pain—not yet, anyway. The wound wasn't such a bad one, but the muscles were torn and he couldn't walk. He bandaged the wound himself.

"Does it hurt?" Porter asked. Porter was a little shaken by the strafing. He had not expected it, and it preyed upon his mind. He believed that it was his fault, for it was he who had considered the wood a safe place; he had brought the platoon there.

"It don't hurt yet," Hoskins said, "but it god-damned well will."

"It's a Purple Heart, Sarge," Rivera said.

"Shove it," Sergeant Hoskins said. "Next Messerschmitt pilot I see I'm going to shoot all by myself. Bastards."

"What are you going to do?" Porter asked.

"Stay here, for God's sake," said Hoskins. "What the hell did you think I was going to do? Get up a god-damned football game?" The wound had angered him and made him loquacious.

"Giorgio got shot in the shoulder," Porter said.

"Who the hell cares?" said Hoskins.

Archimbeau sat looking at Trasker. Friedman came over and patted his shoulder. "He was a good guy," Archimbeau said.

"Okay," said Friedman.

"No Tibet," Archimbeau said.

"Okay."

"I wish Halverson would show up," Sergeant Porter said.

The platoon was spread out, sitting against trees. They felt beat up. Everything seemed to be going wrong. Nothing good had happened. It had been bad in the hollow and it was bad under the trees. The platoon wanted to move. The men were restless. They didn't care where they went; they just wanted to be on the move. Each knew that events were taking place that were bypassing them; they were in a stagnant pool, and all around them flood waters were rushing toward an unknown and dangerous destination. One or two of them, for want of something better to do, were eating C Rations. Everyone was keyed up.

"We can't stay here all day, Eddie," Sergeant Ward said.

"I know it, for God's sake," Porter said. "But what can I do?"

Sergeant Ward thought a minute. "I don't know," he said.

"How's Giorgio?"

"He can walk. It's not too bad."

"Hell of a thing."

* * *

Rivera was talking to Private Rankin, who was an automatic rifleman.

"You want to live here?" he said.

"I didn't say I wanted to live here," Rankin said.

"It's a nice country," Rivera said. "Full of opportunity. Just look around you. Opportunity, that's the big thing."

"The hell with the country," Rankin said."

"That's a lousy way to talk about a country where you're a guest. They'll kick you the hell out."

"No they won't," said Private Rankin.

"Do you know who you're fighting?" Rivera asked.

"They never told me. Germans."

Rivera spat on the ground. "That's all I want to know."

Rankin didn't understand him. "You're screwy," he said.

"It's life, said Rivera.

Archimbeau was walking around with his hands in his pockets, kicking dead leaves. His rifle was slung over his shoulder. "We were the same draft board," he said. "The same day."

"Forget it," Friedman said. He left Archimbeau and walked over to Rivera.

"Go away," Rivera said. "A butt."

Friedman gave him a cigarette. "Arch is taking it hard."

"Nobody dies," said Rivera. It was a platoon cliché.

Sergeant Porter had just about made up his mind. There was nothing for it but to move on. It was the best thing to do. There was no sense in waiting for Halverson, because Halverson obviously wasn't coming. He wondered what was keeping Tyne; probably he was holing in, figuring that the planes would be back. Holing in, that is, if the planes hadn't got him, too.

There was a sound of someone coming through the bushes. Porter pointed his carbine in the direction of the sound. "Halt," he said. The movement stopped. "Who's there?"

"Tyne."

"Well, come on, for God's sake. Where have you been?"

Tyne came into view. The platoon looked at him with interest. Some of the men came over to him. "What happened?" Porter asked.

Tyne was still smoking his cigarette. Before answering he took out another and lit it from the stub of the first. He noticed that his hand was trembling; so did the men around him.''

''Halverson's dead,'' he said.

''God damn,'' Porter said. ''What happened?''

''Machine gun got him.''''

''Plane?''

''No, the one that was down there.''

''Bad,'' Porter said.

''McWilliams is dead, too. The plane got him. And the lieutenant died.''

Porter frowned. It was up to him now. ''That does it,'' he said. ''Trasker's dead here. Hoskins and Giorgio got wounded.''

''I've got the lieutenant's map case.''

''Get it from the barge?''

''No, I had it all the time. I was going to give it to you.''

As Tyne handed him the case Porter stared at it as though he could not believe it existed. It was a shiny new map case; Lieutenant Rand had never really had a chance to use it. The leather gleamed, but in one place there was a long deep scratch down the side.

''What's in it?'' Porter asked.

''I don't know,'' Tyne said. ''Look and see.''

Porter unbuckled it and looked inside. He pulled out two pieces of paper. One was a detail map of a limited area; the other was a rough penciled sketch of what looked on first glance like a road junction.

Slowly and deliberately Porter fell on his knees and spread out the large map. The whole platoon gathered around him then, those nearest the map falling on their knees, too, and those behind them looking over the first rank's shoulders. The map was of the district where they were. There was the seacoast. There was the beach. There was the wood where they were. ''There's the road,'' Porter said. He put his finger on it. Judging from the map, it was about a hundred yards to the south of the little wood. Halverson's calculations had been slightly off.

''Where's the farmhouse?'' Tyne asked.

Porter traced the road with his forefinger. ''Here,'' he said. ''This must be it. It's the only house. Let's see, where's the scale? It's about six miles, all right.''

''Nearer seven,'' Ward said. ''What's the other thing?''

The penciled sketch was spread out over the big map. ''It's the farmhouse,'' Porter said. ''What's that?'' He pointed toward a series of concentric broken lines.

''Rocks,'' Tyne said. ''High ground.''

''It's marked for a machine gun,'' Porter said. ''One of the farm buildings is marked for a machine gun, too.''

''That's me,'' Rivera said. ''I like to work indoors.''

''There's no god-damned orders,'' Porter said. ''Just this.''

''Have to do,'' said Ward.

''He must have swallowed the orders,'' Porter said. ''Too many secrets in this bloody war.''

''Porter,'' Hoskins called. ''Bring it over here and let me see it.''

''Porter picked up the two maps and carried them over to where Hoskins was sitting with his back against a tree. Hoskins took the map, and as he studied it he grimaced. His teeth showed black between his lips.

''Giving you trouble?'' Porter asked.

''It will,'' Hoskins said. ''That bridge.''

''What about it?''

''You'll have to blow it.''

Porter frowned over the map. ''Yes. Blow it,'' he said.''

''You have to use grenades. They'll bring up stuff over that bridge.''

''Your leg hurting now?''

''Son of a bitch. God-damned Heinie bastards. Grenades will do it, all right. Take time, though.''

''Hoskins tossed the maps aside as though he were annoyed with them. ''Leave me some water,'' he said. ''I may be here quite a while.''

''Want someone to take you down to the beach?'' Porter was solicitous. He hated to lose Hoskins.

''Like hell. They'll be strafing that place for weeks. I'm going to stay right here.''

''What about Giorgio?''

''The hell with Giorgio. Jesus, Porter, you're in command. Don't ask so many christly questions. Leave me alone.''

Porter picked up the maps and walked back to where the platoon was gathered. He folded the maps and put them carefully back in his case. ''Cousins, go ask Giorgio if he can get back to the beach by himself,'' he said.

As Cousins rose artillery fire came to their ears from the north. It was light stuff, coming from inland. As they listened they heard shells exploding nearby. A machine gun began far away; another joined it. The battle was beginning.

"We've got to get moving," Porter said. Another shell exploded quite near them. A few of the men ducked involuntarily.

Cousins came back. He had been eating his rations before Tyne had returned, and now he was sucking on a lemon drop from the ration. "Giorgio says the hell with the beach," he said. "He wants to go along."

"He can't go along," Porter said. "They'll be setting up a hospital here pretty soon. Tell him to stay here."

"Tell him yourself," Cousins said. "You've got the rank."

Porter stared fiercely at Cousins, opened his mouth to say something, and then walked over to Giorgio. "You'd better go down to the beach, Giorgio," he said.

"Listen," Giorgio said, "I'm wounded. I got privileges. I don't want to go down to the beach. I want to go along."

"You can't go along. You won't do any good. You can't do anything."

"Oh, for Christ's sake."

"Go on down to the beach."

"I'll stay here with the sergeant."

"Suit yourself," Porter said. "Tyne, where are the binoculars?"

"Oh, God," Tyne said, "I forgot them. McWilliams has them."

"The only pair we had," Porter said. "They aren't doing him any good."

"I'll go back, Tyne said.

"Never mind," Porter said. He walked over and picked up his carbine, which he had laid down while he was going over the maps. "Let's go," he said. "We're going to move."

"For Christ's sake, roll Trasker over," Hoskins said. "I don't want to have to look at that mug for two days."

Archimbeau rolled Trasker's body over. His face was set as he did it.

"Sunny Italy," Rivera said. He picked up his barrel. "A little hike."

"You should have to carry this," Friedman said. He was an ammunition carrier. He did not like the job.

"I am happy with you, dear," Rivera said. "You make me very happy."

"After the war I will cut you dead on the street," Friedman said.

"After the war I will never go to Jersey City to give you a chance to cut me dead," said Rivera.

"Listen," Porter said. "When we hit the road we'll go in three squads. We'll bust Hoskins's squad up. Corporal Kramer, divide them in three. My squad will go first. Archimbeau and Cousins will be scouts. Rankin, follow them. Ward, you take the second squad after me. Tyne, you take the third. Kramer, you're Tyne's assistant squad leader. You bring up the rear. Get it?"

There were murmurs of assent.

"Now, for Christ's sake, keep your eyes open. God only knows what might be coming down the road. If they bring—" A shell struck near the wood. "If you hear me blow my whistle, head for cover. And I mean cover. Keep your eyes open for planes. They may try to shell the road, too. I don't think they're wide awake yet, but they're going to be . It's a stinking situation. Right?"

"Right!" chorused the platoon.

"Then let's go."

Archimbeau and Cousins started out, and Rankin followed them. While the file of men was moving out Tyne stood uneasily, watching them. A little, seedy man named Johnson slipped over to Hoskins and handed him a letter. "Mail this for me, will you, Sergeant?" he said. Hoskins took it silently, and Johnson slipped into his place in Ward's squad.

Tyne went over to where Hoskins was lying. "How is it, Hosk?" he asked.

Hoskins smiled faintly. "It'll keep," he said. "I've got it on ice."

"Take it easy."

"Tyne, you're a smart apple," Hoskins said. "Keep your head."

"I'm the boy," Tyne said.

"I mean it. Keep your head. You may need it."

"I always have."

A grimace twisted Hoskins's face. "Bloody leg," he said. "I ran into an Australian in Tunis," he said, "and they slugged one into his leg at Mareth. He was always going to walk with a limp. That's a hell of a way to be. Ruins you with the army."

"You'll be all right, Hosk."

"You're a smart apple. Keep your head on."

Tyne took his canteen from his belt. "Better hang on to this," he said.

"I forgot. Thanks," said Hoskins. "Keep your eye on Porter. I think he's going to crack."

"How do you know?"

"I've seen them crack, for Christ's sake. He's a good man, but I think he's going to crack. That's the way it goes. He's got a lot on his mind. Keep your head on."

"Okay, Hosk."

"The last of the three squads was moving out. Tyne took up his place at the rear. He was the last man in the platoon. "See you around, Hosk," he said.

"Yeah," Sergeant Hoskins said. "Around."

The platoon wound through the wood, circling trees, stepping over bushes. Tyne caught one legging in a low thorn and very nearly tripped. He slashed at the thorn with his bayonet. Once he looked back, but he could no longer see Hoskins and Giorgio. They were out of sight behind the trees. When he thought of Giorgio he had to smile. He was an Italian, and his father was fairly fresh from the old country, yet all Giorgio would see of Italy was a beach and a little wood. It was ironic. Tyne, of all the people in the world, had never expected to be in Italy. He had never had the slightest urge to travel; on the contrary, he was a one-town man. Rhode Island might be tiny and Providence might not be much as cities go, but it was all that Tyne wanted. If a war had not come along and pulled the pins from under the quiet life he had led and had wanted to lead, he might have been contented with an existence that contained as its travel itinerary, three trips to New York City and one two-weeks' sojourn in the Great Smokies. Yet here he was, moving in toward the heart of an enemy country, a country that was a far cry from Rhode Island and Providence, and all the rest of life. Tyne was caught up in a maelstrom, and, though he did not know it, he wanted nothing more in the world than to be able to cry out for help.

They came out of the wood to a rough and dusty field. The sun had already dried the dew, and their feet kicked up small clouds of baked earth. The road cut through the dry field, running toward the northeast. It was little more than a cart track—two deep ruts running through the dull grass. They turned into it in two files, one walking on each side of the road. It was bad going. Carts had passed over the road in wet weather; their wheels had sunk into mud, and the mud had dried, leaving deep welts. To their left the artillery pounded on. Shells were falling behind them and to the north, along the beach and among the ships. The machine guns sang like locusts in a summer sun.

They were all frightened. The barrage could not be trusted; it was landing on the beach at the moment, but it might start moving inland at any time. They kept glancing anxiously behind them, as though they were afraid the barrage would move if they didn't watch it. The sun was beginning to bother Porter. He hated heat, and now, with the equipment he was carrying, sweat ran down his face and left pale rivers in the grime along his cheeks. He was still surprised that the sun could achieve so much heat so early in the morning. The six miles ahead of him became an infinity of miles. Before he had gone three hundred yards along the road he was tired. He shifted his carbine from shoulder to shoulder. From time to time he would glance behind him, not so much to watch the barrage as to check on the platoon. The road led up to a slight rise, and from this he could see the beach and the ships lying offshore. Barges were teeming around the transports. Obviously more men were coming ashore. That was the reason for the barrage. In that case, it would probably stay where it was. It wouldn't chase them.

* * *

"It could have been something else," Rivera said to Friedman. "It could even have been the navy. They looked at me and said, 'Here's a guy that can walk.' They finished me, all right."

"Everybody walks," Friedman said. "Even monkeys."

"There are limits," Rivera said. "Plenty of limits."

"I've been thinking," said Friedman. "How long have we been in the army?"

"Jesus," Rivera said. He spat into the dust.

"Look at Hoskins. He gets a lousy little dig in the leg. He's out of the army. But he doesn't want to be out of the army."

"Justice," Rivera said."

"Where are we going, Rivera?"

"I am going some place where I can set up this weapon," Rivera said. "And then I am going to shoot this weapon. I am not going to walk any more."

"There are limits," Friedman said.

Why didn't they use paratroops? Porter kept asking himself. The farmhouse, whatever its uses, was far enough inland to use the paratroops. It would have been the most natural thing in the world—just fly over, scatter a few, and let them hold it. God knows it would have saved time, lots of time. As things stood it was nearly ten. Valuable hours had been wasted, had been allowed to run down the drain. Time, that was so precious, had been spent recklessly. It was bad, bad all the way through. They wouldn't reach the farmhouse before noon.

No worries crossed Tyne's mind. For the first time that morning he felt fairly relaxed. As long as he was moving he was quite content. As he walked he looked about him at the country. The land was fairly level, but he figured that in about a half an hour they would run into rather rough-looking foothills. There was little vegetation. It was almost as though the wood where they had stopped had been a freak. A ditch, obscure and ill defined, ran parallel with the road, about fifty feet away. It looked like a trench. In a pinch it could serve for one.

To a man marching in the sun time becomes as static as the shimmering horizon. It surrounds him and presses on his shoulders. He moves, but time stops. Seconds swell to giant size and minutes are immensities. The body conditions the mind's knowledge of time—it flies in pleasure, it crawls in pain. And on no one does its weight fall more heavily than on the soldier. Yet as the platoon wound carefully along the dusty road time warred with itself. It crawled when the men thought of their march, it ran insanely when they thought of their objective. Over them hung the fear and the threat that something was going to happen, that *Something* was going to happen. They did not feel that they could move fast enough to beat time to the punch. In a normal route march a man can let his faculties go dull, he can become numb. He can slog on, unaware of his surroundings, unaware of anything save the back of the man who slogs in front of him. But under fire, during a landing, during an advance, he must keep continuously on the alert. He must seek out rocks and trees and attempt to see through them. He must recognize that there is an enemy very near at hand and that even the landscape can rise up and kill him.

"Suppose this road is mined, Sergeant," Cousins said over his shoulder.

"Don't worry about it," Porter said.

"Okay," said Cousins. "Not till after."

In the second squad Privates Carraway and James were discussing music.

"That's one thing I want to do when I get back," Private Carraway said. "I want a nice collection of records."

"I knew a guy must of had millions of records," said Private James. "Millions, that guy had. He worked in the NBC studios. He had all kinds of autographs. You couldn't name anybody he didn't have an autograph. They even used to sign his records. He had a record of the Andrews Sisters with all three of their autographs. That's the kind of life."

"Just the music is all I want," Carraway said. "I got one collection, but I want a big one. I got all the Bing Crosby records except the last ones."

"You know Russ Columbo? My sister used to be nuts about Russ Columbo. She stayed in her room all the time the day he died."

"Too bad. When'd he die, anyway?"

"Hell, I don't know. Must of been ten years ago. She was a kid. She's married now."

"Her husband in the army?"

"Beats me. I never heard from her."

"Maybe he's in a war plant."

"That's the life, the war plants. Two hundred bucks a week they drag down."

"The hell with the dough. I'd just like to be able to go home at night."

"If I hadn't gone in the army I was going to California."

"Have a job there?"

"Naw, I just always wanted to go to California. Out with the movie stars."

"There was an old Crosby picture in Tunis. I hope nothing happened to those records."

Archimbeau felt resentful, though he couldn't quite tell why. As he walked he scuffed and kicked at dry clods of soil. He was carrying his rifle loosely in his right hand, carefully balanced between stock and barrel. As he advanced he kept turning his eyes from right to left and back again. He was angry at the terrain. It was all alike. Dry as dust. And when it wasn't dry as dust it was wet, and when it wasn't wet it was cold. But it all seemed to be the same country. From his left-hand pocket he took a stick of gum and held it with his hand while he tore away the paper with his teeth and pulled the long flat stick into his mouth. As he chewed it he thought of Trasker, and Trasker's jaw. Nothing to it. He never knew what hit him. A good guy. What had happened in that ravine was his fault. He had tripped Trasker in the dark. Trasker never knew. Meant to tell him. Always meant to tell him.

Allied planes were over the beaches, flying very high, back and forth. They would fly five miles toward the north, bank, and come back down again. Beneath them the shells were still exploding on the beach and in the water. They were dangerously near the platoon—really within ducking distance—but there was no time to be wasted dodging shells. There was no time to be wasted on anything. Ahead of the men, like an abyss, stretched the next two hours. But it was not a dark abyss, for the sun was shining very brightly.

As a matter of fact, it was out of that bright sun that the Focke-Wulf came at them.

5

THERE WAS SO MUCH noise that it was almost impossible to hear it. The planes to the south and the artillery fire and the occasional chatter of a machine gun made hearing difficult. Archimbeau spotted the Focke-Wulf by instinct more than anything else. Ahead of him, in the sun, he caught an odd flash in the sky, a flash not of gold but silver. He did not even wait to ascertain exactly what it was. He threw up one hand, turned his head over his shoulder, yelled "Plane!" and made for the ditch.

Sergeant Porter blew his whistle, and the platoon broke for both sides of the road. Most of them made for the ditch. A few bolted for the open field on the other side of the road. As the men scattered the plane's machine guns opened up. Two men who were making for the field seemed to trip clumsily and went tumbling down. The rest of the platoon made it.

The plane flashed past. It was a Focke-Wulf all right, a dirty scum of a double-tailed Focke-Wulf. Tyne saw the pilot wave his hand to them as he flashed past. He continued on down the road, banked to the north, and went after the beach. He had come in very low, the way the three Messerschmitts had, over the foothills. It was only by the grace of God that Archimbeau had seen anything. It was pure luck."

"Anybody hurt?" Sergeant Porter yelled up and down the ditch. "Anybody hurt?"

"All right down here," Tyne said.

Porter came scrambling down to where Tyne was crouched. "Did you see that?" he wanted to know. "Did you see that? Right out of the blasted sun. The dirty bastard."

"There's some wounded across the road," Tyne said. " My squad, I think. I'd better go over."

"Wait a minute. He may be back."

"I'll take my chances," said Tyne. He climbed out of the ditch and ran across the road. Five men were lying over there. "Who's hurt?" he said. One of the men was lying on his back. Tyne went over to him. It was Private Dugan, quite past hurting.

"Smitty got one," a man said."

"Get the hell over in that ditch," Tyne said. "Where's he got it?"

"Arm and shoulder."

"Give me a hand with him. Get the hell into the ditch."

Tyne and Private Phelps picked up Private Smith. The other two men ran across the road and leaped into the ditch. One of them picked up Dugan's rifle as he ran.

"He's out," Phelps said.

"Never mind." They brought Smith across the road and lowered him into the ditch. "Dugan's dead," Tyne said to Porter.

"I know."

"Look at that Jerry," Private Friedman screamed.

The Focke-Wulf was making an Immelmann to come back along the beach. It was just a speck in the sky, far to the north. Above it, almost leisurely, three Allied planes swung out of formation and went into a steep dive. The Focke-Wulf pilot didn't seem to see them. He dipped his nose and came back down toward the south. The three Allied planes, whatever they were, hit him all at once. He saw them too late and tried to pull his ship up in a steep climb. They got him while he was starting it. The Focke-Wulf seemed to nose straight up, stopped, hovered a bit, and then fell back down again, going into a spin and exploding as it hit the water. The three planes went into a graceful climb, on their way back to join the formation.

"Beautiful!" Friedman yelled. "Beautiful, beautiful."

"No more waving for that baby," Tyne said.

"Did he wave?" Porter asked.

"I saw him. Probably the bastard was grinning, too. Always leave them laughing."

Smith's wounds weren't serious, but they would be painful. The sulfa was out and was going on, but Smith would be out of action for quite a while. "What the hell can we do with him?" Porter asked. "Can we leave him here?"

Tyne looked up and down the road. "We'll have to," he said. "Can't take him with us."

"Nobody'll find him."

A frown of concentration appeared on Tyne's face. "The best thing we can do is wait till we get as far forward as we can, then send a man back. Things may be cleared up down here by then. The guy can bring back the stretcher-bearers. They can take care of Hoskins and Giorgio, too."

"Okay," Porter said. "You pick a man."

"There's no hurry."

"Think we'd better get on with it."

"I'd wait awhile if I were you. There may be more where that came from." Tyne gestured down the road, where the Focke-Wulf had gone into its last spin. "Better take a ten, anyway."

"Tell 'em, will you?" Porter said.

Tyne walked down the ditch. "Take ten," he said over and over.

"Can I smoke, Corporal?" Rivera asked.

"Burn," Tyne said.

"Butt me, Friedman," said Rivera.

The dial on Tyne's watch told him they had been moving for twenty minutes, more or less. That means a mile, roughly—a mile away from the beach and a mile away from the shells. Five miles to go to the farmhouse. Tyne was beginning to get worried about tanks. The Germans, in the time they had had, could have brought tanks all the way from Rome and played a few games of red dog on the route. Perhaps the enemy tanks had already arrived by another road and were joined where the machine guns and small-arms fire could be heard. There must have been more roads leading from the beach, and more important roads into the bargain. Otherwise they would never have sent a single platoon to hold one road, especially at such a great distance from the point of landing. The whole thing, Tyne decided, would make a nice problem to mull over in his old age—if, as, and when. Surely the road they were on could not be of much importance. They must be getting the tanks ashore by now, and if the road had any value the tanks would be trundling themselves along it. It was almost certain that the tanks were aiming northeast. The platoon's job, in all probability, was to go to the farmhouse, blow the bridge, and thus make any counterattack impossible. That must be it, surely.

During the break many of the men were getting at their rations. Tyne began to feel hungry again. He opened a tin of cold hash and ate it with relish. He had not had much of it lately; it was only when a man ate it day after day and meal after meal that the hash became unbearable. Then one was just as apt to throw it away as eat it. The hash was, of course, supposed to be eaten warm; but whoever had put it up had neglected to include smokeless firewood, or firewood of any kind, or leisure. One ate rations only when one was in a hurry; otherwise the thing to do was scrounge. In Sicily it had been watermelons and neat, small tomatoes. Here there was (or seemed to be) nothing. Only brown grass and dry mud. Nothing palatable at all.

Rivera and Friedman, too, were eating hash, loudly and with the gusto of Socrates taking the hemlock.

"You know where they get this stuff?" Friedman asked.

"Yeah," said Rivera. "I know where they get everything."

"Where do they get this stuff?"

"You know the sewers?"

"What sewers?"

"Any sewers. The Hoboken sewers."

"How do you know? You got a brother works in the sewers?"

"Never mind my relations. You want me to tell you how they get it out of the sewers?"

"No. I'm eating it, for Christ's sake."

"We should be in the Heinie Army."

"They wouldn't take me," said Friedman. "Why should we be in the Heinie Army?"

"The god-damned food. It's good food."

"How the hell do you know. You a spy or something?"

"How about that HQ we walked into in Sicily? Wine on the table. Steak. A picture."

"It was Officers' Mess."

"So what? Do our Officers' Mess get wine on the table? Do they get steak? The Heinies are really eating."

"They won't be." Grimly.

"Listen, chum, in three years the whole world will be eating C rations. I got it from a friend."

"Give it back to him. I ain't interested."

"Don't you think of nothing but your gut? You're fat, Friedman. You're a chunk, Friedman."

"What the hell. First thing I'm going to do when I get home is eat the god-damnedest biggest meal any guy ever ate. I wouldn't even tell you what I'm going to have. You're too insensitive."

"Butt me, Friedman."

"Listen, Rivera, all I been doing is feeding you fags. You think I bought out the American Tobacco Company or something?"

"Butt me."

"Ah, for Christ's sake."

"What do you get out of it, Friedman?"

"Out of what?"

"The business."

"What business?"

"This business."

"I ain't a member of the firm."

"You saw that Focke-Wulf."

"Yeah."

"He was after you."

"I wasn't in when he called."

"How about a match, for God's sake? There'll be another one right along. Any minute now."

"I won't be in then, either."

"Friedman, you're a draft dodger. You're yellow, Friedman."

"That's what I am, all right. Hold that match."

* * *

Sergeant Porter was crumbling a clod in his hand. He broke off a small piece of it, crumbled it in his palm and then let the fine dirt sift through his calloused fingers. He counted the number of pieces he could break from each clod—good-sized pieces, about an inch through. From one clod he got seven; from another nine. There were no more good-sized clods near him. He did not feel like getting up to find one. He felt, as a matter of fact, bored and listless. Events seemed to have moved past and beyond him. Sergeant Porter was completely out of his depth. The dry hot plain stretched around him, full of an emptiness that gripped him around the throat and made him afraid. It was hard to say just what was the matter with Sergeant Porter.

Perhaps he had had too much war. Certainly he had had a lot of it—nearly a year. Scenes from Tunisia and Sicily kept flashing before his eyes. Men vary in the amount of war they can take. Some are good only for one action, others can stand it for years. But when a man gets enough of it, when he gets fed up, when he begins to tremble slightly and shift his eyes around or tremble slightly and stare eternally at one fixed spot, there is only one thing to do. Pull him out of the line and ship him back where the steak grows on trees and the only noise is that of the sunset gun. He may be some good there, but he'll be through in the line.

That was almost the way it was with Porter. He was a good man, but he had run his course. He had seen a lot of action and he had gone through it with his head down and his eyes open. But he had reached what amounted to the end of his rope. He wasn't beginning to tremble yet, but he was getting the shifty eye, the eye that doesn't know what is waiting behind the tree or on the other side of the deserted house. Any soldier is expected to have an eye like that, but when they reach the end of the tether the thing that is waiting on the other side of the tree or the other side of the house has become inhuman. It is no longer an enemy—living, breathing, capable of death—but it is *The* Enemy. And Porter was beginning to get that feeling. It was growing on him day by day, it was keeping him awake at night. He was beginning to see things out of the corner of his eye.

Sergeant Porter was, as a matter of fact, ready for the cleaners. He was a good man, but he had reached the end of the tether. All that remained was for the tether to break.

"I've got a hell of a headache," Porter said to Tyne. The latter had come back from calling the break and was sitting beside his platoon commander. "A lousy headache."

"Tough," Tyne said.

"You trust this operation?"

"How do you mean?"

"You know. I don't like the ring of it. It doesn't ring true. There's something funny about it."

Tyne told him what he thought of it: that to blow up the bridge at the farmhouse meant protecting the flank, that a fast-moving small body of men could get through quicker than anything else and accomplish the mission.

"It sounds all right," Porter admitted. It seemed to Tyne that Porter had shriveled somehow. He didn't look as burly as he once had; he didn't even look as solid as he had early in the morning.

"It's the only thing," Tyne said solemnly. "As I see it," he added.

"Everything's been screwed up ever since we started," said Porter. "First we lose the lieutenant, then McWilliams, then Hoskins, then we get machine-gunned. It's all been bad."

"You've got to expect the machine guns," Tyne said. He thought of McWilliams. There had been a lot like McWilliams. Smith was groaning a little, but he was smoking a cigarette at the same time, so it couldn't be too bad. Smith was out of it for a while. The groans just meant that he was working for his Purple Heart. There were many men in the army who would be glad to be in Smith's shoes.

"I don't like the responsibility," Porter said. "It's not a sergeant's job. If I'd wanted the responsibility I'd have been an officer."

"You're stuck with it," Tyne said. He saw Porter's point, however, It was no joke, getting through to that farmhouse. Anything might happen. He was still worried about the tanks.

"Tanks," he said aloud.

"Huh?"

"I hope to God they don't send tanks along here before we get to that farmhouse."

"Jesus, you think they will?"

"You never know."

"We'd better get moving, hadn't we?"

"I think we had. If I were you I'd keep off the road. Let's take it along the ditch. It seems to follow the road pretty well; as far as we can see, anyway."

Porter considered for a moment. "Okay. What about Smith?"

"I'll talk to him."

With an effort Tyne rose to his feet and went over to where Smith was lying in the ditch, his pack underneath his head. "How you feeling, Smith?"

"In the pink, in the pink."

"Think you can stay here by yourself for a while?"

"Leave me some butts."

"Sure you'll be all right?"

A low groan. "Sure, Corporal; just leave me some butts."

"Someone will be coming to pick you up." Tyne took his pack of cigarettes from his pocket and gave it to Smith. It was nearly full. "He'll stay," he said to Porter when he went back.

"We'd better get started, then," Porter said.

He blew his whistle. Grumbling, the platoon rose to its feet.

Porter walked to the head of the column. "We'll stick to the ditch this time," he told them. "Keep the same formation, but stick to the ditch."

Casually the squads gathered together. Tyne took up his place as last man in the column. He listened to the sounds of battle to the north. They had increased perceptibly in volume. The battle sent its noises out in three sections. From far inland came the dull throb of enemy artillery, two or three miles inland from the beachhead was the sound of small arms, grenades, machine guns, and mortars, and from the sea came the thunder of the ships' guns. Added to this and forming a blanket for it was the hum of aircraft circling endlessly over the beach. Tyne imagined that it was wooded country where the small-arms fire could be heard; there must be a lot of sniping going on. That was the main engagement; there could be no doubt about it. The platoon was completely out of that phase of the action. He was convinced that their job was to prevent any flank attack, and he wondered incuriously if Porter had accepted his theory. The way Porter was acting, it looked like he would accept a theory that said the road they were on led to Gettysburg, Pennsylvania.

Tyne started to reach for a cigarette, then realized that he had given all he had to Smith. He walked over to where Smith was lying in the ditch. "Can I bum one of those butts back, Smitty?" he asked.

"Help yourself, Corporal," Smith said. Then: "How long you think I'll be here?"

"Beats me," Tyne said. "It shouldn't be long, though. There'll be plenty of company coming up this road pretty soon."

"What company?"

Tyne grinned. "Any kind you want. Take it easy, Smitty."

He walked away. "If I want anything I'll ring," Smith called after him. He had forgotten to groan.

Up front Porter blew his whistle. The platoon started to move. They could make time along the ditch just as well as on the road; as a matter of fact, it was easier going, because it was level. There were no dry clods of mud and no ruts. They stepped out briskly. It could almost have been a route march. But every man's ears strained toward the thundering hell to the north, and every man's mind strained ahead of him. Tenseness was in every face. Uneasiness had pervaded the whole platoon; now none of them liked the situation. Each spine was possessed of an unnatural rigidity; they were all stiff and uneasy. They had begun to fear the road that ran along by the ditch. It had taken on proportions beyond any intentions of those who had once driven their carts and wagons over it. The road ran, a skinny, unsatisfactory ribbon, toward the crouching Unknown, the dangerous future. Over it at any time might appear a motorcyclist or an armored car or a tank. The next five miles were full of terrors.

Before them stretched a series of little hills, wooded in patches. They were getting away from the level ground that merged with the beaches. Somewhere in this district was a great plain, but they did not seem to be anywhere near it. Nowhere could they see any signs of life—either houses or fields or men. Only the ditch and the crude road proved that this was inhabited country. If it had not been for the sounds of battle a great and utter silence would have hung over that place.

Behind them three P-38s crossed the road, flying low, heading for the firing. Strafe job, Porter thought as he watched them pass and vanish over the low hills. He wished that three of them would roar up the road ahead of the platoon and see what was going on. But then, he decided, if anything was happening up there one of the planes would have noticed it. He felt slightly comforted by the number of Allied planes over the beach. It was obvious that they had air superiority, and that meant a lot. It could mean everything. It might even save them, though Porter could not say, even to himself, what it would save them from. All he had was a half-formed idea that they were walking into trouble. He did not know why he felt that way; all that he knew was that he did. It was an emotion that could not be called fear, because Porter was not afraid, not in the strict sense of the word. It was merely that he had developed an extraordinary sense of suspicion, which in its way can be more paralyzing than fear.

Porter had at last reached the stage where he hated to do anything. He could no longer bring himself to move of his own accord; he had to have someone else urge him on. He was not, however, completely passive. On the contrary, he preferred to force the issue by asking the other man leading questions. What did he think should be done? Should such and such a thing be done in such and such a way? He could no longer put his brain to work; he had to have a middleman between his body and his mind.

The gunfire made Porter nervous. Irresistibly he found himself drawn to it. Gunfire was understandable, dire though it might be. It was identified with men and actual happenings; there was nothing secret about it. You could hear the shell coming, you could see the sniper in the tree, you could lie under the machine-gun's swath. But moving toward an unknown destination through secretive country was hard. Porter wished desperately that Halverson were not dead. Perhaps, he thought, he wasn't dead at all. There was no confirmation. McWilliams couldn't have seen him.

On a sudden impulse Porter dropped out of the column and waited until Tyne came abreast of him.

''What's the matter, Eddie?'' Tyne asked.

''About Halverson,'' Porter said. ''Did McWilliams see them bring him in?''

Tyne thought a moment. ''No,'' he said slowly. ''He said Tolliver told him.''

''Who's Tolliver?''

''He's a guy in B Company.''

''Never heard of him.''

''He must have been a friend of McWilliams.''

''Did he know Halverson?''

''He must have. He said he saw Halverson.''

''And he said Halverson was dead?''

''That's what Mac said.''

They walked on in silence for a minute.

''Bill,'' Porter said, ''suppose Halverson isn't dead. Suppose this guy had him confused with somebody else. Suppose there was somebody who looked like him.''

''Suppose there was.''

''I don't think Halverson's dead, Bill. What do you think?''

"God damn it, I don't know. All I know is what Mac told me."

"I don't think he's dead, Bill."

"I hope he isn't. I don't wish any hard luck to anybody."

"Sure as hell, he's going to show up here. I'll bet you anything he's trying to catch up with us now. They can't knock off a competent bastard like Halverson. Guys like that come through every time."

Tyne studied Porter's face. "Do you want to stop and wait?" he asked. There was a suspicion of sarcasm in his voice.

"No, that wouldn't do any good," Porter said seriously. "I wish to hell he was here, though."

"Give me a cigarette," said Tyne. He took a deep mouthful of smoke as he watched Porter jog heavily back to the head of the little column.

Archimbeau was plotting the course of the war as he strode along. He was trying to improve on the fact that he expected to fight the Battle of Tibet eventually, and he was trying to remember geography that had slipped his mind in the eighth grade. There was, he was sure, a country east of Tibet, but he was god-damned if he could think of it. All he could think of was Afghanistan, and as he remembered it that was somewhere around India. Victor McLaglen in the movies was always fighting around there. He had the itinerary down pretty well up to Tibet, though. Archimbeau, who did not, in all seriousness, expect to see the shores of the United States for three years, wondered where he would have gone if he had been sent to a place like New Guinea. Probably to some of those islands and then to Burma or some place. He wished he had an atlas; first chance he had he'd get one.

"Hey, Cousins," he said. "What comes after Tibet?"

"What comes where after Tibet, for God's sake?"

"In the war. Where we going to fight the war after Tibet?"

"How the hell do I know? In bed."

"There's a country. I can't think of its name."

"There's a million countries I can't think of their names."

"All right, I just asked. Forget it."

But Cousins had suddenly lost interest in Archimbeau. Over on the left, about five hundred yards away, he saw two figures coming toward them.

"Arch," he said softly. "Look."

Archimbeau looked. And as he saw the figures Cousins turned and went running back to Sergeant Porter. He crouched a little as he ran.

6

"WHAT THE HELL are they?" Sergeant Porter asked.

"Damned if I know," Cousins said. "Too far away."

"Ward," Porter said. "Take a couple of men and go down and see."

"Johnson, Riddle," Ward said. The three of them cut away from the ditch, crossed the road, and moved over the field.

"Take it easy," Porter said after them.

Sergeant Ward had a grenade in his hand and his carbine crooked under his left arm. The figures had disappeared in a little gully. "Fan out a little," Ward said.

Johnson and Riddle fanned out as Ward broke into a trot. They picked up the pace from him. Suddenly Ward flung himself down on the ground; the privates followed him.

Two hundred yards away the figures appeared again. They were men, walking fast. Every ten seconds one of the men would look behind him as though he feared pursuit. They were Italian soldiers, evidently unarmed.

Ward rose to his feet and whistled at them. They looked in his direction and stopped dead in their tracks. One of them started to run. The other man said something to him, and he stopped uncertainly. Then he came back. Ward made a gesture for them to come to him. They hesitated for a moment and then, without a word passing between them, they simultaneously broke into a run.

Ward, as they came up to him, looked them over calmly. They looked dead beat. Both had three days' worth of beard and their uniforms were torn and dirty. One man had torn the leg of his pants, and through the hole Ward could see a blood-soaked bandage.

When they came within ten feet they stopped running, smiled, and burst out into loud exclamations, one man's words running into the other's. One of them was just a kid, not more than nineteen; the other, with the injured leg, was about thirty.

"You speak English?" Ward asked the older man.

They both shook their heads violently in the affirmative and went on talking Italian.

"Oh, hell," Ward said. He gestured for the men to follow him and started back toward the platoon. Johnson and Riddle fell in silently behind the Italians.

"Couple of wops," Ward said to Porter as he came up to the ditch.

''Yeah,'' Porter said. ''They speak English?''

''Damned if I know.''

''We'll find out,'' Porter said. ''Hey, Giorgio!''

''Giorgio got wounded,'' Archimbeau said.

''What's the matter with me?'' Porter said. ''Yeah. Tranella!''

Tranella, a dark little man from Ward's squad, came over. ''You want me, Sarge?'' he asked.

''Can you talk Italian?''

''Sure I can talk Italian.''

''Talk to these guys.''

''What'll I say?''

''Ask them where they come from, for Christ's sake.''

The two Italians were standing awkwardly, still grinning at nothing. Tranella looked calmly at them. ''Where are you from?'' he asked in Italian.

The two men gave loud exclamations of joy. The elder came over to Tranella and clasped him around the shoulders. *''Un compatriotto!''* he said.

''All right,'' Tranella said. ''Where are you from?''

''Turin,'' the man said eagerly.

''He says he's from Turin,'' Tranella said to Sergeant Porter.

''Where's that, for God's sake?''

''Up north. 'Way up north.''

''I don't mean that. Find out where he's coming from now.''

''Oh. Where are you coming from?''

The Italian waved his hands toward the north. ''There is a battle up there,'' he said. ''We are running away from the battle. Before that we were running away from the Germans. We are no longer fighting.''

Tranella translated.

''Ask him what's going on up there.''

''What did you see of the battle?''

''Ah, we saw much of the battle. We were lying along the road and we saw the tanks go by. We heard the firing.''

''What tanks?''

''The German tanks.''

''He says they were lying along a road and they saw the Germans bringing up some tanks.''

''Did the tanks go back again?''

''No, they did not go back again.''

''One went off in a field,'' the younger man said.

''Yes,'' said the older man, ''one went off in a field. It was one of the big ones, the Tigers.''

''In which direction did the Tiger go?''

''Toward the sea,'' the older Italian said.

''Going toward the beach, Sergeant.''

Porter looked back, along the road they had come. ''When was this?''

''When was this?'' Tranella translated.

''One hour ago,'' the man said. ''Two hours ago. I have no watch. Neither of us has a watch.''

''He doesn't know for sure. A couple of hours ago, maybe less.''

''Ask him if he saw any Germans.''

''Did you see any *tedeschi*?''

''I saw only the tanks. But there are many roads up there. There are many roads the *tedeschi* could use.''

''Only the tanks, Sergeant.''

''God damn it, Tranella, see what you can find out. Ask him some questions.''

''I am, Sergeant.''

''Well, find out something.''

''Ask him if he knows this country,'' Tyne said.

''The corporal wants to know if you know this country.''

The older Italian smiled at Tyne. ''I am from the north, but I know this country. I was once stationed here. I have maneuvered in this area.''

''He says yes.''

''Good,'' Tyne said. ''Where's the map, Eddie?''

''What map? Oh. It's here.'' Porter passed him the map case.

''We have here,'' Tyne said as he unfolded it, ''a map of the area. Tell him that, Tranella.''

Tranella told him. The Italian nodded vigorously. ''I too am a corporal,'' he said. ''I have handled maps.''

Tyne spread the map out on the brown grass, where it developed pointed little hills of its own at the folds. ''We are here, I think,'' he said, putting a dirty finger at a point along the road. ''Ask him if I am right?''

''Are we where the corporal has put his finger?''

The older Italian fell on his knees beside Tyne and the younger one crowded over his shoulder. ''Yes,'' he said, ''we are there. Perhaps a little farther on. There is where the battle is.'' He pointed to a road junction at the far left of the map. ''And here is where we saw the tanks.''

''Is it bad country?'' Porter asked.

''The sergeant wants to know if it is bad country.''

''It is good country for defense. We have defended it up there in the maneuvers. It is rough. There are many ravines. The rain makes them. This road will take you to country like it.''

''It is very dusty,'' the young man said.

''Have the Germans many men there?'' Tranella wanted to know.

''Who knows?'' said the older Italian. ''Who knows about the *tedeschi*? They have beaten us. Everyone has beaten us. We are no longer soldiers.''

''He says he don't know how many Germans are around,'' Tranella said.

''There were many *tedeschi* in this place,'' the Italian said, pointing to a town. ''But that was five months ago. Who knows now?''

''The Germans are everywhere,'' the younger man said. ''I myself have killed *un tedesco*.''

''This young guy says he's knocked off a Kraut,'' Tranella said.

''Ask him where,'' said Porter.

''Where'd you kill the German?''

''I killed him in Capua. I hit him with a rock.''

''We have left the army,'' the older Italian said. ''We are going south. He has relatives down there.''

''An uncle,'' the young man said.

''We have to hide sometimes,'' the older said. ''I think the Germans would kill us if they found us. I did not want this war.''

''Nor I,'' the young man said.

''Things are different in the north,'' said the older.

''My people are from Milan,'' Tranella said. ''They have told me about it there.''

''Then you know what things are like there,'' said the Italian. ''We are working people. We did not want the war. We did not want the Germans. They give you no choice. Now we can not go home. The Germans cover the north like beetles.''

''They won't,'' Tranella said.

The older man shrugged. ''It is hard to say. They are very difficult.''

''He's griping about the Germans,'' Tranella said.

"For God's sake," said Porter, "do you think we've got nothing to do but sit around while he tells us what's the matter with Italy? We know what's the matter with Italy. Find the hell out about that farmhouse."

"This farmhouse here," Tyne said. "Ask him if he knows anything about it."

Tranella pointed to the house on the map. "Do you know anything about this farm?"

"The Italian studied the map carefully. "I don't know," he said. "It is hard to say. This is not one of our maps. Yes, I remember that place. I remember that bridge. That is a nice farm."

"Ask him what kind of bridge it is."

"What kind of bridge is it?"

The Italian looked puzzled. "That I do not remember. It may be wood. It may be steel. It may be concrete. There are so many bridges."

"He don't know," Tranella said.

"Ask him does he know where I can get a pizza," Rivera said.

"Shut up," said Sergeant Porter.

"I can tell you one thing," the Italian said. "Inland there are many *tedeschi*."

"He says there 're a lot of Krauts a few miles along," Tranella said.

"How many?"

"Who can tell? Everywhere there are many."

"He says he hasn't got any god-damned idea."

"I would like a cigarette," the older Italian said.

"I, too," said the younger.

"Now they both want butts," Tranella said.

"Give them a couple," Porter said.

"Out of my own, for God's sake?" Tranella said.

"Give them a couple," Tyne said.

Tranella gave each of the Italians a cigarette and lit them for them. They inhaled deeply and luxuriously.

"Good," said the younger. "Good tobacco."

"The best," said the older. "Well," he said to Tranella, "now we are your prisoners. We shall follow you."

"He says they're our prisoners and that they're going to come along," Tranella said.

"The hell they are," Porter said. "We aren't at war with Italy any more. They can go where they god-damn please."

"You can go," Tranella said.

The older man gave a gesture of surprise. "But where can we go?" he asked. "We have no money. The Germans will get us."

"They're your friends," Tranella said.

"We are hungry, too," said the older Italian.

"Now the bastards say they're hungry," Tranella said.

"Give them some K ration," Porter said.

"They can take this," Rivera said. He tossed a can of K ration to the older Italian. "When they get a mouthful of that crap they'll wish Italy never went out of the war. They'll think twice about the Americans next time."

"Tell them they will be safe here," Porter said.

"The sergeant says that you will be safe here," Tranella said. "No Germans will come here."

"We would rather go with you," the older Italian said.

"It is an order," said Tranella. Then, to Porter: "God-damnedest people I ever saw."

"We might as well go on," Porter said to Tyne.

Tyne carefully folded the map and put it back in the case. "We might as well," he said.

"Thanks, Tranella," Porter said.

"Any time, Sarge." Tranella wandered back toward the rear of the little column. The Italians remained standing where they were, confused and uneasy.

"We don't know any more than we did before," Tyne said. "Not a damned bit more."

"Did you expect to?" Porter wanted to know.

"They might have known something."

"They never know anything. I've seen too many of them come in. They know all about the private lives of their god-damned lieutenants, but they don't know anything else. They never know anything else. You always draw a blank."

Porter blew his whistle and the column started off again. "Stay up here with me, Bill," he said. "I want to talk to you."

The Italians stood watching the platoon pass them. They were still watching as the last men disappeared over the crest of a small hill. The older one still had the can of K ration clutched in one hand.

"That's the Italians for you," Rivera said.

"What's the Italians?" Friedman wanted to know.

"All give and no take."

"What nationality are you, Rivera?"

"I'm a god-damned Irishman. What did you think I was?"

"I was just wondering, that's all."

"So help me God, I hope I never see another Italian after this war. I never want to see another one. My God, in Tunisia they were even surrendering to generals."

"How many surrendered to you?"

"All the ones that surrendered to me were dead. A guy in my position never sees any live ones."

"You're a tough baby, Rivera."

"I sure as hell am."

"What are you going to do after the war?"

"Join a mob. I'm a mobster."

"What did you do before the war?"

"Friedman, sixty million times you asked me that. I was an undertaker. I undertook stiffs."

"How'd you like the job?"

"It made my hands smell."

"Why don't you join the Graves Registration Squad of the QMC? That's right up your alley."

"I can't spell, for God's sake. Judson, you look like a bright boy. Why don't you join the Graves Registration Squad of the QMC?"

"How's the pay?" Judson asked.

"Lousy."

"Is there any future in it?"

"What the hell do you care about the future?" Friedman said. "You ain't even living in the present."

"That's right, Jakie," said Rivera. "You're a smart apple, Jakie. A character reader. A reader of character."

"What do you mean I ain't living in the present?" Judson demanded.

"I'll ask you," Friedman said. "Where are you now?"

"Italy."

"How do you know you're in Italy? You seen any signposts in Italian?"

"We landed in Italy."

"How the hell you know you landed in Italy? Just because somebody told you? You believe all you hear?"

"I just seen a couple of Italians."

"In Tunisia," Rivera said, "you seen a million Italians. Was that Italy? Naw, it was Tunisia. You're ignorant, Judson."

"All right," Judson said, "if we ain't in Italy, where are we?"

"Sunny France," Friedman said. "Marching up to Armentières. Where the hell did you think we was?"

"Italy," said Private Judson stubbornly.

"I give up," Friedman said.

"So do I," said Rivera. "If the privates are dumb, Jesus, think what the generals must be like. I'm going to get out of this army."

"Me, too," Friedman said. "Move over."

In the second squad Privates James and Carraway were discussing art.

"The *Saturday Evening Post* has the best cover," James said. "That guy. What's his name? Norman Rockwell. He can draw covers to beat all hell. He had some covers about the army."

"I'll take a camera picture any day," said Carraway. "Drawing's okay, but it ain't real. I like things to be real."

"Jesus, this guy Rockwell made it look just like a picture. I used to look at them. It looks just like a picture, I used to say. You'd never of known it was painted."

"He should of took a picture and saved time."

"Ah, you can't get the touch in a picture," James said.

"Drawings was all right when they didn't have cameras," said Carraway. "But now they got cameras, so you don't have to draw."

"That's screwy."

"Why is it screwy?"

"You might just as well say that now they got moving pictures so there's no sense in taking regular pictures. You might just as well have a movie on the cover of a magazine."

"Someday they'll have it, maybe."

"Naw, they won't. Maybe they'll have movies that'll smell, though. Maybe the scene will be in a garden or something and you can smell the flowers."

"I'd like to see one of them laid in a brewery right now," Carraway said, "so I could smell the beer. If a guy came along right now and said, 'What'll you give me for a can of Ruppert's?' I'd give him my god-damned rifle and my god-damned bayonet and even my god-damned pants."

"You don't need pants in this climate, anyway. Except at night."

"The British got the right idea. They ought to issue us some of these short pants, too."

"These uniforms is the worst I ever ran into."

"You never ran into any others."

"When I come into the army they were issuing blue fatigues. That's how long I been in the army."

"When I come into the army they were issuing muzzle-loading rifles. That's how long *I* been in the army."

Sergeant Porter and Corporal Tyne slogged along in silence. Porter kept his head down, as though he were studying the ground before his feet. Tyne kept his eyes straight ahead, watching the backs of the scouts, Cousins and Archimbeau. Occasionally he looked sidewise at Porter. The thought of the two Italians kept running through his head.

He knew very little about Italy, but when he considered it he imagined that he probably knew as much about it as he did any other country, excepting his own. Italy, England, France, and Germany—those were the countries Americans knew best. Tyne did not hate Italy, nor did he hate the Italians. He merely ignored them. Some of the men, he knew, hated them—not necessarily because they had killed their share of Americans, but because they were cowards. They ran. They always ran. A soldier could hate the Germans, but he would respect them at the same time. He would respect their stubborn bravery and their cunning and their battle wisdom. But the Italians had none of these negative virtues. The Italians had nothing.

The two ex-soldiers had, in a way, been pitiful. They had been cast out on a world that they could no longer comprehend. And yet it had been a world they had helped to make, a world they had probably wanted to make, a world of confusion in which they and millions like them would have been the only elements possessed of power and will, or at least possessed of leaders who were possessed of power and will. But now the leaders were gone and the power and the will with them. What remained was chaos and ashes, a country shattered and a people lost.

"Bill," Sergeant Porter said, "did you ever have the feeling that something was going to happen to you?"

"I have it all the time."

"I've got it now."

"Don't worry about it."

''But I've never had it before. I don't like it. Something's happened to me.''

''What?''

''I don't know. Look: if you have to, will you take over?''

''What about Ward?''

''I want you.''

''Sure, Eddie. But don't worry so damned much. Everything's going to be all right.''

''Everything's always all right,'' Porter said. He went back to staring at the ground.

He was beginning to frighten Tyne a little. Something was evidently the matter with Porter. It was as though he were in a vacuum, as though someone had put him in some great bottle and then had drawn out all the air. Porter was lifeless, limp. He seemed unable to form an opinion any more. Tyne rapidly ran through the places where he had seen Porter in action, where he had been most intimate with him. The places framed themselves like signposts in his mind—Tebessa, Gafsa, Bizerte, Gela, the hills of Sicily, and now here. There was a definite change in the man, a definite and dangerous change.

''Ward might not like anything like that,'' he said. He was trying to draw Porter out.

''Why shouldn't Ward like it?'' Porter demanded. He did not raise his eyes from the ground. ''There's no reason why he shouldn't like it. He has his job.''

''We all have our jobs,'' Tyne said.

Said Sergeant Porter, ''I don't feel well. I feel god-damned lousy. My head aches.''

The ditch stopped abruptly, for no apparent reason. They were coming into lightly wooded country, of rather sharp slopes. Here and there a great boulder could be seen. The trees looked ancient and gnarled. None of them were very large; it was as though they could not draw enough sustenance from the soil and were sentenced to be forever stunted. There was an air of strain about the trees, as though they were striving to increase themselves, to swell in size, under impossible and unreasonable conditions.

When the ditch stopped, Archimbeau swerved over to the road without awaiting any command. The rest of the column trailed after him. As far as Archimbeau was concerned they might just as well walk on the road as anywhere else. It made no difference to him. It was all the same country, all the same war. The same dangers were everywhere. He did not expect any more planes to come over. Allied planes were covering the territory pretty well; they were passing over the column frequently now, and if anything went wrong, either on the road ahead or around them, the planes would spot it. As far as Archimbeau was concerned the operation had developed into an automatic business. All they had to do was get to where they were going, do what they had to do, and then relax. It was simple; it was as simple as anything ever was. It was as simple as the Battle of Tibet would be. That was always the way it was in the army. Things looked complicated as hell, but when you came to do them they were simple. Archimbeau thought of Trasker—the suddenly stilled voice, the smashed jaw, the bereft body. Death was like that.

"Cousins," he said, "you married?"

"Naw," Cousins said. "Why the hell should I be married?"

"After the war I'm going to get married."

"Okay. Go ahead."

"Honest to God, if I had a wife now she'd be sending me things. Cookies, maybe. Maybe a sweater. I haven't got a package since I come overseas."

"I haven't got a package either," Cousins said. "What the hell good is it anyway? You open it and you got to give something to everybody you know. There's no percentage in that. I'm just as happy. If I was married I'd have to be sending money home all the time, too. And God knows what my wife might be doing. The hell with it."

"When I get to Tibet," Archimbeau said solemnly, "I'm going to marry a Tibet woman."

"Okay," Cousins said. "Go ahead."

Time stopped in the sound of the moving feet. The clocks ran out. The sun stood still. The world contracted. To the north the battle, the battle that had not yet touched them, went on. They were a part of it and yet not a part of it. For the moment they were still individuals, because their group was small enough for them to be individuals. They had not yet become part of a huge and heaving mass. Each man was recognizable as himself. The platoon was part of a larger pattern, but it had not yet lost its identity. The battle whose noises rolled over the little hills at them was still standing and watching them go about their essential business; it had not yet beckoned them to come. They had been in an enemy country for five hours, and they had not yet seen an enemy.

7

THEY COULD HEAR the motorcycle coming over and above all other noises. Singly and in pairs they turned to look at it. None of them considered the possibility that it might be an enemy motorcycle; it was coming from the direction in which they had come, and it had to be one of theirs. It came slowly for a motorcycle. The rider was obviously having trouble with the rutty road. He jazzed his motor, modulated it, and then jazzed it again. Over the sound of the motorcycle they could hear Porter's whistle demanding that they halt. They halted, raggedly.

The rider bounced up to the head of the column and stopped by Sergeant Porter. He cut his motor. He was a sergeant, too.

"What's cooking, Jack?" he said to Porter.

"All quiet so far," Porter said. "Where you from?"

The rider ignored the question. "What's up this road?" he wanted to know.

"Damned if I know," Porter said. "Where you from?"

"I'm looking for the 25th. You seen the 25th anywhere?"

"The 25th what, for God's sake?"

"Infantry."

"Never heard of them."

The rider looked puzzled. "They were supposed to be up this road," he said.

"Anything can be up this road," Porter said.

"There are some other roads running from the beach," said Tyne. "They run right through the battle area, according to the map."

"Jesus," the rider said, "I didn't know there were any other roads. They just told me to go up the road. They didn't say anything about more than one. What the hell, that's the army." He lit a cigarette.

"What's it like on the beach?" Porter asked.

"Okay," the rider said. "A little rough. They're shelling the god-damned place. Was that your man I saw down the road?"

"What man?" Porter asked.

"A little guy with a smashed-up shoulder."

"Yeah, he's ours. He all right?"

"Damned if I know. I just saw him sitting in a ditch. He didn't complain."

"Did you see a couple of Italian soldiers?" Porter asked.

"Christ's sake, they still fighting?" the rider asked.

"No, we just ran into them down the road."

''Didn't see them. What're you looking for up here, anyway?''

''Objective's a farmhouse,'' Porter said. ''About three miles up the road.''

''Anything up there?'' the rider asked.

''Damned if I know.''

''Want me to take a run up and see?''

''I thought you were looking for the 25th,'' Tyne said.

''They'll keep,'' said the rider. ''It's not important. Nothing's important in this god-damned war.''

''It'll be damned nice if you'll scout a couple of miles,'' Porter said. ''Take a lot off my mind, anyway.''

''Okay,'' the rider said. He flipped away his cigarette. ''This is the first time I've been to Italy. I got to see the country.''

He shoved his machine in gear and roared away up the road, vanishing over the brow of a hill. The platoon resumed its march.

''I feel better,'' Porter said. ''Maybe I should have told him it was the farmhouse by the bridge. You think I should have told him that, Bill?''

''It's the only farmhouse there is,'' Tyne said. ''He can't miss it.''

''You can always miss,'' Porter said. ''But I feel better. If the road's clear it might be all right after all. How long do you think it will take him to get back?''

Tyne considered. ''Fifteen or twenty minutes,'' he said.

''That's the kind of a job to have,'' Friedman said. ''A nice shiny motorcycle and a nice shiny carbine. No walking. Solid comfort.''

''Between you and me, Jakie,'' said Rivera, ''motorcycles scare hell out of me.''

''I didn't think you were scared of anything.''

''Women and motorcycles, Jakie. A butt.''

Wearily Friedman passed him a cigarette and a match. ''When I run out of butts,'' he said, ''you'll be in a hell of a mess.''

''I'll find a new friend,'' Rivera said.

''I'd still like to be sitting in his boots,'' said Friedman.

''Whose boots?''

''The guy on the motorcycle. It's a life.''

''What are you, Friedman, a lousy hero?''

''I like my comfort.''

''Those guys are dead pigeons. High mortality rate.''

''So what?''

"That was the first sergeant I ever saw on a motorcycle. Most of them are lucky if they live to make corporal."

"Do you think you'll ever live to make corporal?"

"Baby, I just want to live long enough to make civilian."

"You've got no imagination, Rivera. You're a lump."

"Okay."

Sergeant Ward was thinking of apples. He didn't know why; he just happened to be thinking of apples. They made a wonderful picture in his mind—huge, red, and juicy. He thought of the different varieties, Baldwins, McIntosh Reds, pippins, russets. He imagined he was cutting one with a knife, the creamy flesh showing wet as he opened the halves. And the funny thing about it was that Ward didn't like apples very much. Occasionally he would eat one, but he wasn't one who went overboard for them. He'd take a pear any day. But right now it was apples. Pears were yellow and the country was yellow; the combination was bad. But apples were red and wet and cold and juicy. Sergeant Ward could feel the sweat oozing through his woolen shirt; the damp cloth clung to his back. It had seemed hardly warm enough last night, and now it was killing him. Stupid. Apples.

There were more trees, and from the crests of the little hills gaunt, rain-formed gullies cut down to the hollows. Incipient serious erosion was everywhere. With his practiced farmer's eye Sergeant Ward studied the soil. He did not like it. It looked old and tired and worn out. Soil was like a body. If you didn't take care of it it would die. There was too much dead soil in the world. For nearly a year Sergeant Ward had been studying the earth. Most of what he had seen had been bad. There were some rich places in Tunisia. They took care of it there; they had taken care of it for centuries. Those were the people who really grew things, who wanted to grow things, who made things live for them. The soil in this small part of Italy was dry and barren and lifeless. Perhaps too many soldiers had walked on it. They had been walking on it for many, many years.

Sergeant Ward was a farmer, and he was also a man of strong opinions that, once formed, were changed only by an Act of God or his wife. He had nearly formed the opinion that Italy was a barren country. He could do it on just what he had seen since he had landed. And though he might spend the rest of his sojourn in Italy walking around in lush gardens and vineyards, he would never change his opinion. He would take it back to Vermont with him. He would spread it wherever he went. Sergeant Ward was not one to take the long view.

"It's time that rider was coming back," Porter said.

Tyne looked at his watch. "He's only been gone ten minutes."

"It seems longer."

"Take it easy, Eddie. It's a long war."

"I know. But everything takes so damned long. Nothing ever happens when it should happen."

"We're doing all right, Eddie."

He was not, of course, sure that they were doing all right. He wasn't sure of anything of the kind. On the contrary, he was worried about the whole business. Not in the way Porter was, though. Porter was more than worried: he was rattled. But Tyne had the natural worries of a careful man. He knew that it was possible for things to go smoothly, but the wisest thing was to take it for granted that they wouldn't. You couldn't go wrong that way. Then, if they turned out to be smooth after all, you felt so much the better. It was not the best philosophy in the world, but it worked.

"It's taking him a long time, Porter said.

"Take it easy, Eddie," Tyne said again.

"It's always the same," Porter said. "Nothing ever happens right. It's always been that way. It always will be that way. You wait for someone and he never shows up. You tell somebody to do something and he does it wrong. It's never going to be any different. Never. They put me on to this job, and I didn't want it. It isn't my responsibility. I don't understand this war. Everything's crazy. Nothing's gone right today. It's not going to get any better." He spoke in a flat, taut monotone that did not carry beyond Tyne's ears.

"You're worrying too much, Eddie," Tyne said soothingly. "There's nothing to worry about. It'll go along. It was worse in other places."

"In other places we knew where we were going," Porter said.

"Sometimes we didn't."

"We thought we did."

"This is a tough road. That rider can't make any time."

"They can always make time if they want to make time. Bill, I'm scared of the tanks."

"Why?"

"If they catch us on this road they've got us cold. Like mackerel."

The same idea had passed through Tyne's mind and had worried him. It was perfectly true; they'd be duck soup for tanks. Even one tank, for that matter. It could come up over one of the hills and be on them before they'd have time to scatter. And all they had was grenades and damned little cover. Tyne didn't relish the thought of the tanks. "There probably isn't a tank within five miles of here," he said. "They're all over where the noise is."

Porter stared at the ground. He did not answer.

"I wrote a letter to my wife," Private Johnson said to Private Riddle.

"All right," Riddle said.

"I wrote it in the landing barge. Hard as hell to write something when you can't see it."

"Why didn't you wait till daylight?"

"You never can tell," Johnson said. "A man doesn't want to take no chances. I even wrote the envelope in the dark. It looked good."

"How the hell do you know it looked good?"

"I saw it in the daylight. Then I gave it to Sergeant Hoskins."

"What for, for Jesus' sake?"

"To mail for me."

"That old bastard'll probably tear it open and read it. He's probably reading it right now," Riddle said.

"Aw, he wouldn't do a thing like that."

"You never know what a sergeant will do. They do some goddamned funny things."

"He wouldn't do that."

"How do you know he wouldn't? Maybe he thinks there's money in it. Maybe he's using it for a bandage. He's got a bullet hole in him. Maybe he stuffed it in the bullet hole."

"You're crazy. You can't stuff paper in a bullet hole."

"How do you know you can't?"

"It crinkles."

"Jesus, what a dope. The next time you get a bullet hole in you, stuff some paper in it and see how it feels. Then you'll know."

"I never had a bullet hole in me."

"Wait'll you get one, then."

"Cut that stuff out, Riddle," Sergeant Ward said. "If he mailed a letter, he mailed a letter. Leave him alone."

"I was just kidding, Sarge," Riddle said.

"You got a mean streak, Riddle. Somebody's going to paste you one of these days."

"I'll wait," said Riddle. "Okay, Johnson, you mailed your letter." Then, in a whisper: "But you never know what sergeants will do."

"They won't do anything," Johnson said.

The battle seemed to be increasing. More artillery could be heard on both sides. The guns sounded deeper and more dangerous. The platoon was now far from the danger area. It was as though the country had taken the men in and hidden them. They were surrounded by a near silence, over which the noise of the battle seemed faint, foreign, and far away, as though it were coming to them over water, as though it were not their quarrel. It was the road that might betray them to the war. It was the one way out of the silence, their one link with the outside world. Over it the rider had gone, vanishing from what they knew into what they did not know. Impatiently they waited for his return. They did not talk to each other about it; rather the feeling was understood. The most important thoughts never have to be spoken.

The rider was late. He was overdue. They strained to catch the sound of his motor, roaring toward them out of the unknown country before them. Over their heads the trees reached out, trying to touch each other across the road. The trees were larger now, and of a different variety. Their branches were clean and lithe, but their trunks were warped and gnarled, as though they had hard births. The whole country looked as though it had fought to come alive; either that or had lived too long. They all thought that, though none of them could have put it into words. With an instinct like that of animals, they could be satisfied or dissatisfied with a landscape on sight. They could see the whole thing as one great panorama, with everything in its place, without knowing what it was about the view that they disliked.

"I suppose you still think he'll be back," Porter said.

"He may have gone further on than we thought he would," Tyne said. "Or he might have got a flat."

"He didn't go too far and he didn't get a flat," Porter said. "He ran into trouble. Did you hear any firing?"

"Didn't hear a damned thing."

"He ran into trouble."

Exasperation surged up in Tyne. "For Christ's sake, Eddie," he said, "I don't know what's the matter with you or what you're thinking, but you're going to have everyone with their tongues hanging out if you don't snap out of it. What the hell's the matter?"

"I don't know." Porter brushed his hand across his forehead under the helmet. "My head aches."

"Are you sick?"

"I don't know. Leave me alone."

"Okay."

"Still want to be on a motorcycle, Ugly?" Rivera asked.

"Sure," Friedman said. "It's a life."

"In that guy's case, the question is—is it a life?"

"He's probably sitting under a tree somewhere, reading a book."

"Friedman, it's optimists like you that cause all the trouble in the world. Where would he get a book?"

"How the hell do I know where he'd get a book?"

Friedman took out a package of cigarettes, removed one, crumpled the package, and threw it away. "I'll let you watch me," he said.

"Open another god-damned pack," Rivera said.

"All I got, baby."

"A drag, then."

"I'll consider it."

"What's the point of having a motorcycle if they knock you off every time you get on to it? And if they don't knock you off you smack into a wall in the dark and knock yourself off. What's the point? Where's the percentage?"

"It's all in how you look at it," Friedman said. "A motorcycle is a civilized way to travel."

"We ain't in civilization," Rivera said. "We ain't anywhere. A drag."

Sighing, Friedman passed over his last cigarette. Rivera took a deep pull at it. "Take it easy," Friedman said. "Take it easy."

"I'm a hard man," said Rivera.

Time moved on to the sound of boots on earth. The minutes drummed by. As they passed Tyne realized that the rider would not be back, that he might never be back. In the time that had been allotted to him he could have gone to the farmhouse and a couple of miles beyond. Probably the platoon would never know what had happened to him. He might have found a road that turned off, though there was no road marked on the map. Perhaps he had run into trouble beyond the bridge near the farmhouse, for beyond that bridge the road forked, and the Germans always were hell on crossroads.

It was odd, Tyne thought, how many people you met in the army who crossed your path for perhaps only a few seconds and then went on, never to be seen again. He could remember countless occasions and countless faces and countless voices. You never forgot the faces. In peacetime you could go into a store and talk to a clerk, but by the time you had left the store you had completely forgotten the clerk's face. It was different in war. You might see a man's face in the flash of an exploding shell or in the cab of a truck or peering out of a slit trench, and though you had never seen the face before and never would see it again, you couldn't forget it. War left impressions of unbelievable sharpness. It was almost as though men, in losing identity, gained identity. Their faces and voices became intense. They clung to the mind. They were like the hands of drowning men, reaching out of the water, refusing until the end to be devoured.

"Take a break," Porter said. "Tell them to take a break." Abruptly, without blowing his whistle, he turned off the road and strode in among the trees.

Tyne turned back to the column and held up his hand. "Take a break," he said in a loud, clear voice. "Take a break," he called ahead to the scouts.

The platoon moved off the road and into the trees. "Keep well back from the road," Tyne said. He did not want to take any chances of something coming along and nailing them. "Archimbeau, you stay out close to the road. If you see that rider coming back, wave to him." This last was for Porter's benefit.

Mumbling, Archimbeau walked back and settled down behind a bush close to the road. He had made up his mind that every dirty job in the army was his personal property. He never missed. In the early days when they had wanted another KP it had always been Archimbeau who had been chosen. He had pulled guard more than anyone else in the outfit. He was always at the head of the column, where it hurt. And he was always crawling off on his belly somewhere. Sometimes Archimbeau wondered if he could stand it until the Battle of Tibet. That was a long time to hang on. He thought sadly of a set of corporal's stripes. In a decent outfit a guy who'd done all the work he had would be a corporal easy. Even a sergeant, with luck. But it was just like this lousy outfit to leave you hanging around for years with nothing to show for it but calluses and bunions. A lousy outfit like this never even got around to replacing officers. Too god-damned economical. Solemnly Archimbeau spat into the bush, directly in front of his eyes. He decided he didn't like Italy any better than he liked any place else. They could have it. He'd had it already.

Tyne went over to where Porter was sitting under a tree, his head in his hands. He sat down beside him.

"Feel bad, Eddie?" he asked.

Porter raised his face from his hands. "Lousy," he said. "I don't know what the hell's the matter with me. I never felt like this before."

His hands were shaking slightly as though he had a fever. Tyne noted the fact and pursed his lips. "Maybe you'd better not go on," he said.

"Oh, hell, I've got to," said Porter. "They gave me this job and I've got to do it. It'll be all right."

"We'll get through," Tyne said. His voice carried as much conviction as he could manage. For the last half hour he had been getting that old Lost Patrol feeling, though there was really no reason for him to have it. The platoon was anything but lost. They knew where they were, and even if they didn't they could damned well find out by going toward the sound of the guns. Listening to the artillery, he noted that the fight was keeping within what seemed to be almost like defined boundaries. It did not appear to be spreading at all. It was odd that there were no flank movements of any kind. Or was he, himself, part of a flank movement? The Lost Patrol feeling he blamed on Porter. He was the one who was doing all the worrying. Everyone else was keeping his head. He suddenly felt very angry at Porter. When he said something like "We'll get through" he felt like a damned fool. This wasn't the movies.

"Something's up with the sergeant," Rivera said. He was lying on his stomach with his helmet off. His black hair was soaked and curly with sweat.

"Which sergeant?" Friedman asked.

"Porter."

Private Cousins was lying with them. "I noticed it," he said.

"Nobody tells me nothing," Friedman said.

"Keep your eyes open," said Rivera. "If you weren't smoking your last butts all the time and getting smoke in your eyes you might know more about what's going on."

"What's the matter with Porter?"

"How the hell do I know? I ain't a doctor. He's just acting funny, that's all."

"Working for a CDD," Cousins said.

"I'm a Section 8 man myself," Friedman said.

"You said it, honey," Rivera said. "Any time you want a certificate signed, just tap me on the shoulder."

"With an ax," Friedman said.

"The sergeant's been acting funny all day," Cousins said.

"This is a hell of a platoon," Rivera said. "In one morning we've lost one lieutenant and two non-coms, and have got another non-com feeling lousy. This platoon is hell on non-coms."

"Now I know why they want me to keep on being a private," Friedman said. "They want to spare me from grief."

"That sure as hell is the reason," Rivera said. "You can't say they ain't thoughtful."

Sergeant Ward came over and sat down by Porter and Tyne. "What's the matter, Porter?" he asked. "Feeling bad?"

"He feels lousy," Tyne said.

Porter had put his head back in his hands. He did not look up when Ward spoke.

"What's the matter?" Porter wanted to know.

Tyne shrugged.

"A guy can pick up anything in this kind of country," Ward said philosophically.

Porter raised his head. "Ward," he said, "if I can't go on would you mind if Tyne took over?"

Ward pulled out a dry blade of grass and placed it between his teeth. He stared out toward the road and turned the blade of grass moodily over in his mouth. "It don't make no difference to me," he said. "I don't care who's boss."

"Tyne's a good man," Porter said.

"I know he is," said Ward.

"You can work with him."

"I know I can."

"You can go on, Eddie," Tyne said.

"I don't know," said Porter. "I feel funny. I don't even know whether I'm sick or not. I just feel funny. Did you ever feel like you wanted to lie down and never get up?"

"Sure I have."

"That's the way I feel. Like I wanted to lie down and never get up."

"A guy gets tired after a while," said Ward. "You've been at it a long time."

"We've all been at it a long time," Porter said.

"Why don't you lie down a while, Eddie?" said Tyne. "You might feel better."

"I need a drink of water." Porter fumbled at his canteen and pulled it out of its cloth case. He pulled the canteen cup away from the bottom and unscrewed the top. That was one of Porter's idiosyncrasies: he never would drink from the mouth of the canteen, preferring always to use his cup. "Maybe I'd better lie down." He drank some water, screwed down the cap of the canteen, and laid cup and canteen beside him. Then he stretched out by the tree.

Ward ran some of the soil through his fingers. "Poor dirt," he said. "Poor country."

"Maybe if I rest," Porter said. He closed his eyes.

Archimbeau had watched the bubbles on his spittle for a long time. They fascinated him, reminding him of things insects made in the early morning at home. If you went out in the fields early you could see them. Spider spit, they were called. He didn't think spiders made them, but he supposed they could if they wanted to.

Suddenly Archimbeau pricked up his ears. There was the sound of a motor down the road, coming toward them. It didn't sound like a motorcycle, but that didn't mean that it couldn't be. These little hills could fool you. He raised himself on one knee and peered over the bush. In the direction of the farmhouse the road rose to a slight crest and then dipped. Beyond the dip, perhaps a hundred yards away, was another, slightly higher hill. He could see the crest of it. And as he looked out from behind the bush he saw, poking over the brow of the far hill, not a motorcycle, not a tank, but a lovely gleaming new armored car. It was German, and what it was doing moving over the road in their direction Archimbeau didn't wait to ask himself. He spun around, cupped his hands, and yelled "Armored car coming. Enemy armored car. Take cover!"

Then he fell flat behind his bush and took a grenade out of his pocket. Behind him the platoon scurried for cover.

8

SOMETIMES IT ALMOST seems as though a man can throw up cover and concealment in his imagination and have it work. He can lie flat on the ground and will that he won't be seen, and he won't be. It is almost as though he could make himself invisible just by willing it. This is the last, most desperate cover of all, but it works a surprising number of times. If you have time you can fix things so that no one would ever be able to find you, but you've got to have the time. Even an hour can mean a lot. But it's when the planes come down or they come over the hill and surprise you that you start trying to push your face and stomach into the ground. When there's nothing over you it becomes necessary to will things. Otherwise you're a gone goose.

That was the way it was when the armored car came poking over the hill. The platoon heard Archimbeau yell, and then they dived for the trees. There wasn't time to do anything else. They threw themselves behind the trunks and put their heads down and hung on. All of them, that is, except Porter. When he heard Archimbeau's warning he merely rolled over on his stomach and burst into tears.

Tyne was behind a tree that was perhaps six inches thick and some three feet away from where he had been sitting. On one side of him Ward lay with his carbine beside him. He had his chin on the ground and was peering out toward the road. Tyne was conscious of Porter's body, lying completely in the open. Near the road he could see the soles of Archimbeau's feet where he lay behind his bush.

The armored car was a small one, used for light reconnaissance and carrying a crew of two, with one machine gun poking out of a sawed-off turret behind the driver. Archimbeau watched it come toward him. The car was battened down completely, and the crew must have been pretty confident that there was no one around, because the turret was keeping still. If they'd been worried they'd have revolved it. The car was traveling slowly, taking its time. Archimbeau watched as it came closer. He prepared to pull the pin from his grenade. Then, thinking better of it, he held off. The armored car came abreast of him and roared on down in the direction from which they had come. Archimbeau whistled lightly between his teeth. He looked up the road. Nothing. He scrambled around and crawled back on his belly to where the platoon was hiding behind its trees.

He saw Sergeant Porter lying on his stomach, facing away from the road. "Jesus Christ, Sarge," he said. "That was close."

"Leave him alone," Tyne said. "He's sick."

They spoke in whispers, as though the crew of the armored car might hear them and come back. "What's the matter with him?" Archimbeau demanded.

"Sick," Tyne said. He came out from behind his tree and crouched down by Archimbeau. The platoon was beginning to show its heads again, peering out one and two at a time from behind the trunks and bushes that had served for concealment.

"Just that one?" Tyne asked.

"Guess so," Archimbeau said. "I almost threw a grenade at him."

"Good thing you didn't. What do you think, Ward?"

Sergeant Ward sat up behind his tree. "Damned if I know," he said. "I don't like it none."

"Go on back, Archimbeau," Tyne said. "Keep your eyes open."

"Why do I always have to pull this stuff?" Archimbeau demanded. "How about somebody else for a change?"

Tyne was taking grenades out of his pocket. "Okay," he said. "Get someone else."

"I'll do it," Riddle said. "Here, Arch, watch this god-damned gun. It gets in my way." He tossed his rifle to Archimbeau, who caught it in mid-air. Then he crawled back to the bush behind which Archimbeau had been hidden.

"I don't think there's more than one," Tyne said. "If they were sending a column along they wouldn't start it with a lousy armored car. It's just looking around to see how things are holding up down here. It'll be coming back this way pretty soon." He had completely forgotten Porter in the problem of the moment. Already he had reached the decision that the armored car would have to be got out of the way. He wasn't sure exactly how, though. Probably grenades would have to do.

"It'll be back all right," Ward said.

"I don't think we've got a hell of a lot of time. But we can probably knock it off with grenades if we're lucky. Those jobs don't weigh more than a couple of tons. A grenade under her belly ought to lift her right off the road. It'll shake up the driver, anyway."

Ward was toying with the bolt of his carbine. "How about machine guns?" he asked.

"The tires," Tyne said. "We can get the tires. I don't know how much armor those babies carry. I've never seen one before."

"They didn't have anything like that in Africa," Archimbeau said.

"Old stuff," said Ward. "They got a lot of old stuff they're starting to use."

"It looked new."

"Paint."

Porter lay with his face in his hands. His bulky body heaved softly. Tyne shook his shoulder. "Eddie," he said. "Eddie."

"Leave me alone," Porter said. He jerked his shoulder under Tyne's hand. He was bad. It wasn't shock or anything like that. It was just a piling up of war. Porter had lived on his nerves for a long time, but he wasn't going to live off them any more. Porter was through, done. It had come quickly when it came. Yesterday he had been all right; now he was finished. It comes as fast as that when it does come. Porter had had his share of it; now he was for the cleaners.

"Leave him alone, Tyne," Ward said. "Nothing you can do."

"No," Tyne said. "What's the best way to work it? How about your squad? Set them down by the road, as close as they can get, and throw grenades on the whistle. Just on this side of the road, though. They'll be tossing grenades in each other's laps. Rivera!"

Rivera's black head, helmetless, poked up from behind a decaying stump. "What's up?"

"Come here, Rivera."

The addressed rose and came over in a crouching run. Behind him Friedman's eyes watched him go. Rivera flopped down beside Tyne. "Got a butt, Corporal?"

"No. How's your gun, doughfoot?"

"Okay."

"Set it up down there." Tyne's finger pointed to the fallen trunk of a tree a few yards from the road and about fifteen yards from where he was sitting, toward the east. "That car's coming back. We're going to try and get it with grenades. Now, when the grenades go off you let the car have it with all you've got. Rake it. *Compris*?"

"Yeah. Sure."

"Get it up in a hurry. Damn little time."

"Right." Rivera went back to his stump.

"Better line up your squad, Ward," Tyne said.

Ward got to his feet. "Okay, my squad," he said. "Off and on." Here and there a man rose to his feet and came over to join his sergeant.

"I got a job," Rivera said. "They just hired me. A hundred bucks a minute."

"It ain't enough," Friedman said.

"You coming?" Rivera asked.

"You mean I'm invited?"

"I got a silver-plated bullet with your name on it. Your name's Appleglotz, ain't it?"

"Yeah," Friedman said. "That's me, all right."

"Then you're invited."

"Then I'll come."

"That's good. Especially seeing as you've got the ammo."

"Now, you'll get a whistle," Ward said. "And so help me, the first bastard that throws before he gets the whistle will get a grenade right between his teeth. And for God's sake, throw straight. You won't get another chance. Johnson, you understand?"

"Yes, Sergeant."

"All right, then, You here. Randolph, you here." Quietly Ward went about placing his men. One at a time the whole squad stretched out flat. Each man had a grenade in his right hand and another lying beside him. Tyne watched Ward place his men. So far the operation looked good. "Archimbeau," he said. "Watch Porter. Don't let him run around." He went over and joined Sergeant Ward. "Listen," he said to the rest of the platoon, "don't anyone else throw anything. Nobody at all, understand. We'll have enough men throwing things as it is. Just stay back where you are and hang on. You'll find out what happens soon enough." He turned to Ward. "Anyway, we know what happened to that rider."

"Sure do," Ward said.

"The only thing is, did they get him before he got to the farmhouse or after he'd crossed the bridge?"

"For all we know he never crossed the bridge."

"Well, if they've got armor at the farmhouse we might just as well call the war off. I've got to pick myself a tree."

"Remember," Ward warned his squad. "On the whistle."

The platoon settled down to wait. Dimly between the trees the throb of artillery came to their ears, but they ignored it. They tried to hear over it, tried to catch the sound of a motor near at hand, the sound of the armored car returning up the road. The car couldn't have gone too far down; as it was it was more or less protected by the trees, but if it came out in the open country, by the ditch, one of the planes would be certain to see it. The crew of the armored car probably knew that; they'd go down as far as they figured it was safe to go and then they'd turn around and come back. They were just looking around, that was all, fronting for a far more powerful force farther inland.

It was a problem, the armored car. Tyne ran over in his mind the pros and cons of smashing it. Now that he had made all the decisions he wasn't sure that the decision to stop it was the right one. If the car didn't come back, whoever was up the road would think it funny; they might even send out a more powerful force to see what had happened to it. They could probably be sure that it wasn't the planes, because if the planes had come down on the road the Germans would have seen them; they'd have known what had stopped their shiny new armored car. But if the car didn't come back and there was no reason for its not coming back—no reason that the Germans could see, that is—they might choose to conduct a little investigation, with three or four tanks, say, and then it would be good-bye platoon. On the other hand, if they let the armored car go back it might report everything clear, and then the heavy armor might come along anyway. It was a ticklish thing for a man to make up his mind about. Tyne decided the best thing to do would be to get the car, because while the Germans were wondering what had happened to it the platoon might be able to get where it had to go. If the German armor was still on the other side of the river they had a good chance of success; if, however, the enemy was on the seaward side, it didn't much matter one way or the other. Once they knocked off the armored car they'd have to make time—good time. And they'd have to go through the woods into the bargain. They couldn't take the chance of meeting more vehicles on the road. They couldn't take any more chances at all.

Sun streamed through the trees and touched the dull barrel of Rivera's gun. He had wheedled a stick of gum from Friedman, and he felt rather better about things in general. He sat with his legs around the gun, a brand-new belt running through it, waiting. Occasionally he would pivot the gun an inch or two either way. "Ever go to Coney Island?" he asked.

"All the time," Friedman said. "Some joint."

"You ever shoot those electric guns that shoot down the airplanes?"

"Sure. I'm a shark at that stuff."

"You want to know a secret, Friedman?"

"You ain't got any secrets. You're an open book. You ain't bright enough to have any secrets."

"This is a secret, Jakie."

"What the hell is it?"

"I never could hit those airplanes. I used to miss those airplanes all the time."

"Maybe I'd better go away," Friedman said. "Maybe you ain't safe to be with. How'd you get to be a machine gunner?"

"I bribed a guy."

"I want a transfer."

"Friedman, it's too late. You're stuck with me."

"Where you going to get that car, Rivera?"

Rivera licked his thumb and touched it on the barrel of his gun. "I'm going to get every god-damned tire she's got. I'm going to aim for the knees. Then I work north."

"You think this stuff will go through armor?"

"Never has yet. You can't tell, though. Did you get a good look at that jalopy?"

"Pretty good."

"It looked old to me. It looked like they been saving that car for the last quarter. The old college try."

"It's still armor."

"You know Biddy Sims?"

"Corporal in B Company?"

"Yeah."

"What about him?"

"He got one of those big bastards with one of these babies. Explosive bullets. He just kept pounding away at the front of it. You pound away long enough and you're sure as hell going to get a few through the slits."

"I didn't know Biddy did that."

"He's a quick boy."

"Where is he now, anyway?"

Rivera waved an expressive hand in the direction of the artillery fire. "Down there, I guess. Maybe we been listening to him all morning, for all we know."

"Maybe he's going to listen to us for awhile now."

"You said it, Jakie boy."

Archimbeau studied Sergeant Porter's back incuriously. He could not understand what had happened to Porter; it was something beyond his comprehension. Wounds were simple. If a man was wounded he might yell or groan or keep his mouth shut, and whatever he did you knew what was the matter with him. But it was different with Porter. As he watched his big, heaving back Archimbeau was afraid, more afraid than he had been during the whole campaign. There was something terrible about the way Porter was crying. If he had been wounded it would have been a different story, but there was nothing the matter with him. He didn't have a mark on his body. It was as though something evil had entered him and shaken him the way a child shakes a rag doll and then thrown him down. Archimbeau felt that he would rather have been given any dirty detail than the one he had. He did not like to be with Porter. He felt that he had to do something. For a long time he stared at the sergeant's back; then he went over and lay down behind the tree that Tyne had been behind when the armored car had first come along.

The tears trickled through Porter's grubby fingers and dripped into the dry earth. Porter did not know why he was crying; he was hardly aware that he was crying at all. He had lost all track of the platoon and the objective and the war. He was beyond all of it. He dug the fingers of one hand into the ground. He wanted something solid under him; he was tired of ideas and orders and the unknown. He was tired of guesswork and waiting and wondering if what was going to happen was what should happen. He had taken refuge in himself, and nothing would shake him out of that secret lair. Sergeant Porter had taken unto himself the final cover, the last concealment. He was unaware of the armored car; he was unaware that it was day, and that there were noises in the distance, and that he was human. All that came through his consciousness was that he was very tired and alone.

Over his shoulder Tyne looked at Porter. Nothing he could do. He fingered the whistle in his hand and then watched Riddle. Riddle had the best view of the road of any of them. He was peering anxiously down the dusty tracks; occasionally he would look back and shake his head. Nothing. Tyne's mind flashed ahead to the farmhouse. He tried to picture it. Must have a look at the map when this was done. There was no compass in his pocket; he had lost the one he had in Sicily and had never replaced it. Probably Ward would have one or, failing that, Porter. They'd have to go by compass through the woods. Tyne imagined that they had about a mile to go—certainly no farther. With luck they would be in the farmhouse within an hour.

The arms of Private Riddle suddenly tensed and he reared up on them, peering out beyond his bush. He's heard something, Tyne said to himself. He saw Ward staring at Riddle intently. Riddle turned toward Tyne and nodded his head in the affirmative. The armored car was coming back. "Easy," Ward said in a low voice. His squad clung to the ground, their faces set.

Riddle went flat again. He laid his face on the ground so that there was a mere narrow slit between the grass and the rim of his helmet. From twenty feet away he would have resembled a small, remarkably smooth stone. In the slit between grass and helmet he framed the armored car as it came into sight. It was still battened down, but the turret was motionless; evidently the suspicions of the crew were lulled. They had gone down to the edge of the open country, had observed, and had seen nothing. Now, on their way back, they were taking it easy. The car was moving at about twenty miles an hour, heaving as its wheels rose and sank in the ruts.

It came closer. Rivera, behind his log, bent over the machine gun, lining the armored car up. He was humming under his breath—not a definite tune, but simply a low murmuration of three or four notes. He sighted along the barrel and picked up the right front tire of the armored car. He held his sights there.

It was necessary to give the car ten seconds' leeway. Tyne closed his eyes for a fraction of a second in silent prayer that everything would go well. The car was almost at the spot he had picked. It was traveling at the speed he wanted it to travel. He counted slowly to himself. One. Two. Three. He brought the whistle swiftly up to his lips and blew it as hard as he could.

Tyne was conscious of many arms moving back and throwing missiles. The noise of the car seemed to become deafening. He knew that he should put his head down, but he couldn't bring himself to do it. The armored car suddenly picked up speed. The driver had seen the grenades. Now it was directly abreast of him. He realized that, unknown to himself, he had been counting aloud. "Nine," he said. As he said it two of the grenades went off, one a few feet behind the car and another directly under it. The car rose like a bucking horse and fell back heavily. The nose pointed toward the side of the road. And even as it hit, the road exploded in a sheet of flame as the other grenades went off. Rivera's machine gun began its chatter. The car disappeared in smoke. Tyne felt something smash against the side of his helmet—probably a stone or a bit of steel. He tried to peer through the smoke. It was clearing, very slowly. Bits of rock began falling around him.

"God damn it," Rivera shouted. "God-damned smoke. Any time

you get a bead on something the god-damned smoke comes along.'' He was firing blindly. Friedman tapped him on the shoulder. ''The corporal says to hold it,'' he shouted in his ear. Rivera looked toward Tyne. The corporal was standing up, waving at him. He released his finger from the trigger.

The smoke had cleared around the armored car. It was lying on its side. One wheel was spinning idly. The belly, facing them, was bent inward. There were no holes in it that they could see. ''Rankin,'' Tyne said. ''Put a few shots through one of the slits.''

Rankin hopped to his feet, his tommy gun at the alert, and trotted out to the armored car. He put the gun in the driver's eye slit and pulled the trigger. Lead smashed against the car's interior as he moved the muzzle up and down. He put about thirty shots into the car. Probably the two men who made up the crew had been alive when he started shooting; if so, they were not alive now. The platoon had no time to take prisoners.

Tyne walked out to the car, Sergeant Ward at his heels. Two members of Ward's squad started to follow them. ''Stay where you are,'' Tyne said. ''There's nothing out here you haven't seen before.''

He bent down and peered through the driver's slit. It was full of smoke inside; all around there was the bitter, acrid smell of burned powder. Dimly he could discern two crumpled figures. He suddenly realized that a hand was hanging limply very near his eye. There was a huge ring on the index finger. ''Funny place to have a ring,'' he thought. It was a red stone, perhaps a ruby.

Straightening, Tyne looked up the road in the direction of the farmhouse. ''I don't know whether they heard all the noise,'' he said, ''but whether they did or not we'd better get the hell out of here. There's more where this came from.'' He kicked the car gently; it gave off a hollow sound. ''You got a compass, Ward?''

''Think so,'' Ward said. He reached in his left pocket. ''Yep, here's one. Good one, too. Never had a bit of trouble with that compass.'' He gave it to Tyne. Together they walked back into the woods.

''Get that gun down, doughfoot,'' Tyne said as he passed Rivera.

''Some smoke screen,'' Rivera said. ''Like a christly battleship.''

''That car's probably full of holes,'' Friedman said.

''Like a cheese,'' Rivera said. ''Like a god-damned cheese.''

''I'll bet you never put a hole in it.''

''I never miss.''

''How about the airplanes at Coney Island?''

"That was Coney Island. Those were airplanes."

"Okay, Rivera, you're a terror."

"I sure as hell am."

"I've got to take a look at the map," Tyne said. "Got to get some sort of beam on that house."

"Porter's got it," Ward said.

"I know."

He bent down and opened the map case, which was lying at Porter's side. From it he pulled the map of the surrounding country, opened it, and spread it on the ground. It seemed that this was the fiftieth time that morning he had spread out the map. By rights it should have been frayed and torn, with all the handling it had received. But it was new and neat and glossy. The only mark on it was a fingerprint in blood. That had probably come from Hoskins.

"I'm a killer, all right," Rivera said. "I don't know what this platoon would do without me."

"Win the god-damned war," Friedman said.

"That's right," said Rivera. "Win the god-damned war."

9

"IT'S WOODS ALL the way," Tyne said, "if we're where I think we are."

"It looks right," Ward said. He wiggled his finger along the map. "The road twisted like hell in here."

"All level till we hit this field in front of the farm," Tyne said. "What's the course?"

"West-south-west, I guess," said Ward. "I'd hold it right on there. Just about a mile to go."

Tyne measured with his index finger. "Just about. Take us a half hour if we move fast and hit it right."

The river cut around the farm and came toward them, about a quarter of a mile from where they were. If they got too far off in that direction the river would put them right; on the other side was the road. They could hardly miss it. "How do we line up now?" Tyne said. He surveyed the platoon. "Craven."

Craven, a sad-faced man, came over, swinging his helmet in his hand. He was nearly bald. "Take over my squad, will you, Craven?"

"Sure, Bill."

"Johnson, you stay here with the sergeant. Can you spare him, Ward? Okay. Stay here with the sergeant. Don't let him do anything. Just keep him here. Understand?"

"What if he tries to go somewhere?"

"Don't let him."

"How?"

"I don't care how. Don't let him, that's all. Wait a minute." Tyne bent down by Porter and shook him gently. "How are you feeling, Eddie?"

Sergeant Porter's nails dug into the ground. There was no other answer.

"Okay, Johnson," Tyne said. "Watch him. Arch, you and Cousins get going. If you see anything, just shoot. Let's go."

The scouts moved out into the woods. "You got the direction, Arch?" Tyne called after them.

"Can't miss," Archimbeau called back. Tyne fell into his place at the head of the column. To the sound of feet on leaves they moved through the woods, past Porter, past Johnson, toward the exploding war.

They all felt better somehow. The fact that they had knocked out the armored car had cheered them considerably. It no longer mattered that they weren't exactly sure where they were going or what they would find there. They had seen their own powers redisplayed. The morning had been bad, entirely bad, until they had run up against the car. Now the balance had shifted. They were no longer oppressed by what awaited them up ahead. They felt that they could handle it, together or singly. They had their morale back.

Not that they had ever really lost it. They had simply been a little uncertain of themselves. They were out of practice. But all in all they were a good platoon, a very good platoon. They worked well together; for the most part they understood each other. That was an essential. In its way war is like a lethal game of football. The squad is a team, the platoon is a team, the company is a team. So are the regiment and the army. It is no longer enough to kill two of them before they kill you: the thing is to kill two of them and stay alive.

Moving between the trees, Archimbeau felt that he had had a bad morning. First there was Trasker and then the sergeant. He had almost forgotten Trasker now. What had happened to him had been a natural thing. It might have happened to anybody. But the sergeant haunted him. Any wound that was not caused by some external object terrified

Archimbeau. ''I am not afraid of drunks,'' his mother once said, ''but I'm afraid of crazy people.'' So was Archimbeau, the dutiful son, the lonely bachelor. Dimly he wondered if Porter had gone crazy. He knew it wasn't shell-shock, because he had seen guys get shell-shocked, and when that happened it was because a shell had hit near them. Simple, like everything else in the army. Simple, like the road to Tibet. But no shell had hit near Sergeant Porter. He had just gone off for no reason. Still, Archimbeau always thought that crazy people ran around with knives. Maybe the sergeant wasn't crazy after all. Maybe he was just sick.

He was not keeping a very careful watch. For one thing, there wasn't much you could hide behind the trees, and there were no bushes to speak of. For another, he had decided that there was nothing on this side of the river. He didn't know why he had reached this decision; he just felt that it was true. Archimbeau was a great man for intuition.

''Did you ever go camping when you was a kid?'' Rivera asked.

''Every time we get in a bunch of trees you ask me that same question,'' Friedman said.

''Every time I get in a bunch of trees I remember it,'' said Rivera.

''For the millionth time, no, I never went camping when I was a kid. I lived in the city.''

''I lived in the city, too, for Christ's sake. I got on a train.''

''You told me.''

''Well, I'm telling you again.''

''You're a juke box, Rivera. Somebody keeps putting nickels in you.''

''I ain't talking to you any more. Hey, Judson, you ever go camping in the woods?''

''What woods?''

''Get that, will you? Any woods.''

''Naw.''

''Judson, you don't know what you missed. You ain't ever lived until you toasted a mickey over the coals. It ain't like the army crap. You can sit around a campfire, see, and shoot it all night if you want to. You can go fishing. All that kind of stuff.''

''Outdoor man,'' Friedman said.

''Next time they make you a civilian, Judson,'' Rivera said, ''try a camp in the woods. Just tell them I sent you.''

"Tell who?"

"The birds and the bees. Didn't your old man ever tell you about the birds and the bees?"

"Naw."

"You hear that, Friedman? Judson never heard of the birds and the bees."

Friedman was on firm ground now. "Terrible," he said.

"Shall we tell him?"

"Maybe we better."

Rivera held out his hand. "Give us a butt, Judson, and we'll tell you all about the birds and the bees."

"I ain't got a butt," Judson said sadly.

In his mind Craven was trying to frame a letter to his sister. He figured that if he could think it out now he could write it later from memory and save time. "Dear Frances," he began. "This is the first letter I have written you from Italy. I am now sitting down in an old farmhouse. We have just blown up a bridge near here . . ." No, that wouldn't do. Best to keep it indefinite. "Dear Frances, I am writing this from somewhere in Italy but I don't exactly know where because we have been moving so fast that I haven't had time to read the signs." No, cross that out. "—Because we haven't seen any signs. For all I know it isn't even Italy but it will do until the next country comes along. It is a bright, sunny day, very warm, so maybe I am in Sunny Italy after all (ha, ha) and if I am I'll send you a barrel of Chianti." No, "Cianti." Neither way seemed right. That was the hell of foreign words. Italian was as bad as French.

He turned to Private Tinker, who was walking beside him. "Tinker," he said, "how do you spell 'Chianti'?"

"What's that?"

"It's a wine. A wop wine."

"Never heard of it."

"What's the matter with you? Don't you drink?"

"Sure I drink," Tinker said. "You've seen me drink. I never heard of the stuff, that's all."

"It's a red wine. You drink it with dinner and stuff."

"The hell with this wine junk. When I drink I want to feel I been drinking something. Applejack. Rye. That's the stuff."

"Don't you think I know it, for God's sake?" Craven said. "I was drinking that stuff when they were feeding you milk. I just wanted to know how to spell it, that's all."

''Why?''

''I'm writing to my sister.''

Tinker stared at him. ''What do you mean, you're writing to your sister? You're walking through some god-damned woods, that's what you're doing?''

''I'm writing the letter in my head, see? Then when I get a minute I just put down what I remember in my head, and the letter's all written. It's the best way.''

''Jesus,'' Tinker said, ''what a system. Does it work?''

''Sure,'' said Craven.

''You just make up the letter in your head while you're walking and then write it down later?''

''Yeah.''

''Hey, that's pretty good. Maybe I'll try it. It works, huh?''

''Every time.''

''Suppose you got a bad memory?''

''You got a bad memory?''

''I got a good one.''

''Then why you worrying?''

''I'm not. I just wondered. What was that word you wanted to spell?''

''Chianti.''

Tinker wrinkled his brow. ''Never heard of it,'' he said. ''They don't have it in St. Paul.''

The easiest thing would be to forget it, Craven decided. The easiest thing would be to begin again. ''Dear Frances, I am writing this letter from Somewhere in Italy, but I don't know where because they haven't told me yet. I am well and hope you are the same. Did you get a letter from Frank?''

There were little bare patches in the wood, as though someone had chopped down a dozen trees and dug out the stumps. Once they passed the foundation of a house, covered with dry grass. Time had played with it, and the forest had taken over. It was impossible to tell how old the house was. Tyne studied it carefully as he went past. Italy, he knew, was full of ruins. Rome had the most of all. Perhaps the foundation was that of a Roman house, and perhaps they were the first who had seen it in two thousand years. But people had been in the woods since then. Here and there a stump stuck from the ground, and once he saw a faded piece of paper. Tyne remembered the ruins in Tunisia, standing by themselves miles from any human habitation.

Little Arab boys had sold them Roman coins. Statues had been found around the broken temples, and once a doughfoot, digging a slit trench, had broken through into a Roman grave, the grave of a woman. Time had left of her a pot of money and a few hairpins. It was enough; it was a memorial.

He looked at his watch. They had been on the move nearly a quarter of an hour; nearly halfway on the last lap. When he thought of the farm he felt his spine tingle, as though somewhere in his body there was a buzzer that was a warning.

He had always had that feeling when something was about to happen. First the buzzer would go and then he would feel weak. He wiped the sweat from his forehead; it had run down into his eyebrows and from there was finding its way into his eyes. A tingle and a weak feeling. It was not necessarily a warning of danger. It was, on the contrary, the body preparing itself, releasing reserves of energy and strength—nothing more than that. Tyne certainly did not feel afraid. He felt rather giddy and lightheaded and confident. The giddiness was part of the weak feeling. It would pass. But the confidence would stay with him. Only when the platoon had done what it had been sent to do would the confidence leave him. Then he would sink into a melancholy. It was a reaction, and it had happened to him before. He was powerless to stop it. But while he had the confidence he would put it to good use.

Archimbeau, he noticed, was getting too far ahead. He seemed in a hell of a hurry to get somewhere.

Privates James and Carraway were talking about life.

"If you aren't on the ball, you haven't got a chance," Private James said. "You got to be smart these days."

"I don't know," said Private Carraway. "Look at the freaks in the circus."

"Aw, they don't count. They're freaks."

"They ain't smart, but they pull in the dough."

"I mean the average guy."

"The average guy ain't smart, for Christ's sake."

"That ain't what I'm trying to say," Private James said. "I mean that the competition is tough. If you don't keep on the ball some bright boy is going to slip in and nab your job. That's life. That's what I was trying to say."

"If you're good nobody's going to take your job."

"That's what I mean. You got to be good."

"You can be good and still be a dope," said Carraway.

"How do you get that?"

"All right, suppose you can run a machine better than anyone else. Do you have to have brains to run the machine? Naw, you don't need any brains. It's a purely mechanical process. Anybody could learn to do it."

"All right, let's get back to where I was in the first place, then. The competition is tough."

"All right, it's tough."

"Life ain't no joke these days."

"All right, it ain't a joke. Was it ever a joke?"

"How do I know? I haven't lived all the time."

"How do you think a guy would like it, living all the time?"

"I wouldn't like it," James said. "You'd get in a rut."

"How do you mean?"

"History's all the same. Life's all the same. You'd be doing the same thing all the time, over and over again."

"I'd like to try it, just the same," Carraway said.

"There'd still be the competition."

The sun was soaring toward the highest reaches of heaven. It blazed down malevolently. Their helmets became like ovens; their clothes stuck to their bodies. They were bathed from head to foot in their own perspiration. When a man is uncomfortable, through either heat or cold, he finds it hard to think consecutively. His thoughts come in flashes. He is too conscious of his ever-present discomfort. The body, as always, thwarts the mind. The minutes develop a talent for moving slowly, for crawling around the face of the clock. Everything seems to stand still. The whole world simmers in a gigantic pot. The air actually has weight and body, and it seems to stagnate, like still water. Smells have a dull, unpleasant pungency. It is difficult to think of food. Anything with an odor repels one.

Yet Sergeant Ward still thought of apples. They were becoming a mirage, dancing in front of his eyes, dripping with juice. He would gladly have given three months' pay for a cold apple, a big red juicy one. There was nothing cold he could have. The water in his canteen was tepid, and so was all the ration he carried. The thought of apples taunted him, and to get it off his mind he thought of other images—of a cold well and of cold well water, of cider cold and fresh from the jug, of ice cream. The new images did not help him. If anything they made things worse, and when he cast them out of his mind the idea of apples still flaunted itself and would not be shaken out.

"Like to have an apple," he said to Riddle.

"Yeah," Riddle said. "What I wouldn't give for a beer. A nice cold glass of beer. Just one."

"I been thinking of apples all day," Ward said.

"Apples and oranges," said Riddle.

"Funny thing is, I don't like apples."

"A guy always wants something when he can't get it."

"Yeah."

The funny thing was that they were not very much concerned with what was facing them ahead. Each had his own problems, his own desires and wishes. They kept these personal things uppermost in their minds, as they had always done ever since they came into the army. The war was incidental to a man's thoughts. It entered into them, of course, but it did not take them over bodily. There had been too many years of life, too many memories, before the war had come along. A man could exist on these memories, he could withdraw into them, he could construct them into an unpierceable shell. They were his defense against the violence of the world. Every man in the platoon had his own thoughts as he walked along, and they hovered unseen over the little group, an indefinable armor, a protection against fate, an indestructible essence.

"It's a good thing they invented trains for traveling salesmen," Rivera said.

"All right," Friedman said. "Kill me. What's the gag?"

"No gag," said Rivera. "But if they didn't have trains all the traveling salesmen would have to walk. A hell of a job that would be."

"You're a traveling salesman," Friedman said. "And you ain't been taking any trains lately."

"What do you mean, I'm a traveling salesman? I'm a murderer."

"You're a traveling salesman. You're selling democracy to the natives."

Rivera was silent for a moment. "So that's what I am, huh? Well, what do you know. Where'd you get that crap, Jakie?"

"Out of a book."

"A book."

"You're a decadent democrat, Rivera."

"That what I am, all right. But to get back to traveling salesmen, how many of those Joes do you think would of become traveling salesmen if they'd had to walk everywheres?"

"I don't know," Friedman said. "I never knew a traveling salesman."

"Maybe I'll be one after the war," Rivera said. "You get to cover a hell of a lot of territory."

"Baby," said Friedman, "you've covered a hell of a lot of territory, and you ain't nothing."

"Friedman," Rivera said, "I been good to you. Every time you needed it I always gave you my last franc. I treated you like a brother. And every time you get the chance you needle me up the back. What kind of stuff is that?"

"I'm anti-social," Friedman said. "I got gap-osis."

"Maybe you should go off somewhere."

"Where?"

"How should I know? I treat you like a brother and you stick a knife in my back. He's a crumb, ain't he, Judson?"

"Everybody's a crumb," Judson said. "I wish I was home in bed."

"Anybody who would sleep in the noontime is a dope," said Rivera.

"He's a dope," Friedman said.

If the bridge was steel, Tyne thought, they'd really have a job on their hands. They'd have one if it was concrete, too. If it was wood, though, it shouldn't be too much trouble. He ran over the possibilities in his mind. There was a chance that the bridge might already have been bombed and the Jerries only had a makeshift job crossing the river. That was a very good possibility. The planes had been bombing around this area for a couple of weeks. If they had knocked out the bridge and it had been repaired they could be sure it would be a wooden affair.

Suddenly it dawned on Tyne that there had actually been no orders given to blow up a bridge at all. It had been decided within the platoon that the bridge had to be blown. It was very strange. Certainly if they had wanted to blow the bridge they would have sent the planes, or, failing that, a bunch of demolition boys from the Engineers. It was damned queer. Tyne felt that he had to run over the entire situation again.

There was a farmhouse. That was certain. What was uncertain was whether or not the farmhouse was occupied by the enemy. That was point one. And there was a bridge. That was certain. What was uncertain was whether the bridge had already been blown or not. That was point two. And there were several courses of action. If the farmhouse was unoccupied and the bridge hadn't been blown, they would have to blow the bridge and occupy the farmhouse. If the farmhouse was unoccupied and the bridge was blown, they'd merely have to occupy the farmhouse and see that no one built up the bridge again. If the farmhouse was occupied and the bridge was blown, they'd have to take the farmhouse and watch the bridge. That might not be easy. And if the farmhouse was occupied and the bridge was unblown, they'd have a good-sized chunk of hell, sitting up warm and wicked, right in their hands. Four possibilities. Tyne tried to reason out the one that was probably right. He wanted to wish that the bridge was smashed to bits and the farmhouse was empty, but that didn't hold water. The armored car had either come from the farmhouse or over the bridge, so it was safe to say that something ran across the water. The armored car would have had to get to the farm in the first place. And in that event the farm was occupied and the river was bridged. The more Tyne ran the picture through his mind the darker it became. At last he had reached the conclusion that the farmhouse might very well be occupied, and that there was some sort of bridge over the river. The Germans were never men to pass over river crossings.

He suddenly whirled and strode back to where Ward was bringing up his squad. "I've been thinking it over," he said. "I think we're going to run into trouble."

"I thought that all along," Ward said quietly. "Jerry's smart. He isn't missing a trick."

"I think they've got someone in that farmhouse," Tyne said.

Ward spat solemnly. "That's what I think," he said. "They probably got a machine gun in every god-damned window in the place."

"They've got something across the river, too," Tyne said. "I don't think it's a regular bridge, but they've got something."

"Yeah," said Sergeant Ward. He was a man of opinion.

Tyne went back to his place at the head of the column. Archimbeau was getting even farther ahead. Tyne broke into a run, caught up with him, and caught him by the arm. "Take it easy, Arch," he said. "Don't get too far ahead."

''Didn't know I was,'' Archimbeau said. ''I was almost asleep on my feet. I didn't get any sleep at all last night.''

''Well, keep awake now.''

''Okay. Say, Corp, do you think I'll make Pfc by the Battle of Tibet?''

''Sure. They'll make you a general.''

''That's all I wanted to know. How much farther's this farm?''

Tyne looked at his watch. ''We ought to be breaking into the field below it any time now. Keep your eyes open, for God's sake, and stop when you see the field.''

''Right.''

On his way back to his place Tyne winked at Rankin. ''How's it going, Tim?''

''I been here before,'' Rankin said.

By mutual consent, without any command being spoken, the men talked in whispers. They knew that they were approaching their objective. They walked more lightly and they began to look around them, peering through the trees as though they expected to see someone. The woods had suddenly become dangerous. No one could say at what point they had taken on a menacing aspect, but it had happened in a twinkling. Perhaps it had been when Tyne had run up toward the scouts. Any unforeseen movement could put a man on his guard or on the alert. Tenseness came over them, and their legs felt stiff. They almost seemed to walk stiff-legged, like angry dogs. The war had finally caught up with them.

Rankin looked at his tommy gun. It was beautifully oiled and in perfect condition. Rankin took good care of his gun; he treated it as though it were a highly sensitive infant. He slept with it cradled beside him. There was only one thing about it that made it stand out, however. Scratched on its barrel were eleven lines. The eleven lines stood for soldiers of the Third Reich—for ex-supermen—moldering into dust in Tunisia and Sicily. They were Rankin's certains; he never counted the probables.

''Some day,'' Rivera said, ''I'm going to walk into a country and they're going to put out a rug that says 'Welcome' and they're going to let me walk in on it. That's what I'm going to do some day.''

''When?'' Friedman asked.

''Next Tuesday, for Christ's sake. How the hell do I know when? In 1983.''

"I'll look you up then."

"This is a hell of a way to see Europe."

"Ah, if it hadn't been for this war the nearest you'd ever of got to Europe would be the Staten Island ferry."

"Anybody can go to Europe. I know a guy worked his way over on a cattle boat."

"Why?"

"He wanted to see it."

"He must have been a hell of a dope."

"He was my cousin."

"Then I know he was a hell of a dope."

"After we get up to this farmhouse I'm going to take you out in the dung shed and beat the bejesus out of you."

"What with?"

"The barrel of this god-damned gun."

"Okay. I thought you were going to really get tough."

"That farmhouse is sure as hell full of Krauts."

"It sure as hell is."

"Friedman, I'm glad I brought this gun along. I'm glad they gave it to me."

"Between you and me, old boy, I am too."

"A butt."

Friedman sighed. "I can remember the days when I had one," he said.

Archimbeau's arm went straight up in the air and he stopped in his tracks. Every man in the column fell suddenly silent. Tyne walked ahead. "Coming out of the woods," Archimbeau said. He pointed. In the direction of his finger, perhaps fifty yards away, Tyne could see light through the trees and a gentle brown slope. "That's it, all right," he said.

Ward came along. "On the nose," he said.

"On the nose."

"What do you think?"

"I don't know yet. I'm going up and take a look. Arch, you come along."

"Take it easy," Ward said.

Silently Tyne and Archimbeau moved through the trees. Tyne carried his rifle loosely in his right hand; Archimbeau had his on the sling. As they moved away from the platoon the wood seemed to open up like a flower. Light streamed in on them, reflected from the field. They walked slower and slower. Once Tyne thought he caught the glint of something far up in the field—it could have been a helmet—and he stopped in his tracks. It was almost as though he were sniffing the air. Then he moved on, more cautiously. Archimbeau followed closely at his heels.

When they were almost at the edge of the wood Tyne could see an old wall, made of some kind of stone and mortar, running along the fringe of trees. He fell on his belly and wiggled the last few yards to the wall, Archimbeau crawling behind him. And then, when they were both safely behind the wall, Tyne cautiously raised his head and peered out on the field—a brown world, full of high brown grass and the sighings of late insects.

10

THE FIELD WAS a hill that stretched a hundred and fifty yards up to a farmhouse with a red tile roof. Here and there a boulder marred its surface, and there were patches where the grass lay flat. It looked as though it had been trampled. Tyne counted four out-buildings; it was quite a large farm. The house had been painted or whitewashed quite recently. He could see no movement around the buildings. "I wish to God I had those binoculars now," he said.

"Can you see anything?"

"Not a damned thing."

"How about the windows?"

"Sun's on them."

To the right the wood curved around, along what evidently was the bank of the river. The wall seemed to stop down there. "I wish I knew," Tyne said. "I wish to God I knew."

"Knew what?" Archimbeau asked.

"Nothing. Let's go back."

They moved back on their stomachs. After a while Tyne stood up. Archimbeau also rose, and they broke into a fast walk. The platoon was waiting for them. Half the men were sitting or lying down; the rest were leaning against trees or just standing around. "How's it look?" Ward said.

"Quiet. But I don't like it. Too quiet."

Ward nodded. "They're bad when they're too quiet."

"Craven," Tyne said. He fell on his knees and picked up a stick. Craven came over to where he was kneeling, and Tyne drew a rough line along the ground. "There's a stone wall that runs along here for about two or three hundred yards, probably between the road and the river. There's a clear slope up to the farmhouse from the wall. Not much cover. The wall seems to stop where the river curves around the farm, but there are trees running along the river bank. There doesn't seem to be any movement among the farm buildings. It's hard to tell just what the story is. If I had a pair of binoculars I'd have been able to see more."

"Think there's anyone there?" Craven asked.

"That's what I don't know," said Tyne. "Anyway, we aren't going to take any chances. We'll send a patrol up first, four or five guys."

"I'll take it," Ward said suddenly.

"I may need you here," Tyne said.

"I want to take it," Ward said.

Tyne studied his face. "Okay," he said. "You take it. Pick yourself four men."

"I'll go," Rivera said.

"No, you won't, doughfoot," Tyne said. "I need your little instrument."

"I want four volunteers," Ward said. "Four Congressional-Medal-of-Honor-with-ten-oak-leaf-clusters volunteers."

"Any extra pay?" Rankin wanted to know.

"Naw."

"Then I'll go anyway," Rankin said. "Just to make them feel ashamed."

"I'm a hero," Cousins said. "I been up front all day. I might as well stay there."

"I'll go along," Tranella said.

"The first guys that get to that house will get the wine," Tinker said. "I'll go."

"Okay," Ward said. "That's four."

"Pass out the Purple Hearts, mother," Rivera said.

"All right," Tyne said. "We'll go up to the wall in column, then fan out when we get there. The wall's three feet high. There's plenty of room. But don't let me catch any son of a bitch sticking his head up in the air. When you fan out keep about five yards apart. Craven, you take your squad down toward the road. Riddle, you take Ward's squad down toward the river. My squad will stay in the center. Rivera, you take your popgun down by the road, so you can keep your eye on the farmhouse and the road at the same time. Got that, doughfoot?"

"It's in my head," Rivera said.

"Keep it there. And remember to cover if anyone needs it."

"Okay, chief."

"Let's go." Tyne moved through the woods. The platoon straggled after him, moving as silently as Indians. As Tyne came nearer to the field he was struck with the same feeling of the wood's unfolding like a flower that he had had the first time. He hit the dirt at almost the same place as before. One by one the men flopped down after him.

He stopped at the wall and directed traffic, to right and left. The men wiggled along the wall or moved at a crouch, careful not to hunch their backs too high. Ward and his volunteers hugged the wall near Tyne. "Might as well go over right here," Ward said.

Tyne considered a minute. "I guess so," he said. "Maybe we're getting worried for nothing. Maybe there's no one up there after all."

"I think there is," Ward said.

"What are you going to do?"

"Well," Ward said, "if we can get within grenade-throwing distance we'll be all right. Let me take a look and see." He raised his head a little over the wall and studied the terrain. When he pulled his head down again he was frowning. "Don't look too good at that," he said. "A few boulders, but not a hell of a lot else. That grass won't do much good."

"It'll help." Tyne said.

"Yeah, it'll help."

Most of the men were in position. "We'll wait till Rivera gets his gun up," Tyne said. "Give him five minutes. If anything goes wrong he'll cover you."

"If anything goes wrong, shoot for the windows," Ward said. "That's where they'll be. They like the windows."

"I know."

Warily Tyne took another look over the wall. Things did not seem to have changed. Nothing had moved around the farmhouse. The windows still reflected the sun. Certainly there was nothing about the farm to arouse suspicion. But that was the way it always was. The things to watch out for were the things that looked innocent. That was the principle of booby traps.

"Why are you so anxious to take a patrol?" Tyne asked.

"I don't know," Ward said. "I just am."

Down at the far end of the woods, by the road, Rivera and Friedman were finishing setting up the gun. "You can hit anything from here," Friedman said. "They ought to have portable walls to go with every war."

"I'll see they have them next time," Rivera said. "I wouldn't want you to be disappointed."

"This is a pretty good spot."

"It'll do for awhile. I ain't planning to raise a family here."

"How's the farm look?"

"I'll rake that joint."

"I think it's okay," Tyne said. "Got enough grenades?"

"Yeah," Ward said. He studied the four men who were to go with him. "We'll stay five yards apart," he said. "And keep on your gut, for God's sake. Spread out, now."

The four men strung themselves along behind the wall. "Good luck," Tyne said.

"The same to you," Ward said. He looked to the right and left. "Over," he said. He leaped over the wall and lay flat in the grass. The other men followed him.

All up and down the line of the wall there was silence. Silence hung over the farmhouse, too. Far away could be heard the dull rumble of artillery, but it was cut off in great measure by the intervening woods. Ward hugged the ground, listening. He could see none of the other members of the patrol because of the high grass. Now he wished he had not had them stay five yards apart. A guy could wander away, especially if he was on the end. Stiffly Ward began to move forward.

The patrol had a long way to go. He moved fast. Near him he could hear the other men moving forward. Beneath the grass the ground was rough. It stuck to his sweat-soaked fatigues. He seemed to grate on the earth as he crawled along. A boulder reared before him, and he skirted it. As he did so he caught sight of Tinker in a bare patch. He winked at him. Tinker licked his lips with his tongue and made a half-wave.

* * *

Tyne slowly raised his head over the wall. The patrol was moving steadily up the slope. He could see two figures; the other three he could locate only by the waving of the grass. One of the figures was in a bare patch, the other was behind a boulder. They had gone perhaps fifty yards.

Suddenly, as though by instinct, he knew that something was going to happen. It was like those times when people see a man who is actually dying a thousand miles away. One moment everything was all right, and the next Tyne wanted to yell out for the patrol to come back.

He saw smoke drift from one of the windows of the house, and the next minute the noise of a machine gun came to his ears. The Germans had opened up. The farm was occupied, all right, very well occupied. Tyne jerked his head down, looked at the man nearest him, and shook his head. "God damn," he said over and over again. "God damn. God damn. God damn."

The machine gun had started up so suddenly that it had taken Ward by surprise. Off to his left he could hear bullets hitting the ground and singing away. It was too hot a place, much too hot. "Go back," he yelled. "Patrol back." He turned around and began to crawl down the slope. He could see the wall beckoning to him. It was hard to believe that anything so near could be so far away. He passed the boulder again and saw Tinker again, crawling back with him. This time he did not wink. He hugged the ground as a line of bullets parted the air over his head.

Slowly Tyne peered over the wall again. Why the hell didn't they come back? But they were coming. Good. He could see the grass waving as they worked their way toward the wall, and he could see the grass swaying as the machine gun traversed it. "Tell Rivera to let her go," he said to the man on his left. The word went down the line.

Ward was wondering why Rivera didn't open up. He was cut off from the rest of the patrol, and he didn't know whether or not any of them had been hit. He was conscious only of his own efforts and the wall luring him on. His mouth was very dry, and he regretted coming out with the patrol. There had been just a chance that the farm had been unoccupied. He had known the chance was slim—he hadn't believed it himself, but he had wanted to take it. He dug dirt again as a row of bullets passed over him.

"Jesus Christ, here goes," Rivera said. The gun jumped and shivered before him. Far away, along the wall of the house, Friedman could see dust rise as the slugs cut into the mortar. "Get that bloody window," he said. Rivera obligingly lowered the muzzle of the gun an almost imperceptible distance. Bullets smashed through the window and into the house. The German machine gun went suddenly silent.

"Let me be the first to congratulate you," Friedman said solemnly. He held out his hand.

Ward heard Rivera's gun go into action. It was home and music to him. He stopped and listened. He was almost certain he could hear Rivera's slugs smash into the side of the house. Behind him the German machine gun went dead. He raised his head and took a quick look over his shoulder. Dust and mortar were flying from the house and glass spattered from the windows as Rivera raked it back and forth. Ward grinned mirthlessly. Rivera kept his finger on the trigger. Might as well make a run for it, Ward said to himself.

He calculated the distance to the wall. It was perhaps twenty yards, an easy run. Ward did not bother to think the situation out in any detail. There wasn't time. He suddenly stood upright in the field. "Cousins, Rankin," he shouted. Everybody over the wall." Three figures rose up from the grass. They all bolted for the long wall. Rivera's gun chattered on. Five yards from the wall Sergeant Ward heard rifle fire from the house. He leaped to the right and zigzagged back again. He went over the wall head first, in a giddy dive. Cousins and Tranella leaped after him. Tinker was slow, at least two yards behind the others. He wasn't zigzagging. As he reached the wall there were three scattered shots from the house. Tinker tossed his rifle in the air and fell forward against the wall, his body half crawling up the rough stone. His hand hung over the top. Far away, on the left, Rivera's gun stopped firing.

Ward lay flat for a moment. His leap had nearly knocked the wind out of him, and he gasped, trying to catch his breath. Tyne crawled over to him. He patted Ward's sweat-soaked back. "You shouldn't have tried it," he said. "You just shouldn't have tried it."

Ward sat up. "Everyone get back?" he asked. He took a deep breath and looked around him.

"They got Tinker," Tyne said. "And I think they got Rankin. Rankin didn't come back."

"I thought there was only three," Ward said. "Jesus, is that Tinker?" He was looking at the hand that appeared over the wall.

Tyne nodded.

"Why don't you pull him in?"

"What's the use? He's dead."

"How do you know he's dead?"

"I can tell when a man's dead."

"Oh, hell," Ward said. "What a god-damned mess. What a bloody, god-damned mess."

"It could have been worse. They could have waited until you were all up there and then let you have it. It could have been a hell of a lot worse."

"It's bad enough," said Ward.

Tyne looked at Cousins and Tranella. "You all right?"

"In the pink," Tranella said. Cousins nodded.

"Tough luck," Tyne said. He turned back to Ward. "Now we've really got a job on our hands."

"Yeah," Ward said.

"There's no element of surprise, and they've got us cold. They know where we are and where we want to get to, and they probably know every way we'll use to try and get where we want to go. They've probably got a machine gun in every window of that house. No one could get near enough to use a grenade."

"I wish to Christ we had a mortar," Ward said.

"It never happens the way you want it to happen," said Tyne. "If we had a mortar there'd be nothing to it."

"But we haven't got a mortar."

"No."

"How about waiting till dark?"

"We can't wait till dark," Tyne said. "We've got to get in there and get in there fast. I wish to God I could make them think we've got a mortar."

"Yeah," Ward said. "But how?"

"Nothing we can do."

Rivera spat on the barrel of his gun. The spittle rolled down, sizzling. "I'm a marksman," he said. "A marksman first class."

"I wonder who they knocked off," Friedman said. "Too damn far away to see."

"I hope it's Ward," Rivera said. "Ward gives me a pain in the pratt. All the sergeants give me a pain in the pratt."

"Tyne's all right," Friedman said.

"Yeah, Tyne's all right. But he ain't a sergeant."

"He probably will be."

"Then he'll give me a pain in the pratt."

Friedman stared down along the wall. The figure lying against it puzzled him. Within him he had a desperate urge to know who it was. He liked some men in the platoon better than others; he didn't want the body to be that of someone he liked. As a matter of fact, he didn't want it to be the body of anyone he knew, anyone he had worked with. "He's a big guy, whoever he is," he said.

"There's somebody else out in the field," Rivera said noncommittally.

"I know it. Didn't see him get hit, though."

"Ah, it was beautiful. The way I messed up that house was beautiful. I could do that fifty times a day."

"You'd better keep your eyes open," Friedman said, "or they'll be sending a halfback around this end with a grenade stuck in his mitt. They'll only have to do that once a day."

"The hell with it," said Rivera. "I've seen them coming around my end by the millions. They never gained a yard around my end. I'm indestructible. Nobody dies."

"Okay, corpse," said Private Friedman.

It was up to Tyne. Responsibility weighed on his shoulders and creased his forehead. Cautiously he raised his head over the wall, behind Tinker's hand. The farmhouse was quiet again. It might have been a farm on a normal busy day, with all the men out in the fields and all the women in the kitchen. It did not look like a theater of war. It seemed quiet, peaceful. It reminded Tyne vaguely of pictures he had seen on calendars in garages and grocery stores. You could sit in that place on the side of the road and be a friend to man.

T-z-i-n-g-g-g. He hit the ground as a bullet ricocheted from the wall and went whizzing off in the woods. "Close," he said. "Somebody up there's careless with firearms." Cousins grinned appreciatively, and Tyne felt better. The joke was an old one, but he supposed it was what he should say under the circumstances.

"They've got us cold," he said to Ward. "Pretty and cold."

"It's no place for a gentleman," Tranella said. He held up one hand. "Please, teacher, can I leave the room?"

"You and Tinker," Ward said. Tranella's hand came suddenly down, and he swallowed.

''We should have given you some cover too,'' Tyne said.

Ward shrugged. ''What the hell, it wouldn't have made any difference. All I hope is they haven't put through a call to send a couple of tanks. That would really screw us.''

The thought of tanks chilled Tyne. He caught himself. ''I don't think they will,'' he said. ''We've got a lot of planes around here. They're probably afraid the planes would see the tanks.''

''What makes you think so?'' Ward asked.

''I just got a feeling.''

''I just got a feeling, too,'' Ward admitted. ''I wonder if Rankin's dead.''

For a moment Tyne had forgotten Rankin. Now he found himself remembering him with some embarrassment. ''God, I don't know,'' he said.

''He's safe where he is, I guess. He can hang on.''

''Yeah, if anyone can hang on Rankin can hang on.''

Privates Carraway and James were lying on their stomachs, talking about nature. Private James had a leaf in his hand. They had developed, over a period of months, a core of hardness to anything that might happen. Already they had forgotten Rankin and Tinker. It was as though they had never existed. ''Now take this leaf,'' Private James said. ''Look at the complications. Think of all the trouble it took to make this leaf. You never saw nothing as complicated as that.''

''I'm as complicated as that,'' said Private Carraway. ''The human body is the god-damned most complicated thing in the world.''

''It ain't no more complicated than this leaf.''

''Ah, sure it is. That leaf's just a little thing. The human body's a lot bigger.''

''That's what I mean,'' said Private James. ''It's got a lot more to be complicated about. This leaf ain't got anything to be complicated about when you come right down to it.''

''What's so fancy about it?''

''Look at the veins, for instance.''

''You mean to tell me that leaves' veins is more fancy than human veins?''

''I didn't say that. I only said look at them.''

''All right,'' Carraway said. ''I'm looking at them. So what?''

"They're fancy."

"Ah, for Christ's sake," Carraway said. "I got no time for nature study. There's a war on."

"Never heard of it," said Private James innocently. But he threw his leaf away.

The map came out again, and again was spread on the ground. "The trouble with this map is that there's no detail about the farm," Tyne said. "It says the wall stops down by the river, but we knew that anyway. It doesn't show anything new at all. We might just as well toss it away."

Craven had crawled over to see what was going on. "How about the river?" he asked.

"What about it?" Tyne wanted to know. He ran his finger over the blue line on the map that marked it off, as though by the mere pressure of the flesh it could actually become water.

"Maybe we can circle the farm by the river," Craven said. "We can crawl along the bank."

The map once more became the object of study. How dead the symbols are! Tyne thought. They are meaningless, like flies crawling on a wall. He looked at the little black rectangles that signified the farm buildings, then at the elliptical lines that stood for the wall. They were cold and empty. "The only thing is," he said, "we don't know what they've got on that side of the farm."

"There's one way to find out," Ward said.

"What's that?"

"Send a patrol."

Tyne shook his head violently. "No," he said. "There isn't time any more. We've got to get in there, that's all."

"How about forgetting the farm entirely?" Craven said. "How about just crawling down the wall, then wading along this bank of the river until we get to the bridge and then blow her?"

It sounded good. "Idea," Ward said. Tyne stared at the map without speaking. He was looking at the location of the bridge. Whether it had been blown or not would make little difference to its position. If it had been blown the Germans would have put up some sort of pontoon affair right beside the old one, so that they could run back on to the road again. It looked as though there might be a bit of rock between the farm and the bridge; there was just a chance that it couldn't be seen from the windows. And there was also the chance that the Germans had no defenses around the bridge. Perhaps they thought the farmhouse was enough protection. The Germans were so methodical that they always left something undone. They were too methodical. "It doesn't sound bad," he said.

"Hell, no," Ward said. "Best thing we can do."

"We've got to work fast," Tyne said. He looked at his watch. "Damned fast."

"Well, let's go," said Ward. "Best thing's a patrol. Four or five men."

Tyne was dubious. "I don't know," he said. "Perhaps there ought to be more. If there is anyone on the bridge four or five men can get tied up very nicely. I'd rather send two big patrols. Say ten men in each. Send them one after the other. Then if the first one gets jammed up the second one can pitch in. That's the most logical thing."

"Whatever you want," Ward said.

Tyne folded the map very carefully. "The best thing would be a diversion. How long do you think it would take to get over around the farm, Ward?"

"Ward thought for a moment. "Ought to allow about half an hour," he said. "Yeah, just about a half an hour."

"That's fast moving," Craven said.

"All right." Tyne nodded agreement. "What we'll do is this. Ward, you take one patrol and go first. Craven, you take the other one. I'll stay here with the rest of the platoon. We'll give you exactly a half an hour. Then we'll hop over the wall and head for the house. You'll know when we start, because I'll put Rivera to work. You can't help but know. The Krauts will think we're coming up on this side, and they'll pay us all the attention. Then you blow the bridge. As soon as we hear you blow it we'll all get up and rush the joint. How does that sound?"

Two vertical lines appeared at the bridge of Ward's nose. He was running the idea over in his head. "Yeah," he said finally. "It sounds right. How about you, Craven?"

"I don't know," Craven said. "I think they ought to start after twenty minutes. Then the Heinies might not pay so much attention to what's going on behind the house."

''You're right,'' Tyne said. ''I never thought of it. Well, that's the story, then. I guess it's about the best we can do.''

''You've cut yourself out a tough job,'' said Ward.

''Suicide,'' Tyne said. ''I'm a hero. We're all heroes. This'll mean the Good Conduct Medal.''

''What the hell,'' Craven said. ''It might be a breeze.''

''It might be,'' said Tyne. ''But I don't think so.''

The men were lounging behind the wall, taking it easy. They didn't seem very much concerned about what was going to happen. Some of them were at their rations. A man can get hungry almost anywhere, under almost any circumstances. The stomach is a sensitive instrument, the seat of many things besides hunger, but it is still a very demanding instrument. Condemned men can eat a hearty breakfast, at least for the benefit of the yellow press. The soldier, who does not necessarily consider himself condemned to anything more than utter boredom, can eat a hearty meal at any time. The men were not even interested in Tinker's hand, poised above the wall. They had seen such things before. It was very much like going to a bad movie for the second time. It was wonderful what could bore them after a year of battle.

They thought of the farmhouse dispassionately. When Ward came among them, picking out his patrol, they were not moved one way or another. What they were about to do was merely a job, and they had probably been on worse jobs before. That, in itself, was one way to make things seem better. Cousins, for instance, swore that none of the action he had seen—and he had seen a great deal—had been comparable to the Louisiana maneuvers. The idea was to convince yourself that nothing that could come could possibly be as bad as what had gone before. You could last that way; you could last a long time that way. They went with Ward and they went with Craven, and the men who were to go with Tyne went to him calmly. It was the war. It was the job. It was *their* job. Get it done and then relax, that was the thing to do.

Tyne talked to them and they listened. The plan was simple, beautifully simple, the sort of simple thing that could easily go wrong. They listened carefully, nodding their heads occasionally, letting Tyne's words sink in. And when he was through they sat looking at him or studied their rifles or rubbed their hands slowly together as though the joints were aching.

11

"SOMEBODY'S COMING UP here," Friedman said.

"Maybe it's Marlene Dietrich," Rivera said. "Has he got legs?"

"I can't see," Friedman said. "It's the way they walk in the army. It's Joe Jack."

Private Jack came crawling toward them, sometimes rising to his feet and going into a crouching run. He often acted as company runner, and it was his proud boast that more bullets had missed him than anyone else in the army. He had a charmed life, had Private Jack.

"Why the hell they always stick you out in left field?" he panted as he came up to the machine gun. "Why don't you ever hang around where a guy can get at you?"

"There are three ways to do things," Rivera said solemnly. "The right way, the wrong way, and the army way. It's the army way to stick me out in left field. What you got, Joe?"

"Message from Tyne," Jack said. He passed over a folded paper.

Rivera opened it slowly. "Wish I had my glasses," he said.

"Cut it," Friedman said. "What's he say?"

"*'Doughfoot,'*" Rivera read. "*'Two patrols going try go round farm via river. I taking rest platoon over field. When blow my whistle synchronize watch 1215 hrs. Five minutes after going up field on dot. Give cover 15 seconds before. Give cover up field. Remember, cover at 1219 and 45 secs. Hope ammo holds out. We are going all the way.'* That's all."

"How's he sign it?" Friedman wanted to know.

"*Tyne, Cpl., U.S.A.,*" said Rivera.

"Formal, ain't he?"

Rivera looked at his watch. "If this thing is right it's only two minutes to 1215. The patrol's left, Joe?"

"Yeah, they left before I came here."

"Okay, hop back and say we're all set. Tell Tyne I said good luck."

"I'll tell him, Rivera." Jack turned and started back in his crouching run. Rivera looked carefully at the dial of his watch. "Nobody dies," he said. "How's the ammo?"

"It's been worse," Friedman said. "And it's been better."

"Tyne really cut himself a piece of cake," Rivera said. He studied the note. "Hey, Friedman, what's this mean? *'Five minutes after going up field on dot.'* I don't get it."

"Let's see the note," Friedman said. He took it and peered closely at it. He read it over several times. ''Oh, I get it,'' he said. ''He means that five minutes after he blows his whistle they're going up the field. He wants you to go to work fifteen seconds before.''

''That it?'' Rivera took the note back. ''Suppose they'll give me money for overtime?''

''Ah, sure,'' said Friedman.

''Jesus,'' Rivera said, ''that's a tricky business.''

Friedman looked glum. ''Looks like we'll be getting a new platoon pretty soon.''

''Yeah,'' Rivera said. Then suddenly the mask of lightness dropped from his face. He looked worn and angry and his dark eyes flashed. ''God damn it,'' he burst out, ''why don't they ever give them a chance? They never get a chance. We're the dirty god-damned Infantry and they stick us in everywhere. Jesus, there's a hell of a lot of good men going down in the war. Why don't they let us alone? I wish to God that I had every Nazi right in the palm of my hand. I'd crush them to a pulp. Why the hell don't they let us alone?'' He subsided as quickly as he had begun.

''Yeah,'' Friedman said.

Rivera looked at his watch again. ''It won't be long now,'' he said. ''A whole new god-damned platoon.''

Tyne watched the patrols go, wiggling along by the wall, their backs turned toward him. He wondered vaguely how many of the faces he would ever see again. Then he shook himself. That was the wrong kind of idea to have. It was just a job, that was all, just a job. Like any other job. It wasn't any more risky than working in a steel mill—not even as risky, perhaps. It was all in the point of view. The twenty-five men who were to go up the field with him were spread up and down the wall, three yards apart. Their faces, or those of their faces that he could see, looked set and tired. He glanced at his watch. Two minutes to go till 1215. He looked up to see if he could see Jack. There was no sign of him. Behind his head, with a foot of wall between them, Tinker's hand reared limply toward the sky. Tyne was vaguely conscious of it, as though it were trying to touch his back.

Ward had gone off almost carelessly. So had they all. That was the only way to go, as though one would be back in a few minutes, as though one were just running down to the corner for a paper or to make a phone call. When it was done that way it was easy. And it was always that way; the dragged-out good-byes were always reserved for the movies. Tyne knew, however, that Ward did not expect him to get across the field. Ward thought he was throwing himself away. They had argued about it, not in so many words. Ward had said he thought the two patrols would be enough, without any diversion. Craven had thought the same thing. But Tyne was in command of the platoon. He thought a diversion was needed, and a diversion there would be. He was not afraid. He was not even worried. Everything, he kept telling himself, was going to be all right. Everything was going to be just lovely.

Silently Ward slid into the river. Now that he was down there things looked better than he had hoped they would. There was a solid screen of reeds and bushes between them and the farmhouse. It looked clear ahead. The river was not more than seventy-five feet across, but it was deep. Even by the bank he went in to his ribs. But as set-ups went, it didn't look too bad. Tranella splashed down behind him. Ward whirled around. "Take it easy, for God's sake," he whispered.

"Sorry, Sarge," Tranella said. "Slipped."

"Well, don't slip again."

The patrol moved forward through the water. Ward carried no rifle. He had a .45 in his left hand and a grenade in his right. Only three men in each patrol carried rifles. They were more in the way than anything else.

Behind Ward's patrol Craven entered the water, catching his breath as he did so. He was still trying to write that letter, but it kept taking curious twists in his mind. Right now it read: "Dear Frances, I am just back from going swimming in a river somewhere in Italy and we have just blown up the bridge so that anybody who tries to cross the river will have to go swimming, too." He was composing the letter subconsciously. Perhaps he ought to write one for Tinker, too. Tinker had been interested. "Dear Mom, I am now sleeping against a wall Somewhere in Italy. It isn't very comfortable but a man has to lie where he can these days. If you ever get to Italy you must come and see me for I am always going to be here." He caught at a bush to steady himself as his foot stepped on an object under the water. Then, steadied, he waded on. The water was strangely cold for such a hot day. Or perhaps it seemed cold because the day was so hot. Craven wasn't sure. It was hard to be sure of things.

Tyne saw Jack coming toward him, coming back from Rivera. He had made good time, but there wasn't a lot to spare. He looked at his watch. Forty seconds to go before he blew his whistle. The patrols had been out for fifteen minutes.

"How'd it go?" he asked as Jack came up to him.

"Rivera says it's okay," Jack said. "He said good luck."

"Nice of him," Tyne said. He looked at his watch and put the whistle to his lips. Every other watch was synchronized; only Rivera had to be checked. A few of the men were studying their own watches as though they expected to be surprised when Tyne blew his whistle. He puffed out his cheeks and let go.

"Right on the nose," Rivera said. "Even the lousy second hand was right on the nose."

"That's not an army watch," Friedman said. "What kind of a watch is that?"

"Just a watch," Rivera said. "It works."

"I'm slow."

"How much time is it now? Oh, yeah, four minutes, forty-five seconds. Honest to God, I'm going to cut that house right in two."

"If the ammo holds out," Friedman said.

"The ammo had better hold out," Rivera said grimly.

On the river the two patrols heard Tyne's whistle sound, faint and far away. Ward looked at his watch. Tyne was right on time. That meant five minutes before the diversion. He calculated that they were already behind the farm. There was a bend in the river less than fifty yards away, and from the bend they would be able to see the bridge. The river, he noted, curved almost entirely around the farm. Everywhere there was silence. They made surprisingly little noise as they moved ahead; much less noise, as a matter of fact, than Ward had expected. That was good. So far things had been successful. With just a little bit of luck they might stay that way. Ward was beginning to believe that the Germans had been so interested in the farmhouse that they had entirely forgotten to watch the river or the bridge. That was what they got for being so interested in windows.

For another thing, he did not believe that German fire covered every field of view from the house. He had a feeling that there were rocks up ahead, between the house and the river, and that it would have been impossible for them to cover anything in that direction. Time would show soon enough whether or not he was right. Ward wondered if he could pull the pin out of a grenade with his teeth. He had never done it before.

* * *

"How do you feel about things, Arch?" Tyne said to Archimbeau.

They were sitting three yards from each other. Archimbeau was chewing moodily on a straw he had picked up.

"It's a long war," Archimbeau said. "That's all I know about it."

"Still worried about Tibet?"

"Sometimes I think we'll never get out of the army. Honest to God, that's what I think."

"I used to think I'd never get in it. So I figure I'll get out of it some day. It could be worse."

"I don't know how," Archimbeau said. "You don't know. You don't get all the stinking details."

"I've got a stinking detail right now," Tyne said.

"Who hasn't? But what the hell. Maybe we can sleep all day tomorrow. Maybe Germany'll surrender tomorrow. Who knows?"

"Who knows?" Tyne said. He crouched and moved up along the wall, checking the men over, asking them if things were okay, making sure that everything was going to run smoothly. "Remember," he told each one of them, "when you hear the bridge blow, get up and run like hell for the farm." That was very important. When the Germans heard the bridge go they were going to be a very surprised group of young men, and it was necessary to take advantage of that surprise. If that went well, it was half the job. They all seemed to know that.

Tyne spoke to every man of the twenty-five. As he came back to his position beside Archimbeau his stomach was screwed up in a tight knot. He felt slightly ill and slightly dizzy. It was rather hard to breathe. He knew that they were all going through the same symptoms. It was the natural thing; it was expected.

He looked at his watch. 1219. Forty-five seconds to go, forty-five seconds before Rivera opened up. He crouched on one knee, facing the wall. Men on either side of him were doing the same thing. He had a sudden urge to write a letter, but he didn't know to whom he wanted to write. Desperately he wanted to put words on paper, but for the life of him he couldn't think of a recipient. There were so many people he would have liked to write to. Words welled up inside him. The desire to write was superseded by a desire to talk to somebody. He looked casually at Archimbeau and winked. Archimbeau winked back, his mouth twitching as he did so. Fifteen seconds to go.

The sun burned down with a radiance fiercer than ever before. It was as though someone had flipped a switch and turned it on full power. It was a most peculiar sensation, to feel the sun grow suddenly hotter. Tyne wondered if anyone else had noticed the phenomenon. He was on the point of asking Archimbeau if he had noticed it when Rivera's gun suddenly started firing.

It chattered off on the left like a riveting machine. It sounded like the pneumatic drills Tyne had heard countless times in countless streets. And as it chattered on, the German machine gun began to fire, too. Good. They were looking for Rivera. That would give them time to get over the wall.

Ward heard the machine gun and jerked his head up. They were just rounding the bend, moving very carefully. Before him he could see the bridge, a pontoon affair with about six or seven floats under it. There was no one around. They were going to get it sure as hell. Ward grinned to himself. His finger tightened around his grenade. He began to move a little faster through the water.

"Fifteen," Tyne said aloud. He stood bolt upright, blew his whistle, and leaped over the wall. Three men came over after him. As he went over the wall one of his outstretched feet struck Tinker's body, and the body collapsed on the earth. Tyne hit the dirt and dug his nose in, listening. The German machine gun had switched in his direction. It was traversing the wall. Bullets cut into the stone over his head and then passed on.

The German machine gun went silent. Either Rivera had hit it or they were changing belts. Two or three scattered rifles fired from the farm. Cautiously Tyne began to worm his way forward, over the same ground that Ward's patrol had covered a short while before. Through the grass he could see Archimbeau working ahead. Archimbeau had perhaps two yards' lead on him. He must have given a devil of a jump over the wall.

"Damned thing's stopped," Friedman yelled.

Rivera suddenly stopped firing. "I put enough god-damned lead in that thing to sink it," he said. "No wonder it stopped."

"They didn't find Baby," Friedman said.

"Nope," said Rivera. "They didn't find Baby." He opened fire again.

It was hard for a man to think as he crawled over the earth. All Tyne's thoughts were strangely disconnected. The farm seemed very far away. The work at hand no longer pressed on his mind. All that was automatic. What did bother him, though, was the fleeting ideas that flashed through his brain and then vanished. He found himself reviewing the whole day in snatches. He saw Porter's face, twisted, and Hoskins's face, set. He saw Trasker with his jaw gone and McWilliams with his hands stretched out as though they would protect him from the plane. It seemed to him that McWilliams had been dead a very long time—that he had been dead for an eternity and that for eternity he was doomed to go through that same impotent action of stretching out his arms. Sometimes Tyne could not distinguish the living from the dead. Faces had a tendency to run together, to blur, to become indistinct. They became as confused and as difficult to explain as the battles they had been in. They ran together like letters of ink in the rain. They had no real identity. They were swallowed up in a mist, in a vapor.

And so were Tyne's thoughts. One moment he saw himself sitting by the fire at home; the next moment he saw himself, as though from a great distance, crawling over a muddy plain. He did not recognize the landscape as a real one. He had never fought in such a place. But the landscape was familiar for all that. It was the landscape of dream. He had been moving through it for years; he would probably never find his way out of it.

The German machine gun started up again. It was firing into the grass ahead of them now. Either the gunners were bad or they were taking their time, playing with them. Tyne looked at Archimbeau again. He was creeping doggedly ahead, his eyes fixed before him, his mouth slightly open. Tyne wondered if he were breathing through his mouth, and then he realized that he himself was. Silly. He crawled on.

The patrols were nearly at the bridge. It was deserted, absolutely deserted. Ward felt a glow creeping over him, engendered by the approaching destruction. There was something fine about destruction; it released something in him. Perhaps it was because, as a farmer, he had spent most of his life cultivating things, building them up. It was the attraction of opposites, an outlet for several kinds of energy. He looked forward with great glee to using his grenade. The mission was so easy that it was almost laughable. Ward had an urge to burst out in guffaws. It was all so god-damned funny. They were going to blow up a nice German bridge. It was like little boys on Hallowe'en, stealing the parson's gate. Just like Hallowe'en.

* * *

"Damned foolish thing to do," Tyne said aloud. But he didn't know what was foolish or why he said it. He looked back at the wall and judged from his position that they were almost where Ward had been earlier. They still had a long way to go, a hell of a long way. Nothing was slower than crawling, nothing in the world. How long would it take to crawl around the earth? A hundred years? A thousand years? He ducked as the machine gun spat over his head. He almost asked himself why they didn't depress the gun a little. It would be so easy.

Ahead of him he caught sight of a body, dark against the brown grass. He thought that he had been crawling where someone had been before, but he hadn't been sure; a cow might have come through the field. The body must be Rankin. He was possessed of an intense desire to know whether or not Rankin was still alive. He very nearly rose to his feet in his haste to get to the body.

Rankin was lying face down. With an effort Tyne managed to roll him over, but even as he rolled him he knew that he was dead. A dead body is completely devoid of any buoyancy. It is a mere lump. Rankin had a hole in his neck and a hole in his chest, and he had holes in his back, also, where the bullets had entered in. His tommy gun lay beside him. Tyne cast an anxious glance at Archimbeau, to see that he didn't get too far ahead of him, and picked up the tommy gun. There was blood on it, covering the notches that marked Rankin's kills. Tyne laid his own rifle down beside Rankin and started crawling again. He took the tommy gun with him.

How were they making out—all the faces, all the bodies? How were Cousins and Jack and MacNamara and Peterson and all the rest of them? Did they feel the way he did? Were they thinking the way he was thinking? They had come a long way to the war, and it would be a long way back. Over their heads and before their eyes the machine gun sent its bullets in their vicious arc. It was death, alive and spitting. For all Tyne knew, some of the men had been hit already. There was no way of knowing. No way at all. Pictures flashed across his mind and were gone before he could grasp them. Everything speeded up; the world was moving at a dizzy pace. He could not keep up with it. It was going around faster and faster. In a minute it would fly away.

A dull explosion came from behind the farm. Then another and another. The bridge. Ward.

And then everything that had been moving so fast stopped dead. The world stopped. Time stopped. The war stopped. The German machine gun stopped. What had spun so fast, what had nearly hurled Tyne among the stars was stopped dead, with such a violence as to shake his body the way a woman shakes a mop from a window. His mind became clear as polished glass. Everything in his life had led up to this moment. It was his. Nothing could take it from him.

Slowly, almost gravely, he rose to his feet and blew a blast on his whistle. Men rose all around him. He saw them sharply in the shimmering air. He broke into a run. Beside him he saw Archimbeau start to run too, and then suddenly stumble with a surprised look on his face and go tumbling down like a sack, on his way to the Battle of Tibet. Tyne knew that he was running gracefully toward the farmhouse, the mysterious farmhouse, the farmhouse that was waiting to gather him in and hide him from the world. Its windows were eyes, and they were looking at him, studying his every move and the movements of the men with him. The farmhouse loomed up, and it was waiting.

Behind it there were two more explosions, and somewhere in the next world Rivera's finger was on the trigger of his gun and he was singing.

They were all singing. All of them.

"It is so easy," Tyne said aloud as he ran. "It is so terribly easy."

STEPHEN VINCENT BENÉT

A Judgment in the Mountains

The news broadcast ended—the man sitting in the chair turned the radio down. Things were much the same. In France, more hostages were to be shot by the Nazis. In Poland there was a reported outbreak of sabotage. In Yugoslavia, guerrilla warfare continued. In Norway—

"I can't get the feel," thought the man, "though it's a good radio. It's so near and so far off. It comes right into your house and yet your mind is blurred. What's it really like for those people? To be free, one day—and the next day, invaded, conquered, fighting underground?"

His hand moved toward the radio and dropped again. He stirred restlessly in his chair.

"Read the books," he thought, "read the books. But even they won't tell you. Supposing it happened here, right here in the mountains? Are we tough enough? Of course we are. But we did have traitors in this country, though they didn't call them Fifth Columnists then—yes, even in the Revolution, we had Arnold. What beats those people—what will always beat them in the end? And how would the folks I know act—just supposing it happened here?"

He slipped deeper into his chair, closed his eyes and thought.

THE CAR STOPPED in front of the dusty country store and the two men got out. They were both in uniform.

"It is still my opinion," said the spectacled man, as if continuing an argument, "that more force should have been employed. It is still my opinion that it is unwise to proceed in this manner."

"My orders are to investigate an accident, not to irritate the feelings of the local population," said the other man. "If you have other orders, you will please show me your authority."

"You know what my orders are," said the spectacled man. "I must report upon the physical and psychological status of these peasant communities and their reaction to our propaganda forms. I agree that a certain winning of confidence is always advisable. Nevertheless, with peasants, a show of strength is a show of strength."

"Oh, we could have marched in," said Lon Stacey wearily, "but then they'd freeze and you wouldn't get anything out of them. I know these people, you see—I was raised among them. That's why I brought two men instead of the whole escort." He stared up and down the deserted street. "As it is," he said, "there's not even a dog in the street. That's not so good—that means they're out in the laurel. We'll be lucky to find our man."

"Please?" said the spectacled man.

"Your objection is noted," said Lon Stacey. "We will proceed."

He turned and gave certain orders to the two men with light machine guns in the front seat of the car. They were to keep in touch with Captain Lenz by two-way radio and under no circumstances to allow civilians to approach the car. He gave the orders firmly, in the foreign tongue, as always a little surprised that they would be obeyed. But they would be obeyed, just as orders to fire the town would also be obeyed. It made a man feel powerful to know that—powerful and sure.

He turned back to the spectacled man.

"Are you satisfied?" he said. "Or would you prefer to return to the escort? I am going into the store."

"It is your country, not mine," said the spectacled man less stiffly. "Nevertheless, though all seems quiet, I have known peasants to do very irrational things."

"These are not peasants," said Lon Stacey. He walked firmly up the two cracked steps, across the sagging porch and into the store. It was such a store as he remembered from childhood—the long room, cluttered and untidy, smelling of cloth and kerosene and pickles and tobacco, and dim when you first walked into it out of the sun—the wonderful store where the candy and the bought goods were. He had been away from such stores for a long time; he had not imagined the memory would be so strong. He stood for a moment in the doorway, drinking in the smells. They were still the same—the sticky candy was still in the glass jars. They were still the same, though most of the shelves were empty.

"I'm a comin'," said a voice from the dimness at the back of the store. "Don't you rush me now—I'm a comin'!"

An old man emerged from the dimness and the darkness—a square, puffing old man in worn clothes with a fringe of white hair that stuck up around his bald head. "Well, howdy, folks—howdy, folks," he said in his soft voice.

"Hail to the Leader!" said the spectacled man. He turned to Lon Stacey and spoke in his own tongue. "Is this the man?" he said. "He suggests the petty-owner type but his repetition of words is that of the peasant. Will you do the questioning or I?"

"I will do the questioning, please," said Lon Stacey with irritation. He turned to the old man.

"I am Captain Stacey," he said, "of the Bureau of Political Affairs. I am here on duty with my colleague, Captain Schildmesser of the Army of Occupation. You are John Quayle," he continued, "Number 241 on our lists. You are a responsible and law-abiding citizen and so far have carried out all instructions."

And what nonsense it is to talk to a man that way, thought Lon Stacey as he spoke. *But if I don't, that spectacled bugaboo will put it down in his notebook and report it. That's why they sent him with me, of course. They never trust you, no matter how many proofs you give.*

But he did not say what he thought, for the old man was already nodding vigorously.

"Yes, sir," he said. "That's me—John Quayle—and John Quayle don't do things halfways. Put the picture up and everything."

Lon Stacey glanced at the well-known picture of the Leader. Yes, it was there, on the wall. He saluted solemnly for the spectacled man's benefit, and was glad to see the old man sketch a ragged salute as well.

"Yes, sir," said John Quayle, "right up there where folks can see it. Shows where a man stands. Used to have Washington up there—calendar. But I reckoned I'd better take George down and put him up. Yes, sir, I reckoned that when I first heard about the troubles." He chuckled wisely and Lon Stacey felt a little sick.

"I do not understand all he says," said the spectacled man. "It is the dialect—of that I was not informed. But you are right—we will have no difficulty here, with such a man. Does my presence embarrass him?"

"I think he would talk more freely—" said Lon Stacey.

"Then I will go to the car," said the spectacled man graciously. "There is much I must write in my notes—my report must in order be. My own observation will come later."

He clicked heels, saluted and left, with another "Hail to the Leader." The old man waited till he had shut the door.

"One of them?" he said in a somewhat breathless voice.

"Yes, one of them," said Lon Stacey.

"Well, now, he looks human, at that," said the old man. "First one I've seen," he said. "But I reckon we'll be seeing more. Yes, sir, even at Rabbit Run. Well, what I always say is—men must move with the times."

His eyes, bright and old and sly, looked wisely at Lon Stacey and the latter again felt a sick taste rise in his mouth. He had known, in his youth, so many old men like John Quayle. And, right or wrong, sensible or not, you did not expect such eager collaboration from such men. He collaborated himself and had from the first. But that was from reason, conviction, common sense—a thousand things that the old man could not know.

He sat down in a chair, hitched it forward, and got on with his job. His voice slurred back to the accent of the mountains.

"Well, now, Mr. Quayle," he said, "I've come for some information and I reckon you're just the man I'm looking for. You're the postmaster here—"

"And justice of the peace. And notary public," said John Quayle with a chuckle. "Oh, they all know John Quayle—they all know Quayle's store. Why, I've had folks come from Vinegar Bend just to trade. That was when there was trading, of course."

"That'll all get fixed," said Lon Stacey, "just as soon as things settle down."

"Don't I tell them that?" demanded John Quayle. "Don't I say all the time—well, now, even if the valley folks got whipped and we got a new government—why, we're bound to take things the way they are. All the same, I'd like some store goods," he said, his eyes regarding his empty shelves. "I surely would like some store goods. It would make folks more contented."

"Would you say they were restless now?" said Lon Stacey easily.

"Why, no, captain," said the old man; "no more restless than usual." His eyes were shrewd. "Of course there's bound to be a wonder," he said, "when government men come in. There's just bound to be."

He paused as if he had asked a confidential question, and Lon Stacey instantly saw his own mission.

"Forget about that," he said. "Yes, I brought in government men. But they're soldiers—they wouldn't know a still or a worm if it was right in front of them. No, there'll be no trouble about that."

"Well, I'm glad to hear that," said the old man. "No revenuers?"

"No revenuers," said Lon Stacey. He remembered a discussion

with the spectacled man on the psychological advantages of an alcoholic peasantry. "No, that's done with."

"And that's good news," said John Quayle, "though it ought to be spread." He slid farther down in his chair. "I won't deceive you," he said; "there ain't many folks in town. Not since we got the word. They feel safer out in the laurel. It's always been that way in the troubled times. I keep telling them it's all settled, but they won't believe me yet. Now, maybe, if a man like you spoke up to them."

"That's one reason I'm here," said Lon Stacey.

"Then I'll send the youngster around," said the old man. He put fingers to mouth and whistled. "Never there when you want him," he said plaintively—and yet, in a moment, the shy, wild boy was there, staring silently at Lon Stacey. He could not have been more than twelve and he moved as shyly as a deer.

"Now, Jesse," said the old man comfortably, "you tell the folks I want them. Tell them all the way up to Green's." He nodded when the boy had left.

"There," he said, "they'll be in. Or most of them."

Lon Stacey did not question the magic that could summon men and women from the laurel at the shrill of a whistle and a word to a boy. That was something the spectacled man could not possibly understand, but he understood it.

"I'm obliged," he said.

"That's all right, captain," said the old man. He lowered his voice. "And now, what's the real trouble?" he said.

"It's three airplanes," said Lon Stacey. "Crashed in the mountains. The last one was a big transport."

"Poor souls," said the old man sympathetically, "poor souls."

"It could only have been an accident," said Lon Stacey carefully. "There are no American fighter planes left east of the Mississippi. But—the men had parachutes. Some should have escaped alive." He looked at the old man closely.

"Well, you know how it is in the laurel," said the old man.

"I know how it is," said Lon Stacey. "But—they don't like it." He recovered himself. "We do not permit such accidents. We must have information."

"There was them two government men got lost on Old Baldy, years gone by," said the old man reflectively. "You know about that, if your name's Stacey. And yet nobody laid a hand on them till they died. But they didn't know the hills."

"Now, listen to me," said Lon Stacey, and tapped his knee. "This isn't revenue or government. The country is conquered."

"Yuh, I heard about it on the radio. Heard all about it," said the old man in a flat voice.

"Conquered," said Lon Stacey. "Just the way the South was conquered after the war. Only, this time, it isn't even our own kin that's conquered. So we've got to do our best and accept it. I'm doing my best."

"No Yankees was kin of mine," said the old man, "though I'll admit some of my kin took up with their side."

Lon Stacey beat his fist in his hand.

"It's a fact," he said. "It's happened. We thought it couldn't happen but it did. Well—these men were in uniform. It must have been an accident. It's bad flying over the mountains, and the pilots were foreign. But if some of them 'chuted down and afterwards—" He stopped.

"You mean if somebody's finger got a little easy on the trigger," said the old man. "You mean if they got to a place—and being foreign, let's say, scared the woman of the house, and then—"

"Yes, that's just what I mean," said Lon Stacey. Something stuck in his throat. "There would be a reward, of course, for information," he said.

"In store goods?" said the old man. "The new money's no use to a man."

"In store goods, if you like," said Lon Stacey. He saw the old man's eyes rove around the empty shelves.

"Well, now," said the old man, "I don't know a thing. And I can't show you the place. But the Green boys—they're a headstrong and godless lot. Owe me money. I don't say if you looked on their place you'd find what you want. But I don't say that you wouldn't. And one of the Green boys may be in tonight. But there's five brothers—and I reckon you'd want them all."

"Yes," said Lon Stacey grimly, "I'd want them all."

"Well," said the old man, "they're troublemakers. Troublemakers. No kin of mine. All the same, I wouldn't want it known. You got plenty of men?" he said doubtfully.

"Well, we didn't bring any tanks," said Lon Stacey lightly, "but my escort's camped down by the run. You needn't worry about that."

"Uh!" said the old man. "Well, I seen them tankers once. First part of the war. But they don't suit mountainy roads. They get stuck and waller and spit stones." He laughed a high old man's laugh. "Funny how they do that."

"They aren't so funny in action," said Lon Stacey.

"That's right," said the old man. "Must be terrible things—in the lowlands. But up in the mountains it's different. It's like the airplanes. They'll fly above you, just like a bird on the wing. But once they hit the side of a mountain—why, it's just a crash and a flash." His head nodded with the drowsiness of age. "What was I sayin'?" he said. "Well, it's darkening now. Mrs. Quayle'll fix us supper—you and the foreigner. And then you can have your meeting and I'll figure some more about the Greens."

It was going very well, thought Lon Stacey later. It was at least a first step, and first steps were important. They had drifted in from the night, the lean men with tanned faces, the women in cotton dresses, the shy and silent children—his people that he knew so well. Not many, to be sure, and many more women than men—but enough for a start.

They had listened to his speech—they had seen Captain Schildmesser's moving picture—the moving picture so skillfully displaying the irresistible might of the New Order, so efficiently shown by Captain Schildmesser on his portable machine. There were one or two sequences in the picture he must discuss with Schildmesser—particularly the one where the treads of the tank ran over the American flag. That might be good for audiences in some countries, but not for this one, though there had been no comment except a low sound.

After the picture and the speech, he had moved among them, talking their language, the language his boyhood remembered. Now they were slipping away again, as silently as they had come—but that was all right, too; he knew his people and their habits. They would have to talk him over among themselves even though he was a Stacey—he had been away so long. But, in time, he'd get them back to the town.

He felt less troubled in mind than he had in a long time. It was one thing, sensibly, hardheadedly, to work for the invaders and the New Order—to be, yes, what books called a traitor. He would face the word; he had faced it for some time now. Still, it was an uncomfortable word to keep in your mind. But there surely could be no treachery in what he was doing now. A scattered group of mountaineers could not possibly stand out against the vast mechanism so efficient to the last detail, from the fleets of bombers to Captain Schildmesser's portable projector. And except for the timber, the mountains held little enough that the New Order wanted.

His cheeks flushed for a moment. You couldn't be governor any more—you couldn't sit in the Statehouse, under the seal of the state. All those things were being very carefully and methodically obliterated. But it was quite possible that he could be District Leader—District Leader of all the mountains. They could put one puppet or another in the lowland cities. But, here, they would have to have someone who knew the hills.

He had come a long way for that—a long way with many turns in it. He'd put up with a lot of things. Yes, he'd eaten crow. And yet, he had always been right—that was what had not been understood. The rules that bound ordinary men should not apply to Lon Stacey. If they'd only recognized that—the people who had laughed at him once—why, he might have been on their side. But they hadn't recognized it—they hadn't let him get ahead fast enough. The old men who sat around country stores and thought him a crack-headed youngster—the teachers at the university who talked about tradition and fairness when they should have talked about Lon Stacey—old Judge Mason, with his soft voice, cautioning him publicly in court—the girl with the dark eyes saying, "I've tried to care for you, Lon. But I guess the only person you care about is yourself." How many of them there were, and all so wrong! He had had to have the money and the power—it had been a necessity of his nature. But once he got them, he had meant to do excellent things. Only, they'd never let him get that far. The New Order was wiser—it recognized that certain men were born to rule.

He noticed the spectacled man inconspicuously beside him.

"Well," he said, "are you satisfied?"

"They are very silent," said the spectacled man. "The group reaction must have a very low index. They show no emotion even at the film. I have been in many occupied countries—there is always a certain silence, to be sure. But here, there is an interesting difference. What about the chief matter?"

"I will have information tomorrow," said Lon Stacey confidently.

"If so, you will have been very useful," said the spectacled man with bleak approval. "I must confess that I was dubious. This group, it is somewhat a problem. It is backward yet, one gathers, undisciplined. We cannot permit an armed populace in the land to stay—yet the land it is very wild and would not attract our good settlers. Establish strong posts we must, and many landing fields. That is primary. But the problem remains. Perhaps transplantation might solve—one has not yet decided."

"Did you ever stir up a wasp's nest?" said Lon Stacey suddenly and sharply. "They want to be left alone."

"Well, that is not your business," said the spectacled man coldly. "Your business is to keep them quiet till we have decided. Now what do we do?"

"We stay in the house for the night," said Lon Stacey with satisfaction. "Braun and Kopp will guard the car and the equipment. There's a shed at the back—the old man used to have a service station."

The spectacled man nodded. "Yes, that makes a good impression," he said. "To stay for the night. They sometimes become talkative and unguarded. One can then observe the reactions. It is necessary to drink alcohol?"

"Well, I'm going to have a pull at the jug," said Lon Stacey. "It'll show them—well, you wouldn't understand that. But you can suit yourself."

The spectacled man sighed. "It blurs the reactions," he said, "yet one finds it sometimes necessary."

In the back room it was more comfortable and there was a clean fire on the hearth. It was a long time since Lon Stacey had sat in front of such a fire. It was a long time since he had drunk the liquor of the mountains. He sucked meditatively at his glass. In the morning the machine would grind on, and he would make John Quayle betray his neighbors. But surely there was time for that, in the morning. Now, he seemed to have slipped back in time—slipped back to the days of boyhood, when the air was clean and both sunrise and sunset good and there were no other people but his people. The only jarring note was the spectacled man, writing his notes by a lamp in the corner. But the rest were right—John Quayle and the other old man called Uncle Billy Hite—the woman who had served the good meal and the shy boy.

"Tell us a tale, Uncle Billy," said John Quayle comfortably. "The night's young yet and we've got company and it's a good night for tales."

Lon Stacey smiled to himself. He had known the other old man must be a taleteller ever since he first stood in the door, tall and gaunt as a wintry pine. If he told his tale now, Lon Stacey would take it as a sign—a sign that, in spite of all, he was accepted again among the mountains.

"I used to know a tale myself once," he said cunningly. "Maybe, if you told your tale, I could recollect it."

"Well, now, mine's an old-fashioned tale," said Uncle Billy. "You see that rifle on the hooks there?"

"I see it," said Lon Stacey. *And Schildmesser sees it too. And "we cannot permit an armed populace in the land to stay." But I can take care of Schildmesser in time. I think I can.*

"Well, that's the kind of rifles they used and they drew a long bead," said Uncle Billy. "I'm telling the tale as it was told to me—the tale about Major Ferguson and the colonels."

"It is a telling of a war?" said the spectacled man, making a note in his notebook.

"Ayuh," said Uncle Billy Hite. "It was far back and long ago, but the times were troubled like these. Yes, troubled times. But I'd best tell you of Major Ferguson first. A slight little hellion he was, with a pale face, but the best shot in all King George's Army. He used to walk through the king's forests in England, knocking down the gray squirrels, and they'd fall like leaves before his shot. Ayuh, he was a man, Major Ferguson. Though the Devil was his uncle, he was a man."

"He was a man but we had better," said John Quayle suddenly and deeply.

"Now, that's true," said Uncle Billy. "But I'm talking first of Major Ferguson and the shooter he was. He was this kind of shooter. They had no guns in those days but the guns that loaded at the muzzle—and well they shot. But Ferguson made one that loaded at the breech and the Devil helped him make it all one long black night, with the bellows blowing and the coals blazing. And when it was finished, the Devil gave it to him and he took it up, red-hot, and tested the weight and the balance in his hand. How could he do it? Why, the Devil put a charm around his neck and no harm could touch him unless the charm string broke." He paused and looked at the fire.

"This is very superstition," said the spectacled man, in his own tongue. "Are they truly believing in devils and magic? That is to be noted."

"It happened as he says," said Lon Stacey, while the spectacled man looked at him oddly. "Go on with your story, Uncle Billy."

"Ayuh," said Uncle Billy. "Where was I? Well, now he had his gun—his gun that loaded at the breech—and he went to the Tower of London to show it to the kings of the world—he was full of pride, that slight pale man. And there they were in London, the King of England and the King of Spain and the King of Denmark and all the kings, for they'd been invited to see it. He showed it to the King of England and when the King saw how it shot, he took off his crown and wiped his forehead. 'Major Ferguson,' he said, 'I'm a handsome shot myself. But you're the best shooter that's been seen in the world.'

" 'I will not deny that, King,'' said Major Ferguson, for he was full of pride.

" 'Yes,' said the King. 'So ask of me what you want and it shall be granted.' Now he thought Major Ferguson would ask one thing or another, like diamonds or pearls or the hand of his daughter, Fair Ellen, and those he'd have been glad to give.

"But then up spoke a puny little king who'd come in by the back door. I forget what he was king of, but he'd only gotten the neck of the rooster at dinner, and so he was angry.

" 'Major Ferguson shoots right well,' he said, 'yet I hear there are men in America who shoot better than he.'

"The King of England's face grew as black as a thundercloud, for those were the Revolution times and he did not want to hear about the men of America. But before he had time to say a word, Major Ferguson spoke up.

" 'Then, King, let me go to America and fight in your wars,' he said. 'And there'll be a shooting match the world has never seen before.'

"So Major Ferguson came here, and that was a time, when he came. There were fighters in the King's armies but none like Major Ferguson.

"When he and the men he had trained with the Devil's gun went across a county, the crows and the buzzards had good pickings. He did not leave a stone on a stone or a log on a log or a corn patch growing in a clearing.

"So at last he came to the mountains, he and his men. They were not all Britishers, his men. There were men of ours who had turned against country and kin. That is true and I'll say it. And the word went through the mountains that he had come.

"Now that was a different fighting from the way it is now. It was a different fighting. A man could fight for a while and then go home and make a crop. And nobody thought the worse of him. But Major Ferguson and his men, they fought winter and summer, day and night. So they were hard to handle."

"It is always the same story—the ready and the unready," said the spectacled man. But Uncle Billy Hite did not seem to hear him, for he went on:

"The word went through the piny woods and the laurel—the word that Ferguson was coming to root and burn in the mountains as he had rooted and burned in the lowlands and the valleys. And that was a strong word.

"So they gathered from the runs and the creeks and the folds of the mountains—they gathered the riflemen. They gathered from Cub Run and Thunder Run and all the runs and the clearings. They gathered under the colonels—the brushwood colonels they'd chosen. They weren't dressed up fine and handsome like Ferguson's men—they were dressed in their shirts and their pants, and for some of them it was a fifty-mile march and for some a thirty and for some more and for some less. And no one man commanded them, though the colonels commanded as they could. But they slipped through the woods like deer, and if some of them went hungry on the road none went short of powder or shot. For this was the big shooting match that they had with Major Ferguson, and it was a long time due.

"Now when Major Ferguson got to King's Mountain, he heard about the gathering of the colonels and he might have turned back. But he did not, for, devil or man, he was bold. He sent word that this was King's Mountain and he was king of the mountain and meant to stay there. And the colonels heard that word and closed in through the woods. They closed around him in a circle.

"You can still see where he and his men stood on the top of King's Mountain. And you'd think it a good place to fight. For, on the top of the mountain, the ground lies open, and it's hard to rush open ground against good shooting. But that wasn't our way of fighting.

"It was dusk when the fight began, and all night long the mountain rang and blazed with the shooting—the great shooting match that we had with Major Ferguson. There were fine shooters on both sides and they didn't waste lead.

"He used every trick of warfare, did Major Ferguson. He charged his men into the woods and drove the colonels down the slopes of the mountain. But the colonels gave in front of him, like a branch of willow that bends under your hand and springs back again, and, as soon as the charge was over, they were on his heels again, like dogs on the heels of a bear. Then he drew back to his lines and tempted them to cross the open ground. But they would not cross it—they stayed hid behind the trees and poured in the lead.

"So it went on all through the night, the great shooting match Ferguson had asked for. And when the morning light came, there was still no outcome. For no bullet had touched Major Ferguson—and that was the Devil's charm around his neck. And yet, while he lived, he would fight and his men would fight.

"Now there was a young man named Abner Hite and this was his first fighting. He could shoot the eye from a squirrel, but he was a peaceable young man and killing men troubled his mind, though he knew it had to be done. So, though he'd fought all right, other folks had fought better. But now there was the morning light and the grayness in the air and he looked at his weary kin and knew something had to be done. He stared through the grayness, because he had sharp eyes. And sure enough, over there on the cleared ground was a pale-faced man in King's uniform—a long, fair shot. He had just one bullet left and he'd scratched a cross on it, for he was a praying man.

" 'In the name of God and liberty,' said young Abner Hite, and fired. And when the light smoke cleared he saw the man in uniform throw up his arms and cry out like a lost soul. For the bullet with the cross on it had cut the Devil's charm string and gone through the flesh of the throat—and that was the end of the great shooting match and the end of Major Ferguson. And the youngster who ended it was my father's father's father, Abner Hite, or that's the way I heard it. But once a year, on King's Mountain, there's a thunderstorm that roars and flames. And if you're bold enough to walk out in that storm, you can see Major Ferguson, stamping up and down the mountain, looking for his lost charm—the charm the Devil gave him. And if you'll face him and question him, you'll get fortune and riches—and yet they won't prosper you. For when it's dawn, he sinks back into the mountain—and if you follow his ways you'll sink after him. But the mountains, they keep on."

He ended on a long, sighing breath, and the room, for a moment, was entirely still. Then there were sudden shots and Lon Stacey sprang to his feet. He saw the spectacled man stare about him wildly—he saw Uncle Billy Hite sweep the rifle from its hooks. Then there was a sparkle in his brain and a rush of darkness.

When he awoke, after a certain time, he was propped in a chair and there were ropes around him—for a moment he wondered why.

"Take it easy, Lon," said John Quayle's unperturbed voice. "The folks won't be back for a while yet. Then we're bound to finish, of course."

"You fool," said Lon Stacey wearily. "Do you know what you've done? They've burned whole villages for less."

"Yes, sir, that was in the screen picture," said John Quayle. "That's what helped us make up our minds. Though I reckon they were made up." He followed Lon Stacey's glance. "If you're looking for that foreign man"—he said mildly—"well, you hate to shoot a man with glasses—doesn't seem right. But he tried to lay his pistol gun on Mrs. Quayle. And your folks with the big car—well, they had their chance. But it takes men used to the night to shoot in the night." Lon Stacey's brain slowly digested these incredible facts.

"I'd have heard the shots from the run," he said dully; "I'd have heard those."

"Not with the wind the wrong way," said John Quayle. "And it was the wrong way. They stood up pretty well, at the run. They killed Tom Green and John Starling and wounded more. But the boys were all around them—yes, all around them. Then they tried to get away in the trucks—but if they switched on a light, the boys would shoot it out, and when they drove blind, they smashed up. So that's what happened at the run," he ended equably.

"But it can't be," said Lon Stacey.

"Well, you heard Uncle Billy's tale," said the old man. "I reckon Major Ferguson thought it couldn't be at King's Mountain."

Lon Stacey wet his lips with his tongue. "All right," he said, "you've wiped out a platoon—you may have. They'll send a division—and tanks. They'll cover the sky with planes. You don't know what they can do!"

"Oh, we know they don't act like human beings," said John Quayle. "We know that. But this is the mountains. They can drive the tankers up and down—but where to? They can drop their bombs on this store—but I'll be out in the laurel. They can fill the roads with the soldiers—but a man that knows how to kill with one shot, if he's hid right, can kill with one shot and get away. We don't aim to fight in armies. We just aim to fight."

"They'll starve you out," said Lon Stacey. "They'll burn the woods with fire bombs."

Then he stopped, for he knew his words were useless—he had known it, he thought, since the end of Uncle Billy's tale. His people were his people; once they made up their minds, they did not change their minds. They had made up their minds to fight and they would fight. And it was true what the old man said. The men and women had taken to the laurel as they had in days gone by. The tanks might wallow and roar on the mountainy roads—but there would be a shot and a shot, coming from nowhere, fired by huntsmen who never wasted lead. Secrecy, silence, camouflage—these things were not new to the mountains. It would be a great resistance. It might even win, in the end, with the West still holding out.

He looked at John Quayle without rancor. "You'll be hanging me, I reckon," he said. It was not really a question.

"Couldn't do much else," said John Quayle. "Now, could we, Lon?"

"No, I reckon not," said Lon Stacey. "Not to a man that turned against his kin. But there's good blood in the Staceys."

He spoke easily, secure at last, for he was home. It had taken him a long road to get there—a long winding road, full of turns and betrayals, but this was the end of it. And the end would have been death, in any case—he knew that now with clarity. He couldn't have stood men like Schildmesser very long, once he'd seen the way they looked at his people. It was better to die by the hands of your own kin—and have a ballad made of you, when it was done.

I'll tell you of Lon Stacey,
A man you all knew well;
I'll tell you on Lon Stacey
And how Lon Stacey fell.

He turned against his kinfolk,
A traitor he became;
I'll tell you of Lon Stacey—

Yes, that's the way it would be—Uncle Billy Hite would make it, or one of the Greens, or some boy yet unborn. They would sing it in rooms like this and he would be remembered. It would be a queer fame, but it would be his own.

Now the gray light was coming through the window and there were men outside. He saw them as they trooped in silently—the man with the bandaged head and Uncle Billy Hite, the shy, wild boy of John Quayle's, staring at him; and Tom Green's brother with a long rope over his arm. A bearded man stood quietly in front of him.

"This here's your Cousin Abner, the preacher," said John Quayle. "He'll pray with you—it's his duty—if you feel like praying. We're bound to grant a man that."

Lon Stacey shook his head.

"No, thanks," he said. "Thanks just the same, Cousin Abner. But I never was much of a praying man. You just pray for the States. That'll do. And when Uncle Billy or somebody makes the ballad, they might put in that I once was a loyal man. I don't reckon that'll hurt the ballad." He grinned for a moment at the quiet faces. "I got just one request," he said. "Bury me near the run—I always did like the sound of running water. But not next where you buried the foreigners. They never did understand our breed of cats."

Then he stood up stiffly, for John Quayle had loosened the ropes that held him to the chair. His hands were tied behind him and they took him out of the door to the justice of the mountains.

AT SEA

JAMES A. MICHENER

Coral Sea

I AM ALWAYS astonished when an American says, "The Coral Sea? Where is that? I never heard of the Coral Sea." Believe me, Australians and New Zealanders know all about it. The battle we fought there will be in their history books for some time. Perhaps I can explain why.

In mid-April of 1942 I was one of a small group of officers who went ashore on the extreme eastern tip of Vanicoro Island, in the New Hebrides. We carried with us a broadcasting station, enough food for two months, and twelve enlisted men who knew how to repair PBYs. It was our intention to make daily reports on the weather and whatever other information we obtained. The airplane repair men were to service any flying boats forced down in our large bay.

Admiral Kester personally saw us off in the tiny tramp steamer which took us north from Noumea. "We can't go back any farther," he told us. "Take along plenty of small arms and ammunition. If the worst should come, destroy everything and head for the high hills of Vanicoro. I don't think they can track you down there. And you can depend on it, men. You can absolutely depend on it. If you can stay alive, we'll be back to get you. No matter what happens!"

Ensign Aberforce, our radio expert, hurried out from the meeting with Admiral Kester and somehow or other stole an emergency pint-sized radio transmitter. "If we go up into the hills, we'll be of some use. We'll broadcast from up there." Each of us strapped a revolver to his belt. We were a rather grim crew that boarded the rough little ship.

At Vanicoro we were thrown out upon a desolate, jungle-ridden bay where mosquitoes filled the air like incense. Of those who landed that day, all contracted malaria. No one died from it, but eleven men ultimately had to be evacuated. The rest of us shivered and burned with the racking fever. Not till later did we hear about atabrine.

We built lean-to's of bamboo and coconut fronds. A few venturesome natives came down from the hills to watch us. In silence they studied our rude efforts and then departed. Centuries ago they had learned that no one could live among the fevers of that bay. Nevertheless, our shacks went up, and on the evening of our arrival Aberforce broadcast weather reports to the fleet.

Six times a day thereafter he would repair to the steaming shack, where jungle heat was already eating away at the radio's vitals, and send out his reports. On the eighth day he informed Noumea that we had withstood our initial Jap bombing. A Betty came over at seven thousand feet, encountered no antiaircraft fire, dropped to two thousand feet, and made four runs at us. Radio and personnel escaped damage. Two shacks were blown up. At least the Japs knew where we were. After that we were bombed several more times, and still no lives were lost. By now we had dug a considerable cave into the side of a hill. There we kept our precious radio. We felt secure. Only a landing party could wipe out the station now. The second, smaller set we buried in ten feet of earth. A direct hit might destroy it. Nothing less would.

As men do when they have been frequently bombed, we became suspicious of every plane. So we ducked for foxholes that afternoon when our lookout cried, "Betty at four thousand feet." We huddled in the sweating earth and waited for the "garummmph" of the bombs. Instead, none fell, and the Betty slowly descended toward the bay.

Then a fine shout went up! It wasn't a Betty at all. It was a PBY! It was coming in for a water landing! It was a PBY!

The lookout who had mistaken this grand old American plane for a Betty was roundly booed. He said it was better to be safe than sorry, but none of us could believe that anyone in the American Navy had failed to recognize the ugly, wonderful PBY. Slowly the plane taxied into the lagoon formed by coral reefs. Since none of us had experience with the lagoon, we could not advise the pilot where to anchor. Soon, however, he had decided for himself, and ropes went swirling into the placid waters.

Our eager men had a rubber boat already launched and went out to pick up the crew. To our surprise, a New Zealand flying officer stepped out. We watched in silence as he was rowed ashore. He jumped from the rubber boat, walked stiffly up the beach and presented himself. "Flight Leftenant Grant," he said. Our men laughed at the way he said *leftenant,* but he took no notice of the fact.

His crew was an amazing improvisation. One Australian, three New Zealanders, four Americans. The Allies were using what was available in those days. Our officers showed the crew to their mud-floored quarters.

"I'm reporting for patrol," Grand said briefly when he had deposited his gear. "The Jap fleet's on the move."

"We heard something about that," I said. "Are they really out?"

"We think the entire southern fleet is on the way."

"Where?" we asked in silence that was deep even for a jungle.

"Here," Grant said briefly. "Here, and New Zealand. They have eighty transports, we think."

We all breathed rather deeply. Grant betrayed no emotion, and we decided to follow his example. "I should like to speak to all of my crew and all of your ground crew, if you please." We assembled the men in a clearing by the shore.

"Men," Grant said, "I can't add anything which will explain the gravity of our situation. That PBY must be kept in the air. Every one of you take thought now. How will you repair any possible damage to that plane? Find your answers now. Have the materials ready." He returned to his quarters.

We did not see much of Grant for several days. His PBY was in the air nine and ten hours at a stretch. He searched the water constantly between New Hebrides and Guadalcanal. One night he took off at 0200 and searched until noon the next day. He and his men came back tired, red-eyed, and stiff. They had done nothing but fly endlessly above the great waters. They had seen no Japs.

In the last few days of April, however, action started. We were heavily bombed one night, and some fragments punctured the PBY. Early the next morning men were swarming over the flying boat as she rode at anchor in the lagoon. That afternoon she went up on patrol. As luck would have it, she ran into three Jap planes. The starboard rear gunner, a fresh kid from Alabama, claimed a hit on the after Jap plane. The Japs shot up the PBY pretty badly. The radio man, a youngster from Auckland, died that night of his wounds.

Grant came to our quarters. "The Japs are out. Something big is stirring. I must go out again tomorrow. Mr. Aberforce, will you ride along as radio man?"

"Sure," our expert laughed. "I think I can figure out the system."

"I'll help you," Grant said stiffly. There was no mention of the radio man's death, but in the early morning the leftenant read the

Church of England service over a dismal mound on the edge of the jungle. Some native boys who now lived near us were directed to cover the grave with flowers. There the radio man from New Zealand, a little blond fellow with bad teeth, there he rests.

That afternoon there was further action. Grant sighted a collection of Jap ships. They were about 150 miles northwest of the Canal and were coming our way. All transports and destroyers. The heavy stuff must be somewhere in The Slot, waiting for the propitious moment.

Aberforce blurted the news into his microphone. He added that Jap fighters were rising from a field on some near-by island to attack the PBY. We heard no more. There was anxiety about the bay until we heard a distant drone of motors. The PBY limped in. It had received no additional bullets, but it was a tired old lady.

Grant called the ground force to attention as soon as he landed. "It is imperative," he said in the clipped accents which annoyed our men, "that this plane be ready to fly tomorrow. And you must show no lights tonight. The Nips will be gunning for us. Hop to it, lads!" He turned and left. The men mimicked his pronunciation, his walk, his manner. All that night our men urged one another, "Hop to it, lad! Come, now, there! Hop to it!"

It was difficult to like Grant. He was the type of New Zealander who repels rather than attracts. He was a short man, about five feet eight. He was spare, wore a bushy mustache, and had rather reddish features. He affected an air of austere superiority, and among a group of excitable Americans he alone never raised his voice, never displayed emotions.

Unpleasant as he sometimes was, we had to respect him. That evening Aberforce, for example, told us three times of how Grant had insisted upon going closer, closer to the Jap vessels. "The man's an iceberg!" Aberforce insisted. "But it's grand to ride with him. You have a feeling he'll get you back." Grant, in the meantime, sat apart and studied the map. With a thin forefinger he charted the course of the gathering Jap fleet. Inevitably the lines converged on the New Hebrides . . . and on New Zealand. Saying nothing, the flight leftenant went out along the beach.

"Throw a line, there!" he called. "I'll have a look at how you're doing." It was after midnight before he returned.

Early next morning there was a droning sound in the sky, and this time our watch spotted the plane correctly as another PBY. It circled the bay and landed down wind, splashing heavily into the sea. We were accustomed to Grant's impeccable landings, in which the plane actually felt for the waves then slowly, easily let itself into the trough. We smiled at the newcomer's sloppy landing.

The plane taxied about and pulled into the lagoon. "Tell them to watch where they anchor!" Grant shouted to the men on his plane. "Not there! Not there!" He looked away in disgust and went into his quarters. A moment later, however, he was out in the early morning sunrise once more. A youthful voice was hailing him from the beach.

"I say! Grant!" A young flight officer, a New Zealander, had come ashore.

"Well, Colbourne! How are you?" The friends shook hands. We were glad to see that Colbourne was at least young and excitable. He was quite agitated as he took a drink of coffee in our mess hut.

"We won't come ashore," he said. "We must both go out at once. There is wretched news. The entire Jap southern fleet is bearing down upon us. You and I must go out for the last minute look-see. This may be the day, Grant. We've got to find where the carriers are. I have orders here. They didn't send them by wireless. But fellows! There's a chance! There really is! I understand Fitch and Kester are on the move. I don't know with what, but we're going to fight!" The young fellow's eyes sparkled. After the long wait, we would fight. After Pearl Harbor and Manila and Macassar and the Java Sea, we would go after them. After one string of crushing defeats upon another, the American fleet, such as it was, would have a crack at the Japs!

"What is happening at home?" Grant asked, apparently not moved by the news.

Colbourne swallowed once or twice. "They are waiting," he said grimly. "It has been pretty well worked out. The old men—well, your wife's father and mine, for example. They are stationed at the beaches. They know they dare not retreat. They have taken their positions now." He paused a moment and took a drink of our warm water. We waited.

"The home guard is next. They've been digging in furiously. They occupy prepared positions near the cities and the best beaches. The regular army will be thrown in as the fighting develops. Everyone has decided to fight until the end. The cities and villages will be destroyed." He paused and tapped his fingers nervously against his cup.

"Many families have already gone to the hills. Cars are waiting to take others at the first sign of the Jap fleet. My wife and the kiddies have gone. Your wife, Grant, said to tell you that she would stay until the last.'' Grant nodded his head slowly and said nothing. Colbourne continued, his voice sounding strange and excited in the hot, shadowy hut. We leaned forward, thinking of Seattle, and San Diego, and Woonsocket.

''The spirit of the people is very determined,'' Colbourne reported. ''A frightful Japanese broadcast has steeled us for the worst. It came through two nights before I left. A Japanese professor was describing New Zealand and how it would be developed by the Japs. North Island will be a commercial center where Japanese ships will call regularly. South Island will be agricultural. Wool and mutton will be sent to Japan. Maoris, as true members of the Greater East Asia Coprosperity Sphere, will be allowed special privileges. White men will be used on the farms. The professor closed with a frenzied peroration. He said that the lush fields, the wealth, the cities were in their grasp at last. The day of reckoning with insolent New Zealanders was at hand. Immortal Japanese troops would know what to do!''

No one said anything. Grant looked at his wrist watch. ''It's 0630,'' he said. ''We'll be off.'' He started from the hut but stopped. ''Aberforce,'' he asked, ''will you handle the radio again?''

Aberforce, somewhat subdued, left the hut. Colbourne and Grant went down to the rubber rafts and were rowed to their planes. The newcomer was first to take off. He headed directly for the Canal. Then Grant taxied into free water. His propellors roared. Slowly the plane started along the smooth water. Then it raised to the step, like a duck scudding across a still pond. It poised on the step for a moment and became airborne. It did not circle the bay, but set out directly for the vast Coral Sea.

All day we waited for news. I helped to code and transmit the weather reports Aberforce should have been sending. About noon a cryptic message came through the radio. It was apparently Grant, using a new code. Later a plain-word message came from the south. It was true. The Jap fleet was heading for our islands!

I issued the last rounds of ammunition. We dug up the tiny transmitter and drew rough maps of the region we would head for. Reluctantly we decided that there would be no defense of the beach. Each of us studied the native boys suspiciously. What would they do when the Japs came? Would they help track us down?

At about four o'clock in the afternoon Colbourne's PBY came back. His radio was gone, so he rushed to our set and relayed a plain-code message to the fleet: ''The Jap fleet has apparently formed.

What looked like BBs steamed from Guadalcanal. Going westward. No carriers sighted. Little air cover over the BBs. But the fleet is forming!" He then continued with a coded description of exactly what he had seen. Before he finished, Grant's plane came in. It was smoking badly. The entire rear section seemed to be aflame. At first it seemed that Grant might make his landing all right. But at the last minute the crippled plane crashed into the sea. It stayed afloat for several minutes, at the mouth of the lagoon. In that time Grant, Aberforce, and four of the men escaped. The co-pilot was already dead from Jap fire. Two men drowned in the after compartments.

We pulled the survivors from the sea. Aberforce was pale with cold and fear, cold even in the tropics. Grant was silent and walked directly in to consult with Colbourne, who stopped broadcasting. They consulted their notes, compared probabilities and started all over again. It was now dusk. When the message was finished, Grant went down to the seaside with his crew and read once more the burial service. Aberforce stood beside him, terribly white.

That night we had a wretched scene at dinner. We didn't serve the meal until late, and as soon as we sat at the table, Grant announced that tomorrow he would fly Colbourne's plane. To this Colbourne would not agree. Grant insisted primly that it was his right and duty, as a senior officer. In the end Colbourne told him to go to hell. Grant had crashed his damned plane and wrecked it and now, by God, he wouldn't get the other one. The younger man stamped from the room. Grant started to appeal to us for a decision but thought better of it.

In the morning Colbourne and his crew set out. We never saw them again. They submitted only one report. "Entire Jap fleet heading south."

All day we sat by the radio. There was news, but we could make nothing of it. That some kind of action was taking place, we were sure. We posted extra lookouts in the trees. In midafternoon an American plane, an SBD, lost from its carrier, went wildly past our island. It crashed into the sea and sank immediately.

Two torpedo planes, also American, flashed past. Night came on. We did not eat a regular meal. The cook brought in sandwiches and we munched them. No one was hungry, but we were terribly nervous. As night wore on, we gave up trying to work the radio. We had long since surrendered it to Grant, who sat hunched by it, his hands covering his face, listening to whatever station he could get.

Finally, he found a strong New Zealand government transmitter.

We stood by silently waiting for the news period. A musical program was interrupted. "It can now be stated that a great fleet action is in progress in the Coral Sea, between forces of the American Navy and the Japanese fleet. Elements of the Royal Australian Navy are also participating. It is too early to foretell what the outcome will be. Fantastic Japanese claims must be discounted. Word of the impending action came this morning when monitors picked up a message from a New Zealand Catalina which had sighted the enemy fleet." The broadcast droned on. "The nation has been placed on full alert. Men have taken their places. In this fateful hour New Zealanders pray for victory."

At this last Grant impatiently snapped off the radio and left the hut. Soon, however, he was back, hunched up as before. He stayed there all night and most of the next day. By this time we had fabricated another receiver. A wonderfully skilled enlisted man and I sat by it throughout the day. Heat was intense, and a heavy stickiness assailed us every time we moved. Once I looked up and saw Grant down by the shore, watching the empty sky. He walked back and forth. I stopped watching him when I heard the first real news we had so far received. American fleet headquarters officially announced that the full weight of the Jap fleet had been intercepted. A battle was in progress. Our chances appeared to be satisfactory.

A wild shout from the other radio indicated that they had heard the broadcast, too. Immediately fantastic conjecture started through the camp. At the noise Grant walked calmly into my hut. "What is the news?" he asked. I told him, and he left. But in a few minutes he was back and elbowed me away from the set. For the rest of that day and night he was there. Once or twice he drowsed off, but no one else touched the radio for sixteen hours.

At about 1900, after the sun had set, we heard two pilots talking back and forth. They were over the Coral Sea. They had lost their ship. Or their ship had been sunk. The encouraged one another for many minutes, and then we heard them no more.

At 0500 the next morning a coded message came through calling on all aircraft to be on the alert for Jap ships. This message goaded Grant furiously. He stomped from the hut and walked along the beach, looking at the spot where his PBY had gone down.

By now no one could talk or think. We had been three days in this state of oppressive excitement. Three of our men lay dead in the bay; an entire plane crew was lost. And we were perched on the end of an island, in the dark. We were not even doing our minimum duty, for our planes were gone. All we could do was sit and wonder. There was much discussion as to what the cryptic message about Jap ships meant. Could it be that the Japanese fleet had broken through? In anxiety we waited, and all about the silent jungle bore down upon us with heat, flies, sickness, and ominous silence.

At 1500 we intercepted a flash from Tokyo, announcing our loss of the *Lexington,* two battleships, and numerous destroyers. So frantic were we for news that we believed. After all, we *had* heard those pilots. Their carrier *could* have been sunk. The news flashed through our camp and disheartened us further.

It was at 1735 that Grant finally picked up a strong New Zealand station. An organ was playing. But something in the air, some desperation of thought, kept everyone at Grant's elbow, crowding in upon him. Then came the fateful news: "Profound relief has been felt throughout New Zealand. Admiral Nimitz has announced that the Jap fleet has been met, extensively engaged, and routed." A fiery shout filled the hut. Men jumped and clapped their hands. The radio droned on: ". . . losses not authenticated. Our own losses were not negligible. Carrier aircraft played a dominant role. At a late hour today the Prime Minister announced that for the moment invasion of New Zealand has been prevented." Three Americans cheered wildly at this. The New Zealand men stood fast and listened. ". . . so we have taken the privilege of asking a chaplain of the Royal New Zealand Air Force to express our gratitude . . ." Grant was drumming on the radio with his fingers. He rose as the chaplain began to intone his prayer. Others who were seated followed his example. There, in the silence of the jungle, with heat dripping from the walls of the improvised hut, we stood at attention. ". . . and for these divine blessings our Nation and its free people . . ." One by one men left the hut. Then it began to dawn upon them that the waiting was over. Someone began to shout to a sentry up in the tree.

In disbelief he shouted back. Soon the land about the bay was echoing with wild shouts. One young officer whipped out his revolver and fired six salutes in violent order. Natives ran up, and the cook grabbed one by the shoulders. He danced up and down, and the native looked at him in wonderment. In similar bewilderment, two New Zealand enlisted men—beardless boys—who had escaped from Grant's wrecked plane, looked over the waters and wept.

Grant himself disappeared right after the broadcast. Others hung about the radio and picked up further wonderful news. Commentators were already naming it the Battle of the Coral Sea. From Australia one man threw caution far aside and claimed, "For us it will be one of the decisive battles of the world. It proves that Japan can be stopped. It proves that we shall be saved."

Grant was late coming in to chow. When he appeared, he was neatly washed and shaved. His hair was combed. In his right hand he held, half hidden behind his leg, a bottle. "Gentlemen," he said courteously, "I have been saving this for such an occasion. Will you do me the honor?" With courtly grace he presented the bottle to me and took his seat.

I looked at the label and whistled. "It's Scotch, fellows!" I reported. "It's a fine thing for a night like tonight!" I opened the bottle and passed it to the man on my right.

"After you, sir," that officer said, so I poured myself a drink. Then the bottle passed and ended up before Grant. He poured himself a stiff portion.

"I believe a toast is in order," an American officer said. We stood and he proposed, "To an allied victory." Americans and New Zealanders congratulated him on the felicity of his thought. Another American jumped to his feet immediately.

"To the men who won the victory!" he said in a voice filled with emotion. No one could censure his extremely bad taste. We knew it was unseemly to be drinking when Colbourne, Grant's fellow pilot, and so many men were missing, but we had to excuse the speaker. It was Ensign Aberforce. After that display no more toasts were given.

Instead we sat around the hut and talked about what we thought had happened, and what would happen next. It might be months before we were taken off Vanicoro. Through all our discussions Grant sat silent. He was, however, drinking vigorously. From time to time someone would report upon late radio news, but since it was favorable news, and since one doesn't get whiskey very often on Vanicoro, we stayed about the table.

At about 2300 the radio operator got a Jap broadcast which he turned up loud. "The American fleet is in utter flight. The American Navy has now been reduced to a fifth-rate naval power. Our forces are regrouping." At that last admission everyone in the room cheered.

It was then that Grant rose to his feet. He started to speak. Surprised, we stopped to listen. We knew he was drunk, but not how drunk. "Today," he began in a thick voice. "Today will undoubtedly be remembered for years to come. As the gentleman from Australia so properly observed, this was one of the decis—. . ." He stumbled badly over the word and dropped his sentence there.

"If you have not been to New Zealand," he began, and then lost that sentence, too. "If you were a New Zealander," he started over with a rush, "you would know what this means." He took a deep breath and began speaking very slowly, emphasizing each word. "We were ready to protect the land with all our energy . . ." His voice trailed off. We looked at one another uneasily. "From the oldest man to the youngest boy we would have fought. It was my humble duty to assist in preparing the defenses of Auckland. I issued several thousand picks, crowbars, and axes. There were no other weapons." He reached for his whiskey and took a long, slow drink.

"My own wife," he resumed, "was given the job of mobilizing the women. I urged her to go to the hills . . ." He fumbled with his glass. "In fact, I ordered her to go, but she said that our two children . . ." He paused. It seemed as if his voice might break. A fellow New Zealander interrupted.

"I say, Grant!"

Leftenant Grant stared at his subaltern coldly and continued: "There are some of us in New Zealand who know the Japs. We know their cold and cunning ways. We know their thirst for what they call revenge." His voice grew louder, and he beat the table. "I tell you, we know what we have escaped. A heel of tyranny worse than any English nation has known!" He shouted this and upset his glass. Two officers tried to make him sit down, but he refused. He upset another glass defending himself from his friends. We wanted to look aside but were fascinated by the scene. Grant continued his speech.

"Gentlemen!" he said with a gravity one might use in addressing Parliament. "Especially you gentlemen from our wonderful ally. I pray to God that never in your history will you have an enemy . . . will you have an enemy near your shores!" He paused and his voice took on a solemn ring as if he were in church. His drunkenness made the combined effect ridiculous. "I pray you may never have to rely upon a shield like this." He surveyed the tiny shack and our inadequate materials. We followed his eyes about the wretched place. The radio that was pieced together. The improvised table. The thin pile of ammunition. Grant's voice raised to a shout. "A shield like this!" he cried. He exploded the word *this* and swept his right arm about to indicate all of Vanicoro. As he did so, he lost his balance. He grabbed at a fellow officer. Missing that support, he fell upon the table and slipped off onto the floor. He was unconscious. Dead drunk.

JACLAND MARMUR

The Kid in Command

ONE WAY OR ANOTHER, it has happened before. It will probably happen again. It will probably happen again. Maybe off the African coast, in Stephen Decatur's gunboat a hundred and fifty years ago, a seaman was faced with a choice like that. From Tripoli to Okinawa, one bloodstained beach is like another—they are all so far from home. So this doesn't belong to a time or a place. It belongs to the men of the fleet. To destroyer people, mostly. This kid was one of them.

They didn't know him in the U.S.S. *James Blake*. He didn't belong to that ship. She was lean and long, the *Blake*, sea-stained and battle-gray. Detached from Desron Twelve, she was steaming south and west along the rock-scarred Korean coast, coming down alone from bombardment missions in the north. Thin smoke haze trailed her funnel lips—her radar sweeping, westing sunlight washing all her starboard gun tubs. She was heeling in the ground swell, twin five-inchers midship trained, her signal yardarms bare when she stood past Yonte Cape, needing replenishment and rest. Tin cans are always overdue for replenishment and rest. This kid was too.

Russ Dobson saw him first. Dobson was on the fo'c'stle head, his chief's cap tipped far back. He was growling disapproval about the pelican hook and the cable stopper. Somebody soon would feel his wrath. Chickman and the others up there weren't worried, though. Bosun's mates were always growling, especially twenty-year chiefs. To hear them, these days nobody did things right. Chickman grinned.

"Okay," said Chick. "We'll watch it, chief." And then, the wisdom of half a hitch behind him, he instantly picked the breeze up where they had left it off. "All right, you tell me, Pink. Your grandpa won a war. My old man too. And here we are again. You tell me why."

"I wouldn't know," admitted Pinkerton. "Ask Dobson here. The chiefs know everything."

"It ain't my trade," growled Dobson, one thick finger thrusting down to point the anchor cable at his feet. "This is!"

The ship's head slipped against a long green swell. The chief looked up in time to see a burst of spray collapsing, loudly hissing as it fell. The westing sunfire caught his cheek, his highboned face like scarred old leather. He kept standing that way, wrinkle-eyed and peering past the ground swell toward the land. It wasn't natural. His harsh wrath should have curled around them long ago, and when it didn't Chick said quickly, "People, Pink; it's people. Saw it in a book somewhere. Ten thousand years ago, all men were hunters. Had to be. It's in the blood. It's like an instinct. Now we're so civilized ain't nothing left for men to hunt—except each other. That's why every—"

"Bridge!" The voice was Dobson's. Hoarse. Explosive. They looked up, alarmed. The chief was facing aft, big head tipped up, four five-inch rifles in the forward gunmounts snouting at him. "Bridge!" he roared. "Man in the water! Starboard bow!"

Chick spun around. His eyes were young and sharp, but he saw nothing. Blue-green water, glitter of late sunlight. Nothing more. Then Pinkerton beside him pointing, "There! Look there!"

Chick saw it then. Dark blob in shadow, halfway to the rocky shore, thin churn of foam behind. Chick thought he saw an arm lift, feebly waving. Man, all right. Hanging on to something, both feet thumping in the flood.

"What's wrong with all them topside lookouts? Someone ought to get chewed out!"

"Ditched pilot! Sometimes them jets go down like stone."

"In a kapok life jacket? That's no fly boy, Chick!"

It wasn't. Pinkerton was right. They could hear quick voices from the bridge. The *Blake's* bows tipped, knifed deeply over in the swell. Ensign Burnham was striding forward, Dobson already halfway down the weather deck to meet him.

When the chief came swaying back, his gravel voice was barking. "All right, sailors, let's get hot! They'll lay him alongside. Starboard bow. Won't use the whaler. Pink! Small line up here. Net ladder, too! He—"

"How about Wesley, chief?" Pinkerton didn't want to miss any part of a thing like this. He complained, "It ain't my watch."

"Maybe it ain't his, either, down there in the water! Move!" Dobson looked quickly out across the cold and glittering flood. What he saw made memory stab at him. His head shot back. ''Corpsman up here, Chickman. On the double! Get the chief. And blankets. Move!''

They could see him clearly now. Mat of dark hair, his white face drawn, he kept dipping under, clinging to a half-washed timber with one arm. Every time his head came up, he gulped in air. He knew what he was doing, and his eyes were always open.

Dark eyes. Nothing hopeless in them. No despair. Not there. They kept glowing up at the lean tall hull, the noisy enormous bow wave bearing down upon him.

On the *Blake*'s forecastle deck, they lined the chain rail, peering down. Dobson had the heaving line all ready in two skillful coils, his scarred brown cheek against the light, watching how the water narrowed in between. He was gauging speed, the distance, angle of approach. Only once he shot a quick glance aft. Looking upward, he could see Commander Rathbone's head and shoulders just above the splinter shield against the bridge wing. Dobson saw the captain's head turn, saw his lips in movement to his talker.

Something flicked across the chief's gray eyes, like pride or recognition. He looked back and down at the water again. He was reassured. The skipper had the conn himself. They wouldn't overrun. When he felt the *Blake*'s deck shudder underfoot at all astern, he snaked the line out smartly. And the kid down there caught hold.

That's how he came aboard the U.S.S. *James Blake*. He couldn't make the rope rungs by himself. He tried. The best he could do was hang there, eyes uplifted, blue lips mumbling something no one heard. When they hauled him inboard, he did not collapse. Water draining from his tattered dungarees, he staggered. Then he turned his head. He didn't see Mr. Burnham. He saw Dobson first. He recognized the chief's cap.

''Commanding officer!'' he chattered. ''Chief, I got to see—''

''Sure, kid, sure.'' They were pulling the kapok life jacket off him. The corpsman's kit was open, a tube of morphine in his hand. ''Shock,'' the medic was saying. ''Bound to be. The blanket, Doyle! He'll—''

''Commanding officer!'' The kid still chattered. ''Got to see him! I—''

''Sure, kid, sure.'' The medic reached out, morphine needle bare. ''Must have been rough,'' he soothed. ''Tell us about it later.''

''No!'' The kid pulled his arm away. He wasn't chattering any more. ''Commanding officer!'' he cried again, his voice a little wild. ''Now.''

He thrust them all aside. He was swaying aft. He must have been a tin-can man himself. He knew exactly where the captain was. He went staggering up all the ladders, past the signal bags. Ensign Burnham was mumbling vague apology up there about a dripping enlisted man bursting to the bridge like that. The kid didn't know it. Dobson's arm was around his shoulders, as much in support as in restraint. The kid didn't know that either. All he saw was Commander Rathbone, tall before him, binoculars against his chest. The kid shook off the chief's large arm. He came erect. He knew the captain right away.

''Hanford, sir,'' he said. ''John Hanford, bosun's mate third. Captain, I need help.''

''Well, son, you'll get it. There's no need to barge up here. The corpsmen know their trade.''

''Not that, sir. I'm okay. But I got fourteen men back on that beach, six of them wounded, two of 'em bad. I tried to signal with a mirror and some fire bursts. Couldn't reach you. They're my people. If I don't get 'em off, they'll fry! I need—''

''Do you mean to say you swam out here to intercept this ship?''

''Yes, sir, I did.''

''Who is your commanding officer? Who sent you?''

''No one sent me. The way I figure, I'm in command myself.''

''You!'' Commander Rathbone snapped the word out and stopped short. Eyes cold and narrow, he appraised the swaying youngster for an instant, while above the chatter of the signal halyards and the sobbing of the sea the murmur swept through all the people on his bridge. Battle fatigue or shock, they thought. They thought the kid hysterical. Maybe the skipper of the *James Blake* thought so too. ''Son,'' he was asking sternly, ''what's your ship?''

''I was in the *Talbot,* sir. Took sick. I got detached to hospital. Contagious ward. I—'' The kid must have seen the captain's black brows lift. ''Mumps!'' he spat out bitterly. ''I had the mumps!'' Then his voice rushed on. ''I was rotting in the personnel pool at Pusan, waiting orders, when this mission came along. I volunteered.'' He took a forward step, eyes burning. ''Captain, there ain't much time left. I got an hour. Maybe two at most. As soon as it closes down real dark, them people are gonna get slaughtered. Maybe the Gooks are bringing mortars up right now. I got to get 'em off that beach! I need—''

The captain's hard voice broke in, "Son, you need to make more sense."

"Sense? All right, sir, sense! We put an army demolition team ashore to blow a tunnel and a bridge. Last night. I was in the landing party. We blew it. Then we got jumped. Must have been a whole platoon. Offshore, in the LCM, I guess they saw the fire fight. I saw Lieutenant Darby start her in to get us off, both motors open wide. Then the LCM blew up. Mine, maybe. I don't—"

The captain's voice cracked out, "Supporting ship! What name?"

"Code call was 'Dingbat Four.' I think we were supposed to rendezvous with her tonight. I don't know when or where. We never had a chance to call her. Radios all smashed. The lieutenant, Sparks, and the chief got killed. The army captain too. We knew we couldn't hold out where we were. Not as soon as it got light. Beach too exposed. No cover. So we had to leave the dead. We took our wounded with us. They kept sniping at us, but we made it. We dug in." The kid made a wild, vague gesture toward the land. "There!" Then his voice rushed on. "It's a good position, sir. Rocky. Right back against the beach. They can't reach us except across an open pass. Corporal and a private first class have got it covered from a forward boulder. I got three men on each flank. Good cover. We got weapons, some grenades left. They tried to overrun us twice. They won't try again till dark. After that, they're cooked. I got an hour, captain. Two at most. If I don't get 'em off in them, they'll fry."

It poured from him. It drained him nearly dry. Dobson wasn't looking at the kid. The chief was looking at the captain, saw the glitter in Commander Rathbone's eyes. He heard the skipper's hard voice saying, "This ship is under orders for squadron rendezvous. Do you really expect me to—"

"Yes, sir, I do!" The kid's eyes glowed. He was a bosun's mate third, and he cut a three-striper short. He broke into a full commander's speech! Ensign Burnham blinked. Not Dobson. Something glowed inside the chief. He still kept looking at the captain, hearing that kid rush on: "I don't mean to be disrespectful, sir. The navy put them people on the beach. When I saw this tin can standing down, I told them the navy would get them off. I'm navy, sir. Enlisted navy. I was the only rated man left alive. The way I learned it, I took charge. I figure I'm in technical command. Those people are mine. I got to get 'em off! That's why I swam out here. I need your help. I need—"

The glitter was growing stronger in Commander Rathbone's eyes.

"For a bosun's mate third," he murmured, "you have taken a lot for granted."

The kid's whole body sagged. An instant only, though. His dark eyes shot out toward the beach. His voice came taut, its calmness terrible. "I didn't shove out here to save my own skin. Lolly will think so for sure, when he sees this can steam off. And them people will fry." He made half a turn toward the after bridge. "I'm a pretty strong swimmer, sir. I'd just as soon fry with them. I request permission to leave the ship."

He meant it! He meant to rejoin his people the same way he had come. He meant to go back where he belonged. He was halfway to the signal bag when Commander Rathbone's voice snapped at him, "Hanford!" The kid turned slowly. "You will want the motor whaler, son," the skipper said. "How many men?"

"Five, six. No more. Be in the way, sir." The kid came striding back, excitement burning in his eyes. "Ammo, sir. And a medic. We got to have covering battery fire when we start to retire. I figure—"

"Simmer down now, son. You want dry clothes. . . . Mr. Burnham, get the gunnery officer. Have the whaler called away."

"Aye, aye, sir." Ensign Burnham's voice was dry. He didn't approve. He thought the captain's treatment of enlisted personnel entirely too unorthodox. "Captain, I would like to go," he said.

"No," Commander Rathbone shook his head. An odd smile touched his lips. "This seems to be an enlisted man's operation." He looked at Dobson sharply. The chief looked back. A flash of understanding passed between them. "Dobson," the skipper asked, "do you want to take the boat?"

"No, sir, I don't." Then Dobson grinned. "But I will."

"Good." The captain knew what Dobson meant. No one wanted to get himself killed. "You bring these people back."

That's how it was. The last cold light was draining from the water when the U.S.S. *James Blake* put her whaleboat smartly overside. The land looked dark, some sunfire still along its ragged peaks, white curl of surf along the rocky beach. Hanford, in the stern sheets with the chief, looked back and up. From down here where the sea noise was, the ship looked huge, sharp-angled, bristling with her armament. For moments he could see the shapes and faces of her topside people and he thought Commander Rathbone's cold blue eyes were boring at him from above the bridge-wing splinter shield.

Fear touched him. He could feel the spasm of it at his stomach's pit.

He felt the boat slide down along the steep flank of the ground swell, tossing sprays before she surged. Then he could see the *Blake*'s three gunmounts stir. They turned together toward the land. The gun snouts lifted all in unison. Six rifle barrels, long and deadly, hovered up there, hesitated, lowered, and then suddenly hung still. The ship receded with them, gently swinging. But the rifles kept on pointing where he'd told them to. Lieutenant Gridley had it all triangulated. Hanford felt the spasm in his belly twist, hurl upward in sharp pain. Fresh rated. Third-class. How much did he know? Suppose he'd told it wrong! He swallowed hard. He wanted to cry out. They ought to check again. They couldn't. They were halfway to the beach already, and they didn't have much time. The kid turned forward, swallowing again.

"We get two hundred yards offshore, they'll open fire," he said. Voice sounded funny. Was it really his? He tried again. "Spaced salvos. Call fire when we need it. The Old Man said we better do it fast."

"Right!" The voice was Pinkerton's. "Sure wish we had a walkie-talkie radio." Pink didn't have the watch, but he was there. "You got the right word on the signals, Flags?"

"I got 'em. You all better get 'em too." The quartermaster chuckled. "Maybe I'm just striking for a Purple Heart. If I make it, someone else has got to take these flags. Chick, you better say again."

"Okay, Buzz." Chickman started rattling off, "All horizontal, shoulder-high and still: Commence Again. Aloft, both waving: Raise the Range. Both at the shoulder, waving downward; Lower Range. One flag out right and shoulder-high: Come Right. And left, the same. That right, Hanford?"

"Yeah, Chick, yeah. That's right." The kid could only hope his voice was sounding better now. He wasn't sure. "All spot calls are for fifty yards."

"Fifty? You nuts? Lieutenant Gridley can shoot, but you sure sliced it close!"

"He said he'd try."

"Okay now. Better knock it off." The gravel voice was Dobson's. He spoke out at last. "That beach looks rocky foul. Where's your sandspit, Hanford? See it yet?"

The kid peered forward through the bow spray toward the land. It looked different, from a landing boat. That tin can's cold-eyed skipper should have sent an officer. You had an officer, he told you what to do. The chief was here, though. He looked like he had his twenty in already. He looked tough. The kid was glad the chief was there.

Then suddenly his dark eyes narrowed and he flung his arm out, pointing, crying, "There! Between those offshore boulders, chief! Sandspit. Gravel bottom We can—"

"Tell the coxs'n, son. Don't growl at me." Dobson's voice was gruff. "You got the conn."

The kid looked up. Swiftly. Dobson's big head never stirred, eyes on the beach, his cheek like saddle leather. What the devil was the matter with him! Wasn't he the chief? First twinge of anger stirred in Hanford. Then his eyes flew landward and cried, "Come right! You see that sandspit, coxs'n? Bring her—"

"Got it, Hanford. We're on rails now. Shoreside liberty party! Here we go."

A ragged crackling reached them from the land. They stiffened in the whaler. Small-arms fire! The beach was in clear sight now, boulder-strewn, reaching inland like a funnel narrowing. Up there they saw quick-licking points of orange fire, the smoke bursts punching out. Hanford thought dark shapes were stirring there. Twenty. Thirty. Panic touched him.

"You see 'em, chief? That's where they are! They see the ship. They see us too. In a minute they'll start screaming. They'll charge out. We got to pin 'em down! Lolly and the corporal are behind that forward boulder up there by itself. They only got five, six grenades left. They'll get overrun! Why don't the ship start—"

"Simmer down. You said two hundred yards." Dobson's gravel voice was calm. "Lieutenant Gridley knows two-zero-zero when he—"

Explosion cut him short. It came from far astern. Enormous-sounding, its blast and concussion rocked the whaler. They could feel the air compress aloft. The kid's head spun around. He was in time to see six five-inch rifle muzzles drool out smoke. First salvo from the U.S.S. *James Blake!* Shells on the way. First shells to help his people. Low across the wine-dark water he could see the ship's slow heel and her recovery. Gray silhouette against the sky, sea-scarred and battle-gray, white feather of a bow wave at her eyes. Tin can out there! The kid belonged in tin cans. He could see her three twin-mounted guns all stirring down, then up in perfect unison, director holding on the target, compensating her slow roll. Then shellbursts crashed against the land. Fear welled up in him. If they'd struck too close! If he had told it wrong! His eyes flew shoreward just in time to see erupting dust and rubble.

"Oh!" he screamed. "Right on!

"Then leave her be," growled Dobson. "Don't look back. She'll do what she's supposed to. Don't look back!"

"Sure, chief. Okay." The beach was rushing toward him now, black tide-washed boulders on each side. Astern he heard the second salvo crash out from the *Blake*'s main battery. Clean-spaced shooting. Fire-cover for the landing. Fire-cover for the men. And Hanford told the chief, "I think we better get the wounded first. We better bring the medic, chief. I'll show you where—"

"Don't show *me!*" Dobson spat it out. "You told the Old Man you took technical command. That's fine!" Then all at once the chief's voice lost its harshness. When the kid looked at him, half a grin twitched past the muscles of that big, scarred face. "It's your show. Son, you name it and we'll do it. You're in charge."

He meant it. He was asking for his orders from a frightened bosun's mate third-class. It wasn't fair! The kid had asked for help to help his people. He had never asked to carry the whole load. Resentment stirred in him. The big man kept on looking at him, eyes like steel. Then anger flamed in Hanford, anger drowning out the fear.

"Okay!" the kid cried. "Cut the engine. Beach her, coxs'n!" Voice wasn't sounding funny to him any more. It was his own. It sounded savage, full of wrath. The chief's grin broke, but Hanford didn't see it. "Two of you stand by the whaleboat. Hit for cover, all the rest. Keep that ammo dry. You watch me, Flags. All ready? Jump, then! Here we go."

That's how it was. The kid took charge. He had to. And he knew he had to do it fast. They brought the wounded to the whaleboat first. The kid remembered that. How could a man forget how wounded look along the shell-pocked beaches far from home? The rest was not so clear. It got mixed up in gunfire, in erupting shellbursts, in the nearer, deadly chatter of small-arms and automatic fire. He knew the *Blake* was out there. Offshore, hovering in smoky sea haze, she looked gray and narrow, flame tongues spearing from her in slow rhythm.

Hanford heard the five-inch common whining overhead before each salvo slammed against the land in deafening explosions. They crashed where he'd told them to. Up past the narrow tip of this funnel-shaped and rock-strewn beach. Up past the boulders there where Lolly and the corporal were. Time they retired. What were they doing up there? Suddenly he knew. He saw the two shapes, dark against the land. They darted out from cover, two arms swinging back to hurl grenades, then instantly dived for the ground again. Salvo from the *Blake* slammed far beyond them. Flame bursts and erupting debris. Far. Too far! Before the hurled earth settled, dark specks leaped from cover, burp guns spurting. Lolly and the corporal were pinned down.

"Flags!" the kid cried. "Signal! Lower the range! Quick!"

The quartermaster leaped erect flags at his shoulders, both out horizontal, waving downward rapidly. Next salvo from the *Blake*—where would it burst? Could the lieutenant, back there far away in the director, spot two flimsy buntings on a distant beach? Could he bring that deadly gunfire lower? Only fifty yards? Maybe Hanford wondered. Maybe not. He sprang up. He was crying, "When I get there, Flags, you watch me! We'll start back. You see us running, wave again. Down fifty more! I'll—"

"You nuts? You know what splinter-bursts of five-inch shell can do?"

Maybe that was Dobson. Hanford didnt' know. He didn't care. The anger swirled in him. Chief handed him the load. Too late to take it back. He had to pin those devils with the burp guns down for long enough to get the corporal out. And Lolly. Lolly, grinning slyly when he'd said he'd swim out to the ship for help. Lolly thought he'd save his own skin if he made it. Didn't like the navy. Lolly never thought he would come back. Well, here he was.

"You heard me, Flags! You do it like I said!"

The kid's voice curled. Then he was racing over broken ground. He thought some others ran beside him. Pink and Chickman? Never asked them. What would they be doing here? And Dobson. Was that him, that big hulk, lumbering along and grinning with a carbine at ready? Hanford didn't know. He saw young Lolly on the ground behind a boulder, and the corporal kneeling. He dived in beside them.

"Well," said Lolly, looking upward, face all twisted. "If it ain't navy!" Lolly tried to grin. "You did come back. Navy, I never thought—"

"Sure, Lolly; sure. You're hurt. We're shoving off. I'll carry you."

"Keep down! *Blake* salvo on the way!" The voice was harsh. The gravel voice was Dobson's after all. Then shellbursts and eruption, deafening and close. That tin can out there gave you what you asked for! Maybe it would keep those devils quiet for a while. How long? Before the rain of debris ended, the harsh voice again: ''Now! On your way!''

That's what the kid remembered best. Big, hulking man with gravel in his throat, half-crouching, Pink and Chickman on each side, all spraying bursts of automatic fire. Covering him. Moving backward with him while he staggered down a beach to where the whaleboat was. Lolly draped across his shoulder. Corporal limping. Salvo from the *Blake* again. Must have come down fifty more. Shellfire walking closer to the water's edge. Then stillness. Startling and abrupt. Who could believe such stillness? Voices murmured in it. Slap of water and an engine's drone.

Then suddenly he knew. The beach was fading into the distance. He could not remember clearly when they launched. He knew they must have, though. Gray shape ahead. Sharp-angled, full of gun tubs. Rocking on the ocean. Looming in the sea haze. Blotting out the dusky sky. Destroyer U.S.S. *James Blake*.

''Did we get 'em all, chief?''

''Yeah, son, all. Except Lolly. The Pfc is dead.''

The kid said nothing. He just blinked his eyes. Someone has to pick the chit up. This time it was Lolly. Lolly didn't think the kid would ever make it. Lolly never thought he would come back. Hanford blinked again. Then at last he murmured, ''Anyhow, he knew.''

No one heard him. They were rounding to. Looming wall of gray steel towering above the whaleboat, faces peering down, the noisy slap and sob of water in between. Then they hooked on. Hanford staggered when he reached the deck. It was too solid underfoot. He kept babbling profound worry for his wounded. Man who took charge had to worry. It he didn't who else would?

''Sir, we brought them all,'' the kid was saying. He was talking to a man with cold and Spartan eyes who had binoculars against his chest. He was giving his report to the commanding officer. It was correct and proper that he should. ''All except the Pfc,'' he blurted. ''Lolly got hurt bad. I carried him myself. I wanted him back most of all. I'm sorry, sir. He died. Beefy's hurt bad too. I wouldn't want to lose—''

''They are being cared for, son. They'll be all right.''

''Thank you, sir.''

''I am sending a signal to Dingbat Four. I thought you would like to know.'' The glitter showed again in the commander's eyes. He still remembered how a bosun's mate, third-class, fished dripping from the water, fiercely asked his help for people pinned down on a hostile beach, demanding it because he was the man in charge. A slow smile touched the captain's lips. He spoke with clarity. "As one commander to another, son—you did all right." The kid just blinked his eyes. Commander Rathbone seemed to understand why he still stood there, swaying. "Son," he said with gravity, "you are relieved."

"Thank you, sir."

The kid's voice trailed off thinly. When he heard those last words, suddenly the load fell from him. When the burden dropped, he sagged. He thought someone suppported him. It looked like Dobson, but he wasn't sure. It seemed to him the voices kept on murmuring, and he was sure he saw young Ensign Burnham frown. Couldn't help it. All the ladderways on this tin can were too unsteady. They kept rocking and he had to watch them with great care. Something told him he was in the wrong place. Chiefs' compartment? He didn't belong there. And the voices were still murmuring.

"Pretty crowded for'ard, sir. I put him in my bunk." Hanford recognized the gravel voice. Dobson didn't sound tough, after all. "Shut-eye's all he needs. He'll do."

Hanford thought he grinned. He'd keep awake. That's what he'd do. He knew the skipper was down there too. He'd lie there, listening. He'd play it cute. There was something funny between that tall three-striper and the big-faced chief. Now and then you saw it. Not too often. Mostly between old navy CPOs and some scrambled-egg-capped officer. Like Dobson here and this commander. When they looked hard at each other, something flashed between. Quick as lightning, cold as steel. Something they both recognized.

"Mr. Burnham seems browned off," the skipper said in a voice too still and quiet for a tin can's bridge. "The ensign is fresh from the academy, chief. He doesn't approve at all. He doesn't approve of you either, Dobson, letting that kid take charge." Commander Rathbone chuckled. It was a most astonishing thing to hear from that cold-eyed man. "Did you ever hear about the destroyer *Perry*, chief? The *Perry* was tied up at Mare Island Navy Yard in 1906. My father was an ensign then. After the earthquake, the whole Frisco waterfront was burning. My father says the commandant sent every man he could down bay to help. For several hours, on one of those days, there wasn't a soul on board the *Perry* except a Chinese wardroom steward. The mooring lines were in need of quick attention on the tide, and he took charge. Good job he did. The point is, chief, that for those hours a Chinese by the name of Sing Hoy had the honor of being in technical command of a fully commissioned ship of war of the United States Navy. I must tell Mr.Burnham about it.'' Commander Rathbone chuckled again. ''If a Chinese steward's mate can pick up the chain of command—so can a bosun's mate third.''

''Seems like when it's needful, sir, somebody always does.''

''Yes. Let's hope somebody always will. Do you think I ought to fly Tare Victor George at the yardarm for him, chief?''

''Operation completed? No, sir, I don't.'' Dobson's voice was quick and flat. ''Not on this lousy coast. They ain't gonna finish it here. They ought to, but they won't. It ain't completed at all. We're gonna have to do it all over again.''

''Maybe, Dobson, maybe.'' The skipper was looking down at the kid. ''Name's Hanford,'' he was saying. ''John Hanford, isn't it? Said he was waiting orders. I intend to ask for him. Make a good man for your division, chief. Be a good man for the ship.''

''Yes, sir. He would.''

''I wonder how old he is.''

''Looks like maybe—'' Dobson's voice cut short. When it spoke again, it sounded almost harsh. ''Sir,'' it said, ''I hope he's way past twenty-one!''

''Why?''

They were looking at each other now. Hanford should have seen it. Tall three-striper, tin-can skipper in fresh khakis, scrambled eggs along his cap's peak. And the chief in dungarees, named Dobson, big man with the face like leather, scarred by conflict. They were staring at each other, blowers humming in the chiefs' compartment, sea noise sounding faint and muffled. They were silent for an instant. In that instant the quick lightning flashed between them. Hanford should have seen it. Tarawa and the 'Canal were in it. Saipan and the Okinawa picket line. Things half-forgotten leaped up; all the perished comrades who were deathless rose, all crying glory and enormous tragedy. Respect was in it too. Respect for dignity and competence.

Then suddenly it passed. The lightning flickered out. And Dobson grinned. Dobson had three daughters and no sons. Just like Commander Rathbone. Dobson didn't mind. The captain did. It was the first time in a hundred years no Rathbone son was at Annapolis or in the

Line. The skipper was always prowling for some likely youngster he could sponsor. Dobson grinned again.

"I hope," he was repeating, "I hope he's way past twenty-one. Kid like that, sir, wouldn't feel right in a wardroom. Just like me. He'll ship over. Bound to. He's enlisted navy. He'll—"

"And the first thing stateside, Dobson," snapped Commander Rathbone, "you intend to introduce him to your youngest girl!"

"Yes, sir, I do. I sure do." Then Dobson's broad grin faded. "He will make a darn good chief, sir," Dobson's gravel voice said firmly. "Good chiefs ain't too easy nowadays to find."

The kid had never heard a word of it. The kid was fast asleep.

TOM YATES

The Living Torpedo

THE SUBMARINE *TRICORN* was fifty hours out, and two degrees south of the Arctic Circle at noon that day. She was at a depth of two hundred feet, traveling on a course taking her steadily in toward the Norwegian coast, when Rogers called Harris and Ryan to the wardroom and opened their orders.

He began reading aloud, " 'You will attack and destroy the German battleship *Prinz Wilhelm* now lying in Nordkyn Fiord . . .' "

He read slowly on through three closely typed pages of instruction and information, and there was a long silence when he had finished. Ryan and Harris were trembling very slightly, and Rogers felt himself sweating in spite of the dank chill of the oil-tainted air.

"It won't be very comfortable," said Rogers at last.

"Nothing's comfortable in this water," said Ryan. He eased his stocky body away from the bulkhead and sat on the forward bunk next to Harris. "Thirty-two degrees is just on freezing point," he said.

Rogers got up from the narrow bench and peeled off his dirty jacket with the stripes of a commander on the sleeves. He tossed the jacket into a corner.

"I don't envy you," said Rogers. "The Germans have been hiding the *Prinz Wilhelm* in this fiord for over a month now, and they're bound to be expecting trouble." He picked up the orders and studied them again. "The Norwegians who sent us the dope about the defense nets report that explosive charges are being dropped all round the ship if the Kraut submarine detectors pick up as much as a shoal of fish. They must be pretty jittery." Rogers pulled out the empty water carafe from its socket on top of the sideboard, stared at it, then pushed it across the table. "Harris," he said, "nip along to the messroom and get some water, will you?"

Harris stood up—a slight, almost delicate-looking figure in soiled dungaree trousers and a thick, white diver's sweater. His dirty, laceless sneakers slopped on the threadbare carpet as he made for the curtain dividing the wardroom from the alleyway.

''Get some out of the galley, Bogey,'' said Ryan. ''It's quicker.''

Harris nodded, and they heard the hurried slip-slop of his shoes receding.

''A man of few words, our Harris,'' said Rogers.

''He can be loquacious at times,'' grinned Ryan. ''When I started off training—in ordinary diving dress—I had to attend him while he did an emergency job on some ship's screw. I let him fall ten feet, and what he told me when I got him up and got his helmet off was an education.''

''I can quite imagine,'' said Rogers dryly.

Ryan chuckled. ''I was green to this human-torpedo game, then. I told him that that was no way for a seaman to talk to a lieutenant.''

''What did friend Harris have to say to that?''

''He pointed out that being killed underwater by me wouldn't be any more pleasant for him if I were an admiral, let alone a lieutenant. And a reserve lieutenant at that. And, as he was a qualified diver and I wasn't, he was the best judge of the capabilities of whoever was attending him.'' Ryan smiled. ''I had to admit the justice of his argument. And after that, we decided to team up together on the jeeps.''

''He's a good boy,'' said Rogers.''

''We're all good boys . . . or we'd better be,'' replied Ryan, as Harris returned.

Rogers poured the glasses from the carafe.

''Here's luck in water!'' said Rogers, and emptied his glass. He set it down with a sigh.

''Do you think you've got everything taped?'' he said.

Ryan put his glass down and leaned back on the bunk with his eyes half-closed. ''You launch us three miles off the mouth of the fiord at eleven o'clock tonight,'' he said in a flat monotone. ''We run in those three miles, course about east-nor'east, and another two and a half up the fiord until we come to the antisubmarine boom. This should take about two hours. Right?''

Rogers nodded. ''Your part now, Harris,'' he said.

''Boom consists of three nets. Antisubmarine net with a wide mesh—we'll get her through that, Alan . . . sir. Then two antitorpedo nets made of small, intermeshed rings. We'll have to get under them, unless we can find a gap somewhere. Nets are about two hundred yards apart.''

''Yes. There's a point there,'' said Rogers. ''The German nets are sixty feet deep from top to bottom, and, according to what charts we've got, even at high tide there is only about sixty feet of water in that stretch of the fiord where they're laid. You might have trouble getting under."

"No chance of going round the end, sir?"

"Not a hope," replied Rogers. "They're carried right up the beach."

"As usual," said Ryan. "Right! Then we've got about a quarter of a mile to go before the next lot."

"That's it," said Rogers. "About five minutes' run. . . . Harris?"

"Two more intermeshed antitorpedo nets enclosing the *Prinz Wilhelm* in the form of a rectangle. Nets are about twenty yards apart, and a hundred and fifty yards from the ship's hull at the nearest point."

"Yes." Rogers agreed.

"Just how you are going to get through those two, I wouldn't know," he said then. "They're also sixty-foot nets, and apparently there is only fifty feet of water where *Prinz Willie* is lying. Your best proposition would be to tackle one of the corners, I think. There's bound to be a small gap somewhere."

Harris tugged gently at his right ear. "The only other thing is the submarine detectors," he said.

"You'll just have to be careful, that's all." Rogers grinned at him, but his eyes were doubtful. "If it's any comfort to you, what German gear we have captured isn't as good as ours; and, as you know, even ours doesn't always pick you up."

"Fair enough," said Harris.

"Well, that's that," said Ryan. "Apart from a head wind and sea, and freezing water, the run-in is a piece of cake."

"Um-m," said Rogers. "You'll set the fuse for five o'clock, Harris, eh?"

"Yes, sir. Head to be attached to the keel plate under the engine or boiler room."

"That's the ticket. The whole job should take about five hours. Two hours in, an hour for the nets and placing the head, and two hours to get out again. That'll leave you one hour's spare oxygen in your breathing sets in case of accidents."

There was a short silence.

"I mean—" began Rogers.

"Quite, sir," said Ryan. He spoke rapidly. "The rendezvous with *Tricorn* is at the spot where you launch us. You'll surface at three-thirty A.M., and dive again at four-thirty, whether we're there or not."

"That's it, I'm afraid. I can't leave it any later. We'll flash a masked green light in the direction of the fiord while we're waiting, but it will be visible at one mile only. So don't panic if you don't pick it up first shot. I think that's about all," he said. "What torpedo are you riding?"

Harris smiled faintly. "Number Six, sir. *Lucretia*," he said.

"*Lucretia?*"

"She took us down to a hundred and twenty feet the first time we rode her, and we both had a bad go of oxygen poisoning before we could get her up again," explained Harris."

"I see. Well, here's luck," said Rogers, and then, for the first time, showed signs of awkwardness. "I know, of course, that—Look, I don't need to impress on you guys the importance of sinking this battlewagon," he said at last. "If you bring it off—Well, you know what I mean. Morale back home, and freeing some of our ships from watching for her, and one thing and another." He looked around vaguely. "But I certainly don't envy you," he said again.

"It'll be all right, sir," said Ryan.

"No trouble at all," affirmed Harris.

"I hope so," said Commander Rogers. "Well, I'm going to take her up to periscope depth and have a squint round. You fellers had better get some sleep. I'll see you are shaken in plenty of time."

Harris woke slowly. He felt sluggish, and there was an unpleasant taste in his mouth. The sumbarine, submerged since she had surfaced to charge batteries at midnight the night before, was very cold; the air, damp from the sweating hull, was dead and badly vitiated. There was an electric silence, intensified rather than broken by the almost inaudible hum of the motors as they crept in toward the enemy coast at a depth of ninety feet.

Ryan appeared through the tiny doorway in the watertight bulkhead. He, too, had been sleeping. He looked drawn and nervy. Harris could understand it. There was a void where his own stomach should have been.

They knew fear. All the jeepmen did. There were so many things that could go wrong, even before they got near the enemy. A breakdown in the breathing appartus in deep water. The constant risk of being trapped in the toxic zone below thirty-three feet, where oxygen poisoning crept on you. First one's lips quivering, then twitching spasmodically, so that one could not grip the mouthpiece and suck in the essential but deadly oxygen. Then the whole body shaking, shuddering violently, until it went into convulsions, and one died a dreadful death alone in the cold, hostile depths. There were isolated fresh-water patches from mountain torrents that sent the jeep plunging toward the bottom while they struggled madly to adjust oxygen supplies and to clear their ears against the tremendous, rapidly increasing pressure of the water. A breathing bag, torn on the barnacle-encrusted nets, injecting a rush of icy water, instead of warm oxygen, full into the lungs with a blinding shock.

And always the persistent fear that perhaps, when real danger came, their courage would fail, and they would succumb to the lurking panic that constantly sought to master them.

Down in the submarine they thrust these thoughts aside. It was always like this before a dive, and nothing ever happened. But it might. Jimmy Spears had blown his lungs to shreds, and Ted Winship had drowned in training. And this time it was the real thing. If they got into trouble below, there could be no help, no hope for them. And if they were detected they would be showered with depth charges, and met with a hail of bullets if they surfaced. And they had no defense.

Ryan cleared his throat. "Half past ten, Bogey," he croaked. "Won't be long now."

Harris grunted, and forced a smile. Together they bent to examine their gear for the last time. The one-piece suits with the skirted opening in the belly where they struggled in. They were of light rubberized fabric, with a heavy, sponge-rubber headpiece or hood with a black rubber gas-mask facepiece cemented on the front. There was no air in the suits when they dived. A tube ran from the mask to the breathing bag, and connected to a rubber mouthpiece that projected inside the dress. This was gripped between the teeth, with a shield between lips and gums making an airtight joint through which to suck the oxygen. The suits were dry and freshly chalked along the seams where extra solution had been rubbed in, and they stank of rubber and disinfectant.

They went over the webbing harnesses that fitted over their shoulders and belted round their waists. They each carried a weighted, rectangular, black rubber breathing bag, or lung, high up on the chest; and a cage containing two alloy bottles of oxygen at high pressure that rested low on the back. The lung and the bottles were connected by a flexible tube, and a by-pass valve was fitted to enable a burst of high-pressure oxygen to be injected into the bag at will. One liter of oxygen per minute flowed constantly into the bag.

They examined the rope laces of the weighted canvas boots. The long knives were greased. Everything was ready, and, as they completed their inspection, they heard quiet orders being given in the control room:

"Break down. . . . Dead slow. . . . Up to periscope depth."

They felt the boat tilt slighlty; then came the gentle upward pressure of the deck as she lifted. She straightened onto even keel again.

"Up periscope!"

They looked at each other. Ryan took a little phial of tablets from his pocket, and they swallowed three each. Harris gave Ryan a cigarette, and put one in his own mouth. The match burned feebly in the stale air. Their tension mounted in the long silence.

Rogers came as the boat dived again. "We are on the spot, men," he said, "and there's a gale blowing up top." He hesitated for a moment, then held out a signal form. "I've got some bad news, I'm afraid," he went on. "While you were sleeping I received a retransmitted message from a recco plane. It warns us that the Germans are sweeping the nets around the ship with a searchlight."

"A searchlight!" ejaculated Harris.

Ryan sat down heavily, and drew hard on his cigarette. Harris gazed blankly at Rogers.

"Things look a bit doubtful," said Rogers. "They've got their boats patrolling their nets, too, and a launch on the center net of the boom defense."

"It seems almost as though something had leaked out in Norway," said Ryan thoughtfully.

"It's possible that they have been tipped off," Rogers agreed, "but they can't know exactly what they are looking for." He avoided their eyes carefully. "The question is: Are you going to chance having a stab at it?"

Ryan frowned down at the steel deck, then looked at Harris. Harris smiled faintly back at him.

"Nearly time we got dressed, isn't it, Alan?" he said evenly.

Ryan nodded.

Rogers opened his mouth to speak, then closed it again. He gestured toward the suits.

"Okay. Hurry," he said.

They stripped, and the two dressers took their clothes, their paybooks and their identity disks. They pulled on union suits of pure, heavy silk, and silk socks. Similar suits of soft, closely woven wool, and woolen socks. Then two heavy white sweaters, two pairs of long underpants, and two pairs of thigh-length stockings of the same heavy white wool.

They sat down, opened the skirts of the suits and forced their legs in, pulled the suits over their shoulders and thrust their arms down the sleeves, hands through the tight rubber cuffs. Wrist bands adjusted, they ducked their heads inside and forced them up through the narrow necks into the rubber helmets.

The attendants folded the skirts and clamped them, making a watertight joint which they tucked away, buckling the folds of the suit over all. The high boots were laced tight, a long sharp knife in a metal sheath tucked into each one. Nose clips were fixed tightly over the nostrils, and when mouthpieces were comfortably adjusted, the helmet straps were pulled tight. Finally, the visors, heavily coated inside with an antidimming compound, were closed down and clamped tight. The were ready as far as they could be.

The boat slanted suddenly, and they felt her rising again. There came a noise of rushing water and the sound of waves slapping against the outside of the thin hull. She leveled and began to roll slowly.

The attendants picked up the harnesses, and the divers clumped in their heavy boots along to the control room. As they arrived, the order, "Divers and dressers on the bridge!" came down the voice pipe. The attendants started up the steel ladder. Ryan and Harris took one last look round the control room, dim in the red night light, and followed. They were both sweating profusely now, and as he struggled through the lower hatch into the conning tower, and clambered up toward the bridge hatch, Harris reflected grimly that they would pay for it later.

On the bridge the gale hit them. The night was black. The wind, howling out of the east, whipped the sea into sharp, choppy waves which were flattened almost as soon as they were formed. Ryan saw, and cursed softly into his mask.

The jeep was being dragged out of its cylinder as they shrugged into their harnesses. The breathing tubes were connected to the face-pieces, the bottles opened and the soft hiss of oxygen started. They closed the exhaust valves at the bottom of the bags and sucked them empty of air, coughing slightly from the fine dust off the carbon-dioxide absorbent canister, expelling the air by switching the mouthpiece cocks alternately from air to oxygen. Then they cracked their bypass valves until they were breathing pure oxygen.

Down on the casing they were alone with the jeep. Harris waved a hand when they were ready, and saw the head on the bridge duck toward the voice pipe.

For a moment nothing happened. Then there was a roar of escaping air. Fountains of spray leaped high from the vents, and they felt a wave of unreasoning panic as the casing deck sank beneath them. The suits contracted and gripped as the water swirled about their knees, then their waists. The long torpedo with the detachable head bobbed free of the cradle, the top of the body just above the racing waves.

They scrambled astride it, crouching behind their rounded shields; Ryan at the controls and Harris behind. Ryan flicked the throttle, and they moved slowly away from the submarine. Fifty yards off they stopped, and, opening the sea cock, Ryan started the pump. Slowly they sank into the black water. Harris threw the lever that opened the main ballast tank in front of him, and they dropped a foot, suddenly.

Carefully Ryan judged his time until, with their eyes just level with the surface, and the machine weighted with water until it would lie motionless, neither rising nor sinking, he switched off the pump and closed the sea cock.

Harris twisted to face the submarine and gave a momentary blink of the underwater flashlight. The figure on the bridge disappeared.

The dim black bulk surged slowly forward. Great gouts of water and compressed air spurted from the tanks, and the sea boiled white as the last of the deck submerged. The conning tower tilted, diminished slowly, vanished. The periscope standard left a streak of white water, then was gone. There was a smooth, swirling patch in the broken seas.

The gale whistled in their helmet exhaust valves, and the icy waves battered at them. The jeep rolled wildly. Oxygen hissed sibilantly into their breathing bags. They were alone, and each began the long, lonely battle against his own fear.

They were cruising with their eyes just above surface, the windblown waves smacking full into their faces. They were well up the fiord, and they could see, dimly, the hills on either side, looming an intenser black against the blackness of the sky.

The luminous dial of the clock on the instrument panel showed one o'clock. They had been away two hours now, and already their hands were numb and swelling, their feet and legs dead and cramped. The clothing under their suits, dampened when they had sweated in the heat of the *Tricon*'s belly, had long ago chilled through; the penetrating cold creeping through the woolens, slowly freezing and numbing. Only two hours gone.

Ryan crouched over the controls, concentrating on keeping a steady course, wondering and worrying how much farther they had to go before they reached the boom.

Harris, while his eyes kept ceaseless vigil, had blanked off half his brain and was thinking of Janet and his next leave. He had found this the only way of enduring the long run-in before he did his part on the nets and the ship's bottom. It kept his mind off things that might go wrong, off the cruel cold, and stifled the ever-present thought that the slightest false move would bring the shattering depth charges to crush them to pulp in their suits below. Just keep on thinking of Janet.

Faintly, borne on the wings of the gale, they caught the restless, eternal clanging of the net buoys as they jostled and bobbed against one another on the hurrying waves.

There was a sudden blinding flash up the fiord, and the *Prinz Wilhelm*'s searchlight swept deliberately along the nets hemming her in. The glare reflected momentarily on the buoys of the boom nets two hundred yards ahead. Then the light died, leaving a denser blackness.

Ryan sighted his compass, waved his hand and pushed forward on the joy stick. The jeep tilted, and the roar of the wind was shut off abruptly as she slid below in a long, steep glide. They dived deep, charging their bags with short blasts from the bypasses; blowing their noses hard against the nose clips to relieve the agony of uncleared ears; letting quick spurts of oxygen past their lips into the helmets to keep the masks from crushing in on their faces.

At sixty feet they leveled out in a cold black world that pressed in on them fiercely. They moved in a cloud of phosphorescent sparks, leaving a comet tail behind them. For some minutes Ryan kept her at full speed, then throttled down to half. Seconds later they felt the cushioned bump as they met the first net. Ryan switched of, and they clambered stiffly along the head to the net, and hung there like two grotesque spiders while they struggled to force the jeep through the mesh. After what seemed an age, they succeeded, and the machine lay there, still, with just the slightest tendency to rise. They climbed aboard again, and dived toward bottom. It was nearer than Ryan thought, and they bumped badly at sixty-eight feet.

They skimmed along, barely clear of the rocky bottom. They went on and on across the two hundred yards between the nets. Then startlingly—ghostly, phosphorescent and weed-grown—the second net swept out of the blackness over their heads, clear by a foot. Somewhere, nearly seventy feet above them in the clean cold gale, a boat was floating; German seamen huddled together for warmth, watching for a vague menace.

Ryan looked again at the clock. One-eighteen. They had been nearly seventy feet down for seventeen minutes. His breathing was shortening, and he prayed silently that they would not be held up too long on the last net. He could not stay much longer at this depth.

Harris, in the rear seat, lay over the ballast tank, alternately swearing and praying into his mouthpiece. The cold had crept up his thin, wiry body until it had reached his waist. Icy daggers of pain stabbed through the small of his back, his kidneys aching until he could have wept with the pain. Confined in his suit, alone in the vast blackness, he struggled desperately with the almost overwhelming temptation to charge his emergency buoyance bag, shoot to the surface and flash the torch until a patrol boat came and picked him up. To risk the prison camp . . . or a bullet. Anything was better than this.

They struck the third net hard. Harris pulled himself off and reeled along the ocean bed like a man in drink. Ryan, although more fleshy than Harris, was also feeling the chill beginning to creep up his spine, and he was thankful for the break from sitting still in the frigid water.

Until they got forward and examined the net. Five rows of rings rested on the bottom in a tangled heap. The rest of the net vanished upward in the darkness, a rigid steel wall.

Somehow those five rows of foot-wide steel rings, inert there on the bottom, had to be lifted clear while the jeep was passed underneath. Somehow they had to support a weight of some hundred and fifty pounds each, four feet off the bottom, and move the jeep at the same time. In pitch-blackness, hampered by the constricting but vulnerable dress and breathing apparatus, they had to struggle with a mass of heavy, hopelessly entangled steel rings and the twenty-seven-foot length of the torpedo.

They went in opposite directions along the net, searching for a gap or gully in the sea bed where there would not be such a great mass of net. They returned knowing that there was not a foot of difference in depth all the way across that deeper section of the fiord.

They wept tears of rage and exhaustion. The net slipped and tore from their hands. Isolated rings hung down, and, as fast as they gathered one up, two more would fall in its place. They snagged on the breakwaters, they caught on the controls and jammed there. The whole weight fell across Harris's saddle, and they had to rest before they could start to raise it again. They labored and strained and sweated in the darkness, heaving and tugging like madmen. They ran insane risks of tearing the lungs on the clustered barnacles, of being trapped under the net. Their numbed hands were torn to ribbons, lacerated until they felt the pain even through the numbness. They got the jeep through, but they were in a bad way.

They had been almost seventy feet under water for three quarters of an hour. Their jaws were shuddering, their quivering lips letting go oxygen that their heaving lungs demanded.

They fell rather than climbed aboard the jeep, and, fighting off oblivion, Ryan sent her reaching full speed for the surface in a steep climb. For ten minutes they lay there, heads just above water, until their lips steadied, the panting stopped, and the poisoning oxygen began to work out of bloodstream and tissue. Until the cold began to creep on them again.

They waited for the searchlight to sweep round, and Ryan lined his compass on the nearest corner of the antitorpedo nets in the flash. Then they forged ahead once more, with a quarter of a mile to go to the last barrier.

They were a bare two hundred yards from the nets when the searchlight flashed again. A cutter, the crew pulling silently and slowly, was silhouetted before the light died. They dived to fifteen feet at half speed, down into the dead silence below. They hit the net, and Ryan held on while Harris worked along the rings and located the corner. As he fumbled in the darkness, the black water glowed into a deep emerald as the enemy searchlight passed over the surface. In the dim light Harris saw the corner. Where the joint of the net came, there was a gap a foot wide that extended down to his level at fifteen feet.

He thought, *O God, we'll never get out of this;* and there came the rush of desire for the clean air above, the surging, fear-driven instinct that fought against putting any more obstacles between himself and safety. The words *Attack and destroy . . . attack and destroy* began running through his mind, over and over in crazy repetition, and the saliva began dribbling and bubbling in his mouthpiece. He gripped desperately at the cold steel of the net, and fought to retain his failing courage.

At last he went slowly back to the jeep, and together he and Ryan dragged the machine to the gap and forced it through. The net's own weight, stretching to the bottom, kept it rigid, and they had to lever and strain before it gave way to them.

A wire rope, part of the moorings, ran between the outer and inner nets, and they pulled themselves and the jeep across the intervening space on this. The corner of the inner net had a corresponding gap that was, if anything, slightly larger. They struggled again, cursing the total blackout that followed each flash of the lights, venting that fierce nervous rage that seizes the diver when the slightest thing goes wrong.

At two-fifteen they were through. Ryan steered about twenty feet away from the inner net and parallel to it. The *Prinz Wilhelm* was a hundred and forty yards or so to their left. They ran for a few minutes, then Ryan eased down to dead slow and brought their heads to within two feet of the surface. He waited until the light swept over them again, then poked his head above water for a split second. The massive hulk loomed up, blotting out the frosty brilliance of the stars. They were amidships, abreast the towering funnel. Ryan ducked back and sent the jeep into a steep dive, turning in toward the ship.

They hit the side glancingly at twenty-five feet. As they touched, Ryan switched off, and Harris, a flat multiple magnet in each hand, gripped the torpedo with his legs and began pulling the machine down the hull.

At thirty-three feet the side began to sheer in to form the bottom. They worked in under the bilge keel, which projected a yard or more. Then, with the depth gauge showing forty feet, they were right under in the suffocating blackness, clinging with the magnets to the vast, almost-flat bottom.

Harris, holding on to both magnet lanyards with one hand, felt around above his head until he found a double row of rivets. They would be holding a small rib inside the hull. He started again with his magnets, placing them as gently as he could, hand over hand, following the rivet line. He had no other means of sensing direction in this unfamiliar territory, and they were in such blackness that they could not even see the inside of their masks. Without a lead to the center line of the ship, they would wander, possibly for hours, before finding the vital keel.

Harris went slowly on until, beginning to think that he had missed it, he felt the thick, heavily riveted keel plate above his head. He plugged the two magnets against the plate and lashed the lanyards to the rail across the ballast tank, anchoring the jeep firmly. They were right where the charge would break the ship's back and flood the machinery compartments above them. They could hear the boiler-room noises clearly. The slow, soft hiss and click of a pump. An occasional clang or clatter that brought their hearts to their mouths. They were preparing to blast the men that made those sounds into eternity, and the thought brought to their minds the measure of the mercy they could expect if they were discovered.

In spite of their exertions on the nets, the cold had gripped them again. Harris turned around with difficulty, his frozen lower body obeying his will only with immense effort. His brain, beginning to be affected by the cold and the oxygen, worked slowly. He had to think hard before he knew what he wanted to do, then force himself, step by step, to do it. There were more magnets in the locker behind him, and he lifted them out, all clinging together in a tight bunch. Painfully he detached the two spares, replaced them, and twisted the lanyards of the other two round his left wrist.

Then he slid out of his seat and pulled himself forward. When he reached the head he paused for a moment and checked, once again, the position of the keel above the jeep. Satisfied that the head was directly below the plate, he clamped on the magnets and lashed the lanyards to the securing rail along the top of the head. Again he had to pause. . . . To stretch his cracking muscles against a cramp that had suddenly seized his loins. To fight a dread, a violent spasm of fear, that swept him—bidding him, while he could still move, to get out from under the huge mass above him. To get to where he could surface quickly in case of trouble. He had to hang there in the thick darkness for seconds that felt like hours until, having checked the blast of his bypass valve and made sure that his deadened hands could still work the tap, he was able to conquer that piercing stab of fear.

Slowly he worked his way along the head. He found the fuse switch and removed the protective cover, which he tucked into his left boot. Each movement took an age, his senseless fingers feeling again and again before he could be sure that he was doing what he wished. His thumbs would not stay rigid, and he had to clasp his fist around the switch before he could move it. He counted the clicks. Half an hour, an hour, an hour and a half, two hours, two and a half. Set for five o'clock. He could not feel the raised figures on the fuse face, and he had to risk flicking the torch on the dial. Two and a half hours.

He made his way back to the joint between the head and the body, and hung on Ryan's leg shield. Then he pulled the securing pin out, lifted the lever and detached the head. It floated gently upward until it nudged the keel plate.

Deprived of the slight buoyancy of the head, the jeep body tilted forward a little. As Harris worked aft toward his seat, Ryan opened the sea cock with trembling, fumbling hands, and pumped enough water out of the foremost tank to compensate for the loss.

As he settled himself, Harris removed one of the two magnets supporting the body, and banged Ryan on the shoulder. He felt the slight vibration as the motor started, and wrenched the other magnet free. They dropped, leveled; then, as they cleared the ship's sphere of magnetic influence, and the compass steadied, they steered for the net.

They missed the corner, and it took Harris seven precious minutes to find the gaps. They carried a coil of light rope in the locker, and he climbed up and along the net with the end made fast to his belt while Ryan kept the slack in hand. By the time they had once again forced the jeep through, both men were exhausted. It would be nerve only from then on. Frozen, physically almost finished, minds numbed with cold and oxygen, they were as good as beaten.

As they cleared the antitorpedo nets, Ryan sent the torpedo down to thirty. He timed the dive by the clock, and did not surface until they were four hundred yards away—within easy distance of the inner boom net.

There seemed to be a lull in the gale when they surfaced, and the waves were now beating on their backs. Ryan looked again at the clock: two forty-seven.

He had to force his sluggish brain to think. They had been two hours running in, and three quarters of an hour getting through the three boom nets. It was thirteen minutes to three now, and *Tricorn* would dive at four-thirty sharp. They had a following wind and sea which would cut their cruising time down the fiord considerably, but even then the most that they could allow for clearing the boom was twenty minutes.

It was impossible. Apart from the time factor, Ryan knew—they both knew—that they could never survive another breakthrough on the inner net. When they had tackled it before, they had been comparatively fresh. Now they were dead-tired, and, furthermore, the tide was ebbing and had probably dropped about two feet already. The mass of netting on the bottom would be even greater now. The only hope was to risk going over the top. That or give the game up.

Ryan steered for the shore. The buoys took the weight of the nets, and in shoal water the greater part of the net rested on the bottom, rendering it easier to force a passage between the buoys. The great danger lay in being sighted while the jeep was showing above surface, half over the net. But the chance had to be taken.

He crept in at seven feet below the hissing waves. When they hit the steep beach, he came up, bringing their heads above water, and turned down the fiord until they came to the buoys. He stayed with the machine while Harris went exploring along the net. He was back in a matter of minutes, and hung on alongside the body, steering. They struck the wire jackstay supporting the net between the sixth and seventh buoys. It was sagging almost two feet in the center, and it would be necessary to blow the main ballast tank and pump the internal tanks dry to get her over.

Harris maneuvered the nose of the body onto the jackstay while Ryan lay in the water working the pump controls. The jeep rose out of the water higher and higher. They could hear, plainly, the engine of the German boom-patrol boat on the center net.

They timed their effort with the intermittently flashing lights of the *Prinz Wilhelm*, and, as one glare died, Ryan blew the main tank. The jeep heaved out of the water and floated like a duck on the surface. With frantic haste they dragged her over the wire. It seemed impossible that they could escape detection. But they had vented the main tank and were pumping in again before the next flash came from up the fiord.

As the jeep sank into the water, they climbed aboard again, and Ryan made another laborious calculation. The center net had been about six feet off the bottom when they had come through. There would still be a space of some four feet if they were lucky. If they turned her on her side—

They cruised to the center of the fiord, eyes just showing. Ryan delayed the dive as long as possible; then, as the buoys came in sight, pushed her nose down and dropped almost vertically. He pulled her out at sixty, and they went down the last few feet on the net itself. It was a tight squeeze, and although they took only ten minutes to get her through, their depleted reserves were already fighting a losing battle against a recurrence of oxygen poisoning. They rose swiftly to ten feet, and despite his swimming head, Ryan kept her there until they came to rest on the last net.

Easily as they had cleared the antisubmarine net on the way in, it nearly broke them going out. Their limbs and the lower part of their bodies were practically useless, their muscles ineffectual, their heads aching to bursting point. But to give up at this stage was unthinkable, and, in spite of their exhaustion, they finally thrust the jeep out to the safe side.

They kept at ten feet for five minutes, and surfaced some four hundred yards clear. They blew the main tanks and pumped out every ounce of interior water ballast, bringing themselves high out of the water and presenting a greater area to the following wind.

Harris looked back. The searchlights were still sweeping the nets around the *Prinz Wilhelm,* and down the wind came the faint chugging of the motorboat, still watching the boom nets.

Their bodies were finished. The nose clips pressed intolerably on nostrils worn raw, and their jaws were aching from the continual grip on the mouthpieces. The rubber cuffs of the suits bit into their swollen wrists, inflicting further agony on their already tortured arms.

Tricorn was somewhere in the blackness, six weary miles away, but they were singing to themselves inside their masks as they set off down the fiord.

At four twenty-five that morning, the signalman of the *Tricorn* stopped flashing his shaded light and reported a white light appearing off the port beam. Rogers steadied himself against the periscope standard and trained his night glasses. . . .

They had to lift them aboard. They hoisted them up onto the bridge and lowered them gently down, through the conning tower, into the control room.

As they came out of the water, their torn hands streamed blood, and in the comparatively warm air of the hull the pain of returning circulation broke through their stupor, making them groan in agony.

The attendants stripped off their suits, cutting away the cuffs to get the sleeves over their distorted hands. They sat shuddering in a pool of water, propped up on the steel deck plates, while the coxswain trickled fiery-neat rum between their locked jaws.

They were both beyond speech. Rogers questioned them gently, and Ryan managed to hold his thumbs up. Harris pointed weakly to the fuse cover that had fallen from his boot, and held up the finger and thumb of one hand. Then they both went suddenly and solidly to sleep where they sat.

Tricorn dived at four-thirty A.M., precisely. Commander Rogers sat motionless in the cramped wardroom, scarcely breathing. He had his wrist watch on the table before him, and he watched the second hand on its tedious journey round and round the dial. Slowly the minute hand crawled up to the hour, and the lines on Rogers's face deepened.

Even at the distance of ten miles they felt the tremendous concussion of the half-ton torpedo warhead that shattered the mighty *Prinz Wilhelm* into a flaming ruin.

Rogers exhaled gustily, and his eyes closed for a moment. Then he methodically strapped his watch back on his wrist. The jeepmen, bandaged and blanketed, were dead asleep in the two lower bunks, and Rogers's eyes softened as he looked at them. Then he picked up his cap and went back to the control room.

STEVE FRAZEE

The Crew of the Foraker

THEY WERE TAKING Jack Muirhead to the brig on Samar. The crew of the *Foraker*, an old destroyer escort now, watched with a quietness that was not healthy. Sullenly we watched, crowding the quarter deck as close as we dared, standing on the torpedo deck, sitting aft on the depth charge racks. Signalmen and quartermasters stalled around the flag bag, staring down.

Lieutenant Naylor, the gunnery officer, was in charge of the detail. "Blubber" Naylor. Whatever he thought of the captain's decision he held it tight behind the fat folds of his sweating face, behind blue, tired eyes. But we could guess what Naylor thought; he had been aboard too long to keep his mind a secret.

Muirhead stood between Pete Macdonald and Joe Burgener. The shore patrol bands were on their arms, the .45's against their hips. Their faces cursed this duty. They were Muirhead's cousins. Jack Muirhead was a bean pole of a man, a long red neck, bristly sandy hair and freckles standing sharp against his pale, defiant face.

Ten days before he had laughed when a fat man playing tennis at Manus in the Admiralties rushed hard for a lob and fell over the net. All the liberty party from the *Foraker* laughed, but Muirhead was the only one who could not stop when the fat man limped over and asked some questions.

He was a big shot in the beach command. His complaint and request for punishment came later, when the *Foraker* was in Leyte. It listed "disrespectful attitude, insubordination, and cursing an officer." Muirhead had cursed, while trying to explain why he could not stop laughing, and how funny it was to see a paunchy man in white shorts crashing over a tennis net.

Our old captain, who had taken the *Foraker* out of Norfolk on her shakedown to Bermuda three years before, would have thumbed his nose at the beach. He was gone. Our present captain revoked the next five liberties of the entire party involved, and he broke Muirhead to seaman second and gave him five days in the brig.

There were thirty-one of us North Carolinians on the *Foraker* and if we were not all Muirhead's cousins, or even each other's cousins, we were still all North Carolinians. When it comes to war the South is always there, and North Carolina is in front.

We scratched our heat rash and watched. The *Foraker* rolled to the long movement of the gulf, and the old, old odors of the Philippines crowded in on us.

Naylor looked at the escort. He nodded toward the ladder. A wildness came to Muirhead's face then. He stepped away from the lifeline, into the clear space of the quarterdeck where the petty officer of the deck waited to take Naylor's salute.

"I ain't a-going," Muirhead said.

Naylor was from the stony hills of Vermont, and Muirhead was a mountaineer too; and it seemed that Naylor understood. But Naylor had the navy's duty, as the captain saw it. He looked at Muirhead sharply, and then he looked at me and big Joe Clegge. We were Muirhead's real cousins. Naylor looked at us, and it was like an order.

We stepped out on the quarterdeck. Clegge said, "You got to go, Jack. You're going without any fighting trouble. Get in the boat."

"I ain't a-going!"

Clegge was a naturally ugly man, burly, blistered, with his red hair receded half way back on his head. His face was lumpy. His eyes were small and cloudy. He pushed his face close to Muirhead. "Go on, Jack. You've got to!"

"No!"

Naylor glanced at the boat davits.

"Wait a minute, sir," I said. Seeing a drunk hoisted by the davits was one thing; the thought of Muirhead, subdued, bound, lowered over the side, was another thing. "Can Clegge and I go ashore with him, right up to the door of the brig?"

Naylor said, "You have my permission to ask the exec."

I went straight to the captain instead. He was at his desk, in his skivvies, a round little man with buck teeth that gave him the appearance of smiling even when he was getting ready to squeal about something.

"There's no reason why you and Clegge should go ashore with Muirhead," he said.

"But maybe we can keep him out of trouble."

''He's already in trouble. That's all.'' The captain rapped his pen on the metal desk. ''Did you clear your request through Mr. Barlow?''

''No, sir. I—''

''You've heard of the chain of command.'' The captain glanced over at my right arm.

''Yes, sir, but—''

''That's all.''

''If you'll let me explain, sir, about how we do things back home—''

''My God! If you hillbillies had been half as stubborn at fighting as you are at talking, the Civil War would still be going on.'' The captain's lips writhed away from his buck teeth. ''You're on report!''

''What for?''

''Sir!''

''What for—sir?'' I could have killed him for his remark about the Civil War.

''Insubordination. Get out!'' He followed me as far as the ladder aft of the yeoman's office. ''What's the delay there, Mr. Naylor?''

Naylor came forward to the bottom of the ladder. ''I recommend you allow Clegge and Donaldson to go with the party, Captain.''

''Carry out your orders, Mr. Naylor!''

Macdonald and Burgener put Muirhead in the boat. It was a filthy thing to watch, to see him lowered with the blood coming down across his forehead. Macdonald pulled a white hat from the water and set it on the prisoner's head. Naylor went down the ladder after the boat crew pulled away from under the davits. He bumped to a seat in the stern sheets and sat there with his face and shirt adrip with sweat, ugly with his thinking.

On the *Foraker* the rest of us stalled too long. The captain pattered down the ladder in his slippers. He bounced along the deck and went to the controls of the public address system.

''All hands hear this. In view of the extremely bad attitude of enlisted personnel, the next two liberties of all sections are revoked.''

We went then to our work stations. We were not ready to kill the captain, not yet. Some of us were ready an hour later when word came from the beach about Jack Muirhead. He blew his top after our men turned him over to the regular shore patrol. On the way to the brig in a jeep he jumped out, right in front of an oncoming truck.

He died on his way to the hospital.

* * *

I stood my mast for insubordination while the *Foraker* was slipping through the San Bernardino Straits. The hills come down steeply to the water there. From a distance the rank, strange vegetation might be pine trees on the hills of home, back there where Muirhead and thirty others of us had come from, driving our old cars or walking from the mountains to enlist in a war for freedom, against injustice.

We knew that the *Foraker* was not the United States Navy; but it was the part of the navy we had to live with.

Yeoman Larsen, fat-hipped, lisping, read the charges against me, right on down to the part about the United States then being in a state of war. Jack Muirhead's ancestors had fought against the British at King's Mountain in another war. Muirhead was dead on the beach, dead because of a big-bellied officer who played tennis, who could never have climbed King's Mountain long ago.

And because of the captain, who was much handier than that beach officer at Manus.

"Reduction to gunner's mate third class," the captain said. "The loss of one month's pay, and sixty hours' extra duty."

Chief Bos'n's Mate Shallop watched me like a hawk. He was sloppy in his complete uniform, an old man with nearly thirty years' duty. We all saluted after the mast. Larsen waddled away to do his typing.

The captain cleared his throat. "You thought you and Clegge could keep Muirhead under control, was that it?"

"Yes, sir."

"The S.P.'s in that jeep had authority to do so, and they were unable to handle him. What of that?"

"Yes, sir."

The captain licked his teeth. He went into his stateroom. Shallop began to loosen his uniform, still watching my face. "Don't try anything," he said. "You want to go home some day, don't you?"

That night Clegge, Burgener, and I were on mid watch on the Number Two gun. Larsen and an electrician named Holt were also on the watch. We left them at the gun and went into the magazine just aft. On the deck above us were two more North Carolinians, Bob Pritchett and Jake Gaulden. We undogged the ammunition hatch overhead so they could be in on the conference about the captain.

Clegge sat down on a pile of foul-weather gear and lit a cigarette. "Smoke's drifting up here like it was coming through a stovepipe!" Gaulden said. "Suppose the captain—"

"Suppose hell!" Clegge said savagely. "What's our plan?"

We talked, voices muttering inside the steel walls of the magazine. Gaulden felt better when no more smoke came up. "There's a bad training stop on the port-twenty up here," he said. "If you—" His words had out-reached the thought. "No, there's nothing in that," he said.

"Naylor knows about that stop," Clegge said. "We haven't been able to get a new one. It could be loosened enough to let the gun train clear around. Then—"

"Yeah! Right into the wheelhouse," Pritchett said. "Who the hell wants everything blowing up in his face?"

"It would train right over the bridge too," Clegge said. "Right where the captain leans sometimes when there's trouble. Suppose a plane was coming in—"

"Oh no!" Pritchett said. "Suppose it was coming in low. The gunner would stay right with it and the next thing you know he'd blow his head off when he began to shoot into the wheelhouse."

"It's not much of an idea," Gaulden said. He was Pritchett's loader on the gun.

We spent an hour in the magazine, and came up with nothing. When we went on deck again a convoy was building around us. Larsen said he could see two attack transports and a cruiser off to starboard; and then, overbulging with dope, as a yeoman always is, he said we were going to Okinawa on a big deal.

"There'll be planes up there," Clegge said. "I still think my idea is good."

Trouble came just before the watch changed. A sub made a pass at one of our APA's. We went after him. The ping jockeys picked him up, and then we lost him. We cruised in a prescribed pattern and got contact again. By then the convoy was dropping over the horizon.

We finally got the sub lined out cold.

Clegge was gun captain of Number One. Just aft of the gun was the hedgehog, an anti-submarine weapon that threw twenty-four charges over the bow. Clegge's crew was there now, jammed between a magazine bulkhead and the flash shield of the hedgehog. Most of them braced themselves, but Burgener, the trainer, and Clegge at the controls could not brace themselves until the weapon was fired.

The order came. The sub was dead ahead, cold meat. Clegge spun the switch and the charges looped over the *Foraker's* bow. Instead of sheering off hard to avoid running over the area where the projectiles fell, we held to our course. That was the captain's fault.

Some of the missiles connected on that long cigar under us. Our bow heaved to the explosion. We came down with a shock that threw our screws in the air and left them shuddering; and then the stern fell and the bow heaved again.

Men all over the ship were thrown to the deck. Neither Clegge nor Burgener had had time to get braced hard. They both went headlong into the hedgehog. Burgener got brain concussion. Clegge, who managed to get his hands out in front of him, had his nose spread to his cheekbones.

We went on up to Okinawa. On the second night there Clegge and Burgener were sent to a hospital ship. Burgener never came back. Clegge did, three days later. His facial bones were cracked to the corners of his eyes. The doctors had taken some of the bone splinters from his nose and packed the passages with X-ray film to keep them open for later operations. Every time Clegge accidentally touched the ends of those razor-sharp strips in his streaming nose his eyes went blind with water and his face turned white with pain.

With the rest of us he stayed at the guns. Day after day the planes came in, the ones that streaked and whined, and the old ones that wobbled, heavy with explosives. The navy burned powder day and night. We shot up planes and each other's radar masts, and dropped our anti-aircraft stuff into the army swarming on the beach.

After a while the *Foraker* was sent to the picket line north of the big island to use our radar on the red-balls coming south so that pilots on Okinawa would have more time to get their planes in the air. Destroyers and destroyer escorts, steel splinters rolling on the long blue water, outposts that could not fall back. The enemy did not want us there, relaying dope back to the island.

They came down like bees on a sweating horse.

Sometime during that first week Pritchett discovered that by swinging his twenty hard to port he could ride it past the training stop and make the muzzle bear on the bridge. Clegge kept making temporary repairs so that the other men who had that twenty station there beside the wheelhouse would not kill themselves.

It happened on the sixth day. A disorderly flock came in when the light was poor. A few of them changed their minds and streaked for home. Off to port a can with quad forties crippled an old Betty, which then tried to use the last of its power to crash the *Foraker*.

Our short-reaching twenties began to get pieces of the Betty. That meant it was a matter of seconds—and luck.

Braced against the harness of the gun, his knees bending as he elevated the plunging barrel, Pritchett was putting everything into the plane. It was then the captain's head and shoulders came in view above the bridge.

Pritchett's gun kept swinging, following the Betty to starboard. Then the captain was gone and tracers were streaking the air where he had been an instant before. The Betty wobbled across our beam, and then the starboard guns blew it up.

The captain was dead, I thought. Pritchett had got him.

But the captain was all right. All that was wrong with him was a bruised knee; he had tangled himself in the lead to his phones and tripped a split second before the twenty would have killed him.

During a quiet interval Lieutenant Naylor watched Clegge repair the stop on Pritchett's gun, as much as it could be repaired without a replacement part. Naylor had not learned his gun mechanics from a book. He was hard to fool; but he had said before that the stop might get someone killed.

Still, he was not satisfied. He said nothing. He looked down at me several times. He made us all uneasy with his quiet attitude. We never knew just what he did think about the matter.

A fragment killed him the next day. It was from one of our own destroyers shooting at a low-flying plane going between us and the can. The stream of forties from the destroyer killed Naylor while he was standing shoulder to shoulder with the captain. It also wrecked our radar screen.

There was nothing fair about it. Clegge nearly went crazy thinking about it. Old superstition rode him for awhile and he said the devil was on the captain's side; and then he changed his mind and cursed our luck. He had jerked the film from his nose. Around his eyes the flesh was a filthy yellow color. He looked like a brute.

Without radar we were worthless on the picket line. Our sound head was also wrecked, knocked out when we ran over our own hedgehog charges on the way to Okinawa; and so we were ordered down to Manus for repairs. There Clegge had some more chiseling done on his nose. Ugly as sin to start with, he was something to give a man a nightmare. The ugliness had seeped deep into him, too, for when he returned from the hospital at Manus he said it was our bounden duty to see that the captain did not last out the war.

"We're all deep into it now," he told a group of us, "and by God we're going through with it. When a man like Naylor gets it and a bastard like the captain ain't touched, there's something wrong. We're going to change it."

We did not go back to Okinawa. We did some convoy work to Borneo, and then we went back to the Philippines. It was at San Fernando that Clegge came up with another idea, a very tricky one that no one liked.

All over the harbor natives in outrigger canoes were using Jap hand grenades to stun fish. For two packs of cigarettes I got a grenade from a bum boat. Then we had to wait until the right boat crew had the duty, a crew that included Reese Duckett as cox'n. He was North Carolinian, and Muirhead had been a good friend of his.

Grenades were making hard chugging sounds around a dozen canoes the day the right boat crew started ashore with the captain in the whaleboat. There were plenty of us who watched from the *Foraker*.

Duckett put the boat between two outriggers. Standing at the rudder behind the captain, Duckett reached under his shirt. He activated the grenade and then he leaned down behind the captain. A few moments later he rang the bell for *stop*. He yelled, "Abandon the boat!"

The crew did not question Duckett's judgment, although the bow hook, who was a poor swimmer, hesitated until Duckett yelled again. The crew went over the side. Swimming away from the boat, Duckett shouted again, "Jump out, sir! Grenade!"

The captain stood up. He began to look in the bottom of the drifting boat. By then he should have been blown clear out of it, but nothing happened.

The damned grenade was a dud.

When the captain found it, instead of heaving it as far as he could, he took it ashore with him to show the beach commander. He cursed the natives for their carelessness, and shortly thereafter the beach command put a stop to fishing with grenades.

Clegge could not sleep that night. Once more he said the devil was on the captain's side; and then in the next breath he said the captain's luck could not hold out forever. "We'll get him," he said. "I know we will!"

But we didn't. The war ended, and the captain was as alive and nasty as ever. I had enough of it by then. The war was over, we would be going home soon, so let everything be forgotten.

"No!" Clegge said. "Jack is still dead, ain't he?"

The *Foraker* was one of the first ships to go home. We came into the destroyer base at San Diego. At once we began to gulp up peace in large chunks. The guns rusted and nobody cared. The captain was no problem now. He was drunk every night and gone from the ship most of the day.

It happened one night when Clegge and I borrowed a car from a chief at the base and went out to slice a fat hog. We wound up with two women in the skyroom of a hotel.

This skyroom, with a long bar and tables in an alcove at one side, was full of officers, including a beefy marine major who was trying to start something with two navy ensigns. The lads were not suckering; they grinned at the major and walked out, which left him standing there as mad as a bull with a sore nose.

Just then the captain came in with a girl. He was wearing a new uniform with shining campaign bars. Clegge cursed. "He ought to have a silver star for Jack." His eyes squinted down, and his brain began to grind away once more on the problem of the captain.

"Let's get out of here," I said.

Clegge shook his head.

There were no empty tables and no vacant stools. The captain and the girl came down the bar toward us and stopped at the turn of the horseshoe, standing to order their drinks. I saw then that the captain was about three sheets in the wind. In a moment the marine major made another try for trouble.

He tapped the captain on the shoulder, smiling. "Not that it matters, Commander, but how many admirals' wives did you sleep with to get all the salad?"

The captain turned around. He drew himself up as if dealing out a mast to a seaman second. "You're a disgrace to your uniform, Major!"

The major laughed. He stepped on the captain's feet and flipped his tie from his shirt. "Pardon me all to hell, sonny." He began to stuff the tie back, in the process tightening it so hard the captain's face turned red.

Clegge got up and half dragged me over to the bar with him. "Can we take you some place, sir?" he asked the captain, most politely.

"Two more of the dirty bastards that ran out at the Canal," the major said. He tried to shove Clegge away. He'd just as well have pushed against the wall.

''Can we help you, sir?'' Clegge asked, still giving that big ugly grin.

A marine captain and a gray-haired woman came over when trouble was set. They sort of surrounded the major, talking to him, tugging at him. His name was Ken. They finally led him away. It was all noise and drunkenness and it created very little stir in that room.

''I—uh—a little air would't hurt,'' the captain said.

''We'll be right back,'' Clegge told the girl.

I looked over at our table. Two ensigns who could hardly walk were moving in on the women we'd left there. Folks were really living that night in the skyroom. On the way to the elevator there was Ken once more.

''Just a minute, you swab jockeys, all three of you!''

Clegge pushed him aside. The major cursed. The marine captain grabbed his arms and nodded for us to get the hell out of the place. When we hit the lobby the captain was really sagging. At the time I doubted that he knew us. We put him in the back seat of the car. He grunted and flopped over on his side and that was it.

Before we got in ourselves Ken showed up. ''You clowns sort of got out of line, didn't you?''

''Beat it,'' Clegge said.

The major hit Clegge in the face. I heard the scrambled mess of bones in Clegge's nose break all over again as he fell on the hood of the car. I hit the major twice and then I was flat in the street. From where I lay I saw a big bloody face move in toward the major. There was a smack and a grunt and the major was down.

He got up. He got up too many times before Clegge and I saw that he was done for the evening. We had about enough steam left to crawl into the car. The captain was snoring.

Clegge groaned. ''They'll put that damned film in my nose again!''

We drove down the hill.

''What do we want with him?'' I asked, nodding toward the back seat.

Clegge was driving with one hand. The other was holding a handkerchief to his nose. ''I'll show you.''

''No you won't. We're taking him downtown and dumping him some place.''

Clegge did not say anything. When I knew for sure we were on the road to Tijuana, I turned off the ignition. He hit me before I got the key out, and that was all for a while.

We were bumping up a sandy gulch when I came out of it. It felt as if one side of my jaw were numb. The mixed drinks I had taken did not help matters any. In spite of all the jouncing and the straining of the car the captain was still snoring.

Clegge stopped the car. He got out and kicked a dirt bank. For a moment he stood there in the headlights, feeling his nose. I felt in the glove compartment. There was a flashlight, but it didn't carry weight enough to suit me. Clegge came back to the car and opened the back door.

I got out and said, "Now wait a minute, Clegge."

He started to drag the captain out.

I hit him under the ear as hard as I could. He fell against the car door. "What the hell?" he said.

Once more I hit him. He got the idea then, and then he was mad. I had to beat him because I was afraid of him; and there was nothing to do it with except my hands. He was sore but I was deathly afraid, and so I finally got him.

He was a terrible weight to put into the car. When I tried to turn I got stuck in the sand. By the time I got back to the highway I was shaky and sweating. It did not take long to get back to San Diego.

Clegge came out of it when I almost turned over on a curve. Liberty parties were coming back from Tijuana then and the highway was full of screaming engines.

"What did you do it for?" Clegge asked.

"You damned fool! This is the United States we're in. You were Asiatic!"

"I still am, about him."

I stopped in front of the U.S. Grant Hotel. It was my idea to lay the captain on the curb and let the S.P.s have him. But he sat up when I opened the back door. He got out by himself, weaving a little as he straightened his uniform. He gave us both a bleary but comprehensive look. He knew our names all right then.

"You're a disgrace to your uniforms," he said.

We must have been. We were bloody and battered and smeared with sand. We had lost our neckerchiefs and our hats.

The captain said, "Report back to the ship within forty minutes!" He looked at his watch, and then he started the long walk under the canopy. He was walking straight, brushing at his clothes.

"You're real smart," Clegge said to me. "We're really going to get drunk now."

Sometime during the night we smashed the grille of the car. Clegge said it was the captain's fault. When we started into the base the next morning just before liberty expired, the marine sentries eyed us sourly. They searched us for contraband and started to let us pass.

And then the captain came bouncing along, with only a redness of eye to show for the night. "At 0300 I ordered you men back to the ship."

"Your men, sir?" one of the sentries asked.

"Yes, I'm ashamed to say."

Clegge stepped toward the captain. The sentry barred the way and grabbed Clegge's arm. That started it. We were holding our own until a jeep pulled up at the gate with the officer of the guard.

We got out of the brig the day before the captain left the ship for the last time, on his way to discharge. Clegge went out on the pier, walking all around the pile of addressed gear. And then, uglier than ever as he smiled, he talked to the captain for a few moments. Clegge was still smiling when he came aboard.

We went to the bow and watched the captain walk up the pier, slowly at first, as if he intended to turn and come back. And then he walked faster, looking back at us over his shoulder for a while.

"What did you tell him, Clegge?"

"Nothing. I just asked him if he thought that grenade and one or two other things was accidents."

"What did he say?"

"He blinked and turned sort of green."

"Clegge, for Christ's sake, let's forget all about everything!"

"Sure, that's what I told him."

"You didn't mean it, though!"

"Sure I did." Clegge was smiling at the captain's back. "Look at him, twisting around to see what's behind him. He ain't got anything to be afraid of, has he?"

Clegge laughed.

If I were the captain I would always be looking behind me for the big, ruined face of a man who will never forget what happened to Jack Muirhead.

ROBERT EDMOND ALTER

The Exile

IT WASN'T A VERY serious crime—getting three amorous Kanaka girls gay on square-face gin; inciting a near riot in the market place; insulting trader Vogel's wife; and giving the Resident Commissioner's best constable a bloody nose. But in the RC's angry eye it was worthy of deportation. The trouble was, he had no means of expelling the culprit. The schooner from Port Moresby was not due for a month, and the steamer from Sydney for seven weeks. The RC's sigh reminded one of a stubby steam kettle about to fulminate. He looked up at John Roke who was standing unconcernedly before his desk.

The remittance man was not picturesque, not even noteworthy. A short man, and spare—birdlike. His battered, rusty old suit of white drill hung on his skeletal frame as though it had been dropped there and forgotten. His front uppers protruded generously over his lowers, causing the inevitable cigarette he held in his mouth to hang straight down. His nose was eagled and his eyes indolent, yet when opened wide, they seemed to hold a hint of innocence, which was rather incongruous in a man of his age and breed.

He was one of that bunch that are scattered througout the island world of the Pacific—a derelict man. Living on the doubtful doles from home (but more often on the generosity of the simple Kanakas), he drifted like a rudderless ship, making himself popular with the local natives by entertaining them with his memoirs of the music halls. An *omoo* man—an island-jumper—he was the despair of every RC, but the delight of all Kanakas, half of them referring to him as "brother-in-law."

"Roke," the RC said huskily, "your conduct is abominable. I shan't be saddled with it a moment longer."

The remittance man stirred, his opening eyes suggesting he was deeply shocked to think *he* might be the cause of anyone's unhappiness. " 'Ere, Guv," he said quietly, "it wasn't that bad by 'arf."

The RC tapped a list of charges impatiently. "It states here that you contributed to the delinquency of three Kanaka females."

"Why, Guv, those girls 'ave been drinking *kava* since they was ten. All I did was give 'em a drop of square-face. A sort of celebration, you might say, on the delayed arrival of my dole from 'ome."

The RC ignored the explanation. "It states that they held a drunken brawl among themselves over you—"

"Two of 'em thought they was married to me," Roke murmured sadly.

"—and when Mrs. Vogel complained to you about the disorder, *you* called her a 'fat sow.' And further, when Mr. Vogel came from his store to reprimand you, *you* pushed him bodily into a rattan fish basket. And further, when the constable came to arrest you, *you* hit him in the eye with your fist."

"I think it was his nose," Roke offered helpfully. He scratched the left corner of his mouth and looked apologetic.

The RC slammed his hand flat on the list of charges. "I won't tolerate it!" he cried. "You're a disgrace to the island community. If I could throw you in the lockup, I would."

Both men were silent for a stony moment, both understanding the embarrassing situation. The local jail was small and used only for Kanakas; it wouldn't do to put a white man among them. Roke once more scratched at the corner of his mouth.

"It's a problem all right," he said sympathetically. "Suppose you could send me down to Tulagi in your launch—except that the RC there said he'd dynamite his harbor before he'd let me land again."

The RC said nothing to this. He half turned in his chair and looked at the wall map of the Coral Sea, studying the confines of his own district. After a while, a sort of a warm glimmer came into his eye.

"Roke, I'm going to exile you for three months on Babaul."

Roke elevated both eyebrows dramatically. "'Ere, that's kind of 'ard on me, Guv. That isle's all rock. And you can't even find two goony birds that'll set up 'ousekeeping out there."

The RC nodded. He had the look of a man well satisfied. "Keep you out of trouble that way," he said. "Three months, Roke." He seemed to relish his words. "No gin, no wenches, no market brawls—"

"Easy on the 'ard names, Bishop. No need to carry on with the sermon. Sound like my old dad, you do. But look 'ere—I'll need a gun out there. Say one of those Lee-Enfields you've got. Babaul is too close to Andomi for comfort. You know those Andomi Kanakas, Guv. If they know there's a man alone on Babaul, they'll be out for my 'ead within an hour."

"Now really, Roke. You can't expect me to furnish you with—"

"You don't want to come out there and find me waiting for you with no 'ead, now do you Guv? Look bad in your report, it would," he mused.

The RC's sigh was bone-weary. "Oh, very well," he said testily.

Roke smiled and put a finger to his brow in a sort of salute. "Sporting of you, Guv. Oh, and one other favor. When those three girls come inquiring after me, tell Balatta—she's the tallest—I'm *not* married to her, and tell Suzy—I call 'er that after a girl I once new in Soho—that . . ."

"Clear out of here!" the RC shouted.

Alone, the RC sighed a final time, and in a precise hand, wrote down the date after Roke's sentence: *December 6, 1941*.

The news was old by the time Roke received it, and it came by accident.

The constabulary had landed him on Babaul on the morning of the seventh, had handed him the rifle, a bandoleer of ammo, six cases of canned goods and a can opener, two blankets, and a tarpaulin tent.

Roke stood on the damp beach, hands in pockets, and looked at his supplies with a contemplative eye. "I say, old man," he said to the Kanaka constable, whose nose he'd lumped two days earlier, "you couldn't spare a chap a fishhook."

The constable grinned, handed him a box of kitchen matches instead, and gave the order to put the launch in reverse.

"Thought not," Roke murmured blithely.

He gave them a good-natured wave as the launch ran the shallow coral pass, and then found himself standing alone in the complete silence of mid-ocean solitude.

"Proper Crusoe I am," he said to the nothingness. Then he put a cigarette in his mouth and wasted one of his kitchen matches on it. After that, he shifted his supplies up to a rift in the hillside and set up his tent under a kauri tree. As he worked, he hummed a song he'd learned as a small boy in the Liverpool streets.

> 'Ere we go round the mulberry bush on a cowld and frosty mornin'.
> This is the wy the tyler does, the tyler does . . .

His camp established, Roke treated himself to a cold can of beans. Then, in the early evening, he returned to the lagoon to look his domain over.

In no sense of the term could Babaul be considered a tropical paradise. Small and irregular in size, it humped barren and stark in the center, dead and brittle-looking because of its volcanic origin. Only where its dry slopes met the coralline beach could there be found a spattering of palms, kauris, pisonias, and pandanus. The reef, a treacherous affair to any deep-hulled craft, swung out to leeward and continued on down a chain of rocky islets for two miles. Beyond that was blank sea.

Roke said, "Tsk," and went back to his camp. He curled up in his blankets inside the tent and sang himself to sleep with a song from the distant music halls he'd once known and loved:

> We're looking for a 'appy land where everything is bright, Where the 'angouts grow on bushes and we sty out every night.

On his second day, he discovered a pandan hut on the west end of the island. Sagging at the seams, woebegone-looking and ready for utter collapse, it squatted forlornly in a small pisonia grove. So low was the doorway, Roke could enter only on all fours.

The first thing he saw was the white bones of a long skeleton neatly arranged on the sand. " 'Ello!" he muttered. "You've 'ad a spot of rum luck, old man."

From the complete absence of clothing, Roke decided that the deceased had been a Kanaka—probably an *omoo* man like himself. Squatting on his haunches, he held a moment's eerie communion with the silent stranger.

"Poor old chap. Crawled in 'ere to die of something all by your lonesome. Then the land crabs came and tidied you up proper. None of your ribs stove in, and your pate's still in one piece. What did it to you, mate? The dengue? Old age? Wonder if it's catching?"

The Kanaka's belongings were few: a sack of trade beads, three fishhooks, some line, four old Snider cartridges, a small, sealed glass jar containing a pale fluid, eleven peculiarly short arrows, and a six-foot length of bamboo.

The arrows were made of hard wood. Affixed to each end was a pointed fishbone, sharp, but not barbed. None of the arrows were feathered or grooved for a bow-string. The tip of each bone was discolored. Roke touched the bamboo stick.

"Oh. This is a *sumpitan*—a Malayan blowgun."

He uncapped the jar of pale liquid, sniffed at it suspiciously, then looked at the dead man again. "I'm afraid you were up to no good, old top. This 'ere goo is the juice of the upas tree. It's poison. Maybe you accidental-like pierced yourself on your own medicine."

He took all the Kanaka's effects away with him, and never returned to the hut again. The *sumpitan* and fishing gear he called "proper treasures." After that, he went fishing in the lagoon every morning, and in the long afternoon, he'd practice blowing arrows at the kauris.

It wasn't an active life, but one well suited to his personality. The only thing he really missed was the square-face gin. And when it came to thinking of the Kanaka wenches, Roke would shrug stoically, put his hands in his pockets, and take a long healthy walk, humming:

> "I knew a lydy, her nyme was Sydy, She used to dance at the old by-ooo!"

And the days shuttled by in starry black and bleached white, and late in January, a handful of Kanakas entered the lagoon in a kula outrigger. They brought with them the news of the war.

All of them were semi-civilized boat boys from New Britain. They had thrown over their jobs and were traveling post haste to their homes on Buka, because "plenty little fella Jap come along water, stop altogether. That fella shoot'm all fella Kanaka, shoot'm all big fella white man. Allatime he walkabout—*bang, bang, bang!*"

"You mean war?" Roke cried. "The Nips have declared war on us?"

He stood with the beer-colored water to his knees and scratched at the corner of his mouth, lost in startled wonder. " 'Ere!" he called finally. "I've got to get off this perishin' rock if I'm to do my bit. Put in and tyke me off, *'arry my*."

But none of them knew him as "brother-in-law." And what made it worse, they'd heard that the RC had ordered Babaul out-of-bounds, or *tambo,* for three months. They struck out for the pass as though both Roke and his island were contaminated with leprosy.

The translucent water sloshing his pants, his hands hanging uselessly at his sides, Roke stared at the empty sea, a look of hurt bewilderment in his eyes. "Well," he whispered wistfully, "how am I to do my bit? And me stuck on this bleedin' rock!"

And the days and nights began to cripple by in a manner so slow, it was painful, like a paraplegic learning to stagger-walk from one end of a long hall to another. Roke didn't fish as much now, and his *sumpitan* practice tapered off. He wandered along the lagoon. He waded across the reef beds at ebb tide, looking at the sea. He climbed Babaul's volcanic hump and looked at the sea, and he went down to the windward shore and looked at the sea again. And each night, he would toss another small pebble in an empty tomato can, and each can would represent a week.

And it went on like that until the afternoon of the eighty-seventh day.

He was sitting on a ledge halfway up the hill, watching the sea—and then he saw the sub limping toward the island. It was lagging along on the surface, as graceless as a tugboat straggling back to its harbor berth, but to Roke it looked like the Queen Mary.

He stood up, feeling greatly honored. "Hi!" he crowed. "They've sent the bloomin' nyvy after me, they 'ave. And three days early at that!"

The flood was on the reef; the sub commander had timed his arrival perfectly. The boat chugged through the pass and drifted into the lagoon hush. Roke started to scramble down the hill to the beach, but turned back suddenly and looked at the sub again, frowning. Something was wrong, very wrong.

She was small—too small for the British. She carried a popgun on her forward deck, and the conning-tower platform was roofed, though open at the sides. But her periscopes were out of whack and the snorkel had been sheared off close to the top of the tower. The real trouble, however, was on the after deck. The deck-plating had been peeled back, exposing an ugly, jagged wound.

"Blimy!" Roke breathed. "She's been in a tiff with someone. A plane or gunboat would've done for 'er. Must 'ave been an armed merchantman."

Little antlike men were scrambling from the gun hatch and tower, moving aft to the shell hole. Roke scratched his mouth reflectively.

"She can't submerge with that 'ole in 'er. And even if she could, she'd be blind with her glims out. But those little devils are 'andy; they'll ship 'er in shape in a day or two, and then she'll be off, looking for more mischief." He grunted and made a wry face.

"I could just sit 'ere cozy and quiet, and they'd never know the difference. They'd go off without a 'good day' between us—" He glowered again at the distant sub. "After all, what can one man do?"

He didn't answer himself. He knew that one man might be able to detain the sub long enough for the launch to reach the island. Not that the launch could do much, but it would get the picture and run for help.

"Oh, 'ell," Roke growled.

He crawled down the hill, keeping under cover, and slipped into his camp for the Lee-Enfield and bandoleer. *Should have known better than to expect the Guv to send for me three days early,* he thought. *It ain't in his nature.*

The sun was sinking like a tired, golden-whiskered old man under the navy-blue blanket of the western sea when Roke took up a position in the rocks fronting the lagoon. He estimated the distance at two hundred yards, set his sight, and placed one of the Japanese seamen directly in the sight notch.

The trajectory of the first bullet was too high. All it did was interrupt the work party, bringing them to a crouching suspension. Roke could see an officer up in the conning tower pointing at them, shouting something. He made a correction in his elevation and fired again.

A crouching seaman toppled toward portside, raised a hand, then let it fall. The rest of the party dropped their tools and scrabbled for the gun hatch. The high sing-song voice of the officer ripped after them, and Roke had to grin.

The gun crew was piling onto the forward deck. He put three fast shots into them, scattering them for cover, except for one Japanese who sat down abruptly and clutched his right ankle. Roke could tell from the insane yakitty-yak issuing from the tower that the officer was having a bit of a merry fit.

"Temper, temper," he admonished softly.

They were up to something on the tower, but he couldn't make out what. A moment later, the basalt cliff on his left began to spit rock chips; then he heard the angry *chat-chat-chat* of a heavy machine gun. He drew a bead on the covered deck and rapid-fired three more shots. There was a hesitant pause, then the sand before his shelter began to spurt, one spurt following another, running an irregular pattern.

"Spotted me that time," he said.

He crawled off among the rocks, found fresh cover, reloaded the Lee-Enfield, and looked out at the sub. The light was failing, but it was better for him than it was for them; he was a much smaller target. The gun crew was unlimbering the popgun. It belched a flat *blam* straight at the island.

His former rock fort flew apart, and Roke dug face-into-sand as chunks and shards of basalt went *zip* over the beach. He remained as he was, letting them enjoy themselves with the popgun. They put four shells in the same spot, and Roke muttered, ''Going to punch a ruddy 'ole clear through the island.''

Then the sea swept up the gunfire and there was silence.

Roke peered over the rock. The Japs were launching a large rubber raft, manning it with six seamen. ''Oh-oh!'' he said to himself. '' 'Anky panky.''

He let them draw ten yards from the sub before he opened fire.

The confusion in the small raft was chaotic. One man stood up and went overboard in a backward dive, his hands neatly pressed to his chest. Another folded at the middle, his head swinging down as if to see what his feet were about. A third jumped deliberately into the lagoon, while the three that remained scrabbled wildly in the raft on hands and knees, trying to man the paddles. The raft jerked one way, then another, and finally skittered around in a loose circle.

Black night crowded in as the raft returned to the sub.

Roke decided to call it a day. He broke camp, hiding his gear in the bush, took a can of beans and the can opener, the rifle, and a blanket, and went up the hill to his lookout ledge. There, under the glowing Southern Cross, he bedded himself down for the night.

''Up in a balloon, boys,'' he hummed. ''Up in a balloon. Up among the little stars, all around the moon.''

The Japanese were back at it the next morning, banging and clanging away at the torn skin of their sub. Roke selected a new position among the rocks and opened fire on them again.

Their reply was overwhelming. They cut loose at the island with machine gun and shells. ''Everything but the perishing torpedoes,'' Roke said. They kept him pinned down for the better part of two hours. Every so often, he'd get a shot or two in at the work party, and then the sub would rake the beach. Twice he was nicked by flying rock, once by shrapnel.

Toward noon, he managed to slip down to a coral break that jutted into the lagoon like a damp, purple slag heap, and for a moment, he had the work party right where he wanted them. He cleared the deck with five shots, hitting one of them so hard the man went overboard as though yanked by a line from the lagoon. Then the sub commenced to chop up the coral. Roke scampered back across the beach, sand spurting all around him.

In the late afternoon, the Japanese decided that they would attempt another *tour de force*.

They launched two rafts and boarded them with twelve armed men apiece. Then they started for the shore.

"Uh-uh," Roke grunted uneasily. "Going to 'it me with the grand slam, eh?" He leveled the Lee-Enfield, taking a sight on the foremost raft. "Get gay with me, my lads, and I'll teach you what for." He opened fire, emptying the magazine into the seamen.

For a vivid moment, the men in the raft seemed to have gone mad. The raft stopped dead and everything was arms and legs, kicking and flaying the air and each other, and bodies tumbling into the water.

Roke grinned savagely, watching the results, and reached for the bandoleer. His trembling fingers pick-picked through the empty pouches, coming finally to the last one. Four bullets.

Cold death shouldered into the rock crevice with Roke and looked him square in the face. He straightened up slowly and scratched at the corner of his mouth. He didn't like what he'd just seen. He had never seen it that close before, and never that personal.

" 'Ere's a do," he muttered. "Oh, I'm a proper soldier, I am, expending my bullets like I 'ad the market on 'em."

The second raft had passed the first. It was coming fast.

Roke made a face and went at the bush in a running crouch. He unearthed the *sumpitan*, the eleven little arrows, and the jar of upas juice. Then he dodged back through the coral rifts and secured himself in a tight little niche facing the lagoon.

The first raft was ten yards from shore; the second, only three men paddling, was tagging along in its wake. Roke sat on the sand, his back against coral, put his legs straight out and cocked his feet on a niggerhead, on a plane with is head. He dipped an arrow in the jar, inserted it in the blow gun, rested the firing end of the *sumpitan* in the notch between his feet and placed the other end in his mouth.

The first raft was in the shallows. A stocky seaman, armed with bayoneted rifle, stepped over the side and started slogging toward the beach. Roke sucked in air and exhaled. The little arrow went *ssswit* in the air.

The seaman stopped short, his almond eyes extending. He seemed puzzled. He came two or three steps from the water, then looked down at his chest. He raised his hand and jerked the arrow out, giving it a bewildered look. Suddenly he dropped his rifle, and then he was down in the damp sand, mouth wide open, kicking and screaming in bewildered pain.

Roke had the *sumpitan* loaded again. He spat out another arrow and quickly followed it with two more. The light was poor; the Japanese couldn't see, couldn't hear what was hitting them. A seaman in the raft was clawing at his face, making a wet, gurgling sound in his throat. Another pitched overboard and thrashed on the surface like a shark on a hook, and sank in a boil of bubbles.

Roke spat out arrows as quickly as he could dip, load, blow. When all eleven were gone he grabbed the Lee-Enfield.

But it wasn't necessary. Both rafts were backwatering in sing-song panic. The *sumpitan* had cleared the beach.

When the shield of night settled quietly over Babaul, Roke went down to the shore and secured the dead man's rifle. It was a long, heavy, clumsy affair and contained only eight bullets. He went through the seaman's pockets very carefully but came up with a negative.

"Twelve perishin' shells between me an' eternity," he muttered.

He tried to be flippant about the situation. He shouldered both rifles and walked jauntily up the beach. "Twelve dead Nips, and then one dead Henglishman." But it didn't really work. He hadn't felt quite so abandoned since the day his exasperated dad had said, "Go west, me lad—and don't come back."

They came for him in the night, though it was long past midnight before they infiltrated the kauri woods at the foot of his hill. They didn't take him by surprise because he'd been watching them search the beach in the moonlight for hours. Now they were under cover somewhere below him, and he knew they were studying the shadowy crevices of the cliff face, trying to determine the position of his hide-hold. And they probably would—soon, Roke was fairly certain.

He was lying prone on the ledge, holding the Japanese rifle. The cliff loomed behind him, rising to the summit far above. There was a precariously narrow foot trail leading from the woods up to his ledge, and he kept his eyes constantly on it, and then he waited.

He didn't blame them. After all, he'd been sniping them for two days, and now it was their turn. "Fair's fair," he concluded wistfully.

Then he shut up and shifted into firing position. It was starting. One-two-three dark blurs left the greater blur of the woods and attached themselves to the side of the hill. He could see them coming up the trail—very slowly, very cautiously.

Roke cut loose—*ba-lam ba-lam*—and saw the first man somersault into the darkness, and shifted his sights to the next. But right then, the black woods started winking bright stabs of light. The bullets whocked the rock like angry slaps, and he winced back, hoping that he wouldn't be smacked by the flying rock.

Then a light machine gun opened up, going *bop-bop, bopbopbop,* and someone lobbed a grenade that fell short by forty-feet and went *plow!* with a great mushroom of flame.

"Easy over the stones, boys," Roke muttered softly.

He came up in a crouch and whacked out two more shots at the men on the trail. But there were more of them now—a string of them. He busted up the head of the procession and ducked as the machine gun began jumping rock splinters almost right over his head.

When he looked again, he saw the trail was clear, and that made him feel pretty good. They'd had enough of that for a moment. He waited, hearing them arguing below him. Every so often, a rifle would snipe at him hopefully, and twice, the machine gun gave him some lip service. "Just for the hell of it," Roke said to himself, and he began to grin.

Then he dropped the grin. They were starting up the trail again, and their comrades in the woods were giving them cover with rapid fire. Bullets slapping, rock chips whirring, Roke managed to get a shot off, hitting the lead man on the trail, causing a momentary mix-up. Then one of them yelled, "*Banzai!*" and some others picked it up, and they started to rush Roke's ledge.

Roke emptied the rifle on them and then grabbed for the Lee-Enfield, saying, "Let's break this up, boys." But he could hear the note of desperation in his voice, and he knew he was downright scared, and wished wholeheartedly that he'd gone into the garage business with his dad. "Should 'ave 'ad more spankings in my youth and less preaching," he decided.

It cost him three more bullets to chase the invaders back down the hill. Then he rolled over on his back and looked up at the stars, while the machine gun went to work again on his ledge. And he thought about his last bullet.

He had lived long enough among savages and Orientals to know just what to expect from the Imperial Navy when they finally got their hands on him. And it was a mighty bleak picture. On the other hand, a man could do a tidy job on himself with one bullet and save himself no end of painful grief. But Roke was of the breed who considered that suicide was pretty much analogous to insanity.

"Oh, I've done fool things in my time," he ventured. "But no one's ever said I was *that* mad."

He decided to save the last bullet for the Imperial Navy.

The moon was now trundling off for the west, and shortly, a glossy new sun would be cracking over the Coral Sea, and that would be that. *Either they'll try to take me with another rush, or they'll pull back and blow me out of 'ere with that popgun on the sub.* So when he stopped to think about it, he really didn't have any decision to make. He could just relax and let them decide what was to be done.

"Oh, I've tyken my fun where I've found it; I've rogued an' I've ranged in my time . . . " he hummed reflectively.

It hadn't been a bad life, by and large. He'd been places, seen things, known some nice women, some nice men, and some of both who hadn't been so nice. And if he had made a few enemies along the line, he imagined he would have made just as many had he spent his life back in Liverpool in the garage.

"So I 'ave no kick coming. Might as well be this way as live to be old and tired and lame and sit in a chair all day nursing my aches and pains."

He flopped over on his stomach and peered down at the trail. Empty. "Off drinking saki, like as not," he said. "Could use a drop of bottle courage myself. Some nice, strong Irish, maybe, or a few drams of Scotch."

But it was awfully quiet suddenly. The machine gun hadn't bopped at him in . . . well, how long had it been? He looked toward the west and saw that the sun was lifting the nightlid from the sea with a great blazing sword blade.

Then he heard a whistle blow; a frantic piping in the morning hush, and it was coming from the little sub away down there in the lagoon. Roke did something sour with his mouth. *Calling them back,* he said. *So they're going to popgun me after all.*

Yes, he could see the tiny Jap seamen fussing around the forward gun; could see the two life rafts putting off from the shore and hurrying toward the sub. And now he could see that the sub was starting, very slowly, to move.

"Going to work 'er in closer," Roke said, "for a nice 'ard-by lambasting shot." He picked up the Lee-Enfield with determination and bolted the last cartridge home with a stubborn air.

"You didn't think I was going to sit 'ere and take it, did you?" he inquired. "A lark's a lark, but do you see any green in my eye?"

He stood up and stepped over to the narrow trail. If this was what they wanted—to flush him from his hole; if they had left a sniper down in the woods to wait for him . . . well, then the game was over and the best shot might just as damn well pick up the trick.

Then he started down the trail, holding his breath, waiting for the sniper's shot.

But he stalled suddenly and gawped at the sub. It was making a wild dash for the coral pass.

" 'Ere," Roke wondered. "What in hell's the giddy gyme now?" Then he looked out at the sea.

A British gunboat was coming at the island like a runaway dreadnought, and it didn't wait for the sub to clear the pass before it opened fire. Quick on her helm, she came tearing round in a wide sweep, lobbing three-pound shells with the perky aloofness of a rich lady going down the street dropping pennies on madly scrambling urchins.

The clumsy sub had no show at all. Shell after shell peppered its thin plating, each missile two pounds of whizzing metal and one pound of H.E.

Roke, who had been standing on the ledge, watched the torn-up little sub take its last dive, and gave his late enemies a word in passing.

"We all got to pay the piper, boys," he said quietly.

He shouldered his rifle and went on down the hill.

Two bluejackets rowed him out to the gunboat, and a tired-eyed skipper in a mildly jubilant mood gave him a hand aboard.

"Mr. Roke?" he asked him. "John Roke? The RC asked me to put in and take you off."

"Crikey," Roke said, "what's gone wrong? It's a whole day ahead of time. Is the RC sick?" The skipper looked at him somewhat peculiarly for Roke looked genuinely distressed.

"No, no. I understand that a letter has arrived for you from home, and the RC desired that it be delivered to you personally—immediately."

Roke slapped his hands gleefully, almost like a child. " 'Ere, this is something like! Must be my quarter dole."

Then an alarming thought struck him. " 'Old 'ard a mo. It's not natural for the RC to be that concerned over my welfare. Are you sure there's nothing wrong with the man?"

The skipper made a wry face. "I'm afraid it's not your remittance, Mr. Roke. It's from the War Office. They're calling you up, old chap."

Roke scratched at the corner of his mouth, then grinned and gave a vigorous nod of satisfaction.

"That's more like it," he siad. "Thought for a moment there the Guv 'ad gone of 'is chump."

GEORGE P. MORRILL

Act of Honor

IT WAS ONE of those freak reunions. They happen all the time in the big marble foyer of the New York Port Authority. A massive man in a blue uniform came through the glass door. I was on my way out. I stopped. I put out my hand.

"Hello, Captain von Richter," I said.

His face was the same. Broad-fleshed, red as beef. His jowls a little heavier, perhaps. He still had that innocent Saint-Bernard-dog look that had won him the title of the Boy Skipper on the old Hamburg Line before World War II.

He pumped my hand, grinning. "Is that Fred Callagan, the old college boy?" he said, his voice still thick with the guttural German accent that was so familiar.

Half an hour later, we sat in the Mariner's Loft, a sailors' oasis near Bowling Green. A waiter served ruby-colored wine.

I nodded at the gold stripes on von Richter's sleeve. "I see they didn't sack you for losing the *Black Forest,* Captain."

"Did you think they would?"

"No."

He looked out the window. The harbor lights had come on. A ferry steamed toward Staten Island, glowing like a jewel box.

"Long time ago," he said.

We sat there. *Nineteen . . . no, twenty years ago.* I studied von Richter's face. There was nothing there that I could read—only the heavy Teutonic jaw and the blue, twinkling eyes. There was strength and friendliness in his silence, however. *He's no different*, I thought.

I said, "I've often wondered if you had any—ah—*influence* on the way things came out, Captain."

He stiffened. "I would purposely lose my ship? You think that?"

I drank my wine. All at once the years melted away. I was standing on the rust-pocked deck of the old *Glasgow Queen* in Valparaiso harbor, Chile. It was September, 1939. The news of Germany's attack on Poland had just come down from the radio shack. . . .

I leaned forward. "Remember Captain John Gleason of the *Queen*?"

Von Richter broke into a smile. He raised his glass. "Here's to that little mouse. I forget him when I forget my mother's stick against my backsides."

He was a dried-up nubbin of a man, Captain John Gleason was. Five-and-a-half feet of prickly Scotsman. He had crumply white hair under his blue officer's hat. One of his eccentricities (he had many) was that he despised formal education. Another was that he often wore kilts instead of pants. He liked chess, black cigars—and independence.

"Mister Yankee Doodle?" he barked.

I walked out of the wheelhouse. On the starboard wing, Captain John peered through binoculars at a freighter anchored across Valparaiso harbor.

He spoke through his cigar. "Lower a Jacob's ladder. Von Richter's coming."

I trained my binocs on the vessel, a German tub, the *Black Forest*. She was a sparkler. Her masts were the color of fresh cream. Even her brass doorknobs gleamed like gold. On her afterdeck, the crew was lined up at stiff attention. A thin man with a red swastika on his arm—not von Richter—was haranguing them.

I said, "I don't see Captain von Richter, sir."

"Take the blooming cabbage out of your eye. He's sneaking down the forward ladder. Trying to shake that swine, Schlitt."

Sure enough. The bulky figure of von Richter dropped into a lifeboat manned by Nazi seamen sitting at attention. But at the last minute, the thin man scrambled down the ladder, too.

"Schlitt's coming, sir," I said.

Captain John snapped his cigar in the sea. "My bloody back," he growled.

Captain John had hired me in New York when his regular third mate burst an appendix. At the time, he hadn't known that I was a student at Dartmouth, expelled for a semester for making an explosive stink bomb in the lab. The first inkling he had had that I was a slave to formal scholastics was when he caught me unloading books in my room.

"What goes here, Yank?" he had said.

"Textbooks, sir. I'm studying to be a research chemist."

He had picked up Forbes' *Practical Chemistry*. He had given it a prune-faced stare. "You young birds educate yourselves so you can understand all the clap-trap that people write, so you can pick out what will hurt you the least."

A week later he had borrowed the book from me and had kept it ever since.

The Germans climbed aboard the *Glasgow Queen*. Schlitt, the Nazi ship's "Fuehrer" walked snappily on the bridge, ahead of von Richter. He bowed to Captain John.

"Compliments, *Kapitän*."

He made a speech. The purpose of this visit was friendship. In spite of present international tensions, their great leader wanted world peace. He had ordered German officers to pay respects to British vessels in foreign ports.

"Bloody thoughtful of him" said Captain John.

He ordered Mr. Carruthers, the porky first mate, to guide Herr Schlitt on a tour of the ship. Their footsteps clanged down the ladder. Von Richter leaned forward, his face crimson.

"I must apologize, John. That feller—"

"—is a spy," said Captain John. "He won't find a hell of a lot to report to Berlin here, Von."

He took a chessboard out of his desk. He uncorked a bottle of whiskey.

"I hope there's been some improvement in your queen's knight defense, old chap."

They played chess and drank whiskey. Von Richter relaxed. He loosened his collar. "Like old times, John," he said.

The world was crumbling—but the Scotsman and the German were ancient friends. In Valparaiso, they were known as the Mutt and Jeff of the saltpeter trade. They had bid against each other at stockpile auctions, gone on puma hunts together. Now that von Richter had lost control of his vessel to a tinhorn Hitlerite, Captain John treated him with touching gentleness. He never mentioned the ugly rumors going around the sea lanes—that von Richter's aristocratic family had been wiped out by the Nazis, that von Richter himself was under Gestapo surveillance.

Schlitt returned. He said, "One thing intrigues me, *Kapitän*."

"I can't wait to hear it."

"The forward hold contains the residue of other voyages—machinery, what-not. In Germany we would call that wasteful."

Captain John squinted out his port. Wash cloths fluttered from the *Queen's* rusty foremast. The lady was a tramp. Schlitt's very presence was an insult to the lovable old tart.

"In Britain we call it *abundance*," he said haughtily. . . .

The next day the *Black Forest* moved to the loading quay. Cranes began dumping saltpeter in her holds. Captain John looked, then slammed his hat on the deck.

"I bloody well arrived in this harbor first. This is Schlitt's work."

Indignation flashed around the ship. The news from the radio made the tension worse. Hitler had delivered an ultimatum to Poland . . . the Home Fleet was assembling at Scapa Flow. . . .

"Lower a boat, Yankee Doodle. We'll sink a hook in the commissioner for this."

Valparaiso's streets were hot from the noon sun. Captain John strode to the Chilean Trade Authority, his pipestem legs knocking his red-plaid kilts angrily.

"What's the idee of berthing the *Black Forest* ahead of me?"

The commissioner spread his fat hands. "Herr Schlitt made arrangements by radio."

"Since when was that allowable? Where is the swine?"

It was perfectly legal. As for Herr Schlitt, he had taken some crew members on a tour of the city.

We searched Valparaiso. We rode the open elevators up the steep streets. Below us, the bay twinkled, sapphire-blue. Then I said something which gave me my first glimpse of Captain John's fierce pride in his battered old ship. I pointed to the *Glasgow Queen's* orange-patched hull, then to the *Black Forest's* shiny superstructure.

"We look a bit grubby beside that Kraut job, sir."

Captain John's pink nostrils grew pale.

"I take a damned contrary view of that, Yank," he said.

We found Schlitt's party at Bolivar Beach. Ten big blond youths were flinging a medicine ball around in a circle, while Herr Schlitt, wearing a storm trooper's uniform, directed the exercise.

Captain John scratched a match on his kilts. He lit a cigar. "Asses," he said.

Schiltt ordered his men into the water. He strode over to us. There was a new, scornful curl to his lip.

He said, "Have you heard the news? We are now enemies, *Kapitän*."

Captain John blew a cloud of smoke. "We were enemies the minute you stole my berth, you thieving barracuda."

Schlitt backed up, coughing. "Outside the harbor I teach you a little manners, no?" he shouted.

Great Britain had declared war on Germany. Captain John called a conference of his officers.

He said, "I want a count of all arms on the vessel."

We added up three rifles, the captain's revolver, and an Austrian dueling pistol that Mr. Carruthers had bought in a Valparaiso pawn shop.

Captain John looked at the arsenal belligerantly. "Good. We'll bloody well board Schlitt if we catch him outside a neutral port."

The *Black Forest* finished loading. She steamed out of the harbor, watched by every eye on the *Glasgow Queen*. We moved into her berth. The Chilean dockmaster came aboard and handed Captain John a note. It had three words scrawled on it: *Intern yourself. Please.*

"Von Richter's handwriting," said Captain John.

"Sir, he's trying to warn us of something," I blurted.

He looked at me sourly. "You're a shrewd and penetrating Yankee," he said.

Slowly he tore up the note.

We pulled out, loaded to the marks with Chile saltpeter. Valparaiso faded, like a huge concrete grandstand. We steamed past the palm trees of Punta Gruesa.

The *Black Forest* was anchored a mile offshore. Immediately, she pulled up her hook and followed us into the Pacific.

"What's her game, Yankee Doodle?"

"She's radioing our position to a U-boat," I said.

"Undoubtedly. But I've radioed her position to our boys, too. Look here . . ."

He ran a gnarled finger across the chart. We were moving into the empty waters of the South Pacific. It was doubtful if either England or Germany had armed craft within two thousand miles of us, he said.

"She's behaving strangely, sir," I said.

We turned our binocs on her.

Strangely was right. The Nazi sailors were peeling the canvas off number-two hatch. As we watched, they rigged up a cargo boom. Then they raised the boom.

"Are they opening a *hold*?" said Captain John incredulously.

They were. They began hauling out crates. They piled them in Teutonic order along the deck.

Captain John stroked his stiff, white hair. ''I don't know what's up, but I think we'll leave this territory, Yankee Doodle.''

After sundown, we swung ninety degrees south and put on three extra knots. Half an hour later, the *Black Forest* loomed darkly on our starboard quarter.

''She's tailing us, all right, sir.''

Captain John chewed his cigar. ''Quick thinking, Yank.''

Suddenly a blinker signal flashed on the *Black Forest*:

NO ESCAPE. I HAVE SUPERIOR SPEED. SCHLITT.

Captain John bit his cigar. He had a violent coughing spell. ''T-tell . . . chief to put on . . . a-all speed. I'll show . . . swine some speed.''

The *Queen* leaped ahead . . . sixteen knots . . . seventeen. . . . Captain John had always been proud of her speed. But all at once, smoke rolled from the *Black Forest*'s stack. She came abreast of us, foam flashing at her bows. Then, as our boilers strained every rivet, the *Black Forest* turned a complete circle around us.

Captain John went to his cabin.

We changed course for the Fiji Islands. Captain John's original plan had been to sneak around the Horn and run for England. Now he announced, ''We'll pull Schlitt toward Australia, bit by bit. Then we'll call the Aussie Navy out to nab him.''

Where was the Royal Navy?

Days passed. We sailed into green, tropic waters.

Each morning Captain John stood by the rail and drank his coffee. The *Black Forest*'s mountain of cargo had grown as high as her bridge. Still the winches hissed. . . .

''Radio from Admiralty, sir.''

Captain John read the blue slip. Color drained from his cheeks. He set his cup on the life preserver box unsteadily.

''Yankee Doodle, pray for a storm.''

Pray for a storm. I already had. I had imagined waves crashing over the *Black Forest*, floating off crates . . . pouring in the open hold. I took the blue slip. It said:

IMMEDIATE TO ALL SHIPS PACIFIC AREA. INTELLIGENCE REPORTS ENEMY MERCHANTMEN CARRYING FIVE-INCH GUN BELOW DECKS. CONVERTING TO RAIDERS AT SEA. AVOID CONTACT.

Schlitt had fooled us all. Now the reason for Von Richter's scribbled message was clear. He had wanted us interned in Chile rather than stuck in a German prison—or drowned.

At lunch, Captain John was out of sorts. He snapped at the mess boy. He scowled at his officers.

"We can always scuttle, sir," said Mr. Carruthers.

Captain John's wrinkly cheeks contracted. "I'm contrary-minded to that, mister. I'll ram Schlitt first."

The world news had shaken him. Reports of U-boat sinkings peeped in from the North Atlantic. Poland's disaster grew. The upstart Nazis were striking in all directions, and—shockingly—the mighty British were not striking back.

After dark, we tried to get away once more. We found a fog bank. We swung south in choppy, black waves. The Nazi masts faded out of sight. But in the morning, the fog was gone. A dot on the horizon grew larger. The *Black Forest* pulled abeam of us.

Don't be asinine, signaled Schlitt.

The Germans brought up the five-inch gun. Its mean gray snout dangled from the cargo fall. The *Queen*'s crew prayed for a cable to slip, a boom to crack. The big weapon floated gently down on the deck. German welders started on the gun platform, their torches spitting blue.

"We have twenty hours," said Captain John to the officers assembled before his old-fashioned oak desk, "Isn't there one bloody idee in the lot of ye? Carruthers—you tub of lard—speak up. Yankee Doodle—you smart college baboon—Amurrican citizenship won't save you when the shells start whanging!"

He banged his fist on the desk. A book slid off. He caught it with his knees. It was Forbes' *Practical Chemistry*.

"Are we going to sit . . ." He stopped. His eye fell on an open page. Suddenly he jumped, as if jabbed by a needle. "The manufacture of dynamite," he read aloud.

What followed was fantastic. Captain John went off like a skyrocket. He had an idee, an idee. He waved his skinny arms. He outlined a plan *to attack the Black Forest*. It was utterly mad. But he poked a bony finger on my chest.

"I appoint you head chemist," he howled. "Make dynamite."

"Sir, we need more than Chile saltpeter. Sulphuric acid, glycerin," I protested.

"I got 'em somewhere on this bucket. Carruthers, unload a ton of saltpeter from number four. Chief, see if there's a drum of glycerin in the machine shop."

The ship came alive. Some of Captain John's sparks bounced off on us. I went with him into number-one hold, a catchall for every type of junk. Our flashlights picked out old crates . . . a spare anchor.

"Schlitt would go balmy in a place like this," he said. "What's that?"

A steel carboy lay against the bulkhead. I blew dust from its stencil. *Caution—Sulphuric Acid.*

Captain John did a Highland fling.

We examined the collision bulkhead. It was a huge, steel wall running athwartships from deck to keel. It was built about thirty feet back from the bow. Its purpose was to keep us afloat in case the bow was blown off or punctured.

If Captain John's plan was to work, the collision bulkhead had to hold.

On deck, men lugged pails of yellowish saltpeter. They hoisted a drum of glycerin through the engine-room skylight. The sound of hammers on steel rose from the machine shop. The engineers were hard at work on the crazy rig I had designed for the first step of our process.

"There she be, Yankee Doodle!"

I looked at the rig. The engineers lowered it gingerly beside the pile of saltpeter. It was a cylinder, lined with lead on the inside. The cylinder was encased in planking nearly to its top, sealed watertight. Pipes, valves, vents, and a glass window were stuck on every side of it.

"We attach the fire hose here," said the chief engineer. "Compressor hose here."

"Rube Goldberg would blow his marbles," I said.

"Start mixing," ordered Captain John.

The rig was a "converter." It converted nitric acid and glycerin to nitro-glycerin—we hoped. First, we had to mix sulphuric with the saltpeter to get the nitric acid.

"Watch your skin, boys," I said.

The men wore gloves and gas masks. They dumped the chemicals in a large tub. Smoke curled up.

I read from Forbes' *Practical Chemistry*: "Mix two parts nitric with three parts sulphuric."

It was risky business. The mixture flowed in the cylinder. Grayish fumes swirled behind the glass window. Then the compressor started up, *pum-pum-pum*. Glycerin spurted in. The glass grew warm.

"Water, quick," I ordered.

Cooling water rushed around the lead cylinder. The thermometer stopped at eight-five degrees Fahrenheit.

"Ready to draw off, sir," I said.

Captain John held a glass jug under the pipe. I turned the spigot. *Gluggggggggg*. The jug was full of oily pale-yellow liquid..

"Nitro-glycerin," he said reverently.

By nightfall, twenty jugs of nitro-glycerin sat on bed pillows under the forepeak. Captain John waved at the *Black Forest* and laughed. Schlitt and von Richter stood on the bridge, binoculars turned on us.

"Schlitt would give his storm-trooper pants to know what we're up to."

Sometime after midnight, Schlitt blinked a message:

DEMAND SURRENDER. MY GUN READY BY DAWN.

Captain John sent back:

HAVE YOU SUFFICIENT LIFE JACKETS FOR YOUR CREW?

We took powdery earth from the cook's flower box and mixed nitro-glycerin with it. We packed the black substance in cardboard boxes. Then we knocked off for coffee and saluted King George with upraised mugs. We had done it.

We had made dynamite from our own cargo.

Minutes later, Captain John's voice snarled from the bridge: "Belay that old lady's tea. Set the charge."

We loaded the dynamite in the forepeak, snug against the bow. Mr. Carruthers bolted our three rifles to the deck and ran steel rods from their triggers to the vessel's hull. He plugged the barrels with rags.

He explained, waving his fat hands: "The slightest collision will explode the rifles. Then the dynamite—*boom*!"

A pink dawn rose. Exhausted men lashed bed mattresses on the forward side of the *Queen*'s wheelhouse. Captain John worked with them, his kilts torn and soiled.

The *Black Forest* blinked insolently.

GUN WILL PENETRATE THAT PROTECTION LIKE CHEESE.

"All hands below decks," blazed Captain John. "Carruthers, take the helm. Yank, stand by the telegraph."

We were none too soon. Nazi sailors finished bolting down the five-incher. The big, gray barrel swung around at us. Schlitt signaled:

DO NOT ATTEMPT RADIO OR SCUTTLE. WILL ANNIHILA—

"Hard left!" said Captain John.

The *Queen* heeled over. Through the mattress slits I saw the Nazi gun growing larger . . . larger.

Bam. Something whined past the wheelhouse.

"Steady as she goes, Carruthers," said Captain John with icy calm.

Ka-wrang! The world exploded. I woke up under the gyro-compass. The *Black Forest* loomed through a ragged hole in the bulkhead. Feathers from the mattresses floated in the wheelhouse.

"Duck!" shouted Captain John.

We rammed the *Black Forest* amidships. For a mad second, Schlitt's savage face hung over our deck, yelling through a megaphone. The tiny gold swastikas on his collar winked. Then—*who-o-o-om!*

Our bow blew up. It was like a huge fist punching deep in the *Black Forest*'s guts. The ships heaved up in agony. Metal rained on our protecting mattresses. The vessels fell back, their steel plates grinding.

"Reverse engines, Yank."

My hand pulled the telegraph. Then something slammed me in the head.

I woke up, propped against a lifeboat davit. Down on deck, figures were climbing up a Jacob's ladder. They were German sailors. Our men led them below.

"Stubbed our nose a wee bit, Yank."

Captain John's kilts had been blown to tatters. Mattress feathers stuck in his white hair. He pointed. *Our bow was completely gone*. Tangled steel hung over number-one hatch.

"The collision bulkhead?"

Captain John grinned—a pricky Scot's grin, twisted at the edges. "She's holding. And we kicked a hole in that Kraut aboot the size of Buckingham Palace."

I lay in a canvas deck chair, my head bandaged. Captain John and von Richter hunched over a chess game. Hours behind us floated the oil slick of the sunken *Black Forest*.

Captain John said, "I'm not showing preferential treatment. I keep Schlitt below and you up here for security reasons only."

"Bishop takes the knight," said von Richter, moving his piece.

Their eyes met. A new gentleness came over Captain John. "Why did you let me ram you, Von?"

"You talk foolishness, John."

"I knew you'd be on the right side in a showdown. But I know it was a bloody hard decision. My thanks."

"Bishop takes the knight," said von Richter.

They looked at each other. They were enemies—in nationality. One was headed for a British prison camp. The other for six years of fighting U-boats. But an invisible bond stretched between them like a link of gold.

I sat up. "Sir, you mean Captain von Richter *let* us ram him?"

Captain John winced. He didn't look at me. "That's the trouble with these blooming American college boys, Von. High bilge intake, low RPM output."

And he never let me any closer than that to the secret, whatever it was.

Von Richter lowered his wine glass. Outside, wind gusted a black fedora across Bowling Green. A white-haired man appeared, chasing it.

Von Richter laughed. "About time that feller show up."

The man pounced on the hat, then crammed it wrathfully on his head. He was a gnome-like person, bent with age. But he hopped vigorously to the Mariner's Loft door. He pushed his way in . . . oddly familiar in his walk. . . .

Memory crawled at my stomach. "Why, it can't be . . ."

But it was. Captain John, the ancient, the indestructible. He peeled off his coat. He was wearing kilts. His wrinkly knees poked out below them, red with cold. He shook hands with von Richter. He squinted at me, then put out his hand.

"Mister Yankee Doodle, you're gitting fat as a pig," he said.

He ordered a double scotch and soda. His vessel, the *Liverpool Swan*, had been delayed in docking because the tugs hadn't arrived. He apologized for being late.

Von Richter winked at me. "The tugs take my *City of Bonn* to the berth—*swoooosh*."

"Just like old times," I said. "Remember down in Val when they berthed the *Black Forest* ahead of us, Captain John?"

Stony silence fell on the two seamen. Then von Richter quickly started talking about the *City of Bonn*. She was brand-new. She had everything, fine food, television for the crew. She handled as sweet as a duck in a seaway.

"She was built in Bremerhaven," he said proudly. "By damn, she's as good as anything that floats."

He excused himself to go to the men's room. Captain John eyed me.

He said, "Still plunking your bloody foot in it, eh, Yank?"

"I had no idea he was still touchy about what happened."

Captain John finished his drink. He pulled out a pocket chessboard and started setting up the pieces. "You're still curious about that, aren't you, Yankee Doodle? Well, Von *did* let us ram him. I'm sure of it. He saw through his binocs what we were making. He could have pulled off to a safe distance. Then Schlitt could have blown us to hell with his gun."

"Saw us? Captain, not one seaman in ten would understand anything about making dynamite."

Captain John leaned forward. He whispered, "Do you know Von's mother's name? Krupp. His father was an explosives expert in the family factory."

My mind went back to von Richter on the *Glasgow Queen* after the sinking . . . how he had denied letting us ram him. *"You talk foolishness, John."*

"Von was an anti-Nazi. You knew his two brothers had been murdered by the SS, didn't you? But he was also a proud German." Captain John tapped my wrist earnestly. "He had to make a tougher decision than you or I ever had to, Yank. He made the right one. But his seaman's soul still hates to remember that he gave up his ship."

Von Richter came back. He went on talking about the *City of Bonn*. Such a clean, fast vessel—like a strong horse.

"Good vessel from a good shipyard," said Captain John.

He and I agreed and nodded to Captain von Richter for some minutes more. Then Captain John pushed his king's pawn out two spaces.

"I got a contrary opinion of your blooming chess game, however," he said.

IN THE AIR

WILLIAM E. BARRETT

The Destroyer

1

BRUCE MCNEIL COULD have been anything; a leader of men in politics or business or industry or war. Because he had the urge to destroy where most men have the passion to build, he was a creator of legends. He died four times and in those deaths there lies the story of his life. In the end he was an international incident.

The gods gave Bruce McNeil parents with money, the heritage of good blood, and a sound constitution. They gave him handsome features, a strong body, and courage. They bestowed upon him the privilege of being born in the United States of America. In the grim decades of international unrest during which men of great gifts were often trampled under the feet of dictators, this last was not the least gift of the generous gods.

At the age of ten, Bruce McNeil first tasted the joys of destruction.

The boy who lived next door to him was given a playhouse for his birthday, a shiny thing of painted wood with a green sloping roof and real shutters on its four windows. A boy could enter the front door without stooping, and the house was destined to be a headquarters for the boys of the neighborhood who played together through the long lazy afternoons of a summer vacation from school.

Johnny Dean was proud of his gift, and he was elected president of the newly formed club by acclamation. Bruce McNeil, as a matter of course, was a charter member.

From his own bedroom, Bruce McNeil could look across two yards on that first night of the new playhouse and see it standing proudly in the moonlight. Bruce McNeil had been sent upstairs to bed, but he could not sleep. He stared at the green roof and strange desires stirred in his blood. He was not particularly jealous of Johnny, nor was he envious of the boy's good fortune. After all, he would share the house, wouldn't he?

The thing that stirred viciously in the blood of Bruce McNeil was the awakening urge to tear down, to destroy, to lay waste. For a time he fought against it, a little frightened at the thought of the consequences; then the desire became a fever and he stole softly down the stairs.

There was a hatchet in the basement. Bruce lifted it, weighed it in his hand—and was lost. Desire was so much stronger than the fear of consequences now that there was no longer a conflict. He slipped swiftly across the grass, over the fence, and into the yard next door.

Once within striking distance of the playhouse, he no longer thought of observing caution. He raised the hatchet and attacked boldly. There was a savage intensity in the attack. His breath came fast as the hatchet crashed through the roof, rose and fell again. He hacked at the door and the shutters, oblivious to the quick flashing of lights in the house and the startled cries of aroused adults.

They had to pull him away from the playhouse when they reached him and he struggled against the grip of his father's hands.

He was not whipped. There was a shocked feeling on the part of his parents that this was not merely a lapse in discipline, that somehow it went deeper. His father took him upstairs, sat beside his bed, and talked to him.

He spoke of the folly of envying another boy's possessions and the evil of destruction. Bruce McNeil listened to him humbly, without offering a word in defense. Inside, however, some exultant force shouted and jumped with excitement. He knew that mere envy had had really nothing to do with it.

It was fun to smash things—and he was anticipating more fun on the same order.

He never repeated the mistake of attacking another's property openly, but he sought and found through the years a score of ways in which he could experience the same thrill. He played rough and he hit hard, and there were many "accidents" in which the bicycles or the wagons or the sleds of other boys met with mishaps. Strangely, he was never tempted to destroy anything of his own.

In college he played football.

Bruce McNeil could run tirelessly, he had endurance and a strong throwing arm; but he could not be persuaded to go out for track or baseball. He took to football with enthusiasm.

He was a freshman sensation and he made the varsity in his sophomore year. He played left halfback and he should have been the idol of Cornell. He had everything—everything, that is, which can be measured by the eye of a fan or an expert. He passed and blocked and tackled with precision; when he got the ball he knew what to do with it. To the stands he was, for want of a better term, lacking in "color."

Bruce McNeil did not like to play football and he had no Cornell spirit; he did like the opportunity which football gave him to indulge his appetite for destruction. He did not draw penalties for slugging or unnecessary roughness, but a great many men whom he tackled were hurt. Some of them left their football careers on the field where Bruce McNeil hit them.

He was a lone wolf and he had no known vices. He did not smoke or drink or play cards or chase women. He was a powerful, co-ordinated body, a brilliant brain—and a man with a strange shine in his eyes.

Shine is the only word for it. His eyes did not glow or gleam or glitter; they merely reflected light wetly. Many people were afraid of him, and he could put a curse on a party by merely joining it.

Even that early in his career people around him sensed the fact that he was thinking thoughts which would be horrible to share. He rarely looked directly at a person; he looked off into distance. Out there in the projected mists of his mind there were castles and buildings and bridges toppling to ruin—or a hatchet, perhaps, banging against a wooden roof.

In his last year at Cornell he became more human

He was a big man in his own world, an All-American halfback and a legend that thrilled people who never saw him save as a tiny figure in a big bowl or as a featured name in a newspaper. The glory that was his overshadowed the repellent something which was part of his personality.

He dreamed sometimes now of being a glorious figure astride a world. That dream made him conceited, and conceit, mean though the trait might be, was the vice that humanized him. The college world understood conceit because it held many conceited men. It was willing to overlook conceit in a man who touched glory with such sure hands.

Bruce McNeil rushed girls part of the time now, because their applause was more pleasing than the applause of men. A strange thing happened to him.

He was a senior, at his physical peak and with the experience of two varsity seasons behind him. By all standards, he should have been headed for the greatest season of his career.

He slumped. He was playing for glory where he had been playing for the joy of impact, and the other teams stopped him in his tracks.

Cornell romped all over Buffalo to start the season, but a sophomore back outscored the great McNeil. Niagara, the next opponent, was another setup, and Bruce McNeil showed a flash of his old form, but not enough to excite the crowd. He was taken out of the Richmond game, and Princeton slapped him down repeatedly behind his own line. He made three fumbles against Columbia.

The sports writers were already referring to the "McNeil Myth" and the stands were groaning. All of the strange instinctive dislike of other years flared up now into active resentment, and at last there was something to which the college world could put a name. Bruce McNeil was an overrated bum, a flash in the pan, a washout. He was soldiering and loafing, and he never had any spirit anyway.

McNeil took all of that with a twisted smile. Criticism did not hurt him, and his love of glory was such a new love in his life that he did not miss glory when it died.

He stopped his efforts to mix, dropped the girls from his list, and sat long hours in his room with his eyes on space and his fingers moving carelessly over the strings of a banjo.

He did not play very well and he didn't care. The banjo provided something to do with his hands while his brain went out over the horizons and smashed a world.

He was benched in the Albright game and he had time to think. The shine was back in his eyes and they put him in against Dartmouth. The big green had had a splendid season and it came to the Cornell game with a victory over Yale on the week before. Even conservative writers picked Dartmouth by three touchdowns.

Bruce McNeil beat the Green singlehanded.

From the opening whistle to the final gun, he was a one-man tide. He had not smashed anything for a long time and the hungry thing in his soul rose up and writhed. Corliss, the brilliant Dartmouth quarterback, took the ball on the kickoff and McNeil took Corliss. He was a tawny blur when he tackled, and the whistling breath from the stands was the forewarning of tragedy. Masses of people know instinctively what a single person might be slow in finding out.

The stands knew that Curt Corliss would not get up.

Corliss had a broken leg and three broken ribs, and it was hard to explain that. Nothing in the rule book had been violated, but there was a sudden pall over the game. Violence incarnate had met human flesh in that tackle. There had been more than the impact of bodies and both the stands and the players realized it; behind one body there had been unholy will.

McNeil broke up the first play of the new quarterback, and a few seconds later he intercepted a pass. From then on he was the target of the Dartmouth team. He reveled in the rough, smashing play, and before the day was over he had scored three touchdowns.

Cornell, the underdog, was on top by two touchdowns when the final whistle blew and the stands forgot that they had been shocked. The thrill was greater than the shock. Two other Dartmouth men, however, went to the hospital, and one of them had internal hemorrhages. Both men had collided with Bruce McNeil.

Glory stretched her hand to McNeil again in the week that followed, but he ignored the phone calls from girls and the friendly overtures of the press. The shine was back in his eyes and he was looking forward to the game with Penn.

Penn closed Cornell's season, and Penn had one of its really good teams—a fast, tough backfield and a heavy line. Pitt alone had taken the measure of the Quakers, and Cornell did not compare with Pitt. "Deac" Benson, the Cornell coach, was very solemn about this game, and when he was solemn about anything, he made it a practice to visit each man personally before the game and chat with him. A blocky, gray-haired man, he made a strange contrast with McNeil's Viking build.

"Boy," he said, "it's your last game. Can you give us what you gave us last week?"

McNeil was looking away into distance.

"I'll make out," he said.

There was an expression in his eyes that made the coach uneasy, and Deac Benson was not accustomed to being uneasy in the presence of his own men. He shrugged his shoulders and turned away. The things that he would have said to an ordinary player would have seemed absurd if he said them to Bruce McNeil. He didn't know exactly why they would be absurd, but he knew that they would be.

Bruce McNeil made the Dartmouth game look like a garden party in comparison with the Penn game. He played, as he usually did, without a change of expression in his face, without personal rancor, and with neither oaths nor insults. Something inside of him was indulging in a grand orgy of smash and bang and hammer. That was enough. He was willing to pay for his fun with his own flesh—and he paid.

He was a reeling, bleeding, groggy figure in the final quarter, a bruised and battered brute of a man who had invited all that Penn could deal out and who had been accommodated. There were giant linemen on his neck in every play and husky backfield men aching for a crack at him. A half-dozen times Benson tried to take him out. After a half-dozen refusals, Benson stopped trying.

Cornell slowed with Bruce McNeil, and Penn tied the score at thirteen all. It looked as though the game would end that way, but second wind flowed into McNeil in the closing minutes and Cornell gridiron history was written.

He scored two touchdowns in four minutes, and when he went across the line with the second of the two he didn't get up.

They carried him to the dressing room, and there was a wild and screaming mob outside that demanded a glimpse of him. His name still rolled across the gridiron above the heads of crazy lunatics who tore the goalposts down.

Bruce McNeil blinked, sat up, and shook off the hands of his teammates. He took a wet towel and mopped his face, and Deac Benson was standing before him—the chunky coach who had made a polished player out of him, who had benched him when he wasn't going well, and who had never been able to talk comfortably to him. Benson's face was pale under the gray stubble of beard.

"McNeil," he said, "I wouldn't swap the man you were today for Thorpe and Grange and Ernie Nevers at their best, not with Whizzer White thrown in to boot. It was a last game to be proud of. Cornell owes you——"

Bruce McNeil threw the towel away.

"To hell with Cornell," he said. "I wouldn't work that hard for anybody. I just—liked it. . . ."

His eyes looked past the dressing room and he was looking at something that no one in the room wanted to see. He shed the moleskins and kicked them under a bench. Most men made a ceremony of the last game, of the last time they shed a uniform; some of them cried. Bruce McNeil kicked glory under the bench with the moleskins.

He was looking beyond college. An ax and a wooden house had been the sport of a boy. Rough, tough, fighting football had been the sport of a youth. He was ready to be a man.

2

THE WORLD BEYOND college walls did not permit Bruce McNeil much time for sitting with a banjo and feeding the coiled python of destruction in his soul. He found it tougher than a Dartmouth backfield or a Penn line. He could not destroy and live—and he chose to live. He had never been tempted to destroy that which was his own, and the world of mature men was too well organized to permit a husky youngster out of college to run wild. Life whipped him into line.

The fortune of his family melted in the economic crash of a world, and he had a big body to feed. That powerful body demanded a career of action, and he chose aviation for his career. It took him four years to become a crack transport pilot on a star run. Few men made it as fast as that.

He met a girl named Winifred and she hated him on sight. She continued to hate him for many months, during which he set himself to the task of breaking down her resistance. In the end, she married him. He was, after all, a man who had everything. The only thing wrong with him was the thing that people felt and could not explain. There was a baby at the end of a year. It was a girl. Bruce McNeil could have got along without children, but if there had to be a child, he wanted a boy. He was never interested in the girl.

Nobody, not even his wife, suspected the real reason why he loved flying the huge transport plane from Newark to Washington.

With the wheel in his hands and all immensity above him, he was back in the room at college where he had held a banjo and looked beyond four walls to a world that broke beneath the blows of his brutal imagination. The cabin of a plane, however, was an improvement over a quiet room.

He flew above cities and homes. He could look down upon long lines of jewels which were the lighted streets of cities. He could see proud buildings rearing their bulk above the mass. Beneath him many men scurried like insects and his imagination went down to them. He could picture their terror when their world started to break up—when bombs dropped from his big plane and toppled their vaunting structures about their ears.

Bruce McNeil was a grown man with a dangerous job which he fulfilled faithfully, but he thought as an irresponsible child would think, and his every trip was an orgy of imagined desolation. In a time of peace, he was the eternal bomber and he destroyed Jersey City, Philadelphia, Camden, Baltimore. Times beyond number he blasted the shining white glory of the nation's capital, shattered the gleaming White House, and toppled the Washington Monument into powder.

The python in his soul slept, but he fed it, and for a time he was content. Then one night the python awakened.

The weather started to close in on him after he took off from Philadelphia. The ceiling had been coming down for an hour, but reports from along the line were favorable and he figured on beating the fog into Washington. He had seven passengers, and his record was remarkably clear of cancellations. He was not outwardly proud of his record, nor proud of anything else; but he always protected anything that was his.

"Cinch," he said. "Bet it doesn't get any lower in Washington."

In half an hour he was flying through thick soup. His wing-tips were lost somewhere in the rolling gray stuff and he was flying blind, his eyes intent upon his instruments.

He was all pilot now. The world was blotted out and he had no focal point for his imagination. He was not riding above strings of gleaming beads or masses of light; he was flying in a world of fog. Fog was not an enemy to be smashed. Fog had to be outwitted. It was not his first experience with the grim enemy of the airlines. He had been through it all before. Against such an enemy he was a normal human being. Intense concentration drove the shine from his eyes.

There were seven passengers, a copilot, and a stewardess in the ship; nine lives hanging upon his skill. He did not worry about those lives, but the challenge to his skill meant something to him. The voice of the Baltimore dispatcher came into the cockpit.

"Baltimore to Flight Nine . . . Baltimore to Flight Nine . . . Special weather, Nine . . ."

He had a hundred feet of ceiling at Baltimore. It was higher in Washington. He had three passnegers for Baltimore besides the mail. He was going to set down. He called for the beam and maneuvered over a city that he couldn't see.

Then a weird thing happened.

There was a big fire in downtown Baltimore, a fire that was sweeping over an entire city block. As number nine flew across the city, its powerful engines drumming through the fog, the solid masonry of the mist parted. There was a rift that was like some western canyon, sliced out of ancient rock.

Bruce McNeil saw the flames.

They jumped into his vision out of a gray world, and it was like the sudden flowering of destruction beneath a bombing plane.

The breath dammed up in his lungs and his heart stopped beating. He was like a man who awakens suddenly to the reality of his own maddest dream. His soul was shaken by it. Almost as suddenly as it came, the vison was gone.

The fog closed in triumphantly once more, and he was alone with his instruments and the voice of Baltimore and the beam that would lead him in out of the gray void. He found the beam mechanically and he rode it down—and for the first time in his career, Bruce McNeil cracked up.

The great silver ship roared in, circled the field, hummed confidently as it settled beneath the pallid mist which shrouded the tops of the hangars, then touched hard, bounced, and washed out a wing.

There was a screaming passenger, excited airport crews, and a milling mass of people who had been waiting for relatives and friends to land. Bruce McNeil scarcely heard them, was aware of them only dimly. He was unhurt but he looked unconscious. His eyes were filmed over and he walked stiffly.

"It's all right, McNeil. All right. Nobody really hurt. . . ."

The operations manager was shouting in his ear; pounding him on the back. McNeil paid no attention to him. In that minute he realized that his career was over—not because of a crack-up that could happen to anyone, but because of a vision in the fog that could happen to few.

Bruce McNeil had seen something that he would have to see again. His soul would give him no peace until he saw once more the red flower of destruction beneath his spreading wings.

He shuddered, and the amateur diagnosticians of the airport said that he was suffering from shock. The motor highway from Baltimore was almost as bad as the airways, so they sent him home on a train. His wife made a fuss over him, and he was as oblivious to her as he was to his passengers or the boys in Baltimore.

"I'm tired," he said. "Dead tired. I've got to rest."

"Of course."

Winifred McNeil had had her arms around him and she had felt the coldness of his body. It was as though Death, having come close to Bruce McNeil, was reluctant to move away. She didn't know that McNeil had invited Death in, and that Death sat comfortably in his brain and drew sketches in red crayon, macabre sketches of flame leaping out of a gray background.

Bruce McNeil did not want to rest; he wanted to relax and enjoy those visions, to live again that moment over Baltimore. In the darkness of the bedroom, he lay flat on his back and he could hear the thud of his hatchet hitting wood, feel the smashing impact of his body against other bodies on the football field, see the blazing rosette in the fog.

Then the baby started to cry.

The high, shrill cry broke the spell, and he shook like a heavy drinker awakening from a drunken dream. His wife got swiftly out of bed and moved to the side of the crib. She spoke soothingly and still the baby cried. Bruce McNeil could see her slender figure as a sort of wraith in the darkness, no more substantial than a wisp of fog.

It was the last time that he ever saw her.

She took the baby into the other room, and the baby still cried. Bruce McNeil lay with his fists clenched and tried to block out of his brain the sound of that crying, but the shrill cry broke his mad vision into bits. He couldn't concentrate on it, couldn't call back the thrill of destruction.

Quietly he rose. He knew suddenly what he was going to do, what he had to do. That last picture that he had of his wife shaped his decision. She had been like something unreal, a figure as hazy as those strange figures that blew past his wings at dusk. He would leave it at that. His life was a thundering ship that raced across a world and brushed the clouds in its passing. A cloud had no existence for a ship that had already passed it; so would it be with Winifred.

Bruce McNeil dressed quietly and slipped out of the house without crossing the room where his wife hummed softly to a fretful baby. For hours he walked aimlessly; then he sat on a park bench to wait for morning.

He drew twelve hundred dollars out of the bank at five minutes past nine—and by eleven, he was heading westward on a truck from which he hailed a ride. He was wearing a cap instead of a hat and a gray shirt instead of a white one; beyond that he attempted no disguise.

He He did not need a disguise. Winifred McNeil checked the hospitals before she reported to the police, and it was a week before she discovered the withdrawal of funds from the bank. The personal relations squad, which is Washington's missing persons bureau, posted the name of Bruce McNeil as missing—and there it stands.

It was the first death that the man died. The name will never come down until seven years have passed and his wife has him declared legally dead.

Rolling westward, Bruce McNeil gave no thought to things like that. He did not care. He had a date with destiny.

3

BRUCE MCNEIL NEVER doubted his ultimate destination once he had put Washington behind him. Across the Pacific a world was being blown to bits by men with training such as his. There were targets enough to last a dozen years, and that was not true of Spain. Spain was closer, but there might be interference there; certainly more chance of an American flier being recognized. Dispite the flame that flowed in his veins, Bruce McNeil held himself with the leash of patience.

He must sink slowly into the ranks of mankind's driftwood and be carried to his destination unnoticed.

The gray shirt became dirty on the trek westward, and he did not change it. In Wheeling, he mailed half of his money to general delivery in San Francisco to an assumed name. In St. Louis he mailed more. In Fort Worth he broke the arm of a tramp who tried to rob him while he slept.

He found combat and hazard and an outlet for the cold urge to smash along the road to California. He was big; the muscles rolled on his body like steel ropes, and he was ruthless in the use of those muscles. He got along and men walked wide of him. In San Francisco he bought new shirt.

In San Francisco, too, a man talked loudly in the saloons along the waterfront. He had been paid a lot of money and he had been promised more if he would go to China.

''Mechanics, they want, men that know motors. Hell, Chinkee money is good, ain't it? And them damned Japs!''

Bruce McNeil knew the breed of this fellow: a greedy little coward who wanted the big money that went with a job that might be dangerous, but who had to talk loudly to drown out his own fears. Bruce McNeil bought him a drink.

''I'm a mechanic myself,'' he said, ''and I don't care where I go to get money. How about it, Bud?''

The little man with the big voice became cautious. ''It's a tip that is worth money.'' His close-set eyes narrowed. ''Me, I know. You got to find out.''

''How much money?''

The little man hesitated. ''Twenty bucks.''

''I'll give you five.''

The self-styled mechanic started to laugh; then he saw Bruce McNeil's eyes and the laugh died in his throat. The little man put out one shaking hand.

''Five bucks is okay,'' he said. ''I'll take you to meet a guy.''

The business of recruiting for a foreign army on United States soil is a mysterious business, like bootlegging used to be. It was twenty-four hours before McNeil met the man he had to know. The man was short and husky and he looked like a Russian. He said that his name was Jones.

''So you're a mechanic,'' he growled. ''Ever see an engine like that?''

McNeil looked at the Curtis J-5 that stood on a block and laughed aloud.

''Lots of them.''

''Show me.''

Jones was grim, suspicious, unfriendly. McNeil didn't give two whoops in hell how he was. He showed him. The engine was partly torn down and McNeil was working on it only five minutes when Jones was convinced.

''Okay,'' he said. ''You got a job as a stoker on a steamer, see?''

Their eyes met and they understood each other perfectly. As far as the Russian Jones knew, Bruce McNeil might be a government sleuth. There wasn't much nourishment for a sleuth in an interview like this. Hiring stokers was not a crime, and if Bruce McNeil wanted to be hired as anything else, he would have to jump ship in China and get himself hired. McNeil's lips twisted in a hard smile.

''Jones,'' he said, ''charge them double for me. You've just hired a damned good man.''

The Russian's face was expressionless, but something lighted in his somber eyes.

''I believe that,' he said.

It was all that passed between them. McNeil knew that this man was being paid so much per head for recruits and he rather admired the system. He was no longer impatient. The hungry thing in his soul coiled and waited. He was on his way.

Outside, the little man with the big voice was smoking cigarettes nervously. He fell into jerky step with McNeil.

''How about it?'' he said throatily. ''You think it's a square deal, huh?''

McNeil spat. ''I paid you five bucks for it. I'm not kicking.''

''I know. But a guy can get a long way from home and be gypped by a lot of foreigners.''

''Okay. Stay home.''

McNeil strode, and the little man padded along.

''Guy,'' he said, ''you're big, powerful big. Nobody will gyp you. Me, I ain't so big. If I go, how about being partners?''

Bruce McNeil looked at him. He was in good humor. He had a quiet evening ahead of him in which to feast his imagination uninterrupted, and it had something now upon which to feast.

"What's your name?"

"Parker. Duke Parker, they call me."

McNeil chuckled.

"Sold," he said. "Stick with me, Duke, and you'll wear diamonds."

Parker stumbled and almost fell down. "Kid," he said, "that's swell. I was worried, I was . . . Here. I ain't got all that five bucks left, but I'll give you two bucks back. Charging a partner for something ain't square."

He held out two crumpled bills and Bruce McNeil took them. The partnership idea was a joke to him, and he didn't care if he never saw Duke Parker again, but money was fuel to the hurtling ship that was his life.

He still thought of his life in terms like that. He had not experienced a moment's remorse over leaving his wife and child. He didn't worry about them and he didn't wonder about them. They were gone. Somewhere behind him they had slipped off into space, like the wisps of cloud that brushed his wing-tips in passing. Ahead of him lay China.

It was a week before he was assigned to a tramp steamer, and then word was sent to him in the flophouse where he was staying. Duke Parker was assigned to the same ship and he was almost tearfully happy about it. McNeil suspected him of pulling wires to have it happen that way and he didn't give a damn. He went down into the hold and he stoked coal.

For all of a long, rough voyage, Bruce McNeil slammed coal in the bowels of the ship and he asked for no quarter. Word was passed along to him when they were twenty-four hours out that he could soldier the job if he wanted to—and he cursed the suggestion away. Stripped to the waist, with a giant scoop in his hands and the blasting heat of the hold wrinkling his skin, he found a strange excitement. The coal hissed into the greedy maw before him and the flame stirred angrily when it hit.

He liked that sudden leap of the flame, the towering upshoot of the sparks. There was violence in it and destruction. He could look through the red haze and see visions that moved the blood in his veins like streams of electricity.

Not so the Duke.

The Duke begged off in the first two hours, and he was assigned to a job with the engineer, a job which permitted him plenty of time for loafing and for visiting. He visited Bruce McNeil just once when Bruce was on duty. The man looked up at him and the red glow of the stokehole fires seemed to be reflected in his eyes. The Duke never went back.

"He's a nice feller, but there's something about him . . ."

The Duke shivered, but there was excitement in his fear. If Bruce McNeil was a strange, strong force, Bruce McNeil was also his partner, and Duke Parker had never been troubled with too much imagination.

"None o' those foreigners will do any gypping when they catches a look o' Bruce," he said. "Not any. They won't try their tricks on us."

4

JAPAN, IN THE INTERESTS of world peace and the promotion of trade, was hammering Shanghai into bloody ruin. At Woosung, twelve miles down the river, twenty members of a tramp steamer's crew were being landed under the vigilant eye of a trim Chinese officer and the guard of gray-clad soldiers.

The sullen booming of distant explosions could be plainly heard here, and grim-looking Japanese warships were riding at anchor within sight of Woosung, menacing hulks in the slanting rain. Bruce McNeil's fists clenched. This was it. This was the spot for which he had been born. He could feel the response rise in him, the tiptoe feeling of nerves clamoring for the balm of action.

His brain, however, was alive to subtle dangers.

There were American flying men by the scores over here, washed-out mail and transport pilots, adventurous youngsters, veterans with the itching foot. In such a motley crew, there would inevitably be men who would recognize Bruce McNeil. If there were not, there was still the danger of newsreel cameras. Where American flyers congregated there would be American cameramen.

McNeil shook his head. He did not know whether Winifred had raised much hell about his desertion. It was conceivable that the State

Department would take advantage of an excuse to drag Bruce McNeil back to the States. American fliers in an Oriental war created a problem for the diplomats, and they would be happy over the excuse to make a horrible example out of one of them.

That must not happen. McNeil's forehead furrowed. He had taken the bootleg route out of the United States instead of paying passage on a liner because he jumped the passport difficulty that way. He did not suffer delay and inconvenience, only to be tripped at the last moment. He looked around at his companions. There were many of them whom he had not seen before.

Short and tall and fat and lean, they were the kind of men that a foreign agent might be expected to pick up in a tour of flophouses and saloons. The sole requirement had been that they have mechanical knowledge and skill that would be valuable to the Chinese air force. McNeil's judgment in allying himself with the mechanics rather than the fliers was justified so far. There was no one in this crowd who was likely to know him or care; they were less adventurers than they were men seeking a quick stake through high-pay work. Many of them were swarthy, heavy-featured men; obviously Americans only by adoption, if they were Americans at all. It was this group that gave McNeil his big idea. He beckoned to Duke Parker.

"Stick with me, Bud," he said. "We're going to register in as Russians, see!"

"Roo-shuns? Us?"

"Sure. It's a racket, see. They'll send us to some Russian outfit, and we won't have some Yank over us to run us ragged."

Duke Parker, uncomprehending, smiled with pretended wisdom.

"Sure," he said. "That's a swell idea."

Bruce McNeil grunted. He thought so, too. He had to take Parker with him because the little man talked too much and the man knew his right name. It had been a slip, but it was not too important. There were many McNeils, and, unless he courted attention, nobody who cared would be looking for him in a motley crew of mechanics behind the battle lines of China.

The squad filed through the rain to a huge building that looked like a warehouse. It was painted black. Bruce McNeil towered over the rest of the crowd. He had let his beard grow for the past week and it changed the contour of his face somewhat. It was a blond beard, however, and he did not look Russian.

Inside the warehouse there was a large room with a desk at the far end. A bespectacled Chinese sat at the desk with a bored-looking

American beside him. There was a big ledger and several stacks of printed forms. McNeil tapped the Chinese officer commanding the squad on the shoulder.

"No. No. Not here. No American. Russian. Russki. . . ."

He pulled Duke Parker close to him as he said it and included him in the sweeping gesture. The other men were in a line which stretched to the desk. The Chinese officer looked puzzled.

"No Amelica?"

"No America. Russki."

The officer called a man, spoke to him rapidly in singsong Cantonese, and sent him off on an errand. The mechanic at the head of the line was answering questions being thrown across the desk at him, and the Chinese clerk was writing in his book. Five men had registered and been given filled-out forms before the Chinese soldier came back. He spoke briefly to his officer, and the officer nodded.

Bruce McNeil and Duke Parker were signaled out of line and sent on a march through the rain with three soldiers. The soldiers carried rifles with fixed bayonets. Duke looked at them apprehensively.

"I hope we ain't making no mistake," he said.

Bruce McNeil chuckled. "Leave it to me."

Within a few minutes they were ushered into a smaller building and led upstairs. There were many Chinese soldiers to pass and two Chinese officers. Finally they were led into a room that was heavily hung with draperies of rich cloth. A Chinese in a plain gray uniform without markings was seated behing a carved table. A smoothly shaven man with bushy eyebrows sat on his right.

McNeil and Duke were alone with the two. The soldiers had left them at the door. The Duke's feet moved nervously over the carpet. McNeil looked from the placid face of the Chinese to the scowling countenance of the man beside him. Despite the absence of insignia, both of these men were evidently officers of rank, the one obviously a Russian. The Russian broke the silence.

"You are liars," he said.

Bruce McNeil grinned. "That is right. We are not Russians."

"Why did you claim that you were?"

"Because we are Communists. It is dangerous for us among Americans."

McNeil felt the shudder of Duke Parker at the dreaded word "Communist." It amused him. The Russian was looking a hole through him and the Chinese was leaning back comfortably in his chair, his face blank. The Russian spoke to him in Chinese and he answered briefly. McNeil had the idea that the Chinese also understood English. He paid grudging admiration to such linguists. Except for a certain thickness of voice, the Russian's English was good.

"Communists. And you want to serve under Russians?"

"That is right."

Suddenly the Russian smiled.

"Your wish shall be granted," he said. "I am Alexander Defsky. This is Chu Yuang-fu."

He mentioned the names casually, without titles, as befitted a member of the Soviet, but Bruce McNeil looked at him with a new respect. He knew of Defsky from the press as one of the most powerful figures behind the organization of the Kungchangtang in northern China and Chu Yuang-fu, of course, was the great war lord who had come south to effect a union between the Chinese Reds whom he commanded and the Kuomintang.

Two men of destiny sat in a room and talked casually with humble mechanics. In that fact, McNeil saw something of their stren[illegible] Anything out of the ordinary in the conduct of affairs with foreign recruits was brought to their personal attention, because foreign recruits could become danger spots in their organization. Defsky was amused at two Americans wanting to serve under Russians.

Bruce McNeil understood that amusement. There was no softness in the Russian setup. Soviet mechanics were going to have to hop and like it. Well, that would be too bad for Duke Parker; but when Bruce McNeil was safely into the Russian zone, he'd drop this mechanic nonsense damned fast. Defsky rang a bell on the desk.

A door behind the two Americans opened, and an officer came in with two soldiers. Defsky gave them a command and Chu Yuang-fu raised his hand for a moment's delay. He looked from McNeil to Parker.

"You came to us voluntarily," he said softly. "Be good soldiers."

That was all. Defsky translated his own orders into English. "Three planes will go north in an hour to Pao-an on the Shensi front. You will find your station there."

The officer stepped forward, McNeil and the Duke fell in with the soldiers, and they went out. They were loaded into a small power boat with two obvious Russians and several Chinese. Scooting in and out among junks and small craft flying the flags of all nations, they passed the battleships of the United States, of Britain, of France, and of Japan. They saw great billowing clouds of smoke off the right bank and they could hear distant firing, but no one interfered with the launch and they landed south of Shanghai.

Bruce McNeil was silent, despite the nervous attempts of the Duke to relieve tension with conversation. The smell of death was in McNeil's nostrils. This was the thing that he had dreamed about. He marched to the big Russian transport planes like a man in a trance. There was a great deal of bustle and confusion about the airdrome and everything was camouflaged.

Planes of war and transport planes used the same drome, and McNeil wondered why the Japs did not blast the drome out of existence. His lips flattened against his teeth at the thought. He could have a lot of fun with those sprawling hangars and the barracks and the wall that enclosed them. In his mind he could see all of this wreathed in flame and the vision pleased him.

"I liked that old Chink. 'Be good soldiers,' he says. I never thought of it like that before. We are soldiers, ain't we?"

The Duke was chattering and McNeil let him chatter. A trim Chinese officer snapped orders and they piled into the plane.

There were twelve passengers in single seats, six to a side on either side of the aisle. The pilot and copilot were Russians, blocky men in gray blouses and loose-fitting trousers. Bruce McNeil, sitting behind the Duke, leaned back and let the excitement run in his veins.

They were taxiing out into position when McNeil sensed interference in the smooth flow of his thought. It was like static in a radio.

He looked out. There was only the drab, blurred panorama of rain-swept airport flowing past. He swept his eyes, then, over his fellow passengers.

Unerringly his eyes halted upon a swarthy, black-haired Slav across the aisle and one seat ahead. The man was seated quietly and there was nothing about him to attract attention, but there was no doubt in Bruce McNeil's mind that the distraction he felt was emanating from that one source. It was an instinct with him.

Somehow, he and the Slav were on the same mental wave length. They were both thinking destruction in a purely sensual way, as a sort of indulgence of the mind and will.

It puzzled Bruce McNeil. He did not know why he should be so positive in his own mind about the other man, and he resented the fact that he could not relax because the other man was there.

They kicked away from the drome and climbed high into the murky sky above Shanghai.

He tore his attention from the quiet Slav and looked out at the flattening panorama below. His breath caught.

Through the rain and the mist he saw doll-sized houses and long lines of streets, so like the many American cities that he had seen from aloft. Yes—and unlike them in the way that meant most to Bruce McNeil.

In a score of places, he saw pools of flame.

Smoke wreathed across the face of Shanghai; not the smoke of a throbbing industrial life, but the smoke of agony, of bombs and shells and ripping machine-gun bullets.

McNeil stared fascinated through the slanting rain as the plane climbed. He could see the winding river and the myriad vessels that were anchored there, the buildings that lined its banks—and, flying low over those buildings, the planes of the attackers.

The Russian ship climbed, and Bruce McNeil resented the fact that he was not a part of this destruction. He would drop no bombs into that sprawling city where the smoke flowed and the flames spread in blazing floods; he was part of a remote, disinterested mechanism that was taking him away. He was not even a pilot, merely a passenger.

Suddenly his mind was rubbed blank of thought. He was conscious of violent interference in the strange psychic instrument that was his brain.

He whipped his attention across the aisle and he saw the Slav come to his feet.

The black-haired man's eyes were wild with resolve, his lips drawn back hard lke the carved lips of a gargoyle. Bruce McNeil lurched to his feet. He knew that he was late, even as his muscles responded to the impulse from his brain.

The Slav had a gun in his hand and his finger was squeezing the trigger. He stepped toward the pilot's compartment as he fired.

The pilot died with the first bullet, and McNeil had a flash of the copilot slumped over the controls as Bruce McNeil swung his mighty fist from the waistline into the Slav's jaw.

Bruce McNeil hurdled the body in the aisle and dived for the pilot's compartment in front.

The plane was in an uproar, with frightened men shouting and piling out of their seats. The plane itself was lurching sidewise.

McNeil gripped the copilot's collar and hurled his body backward into the aisle. The horizon was going around the plane like a skidding rope, and he was flung violently against the dead pilot.

They were spinning down upon Shanghai.

5

THE BIG SHIP WHIPPED around in a tight spin, and the pilot's body had fallen forward over the control column. Bruce McNeil had to fight against the pressure of air as he struggled to pull the limp body back. He wedged himself in at length, half-sitting on the corpse of the pilot, shoving it to the back of the compartment with his own body while he maneuvered his feet onto the rudder pedals and tightened his fingers about the wheel.

They had lost a lot of altitude, but they had had altitude to spare when the pilot died. McNeil shoved the wheel forward and ruddered hard against the spin.

The wires screamed above the roar of the engine, and the horizon stopped whirling. They were in a dive. McNeil held that dive, straight down. He could see black roofs, long lines of barricades, a fenced field. When he had flying speed, he pulled gently back on the control column and the ship shuddered.

For a moment he feared that it was about to fall apart, but the moment of maximum strain passed and the ship straightened out.

He was flying over the corner of the Japanese flying field east of the International Settlement and the antiaircraft guns were cutting loose. Puffs of smoke bracketed him and he staggered his flight. His eyes gleamed, but he did not look down. He had no bombs, and it would have been too depressing to look upon targets which he could not hit.

He climbed back into the high lanes of the sky, and two savage little Japanese scouts dived at him. He stood on one wing to avoid the first burst of fire and his hand groped along the control column. He had never flown military planes and his knowledge of gunnery was theoretical, but he did not believe that the Chinese sent a transport plane into such hostile skies without at least a machine gun.

There were gun trips on the control column, and he pressed them experimentally when one of the Japanese scouts flashed across his nose. Green-gray tracers cut the mist and he knew that he had a gun. He did not come remotely close to hitting the Japanese plane, but the mere act of firing at it was nourishment to the hungry demon in this soul.

He flew on, climbing. One of the Japs flew after him and fired another burst and then they both pulled off.

He didn't understand that. They could have brought him down but they were letting him go. It was a crazy war. There seemed to be some queer rules for it. These transport planes had been let alone while they flew above the destruction, but, as soon as one of them came down low, it was blasted. When it started to climb again, it was permitted to proceed on its way.

The other two transport planes had gone on and Bruce McNeil headed this one back to the drome. He landed it easily, and before the wheels stopped rolling there were at least fifty Chinese soldiers around the plane.

''Probably caught most of the action by telegraph from one of their posts,'' he muttered. ''Well, we've got a story to tell them.''

He swung down lightly and a soldier held a bayonet against his chest. There was a lot of excitement as the passengers started to emerge from the cabin. Half of them were sick and one of them had been killed by a Jap bullet. The black-haired assassin had been clubbed by his companions when he came back to consciousness after his knockout by McNeil. He was a sorry-looking object when they hauled him out. Duke Parker stood and stared at Bruce McNeil.

''Jeeze, guy, ain't you something?'' he said. ''Never been nothin' like it.''

McNeil shrugged. An hour later he was telling his story to Defsky and Chu Yuang-fu. When he had finished, they both shook hands with him. The Chinese offered him cigarettes.

''You should have told us that you could fly,'' he said. ''Now tell us your story. It is in strictest confidence.''

McNeil hesitated, then he told them. He said nothing about a wife and child. He told them merely that he was flying the ships of peace and that the call of war became too strong for him to resist. Chu Yuang-fu nodded his head gravely. He understood such things. There were men who were reborn out of past existences too soon, before the earth-bound cravings of a past life had been cleansed from their souls.

''You are a born warrior, my son,'' he said, ''and China's need is great.''

For a half-hour he talked. He spoke of past glories, of the troubles which had come on China, and the great patience of a brave, enduring people. They were fighting now for national existence, and most of those who fought would die of bullets or of old age before the China of which they dreamed could be built; but they were willing to make the sacrifice in order that their sons would be Chinese, not Japanese.

He spat the word ''Japanese'' out of his mouth. He was an impressive old man. With all of his wisdom, however, he failed to comprehend one thing, that the cause of China meant nothing whatever to Bruce McNeil and never would. All that mattered to Bruce McNeil was the license to destroy.

He got that license. He was rewarded in gold for exceptional heriosm and for saving a doomed ship, and he was given a commission in the air service of the Kungchangtang which was fighting the Japanese in the north.

"Some of the new ships are difficult for our men, and we are deficient in the arts of navigation and blind flight," Chu Yuang-fu said slowly. "Russia helps us but little with pilots."

He looked sidewise at Defsky and the Russian frowned.

"There will come a day . . ." he said ominously.

McNeil waited, then he said, "One more thing. The American who came with me—I want him as my mechanic."

Chu Yuang-fu nodded his head. "That will be arranged."

Bruce McNeil felt strangely relieved. He feared to leave Duke Parker behind him. The man's unabashed hero worship of him meant nothing, but the man's loose tongue was a danger.

He had the Duke with him when he left for North China, and the Duke flew many flights with Bruce McNeil that made him regret that he had ever left the United States.

The Russians on the northern front were suspicious at first of the blond giant from America. They assigned copilots to him who were less pilots than guards, grimly watchful men who seemed to be eternally vigilant lest he betray the cause in some obscure way. McNeil laughed at them.

He was having the time of his life.

He flew over columns of Japanese troops and brought them death from the sky. He brought flame and destruction to squat villages, and he blasted trenches that were laid across fields of grain. The country was flat, like the rolling land of Kansas, and there was little cover for the enemy when he caught them in the open.

He did not, however, think of them as the "enemy." He thought of them as targets. The only flaw in his fierce joy was the fact that men in the rear compartments actually released the bombs. McNeil compensated for that by being able to watch the downward curve and the impact. He became expert at bringing his ship into position for dead shots, and he was disdainful of danger. Other ships were hit, but he had a profound belief that his would not be.

He slept soundly at night and he no longer had fierce dreams to make him restless.

Then the new Russian planes came out and changed the whole course of his career.

They came in crates, and there was a mystery about uncrating them. Ivan Rodoff, commander of the Russians, called him into the operations office when the planes had been set up. McNeil had had trouble talking with Rodoff until he found that the man spoke French. McNeil had studied French in college. Rodoff paced the floor when he talked about the new planes.

"Comrade," he said, "they are remarkable. They will revolutionize warfare. We are fools to risk them here, but there is a need to test them under war conditions. Your American manufacturers are doing the same with planes designed for your fighting services. But your Americans have nothing like these."

"What have you got?" McNeil's voice was curt.

For a long minute, Rodoff stared at him.

"A man who betrayed the secret of these planes would not die swiftly," he said. "He would die over many days."

"Okay." McNeil looked into the cruel eyes of the Russian, and there was something in his own eyes that no one, Russian or American, cared to meet. Rodoff sat down at his desk and spread a set of blueprints flat.

"The bomber is always vulnerable," he said, "because it is the heavy ship. It cannot maneuver with the small ship, the fighter. If it is attacked when it does not have escort, it can perhaps be destroyed."

"That's right."

"This new bomber of the Soviet is a terror for the pursuit ship. Listen. In this ship, you are attacked by many scouts. You speak into a mouthpiece. So! There is a loud-speaker in the bomber's compartment and your voice comes there. You say 'Stations!' Immediately all those men who drop bombs go to places prepared for them, little compartments in the wing; each has a machine gun in his compartment. You give them five seconds. During those five seconds, you pull a lever and the gas tanks drop out of the wing. Then you pull another lever and the entire cabin drops out of the ship. You have now a flying wing of great power, of little weight, and of heavy armament. You see!"

There was sweat on the Russian's face as he talked. Bruce McNeil leaned forward and pulled the blueprints to him. He felt a little of the Russian's excitement. There were possibilities in this thing if the engineering was right.

"In less than ten seconds you can rid yourself of half the weight and still retain full power and armament?"

"More than half the weight, my friend. More than half. And the ship is not destroyed. The cabin is standard. A new one can be fitted immediately. New gas tanks can be fitted immediately. You have, of course, a spare tank in front." Rodoff spread his hands. "Lest one of these be captured, we have built into the ship another device. A third lever blows the ship completely apart."

Their eyes met. "A pilot must agree to do that?"

"He must swear to do that if capture is inevitable."

Bruce McNeil nodded. He was seeing a new vision. That night he attended a lecture on the new ship by a pilot who had test-flown it. He took the oath to die with the ship if need be, and he was instructed on the making of necessary control adjustments when the weight was jettisoned.

Russia had a new ship of infinite possibilities, and it came out at a time when Bruce McNeil was yearning for fresh fields. He was tired of bombing the grain and the squat villages and the drab airdromes and the marching troops.

Japan had the right idea. Japan bombed cities.

6

THE LUST TO DESTROY grows in a man's soul. It is never satisfied except momentarily. The destruction of a small thing creates the desire for a larger objective. Bruce McNeil, who had started by swinging a hatchet against a wooden playhouse, was bored now with the bombing of huts and hangars. He flew the new bombers over Japanese bases, always with a vigilant Russian at his side, and he felt a flying man's pride in the way that the big ship handled. Rodoff would not, however, consent to a trial of the gas-dumping and cabin-dumping devices.

"We know that they will work," he said. "They have been tested by our own technicians and passed. The sweat of men is the gold of the Soviet, Comrade, and we do not waste such gold."

McNeil argued in vain, but a day was selected finally for flying the planes without the cabins and the gas tank, both of which were released on the ground. The test took place deep in Chinese territory, and there were two squadrons of scouts aloft to provide against interference. Bruce McNeil, as the outstanding pilot on that front, flew one of them.

"By God," he said, "they have got something."

He was a little bit awed by the way in which the big ship handled when stripped for fighting. The engines were not too powerful for the ship, as he feared they would be. It was a flying man's dream to be aloft in anything which was so sensitive and yet so stable. If he had been able to think in terms of flying as something apart from destruction, he would have found his excitement in the possible future of the big ship. But Bruce McNeil was a destroyer. His mind leaped ahead once more to a dangerous possibility. While he was playing with it, Duke Parker drew him aside for a confidential talk.

"Bruce," he said, "I ain't happy with these Rooshuns. It gets worse and worse, with them not knowing any language worth talking and not eating any grub worth eating—and them Chinks ain't no better. When it comes to eating, it's even worse with Chinks. . . ."

The little man did look unhappy. He had lost weight and there was a dispirited air about him. The bombing thrill which made anything bearable for Bruce McNeil was just an added horror to the little Duke. McNeil had arranged for the man to come along on the bombing parties, and he generally jerked levers in the rear compartment where skilled bomb layers figured the altitude and the speed and the drift. He neither saw the bombs go down nor cared to see them. Today his skinny jaw was set.

"And so I'm goin' home, Bruce. There ain't no money nor no nothing that would pay a man properly for making a Rooshun out of himself. Being a Rooshun is the worst thing can happen to a man, and the next worst is being a Chink. Me, I'm getting to be both and I can't stand it."

Bruce McNeil frowned. He didn't think that there was a chance of the Duke being sent home after seeing the new planes, but there was a chance that they might send the little man back to the Shanghai front. Bruce McNeil didn't want that. The Duke would talk too much about Bruce McNeil. McNeil patted him on the shoulder.

"Stick around a few days, kid," he said, "and maybe I'll get a chance to fly you back to the river. Me, I'd like a little change of scene, too."

"Okay."

Bruce McNeil got rid of him. He wanted time to think. For a long time he sat in a chair that was tilted back, a cigarette burning out between his fingers and the wet shine in his eyes. When he stood up, he knew what he was going to do.

The following morning he piloted one of the big Russian ships over the lines to bomb a motor transport camp which the Japs thought they had camouflaged. Five miles beyond the camp was a battle-scarred Japanese airport, and fifty miles beyond that was a central airport of Japan which the Russians had never had nerve enough to bomb.

Rodoff, because he babied the big new ships, was sending them out one at a time now with some of the older style bombers to fill out the flight. That was his mistake.

The big ship flew to the motor camp but it never bombed it.

When he was close to his objective, Bruce McNeil eased his body in the cockpit. The Russian who was riding with him was sleepy, and the Russians had long since lost their suspicion of Bruce McNeil. He, like themselves, was a volunteer in China's war and he took a more vicious interest in it than even the Chinese.

Besides, his best friend was in the rear compartment when he flew.

"Do you think that the Japs will be surprised?"

McNeil's tone was easy, conversational. The Russian beside him did not even turn his head. He was slumped down carelessly in the cockpit.

"Yes," he said, "they are very stupid at camouflage. I think they will be surprised.

"So do I."

There was a peculiar expression on Bruce McNeil's face, an expression that the Russian never saw.

McNeil's left hand came up from his side, crossed his body, and squeezed the trigger on an army automatic when the muzzle was lined on the Russian's body. His right hand left the wheel and dropped swiftly to the levers under the seat. He pressed lever number two as the startled Russian straightened with a jerk.

There was a click behind the pilot's compartment that was like the breaking of a strong board. McNeil shot the Russian again as the man slumped and then looked down.

The bombing compartment of the plane, with its three men and its bombs, was dropping to earth like a huge coffin. McNeil's eyes followed it down hungrily and the blood raced wildly in his veins as it hit.

The bombs let go with the impact and there was a sheet of flame shooting skyward.

"Good-bye, Duke. . . ."

Communism was repellent to him and that he had been watching for his chance to desert from the time that he found himself assigned to service with Russians.

"But I realized," he said, "that I would need proof of my sincerity when I came to the army of the Emperor. I would have been killed if I had tried to return to the United States, and you would not have received me with trust had I merely fled to you seeking sanctuary."

Heads nodded about the table as this speech was translated. This was logic as the Asiatic knew it. The American told a story that men could believe.

"When I came to you, I brought you a gift that leaves no question of my sincerity. Listen . . ."

McNeil leaned forward, and in slow, precise language that the sharp-eyed translator could understand easily, he told about the great new plane of the Soviet and of what it would do. He was talking to the representatives of a people who had never originated anything but who could copy anything for which there was a model.

In the middle of his discourse he was interrupted and a technical man was summoned.

He went over it again and drew diagrams in reply to shrewd questions. When he had finished the technical man shook hands with him. The others were more restrained.

McNeil's lips tightened.

"You cannot deal with me as with a traitor," he said. "I am an American with a talent for war. I brought my talent to Asia and fell among the wrong people. I sought the people in whom I believed. I do not want money or rewards. I want a commission in the Japanese air force and a chance to fly against the people for whom, unfortunately, I flew against the Japanese."

Dead, shocked silence greeted him; then the colonel stroked his chin. His eyes were doubtful and he spoke hesitantly.

"The matter," he said, "shall be referred to the Emperor."

7

IT TOOK BRUCE MCNEIL a month to convince the Japanese that he was not trying to trick them. He drew plans of the missing cabin, and, when they produced the bits of wreckage that had been recovered near the motor camp, he helped them to reconstruct a model from which engineers at home, with their greater facilities, could construct a similar cabin. It was not until they had seen him in action that they were fully convinced that he was heart and soul with Japan.

With a watchful Japanese beside him, he flew over his old drome and gave the bomb droppers perfect targets for their bombs. The wet shine was in his eyes when the bombs went down and he saw red fury spread over the barracks in which he once had slept.

The Japanese beside him saw the expression on his face and he gave testimony to that expression.

"The man hates Russians," he said. "There can be no doubt of it."

Bruce McNeil did not see the report, but he felt at home with the Japanese and he was confident. It did not occur to him that he had died on the drome where the bombs blasted the Russian barracks, but he had died his second death down there.

Rodoff had not dared to make a report of desertion and of the loss of a prize plane. On his reports there was a report of the bomber's destruction and one line beneath it, read:

"B. McNeil, American, killed."

McNeil would not have cared if he knew. He had adopted the name of Thomas Smith when he came over to the Japanese, and it was a good name. He was not seeking fame, but the gratification of a consuming lust. He wanted to bomb Shanghai or Canton.

In December, 1937, he got his wish.

He was so much better at long-distance flying than his Japanese comrades that he was used as the leader of the flight for the bombing of Canton. Beside him sat the man who was the actual leader; it was significant that Bruce McNeil was not permitted to carry sidearms. The idea amused him and he did not make an issue of it.

He watched his bombs crash into frail, cardboard construction houses and watched scarlet tides of flame sweep the city below him; more thrilling far than the night in Baltimore when the blazing downtown building tore a hole in the gray fog. This was the real article, and there were no firemen down there battling for control of it.

He swooped low, too, and saw his bombs rend frightened mobs in the streets. He felt no pity, only a mounting joy at the monstrous efficiency of it.

As a man, he had almost ceased to exist. He was 90 percent an appetite for destruction and he did not know that the 10 percent still existed. He was to find out—and dramatically.

The Japanese, too, had an invention to test. They did not confide in Bruce McNeil, but they planned to use him. A German in their service had developed a new type of bomb with directional wings on it and a method of releasing it from high altitudes. He claimed deadly accuracy for his invention, even against moving targets.

"It is a naval weapon," he said, "and it will forever settle the question of the airplane's supremacy over the battleship."

Japan was cautious about naval warfare. There had been too much talk of blockades, and a naval incident on the high seas might be the last straw upon the patient back of an outraged world. Yet, indisputably, a new naval weapon should be tried out against a warship; a warship that was in motion and not merely an anchored target.

The wise eyes of the strategists surveyed the field of Japanese operations, and a yellow finger touched the Yangtze River below Nanking.

"Here," a dry voice said, "naval vessels move. On either bank we are engaged with the unreasonable Chinese. An 'accident' would be deplorable but natural. It is the place for the test."

Bruce McNeil knew nothing of what went on within the sanctums of the leaders of the Sun God's armies. He was merely a flying man. He was picked to pilot the test because he had a consummate mastery over any type of airplane, and no nerves.

On the afternoon of December 12 he took off for a flight over the Yangtze at an assigned altitude of sixteen thousand feet. He had a copilot who bore the rank of captain, and the cabin crew included a nervous, bespectacled German. He looked the German over with interest and he was not stupid.

"Something unusual coming off today?" he asked.

The little captain beside him shrugged and smiled. The captain was carrying binoculars and he, like those in the rear compartment, was fairly bursting with excitement.

If what the German said was true, the winged bomb would correct its own deviation from the target after a fall of five thousand feet—and it would be equally destructive whether it scored a direct hit or struck close to a vessel. There was but one bomb.

Bruce McNeil took off. He was flying a Mitsubishi bomber of an orthodox type, a ship with a fairly good rate of climb but with no particular distinction in the way of speed.

Riding serenely on the yellow waters of the Yangtze were several British vessels, the Union Jack whipping in the breeze. On the far bank he could see evidences of fierce fighting between Chinese and Japanese troops. A Japanese war vessel in the river was dropping an occasional shell upon the Chinese infantry positions.

It was a familiar picture and not particularly exciting to the man who had been Death's messenger boy on grim visits to the crowded cities of China. As the ship climbed, details of the ground became hazed over. As they neared sixteen thousand, the Japanese captain started using the binoculars.

Bruce McNeil was bored. This had all of the earmarks of a routine flight in which a bunch of Japs did things which seemed damned important to them and that were a pain in the neck to everyone else. He lolled behind the wheel and kept a weary eye on his instruments. Beside him the captain emitted a sudden sharp yip.

McNeil looked at him, startled. The little man was far over the side, the binoculars glued to his eyes and his body trembling with excitement. Bruce McNeil looked over and could see only the flat, distant contour of the earth. It annoyed him, and his attention swung back to the man at his side.

The Japanese had forgotten his dignity.

"It is true, he said. "It is true. It really does what was claimed."

He was speaking Japanese and Bruce McNeil did not understand him, but if something had happened below him which was interesting enough to shake a Jap out of his pants, then it was too good to miss. He reached over with one big hand, took the binoculars without an apology, and focused on the scene below.

The river and the embattled land came up to him. He saw three Japanese planes darting about like angry hornets; two scouts and a torpedo ship. Below the planes was the river—and in midstream a stricken vessel was heeling slowly over.

Bruce McNeil's breath caught. He knew every one of those Jap planes beneath him as a type and he knew their possibilities, their limitations. There was not one of them that could have destroyed a gunboat on the river, even with the aid of luck—and the Japs did not send ships out on impossible jobs.

"They are a stall, a blind. They are attracting attention so we won't be noticed. We dropped the knockout punch. Something new, something that excited this skibby beside me. And I missed the show."

That was his first reaction; then the glasses focused with attention on the crippled gunboat and his muscles slowly stiffened.

Flying from the mast was the Stars and Stripes. Painted on the side of the vessel were the American colors.

"Yanks," he muttered. "An American ship."

Time stood still and a flag fluttered across the binocular glass; red stripes and white with a field of blue. He looked at it fascinated, as at something that he had never seen before.

The ship was going down and there were men out on the yellow bosom of the river in small boats. Up here in the sky a Mitsubishi bomber was pursuing its anonymous way with an American at the controls, while down there the ship that it had blasted was going to its death in a filthy Chinese river.*

The blood in his veins slowed—where disaster and death had always speeded it. The Japanese captain touched his arm and tried to reclaim the binoculars, but he shook him off.

The Stars and Stripes still fluttered across his field of vision.

McNeil was like a statue in the cockpit. He was not a patriot. He had played football at Cornell but never for Cornell. He had looked at a thousand flags and felt nothing. The stuff from which patriotism is distilled was not in him. He did not fight for causes or sacrifice for ideals.

Still, there was a flag fluttering down there that symbolized life as he had known it.

In all of his years, Bruce McNeil had never destroyed a thing that was his own. He had guarded the things that he possessed, and if they no longer served him, he abandoned them; but, no matter how strong the lust to destroy, he had never gratified that lust upon things that were his.

Beneath him in the river was something that was Bruce McNeil's.

He lowered the binoculars and turned slowly to the man beside him. The Japanese stretched out his hands for the glasses, and Bruce McNeil broke both of his hands at the wrist with a quick grip and a twist. His hands launched then for the other's throat, and they were the hands of a football player, hands that had grown hard on the control columns of big planes.

He wrung the little man's neck as he would wring the neck of a chicken, dipped his hand into the leather holster, and possessed himself of an automatic pistol.

He stood up, away from the controls. It was a stable ship and might reasonably be expected to fly for a half-hour on an even keel if

*On December 12, 1937, the U.S. gunboat *Panay* was sunk in the Yangtze River above Nanking, presumably as the result of bombs dropped from a Japanese airplane. Japan apologized for the incident and paid indemnity, but the "accident" of that day was never explained.

properly set. He faced the door to the rear compartment and kicked it open with his foot.

There were three men inside; the German and two Japanese. They had their eyes glued to binoculars which were set into a table in mid-cabin.

One of the Japanese looked up, startled, and McNeil shot him.

He shot the others while the echo of the report was still thunder in the enclosed space.

For a long ten seconds he stood there with the gun in his hand. The men lay where he had dropped them. He felt no thrill, no sense of elation, no wild excitement in his veins. He had killed before and some strange electricity had run wild in him. Today he felt nothing.

Slowly he turned back to the controls of the ship. He stepped on the body of the man whom he had choked and he took his place under the wheel with a numb sense of having experienced all things; a dull wonder that he was where he was and that he had done the things that were written into the book of his life.

He did not look again at the United States gunboat in the river. It had gone down, he imagined, and the thought did not shock him.

He did not feel remorse that he was connected with the sinking. His entire reaction was that something that was his had been at stake and that he had fought for it.

He spiraled slowly down and he knew now that he had a problem on his hands. He was flying a ship of Japan, but he could not take that ship back. There were corpses for which he could never account. Wearily he turned the nose of the Mitsubishi toward the first airdrome that he had known in war-torn China.

He would go back to the first chapter. The trick that he had worked on the Japanese when he brought them a gift for the Emperor might reasonably be expected to work again. He braced his shoulders and flew south for Shanghai. The airdrome that he had known was still there, a broad rough field with dirty hangars and a high wall about it of pale yellow. He had pulled a Russian ship out of a spin over Shanghai and brought it back to this field, but that was long ago.

Antiaircraft fire blasted him and he flew through it. He slipped the big ship and came in fishtailing. The Chinese soldiers ran out and he came down from the cabin stiffly.

"Send for your commander," he said. "I bring a gift for Chiang Kai-shek."

Some of the old vitality was gone out of him, the natural haughtiness and the will to command. The Chinese soldiers were rougher, too, of coarse fiber. They paid no attention to his demands and showed no interest in what he might have to say. They laid bayonets against him and disarmed him. An officer in a torn uniform intoned a command, and two soldiers bound the hands of Bruce McNeil. They hustled him along with a bayonet prodding his back. When the stone walls of an obvious dungeon loomed ahead of him, McNeil played his last card.

"Chu Yuang-fu," he said. "Get me Chu Yuang-fu."

The soldiers heard him and they handled him less roughly, but they did not reply to him and they did not desist in their obvious purpose. He was rushed down a damp corridor, pushed into a dark cell that smelled of forgotten centuries.

It seemed, at least, that he had been forgotten. He paced for hours, searching his clothes vainly for crumbs of tobacco; he beat one powerful hand against the other. There was no sound from the other cells and no evidence of a world outside until a door creaked and a yellow light gleamed at the end of the cell corridor.

Chu Yuang-fu came down the corridor behind the man with the light.

The Chinese was, as he had been, untouched by time. As before, he wore no insignia of rank. He wore in his personality the badge of a man who is qualified to command and it was enough. Before the cell of Bruce McNeil he stopped.

"You inquired for me?"

He spoke English, but there was no recognition in his eyes. McNeil remembered that this was the man who had spoken of being "a good soldier." He braced his shoulders.

"I have been the victim of outrage," he said. "Captured and forced to serve Japan, I sought the opportunity of returning to China with a gift which would prove my sincerity. I brought to you a Japanese bomber and four servants of Japan who died by my hand."

Chu Yuang-fu looked at him without expression. He turned to the man with the lantern and he spoke in English.

"Get me an interpreter," he said, "who understands Japanese. I do not speak the tongue of Japan."

Bruce McNeil stared at him.

"Hey," he said, "I'm not speaking Japanese. You know it. You . . ."

He broke off at the look in the eyes of Chu Yuang-fu. That look told him that he had become Japanese in the eyes of China, that never again would he be able to speak to a Chinese in any language that a Chinese understood. He spread his hands resignedly.

"All right. I'm a Japanese," he said. "When does it happen to me?"

Chu Yuang-fu bowed.

"At dawn," he said.

The man with the lantern, who had not gone after an interpreter, sensed the end of the interview. He started back along the corridor, and the war lord followed him.

Bruce McNeil watched the retreating light and returned to the bench in his cell.

He did not know that at that moment a Japanese petty officer was writing in the list of the day's casualties the name "Thomas Smith," and that in the Japanese book of death over China, Bruce McNeil's third death was being recorded.

Bruce McNeil knew only in a dim sort of way that he was done with destruction and that the last things he destroyed had given him no satisfaction; that in the end he had found that there were things that were his. Things of vague value: a set of stripes, red stripes and white, and a field of blue.

At dawn they shot him, against a yellow wall at Hungjao.

When he had been tumbled into a shallow hole an officer in a torn coat made an entry in a little book. It was a routine entry, and no future historian will ever find it to link it with an international incident.

"Executed this morning," he wrote, "one Japanese."

LELAND JAMEISON

East from Botwood

IT WAS BECAUSE their armament had been stripped to the minimum to allow weight for extra fuel, and because they were almost defenseless, that they had timed their take-off from Botwood, Newfoundland, so as to get the advantage of all possible darkness over the danger zones of England where they might run into German patrols. There were twelve of them, sleek American-built bombers flying at ten thousand feet, piloted by flying officers and sergeant pilots of the Royal Canadian Air Force who had graduated from training school only last week, and whose wings were therefore almost as new as those of the planes themselves. In loose formation they were racing eastward in a frantic haste to aid Britain.

Fog lay under them now—mile on mile of white mist that blanketed the North Atlantic as far as the eye could reach. At the point of their V, their commander, Squadron Leader Hartley Turner, a tall young man with a lean, hungry face and observant blue eyes, sat easily at his controls, watching his compass and his flight instruments attentively. Through the earphones in his helmet, the squeal of the Botwood beam was a reassuring, monotonous sound that laid down an invisible pathway from Newfoundland to Ireland.

Botwood, Newfoundland—Newfoundland Airport—was two hours behind them now, as they climbed the curve of the earth in a sweeping great-circle course that had already placed them above 51° north latitude. It was late afternoon, local time; eight o'clock, London time; it would be sundown before many hours. Then through the short night they would roar steadily on, to reach England just after dawn.

"And a bloody fine thing if we run into a strong formation of Germans just when we get there," Hartley Turner was thinking. "With only one machine gun and gunner apiece!" He turned suddenly to Sergeant Drake, his gunner navigator, who sat in the cockpit beside him. "What will we do," he yelled against the muttering exhausts, "if the Germans do jump us? We won't have enough strength to drive them off!"

Sergeant Drake was a short, stocky man with steel-gray eyes set in a squarish, cocky, stubborn face. "We'll give 'em the works with the guns we've got!" he exclaimed. "I hope we stumble across some of them!"

"I hope we don't!" Hartley Turner said. He was thinking of the inexperience of the pilots behind him, and he was thinking how important it was that they and their planes be landed safely in England. Every day, every hour almost, put Britain in increasing danger; only planes and more planes, pilots and more pilots, coming in flights from Newfoundland every day the weather permitted their crossing of the North Atlantic, could turn the tide of this holocaust of war. An overwhelming force of Germans, with superior experience and crushing fire power, could easily annihilate this squadron. "We can't afford to let the Germans jump us on this flight," Turner added. His wide mouth twisted in a grim, wry smile. "If they do, I'll run like hell!"

He saw the sharp sidewise glance Sergeant Drake gave him, and saw the look of questioning surprise that crossed Drake's face.

"What do you think would happen if every squadron leader ran from them?" Drake demanded bluntly, and his tone held a suggestion of contempt. "They'd take the British Isles in sixty hours! In war, no matter what the odds, you've got to fight!"

Hartley Turner felt his face grow hot. Sergeant Drake was a man who spoke his thoughts without reflection or restraint, no matter to whom he might be talking. He could do that, being who he was. Of all the heroes of this war, he was the greatest. Already he had shot down eleven German planes and had been wounded, and decorated by the King for conspicuous bravery beyond the call of duty. During his convalescence he had been sent to Canada to instruct students in the British Commonwealth Air Training Plan. It was only because he preferred to fly back to England than cross the Atlantic on a transport that he had been assigned temporarily to Hartley Turner's squadron.

Like most young air-force officers and men, Turner admired him immensely in an awed sort of way. So it was a shock to see that look on Sergeant Drake's belligerent, tanned face. To Turner, the sergeant's good opinion was a priceless thing. But he could see he didn't have it now. The sergeant thought he was afraid to fight.

He wondered if that could possibly be true. He had often considered the probability that he would be killed before this was was over. So many men were being killed; the casualty percentages in the air force were awful to consider. Wanting life intensely, Turner was afraid of being killed, but he did not think he was afraid to die.

He had often worried, too, whether he had the qualities he needed as a squadron leader. He didn't know. He was only twenty-five, but he had had two years as a co-pilot on a commercial air line before going into military training at the beginning of the war; that was the only reason he had been made a squadron leader, he was sure. But that experience did not necessarily qualify him to lead other men into the deadly fighting of this war. Probably Drake thought him not qualified at all.

''It's about time for me to take a sun sight,'' Drake said suddenly, as if, reading the defenses that were building up confusedly in Turner's mind, he did not want to listen. He moved back through the cavernous bomb bay to the rear gunner's cockpit.

Turner sat there, feeling an anger and humiliation that he could not overcome. Ordinarily he did not give too much consideration to what other people thought of him. But this was different; it was immensely different. Admiring him so much, and wanting to be like him, to Hartley Turner it was almost desperately important that Drake's opinion of him be a good one. In some peculiar way, the sergeant's disapproval robbed him of his confidence. And confidence in this war was a vital thing. Without it, any man was lost.

The wind at ten thousand feet was strong from the west; the temperature was thirty-six. Farther on, the squadron might run into ice. Turner wasn't sure he would encounter it, but there was danger. Because of the curtailment of ship's weather reports on account of the war, conditions were not accurately known. The map had shown an indefinite front a few hundred miles west of Ireland.

If the front was there, Hartley Turner hoped it would be mild. The pilots of this squadron knew so little. Of them all, he was the only one who'd had a thousand hours. They'd had only a limited amount of training in formation flying in clouds, and had never slammed into any violent turbulence. If that front was a tough one, it might get them all in trouble.

Holding his course, Turner studied the fog below. They had seen nothing, since shortly after leaving the rocky Newfoundland coast and heading over the sea; the fog had lain in a low wall near the coast, blanketing everything. For the past two hours, every thirty minutes Sergeant Drake had taken a sun sight with his octant, and had projected his sun line to get a cross bearing to check against the widening Botwood beam. It was necessary to maintain a running fix; by the time they reached the Irish coast the beam would be two hundred miles wide.

Now Drake came forward to his seat. Burrowed in his heavy flying suit for warmth against the cold, his collar turned up around his neck, he bent over his chart board for a while.

"At eight-thirty, Greenwich time," he yelled, "our position was fifty-two degrees ten minutes north latitude, forty-one degrees forty minutes west longitude. We're making better than two-thirty."

"How far out of Botwood now?"

"Nearly six hundred miles." Drake looked back at his board a moment. "I make our speed exactly two-thirty-nine—five miles better than before."

Turner nodded, and looked from Drake's tough face back to the instruments. It was a hell of a thing, he thought bitterly, to have a man like Drake think you were afraid to fight. But he said nothing more. Words would never alter that opinion.

He hadn't expected to find a stronger helping wind as he got farther out from Botwood. It was a relief to have it. These planes cruised at well over two hundred at this altitude with normal power output, but he was flying at reduced power to achieve maximum fuel economy. It was more than twenty-three hundred miles from Botwood to London, and it would require all the fuel in the tanks to do that, and still leave a safe margin at the end.

When he transferred the new position to his own chart, Turner was surprised to see that because of his speed he was already north of his track. He turned three degrees to the right. His magnetic variation was still thirty-four degrees west, and it would remain nearly constant for another hour's flying. Every hour he would have to turn a little, to maintain his great-circle track; a great circle was flown as a series of short straight lines. It was a good deal more complicated than the navigation required on the airline flights he was used to.

Working with his chart board in his lap, he checked Drake's last position against previous positions. He checked everything twice. There could be no mistakes now; a mistake now would upset his dead-reckoning navigation later, when they got into that front.

The minutes ticked slowly to hours; the hours dragged past. Turner made no further effort to maintain conversation with Drake. He would have liked to ask about air fighting, about the sergeant's experiences, but, feeling youth's sensitivity to disapproval, he flew on in silence.

The sun dipped toward the western horizon. For nearly an hour now, Drake had been unable to get an accurate sight. "I'll shoot Polaris as soon as it's dark enough!" he yelled. "Until then we'll have to depend on the beam!"

Turner nodded. They would soon be halfway across. The mat of fog was still solid below.

The sun sank behind them, amid a slow, magnificent flush of crimson reds. Daylight merged into twilight—the murky half-light of this far northern latitude in summer. Drake, to be ready to take his star sights when twilight had faded to darkness—as much darkness as would come here at this time of the year—went back once more to the rear gunner's cockpit.

Turner sat there, boring on into the inscrutable curtain of sky. His job was to get these bombers safely to England; he must get them there. He wondered why it made so much difference what Drake thought of him.

Suddenly, every nerve taut, he stiffened to the change in his earphones. They were empty and dead. The Botwood beam had gone off the air.

He listened a moment, and turned up the volume and fiddled with his receiver tuning dial. Static scratched at his earphones, making his ears hurt. The trouble was not in his receiver. But to make sure of that, he flicked on the transmitter of the low-power intra-squadron wireless, and called Flight Leader MacKenzie, "Are you still receiving the beam?"

Mackenzie's voice, hollowly modulated, came back at onec, "It went off about a minute ago. A nice time for it to play tricks on us, what?"

"What do you make your position?"

"Stand by."

Waiting, Turner yelled an explanation to Drake, "We may be in trouble, if we go on without that beam! I can't take chances with a whole squadron of pilots and planes, when they're needed so badly! Do you think we should turn back?"

Sergeant Drake's square face was expressionless, but there was a look of derision in his gray eyes. "You're in command," he said. "But I don't see why you're worried. The beam will probably come on again.'' He shrugged. ''If it doesn't, we'll navigate in without any trouble.''

But Turner could not help feeling worried. He had seen detailed reports on the Botwood range setup, and he knew a prolonged beam failure was very improbable. Yet, it was possible. A main-transmission-line breakdown could have occurred, or some incoming pilot might have neglected to reel in his antenna wire and, crossing low over the hundred-and-forty-foot range towers, might have broken his wire off across the antennae, kicking a relay out and putting the beam off the air until the antennae could be lowered and the obstruction removed. That would take several hours.

''By dead reckoning,'' MacKenzie suddenly said, ''at ten thirty-five Greenwich time, I make out position fifty-three thirty-eight north, twenty-nine fifteen west. But my navigator won't guarantee that. What do you make it?''

''Fifty-three thirty north, twenty-nine fifty west,'' Turner said into his microphone.

''That's pretty close. You going on?''

Turner gave a moment of anxious debate to that question. He should proceed if he could. He believed, as Sergeant Drake did, that the beam would come on again soon. Of course, he thought, he could call Botwood with his high-power transmitter and inquire about the beam—except that such a call would reveal to a listening enemy the presence of eastbound planes over the Atlantic. He decided against that. In a few minutes Drake could get enough star sights to establish beyond question the squadron's position; the sky was still clear. They should now be less than nine hundred miles from the Irish coast; they could navigate that distance by dead reckoning, surely, having established their drift and speed at this point.

''I'm going on,'' he informed MacKenzie. ''We can't be far off, and we'll be running into daylight.''

''Good,'' MacKenzie said in his hollow voice. ''We're all right behind you.''

They roared on toward the retreating horizon. The sun was barely gone, leaving the ash of its flame in the west. Polaris had not yet popped out in the north. Twilight at this latitude lasted a long time in summer. Turner thought he could make out a dark, towering cloud mass ahead now. He should, he knew, descend before he got to the front. But he was impatient for Sergeant Drake to get that shot of Polaris. With it, they could correct their course if necessary, and proceed with rough accuracy. Without it, navigation from here on would be guesswork. To allow Drake to get it, he must maintain his altitude during the sight. He didn't descend.

But Drake never got a fix on Polaris. For suddenly, with frightening speed, the black line up there took sinister shape, and then the clouds seemed to reach out and gulp Turner's plane. The red and green running lights exploded in wet mist.

At once Turner yelled into his microphone to every pilot in his squadron, "Close up formation! Close up and stay closed up! Maintain plane-to-plane contact! I'm reducing speed and turning back!"

He didn't want to turn back, but he knew he must. A dozen pilots and gunners and planes were too valuable to risk. With the beam off, with nothing but dead-reckoning positions for the past hour and a half, with a front ahead, filled with violent shifting winds that would change every factor of drift and speed, it was sheer folly to continue.

He analyzed all the factors involved in a sort of distracted haste, for he had his hands full now. Deep in the clouds, he dared not slow too suddenly, or his wing men would overrun him, perhaps collide with him, certainly become separated from the formation. As the acknowledgments came from the individual pilots, he was putting on carburetor heat and easing his throttles back to reduce the manifold pressure; he was flying his instruments, his legs tensed for rough air that hadn't come yet, but would come at any moment.

Sergeant Drake had given up trying to get a sight on Polaris. He came back to his seat and put his belt on. He asked calmly, "Can you get out on top?"

"Not these clouds!" Turner yelled. He could not turn to look at Drake now; he was too busy. "Check our fuel! This is a front! We're going back!"

He went on flying, every sense actely tensed to the reactions of the instruments. In the stress of the moment, it was impossible for him to look back to make sure the others were close enough to him and to one another to maintain visual contact through this thick, choking mist. His own plane was slowed to one hundred and twenty. He started a slow, cautious turn, inching around. In straight flight it was hard enough for his wing men to follow him through solid clouds; in a turn it was precarious.

But the idea of turbulence harassed him, making his skin feel prickly and cold. If they went into violent turbulence in this close formation, there would be collisions inevitably. He had to get down.

In a front, the lower altitudes were always smoother than high ones. If he got down quickly enough, they might escape the most turbulent air; if they turned back quickly enough, they might never encounter rough air at all. They must hurry—and they could not hurry too much in a turn of this kind. It seemed to take forever.

They had turned about forty degrees when MacKenzie's voice, hollower than usual, yet terse with excitement, came through Turner's earphones, "I'm getting ice! Big!"

"Are you in contact with me?" Turner yelled. His eyes went from his instruments in a quick glance at his windshield. He had been too busy to see it before, but he saw it now. He was getting ice too.

"Contact," MacKenzie said. "But I'm losing you fast, with ice on my windshied."

"Open your windshield," Turner ordered. "All pilots, open your windsheilds before they freeze shut."

He tugged at his own with both hands, letting the plane fly itself for a moment. He yelled at Sergeant Drake to open the glass on that side of the cockpit. Both panels were almost frozen shut already. But Turner got his window open. Freezing wind knifed into his face through the gap, making his eyes water. He ducked his head out of the blast, keeping his eyes on the instruments. Drake was still having trouble getting his panel open.

"Heave on it, man!" Turner bellowed. "Take a fire extinguisher and break it out, if you have to!" Just then the window slid slowly open as Drake, cursing, exerted all his strength. "Check that fuel!" Turner added "We've got to make sure we've got enough to get back!"

They went on down, still in the turn. In Turner's mind was a dread of the planes becoming widely separated; widely separated, they would never find one another, probably, even after they broke out of the clouds. He had been a fool! He should have descended before they ever got to the front. But he had been determined to let Drake get that sight on Polaris. He hadn't thought it was possible to run into such a dangerous icing condition quite so suddenly. He had led his squadron into a trap.

Sergeant Drake, bending forward to read the fuel gauges, turned his head suddenly and exclaimed, "We haven't got enough fuel to get back to Botwood now!"

Hartley Turner sucked his breath in sharply. It seemed to him just then that he was utterly incompetent to lead this squadron. He was the most experienced pilot in it. But there were so many things to consider that he couldn't think about them all.

The Botwood beam, he felt sure, must come on soon. But it might not. Yet whether it came on again or remained silent now made little difference, actually. If he did not have enough fuel to return to Botwood, the other planes likewise would run out before they got back. Front or no front, they now had no other choice than to continue on.

But first they must rid themselves of ice. They were still in the flat, slow turn. "Is each pilot in contact with the one in front of him?" Turner demanded hurriedly. "Acknowledge."

Quickly, beginning with MacKenzie, the acknowledgments came through. They all had their windshields open now. Each one was in contact with the plane ahead.

"I'm straightening out on a course of one-eight zero and increasing descent," Turner said. "Keep your intervals closed. We'll find warm air and go on. I haven't enough fuel now to get back to Botwood."

He heard MacKenzie say, "That saves me a bloody cold swim!" and then there was silence.

Turner eased out of the turn, heading south, planning to parallel the front in an effort to stay out of the turbulence until he had found warmer air and had got rid of the ice. They must avoid turbulence at any cost now. If they encountered it, it would scatter the squadron like dead leaves.

He nosed down still more, very gently, every muscle taut. This sort of flying was the most exacting of any he had ever attempted. It required smoothness and deliberation in every change of speed or direction or level of the plane. They had practiced it while in training, to be ready for night bombing flights. A few times they had lost one another in the clouds, and there had been some near things, with wings actually touching two or three times. And that had been without any overpowering burden of ice, without vision limited to the scope of a small gap in each windshield.

They were at nine thousand feet now. The ice was still forming. It seemed incredible that the air could have become so much colder in such a short space of time. They had plunged into the rear of a major front; there was no doubt of that. And they were deep into it.

They were down to eight thousand feet, and still getting ice. . . . They were down to seven thousand, and the temperature gauge showed no perceptible change. The load of ice was becoming rapidly dangerous. Turner's plane was trembling, and the controls were stiff and rebellious in their response. It required all the strength of his legs to stop the repeated effort to yaw.

They were settling now, not just descending; the weight was that great. Turner eased on more power slowly, so as not to draw away from MacKenzie. The rate-of-climb showed a thousand feet a minute, down. They were at six thousand feet, and then five thousand. The wind was shrieking in through the open windshield, blasting back out of that solid cold mist.

But at four thousand feet, the air-temperature gauge was showing a definite rise.

Sergeant Drake, who had been sitting mute in his seat, pointed at the needle and yelled in a voice that was raucous against the rush of the wind into the cockpit, "Thirty-five now! Getting warmer out there!"

Before Turner could answer, ice was suddenly flung from one blade of the left propeller and struck the fuselage with a violent metallic explosion. Immediately that engine grew terrifically rough, adding its vibration to the trembling caused by the ice on the plane; threatening, it seemed, to tear the engine out of its mount.

Instantly Turner grabbed the prop pitch controls. His impulse was to throttle the left engine, but he overcame that. He put both engines into low pitch. With a series of ear-shattering detonations as more ice slammed the fuselage, the engines growled up to twenty-two hundred revvs. At once the propeller vibration ceased as the props spun their ice off. Turner pulled them back into cruising pitch once more, and went on descending.

A moment later a slab of melting ice loosened from the glass of the windshield made a resounding impact and was flung away by the wind. Still later the plane yawed suddenly and the left wing went abruptly down as ice broke loose from the right one. Then, little by little, the dead weight was lost, and the plane became docile again.

But the squadron was still buried in clouds. With a quick backward glance through each side window, Turner saw that Flight Leader MacKenzie and Flying Officer Johnston were close on his wings. Their running lights, glowing in the thick mist, silhouetted the wings and fuselage in a ghostly outline. It was impossible to see beyond them, to determine whether the others were in position, too; the clouds were too thick.

This sort of formation flying would exhaust any pilot within a short time, Turner knew. His job, as leader, was easy compared with the problems of spacing and altitude and speed that the others must cope with without a moment's relaxation. He wondered if it were possible for them to withstand the terrific strain of several hours under tension like that. He didn't think so. Sooner or later, fatigue would slow a reflex, and a pilot would overrun or lag too far, and there would be a collision or a part of the squadron would become lost.

Yet they had to go on. They must penetrate this front, and ride out its turbulence, and go on, and then let down and find out where they were. Their lives depended on their going on now.

At one thousand feet, Turner leveled off and turned back on his course. He was desperately tired, but he dared not relax. And he dared go no lower, to attempt to get under the ceiling—if there was ceiling here. With the change of barometric pressure between Botwood and here, there might be a wide error in his altimeter now. He knew he was running into a lower pressure, approaching the front; in that lower pressure he might be only five hundred feet above the sea now, instead of one thousand. Grouped close on his wings, the squadron made the turn with him.

With startling abruptness, they slammed into the turbulence, taking the first shock, and the second, and being tossed upward. Fighting his rudder until his legs ached, Turner tried to hold a straight course. He couldn't maintain his altitude. The shocks of the updrafts blasted him to three thousand feet. He was sure he had lost the squadron behind him.

But in a moment of smoother air when he could tear his eyes from the instruments, he saw MacKenzie and Johnston still in there close to his wings. Through his microphone, he called on the others to count off. They answered in prompt order, in dead-tired voices. They were all in formation. Somehow they had managed to ride through that turbulence without being separated.

They hit the rain in the front, a short, hard deluge that dwindled quickly to a steady drizzle. And then the rough air was behind them.

But they were still in the clouds—with their destination almost a thousand miles away.

The Botwood beam had not come on again, and of course there would be no star sights possible in continued weather like this. On the east side of the front, these clouds would tower higher than any pilot could survive without oxygen. They had no oxygen. Their situation was critical, perhaps even desperate, although it was too soon to know that.

For they were lost, with no possibility, at least until daylight, of determining where they were. Even if they managed to get under these clouds, below them would be only the blank, open sea, with no lights, no clues of any kind as to their position. Turner sat there, boring on into the mess of black, wet mist, biting his lips.

Instead of descending, he started, presently, a slow climb. His pilots could not stand the unremitting strain of flying constantly in the clouds, in tight formation. He had to give them relief, if he could.

He went up to two thousand, then to three thousand. Still the clouds were unbroken, solid as a curtain draped from the sky.

But at four thousand feet, suddenly he emerged from the lower overcast; the running lights stopped glowing as his plane broke out into a clear stratum of air. Above them was still another overcast, but here, at least temporarily, they were out of the clouds. Looking back, Turner saw the whole squadron, every running light clearly visible. He counted the planes, feeling thankful and proud of thee pilots who knew so little and yet had come through so much.

For an hour after that, he flew steadily on through the darkness, giving everyone a chance to relax from the strain of that front and the long drag of instrument flying afterward. For himself, he could not relax in the least. The problem was in no way simplified by their having come through that front. He knew the winds had changed, with the crossing of the front, and since then there had been no way of determining their strength or direction. He thought Ireland was within three hundred miles, probably, now. But there was no way to be sure. It was possible that they would miss Ireland altogether, and England, too, unless they could get under the overcast soon. But until dawn came it would be suicide to attempt that.

"See if you can pick up a British broadcasting station on your directional wireless!" he yelled at Sergeant Drake. "We ought to be close enough to hear somebody now! We've got to find out where we are!"

But Sergeant Drake, even after more than an hour of trying, was unable to pick up any broadcasting stations in either Ireland or England. Finally he came back to his seat.

"No luck!" he yelled. "The Germans must be out tonight! All the stations are silent—they're always silent when Jerry's loose! I can't pick up a thing!"

"Keep trying!" Hartley Turner said against the growl of the exhausts.

It was growing faintly light now. Dawn would be here in a few more minutes. Because of the danger of flying into the water—since he had no way of knowing the barometric pressure and his altimeters were untrustworthy until he did know—he was afraid to let down through the overcast below him. The ceiling might be zero. If it was, he would never see the water until he crashed into it. "Keep trying! We've got to pick up a station and find out where we are!"

Drake kept trying. He tried steadily for another hour, tuning his receiver endlessly, listening; tuning and listening. Through his earphones Turner was listening, too, while he held his course—a course that might be taking him straight over England, or south of England, past Land's End, or over Scotland. Sitting up here with the overcast below him, there was no way of knowing. The overcast, he could see now, straining his eyes, was solid and heavy, and it looked as if it reached down to the sea.

They were already well into their last tank of fuel. They cold stay in the air less than two more hours. It was daylight now, a weak, gray, cheerless daylight here between the overcasts. They must be long past Ireland. They should be past Wales, or over England, if their speed had not materially diminished. If it had increased much, they were over the Channel, perhaps almost to France.

The thought of that made Turner desperate. He had to find out where he was. If he went on, and found a hole and let down over France, there would not then be sufficient fuel to return to England—even if he could escape German fighters and get back to the Channel. He would be forced down in France, and the Germans would capture these planes and their crews. He was determined that that shouldn't happen. He had been given the responsibility of delivering these bombers to Great Britain, and he intended to succeed. But it was several minutes before he thought he saw a way he might succeed.

When he did see it, he called Sergeant Drake, and explained in staccato, hurried words, "I'm going to let down—alone. We may be over land, instead of water. I can't risk taking the squadron down and putting twelve ships into a mountain—there are thirty-five-hundred-foot mountains in both Wales and Scotland, and we may be over either one. I'm going to leave the squadron up here with MacKenzie. When we start down, you report our altitude to MacKenzie every thirty seconds. If we stop reporting, he'll know the altitude of whatever we hit and can take the squadron away from there before he lets down. That way, we may lose this plane, but we won't lose the whole squadron."

Drake looked at him with startled eyes. He took a deep, quick breath. "Yes, sir," he said in a peculiar muffled voice.

Quickly, Turner called MacKenzie and explained what he was going to do. "Stay here between the overcasts, flying the same course I'm flying, until I call you down. We can't pick up a station and I'm going to find out where we are this way."

"Here's luck!" MacKenzie said.

"Cheerio," Hartley Turner answered, and nosed down for his descent.

He knew exactly the risk he was assuming, and it frightened him, but he had to save his squadron, even though his own plane might be lost in doing it. One plane was not important, relatively; it would be well spent if its loss enabled all the others to get safely through.

For a moment, flying just above the clouds, he got a sense of the plane's terrific speed, and then the dark wet mist enveloped them. Rivulets of water swirled around the edges of the cockpit windows. Turner snatched his windshield open and tried to peer out into that thick cold blanket. He couldn't see more than a hundred feet ahead. At this speed, if he was lower than a mountain, he would see it but an instant before they were shattered on its side; he would not have time to move a muscle before the crash occurred. Feeling taut and excited, and yet completely self-possessed, he eased his throttles off until his air speed sagged to ninety miles an hour. Then, straining his eyes and trying not to think of what might be just ahead, he went steadily down.

Thirty seconds after they had sliced into the clouds, Drake called MacKenzie. "Thirty-seven hundred feet, course ninety-three degrees true," Drake said.

Hartley Turner held that steady angle of descent. Tension was clawing at his nerves, but now that he had decided what to do, he had no trouble doing it.

"Thirty-four hundred feet, course ninety-two degrees," Drake said. His voice was clipped and harsh.

Now they were below the mountain peaks that were buried in this choking fog somewhere. They might be paralleling a range, or they might be descending into a valley with a high, sheer wall ahead. The only way they could find out was to go on down and see.

"Twenty-eight hundred, course ninety-four degrees," Drake said. There was sweat on his forehead, but Hartley Turner had no time to see it. He was too busy flying by his instruments and snatching glances through his open windshield into the solid mist.

"Twenty-five hundred, course ninety-three," Drake said. "We haven't seen a thing."

Each second seemed to stretch into eternity. Time was measured now only by the crawling needles of the altimeters. They seemed to sweep around their dials, and yet Turner had to look at them to be sure that they moved. The mutter of the engines mingled with the steady, noisy blast of wind into the cockpit. Gravity sucked them toward the earth another thousand feet. It was growing darker under them; something was below, but whether it was level earth or sea or mountains would remain a secret until they crashed or burst out of the clouds.

"Fifteen hundred feet, course ninety-five," Drake said. "Still in the clouds." He turned to stare at Hartley Turner, and his face was pale, but Turner was looking at his instruments and didn't see. "How low do we dare go down?"

"Watch your time!" Turner bellowed. "We'll go down until we find the bottom of this stuff, or hit—"

He didn't finish. For just then they broke out underneath the dark thick clouds at thirteen hundred feet, by the reading of their altimeters, but much lower actually. Under them, in the thin morning light, they saw the sea. Relief turned Hartley Turner weak. And what he saw there on the ocean brought a quick emotion to his throat.

Down there was a convoy of a dozen freighters that wallowed steadily upon their course. Flanking them were two lean, businesslike destroyers that flew the British flag.

Sergeant Drake let out a whoop, but Turner only smiled in a weary satisfaction. That convoy meant that they were close to England; they could find out from a destroyer exactly where they were. Now, with still another hour's fuel in their tanks, they would get in without more difficulty. They had come through, and their mission was accomplished. Tomorrow, these bombers would be ready to do their part in the defense of Britain.

"Call the squadron down," Turner said. "Then get in contact with one of those destroyers and find out where we are."

"Yes, sir," Drake said in a respectful voice, and began to speak into his mike.

Later, when the squadron was winging low above the hills of England, he looked across the cockpit and declared, "I'm going to report the way you let down through those clouds, sir. You deserve a decoration for tonight! I'd not have had the nerve!"

Hartley Turner smiled. He was dead tired, but he felt all right; he felt pretty good, to have sat here in this cockpit for so long.

But he was embarrassed by Sergeant Drake's mention of a decoration, and his statement about nerve. He knew, from having been a co-pilot, that it was always harder to ride through a crisis with some other pilot than to fly through it yourself. He had done the best he could tonight; the only thing that he could think of. But he had only done his job. The real test was still ahead of him, he thought. He wondered what he would do now, if suddenly he saw some German fighters after him.

He knew he had the experience—the tough confidence—that Sergeant Drake possessed. To shoot down eleven Germans and be wounded and still be chafing to meet more! Maybe, he thought, he might develop those qualities that he admired so in Sergeant Drake, if the Germans didn't get him first. The only way to find out was to wait and see.

ARCH WHITEHOUSE

Bataan Landing

CORPORAL PETE COYNE draws his pay regularly as a member of Number 4 Observation Squadron—most of it used to be squandered in the jitney creeps of Manila for refreshment and visual entertainment. Coyne is one of those dog-wagon warriors, and if Number 4 ever gets out of Corregidor and goes into reserve somewhere in Alaska, his first demand will be: "Gimme a Coke an' a hamboiger!"

The war had not made a great deal of difference to Pete. Of course, it had plummeted him into the unwelcome responsibility of a blitzkrieg rating, but he had company—the colonel had been a captain only three weeks before.

Coyne had been massaging the gears of a White half-track when the Japs began dumping five-hundred-pounders into Manila. The boost in pay provided a little extra pocket lettuce to spend on enlarging his informal education, and the transfer to the gun turret of one of their few remaining O-47s gave him the opportunity to try out some of the theories he had evolved from a close study of air adventure as presented in that classic volume *Aces Wild*.

The equipment line-up at Kindley Field was about as impressive as a rube air carnival—what material was left had been dispersed amid the shell craters and spread out under the apitong trees and abaca palms to prevent the Japs from slugging them.

Corporal Coyne was standing by in the shadow of Number 14's port wing. The heat of the afternoon swept across the jagged chunk of volcanic rock jutting out of the waters of Manila Bay, it came down through the tropical overlay of deep green jungle that quilts Corregidor's gray cliffs, and swirled up the dust of the runway and diffused the metal gleam of the three-place observation planes.

Pete ignored the discomfort. He squatted on a rigger's tool chest with his knobby knees locked together and his squirrel eyes devouring the glorious details of a certain Lieutenant Hank Scott's adventure against the Huns somewhere over the Wipers Canal.

"Scott tooled his S.E.-5 into position," the author had penned. *The Fokkers were preparing to slam down on the sluggish Limey crate below. The* Harry Tate *was cold meat unless Scott got there in time. He rammed the spade-grip forward and stood on the rudder bar as the single-seater dived dead on the gaudy Fokker that led the death-pack below. Scott pressed the button, and his guns yammered . . ."*

"Come on! Come on!" a voice yammered above the crash of *Hank Scott's* guns. "We gotter get ridin'!"

"Sure! Yes, sir!" Coyne spluttered and hastily stuffed the book into his back pocket. "Be right there!"

A three-place observation ship can provide more trouble than the eternal triangle. The pilot, Lieutenant Malcolm Breeze, gloried in his post—his sole idea of winning the war was to shoot at anything and everything. Lieutenant Stacy Sewell, his observer, had been an air-traffic man and displayed about as much flexibility of thought and action as one might expect to find in a Pan-Central Air Line timetable. Against these two fate had stacked Corporal Coyne, a romantic if there ever was one.

"Don't you get enough without gorging on that ancient history?" Breeze snorted at him.

"It ain't so ancient," Pete defended. "That's only the last war. Them guys really did a job!"

"How do you know?"

"It says so, here in the book. Them little scouts sure used to pack it to them Fokkers. That was some war, I guess."

"The way those rags write it up, it sure was. Wait till they get through with this one—you won't recognize it."

"But this is straight stuff, sir," Corporal Coyne attempted to argue.

"Let me tell you something, Coyne," Lieutenant Sewell broke in as he lumbered up with his load of operational gear and piled it under the fuselage stirrup. "There's more phony stuff in that old war dope than you can shake a stick at. I know. I've checked it. You put a slide rule on it, and none of it checks."

"Slide rule, Lieutenant?" Pete's face curdled into a dull blotch.

"Those guys diving through zeppelins!" the observer snorted. "Hitting balloon cables to destroy spotting kites! The one about the gunner who was tossed out of an old D.H.-4 and was caught again by the pilot before he hit the ground. They can't do it, Coyne! You can't beat facts and figures. No guy ever flew through a dirigible!"

Coyne was in no position to make his superiors appear ignorant, so he muffled his protestations with his chin piece and snapped the thigh straps of his parachute pack with dull interior rumblings.

''Come on,'' Breeze ranted. ''Let's get on with the war. I got to get me a Mitsubishi. You guys and your arguments.''

''There isn't any argument,'' proclaimed Sewell. ''You can't argue with facts and figures. That's what's wrong with this war—too many people trying to be heroes, and not enough straight figuring.''

''Maybe that's what's wrong with MacArthur,'' Breeze taunted with a sly grimace.

''The only thing the matter with General MacArthur is that he's ignorant of certain facts. That's why we're being sent out again. I'm supposed to find out where the Japs have a secret landing ground. You think of nothing but shooting down planes. Coyne is figuring out how he can become a hero by the standards set in that fool book. I'm the only guy who is acting sane.''

''Do the Japs have any dirigibles for us to dive through?'' asked Breeze in mock seriousness.

''It isn't the spectacular efforts of the grandstanding few who will win this war,'' said Sewell with a patronizing air. ''Knowledge is power. That's why they train us observers.''

''It wouldn't be because you flunked out on primary aerobatics at Randolph, would it?''

''Any dope can fly a plane! Even Coyne could be taught that much.''

''Yeh?'' Pete muttered as he scrambled up the side of the O-47. ''You wait, Mr. Sewell. Lots of swell war pilots began as gunners. There was McCudden, and Bishop . . .''

Number 14 creaked as the crew climbed in; Breeze took the forward seat and kicked in the starter; Sewell, all biff and pencils, was accommodated under the direction-finder ring where he assumed his air of important business; Coyne had to be content with the poor arrangements aft, where he hoped to furnish some measure of defense with a single Browning gun.

The Cyclone engine boomed out and growled at the scream of shells that were coming out of the rifles at Fort Drum and burying their ringed snouts deep in the sands along the Pilar Road.

The Intelligence captain came out of the underground quarters waving a sheet of paper, so Sewell shoved back the hatch cover and leaned out into the prop stream as the two-bar guy barked further orders into his earpiece: "The colonel thinks maybe you have something on this landing-strip idea. There's a hint of camouflage there. He wants you to get another shot at it from about twenty-five hundred, at forty-five degrees."

"Can do!" Sewell agreed with a triumphant gleam.

"We carrying that cockpit camera again?" grumbled Breeze over the radio-panel bulkhead. He gave the Cyclone the octane, and Number 14 rumbled down what was left of Kindley Field. The dust swept up, rolled itself into a huge ball and descended on the .50-caliber ack-ack emplacement. Breeze drew her off carefully, swung over into a tight climbing turn that would have netted him twenty gigs at Randolph Field, and brought her out over the garrulous waters of lower Manila Bay.

The 75-mm. guns tucked away in the jungle area of Bataan pumped out a warning bracket on a speck flashing toward Malolos. Pete Coyne studied the signal and began to fidget with the slide-away gun mounting.

"Take it easy, von Richthofen," Sewell sneered. "It's only a Jap Nakajima. She'll stay there as long as those Gyrines keep shooting. I got to get pictures. Never mind your running up a score!"

"Yes, sir!" Pete nodded.

"Cut back for the east shore," Sewell ordered over the cockpit communication set. "We'll work up from there and follow the road across to Olongapo and down again to Bagac."

"What about that guy the marines are checking up there?"

"Leave him for the fighters. We're getting pictures."

"What fighters?" Breeze argued. "If we dump those guys, the landing strip won't matter, will it?"

"You been reading a book, too?" snorted Sewell.

The sore thumb of Bataan was blotched with shell scars. The road along the east shore was barricaded with felled timber. Gashes hacked out of the apitong and nipa palm suggested gun positions, and scorched vegetation marked where MacArthur's gunners had fired point-blank over open sights into charging waves of Japanese troops as they stormed across the beaches and sought a toe hold.

Breeze circled south of Pilar and waited until Sewell caught the strip and semaphore signals and had charted the new line positions for the squadron map back at Corregidor.

"They're holding on," Sewell muttered. "I don't know how they do it. They were supposed to have been clamshelled out of there ten days ago.''

''Maybe MacArthur ain't seen the facts and figures yet,'' suggested Breeze in dumb monotone.

''Okay. You have your fun with words, but how about getting some work done?''

''Boy, I wish we were over the Burma Road.'' Breeze leveled the O-47 off and headed north. He wished Sewell wouldn't flaunt his devotion to duty so much. He resented being encumbered with two yard birds like Sewell and Coyne. Sewell was bad enough, but Coyne was the prize dope of the first pressing—Coyne and his book!

''Where you heading?'' Sewell jerked him out of his train of thought. ''You'll be relieving Singapore unless you snap out of that stupor.''

The pilot saw he had passed well beyond Hermosa and was dead over the road that leads northeast to San Fernando. The Jap guns were blasting away again, their dirty-white puffballs setting up rough Southern Cross insignia four hundred feet below. The thud of concussion blasted all about them, and the sluggish observation plane lurched lackadaisically in the uneven swell and seemed to be stifling a yawn.

''If you fly straight across, holding a course on the upper end of Subic Bay,'' Sewell suggested, ''I might be able to get a line on that area again.''

Breeze argued, ''All I've seen here is jungle and rocks. You couldn't put an open umbrella down in there.''

''When you're trained in observation,'' Sewell taunted, ''you learn to put two and two together. You don't have to believe anything until you have proved it to yourself.''

''You mean to tell me . . .'' Breeze began, but Sewell shut him off with further attention to the radio panel.

Breeze bridled, but then tightened up. ''Maybe you're right,'' he yelled into his muzzle mike. He had spotted a gray Karigane two-seater below, blotched in against the gaudy verdure of bamboo palm, guijo trees, and abaca fronds. The nose of the O-47 went down with a lunge.

Sewell tried to head off the pilot, but he was helpless behind the radio panel. Coyne began rattling his artillery again, but Sewell slapped him across the shoulders. ''You stay put! Cover our tail. We're being sucked in!''

"This is the way it should be." Coyne grinned. "Just like you read . . ." The pilot was high tailing down so fast Pete was unable to punch out the words; the slip stream sliced his breath away.

The gunner aboard the Karigane saw them in plenty of time; Jap three-inchers rifled opposition long before Breeze was anywhere within range, and chunks of Kobe shell pelted through the fuselage and cut Wailing Winnies in the skin.

"You damned fool!" Sewell yelled.

But Breeze was on his way to glory, his sight stick lanced dead at the fishtailing Karigane, while the Jap gunner poured it back at them.

"Lieutenant Breeze got the right idea," Corporal Coyne reflected.

Breeze pumped a few short bursts, the tracer streaked across the sky and drew chalky lines between the two war planes. He held her steady, but there was a damper of air pressure billowing up from the heated hills and the O-47 bucked like a stallion. It was like trying to draw a bead from the front seat of a roller coaster.

The heavy O-47 almost scraped her belly over the Jap's cockpit covers before Breeze sensed he had missed. With visions of the Order of the Rising Sun, Third Class, the Karigane tossed with his gods and pressed the trigger of his Nambu gun; the 6.5 slugs stitched a wicked line of perforation along the muck-streaked belly of the O-47. The motor retched and coughed as Breeze drew her out of her headlong plunge—a lifetime of hope and fear was compressed into the next ten seconds.

"What the—" Breeze gurgled as he stared about with his mouth wide open. Sewell finished it for him: "You damned fool! You took all he had—cold! I told you!"

They sat constricted and trembled in sympathy with the frantic gasps of the motor. The pilot punched at various adjustments on the Chandler-Groves in a hopeless effort to get her to take it up again. The prop churned over with the sluggish ambition of a dilapidated windmill and ground up enough loose metal to provide a suitable nerve-shredding accompaniment.

Coyne, who had no idea of what had actually happened, reacted normally. He whipped out the Browning again and blasted off a four-second burst at the Jap two-seater below and torched her tanks as she tried to edge around for a front-gun attack.

"That lug was tryin' to get a burst into us!" Pete bawled, and then realized the adventure was jumping the cogs and getting out of the groove.

In the confined cockpit the three men gripped objects that were most familiar; Coyne blinked and clutched the grips of the Browning; Sewell held the ends of his radio panel, his mouth would not form the words he was trying to scream; Breeze clawed at the control column as though he would throttle it for even suggesting there was nothing left.

"We're going—down!" finally spurted out of Sewell. "We're going down—prisoners!"

Bewildered and unbalanced, Coyne again pressed the button of his gun and lashed .30-caliber stuff into the jungle below."

"Shut that damn thing off!"

Pete released the weapon and it hung disconsolately on the mounting. He sought an answer in the jagged outline of their shadow racing along against the green sea of tropical foliage.

"Stow that thing away!" Sewell yelled at him. "It'll crack your noggin!"

The gunner shoved it under the fuselage hump and as he was turning around, limp and resigned, the plane hit.

"Hang on!" Sewell started to yell, but he was slammed with a cruel thud against the radio panel, and Coyne catapulted forward against the cushion provided by the observer's body. The O-47 sliced the tops out of the palms and, with a scream of metal surging through her wings, plunged on to smash up at the base of a tree.

Pete shook himself free and muttered, "Nice of the lieutenant to tell me about the gun."

He crawled through the fracture in the hatch and waited for Sewell and Breeze to follow him.

"Lieutenant!" he called. His eyes straightened out and swept the wreck. "You can't stay there! We gotta get trackin'!"

He tottered about uncertainly, wondering what he was supposed to do next. He sniffed, caught the tang of gasoline, and an unprecedented sense of duty jetted through him. As Sewell's arms came over the edge of the hatch, Pete saw the painful twists of the hands; the observer's face, a mask of uneven planes and streaked with a fine tracery of scarlet, hooked its chin over the cover slide.

Pete climbed up again and dragged out a short ax and cut and slashed with tottering inaccuracy until he had a gash in the side through which he helped Sewell to crawl. The observer got to his feet and then stumbled drunkenly to a curved palm trunk and leaned there with his arms at grotesque angles.

"Both arms—when I braced myself against the panel," he babbled as he slid down the palm butt and rolled over.

"You stay there, sir," Pete suggested dubiously. "Wait till I get Lieutenant Breeze out."

From the jagged wing root the gunner hacked until he had gouged out another panel. The pilot was slumped over, his arms swinging between his splayed knees.

"You sure stopped som'pin, eh, Lieutenant?" Pete wailed.

He then dragged Breeze into the clear and scrambled through the nipa and fern until he had him on his back beside Sewell. There was a deep, grinning gash across the pilot's forehead and blood drooled across the undulations of his face.

Pete loosened the chin piece of the helmet and returned to the plane for the first-aid kit in the observer's locker. He then daubed and fumbled bluntly with gauze pads, bound the wads into place with bandage, and pulled Breeze's ear flaps down and strapped them.

He stripped off his coverall and parachute harness, tossed them aimlessly toward the wreck, and turned his attention to Sewell. Sympathetic reasoning and latent perspicacity dictated his efforts to help the observer. He placed Sewell's lower arms together with the gloved fists cupping the elbows, and bound them with what was left in the first-aid can. Strips of fabric ripped from the rudder completed a bulky but satisfactory support.

"The lieutenant says you can't do it," he muttered, "but *Lieutenant Scott* did it." He stared about him. Breeze was snorting unintelligibly and trying to get up.

"Take it easy, Lieutenant. You got nothin' to worry about."

Breeze struggled to one elbow. "That you—Coyne? Where's Sewell?" he asked thickly.

"Right there alongside you."

Pete watched him with tortured eyes as Breeze peered about.

"Where are you, Coyne?"

"Jees! I'm right here—kneelin' right in front of you."

The bandaged head came up again and stopped, its sponson of gauze trained on the gunner. "But—I can't see you—either of you. I can't see anything!"

"Maybe you got a lot of blood in your eyes."

"It—it isn't blood. I'm blind—blind! I can't see a thing! Holy God!"

Sewell drew up his legs and tried to peer into Breeze's face.

"You got a smack across the head, sir," Pete whimpered. "Maybe it's only just for now. Maybe you got such a headache you can't see, eh?"

"Where are we?" Breeze appealed in a half-whisper.

Coyne dropped to his knees again and crawled forward. He wondered if Breeze was really blind. He waited, watching intently, then he turned slowly toward Sewell. The observer's eyes confirmed the fear that was beating a trip-hammer warning in Coyne's chest. He saw Sewell nod, and he lurched forward suddenly and snatched Breeze's automatic from the hip holster.

"Where are we, Coyne?" Breeze asked again, and then sensed what was happening. "Damn you, Coyne! Come back with that gun!"

Pete rolled away with the big automatic hugged to his belly.

"Why don't you shut up, Breeze?" Sewell hissed through his puffed lips. "The guy's just trying to make you comfortable."

Breeze lay flat on the tangled foliage and stared with sightless eyes at the marquee of palm fronds that swayed gently in the tropical air.

"Thanks. Thanks, Sewell," he sobbed. "Good scout, that guy Coyne. You all right?"

"Sure. I'm swell!"

Half an hour later Breeze struggled up to a sitting position. Sewell was still hunched at the butt of a big palm watching the pilot. "Take it easy," he muttered quietly.

"Where's Coyne?"

"I don't know. He went off, scouting around to see where we are. He'll be back. Thinks he knows this area. Says he drove a half-track on maneuvers here last summer."

"The dopey guy might get away with it yet," Breeze said tonelessly. "God, I wish I could see!"

"Don't worry—you will. You got a smack that gave you an anemic reaction as the result of loss of blood. It's just temporary," Sewell said slowly and thoughtfully.

"Jees! Old facts and figures again. For once I hope you're right."

"They got a lot of that in the other war—temporary blindness."

"You got it figured out now that no one was really blinded, eh?"

"Listen! Here he comes," Sewell warned, "or someone, anyway."

A sweaty figure emerged from the tangle of vines that walled them in. It was Coyne, panting and beaming. "You wuz right, Lieutenant!" he yelled at Sewell. "They got a strip back there—about a quarter of a mile. Planes and trucks lined up. It's blocked out with curtain camouflage."

"I'm not goin' to lay here and rot in this jungle," Breeze growled.

"We can get there in half an hour," Pete continued. "It will be almost dark then. We can torch this wreck, and they'll all come to find out where we hit."

"Where the devil did you read that?" Sewell demanded.

"That's the book again, and maybe Pete has something."

He helped them to their feet with rough enthusiasm. "Anyway, we should burn her, shouldn't we?" he suggested, and fingered for a match. He crossed to the tangle of fuselage, tore open his parachute pack, and stuffed the billowing wad of silk inside the pilot's cockpit. He applied the match and stepped back to watch the flames lick up and eat away the fuel lines that fed the carburetor.

"I don't know why he doesn't have an idea to stick on the wings again and slingshot us off a bamboo tree," Sewell muttered as the flames roared up.

"You wait. I'll bet he's got an idea that has that one beat a mile," Breeze husked as he swayed drunkenly.

"You better keep your packs, eh?" Pete suggested as he came up and took their arms. "They'll be nice for you to sit on, if we get a lift."

As they made their way through the spiny thicket, the hot glare from the burning observation plane threw a gaudy orange-tinted canopy at the sky. Coyne hacked a path and helped them along. The observer walked wide-legged and stumbled now and then, but he plunged on after the encouraging chatter of Coyne, who dragged Breeze through the jungle ahead.

"It's only a little way now, Lieutenant," he said as he steadied the blind pilot. "Listen! You can hear them scrambling through, over there toward the fire. You still got that headache, Lieutenant?"

"I got one that will last for fifty years," Breeze mumbled with his head bent over.

"Maybe we can git some aspirin."

The route was tortuous and winding and it seemed an hour before they came into a clearing. Breeze could hear the metallic activity, and Sewell could see what he had long suspected. The landing strip had been cut through the sparse area of vegetation, and from a series of bamboo poles set along the sides dangled shallow curtains of net and light cloth on which tufts of dry grass, palm leaves, and sprays of ferns had been laced.

"Baby! They can keep pounding our guys for twenty-four hours a day from this hole!" Sewell gasped.

On one side was a collection of trucks, fuel wagons, and light tanks; on the near side, their tails drawn into hacked-out dispersal areas, stood several indistinct planes. Vague figures moved in and out of the lights flickering from small portable tanks.

"What are we waiting for?" Breeze whispered.

"I remember this spot," Pete added. "We used it for a transport park. Maybe we could swipe a truck."

"That's out," Sewell said from a shadow. "There's no road out of here going south."

"That's what I was going to say, sir. The only way out . . ."

"Here we go," Sewell moaned.

"What's he got to lose?" Breeze demanded, as he moved about aimlessly. "I'm willing to go with the guy!"

"Who's going to fly it?" Sewell argued uncertainly. "You—well, you can't see right now, and I got two busted arms. Coyne can't fly."

"Two busted arms?" Breeze sucked in his breath. "But you said you were . . . Then Coyne *has* to. . . ."

"Listen!" Pete whispered. "They're runnin' one up—right down our alley. Maybe if we got aboard, Lieutenant Breeze could get it off—blind, an' we could tell him where to head it."

"Sure!" Breeze added. "All we got to do is get it into the air. We can pile it up anywhere on the other side."

The enthusiasm of illogical thinking beat down any sane view of the situation. For one thing, it was obvious that the blazing observation plane had drawn many of the ground crew from their posts.

Uncertain, but unwilling to be left behind, Sewell followed Coyne and Breeze through the shadows.

"It's one of their Kariganes, sir," Pete confided to Breeze as he led him along. "We can all get aboard, eh?"

"Be a tight squeeze. Which way is she headed?"

"Across the runway. If we can get those Japs out of the way, it will be easy."

"How many guys around her?"

"I can see only two. One in the cockpit, runnin' her up."

"Okay. You get those guys out of there. We'll stay here."

The first Jap was easy. He was bending over the tail, holding it down while the mechanic in the cockpit tested the A-14 motor. A solid smack with the gun butt of the automatic Pete had taken from Breeze brought the Jap to his knees and he rolled over with a grunt.

"An' *stay* there!" Pete growled as he dragged him clear.

Then he moved like a cat to the wing root and climbed up. The puzzled Jap mechanic stared into Pete's gun tunnel and started to shut off the motor. ''No! No! Let her rumble,'' Pete ordered. ''You just get out and give *me* a hand.''

Exaggerated gestures with the gun clearly interpreted his meaning. Now a suety gray, the Jap stumbled down off the wing root in feverish haste, but Coyne collared him and rammed him toward the tail.

''Lift!'' he explained with his hands. ''You lift while I push—compree?''

''Take my arm,'' Sewell whispered. ''Grab me under the armpit—easy. That mug is going to get away with it.''

''All the facts and figures are against it, aren't they?'' Breeze said with a smirk in his voice. ''If I could only see!''

Coyne had the Karigane out and turned around, as Sewell and Breeze reached the wing tip. The pilot felt his way along the trailing edge and was clambering up when another businesslike *thock* thudded somewhere in the darkness.

''An' *stay* there!'' Coyne repeated as the Jap mechanic corkscrewed to the ground.

He came up to the fuselage, grinning. ''I guess Lieutenant Sewell had better take the back seat. I'll stand between you—somehow. Get in, sir. The throttle's on the left side, just like ours. You're headed straight down the runway.''

Breeze fumbled about and instinctively his hands found the control column and the throttle; his feet slid forward and rested on the rudder pedals, which he waggled experimentally.

''She'll fly like a Mack truck,'' he grumbled.

''Get going, Lieutenant. Here comes a mob over from them trucks. You're dead center down the runway.''

''Hey!'' Wait a minute!'' Sewell yelled, as he tried to lean forward. ''How the hell we going to get this thing down again?''

''You can step out if you like,'' Breeze growled.

''Sure. We can, but Coyne . . .''

The rest was drowned out when Breeze eased the throttle up the gate; the 800-hp radial picked it up smartly and she began to rumble down the runway.

''Steady, Lieutenant,'' Pete instructed. ''You're bearing a bit right—and don't take her off too soon, or you'll hit the curtain camouflage. Left sir—*left!*''

''Just like a Mack truck!'' Breeze growled over his chin piece.

''*Left*, sir! You're gonna take her wing tip off!''

The pilot rammed his buttocks down hard and pressed the left rudder. She was trying to clear by herself now. He eased the column forward and felt the wheels thump off the uneven track. Her tail was up and she answered the rudder reasonably fast.

"Good! Hold her now. Hold her down, sir. We got a few more yards to clear."

"Listen, you dopes," Sewell was yelling behind Pete's back. "How we going to get down?"

"Take her away, sir. You're in the clear!" Pete turned in triumph to yell at Sewell, who was jabbing him with his knee. "We got away wid a enemy plane—an' escaped!"

Sewell glared at him in frank disgust. "Sure. We stole an enemy plane. Now figure out how you're going to get it down again. I get two broken legs now, I suppose."

Breeze took the Karigane over the palm barrier with amazing ease. A trickle of tracer crept up from the area where the transport had been parked; ahead, over the knobby nose of Santa Rosa crater, the Bataan line was jeweled with serried gashes of gunfire and the sparkle of signal rockets.

Coyne squatted behind the bucket seat that encased Breeze's back and peered forward for the outline of Mount Bataan. A welter of disjointed thoughts doused the first warm blaze of enthusiasm of having effected an escape.

"You're heading straight down the peninsula, sir," he advised the pilot. "We should be getting some of our own fire soon."

Breeze nodded with resignation. "Can't be helped. Keep me well clear of that crater and then turn me right so that we go past Bataan and out to sea. I'll circle that, and approach Corregidor from the west. That should evade a lot of it—until we get in."

"Sure! Then once you get over the island, you and Lieutenant Sewell kin take to the silk. I'll stay and see if I can get her down."

"You're nuts! You'd splatter yourself all over the island."

"What are we going to do?" the trussed-up Sewell yelled from the rear.

"You got about fifteen miles to figure it out," Breeze barked. "Two of us have chutes, one guy burned his up. I might be able to set this thing down if Coyne could read the instruments for me."

"Some are in American and some in Japanese," Pete said after a glance over the instrument board. "Turn sharp right now, sir."

"Ninety degrees?"

"Sharp right—I don't know how many. . . . There! Now get her straight again. You'll soon be through the two peaks."

"You're through," Sewell said. "Now turn left—ninety, and you'll be heading south down the beach. The island is just around the bend."

After another five minutes of flight Breeze asked, "Where are the flaps, Coyne? We should be somewhere by now."

The gunner leaned over and felt around below the pilot's knees. "They's a hand wheel on this side, sir."

"Oke! I'll give her a twist or two and see what happens."

The wheel proved to be the flap control and the Karigane snubbed into a slower speed on the brake pressure and Breeze drew back the throttle until the engine was only just ticking over.

"You're only about four miles away now, Lieutenant," Pete almost whispered over Breeze's shoulder.

"Oke! Keep me dead on. When we get within a quarter of a mile of the western end, let me know and I'll run across Kindley and we'll see what happens."

The Corregidor searchlights blazed out and fingered into the cumulus.

"What's that?" Breeze said suddenly, sitting upright. A shell arced up from the island fortress and spoke its wrath fifty feet below their port wing tip.

"That's our guns, sir. They got the searchlights out, too," Pete explained.

Sewell edged forward and tried to see around Coyne. He felt himself relax, and he sensed that Coyne *was* going to get away with something.

The Karigane slipped into the long glide with sluggish movements of the wing tips. Another searchlight slapped out from Fort Drum and bathed the Jap plane in swabs of garish silver. The three-inchers from Fort Hughes spanked the course with convulsive gashes in the backdrop of the night.

"I wouldn't waste too much time here," Sewell advised. "You'd better hit the channel between Corregidor and Caballo. If you make a 120-degree turn to the left there, you'll be heading straight down the long runway—if we make it."

For some reason Breeze didn't answer.

"I got it figured out, Lieutenant," Coyne rattled on. "We're at fourteen hunnerd, over the channel now. You bring her around, like he said, an' I'll try to help you in."

"Sure. Any dope can fly a plane. They almost taught Sewell once," Breeze answered. "When we get around and headed for the runway, you lean over, Pete, and put your hand on mine. I'll fly her by the seat of my pants, and you can ease her off when we look like we're going to sock the wheels down."

Coyne beamed. "I'll bet you, I—we—can get her down!"

"I'll bet you can," muttered Sewell with a numb grin.

"Don't let me slow her up to less than seventy. I don't want to spin her in."

Breeze sat steady, his head held in the unnatural tension of a blind man, but under his wad of bandage he was smiling. "Are we still dead on, Coyne?"

"Dead on, Lieutenant. Hold her there."

"You put your hand on top of mine. She's yours, Corp."

The guns from Corregidor blasted at them with furious ambition and the searchlights crisscrossed and attempted to snip them in two with their great silver blades. Coyne hugged close to the pilot's shoulder and breathed the lateral directions.

"Right, gently. We're dead over the shore line now. Keep her there, gently. The runway is dead ahead."

"Air speed, Coyne? What's our air speed?"

"Er—seventy-four. Left—just a trifle."

Sewell sat back, relaxed and complacent. He wondered how long it took to mend two busted arms. He tried to see past Coyne's shoulder again, but the corporal was bobbing about and peering out of the cockpit windows.

"Down to sixty-eight, sir. Just skipping the main hangar. They ain't shooting now. Just looking up at us. Them dumb Gyrines!"

"Right! Take it, Coyne," Breeze ordered quietly. "Keep your hand on mine and ease her back—*ease* her back, when you see the runway racing under the leading edge."

The corporal wound his left arm around Breeze's chest, his right hand on top of the pilot's gloved fist, and jerked and pump-handled the control, but the pilot steadied him somehow. The Karigane ballooned off the pressure set up between the wing and the runway, and Breeze eased her back.

"Now! *Now*, sir!" Coyne gushed. "We're practically—"

The stick went back at the right instant, and her tail wheel touched, levering the front wheels down. The Karigane bounced once, and tried to ground-loop, but Breeze caught her with an aileron and a punch of rudder. She scraped to a stop.

"Nice flying, Coyne," Breeze said quietly. "I'll try to turn her and get her back to the hangar. You check me."

It took fully fifteen minutes to explain everything and get Breeze and Sewell off to the hospital bay. The medical officer kept saying, "It's nothing serious. Temporary blindness caused by the loss of blood and shock. Affects the optic nerves. Form of anemia which breaks down the blood picture. He'll be all right."

Sewell turned on his cot and looked at Breeze, who was flat on his back. The M.O. had gone out to do a check on Coyne.

"Nice going, Breeze," Sewell said quietly.

The pilot turned over slowly and winked. "When did you catch on?"

"When you jerked at the searchlight. I don't think Coyne knows. He thinks *he* landed that plane."

"Good! Don't ever tell him. He did me a very good turn back there."

"When he swiped your gun?"

"Yeh! I was pretty low then. I guess I did a job for him, eh?"

"Guys like Coyne," Sewell observed, "win wars, but they never know it—because of guys like you."

PAUL GALLICO

Bombardier

SECOND LIEUTENANT SALVO JENKINS crouched on his knees in the greenhouse of the big B-31 bomber as the ship, shaking, trembling, and complaining, swiveled into the wind and thundered down the runway for the take-off. This, then, was it at last. The practice days were over. The hunt was on. And he was miserable.

The concrete strip, streaked like scratchy film, reeled interminably beneath the glass nose of the bombardier's bay. Lumbering Annie, wing and belly heavy with her load of gasoline, demolition bombs, and depth charges, took her own sweet time about getting into the air. Of the dangers that might be encountered on the mission, this was the worst moment, the leap into the sky. The B-31 had a reputation for crankiness at the end of the runway.

But Bombardier Salvo Jenkins—aged twenty-two, blue-eyed, slight; his face, beneath the short-cut tawny hair, the face of a child; quick and nervous as a cat in his movements—was not entertaining visions of what would befall Lumbering Annie if she failed to shake loose at the end of the field—the crashing green of stripped trees, the red bricks of the barracks, white faces staring upward, and the final holocaust of flame. His fears and doubts reached far ahead to that moment which might come upon him out over the blue wastes of water, when the success or failure of the mission and all that it meant to his crew would depend upon him alone.

What if he should let them down? He fought off the sickish feeling his thoughts brought on and swallowed to get the dryness out of his throat. This was for keeps. The pilot and navigator would bring him to the target. They could do no more. He was the bombardier. It would be he who must make the kill. Must make it . . . must make it . . . must make it. . . . The words throbbed to the engines beating slightly out of synchronization.

Runway, fence, trees, barracks, and sand waste fell away beneath them. They crossed the white edge of the Atlantic as they climbed into the sky. In ten minutes the target area would begin. To ease his nerves, Salvo Jenkins reached in his data kit for his computer. Pilot Captain Strame had given him his bombing instructions before the take-off. "We'll bomb at X feet altitude and zero-zero-zed speed."

You bombed at low altitude and in a hurry on those sub hunts. You had just so many seconds to lay your eggs from the moment the tin shark was sighted until it vanished to safety beneath the sea. Salvo made his computations, ground speed, temperature, true altitude, checked and rechecked them and set his Rube Goldberg, the Flanick hand sight used for low-level bombing. He loved the Flanick. It was like pointing and sighting a fine gun. If your computations were right, steady eye, steady hand, finger ready on the solenoid switch for firing, you couldn't miss. You dared not miss.

He knew that his figures were correct, but it gave him no feeling of ease or relaxation. If and when the emergency came, he might have to discard them in an instant, and in the trembling space of ticking seconds recalculate entirely for different height and speed. No one could instruct or help him. A fractional error, and chance and prey would be gone. The men upstairs trusted him. If he failed, he could never face them. So this was what it meant to be a bombardier.

But fearful and anguished of nerves as he was, Salvo would not have traded places with any of those above in the ship. The thought of his name in the crew list, chalked up on the blackboard in the squad room, filled him with pride: "Bombardier: Sec. Lt. Horace Jenkins."

He had found excuses to go in there more often than was necessary, so that he could glance up at it. He would catch himself sneaking those glances and would say to himself, "Dawgone it, Jenkins; you're actin' just like a kid. Ain't you evah goin' tuh grow up?"

But the line kept bringing a glow to his heart. There it was, up with the finest crew on the field—Pilot Captain: John (Cappy) Strame; Navigator: Lt. Carl Jorgens; Co-pilot: Lt. Ed Hammond; Engineer: Sgt. James Bradley; the radioman and the gunners. But how his own name stood out—"Bombardier: Sec. Lt. Horace Jenkins." Why, that was himself. That line was the end of a long-ago dream come true—or at least almost the end.

The altimeter needle settled at 1000 feet and stayed there. Automatically, Salvo checked the centigrade thermometer and inspected the green lights glowing on his bomb-indicator panel. Below him rolled the Atlantic, calm, capless, and shimmering in the afternoon sunlight.

The earphones of the intercommunication system crackled and he heard, ''Navigator from pilot: What is the course?''

When the navigator gave it, Salvo checked it with his own compass.

He heard the pilot's brief acknowledgment, ''Roger.''

''Roger.'' Salvo savored the word. It was the airman's response and meant ''Received order.'' Jenkins used it whenever he could in his everyday talk. It was one of the things that set you apart, like the title 'Bombardier'' in front of your name. Instead of saying ''Okay,'' or ''That's right,'' or ''You're darn tootin',' you said ''Roger.'' It was air forces.

They were ten minutes out and flying south over the water, paralleling the yellow-and-green strip of shore in the starboard haze. The mission was yet young and there was a moment's kidding on the interphone.

''What'll you bet the lunch is ham sandwiches again?''

''Co-pilot from navigator: You'd holler if it was caviar.''

''Shut up! You'll wake the bombardier.''

Something seemed to choke the throat of Salvo Jenkins. He was so proud to be kidded by them.

Yes, that was his gang up above. He belonged to them and they to him. He had become a member of the greatest team in the world. In school, at the outbreak of the war in Europe, he had dreamed of someday become a bombardier. But he had not imagined that it would be like this.

As a boy, back on his father's farm in the Greak Smokies of North Carolina, he had yearned for the day when he would go to college and play on a team—when he would belong. But he had been far too slight for football at State University. He could run and play a little ball, but he had never made anything. He had been a wistful wanderer on the fringes of the great who belonged. He admired the football men who had their own talk and felllowship of play and strategy and bruises. Young Jenkins thought the finest thing in the world was the friendship between the star halfback, Swifty Morgan, Ted Jones, who ran interference for him, and Sparky Slade, the quarterback. They did everything together. It was all for one and one for all, and everything for the team.

The pilot called for a crew check-in over the intercommunication, and in his turn Salvo barked, ''Bomber, Roger!'' and listened to the others, ''Navigator, Roger! . . . Co-pilot, Roger! . . . Radio, Roger! . . . Engineer, Roger!''

This was a real team. How they worked together! Each trusting in and dependent on the other. Only this was such a game as none of them had ever played before. And, at the thought, the old pang returned to the bombardier and his nerves quivered again. He was the only member of the crew as yet untried. He was still Salvo Jenkins.

His mind turned back to that awful moment during a patrol flight over the California coast two months ago, when, in one sickening moment of error, confusion and a momentarily jammed lever, he had gone to "Salvo" instead of "Selective," and had dumped two thousand, five hundred pounds of expensive demolition bombs into the Pacific Ocean. And he had picked the time to do it when the general was on board and at the controls of the ship. There had been a truly magnificent explosion, but outside of killing all the fish in the vicinity, it had accomplished nothing but to pin a nickname on him. From that moment on, he was known as "Salvo" Jenkins.

It had gotten around, this really Gargantuan blunder. They knew of it in Texas the same night, in Louisiana, New Mexico, and the Atlantic seaboard the next day, and in Australia, India, and Java the following week; in the primary and advanced schools, the flying fields, the bombing grounds, and the fighting squadrons. News moved swiftly in the air forces. The radio would talk, a transfer would carry the story, or an outward-bound pilot of the Ferry Command, hot with the latest home news, would squat down in Africa, or South America, or the Near East, and say to the gang, "Did you hear about that kid Jenkins from the Eighteenth? Salvoed a ton on a turtle. Had the general riding with him."

The earphones came alive. "Target at ten o'clock. Eight miles."

The left wing dropped slightly and Lumbering Annie turned and then slid downhill a little. Salvo crouched and strained his eyes in the direction indicated. The sparkling water rushed beneath them. "Target" to the Army Air Forces Bomber Command was anything that floated above or beneath the waves. Only after it identified itself did it become a ship. They were still hours away from the area designated by Intelligence as possibly harboring a U-boat, but Salvo's fingers were itching for his levers.

The intercommunication clicked, "Subchaser!"

"Roger!"

She looked like a greyhound, long, lean, slim of flank, blue-gray in color, and flecked with the white hats of her crew. A curving white wake boiled out behind her. The racing ship changed course and charged on as the lumbering bomber dipped her left wing and staggered around her in a wide circle. The hairs at the back of Salvo's neck bristled. The navy was on the hunt too. Was she following a scent with her instruments? If so, there might be work for him to do. In a heap, he tried to remember everything he had been taught.

He saw the subchaser's blinker light flash, and read the code. Up above, Cappy Strame was talking to her with his blinker, too, probably querying whether they were following a trail of sinister submerged engines, distantly beating.

The firefly light from below winked, "*N-O*."

"Huh," said Salvo Jenkins to himself. "They probably wouldn't tell us if they had one treed," and then, in an onrush of loyalty, corrected himself with, "Jenkins, ain't you ever a-goin' tuh grow up? You know the navy's been co-operatin' a hundred percent. But I sure wish she was on a sub."

The black ball of the compass jogged around until they were on their course again, southward. *Just one sub,* prayed Salvo Jenkins; *just a conning tower*. How he'd like to lay an egg right alongside. In his mind he saw the upheaval of the depth charge, the crushed U-boat lurching to the bottom. His imagination took him further. Now he stood on the field, his head cocked a little to one side, and watched the technical sergeant in charge of the ground crew proudly painting a tiny submarine on the fuselage of Lumbering Annie near the tail. One for the team. One for Cappy Strame, the best pilot and the greatest guy who ever lived. One for—The dream broke. What if Salvo Jenkins lost his head and missed?

Again the imagining of failure brought that cold horror to his stomach. So terribly much was at stake. He was just Salvo Jenkins, the kid who had gummed things up the day the general was aboard.

He thought back to the third day after his arrival at Humphrey Field, from the West, discouraged and miserable, and his summons to the office of the commanding officer. The C.O. was a great lanky stalk of a man, six foot six, with a craggy face, beak nose, and an abrupt manner that covered his absorbing passion for his command.

He said, "Lieutenant Jenkins, there is a vacancy for a bombardier in the crew of Captain Strame. I am assigning you to that crew."

"Yes, sir. Did you say 'Captain Strame'?" It was no wonder he had asked. Strame's was the crack bombing crew of the squadron. It had been together for more than a year. It was like the coach calling up a third-string substitute and saying, "Okay, son. You're on the varsity. Go in there and score."

The C.O. sucked at a pipe carved in the shape of a skull, and said:

"Captain Strame asked for you, Lieutenant Jenkins. I don't mind telling you that I questioned his judgment. He could have had any man he wanted. I made that plain. I am going to repeat to you his exact words. He said, 'I'll take the kid, if you don't mind, sir. He's a bombardier. I know all about that Salvo stuff, but it doesn't cut any ice. He's got hunting blood. He signed up for bombardier from way back. He's no washed-out pilot or flop navigator. Ever since he's come into the air forces he's done nothing but eat, sleep, live, and dream bombing. He just wants to bomb. When we get over a target, that's the kind of kid I want at the sights.' "

The C.O. blew a wisp of smoke, studied Jenkins a moment and then concluded, "That's all, Lieutenant."

The big bomber droned along on its mission. The men in her watched their instruments and the surface of the sea. Thinking back over what the C.O. had said, Salvo Jenkins knew that he would never want to succeed for anyone as much as he wanted to succeed for John Strame, not even for Mary Lou Allen, who was pledged to him back at State University ar Raleigh. And he loved Mary Lou with all his youth and yearning and imagination.

Strame was a pink-cheeked, black-haired, black-eyed boy from Alabama who was a born pilot the way Jenkins felt he was a born bombardier. He radiated love for his work, his ship, and his crew. He was as trim and fiery as a Derby race horse. His specialty was flying. The other specialties he left to the various members of his crew. But he expected and accepted nothing short of perfection.

It wasn't the job Jenkins worshiped, but the man, his spirit, and his friendship. It seemed as if Strame was the first person who had ever understood him and had faith in him. Jenkins's fear of letting Strame down became a sweating nightmare that never wholly left him.

He remembered that not even Mary Lou had quite understood him when he explained his great ambition to her. They had sat one night in the rear booth of Mason's drugstore. She wore a muslin dress that was soft and inexplicably thrilling to touch. It smelled of a mixture of warm cloth and flowers. Her presence brought pangs of sweetness to his heart that were nearly unbearable. When he put his fingers beneath her chin and turned her head to him, she gave him her mouth without restraint. It was that night that he told her that he had passed his preliminary examinations and was going to try for a commission as a bombardier.

She looked at him with her wide, serious eyes, contemplating what he had told her. She was not a lion hunter, but, womanlike, she wanted her man to have the best. She said, "It sounds teh'bly exciting, honey." But it was not exciting the way she said it. Then she added, "Swifty and Ted and Sparky are going to be pilots. I mean—"

"Let 'em." Jenkins leaned forward on the table top wet with the circles of their glasses, his face flushing, his young blue eyes shining with enthusiasm. "Anybody can fly a plane. But when they get where they're agoin' to, the bombardier pulls the trigger. That's me."

She had continued to stare at him strangely. He could not decide whether it was because she did not quite understand what a big job the bombardier had, or because she was surprised at him for wanting to be one. He hadn't meant to boast, but the ambition had burned so long inside him, unexpressed, that he had to talk about it.

"It's the most wonderful job in the war, Mary Lou. You've got to have a good bombardier. And it ain't as though anybody can do it. Why, if you know how, you can knock out a battleship from over twenty thousand feet in the air. It's the shooting part, Mary Lou. That's why I know I can do it better'n anybody else. I'm goin' to be the best bombardier they evah had. I'm goin' to sink a battleship."

Of course, he was only a kid of twenty then, or he wouldn't have talked like that. He knew a lot more now. Well, if Mary Lou had not quite grasped the significance of his ambition, she had divined the enthusiasm and the yearning behind it. Her loyal attitude was that if he said so, it must be all right. She had taken his hand and said, "I know you will, honey, a big one."

What children they had been, and how different it all was, now that he was no longer a boy, but a second lieutenant and a bombardier. It was one thing sitting with your girl in a booth and telling her what a big shot you were going to be, and another to be squatting in the nose of a flying ice wagon, out over the Atlantic Ocean, desperately afraid of making a botch of dropping a bomb on an enemy submarine, if you ever saw one.

The heavy ship hit a bump in the air and jarred Jenkins back to reality. Somebody clicked a microphone and said, "Oh-oh!" which wasn't regulations, but got over the idea. Ahead and slightly to the east, a pillar of black smoke boiled up into the sky, a furious, volcanic, writhing thing, as though the ocean were erupting at that point.

Talk crackled on the intercommunication. "Tanker! Got it last night!"

"Roger!"

"Engineer from pilot: Get a picture of her."

"Engineer, Roger!"

They came down to within fifty feet of the surface of the water to let Bradley, the engineer, who doubled as photographer, get a shot. Only the stern of the tanker was visible. The rest was smoke threaded with orange flames. She was already down by the bow and the water around her was burning too. Salvo Jenkins stared hard. It was the first torpedoed ship he had ever seen. Somewhere beneath the surface of the sea, miles away by now, crept the enemy that had done this. And he, Horace Jenkins, was hunting him now, to wipe him out if he could. Somehow it was like being back on the farm when a wildcat would come down from the mountains and get into the chickens. Then you would go out with dog and gun and track him down and kill him.

He remembered suddenly what his father had told him when he taught him to shoot.

"Yuh got to be able to hit what you aimin' at, son," his father had said, "or it ain't no use goin' out with a gun. The dogs kin git you tuh where the cat's at, an' yore legs cain carry yuh there, but it don't do yuh no good if yuh miss."

Here in this strange element, the air, out over the endless wastes of water, the same held true. Pilot, navigator, and radioman would find the quarry if it was humanly possible, and would carry him to it. But once there, they were helpless. Their work was done. He must aim the deadly charge and send it straight to the target.

He remembered the day he had decided to be a bombardier. It was when a British bomber pilot had come to State University to lecture. There had been questions permitted after the talk, and everybody stared when young Jenkins asked, "Who pushes the button that lets the bomb go, sir? I mean is there anyone special who has to—"

"Rather! That's the bombardier. He's the top card in the deck. I fancy we've got the keenest chap in the whole push in our crew. We caught a Nazi supply ship off the coast of Norway once, a big one. He put one right down her funnel from ten thousand. That's bombing, you know. He got a medal for it, and dashed well deserved it. We called him Dead-Eye Dick."

Jenkins' heart beat faster. Dead-Eye Dick! Right down the funnel from ten thousand! Top card in the deck! "That's for me," said young Horace Jenkins under his breath, and from that moment on had hardly thought of anything else.

And all the time these thoughts were racing through his head he was crouching on his knees in the glass nose, straining his eyes onto the glittering surface of the sea to catch the first glimpse of a rising periscope, fingering his instruments, rechecking his calculatons, mentally making his selection of depth charges from the indicator panel, working, studying, fretting, worrying, thinking of Strame and his crew mates and the wonderful team of which they were all a part, and how terribly he wanted to make good for them, to make them as proud of him as he was of them.

They passed over a convoy escorted by a busy destroyer. Abeam of the lighthouse, the navigator set a new course and they wheeled left and headed out to sea, away from the sheltering land.

They saw nothing for a hundred miles but a broad oil slick from sunken tankers, and then they came upon a stubby freighter, all gray under war paint, terribly lonely and nervous, pushing her way eastward. She changed her course as they circled her, and then changed it twice more, rapidly.

Salvo recognized the symptoms of her jitters. Those lone freighters got to thinking, whenever they saw a bomber hovering about them, that there must be a submarine in the vicinity, and immediately began cutting semipanicky patterns to avoid possible torpedoes.

He felt a sudden pity for the solitary vessel. He wanted to call down to her, "It's all right. Don't you worry. We're here." The big bomber spread her wings protectingly over the hysterical ship. Salvo's heart went out to her; she seemed so helpless. That was why they were flying around out there, to watch over wanderers like her, to blast to the bottom of the sea the steel sharks that lay in wait.

Then the ship was gone from beneath them as Lumbering Annie clattered on, sniffing the sea lanes. Salvo understood better now the whys and wherefores of the long training grind that aimed only at perfection. Ground school, long sieges of physics, mathematics, navigation, meteorology, sighting and theory of bombing, the arithmetic of falling bodies, followed by the long weeks of practice with hundreds upon hundreds of missiles dropped from every altitude. He thought of all the mil errors made, never to be recovered, of the fractions miscalculated in the mind, the hundredth part of an infinitesimal error that magnified itself to a hundred yards off the target below and failure. Inevitably his mind returned once more to the culmination of his frailty—the day he had salvoed and wasted his whole load.

Again close to panic at the awesome picture of responsibility that had opened itself out, he reviewed his time from student to bombardier, and wished desperately that he had applied himself even more to his studies.

Legs appeared at the hatchway and descended the short iron ladder, bringing after them Hammond, the co-pilot. He carried a cup of grapefruit juice and a sandwich wrapped in wax paper.

"It's ham again," he said. "I thought we'd plowed all those pigs under years ago." He made himself comfortable in the narrow bay crammed with instruments, levers, tubing, cable leads, petcocks, wiring, and aluminum. "Nice place you have here, provided you've got a can opener to get out of it with," he commented. "Best view in the house."

Salvo munched on his sandwich. The fruit juice felt good in his dry throat. He was glad to have company for a moment.

The co-pilot retailed the gossip from above. "Carl's going to have a fine shiner in the morning. He was taking drift when we hit that bump away back. Good old navigator's drift-meter eye. Cappy's fidgety as all hell. He thinks he smells a sub. Say, I wish I had your job. Why didn't I think of putting in for bombardier? Ride around like an air-line passenger all day and when a target pops up, push a button and Bloo-o-o-ey! Pretty soft."

Salvo said, "Oh, it is, is it?" Of course Hammond was kidding, but through his mind there flashed all the other myriad duties of a bombardier besides hitting his target—the loading of bombs, repair and cleaning of guns, repair of his equipment in the air, knowledge of Morse code, blinker code, flag code, flare code, hydraulic, fuel, and fire-extinguisher system of the ship, as well as a working knowledge of how to fly and land her in emergency.

As he looked at Hammond, Salvo had an instant's temptation to unburden himself of all the doubts and fears and worries that had assailed him since the take-off, to rid his mind somehow of the nightmare of failure that haunted him. But he held it back. That was kid stuff, spilling your guts. The air forces didn't care about what you thought or how you felt. There was only one thing you could do for it—deliver.

"Guess I'll be getting back upstairs to the club," said the co-pilot. "The carburetors want to ice up. In June! So long, kid. If we flush something, don't miss."

Don't miss! Don't miss! That awful refrain. Earlier in the flight, Salvo had prayed for a target, had asked to be allowed to see just one sub. Now his jangled nerves cried for a reprieve. If they would only complete this mission without sighting a target, it would give him another chance—for more study, more practice. Just two hours, just an hour more on the training tower. The next time he would be ready.

He looked at his watch. Four hours under way. They would be turning back soon. He heard Cappy Strame on the interphone, ''Navigator from pilot: Turning back. What is the new course?''

''New course, two-nine-zero, turn now.''

''Roger!'' Then, informally, ''We'll have another look at that freighter on the way in.''

''Roger!''

Salvo saw the big starboard wing dip. The sun, already low on the horizon, floated in an arc around them as they made their turn. The wind had freshened and occasional whitecaps frothed on the sea below.

He was glad, in a way, that they were going to pay another visit to the lonely freighter pushing its way eastward. It might make it cut those frantic circles again, but it would be a comfort to it, too, when those friendly wings flew overhead, watching over it.

An hour passed, and another. Salvo's eyes ached from straining to the sea. The white patches of froth made observation more difficult. His duty was never to take his eyes from the sea below.

The impersonal, colorless, metallic voice of the interphone said, ''Ship at one o'clock. Ten miles.''

Salvo crouched low in his bay to see ahead out from under the glass nose. She was ahead and a little to starboard, a tiny speck on the darkening sea, growing larger as the thundering motors ate up the misty miles. She looked lonelier than ever. One tiny ship, an endless waste of water and sky, a tiring sun swelling and yellow as it neared the horizon and—

''Bomber from pilot: Open bomb-bay doors!''

''Roger!''

''Submarine three o'clock five miles.''

With what seemed like a single lightning movement, Salvo hit the three steel levers to his left, one after the other, but faster than the eye could follow. Doors open! Selective! Depth charges armed!

''Pilot from bomber: Bomb-bay doors open. Hey! We've got something!''

He did not even know he had yelled the last into the interphone. The surface of the sea was rising up to meet him with incredible speed as the big bomber descended, her air-speed indicator leaping forward.

There she lurked, the sub's black form, barely at surface. Already she was tilting forward for the crash dive. A matter of seconds and she would be gone. Salvo Jenkins was as cold as a glacier. His fingers had already pressed the selector switch—depth charges Two and Five, one from each side, two in reserve. He crouched like a cat waiting to spring, his nostrils spread, eyes staring, his rear end waggling catlike as he got himself set.

There were only seconds, but his mind was so clear and keyed and ready that he seemd to know everything that was needed to be known at the same instant, as though there were different compartments in his head, and all of them were functioning independently. He knew altitude, air speed, ground speed, temperature, and time. And he knew at once—had known it from the first instant he had sighted the diving sub and while his fingers were pressing the selector switch—that they would not be able to bomb at the predetermined level. By the time they got there the target would be gone.

He had eyes in the back of his head, in his knees and elbows, and in the seat of his pants. Inside his brain a computer worked like a machine. In the time that the swooping ship drooped fifty feet he knew at what level Strame would make the run, and recalculated. The figures popped up and leaped into place as though he were seeing them on a gigantic screen.

"Bombardier from pilot: On course! Level!"

No time for a verbal answer. Salvo double-clicked his mike. His right hand held the hand sight, swung from its steel shaft, the ring and bead centered on the vanishing conning tower. The fingers of his left hand quivered over the firing switch, hovering, barely touching, moving slightly to keep the barest contact.

Half the conning tower and periscope was still visible, tilting forward. . . . Breath held. . . . Steady aim! Like shooting a gun at a treed wildcat.

The bead lifted inexorably from the sea to the black steel poised there, held—

Just a tightening of the fingers on the solenoid firing switch.

"Bomb away! Okay to turn!"

Two legless gray pigs appeared beneath the glass nose of the ship and drifted downward lazily, shrinking in size like deflating toy balloons. They kept forward pace with the hurtling ship as it raced across the line straight to the sub. The wing had already dipped for turning.

At the precise moment that the bombs met water, the nose of the ship passed over the target and Salvo's vision was cut off.

"Engineer from pilot: Prepare to take picture left side!"

"Engineer, Roger!"

Then the intercommunication seemed to go haywire for an instant as somebody up above yelled "Yahooo!" into it.

Salvo had already selected two more depth charges.

He was a split second ahead of Strame with a new set of calculations when the order came, "Bombardier from pilot: Stand by for second run! We've got him!"

"Bomber, Roger!"

Lumbering Annie swung heavily into a diving turn. The freighter hove into sight again, veering frantically away, black smoke belching from her single funnel. Then into Salvo's view came an expanse of tumbled white froth, as though there had been a sub-sea eruption. In the center of it bubbled a thick yellowish slick from which something black was upthrust. It was the bow of the stricken submarine, poised there for an instant.

Salvo felt no elation. He was too busy. Computations checked, bombs armed, fingers gentling the firing switch, bead drifting onto target, steady—

"Bomb away!"

"Pilot from engineer: Picture taken okay! Oh, baby!"

Salvo Jenkins tried to rememeber what had happened, what he had done, what his calculations had been, whether he had left anything out. He couldn't. He remembered nothing. Lumbering Annie circled and circled. The yellow oil patch grew in size and length, bits and pieces of unidentifiable things appeared in the center. The freighter was stuttering hysterical cheers with her blinker.

Someone came down through the hatch from above and began to beat Salvo on the back, yelling, "Wow! Wow! Wow! Wow" in tune with the thrumming motors.

Salvo Jenkins went back to the orderly room of the squadron to pick up his data kit, which he had left there in the excitement. He felt very tired and a little queer in his insides.

Voices came drifting through from the partitioned office of the C.O. The door was shut, but he recognized the speech of Ed Hammond, the co-pilot. "Say, Cappy. We've got a bombardier, haven't we?"

The hard, crackling voice of the C.O. broke in. "He's your man, John. I was wrong. And glad of it."

Salvo Jenkins wanted to get his brief case and get out of there. But his hands were trembling so, he fumbled it.

Captain Strame said, "That kid's a honey. Say, Ed, that 'Salvo' stuff is gonna be out. From now on we're calling him 'Bull's-eye.' "

Bull's-eye Jenkins got his brief case, but found suddenly that he could not see his way clearly to the door until he stopped and brushed the tears away from his eyes.

"Dawgone it, Jenkins," he said to himself. "There you go, actin' just like a kid again. Ain't you evah goin' tuh grow up?"

DAVID GOODIS

Hawk of the Sudan

THIRTY MILES NORTH of Shambe, in the southern cup of the Anglo-Egyptian Sudan, the British prepared for their big try. They had an army of 175,000 men drawn back on a leash of trucks, motor cars, railroads, and carbine-armed motorcycles. Their plans were a motley of daring strategy, sliced and chopped and blended into one huge gamble. They figured on this big stab into the middle of Ethiopia, cutting deep through mountain and desert and flatland. From the north another English contingent would make a similar move. Between these two sections the Italian army in Ethiopia would be trapped. And if the defeat could reach completion, it would mean a virtual conquering of this land that had once been Abyssinia.

British and Sudanese infantrymen were quite pepped up about the project. On the vast parade grounds of the camp, they gathered in small groups, expressing their grinning optimism.

And the aviation section, centered in the chalked-off circle of hangar and barracks and supply drome and yellow-green tarmac, was likewise enthusiastic.

With one exception.

He was just another flying officer. His name was Lawrence Thate. He was twenty-six years old and he was of medium height and medium weight and his looks were those of nothing more than just another clean-cut young Englishman. He had close-curled blond hair and glinting blue eyes and straight lips. There was nothing about his appearance to indicate a man apart from his fellows.

And, in truth, Thate did not stand out. At least, not down here in the broiling heat of the lower Sudan. Yet in England, as a cadet at a string of military schools, ending up with a lieutenant's commission in the Lancaster Regiment, he had gained for himself a reputation as a brilliant student of strategy.

The trouble was that Thate never had the opportunity to put his knowledge and his theories into actual practice. When the war broke out, he was immediately sent to France and while he was on a truck, riding to the front, a shell exploded somewhere near and that was all he saw of Western Front action. He was in a hospital for three months, and propped up in bed he read about the growing importance of the air arm. And when he left the hospital, he received permission to enlist in the R.A.F. He figured that in a very short while he would be in the thick of things again, and the opportunity would come for him to show what he could do.

But the R.A.F. was not hurrying matters. Quality rather than quantity was the order of the day, and it took a long time for a young pilot to emerge from the training school, polished and ready for actual combat.

When Thate was ready, they sent him down to the Sudan.

And so this was his status now, just another Flying Officer waiting for the call that would throw him into the troubled skies. Already he had tasted the hot broth of combat, in a few transactions over the Ethiopian border. Already he had two victories to his credit sheet. And like his brother officers of the 19th Combat, he should have been quite eager for a resumption of activity, particularly since this was a major offensive.

But Lawrence Thate was most certainly not enthusiastic. Rather was he downright gloomy, pessimistic, and sullen over the situation.

His reasons for this attitude hinged on his background as a strategy scholar. He had studied the geographical, geological, mathematical, and metaphysical aspects of the matter, and he was quite convinced that the staff officers in charge of the projected operation were making a big mistake.

However, Thate kept telling himself to keep his ideas buried. Past experience had taught him the value of silence, particularly for one who became excited easily and had a very hot temper. Many times Thate had started to argue strategy and had wound up flinging fists at his dissenters. The last debate had taken place in the R.A.F. training base at Bristol, and had nearly resulted in a court martial for young Thate. That incident had made him promise himself to refrain from open argument on strategy.

Nevertheless, when he was alone, with his maps and his charts and his calculations, he sensed a throbbing deep within him, a bouncing force that kept telling him of the weaknesses in this big advance into Ethiopia. And he wanted to leap out of his narrow room, and present himself at the squadron office, and tell Group Captain Jenn-Fraws just what he thought about the entire matter.

He was thinking about it now, as he sat on his cot, frowning at the papers in his hands. One was a map. The other was a chart. And the two papers reached a rather glaring conclusion. They showed that the push into Ethiopia would be slowed down by the maze of mountain streams flowing southward. The Italians would have an intense geographical advantage, not only because of the streams, but also since the hills and mountains of western Ethiopia would force the British into a steady, slow, painful climb. Once the Italians maneuvered their artillery into the right emplacements, it would be quite a bloody mess.

Thate did not know what his counterproposal would be. He understood only that the British were making an error that would prove quite costly. He saw a need for a more careful study of the situation, with an emphasis on aerial reconnaissance.

But how was he to put his ideas across?

For many minutes he sat there, staring at his map and his chart, and muttering against tradition and discipline and the high-handedness of his superiors. Finally he stood up and went to the high-boy, opened the second drawer, took out a bottle of scotch.

He gulped long and heavily. He put the bottle down and again looked at the map and the chart. He took up the bottle, tilted his head back. Something sparked within him, became a glow, and the glow was growing.

And he took a third long pull at that bottle.

Thirty minutes later he had a load on. And it was a prize package. It did not make his head spin. It did not make his knees sag. But it did cause his eyes to tighten up, his expression to become one of reckless, alcohol-inspired determination.

He flipped the empty bottle onto the cot. He straightened his tunic, snapped his fingers, and braced into rigidity. Then he marched from the room.

Moving in a straight line, unswerving, unstaggered, he marched from barracks across the hard-packed sand to the squadron office. A burly orderly blocked his path. In very quiet but firm tones Thate told the guard that this was important business, that it was imperative for him to speak to Group Captain Jenn-Fraws.

Behind the desk, the square chunk of a red-faced, silver-haired air officer listened attentively. Jenn-Fraws was an old warrior who had been in the Sudan for almost a quarter of a century. He knew his desert fighting and he knew his air strategy. Most of all, however, he knew his tradition and his discipline. And he looked straight into the eyes of the young Flying Officer and told himself that this sort of thing would have to be stopped before it could run outside the boundaries of British military efficiency.

"—and so, sir," Thate said, "it is my opinion that the matter should be given further consideration, and if—"

"Stop right there, Thate!"

"Uh—what—what did you say, sir?"

"I said stop right there." Jenn-Fraws stood up slowly. The expression of polite attentiveness had changed to one of stern rebuke. In slow, rumbling tones he said, "You have shown unaccustomed effrontery, Thate. You dare to come here and question the conclusion of your superiors. You dare to present yourself before me and jolly well claim that all our plans are just a means of Yorkshire pudding. Out of order, Thate! Bloody well out of order."

"But I've studied this carefully, sir. I—"

"Be quiet!" Jenn-Fraws thundered. "What right have you to study a situation such as this? What qualifies you to place your opinions in direct opposition to the reasoning of your superiors? You—a mere Flying Officer—a mere boy! You—you dare to come here and—it's absurd, it's unthinkable, it's—why, I say, it's downright insubordination—"

Thate was burning. He was standing there, rigid, unblinking. But his eyes were sparking fire, and at his sides his fists were clenched. And he could sense the anger hammering away, taking command of his senses, his impulses.

But now he made a valorous try for self control, saying, "Begging your pardon, sir—I did not mean to show insubordination—"

The group captain was not satisfied with that. He yelled, "You did not mean to? You deliberately stand there and claim that you did not mean to be insubordinate? How else can you explain this action? You surely are not intoxicated—or—or are you? Come here—come here, closer—I want to get a whiff of your breath. Yes, yes, I can see it now. I can see that brightness in your eyes. It tells me all I want to know, Thate. We'll put a stop to that sort of thing here and now. We'll hand you a penalty of five days in the guardhouse!"

"What?" It came out fast, blazing. Thate leaned forward.

"You heard me, Thate. And stand at attention, if you please. Brace, I said—*brace!*"

"To hell with you," Thate said.

Jenn-Fraws almost fell on his back. He winced, shook his head dazedly, wondering if he had heard right, and then he rasped, "What did you say?"

Thate had surrendered to his temper. He didn't care now. He didn't care about anything. His arms folded across his chest and he was saying, "You heard what I said. And you don't have to attribute it to the alcohol. I knew exactly what I was saying, and I meant it."

"Oh, you did?"

"Yes, I did. I'm damned fed up with all this high-handed color and embroidery and tangled-up mess as tradition. We have a lot of old dotards down here who have an idea that they're still fighting the Boer War, or something. They refuse to accept the new theories of strategy. They refuse to realize that a man is flesh and blood rather than oil and steel. They stick their pins in maps and say *go ahead* and then they sit back with their scotch and soda and wait for miracles to happen. Well, I for one, do not believe in miracles. I do believe in common sense. And that's exactly what our staff officers are lacking in, and—"

"That's enough!" Jenn-Fraws yelled. His face was purple. His voice rose to a screech. "You're under arrest!"

That was a bit too much for the group captain, who had a temper of his own. He stepped close to the young officer, and for the slice of a moment his better judgment lost out. His arm was raised, his fist clenched—

Thate didn't wait for the fist to come down. He leaped in, spitting an oath, and his left jabbed deep into the group captain's paunch. Jenn-Fraws emitted a wheezing sound, doubled up—and Thate lifted him off the floor with a sizzling uppercut.

The Flying Officer was completely out of his head now. In Jenn-Fraws he saw a symbol of all that he despised. Here, before him, was the kind of superior officer who would sacrifice the lives of his men rather than cater to a new idea. It made Thate think in terms of blood and hate and murder.

And he was a wildman as he leaped again at the group captain. His fist pistoned out and once more Jenn-Fraws doubled up, staggered against the wall. Thate rushed him, threw a thudding succession of lefts and rights that brought blood from the group captain's nose and mouth.

But finally Jenn-Fraws initiated a counter-offensive. It was not exactly in the rules, but he was not thinking of that now. He saw before him a killer, and he felt like living a few more years.

With that in mind, he grabbed at the side of his desk. His fingers found a heavy marble paper-weight. He drew his arm back and heaved it. The marble block sailed a few feet through the air and made contact with Thate's forehead.

The Flying Officer went to sleep.

Deucedly uncomfortable. Plenty of heat up there on the tarmac. But at least there was light and air and a bit of space to move around in. Here it was dark, and hot in a black, sticky, dirty way. And all sorts of vermin crawled along the walls, hopped from the walls onto his hair and his shoulders and his face and arms and legs. The more he tried to whisk them off, the more they persisted.

He cursed a few times, but that didn't help. He called himself a few hundred different kinds of fool, and even then he didn't come near to describing his brainless move. It all added up to the nasty truth that he had struck his superior officer—had, in fact, tried to knock the group captain's head off. That would mean a court martial, and with the discipline situation as it was these days, it might mean five or ten years in prison.

That would never do.

Especially if the prison would be anything like this hell-hole. He groped in the darkness, found the length of hard, hilly mattress, and threw himself on the cot. For an instant he almost gave in to his despair, and came near to breaking down. But then the anger came again, and with the anger came an intense desire to challenge this dark outlook, to see if he could do something about it, form some kind of plan.

Strategy. That was the word. That was his growing talent, strategy, and maybe it could aid him now. He sat up, moved slowly to the bars of the cell door, stared out at the corridor, where the blackness was broken by a band of gray light flowing from the upper floor of the guardhouse.

His trial was to come up on the morrow. That meant that if he was to do anything, it would have to be done in a big hurry.

He fidgeted with the cell door. Nothing doing. He tested the walls on all four sides. The concrete was stronger than he was. He moved toward the door again. Then he grinned. He had his scheme, and it glowed like an eager candle in his brain.

"Guard!" he yelled, and waited.

In a few seconds the guard appeared outside the cell door. He was the same burly fellow who had been standing at the door of the squadron office when Thate had started his one-man campaign against the General Staff. Now he glowered at the prisoner and muttered, "Well, what do you want?"

"Simply this," Thate said. "I need a witness."

"A witness? What for?"

Thate shrugged. "My court martial comes up tomorrow. The only chance I have is to produce a witness who will prove that I struck Group Captain Jenn-Fraws in self defense."

"Well, what's that got to do with me?" the guard said.

"Simply this. You were standing outside that door. When they brought me down here I recognized you. Perhaps you saw what took place. Perhaps you might have heard the argument, and looked through the window."

"Nothing of the sort," the guard said.

"You're a liar."

"What did you call me?"

"A liar," Thate said, edging venom into the words, telling himself that he had to make this guard become angry—more than angry—boiling to rage that carried a minimum of reasoning.

"Be careful what you say," the guard growled.

"In your eye," Thate said. "You saw what took place in that squadron office. You were looking through the window."

"I certainly was not!"

"You're a low liar," Thate said. "Not only that, you're a coward. You're afraid to appear at that court martial, afraid to give testimony in my behalf. Worrying about your own skin, thinking that the General Staff will make things unpleasant for you. What a low, lying, sneaking hound of a coward you are! What a miserable yellow cur!"

As he said this he moved toward the bars of the cell door, offering himself as an easy target for the guard's wrath. And the heavy fellow was quivering with rage, righteous indignation blended with a furious desire to inflict bodily harm upon this snake in human form.

The guard hesitated, and Thate sneered at him, and that sneer settled matters.

A fist was drawn back, and it came forward fast. Thate was expecting it. As the fist whizzed through the bars, he dodged to one side, and in the same instant he grabbed at it. He caught the guard's wrist, and with all his might he yanked back. Caught off balance, the heavy fellow was pulled against the iron bars. His forehead made a dull thud as it hit against the metal. The guard was staggered. Thate made the most of the chance. He pulled again at that thick wrist, and once more the guard fell against the door, with his head as the point of contact. This time the burly man lost consciousness.

Thate leaned down, reached outside the bars, grabbed at the ring of keys that dangled from the guard's belt.

Out of that cell; down the corridor slowly, carefully. Up the steps, and down another hall—very carefully now—and hearing footsteps coming toward him—waiting, pressed against the wall—with his fists ready, and leaping out as the shadow made a turn, and jabbing hard with the left, crossing the right—grinning as the tingle of a knockout blow throbbed down his arm—moving again—quickly now—toward a door—wasting no time—opening it and walking into daylight.

He still wore his uniform, and despite a day's growth of beard and a patch of gauze and adhesive on his forehead he was quite similar in appearance to the other fliers who walked to and fro across the tarmac. Some of them were conversing with mechanics who were tuning up motors. Some were making check-ups on their flight orders of the day. A jumble of activity swarmed across the tarmac of the 19th Combat.

Thate walked casually toward a line-up of Hawker Hurricanes that were now being warmed up. A few of these planes were already sufficiently tuned, and pilots were climbing into cockpits for take-offs on respective scouting jobs.

Very calmly Thate walked up to a Hurricane, climbed in, and took off.

No trouble at all.

He climbed quickly to 3,500 feet, feinted toward the left, as if to follow a trio of planes that were moving in a southeast direction. He shook his head slowly as he watched them. A fine way to make preliminary scouting maneuvers. The real action was going to take place to the north of Shambe, and as if that wasn't a big enough mistake in itself, they were sending the planes out to scout the southern terrain, where nothing at all would happen.

Thate frowned. Like a hammer-blow it came at him now, and he realized that the fate of this British army was none of his concern. He was no longer a part of it. He was a deserter, running away from his squadron and his army and, automatically, *he was no longer a part of England!*

It struck at him again, and again, and heaviness was in his throat. He wanted to turn back. He wanted to give himself up, surrender himself to that court martial and take what was coming to him.

Yet, if loyalty was a blood brother to justice, the higher-ups were as guilty as he was. Justice would not be their prime goal. They would crush him, grind him down, erasing the merits of his case, and giving thought only to their own stern, unrelenting methods of maintaining tradition and color and military efficiency and their own old worn-out strategy.

Therefore he would not go back. He was no deserter to England. He still would gladly give his life for the Empire. In his own way he would remain true to the cause of Democracy and Freedom. The odds were stacked high against him, but—what did he have to lose?

He turned northward, and gunned the Hurricane to 250 miles per hour. Kept feeding juice until the silver-gray plane was hurtling at meteor speed toward the purple waves that glimmered in the sunlight—in the far distance—the mountain peaks of Ethiopia.

Three olive-green Fiats moved in straight formation at 6,000 feet. In command of the small patrol was Captain Nordeno, a tall, lean man in his late twenties. He had a reputation for sky combat based on his achievements in the clouds of Madrid, where he had met and conquered some of the greatest aces in the International Brigade. And now, in another war, he was continuing his brilliant record. Already, his flaming guns had smashed twelve R.A.F. planes from the blue above Ethiopia.

Nordeno was hungry for additional game. Impatience showed in his glittering jet eyes. This, his fourth patrol in as many days, was resulting in the same monotonous emptiness. The British were not sending their aerial scouts over this sector. Obviously they were rather discouraged by the unpleasant reception that Nordeno and his flying mates had offered on previous occasions. Or perhaps they had other reasons.

The Italian's eyes narrowed. Peering ahead, he thought he saw a dot in the calmness of blue sky. Or was he mistaken?

No! Assuredly it was a dot, growing larger and larger with each second, taking shape.

It was a British plane.

Nordeno muttered his incredulity. A single plane would not be sent over this trouble area unless there was some special mission. And even then, an important scouting job would naturally have some sort of escort. Maybe the Englishman was a decoy. Maybe there were other planes hovering in the high galleries, waiting.

But that was also disproven by a cloudless sky that showed nothing more than the single plane coming on at terrific speed.

Nordeno shrugged, and a thin smile came over his lips. If the Englishman was looking for trouble, then he would most certainly find it. Instinctively the Italian caressed the trigger handles of his guns.

Then he reached out, lifted the speaking tube from its panel placement, switched on the radio that connected him with the other planes. "Crissotti—Frezione—we have a visitor. Let us try and make him comfortable—our hospitality will be most warm."

In the cockpits of their olive-green fighting planes, Crissotti and Frezione were grinning. They also saw the Hurricane, which now was walking up the ladder, grabbing for an altitude advantage. There was no doubt about the fact that the Englishman had seen the Fiats, and was all too eager for a negotiation.

Nordeno said, "Let me handle this little matter, gentlemen. I judge that three minutes of argumentation will dispose of the Hawker Hurricane. If my judgment proves wrong, you can dip your spoons into the soup and take part in the debate. But, of course, my judgment will be correct."

The two other Italians nodded to themselves. They had the highest respect for Nordeno's ability with wings and guns. Now they swerved off to right and left respectively, leaving the field clear for the joust.

Nordeno zoomed up, carefully watching the Hurricane's climb. The Fiat had speed and lift ability and now it was even on the jump-up. Nordeno gunned the ship and it moved in for the initial contact. He faked to the left, but the Hurricane did not bite. Still climbing, the Italian waited for the Britisher to close in. But the Hurricane continued its walk up the stairs, taking its time.

With Thate it was a matter of small choice. He could not turn back. He could not make a landing. He could not go forward unless he felt like fighting. And since he did feel like fighting, he was telling himself that the odds of three-against-one were of minor importance. He would fight and do his best and if they shot him down it would be nothing more than a part of the game.

Yet somehow he felt a lift of confidence as he moved up into the big arena, prepared to make his first bid. This air combat was essentially a matter of strategy, and strategy was the big word in the vocabulary of

Lawrence Thate. He had gained his first two victories by timing and measurement and brilliant anticipation of the enemy's moves. If he had done that twice, he could do it again.

Fear tried to slice into him, but he threw a shield before his senses, and now he was smiling thinly.

At 8,000 feet he made his bid.

He was level with the Fiat, the separating distance being somewhere around 400 yards. He started to the left, banked hard, and carved it into a dive. He held the dive for a few hundred feet and then crawled up, starting a loop. The Fiat whizzed past, about 400 feet beneath him. But his loop was sizzling, and he was out of it fast, and streaking down.

Nordeno heard the bullets, heard the thud of slugs punching into his wings. He rolled out hard, dived, and faded to the right. The Hurricane leveled, turned, and now the Fiat took the initiative.

The Italian plane looped high and wide and came down with guns talking. Thate started his runaway dive, chiseled it into a zoom. He continued the climb for swaying seconds, then tangented to the left, fell over on his right wing, kept going down until he was out of the trouble spot.

They scribbled through the sky.

Nordeno crawled in for a side-burst. Thate took bullets in his wings, was forced to roll-out. But he was up again, and looping once more, and fading out of the loop, and coming in fast and sizzling and punching his gun button at a range of ninety yards, when he was facing the nose of that Fiat.

Bullets sliced through the glass cockpit roof, missing Nordeno's skull by less than an inch. The Italian writhed. And then he cursed. He set his Fiat to the right, started down, and crawled into a tight wing-over. Thate slid by, started his own jab, and then crossed up the Italian by dancing into a wide loop.

Nordeno studied the matter carefully.

Then he was walking up fast, getting the jump on the Hurricane, and grinning as he realized a decided advantage on the move. At 8,500 feet he had his 500-feet height superiority, and that was all he needed. And he pivoted hard to his left, sliding into a neat Immelmann, and then pointed down, diving hard.

Thate looked up, saw what was coming, and knew that his move was a roll-out. That was the only safe way to play it. But there was another maneuver that would, if done right, slide him away from the death spot and place him on the Italian's tail. To do it he would have to wait until the last possible instant, chancing a fatal bullet through his motor or his gas tank or his brain.

He waited. He heard the bullets. He felt the impact as the slugs stabbed into his fuselage, his wings. He heard something crackle through his glass cockpit roof. He saw a splash on his instrument panel. Still he waited.

And then he pointed up!

Climbing hard, twisting over and back into a tight loop; coming out of it fast; spearing down onto the tail of the Fiat.

Desperately the Italian writhed left and right and left and right again. But the Hurricane followed in, close and deliberate, waiting for the moment when the olive-green wings and fuselage would form an ideal target.

Now the range was slightly more than a hundred yards—then 80—70—60—with Nordeno wriggling like an eel, frenziedly trying to slide out of the net. Thate gave him a three-second burst that missed. Another burst and Nordeno tried a roll-out. Thate had anticipated it, and followed smoothly. Nordeno looped. Thate looped with him and crawled closer. Nordeno sweated. Thate grinned. The Italian dived, pulled out hard. Thate was not fooled. He kept moving in close.

It was then that Lieutenants Crissotti and Frezione glanced at their wrist-watches and saw that the three minutes were up. The signal could not have come at a better time. From their perches at 10,000 feet they saw the course that the battle was taking and they realized that Captain Nordeno was having quite a difficult time of it.

Together the two Fiats left their gallery seats and leaped down toward the stage.

Thate saw them coming. He gritted a curse, poured juice fast and thick, and then snatched at a scheme.

Nordeno was still trying to crawl out of the tight spot, and his Fiat was giving all it had. He was diving now, and Thate was still trying to center the Brownings on him. But the Italian was making a runaway that was as neatly conceived as it was frenzied. Yet Thate continued the chase, retained his position behind the Fiat even though the other two fascist planes were now lunging at him from either side. He appeared not to notice them. He continued to close in, and even now he was taking their bullets.

And then like an enraged leopard he veered to his left, swerving away from his pursuit of Nordeno. The acute angle brought him in a prop-to-prop position with Crissotti. The Italian was quite surprised.

Thate was not. This was part of his plan, and he knew how to handle it. He reached out, punched the gun button. The Browning started to chuck lead. Eight streams of fire lanced out from the Hurricane's wings, spat furiously into the nose of the Fiat. The bullets cut through the motor, the gas tanks, the glass cockpit roof, and one of the slugs hit Lieutenant Crissotti between the eyes. He slumped forward, and flames blanketed him as he became a corpse. The plane hurtled down to its last landing.

Nordeno saw that, and shuddered. He knew full well that the thinnest slice of chance was all that prevented him from taking Crissotti's place. But relief catered to fear, and fear gave way to a renewal of rage. The Italian ace signaled to Frezione, and together they climbed for a high diving board from which to leap at the wild-flying Englishman.

Thate wasn't waiting for any time-outs. He pumped juice, and the Hurricane, well warmed to its task, lined up toward the two Fiats.

At 10,000 feet the battle went into its second phase.

The range was 400 yards. Nordeno and Frezione had a height advantage of slightly more than a hundred feet. And now they lunged at the Hurricane, cutting from left and right and pouring bullets as they hit the 200-yard range.

Thate dived, curled it into a loop before the Italians touched his line of flight. He came down hard, swerved to his left, and all this time he was watching, anticipating, finally concluding that Frezione would negotiate for a side attack.

He reasoned correctly. The Italian was turning hard, coming in fast as Thate leveled. Bullets leaped from the Italian plane. The Hurricane dodged out of the trouble line, feinted to the left, and then crossed up the fascist flier with a lightning maneuver to the right. This brought the Brownings in a direct line with the Fiat's cockpit. Bullets zipped from the Hurricane's wings, jabbed out, and danced into the cockpit of the Italian plane.

Lieutenant Frezione screamed. Blood rushed from his nostrils and his quivering lips. His lungs were gushing red wetness, and it was welling from his head now. He was trying to scream louder, but the blood flooded all sound, and Lieutenant Frezione sagged in his narrow leather-lined coffin, waved weakly to the victor, smiled, and died.

Watching the Fiat go down, Thate heard bullet-chukking behind him. He glanced into his rear-view mirror, knew that the lone remaining Fiat was now making its big try. He rolled out fast, kept going down, and still the bullets sang in his ears. The Fiat had played the roll-out with uncanny timing, and now the Englishman realized that this was rum business.

Again he tried a roll-out, and again the Fiat played it correctly, moved in for the kill.

Bullets punched into the Hurricane. Thate squirmed. He saw a line of green flame shiver along his glycol tank. He dived hard.

Nordeno also dived.

The Hurricane was smoking now. It was racing into a weird fire dance, whistling its own death knell.

The Italian pumped more bullets, and smiled wider as he saw the orange lines seep into the mortally wounded engine-bird.

And Thate sweated. He sensed the heat, he sensed the end of everything. Already the flames were forking through the instrument panel, stabbing at his face. The front of the plane was a welter of black smoke and green, gasoline-fed fire. The Hurricane shuddered, stumbled, then leaped high, went over on its back, and plummeted to earth!

Captain Nordeno laughed in low tones. He pulled out of the attack stance, settled himself in a comfortable box seat, and watched the English plane go down, enveloped in a cloak of flame. And then there was a splash of liquid orange fire as the Hurricane hit the ground.

The Fiat made a slow turn, and with the nonchalance of triumph, moved eastard toward its base.

Heat—enough of it to give him the idea that he was in Hades, with devil dancers sowing seeds of fire around him. He groaned, and sensed the rhythm of his heart and his lungs, and he knew that he was alive.

He opened his eyes.

He was curled up on a vast pillow of heavy bush. Thirty yards away he could see the charred mass of wreckage. And he knew that luck had tagged him, that he had been thrown clear of the plane before the flames could consume him, before the terrific impact of crashing could crack every bone in his body.

He groaned again, and sensed a certain amount of pain and stiffness, accentuated by the awful heat. He was exactly seven degrees above the Equator, and on this day the sun was doing its damnedest.

Thate rolled away from the bush, tested his legs. Movement

seemed to help out, and he wriggled for a while, loosening his aching joints. Then he glanced at his wrist-watch, that had a small compass in its dial, and he started his big hike, eastward.

Three hours later he was on a mountain slope. He was tired, and the sweat rolled from him in floods. Time and time again he fell, picked himself up, fell, picked himself up. He thought of all the things that would come in handy at a time like this. At least—a pith helmet—or someone to talk to—or at the very least a canteen.

No use denying that. He was very thirsty.

He started to look around for a stream. There must be a stream somewhere near. All this vegetation—water fed it—and water was around here—somewhere—somewhere—and the sun—it was cutting through his brain—he was so very tired—he fell on his face, rolled over, cursed, struggled to his feet, fell down again—and sobbed. But once more he was moving—crawling now, and telling himself that there was water somewhere near, that he was not so weak and far gone that he could not make his way to water—because he was so very thirsty—and so damned hot and sticky and weak and tired—tired—

Again Thate fell on his face. His arms spread out. He made an effort to crawl forward. His fingers clutched at the black soil, shivered. And the sun beat down on him, and each ray of merciless heat seemed to leer at him as he lay there motionless.

General Briocho was a good listener; particularly when he was hearing the exploits of his air warriors. Although the general was strictly an infantry man, he had at one time been an observer in the Italian Air Force in 1916 when Italy had fought side by side with England, instead of against her.

The general, therefore, was intensely interested in the aviation phase of this war, and he enjoyed no better recreation than to gather his flyers about him and hear them tell of their battles in the clouds.

Briocho, tall and heavy and strong-jawed, sipped at his red wine, tugged at the long black cigar, and listened attentively as Captain Nordeno gave a detailed description, using his hands as imaginary planes, dipping and swirling them in a recounting of the fight.

"He was quite a flyer," Nordeno said. "Crissotti and Frezione didn't have a chance against him. Even I had my troubles. But I knew that sooner or later my superior ability would decide the course of battle."

General Briocho nodded. A few of the other flyers gathered at the table, glanced at each other knowingly. Nordeno's abilities at boasting were even greater than his peculiar talents at controls and trigger-handles.

"And so," Nordeno went on, "he circled—thus—and I went into a reversement—thus—and—"

He was interrupted by the appearance of an orderly, who stepped before General Briocho, saluted briskly, and said, "Major Cianzo sends his compliments, sir. He reports that one of his mountain patrols has captured a British aviator. He asks if you wish to question the Englishman."

Nordeno leaned forward, broke in with, "Where did the capture of this man take place?"

"On a mountain slope," the orderly said. "Near the southern branch of the Sobat River."

"It seems impossible," Nordeno muttered, "but that is precisely the area over which we were fighting." He turned to General Briocho and said, "If I may offer a suggestion, sir, I think it would be feasible to question the Englishman. The very fact that he was alone on that flight gives me to believe that he was on some special mission. He may be able to offer valuable information."

"Quite true," Briocho said. He gestured to the orderly and muttered, "Bring the prisoner at once."

The man withdrew.

There was a certain amount of thankfulness in the mind of Lawrence Thate. He was thankful, of course, for the fact that he was alive. It would have been painful and ironic for him to die there on that mountain slope, scarcely seventy yards away from a stream of cool, crystal clear water. If not for the Italian patrol he would still be there, his fingers clawing in rigidity at the soft black soil.

And so he was thankful. Yet at the same time he was blanketing emotion, replacing it with a realization of what he had stumbled into. He knew exactly where he was. He knew that this immense military camp was less than fifty miles from the border. It was in a strategic position, a placement not known to the British who soon would be marching in this direction utterly unknowing of what awaited them.

And that was only a preliminary to what the actual plans of this Italian army might be. If they had come this far, they might be preparing for their own offensive.

A shudder ran through Thate. He thought of the mountain slopes along the border. He could see the Italian heavy artillery smashing into the British lines; tearing through masses of men, annihilating them.

His thoughts were detoured as he followed the guards up to the rectangular table that was placed outside the headquarters tent. He knew enough Italian to gesture aside the interpreter who graciously offered service.

Thate was introduced to the general, who in turn brought forth Captain Nordeno, saying, "You might be glad to meet your—shall I say—conqueror?"

The Englishman shrugged, while Nordeno smiled blandly. The smile was fast erased as Thate said, "Conqueror is not exactly the correct term. It was a victory for Captain Nordeno, I will admit, but not a complete victory."

Nordeno scowled, and his fists were clenched, and an oath escaped his lips. For a moment it seemed as if rage would dominate him, cause him to leap at the captive flyer. But General Briocho stepped into the breach and quickly changed the subject, saying, "You are willing to provide information?"

"Perhaps," Thate said.

Nordeno moved away from the table, still muttering. The other flyers glanced at him and then glanced at each other and smiled. They knew what the prisoner meant by his reference to an incomplete victory. Nordeno had probably scored his hits while the Englishman had been veering away from a follow-through on one of the other Fiats. Nordeno would, of course, not admit that, but it was probably the case.

The Italian ace turned and stared back, and saw the knowing smiles on the faces of his flying mates. His eyes narrowed and he promised himself that if the victory was not complete now, perhaps it would be quite soon.

At the table, General Briocho said, "Your squadron?"

"Nineteenth Combat," Thate answered.

"Locale?"

"Indefinite," the flyer murmured.

Briocho frowned. "Just what do you mean by that?"

The Flying Officer shrugged. "We never know where our assignments will take us. We flit from one drome to the other, all along the Sudan." He made that sound convincing.

"Now, let us get down to details," Briocho said. "Why were you flying north, over Ethiopia, alone?"

"Reconnaissance," Thate murmured. He knew that he would have to play this delicately. He wanted information as much as did Briocho. If he could only ferret out the facts by squeezing revealing questions from the Italian general.

Briocho was frowning and saying, "That seems absurd. Why would you be making reconnaissance in this area alone?"

Again Thate shrugged. "After all," he said, "we have to cover quite a lot of territory down here, and we don't have many planes. In fact, it surprises me to see that you Italians are gathered here in such large numbers. Our military force in the lower Sudan consists of nothing but small patrols. We don't expect any trouble."

Briocho laughed. "Oh, you don't?" He turned to the flyers and said, "You hear that? They don't expect any trouble. We'll have quite a surprise for them when we cross the border, advance deep into the Sudan, and then push north."

Thate's features were expressionless. But inside he was quivering. The Italians were preparing for an offensive, on an even larger scale than the British army. And the Italians had this tremendous geographical advantage. If word could be gotten to the English contingent, advising them of the Italian push; telling them to hold back, to draw the Italians deep into the Sudan, and then flank them from both sides, cut off their supply lines, and surround them.

Briocho said, turning to the Englishman, "Your information is most valuable. Permit me to express my thanks by offering you the comfort of a tent, rather than an uncomfortable cell. Of course you will not mind if a guard is placed nearby?"

Thate smiled politely and said, "Not at all."

The sky was a ceiling of hot black tar, without stars, without a moon. Through the slit in the front of the tent Thate could see the dots of yellow light, the fires of the Italian camp. Every few moments a shadow blotted out the dots of light. The sentry, moving back and forth.

And the sentry had a rifle. And the monotony of his job made him only too anxious for an excuse to use that weapon. If there was going to be a deal, it would have to be made with finesse and polish and strategy.

Thate frowned at the toes of his boots. Slowly he took out a pack of cigarettes from his breeches pocket, slowly lit up, slowly puffed.

He did not see a second shadow move past the front flap.

He did not see the two shadows huddle closer. Did not hear the low tones that passed between the sentry and Captain Nordeno.

For several minutes Thate smoked and made his mental charts. And then he stood up, ground the cigarette beneath his boot-heel, and made a final review of the plan. Just as he was telling himself that the odds figured out to about a hundred to one against him, and shrugging and figuring that he still had very little to lose, he saw the front flap open to one side.

The sentry stood there, a tall, wide fellow. He held the rifle in readiness, but he was grinning.

"What do you want?" Thate said.

"It's lonely out there," the sentry replied. "Lonely and hot."

Thate grinned, This was a break. The fellow wanted to chat. It meant the discarding of the original plan. It threw Thate's mind into a new channel of strategy, and now he said, "I don't envy you your job. I think I would go off my head, walking out there in the black heat alone, and with that heavy rifle."

"Sentry duty is the worst job in the army," the Italian said.

"I don't doubt it a bit," Thate said. "A man might just as well be in a cell, butting his head against four stone walls."

"That's no joke," the sentry said, frowning.

Thate leaned forward and murmured smoothly, "You seem discontented."

"I am," the sentry replied.

"Well then, why don't you do something about it?"

"What can I do?" returned the sentry.

"Oh, several things."

"Such as?"

Thate studied the sentry's face. And even as he did, he saw a shadow outside. And in that instant he knew. He smiled inwardly. This was bait. But a wise fish knew how to take it off the hook without being caught.

He said, "You are loyal to your country?"

The sentry shrugged. "There are limits to what one will do for any cause."

"Of course," Thate said. "You have reached those limits?"

"With all the heat, the insects, the marching—yes, I have reached them."

"Passed them, I should think," Thate said.

"You are right. I—I have passed the limits of loyalty. I am not contented with things as they are."

"Then there is only one thing for you to do."

"And that is?"

Thate smiled. He looked over the sentry's shoulder, as if someone else had just entered the tent. In a bland voice he said, "Good evening, General Briocho."

The sentry's face went white, and his lips trembled. In that moment he was off guard, and as he turned, expecting to see the general, Thate leaped at him.

A fist whizzed in a straight line, smashed against the Italian's jaw. Thate grabbed at the rifle as the Italian sagged. And then he brought up the heavy stock, and it thudded against the sentry's head. He fell flat on his face, unconscious. Thate still held the rifle, and now he was hurling caution away, and he ran out of the tent.

Nordeno was there, waiting.

"Hello," Thate said.

The fascist flyer gaped at him, started to move toward him. But the rifle stopped the advance.

Nordeno was trying to say something, no words came out of his mouth.

"Your clever little scheme didn't quite work out," Thate said. "You had it in for me, didn't you? You figured that you'd entice me into an escape, and I'd be caught, and, of course, since regulations provide for the execution of any prisoner who tries to get away, you'd finally register a complete victory over me. But it isn't as easy as all that."

"You'll still be caught," Nordeno muttered.

"Not if I use strategy. And strategy is something that I know quite well. Turn around, if you please, and keep your hands high."

"What are you going to do?" Nordeno quivered.

"Oh, nothing very exciting. You and I will take a little walk, and we'll have a pleasant chat."

"You'll never get away with this, Englishman," Nordeno rasped. "Others will see us. You'll be re-captured. At dawn tomorrow you will be shot."

"Really, old man, I hate to spoil your pleasant plans for me, but—just keep on walking, if you please, that's a good fellow. Now, I'm going to count quite slowly up to twenty, and by that time you will have guided me to the nearest plane."

"I cannot do that," Nordeno said. "The air field is miles away."

"It is? That's too bad, my friend, because, unless we reach a plane by the time I count to twenty, I'm going to pull this trigger and Italy will lose a rather fine airman. And now, I begin. One—two—"

Nordeno's knees sagged, and he hesitated. But Thate was counting off those numbers, and the Italian realized that each second brought him closer to death. He quickened his pace, and the Englishman followed.

"Thirteen—14—15—"

Nordeno was moving on the double quick now, hunching low as he broke through foliage, with Thate close behind.

"Seventeen—18—19—"

"There!" Nordeno gasped. "There—damn you!"

Thate looked out upon the landing field, a smooth circular patch in the thickness of the wooded area. Orange lights illuminated the landing field. Fiats and Savoia Marchettis were lined up there, noses pointed toward the west.

"Very good," Thate murmured. "Very good indeed."

"You think so?" Nordeno muttered. "How are you going to get away?"

He had turned, and now his thin features leered at Thate.

And the Englishman frowned in annoyance, and murmured, "You know, Nordeno, I don't like your face. Turn around, if you please, while I concentrate on this situation."

Nordeno turned around, muttering an oath.

And Thate very casually lifted the rifle, brought it down against the Italian's skull. It was not a malicious blow. It was rather a gentle tap, placed with precision and given just enough force to render Captain Nordeno out of the picture for a convenient five or ten minutes. The fascist flyer sagged to the ground.

Thate moved toward the nearest Fiat. He still held the rifle, and when he was less than ten yards away from the Italian plane, he knew that he would have to use it. A mechanic had come out of the hangar, was walking toward that same plane. When he saw Thate he let out a yell, started to race at full speed toward the Englishman, intent on cutting off the escape.

In that faint orange light, Thate knew that he would have to pull the trigger. It was war, and war was hard and cruel and devoid of sentiment. He brought up the rifle, aimed, fired, and the mechanic took a bullet through his heart.

But the shot itself was an alarm. And now men were running, swerving in from all directions. Shouts and curses blended with the siren that screamed from the hangar. Thate leaped toward the plane, climbed into the cockpit and switched on the self-starter just as the first of his pursuers reached the Fiat.

The propeller whirled. But the ship was not warmed up, and for an instant the Englishman figured that it was all over. Already they were swarming about the plane, and one of them had a revolver; was pointing it.

Thate still had that rifle. Quickly he brought it up, fired without aiming. The Italian who held the revolver whirled around twice, and dropped. The others fell back. Upright in the cockpit, Thate fired again and again, the crackling rifle blending with the roar of the Fiat's motor. The Italians were retreating now. Only a few of them carried revolvers, and as they reached for their weapons, Thate shot them down. He was firing with cold aim now, and as the seconds passed he was listening to that motor, telling himself that ready or not he would have to hurry this matter.

A bullet whistled past his head, and he ducked low, sat down in the narrow cockpit, and fed the Fiat a lot of juice. The plane leaped forward. Its motor screeched eagerly, to an accompaniment of raging shouts and curses from the Italians. Bullets spat at the Fiat as it whizzed across the tarmac. But although it took lead in its wings and fuselage, it leaped clear of the ground, its motor seeming to sing a song of mockery at the Fascist horde on the field below.

And Lawrence Thate grinned as he headed the ship westward, toward the Sudan. He knew that he had a convenient head start now, and that if they tried to chase him, they would have a blasted difficult time of it. The thick black sky was a perfect curtain in which to hide.

Not much farther to go. He was arriving at that conclusion by looking at his watch and his compass and his instrument panel. The dial showed him to be moving at almost 250 miles an hour. He figured that less than twenty minutes more of this kind of speed would bring him to the British base north of Shambe.

Suddenly he frowned, listening attentively.

Then he was looking at the rear-view mirror, and it showed him the wing lights of a plane, not far behind him. Those wing lights were powerful. They focused on him now, placed him in a circle of illumination, and then—

Thate heard bullets!

The slugs punched into the fuselage of his Fiat. He squirmed, started a roll-out, and as he did, he realized that a single plane was after him. He knew that this was going to be a rather tepid party, and he leaned forward, switched on his own wing lights, which he had ignored until now for the very well-founded reason of camouflage.

In the blackness the two planes dipped and swerved and sought for convenient attack stance. At 7,500 feet Thate broke out of a loop and lunged hard at the other plane, which was also a Fiat, and carried an insignia that seemed familiar.

Thate missed on that lunge, but as he flashed by, he caught a glimpse of the flyer in that other plane.

It was Nordeno.

The Italian's face was twisted into a mask of rage, and the grimness of his expression made correct harmony with the chatter of his guns as he twisted out of a vertical turn and attacked from the side.

Thate dodged the bullet burst, looped again, and muttered, "So you're out after a complete victory, are you? Well, I'm sorry to disappoint you."

And he went into a renversement, came level with the other Fiat as Nordeno maneuvered for an underside burst. Thate grabbed at the trigger handles, pitched bullets, and the other plane lurched, then twisted into a backward roll, screamed down.

For an instant Thate thought that he had won. He relaxed, and his fingers loosened their hold on the trigger handles.

But the other Fiat pulled out of its dive, carved the run-down into a wide loop. It was above Thate now, and Nordeno was laughing like a fiend. He had the advantage now. In a moment he would lunge down again.

Thate glanced up at the other plane, a night-bird whose lights were set wide and blazing on its wings. And as it came down, Thate rolled to his left. He did not complete that roll. He twisted it into an acute bank, turned almost completely around, and lunged at Nordeno, who was wondering what had happened to that very convenient target.

And while the Italian grabbed for an answer, Thate prepared it.

His fingers once more reached for the trigger handles. His wing lights showed him the enemy cockpit. That was all he needed. He pressed the triggers. Bullets leaped out, walked an invisible wire, and crackled through glass and stabbed through a suede helmet and bounced in Nordeno's brain. He opened his mouth to cry out, and his jaw went rigid. And his eyes bulged.

He was dead.

Thate switched off his wing lights, resumed his course westward. He knew that he wouldn't be bothered by any more pursuers. The others, if there had been any, had given up the chase by this time. Nordeno had kept it up for personal rather than military reasons. The Italian had been intent on settling this matter, and now it was settled.

And very soon other matters would also be settled.

* * *

A few days after the glorious British victory over the South-Ethiopian contingent of the Italian Army, Lawrence Thate was given a D.S.O. and promoted to flight lieutenant in the R.A.F. The medal was pinned on by Group Captain Jenn-Fraws. And an honored guest at the occasion was General Briocho, who had been captured in the midst of his army's complete downfall.

Jenn-Fraws was saying, "For conspicuous bravery, resourcefulness, and most significant—for brilliant handling of a situation calling for the utmost strategy."

As he said that his voice was solemn, but a twinkle was in his eyes, and the left one slowly winked.

General Briocho saw that, and wondered at the reason for it. But he would never know, and neither would anyone else. For that wink was to remain a secret between Group Captain Jenn-Fraws and his favorite flight lieutenant.

J. L. BOUMA

Final Mission

IT IS A DAMNABLE thing, Dane Spencer thought, to come to the end of your combat career and have it fizzle out like a spent cartridge. He turned in the bucket and looked with hungry eyes at the Lightnings flying his wash. Off his left wing, Major Dunn led the formation with the careful precision of a man who had learned the officer's manual well. Twenty-three, this man who had won his rank as an instructor at Kelly Field. And Spencer was aware of intense dislike that bordered on hatred for Major Dunn.

Below, the blue-green heave of the Adriatic was a darker reflection of the sky. The Mountains of the River Po curved in abrupt entrance to the Gulf of Venice. Beyond, past the province of Venitia, lay the Brenner Pass—a deep narrow V carving through the milk-white Italian Alps. And below the Pass, between the towns of Trent and Bassano, the ammunition train was fair game for the sixteen Lightnings. Or would it end up another fluke?

Anger pressed outward against Spencer's chest wall. This was the third time in a week they were going out to bomb an ammunition train between Trent and Bassano. On the previous two attacks they had found the box cars on a siding between the towns.

They had come out of the sun, smashing the column with their 500 pounders, hosing the column with machine gun and cannon fire. But there had been no answering concussions, no earth-shattering explosions to tell them the box cars had been loaded.

They had not been loaded. They had been planted there, empty, at the side of the River Brenta that followed the tracks, and nothing on either side but the lower foothills of the Alps.

Major Dunn led the formation across the coast between Chioggia and Venice, taking them to 20,000 and using evasive action as flak batteries darkened the sky on either side. The corridor was narrow, but it was enough, and Dunn angled down with throttles wide open.

The railroad tracks were thin and glinting copper as they swept past Cittadella. Bassano was twenty miles in the distance, and the Alps towered high and wide beyond. Spencer sighted the columned box cars on the instant that Dunn dipped his wings. They went down for the run, and to Spencer it was a moment when three years of combat were forgotten, for it is never the memories but always the present acts that witness the manner of our living.

They came down in a single stretching line and poured their hot steel to the waiting box cars. Spencer's bombs found the locomotive and blew it in a swelter of angry steel. He pulled back the stick and knew a hollow aching as his stomach sucked against the curve of his spine.

Thirty years old, he thought bleakly. Graying at the temples. Africa and Sicily behind him. P-40s in Africa. Dive bombers in Sicily. And all the hell and terror of a thousand hours fighting the enemy. But a deep, underlying fulfilment had come with the years. Duty performed, and it was not something he wanted to give up for a state-side desk job. He wondered now if the major had considered and put through his application for another tour.

The Allisons howled as he heeled at the top of his climb and looked down. The box cars were splintered firewood, scattered and blazing. They had been empty again. Spencer cursed softly and combed the surrounding terrain. The river glistened beside the tracks. Brush and shrub led to a narrow belt of green forest that met the foothills. Five miles away, Spencer estimated.

He flew toward it as the formation wormed the sky. No roads down there. He banked for the turn and then a glint of silver in the green, a sudden alien reflection that came and went like the snap of an eyelid. Spencer thumbed his mike.

"There's something in that patch of forest, Major. We'd better investigate."

"Rejoin the formation." The major clipped his words and Spencer found anger in them.

He bridled a hot retort and took his deputy lead position. Dunn was new to his job, but Dunn was also in command. And the man had the power to waver his application for another tour. The thought was with him when he saw the fighters.

"Bandits at nine o'clock high."

Six Focke-Wulfes, Spencer saw, angling away from the formation and well out of gun range. He waited for Dunn to give orders for the chase, but the major led the formation toward the coast.

Spencer jabbed his mike button. ''Let's give 'em a run.''

''We're not chasing enemy fighters over half of Europe, Captain,'' Dunn snapped. ''We came here to fly a mission, and we've accomplished it.''

They flew home. After landing and interrogation Spencer stalked across the area toward Squadron Headquarters. The major was in his office, a smooth-faced youngster with eyes that could cut. He listened Spencer out, then looked up, unsmiling.

''We followed orders, Captain,'' he said. ''It was no fault of ours the box cars were empty.''

''We're being played for suckers,'' Spencer said evenly, ''and it burns me up. They know we're after their ammunition, so they set up a decoy and wait for us to bomb it.''

''A decoy, Captain? Those box cars were real enough. At least we deprived the enemy of their further use.''

''I'm trying to tell you they would not send ammunition through unescorted. You don't bag a prize in this war without paying for it. Had the ammunition been down there, we would have met plenty of opposition.''

''Intelligence said it was coming through,'' Dunn snapped. ''Reconnaisance spotted the train leaving the Pass for Trent. Maybe they unloaded there and trucked the stuff to their front lines.''

''I don't think so. Our P-40s stationed at the lines are pretty good at shooting up truck convoys. The enemy wouldn't take the chance on moving it that way. It's my idea thay have a central dump beyond the limits our P-40s fly. They probably draw enough from this dump to supply only their immediate needs.''

''It's not our problem to find such a dump—if there is one.'' Major Dunn impatiently rattled papers on his desk.

''I have a hunch where it's located.'' Spencer quickly told what he had seen in the forest. ''I've been thinking about it all the way back, sir. Whatever I saw didn't belong in those trees. A reflection from metal of some sort. A helmet, perhaps, a rifle barrel.''

Dunn leaned forward. ''Did you see any roads leading to this forest?''

Spencer said he hadn't.

''And are you trying to make me believe they would have thirty or forty car loads of ammunition down there? It's ridiculous, Captain.''

Spencer tightened arms at his sides. ''They could cover their tracks so they couldn't be spotted from the air. The forest is thick, and they could easily camouflage the ammunition boxes so that it would be impossible to see them. Our ground forces keep untold amounts of ammunition hidden in the same way, sir. I suggest we take the chance and bomb that strip.''

The major flushed and his mouth hardened. ''Headquarters has mapped every inch of that terrain. If there's anything unusual down there they would know about it. And I'm not wasting bombs on a wild goose chase. Forget you mentioned it, Captain.''

Spencer bridled his impatient fury. A man had to take chances in this war, but the major wasn't a gambler. He would schedule his missions, his duty accomplished. But the taste for daring wasn't in him.

''Those Focke-Wulfes we saw, sir. I think they were there for only one purpose—to lure us away from that vicinity. They—''

Dunn banged the desk with his open palm. ''You need a rest, Captain. You've flown one tour and have a final mission to finish your second. That brings us down to this request of yours for yet another tour. I'm refusing it.''

''Yes, sir.'' Spencer saluted and turned to the door.

''One moment,'' Dunn stood, his hands on the desk. ''I'm leaving for Naples tonight to be gone two days. I'll want you in charge until I return. You'll receive orders for tomorrow's mission through the usual channels. Lieutenant Bricker will lead the formation. You'll remain here in charge of the office. Is that understood?''

Spencer merely nodded and walked out.

The orders came late that afternoon, and Spencer posted the flight schedule on the Operation's bulletin board. In the morning he presided at the briefing.

''Escort mission to the 55th Wing, Heavy Bombardment. They're bombing the Munich marshaling yards, and you'll rendezvous at-''

He finished and watched them file out in the early dawn. Mae Wests and parachutes slung carelessly across shoulders. Helmets and goggles cocked high as the pilots laughed and shouted and clambered onto the trucks that would take them to the line. Spencer watched and stifled his feelings.

He was on the line an hour before their return. Later he counted them as they flew the pattern before landing. One was missing. He sought out Lieutenant Bricker at the interrogation tent.

''Bandits,'' Bricker said. ''They caught us past the Alps. Two to one. They got Jones.'' He grinned. ''Four of 'em won't be back for chow.''

"Good boy."

Spencer checked the rest of the pilots and returned to the office. Orders had arrived for the next day's mission. He read them and leaned back in his chair.

The main target was an enemy fighter base, twenty miles south from where they'd ruined the box cars the day before. There was a secondary target—a radio station at Belluno. No alternate targets. Spencer stepped to the wall map, studied it carefully.

He went back to the orders that said twenty Lightnings would participate, ten carrying bombs, the remaining ten to act as cover over the main target. There was a distance of forty miles between the main and secondary targets. And in between, filling out to a triangle, was the forest. Spencer's hesitation was only momentary before he picked up the phone and called the armorer sergeant.

"Twenty ships, Sergeant. Maximum gas and ammunition load. And two 500 pounders to each ship."

The next morning Dane Spencer was up before the dawn, and his own name headed the flight schedule. His last mission, and they could break him if they wished.

Nineteen pilots faced him in the briefing room. Spencer advanced to the wall map and pointed with his ruler.

"Our main objective, gentlemen. Lieutenant Bricker will lead his flight across the target. The rest of us will fly cover." He turned to the room. "One run, you understand, Bricker? Then keep going." He pointed with the ruler. "To here, the radio station. Shoot it up good! You have five minutes to do the job. Meanwhile, we'll be strafing the hangars and barracks at the air base. Then we rendezvous at . . ."

The dawn lifted its curtain and exposed the day. To experience it once again and for the last time, Spencer thought. He led them along the narrow sweep of the Adriatic and watched Bricker's element of ten settle off his right wing. Timing was essential, and he hoped Bricker understood. Bricker had to understand!

The morning sun lighted the white crags of the Alps with beacon fires as they crossed the coast. Flak bursts fingered across the sky, sought them out. Spencer increased his throttles and wheeled the Lightning in a dance. The flak mounted in intensity, then died like the last splatter of rain. Spencer dumped the stick and ran down to 5000. The air base, he knew, was across the next rise. He thumbed his mike button.

"Deck level, Bricker, and I want that landing strip ruined so a fly can't set down."

The rest of the escort strung out behind Spencer in a thin line, circling the base as Bricker led his ten downstairs. Spencer looked down. Two hangars. A half dozen barracks buildings. A row of tents. A shop area and the runway itself with its sand-bagged revetments for the fighters. He counted only a dozen aircraft, 190s, by the looks of them, spaced around the shop area. That meant their main strength was on a mission.

Or were they high overhead to protect the ammunition dump? Or was there an ammunition dump?

Spencer shivered in the enclosure of his cockpit. A flash of silver in the green stretch of a forest. Not much to go on. And yet—He remembered a lesson on camouflage, learned long ago in the States.

" . . . and blend your camouflage with the natural terrain. Keep covered any slick surface that might throw a reflection . . . "

Spencer took a quick look across the sky and looked down as Bricker unloaded his bombs on the head of the runway. Fire, smoke, and earth leaped up as the rest followed and smeared the landing strip. The men knew their jobs, and there was your war. Knowing your job and doing it. Spencer took a ragged breath and pointed his props for the hangars as Bricker and his ten raced across the horizon.

Tracers were golden daggers as they found the hangar's roof, leaving behind a lace work of smoke that spread and swirled and revealed the tiny flames beneath. Spencer allowed the run to take him across the shop area. A flexible machine gun down there stung the Lightning's wings before Spencer banked out of range.

He turned carefully dropping the nose, finding the sand-bagged hollow in his sights. He squeezed a burst, watching his fire gather dust puffs that moved in a startling clear line toward his objective. Instinct told him when the target was his, and he fed three .20 mm shells down there that killed the machine gunners and left a shambles.

The parked 190s were next, the barracks, and the panic-driven soldiers who ran with the pride of the Luftwaffe forgotten. A last run on the tower, and then the job was finished. Spencer eased back on the wheel and called his pilots to formation.

Ten minutes were gone. Allow that for Bricker to reach the radio station, five more to destroy it. Spencer led a wide course around

Bassano. Give Bricker another five minutes to reach the rendezvous. Spencer eased back on the throttles and Bassano huddled off his right wing.

There was a tight, unwanted pressure in the pit of his stomach. Major Dunn would not hesitate to throw the book at him when he found out about this day's work. Somehow that didn't seem to matter, and he traced back his feelings and found in them an anticipation that bordered on the unknown.

He'd had the same feeling, he remembered, the first time out on mission. The temptation to search what lay beyond. He had never considered himself a dealer in death. It had been a wanted duty, a task to accomplish, a chance to strike the enemy at his strongest spot.

So it was now. The enemy used considerable ammunition to defend their Gothic Line. And the Brenner Pass was the logical route. Intelligence knew it and confirmed it. And yet they had wasted precious bomb loads and gained nothing.

Now was the showdown. If the enemy was found out, there would be a reckoning. Ten Lightnings with bombs snug beneath their wings, ready for the battle. And Bricker and his men to fly cover, to help in the strafing—if strafing was necessary.

The River Brenta curved like a living snake in the distance, and Spencer consulted his wrist watch. They should hit it right on the nose. And with the proper amount of luck, they would make it.

"Unidentified aircraft at twelve o'clock high, coming out of the sun."

Spencer's breath caught in the tight chamber of his throat. What better confirmation than to know they were being watched? As they had been watched on the previous attack.

"Watch them, but don't pull from formation unless they attack."

It was hard to count them in the yellow haze up there. The sun made glinting darts through the convex curve of the canopy, and Spencer was aware of its warmth. He was sure he had counted twenty of the bandits, circling high, above 20,000, most likely, waiting to pounce at the opportune moment.

The river glowed below them now. The tracks glistened beneath the sun. Off to the left lay the blackened hulks of the box cars they had bombed two days ago. And the forest rose in the distance.

"Those bandits are circling lower," a pilot said. "I think they're getting ready to attack."

Where was Bricker? In trouble? Had they walked into a trap?

Cut in two like they were, Bricker might well be under attack, with no hope of fighting back for the rendezvous. But there was no time to think about it now. There was a job to do, and Spencer mouthed orders in his throat mike and led the Lightnings downstairs.

The strip of forest tilted in crazy angle as he made the turn and lined up its center. It was purely guess work. It was hit and run and see what happens. He sent a preliminary burst through the heavy foliage and watched the tracer suck down and disappear. His hand lay heavy on the bomb toggle release. He was ready to trip it when the incredible happened.

A wide swath opened in the forest's center and revealed a line of light flak and machine guns. It was as if invisible wires had drawn the branches and the puppets below were ready to go into their act.

In the split passage of time Spencer was aware of soldiers pulling branches from guns, a line of camouflaged humps that might be trucks, ribbon-like trenches that contained the unmistakable shapes of boxes. His hand slapped the bomb release.

A tower of earth and broken branches flew up as if thrown from a huge shovel. Spencer felt the twin booms shudder beneath the impact, even as he thumbed his mike:

"Make every bomb count," he shouted. "If you're not sure, try another run."

Try another run! And a curtain of steel pouring from below, and the 190s attacking from above. Spencer dipped his wing straight down in turning. Stay above the strip of forest. It was their only chance. Make the attacking planes brave their own ground fire. But get that ammunition. Hose the blazing tracers and cannon shells and ruin the enemy's dump. Not easy. The ammunition was scattered.

He tipped the nose of the Lightning, disregarding the ground fire and the tracers that burned from above. The Allisons shrieked and clamored and Spencer's eyes were tight slits as his tracers and cannon shells streaked in yellow and red lines to rip into the ammunition trenches. He saw the explosions that followed, the length of the trench a molten river of flames and hazy smoke.

They were flying it wing tip to wing tip, and some of them had blown the trucks. He turned on another run for a flak battery, and watched his steel wipe the gun crew as if a sudden, hot blast of air had caught them and flung them in writhing agony in a furnace of scalding fire.

The Lightning bucked through the inferno and he saw that they had lost two so far. And the forest down there was no longer a green haven. It was a roaring stretch of death, the trees bare and pointing grotesque fingers that shivered beneath the blistering fire.

All but one of the gun emplacements had been knocked out, and Spencer twisted the wheel and ruddered right, aware that half the Lightnings had gone up to offer combat to the 190s. The enemy planes hovered like vultures, he saw. He watched them and cursed and made his final run on the remaining machine gun nest. He swept it clean with the hammering fifties and gutted the wheel for his climb.

Two Focke-Wulfes were chasing a P-38, trying to run it into the ground, and Spencer flipped from the climb and angled a deflection shot toward the 190s. He watched his tracers rip fire from the cowling of the near one, the flames eating back under the prop wash and spread across the canopy.

"Here's your tracks, skipper! Below your right wing where my bombs landed off center."

Spencer looked down. At the tip of the forest, where it was closest to the main line, he saw twin bomb craters in the heavy brush. And the twisted railroad tracks pointing upward.

"Hang on a little longer, boys. Here we come!"

Spencer swung around and saw the twin-boomed Lightnings swing out of the sky and pounce like terriers on the hovering enemy. Bricker and his gang! A tight happy smile drew Spencer's lips across his teeth. He pitched into the battle with renewed fury, using all the wisdom, the little tricks learned in a hundred sky battles.

Another 190 blew and disintegrated under the viciousness of his fire. And then his guns jammed for the last time and were silent. He looked around. The fight had carried them away from the forest. The terrain was dotted with burning aircraft, most of them Focke-Wulfes. The job was done, and now was the time to get out of there. He gave the orders.

"Make a break before we all run out of ammo. Let's go, gang!"

There were fifteen where twenty had started, but the retreat went unhampered. The enemy seemed eager enough to postpone the battle to a later date. Their home base was destroyed and they had another nest to find.

Spencer felt the weariness in his bones as he led the formation across the coast. At high noon he saw a plane streak toward them with the speed of a bullet and disappear toward the Alps. An F-5, a photo ship, he noted mechanically. Probably going over for pictures of the enemy base and the radio station. He smiled grimly.

"Target destroyed, Major Dunn."

Bricker explained his delayed absence at interrogation. "Bandits jumped us after we had destroyed the radio station and were turning for the rendezvous. We had to fight our way back—it took a little time."

"You saw the tracks?" a pilot asked Spencer.

Spencer nodded and stepped to the wall map. "Here," he told the interrogation officer, "the forest is some three or four miles from the main tracks. They had a single track, camouflaged by heavy brush and shrub, running that distance. Our reconnaissance plane made sure the train left Trent before heading for home with the information. After that the enemy ran the train into the forest, unloaded, and came back to rest on the siding, empty. Not a new trick, but one that has probably worked for a long time."

In his tent, Spencer stripped off his flight clothes and sat wearily on the edge of the cot. So now it was finished. The past years were nothing now but memories, and memories served only for the aged. Only good when there was nothing left but a pipe and idle talk. A man couldn't stand that. Not when there was still work to be done.

He looked up at the headquarters' sergeant who had pushed through the tent flap.

"The major just came in, Captain. He wants you pronto."

"Right." Spencer rose and reached for his cap. Now trouble would break loose. Let it. To blazes with the major and his manner of fighting a war. He stepped through the tent flap.

Major Dunn still wore his dress blouse, and the golden leaves on his shoulders twinkled in the lazy sunlight that streamed through the window.

"I haven't as yet read the report on your mission, but I doubt if it is important as disobeying my orders. You remember them, Captain?"

"To remain in charge of the office."

"Correct." Major Dunn strode across the office and back. Tiny muscles jumped across his jawline. "Direct disobedience. You've been long enough in the army to know—"

The ring of the field telephone cut across his words. "Major Dunn speaking. . . . Eh? . . . Yes, sir, thank you, sir. . . . Daring? . . ." Dunn half turned and looked at Spencer while speaking. "No credit due me, sir. . . . No, I was absent from the base. Captain Spencer led the formation. It was his idea something might be going on down there. . . . Yes, sir."

Major Dunn carefully replaced the receiver and for a long moment looked down at his desk. When he looked up, a grin pulled at his lips. "The general from Wing. It seems the reconnaissance plane just returned and brought some startling information. Why didn't you tell me about it?"

"Would it have made any difference?"

The major frowned. "Listen, Spencer, they say a man is never too old to learn, and I'm just starting out. I made a mistake. I should have investigated your suspicions." He drummed the desk in thought. "About your request for another tour—my Operation officer is leaving for the States in a month. It means flying only one out of every four missions, but—" Dunn left the sentence unfinished.

Spencer grinned. "Say no more, Major. Throw in a short leave to Cairo, and I'm your man."

For a second the major grinned. "Your leave starts day after tomorrow." Then his face sobered. "Right now, Captain—orders just came in for tomorrow's mission. I'd like your advice on—"

JACK RITCHIE

Hot Air Pilot

UNTEROFFIZIER BENECKE reported to *Kommandant* Reinholdt. "Sir, the prisoners have started another tunnel. This time it apparently begins under the main kitchen."

"Where is it going?" Reinholdt asked.

"It is still a little too early to tell, sir. But it seems logical that it will turn toward the wall near the northwest tower."

Reinholdt dismissed him. "Very well, Benecke. Keep me informed on the progress."

Kommandant Reinholdt, a gray-haired former schoolteacher who had last heard a shot fired in anger during World War I, turned to *Leutnant* Studt. "*Leutnant*, you seem a bit surprised that I did not immediately order some kind of action?"

Studt, convalescing from a leg wound received on the eastern front and assigned to temporary light duty at Mecklin Castle, admitted as much.

Reinholdt smiled. "*Leutnant,* these men must be kept occupied with something they believe is of importance, and correspondence courses are not enough. It they are not kept busy, they will fall into all kinds of depressions and emotional illness, and this is not healthy. And so I let them dig their tunnels and pretend that I do not know."

He lit a cigar. "One cannot dig silently in this rocky earth, and we have sound-detection devices. We know from the very beginning when a tunnel is started, and where. I permit the prisoners to get within a dozen feet of success and then I have my guards 'accidentally' discover the work. This may seem cruel, but it is not meant to be."

Kommandant Reinholdt walked to the window and looked down at the courtyard. "Mecklin Castle. It was built eleven hundred years ago to keep people out and now we must use it to keep people in. I have here roughly two hundred American officers who are prisoners of war. All of them have been previously apprehended attempting to escape from the conventional camps, and it has been thought wise to transfer them here where the security is greater. They have been quite busy, these Americans, but not one of them has yet managed to escape."

Reinholdt exhaled cigar smoke. "And none of them will. I personally guarantee that."

Captain Charles Hendricks, a big-shouldered man who had been in Mecklin Castle less than a week, moved down the bench to get more of the courtyard sun. "You mean that in almost two years not one of you jokers managed to get out of here?"

Lieutenant Carson shrugged. "So what's the difference now? In another month or so this war will be over and we can all walk out of here without stirring up any sweat."

Hendricks scowled. "How's something like that going to look in the history books? Not a single American bright enough to escape."

Carson regarded him tolerantly. "If you're all hot about getting your name in print, why don't you go over to Section B? I hear they're starting another tunnel."

Hendricks rejected that. "That's not the way to get out of here. Tunnels are for the foot people. Not air force."

Carson, a slight, fair man and also air force, smiled faintly. "We tried smuggling our people out of here under trucks, in garbage cans, disguised as guards—you name it. Nothing ever worked. But you think you got a new idea?"

Hendricks grunted. 'Like I said, for an air force man, there's only one way to get out of here."

"Flying, I suppose?"

"Why not?"

"You got an airplane up your sleeve?"

"No airplane."

"You wave your arms and think positive?"

Hendricks scowled again. "How about a balloon?"

There was a long moment of silence and then Carson said, "You're crazy."

"What's so crazy about a balloon?" Hendricks demanded. "I can see that what this place has been needing for a long time is a shot of imagination. All we need is some cloth for the balloon, a little rope, and a basket for the passenger."

Carson mulled over the idea again. "Damn it," he said finally, "it just might work. We'll take it up with the escape committee."

Captain Hendricks agreed, unsmilingly. ''Just remember that this is *my* baby. *My* idea.''

Carson regarded him mildly. ''Don't worry, Captain, nobody's going to beat you out of the credit.''

That evening Captain Hendricks presented his plan to the escape committee of Section C for consideration and approval.

Colonel Stranahan, a tall West Pointer, cleared his throat. ''What do you intend to put into this balloon to make it rise? We've done some first-class scrounging in our time to get materials for escape attempts, but I just don't see how we'll be able to come up with helium or hydrogen. Do you have any ideas on the subject, Captain?

Hendricks thought about it and colored slighlty. ''No, sir.''

Carson spoke up. ''I understand, sir, that in the old days balloons were inflated with hot air.''

Stranahan smiled faintly. ''Not getting personal, Lieutenant, but where are we going to get this hot air?''

''Why not from a chimney?'' Carson asked. ''This old castle is loaded with chimneys. If we stoke up our stoves, we ought to be able to create plenty of hot air.''

Stranahan rubbed an ear speculatively. ''How are you going to get the hot air into the balloon?''

''We take the balloon onto the roof and connect it with one of the chimneys,'' Carson said.

''Really? And while we're filling this thing with hot air, what are the guards going to be doing? Looking up and admiring us?''

''Well,'' Hendricks said thoughtfully, ''we'll need a night when there is absolutely no moonlight.''

Stranahan agreed dryly. ''Darkness does seem necessary. But you forget that the area would still be lit up by the usual searchlights, area lights, and so on.''

There was a silence until Stranahan himself came up with an answer. ''There are no lights at all during the air-raid alarms. We're blacked out and confined to our quarters. Suppose we wait until one of the alarms and then carry the bag up to the roof and begin stoking the fires. I've been keeping an offhand record of the air-raid alarms for the past few weeks and the length of time we've been blacked out has averaged out to four hours. Is that enough time to inflate your balloon, Captain?''

''I really don't know, sir,'' Hendricks said uneasily.

Stranahan shrugged. ''I guess that's a chance we'll have to take.'' He pondered over the plan a bit more. ''Even uninflated, I imagine the balloon will still be rather large, so we'll sew it together in that tunnel we started six months ago but had to abandon because we hit solid rock.'' He looked at Hendricks again. ''We're fairly close to the border. I suppose that once you get aloft, you'll steer for Switzerland?''

''Yes, sir,'' Hendricks said confidently. ''Head for Switzerland. That was my plan.''

Lieutenant Carson reached for a cigarette. ''You can't steer a free balloon, Captain. It just follows the wind currents. However, the prevailing winds here are south southwest—toward Switzerland—and that's where they ought to take you after all.''

Hendricks addressed Colonel Stranahan. ''With your permission, sir, I think that we ought to keep this strictly a Section C project.''

''We should? Why?''

''Well, sir, we're all air force in this building, and it seems to me that this is particularly an air force project. Suppose some of the other sections decided to imitate us? They might get one of their men out of here before we do.''

Colonel Stranahan nodded. ''I guess you have a point there, Hendricks. Very well, this will be an air force show and limited to Section C. Not a word of this to anyone else. Now . . . what kind of a fabric do we need for this balloon?''

''Silk or muslin, sir,'' Hendricks said. ''I believe I read that someplace, sir.''

Stranahan nodded. ''We'll probably have to coat it with something that won't allow the hot air to escape. But we've got men in this building who can concoct 180-proof joy juice in their still, so I think they ought to be able to come up with some kind of varnish.''

Hendricks was pleased. ''In the Civil War, during the siege of Vicksburg, the women contributed their silk dresses, which were sewed up into a real working balloon.''

Colonel Stranahan sighed. ''We don't have any women here, much less dresses. So where the hell are we going to get silk? Or muslin?''

Finally, Carson raised his hand. ''I believe I have an idea, sir.''

Unteroffizier Benecke saluted. Reinholdt looked up. ''What is it?''

''Sir, the flags have been stolen.''

Reinholdt's mouth dropped open. ''From the flagstaffs?''

"No, sir. Those are still up there. But all the others in the flag locker are gone."

Reinholdt frowned. "If I remember correctly, we had quite a supply. You mean *all* of them are gone?"

Benecke nodded. "The complete supply, including the very large ceremonial flags that we had in case *Der Führer* ever decided to visit. . . ."

Leutnant Studt stepped forward. "Sir, I will search the entire castle immediately."

Reinholdt sighed. "I suppose so. Though when you have been here as long as I have, you will realize that once something has been stolen, its recovery is almost an impossible task."

"But, sir," Studt said, "the flags must constitute a considerable bulk."

Reinholdt agreed. "However, this bulk can be distrbuted into dozens of hiding places. The walls of Mecklin Castle have become almost like a honeycomb." He shook his head. "No, *Leutnant*, once something is gone, it is gone."

"But why should the prisoners want to steal our flags?" Studt asked.

Kommandant Reinholdt smiled patiently. "You must learn to appreciate the prisoner's mentality. He is like a naughty child who will steal anything at all if it is not guarded, even if he has not the slightest use for it. It is simply the principle of the thing."

Lieutenant Carson re-threaded his needle. "I've been thinking about weight."

"What about it?" Hendricks asked.

"How much will this balloon be able to lift?"

Hendricks was irritated. "I don't know. But if it lifts me, that's enough."

"Sure," Carson continued, "but you weigh around 190 and that might bring you down before you get to the Swiss border. Why don't we pick somebody lighter?"

Hendricks regarded him suspiciously. "Like you?"

"No," Carson said, "I wouldn't voluntarily set foot in anything that doesn't have a motor. I mean that in the interest of the project, maybe we ought to send up someone lighter. Like Lieutenant Stebbins from Section E. He's about the skinniest little man around here."

"Forget it," Hendricks snapped. "He's Quartermaster Corps. When this balloon goes up, it's going to carry 190 pounds of air force."

* * *

It was a warm, dark night in early May when the air-raid sirens sounded and the prisoners were secured in their quarters. Hendricks, Carson, Stranahan, and four previously selected men quickly retrieved the deflated balloon from its hiding place in the tunnel and carried it up to the roof. They fitted the bag-opening to a frame over the chimney and laid the bag itself in the long roof-valley.

At 2 A.M., three and a half hours later, Colonel Stranahan heard the faint sound of airplane motors. 'Our planes are coming back,'' he whispered. ''That means we have about half an hour at the most. Get the bag away from the chimney as quickly as possible and hitch up the basket.''

Ten minutes passed before Captain Hendricks eased himself into the basket. ''Let go all the ropes,'' he commanded.

After a half-minute of dark silence, Hendricks hissed again: ''Damn it, I said let go of the ropes!''

There was a hurried conference and then Lieutenant Carson spoke up. ''Everybody *did* let go of the ropes. The balloon's just not taking off.''

Colonel Stranahan sighed. ''Okay, Hendricks, get out. We'll try Carson.''

''But, sir—'' Hendricks protested.

''That's an order,'' Colonel Stranahan snapped. ''We don't have time to argue. Carson, take his place.''

But even with Carson—40 pounds lighter—in the basket, the balloon refused to rise.

Carson climbed out. ''I have the feeling that it's just a question of a few pounds—but I'm the lightest man in the section.''

Colonel Stranahan agreed. ''Well, I guess we'll just have to deflate the balloon again for the time being and figure out how to load it with more hot air the next time we try. I hope we get another chance like this before the war ends.''

''Wait a minute, Colonel,'' Hendricks said hastily. ''Why don't we send up Lieutenant Stebbins?''

''Stebbins? I don't seem to remember anybody by that name.''

''He's in Section E, sir, and just about the size of a jockey.''

''Not air force, is he?''

''No, sir. Quartermaster Corps. But this is no time for intraservice rivalries, don't you agree, sir?''

Colonel Stranahan nodded. ''I guess you're right. Lieutenant Carson, get Stebbins—and hurry.''

Carson darted downstairs, let himself out of a ground-floor window, and crawled in pitch darkness to the next building. Softly, he tapped on one of the windows.

When Carson returned to the roof of Section C, he led a stumbling Lieutenant Stebbins by the hand. "I can't see a thing," Stebbins complained, "but I feel a wind."

Captain Hendricks took his arm and guided Stebbins over the roof. "Just step up and hold onto these ropes."

"What is this all about?" Stebbins asked plaintively. "It feels like some kind of a basket."

Captain Hendricks spoke quickly. "Lieutenant, you are about to become the first—and probably the only—American ever to escape from Mecklin Castle. I don't have time to explain—the all-clear will sound any minute and the lights will come on—but just remember that you have nothing to worry about. This thing will come down as soon as the air in the bag cools, and that ought to be over Switzerland."

Then Captain Hendricks leaned closer to Stebbins' ear and whispered fiercely: "You'll be talking to a lot of reporters soon and there's one more thing I want you to remember. The name is Capt. Charles Hendricks and this whole operation is my baby. My brainchild. If it weren't for me, you wouldn't be here right now."

Hendricks stepped back. "All right, men, let go of the ropes."

There was a sudden whoosh and a thin, rapidly fading scream.

"Well," Stranahan said, "I guess we did it."

Carson agreed. "The way that thing took off, I don't believe it was really a matter of weight after all. I'll bet the basket was caught on something. How high do you think Stebbins will go, Colonel?"

"I don't know," Stranahan said, "but I hope he was wearing a jacket."

One hour after sunrise, Stebbing and the balloon landed in Switzerland.

Two days later, the war ended and *Kommandant* Reinholdt invited Captain Hendricks to his quarters.

"I understand that you were the author of this unique escape," Reinholdt said. "I must congratulate you on your most eye-catching balloon. Undoubtedly your name will go down in history." He pushed a bottle of cognac toward Hendricks. "A drink?"

Hendricks half-filled his glass and drained it. He poured again. "Damn it," he growled, "if I ever get my hands on Stebbins, I'll kill him."

"Now, now," Reinholdt said soothingly. "The war is over. Let bygones by bygones."

"That *damn* traitor!"

Reinholdt shook his head. "He was not a traitor. Stebbins—or Hans Wolff, as our army records list him—was a loyal German citizen performing a distasteful job for his country."

Reinholdt smiled. "I have two hundred bona fide Americans in Mecklin Castle and yet it was your misfortune to choose my camp spy. It is enough to make a man cry, is it not?"

And after a few more drinks, Hendricks did just that.

ARCH WHITEHOUSE

Savoias Out of Sapporo

1

IT WASN'T THAT anything untoward had happened that made Todd Bancroft and Larry Leadbeater cringe. Practically nothing had happened, and you can't take a punch at nothing. You're likely to throw your arm out.

Long before Todd and Larry had reached Sapporo, plenty of nothing had happened and it had happened in large, oval chunks.

"I read once," Leadbeater said, as they followed the railroad from Shiraoi up toward Sapporo, "that these Japs use the same old torture methods their great-grandfathers used. They say they start off by lighting fires on your belly."

Todd Bancroft, pilot of the Seversky Convoy fighter, considered that for several seconds and then supplied further information.

"No, that's the old Afridi trick they pull up along the Northwest Frontier. I think they stick a curved funnel in your ear and pour hot lead down it."

"A lot you know about torture!" argued Leadbeater. "That's Chinese. I think the Japs bore holes in you with things like the Boy Scouts use to light fires by friction. The Death of a Thousand Perforations, I think they call it."

"You've got it mixed up with the Death of a Thousand Cuts," corrected Todd.

"What do they do, run a lawnmower over you?"

Todd gave it up at last and returned to his instrument board, faintly smiling at the knowledge they had both been gagging to keep up their spirits. At times the pair of them seemed to be nothing short of hopeless fools barging about the world with no other qualification but the ability to get into trouble. Actually they were two highly skilled members of the United States Secret Service, and it was informal little conversations of this kind that covered up their thoughts and plans.

For instance, their plane, a modern, high-speed military fighter of long range, had been beautifully camouflaged to appear like any ordinary piece of service equipment used by the U.S. Meteorological Survey. They were in the Far East carrying out secret missions conjured up by a man named Blaisdell who sat at a prosaic desk in Washington, D.C.

"Well, we're sure of one thing," the Leadbeater guy said after another lengthy pause. "Old Yoshida will be at Sapporo, won't he?"

"He should—he and the Russian gal, Olinka Ivanovna, who got away with him."

Leadbeater started to remove the discharge disk from the rotary machine gun which they had christened "Slingin' Sal" when he instinctively looked around as a precaution. He stiffened, gulped, and rammed the disk back on the shaft.

Todd Bancroft, his keen eyes on his instruments and his mind on problems of piloting, sensed that something had happened. As he started to turn his head he heard Larry say:

"Jumpin' spark gaps! Pieplate!"

Bancroft went warm at the throat. His palms perspired as he followed Larry's gaze across the inky-blue sky.

"She's back, the little fool!" Leadbeater was shouting.

Bancroft spotted the wide-winged Koken plane which Sturgis Sands, the girl from Pieplate, Kansas, had purloined to get the famous Professor Deuhl out of Vladivostok and into sanctuary of the Philippines. Now she had risked her life again on another long-distance flight from Manila back onto the stamping grounds of the enemy.

"The little idiot!" growled Bancroft, as the full force of the event struck him.

"That makes it unanimous," said Leadbeater coldly.

"What are we waiting for?" snapped Todd. "Let's call her wavelength."

Larry leaned over and swung the lever on their set while Todd slipped the ear phones on his head and snatched at the muzzle mike. The tubes warmed, and then they learned that the girl aboard the Japanese Koken plane had been trying to call them.

"Hello, Pieplate!" cried Todd into his mike.

"I thought you would never answer," came back over the ether. "Doesn't one of you ride with your set in?"

"Sorry. What's the game, Pieplate?"

"Miss Sands," said Larry. "Don't call her Pieplate!"

"You gave her that name—shut up! Hello, Sturgis."

"You're going through to Sapporo?" the girl asked, and there was an anxious tone to her voice.

"We'll have to now. We're almost out of juice."

"Fine! We've got to find Hallerton. There's something mysterious about Hallerton. If you register at the Imperial Hotel, I'll try to contact you. The Imperial is on the Nishi-Ginza Square and you can get there from the Sapporo airport by taxi very quickly. Stay there until you hear . . ."

"Who's Hallerton?" called Todd, as the girl's signal faded. "Who's this guy? What's up, Pieplate?"

"Plenty!" yelled Leadbeater. "Look, they're shooting at her!"

"Good Lord!" gasped Todd, swinging the Seversky over hard and ramming after the Koken plane. "Nakajimas!"

"Yeah, and they're going to work on her!"

"They've gone to work on her. She's in flames!"

The two Americans stared with straining eyes and watched the Koken monoplane strangle itself in mid-air. Three Nakajima fighters with Japanese Imperial Navy markings on their flanks were pouring flaming tracers and armor-piercing slugs into the floundering, long-range ship as it stalled at the top of a mad struggle to get away.

"Let 'em have some of it," husked Leadbeater. "What you waiting for?"

Todd did not answer, but drew back a lever that opened the ports of the 37 mm. guns hidden in their wings. He tripped in the gear, pressed the firing lever, and a series of cannonading chugs splashed from the wing orifices.

A Nakajima skidded across the sky minus its tail assembly. Another, intent on its effort to splash more lead into the floundering Koken, never saw the Seversky slam at it and pour another salvo of shell-gun ammo into its vitals.

"Good stuff," approved Larry, over Todd's shoulder. "But that doesn't save Pieplate."

"Why the devil doesn't she jump?"

"How do you know she has a 'chute?"

"Of course she has a 'chute—I hope. What's the matter with you, Larry?"

"What's the matter with you? She hasn't jumped yet, has she?"

"How do I know? I haven't seen her jump," argued Todd, taking another long shot at the last of the three Nakajimas.

"Well, how do you know she hasn't jumped? She might have," Larry argued pathetically.

Neither of them had any idea what they were saying. All they knew was that Sturgis Sands, a fellow agent who had more than proven her worth, was going down in a flaming plane.

"I haven't seen a 'chute yet," said Todd mournfully. He had a face like the business end of a vinegar cruet now.

The whole sky was lit up by the flame and glare of two burning planes. One was a Koken, the other a navy Nakajima. But there was no sign of a fluttering white canopy that meant life or hope for a young girl.

The two torches fluttered down toward the rice paddies below. A small river trickled placidly through it all and gurgled over its banks in spots. The Koken, a mere smoking skeleton, fell with a low hiss into a bend of the muddy river.

The two grief-stricken agents circled the spot several times, but there was no sign of life or evidence of hope. They circled wider and tried to find a clearing to get down, but the rice paddies covered miles of territory, and was no place to attempt to land a 300 m.p.h. Convoy fighter.

"I guess that's that," moaned Leadbeater. "What was that all about, anyhow?"

"You've got me. She was just saying that we had to find a guy named—let's see—a guy named Hallerton. Who's that?"

"Hallerton? The name is familiar, but I don't know anyone by that name. That was all our fault."

"Where the deuce did they come from?" demanded Todd, climbing again and reluctantly returning to their original course.

"They could have come from anywhere. What really matters is how they nailed her. Something's slipping in this game somewhere," Larry exploded. "We're just sticking our necks into a noose. Why don't we beat it out at sea and try to get picked up by a P. and O. liner?"

"What about Pieplate? You can't leave her out here."

"Well, did you—did you see her jump or something?"

"No. But something tells me she got out of that mess, somehow."

"Oh. Swell chance!"

"She's not that dumb," argued Bancroft. "She must have jumped. We couldn't see the other side of the glare, remember."

"I guess we go to Sapporo," said Leadbeater with a doleful air. "How will she get out of that mud puddle back there?"

"You tell me. Maybe she's not even in there. A million things could have happened."

"Yeah, but only one did."

Mumbling the rest of the argument to themselves, they settled back glumly for the remainder of the trip to Sapporo. There was an airport there of fairly reasonable importance, although Todd could find no list of the call letters of any radio station connected with the field. So he just went on and trusted to luck to get in.

Sapporo, the official capital of the island of Yezo, was now called Hokkaido. It had a population of more than 150,000, was an important garrison town; boasted an agricultural college, several important saw mills, flour mills, breweries, and flax factories. Even at this unearthly hour of the morning there was plenty of activity discernible.

Smoke stacks belched fire. The main streets were illuminated and cut the city up into shapeless slabs. The railroad yards were touched up with blobs of steam, streaks of fire, and the intermittent glare of open fireboxes. The steel rails gleamed and signal lamps twinkled their red and green warnings.

"Wonder what the hoosegow is like down there?" pondered Larry.

Todd was busy circling the city now, looking for the airport. He studied the Interavia map again and finally checked that the field was located two kilometers north of the widest section of the railroad yard. He swung across the city again and caught the fan-shaped wedge of light that fanged out from a portable landing light.

"Well, they're putting out the carpet for us," Leadbeater said, as he tucked the last important part of Slingin' Sal away.

"You keep your trap shut when we get in and don't start a fight with the first bird you see," warned Todd, lowering the landing gear.

Larry blinked at that, but let it go. Todd needed all his skill to get in, and this was no time for horseplay. The Seversky swished around, caught the wind and headed into the glare that was set across the field for landing. A shadow bar across the lens gave them a chance to keep out of the glare and eventually they touched down gently, scrawnched their cleos, and finally pulled up safely.

A hangar door was open, and a wide oblong of light fell out and formed a ceremonial carpet for them to approach. A number of indistinct figures moved back and forth across the entrance, throwing grotesque shadows before them. The hangar door was pushed open farther, and inside they could see several Nakajima-Douglas transports of the Nippon Koko Yuso Kabushiki Kaisha (Japan Air Transport Co.) around which a number of Japanese mechanics were carrying out routine duties.

"Douglasses?" gagged Larry.

"Sure. They make 'em under manufacturing license over here. These Japs know what they're doing."

"I'll bet they do. We'll know what they're doing, too, when we get in."

A group of mechanics came out and took the wing tips of the Seversky and guided Todd in. The Seversky was inspected with only ordinary interest as the two Americans climbed down. A young foreman in American coveralls directed them to an office on the far side of the building which obviously housed the customs officials.

"Here it comes," said Larry under his breath.

"Shut up! They've been very cordial so far. What do you want them to do at this time of morning? Serve cocktails?"

"Let me alone, that's all. Just a hotel bed, something to eat, and—"

"Sure, I know the rest. You're thirsty."

The customs official was a small, spare man in a neat blue serge suit. He wore the omnipresent tortoise-shell glasses and a snap-brim felt hat. He smiled, lit a cigarette, and began talking, but his voice was pitched so high and he spoke in such rapid tones that it was some time before they could get the drift of his speech.

Todd just stared at him and offered his passports, travel permits, and government credentials on the plane and their equipment. The Jap official ignored them and continued his bleating until finally they sensed that he was presenting some form of formal greeting.

2

"AS WE HAVE HEARD so much of you two gentlemen," the customs official was saying, "we here in Sapporo are most delighted to welcome you and to offer all our services. We appreciate your efforts here and hope you will call on us should you require our assistance in your meteorological work. The Japan Air Transport Company is most interested, I assure you."

"Well, bounce my landing gear—that's right," muttered Larry. "We are in the Meteorological Survey Service."

Todd wanted to kick him in the shins.

"And so, gentlemen," the Jap official went on, "I am most pleased to waive all customs formalities and offer you all our assistance in getting into the city and to a hotel. I have a car outside."

"Well,—thanks," said Todd, watching the Jap stamp their papers and scrawl his name on their passports, "but I guess we can manage, if we first arrange for the servicing of our plane."

"Of course, but you are not leaving at once, surely?"

"No, but we get orders unexpectedly. Certain meteorological situations arise frequently and we have to be on hand to make our computations," explained Todd.

"Where did you learn all that line?" asked Larry out of one corner of his mouth.

"Your plane will be checked and serviced immediately," the customs official said. "Now, may I run you gentlemen into the town? Have you any idea where you wish to stay?"

"We have considered the Imperial Hotel," said Todd.

"I am quite sure it will more than meet your expectations, Mr. Bancroft." Then the Jap made a queer grimace as he shuffled his papers. "I do not suppose you have heard anything further about Mr. Hallerton, have you?" he said, and for the first time they sensed an icy tone of suspicion in his voice.

"Mr. Hallerton?" repeated Todd, trying to remember where that name had come up before. "Mr. Hallerton?" Then it struck him. "I'm sorry, but I've never heard of him. Why, is there anything wrong?"

"Anything wrong?" repeated the Jap. He stared through his thick lenses at the two Americans, studied Leadbeater carefully and then said, "No, I hope there's nothing whatever wrong."

Todd decided to drop the subject and sent Larry out to collect their bags from the plane and give orders for the servicing.

"You know," he snapped suddenly, "we have been getting a rough handling in this area."

The customs man frowned and pursed his lips. "A great many things have been happening in this section and you should have known that it is a restricted area," he said finally. "That is why you have been attacked—or at least fired on as a warning to stay away. I hope you will acquaint yourself with these restricted areas in the future. You should get permission for such flights."

"Don't worry, we will, after this."

The Jap led the way out to his car, a new German Mercedes. He slid behind the wheel after they piled in, pressed the starter, and drove skillfully out of the airport confines. He swung into the main road that led to Sapporo. Both Todd and Larry were silent all the way in, not fully satisfied that everything was on the up and up. That Mr. Hallerton business had them worried.

Sapporo was typically Japan. It appeared to be a weird combination of Bethlehem, Pennsylvania, Harrison, New Jersey, and something designed for a Japanese exhibit at the World's Fair. There were factories, modernistic department stores, smelly warehouses, and Oriental structures all stirred in together. Then there was the Hotel Imperial, reminding one of a midwest cinema minus the billboards. It was built of white marble or terra cotta.

It had an imposing entrance in spite of the early morning chill. There were windows set so that the patrons could sit and look down on the turmoil of the street and the restrained gaiety of the sidewalk. The streets were cluttered with creaking-wheeled carts, wheezing motor cars, bicycles, and rickshaws. Bells rung and tingled. Gongs clanged and vibrated from the most mysterious places. Men in uniform blew whistles and flashed short swords. No one took the slightest notice, and life went on in a strange even tempo.

The customs man pulled up before the Imperial, turned in his seat, and spoke.

"I'm most interested in Mr. Hallerton, gentlemen, and would appreciate any information you may receive on his whereabouts."

"Who the devil—" started Larry, but a nudge from Todd made him convert the statement to, "Who the devil designed this town?"

"We can do a lot for each other, Mr. Bancroft," said the Jap with a steely timber to his voice. "If you hear anything about Mr. Hallerton—well, I think you understand."

"If I do, I'll let you know. I guess he'll turn up in time," Todd said with an innocent gesture.

The customs man jerked in his seat. "You think he will?" he asked with a queer twisting of his lips.

"Oh, no doubt of it. He always turns up," answered Todd, picking up their bags.

"He *always* turns up?" the Jap repeated in a low, choked tone. "What do you mean? Has he been missing before?"

"Missing?" exclaimed Todd. "Is he missing?"

The Jap customs man gave them both a glance that was a cocktail of curdled frozen custard and double-strength vitriol.

"I'm afraid we are wasting our time. I have no use for levity in a case like this."

They got out, thanked the Jap, and watched him drive away in the chill morning.

"Now who is Mr. Hallerton?" they blankly asked each other.

A Japanese boy in oversize uniform greeted them in the lobby and took their bags. Another Jap, an almost exact replica of the customs man, was behind the counter of the office. He greeted them and mentioned their names at once.

"How do you know us?" demanded Todd, deeply perplexed.

"But the lady called and reserved your room, sir," the desk clerk stated. "You are to have room three-o-seven."

"The lady called?" they both said. "What lady?"

"The lady who say she is your secretary. A Miss Sands, her name is," answered the surprised clerk, fairly hissing his words.

That was too much for them. How could Sturgis Sands call and arrange their room for them?

"When did she call?" asked Todd.

"Yesterday—yesterday morning. Nossing is wrong, I hope?"

"Yesterday morning?" Todd managed to get out. "But there must be some mistake. She couldn't know we were coming to Sapporo then. Are you sure?"

The clerk waxed emphatic.

"Positively. I took the message from Osaka—on the telephone."

"Osaka? But Miss Sands was in Manila! That is, I think—oh, forget it. She *could* have been in Osaka. I guess it's all right."

"Of course, gentlemen," beamed the relieved clerk. "The room is the exact one she ordered. We even managed to get Mr. Hallerton's book in time."

"Mr. Hallerton's book?" exploded Leadbeater.

The clerk fumbled with the register a minute, glanced about furtively, and then displayed all the symptoms of a man about to faint. His eyes popped and blazed and his throat muscles constricted to stiff cords.

"What's the matter?" Todd started to say.

"The book—quick, Mister Bancroft," the clerk began, "the book! I have it here—you are to read page three—"

Something swished between Todd and Larry. Something that sizzled and then left a leaden and horrible silence.

There was a scuffle behind them and a low Oriental oath. A figure went quickly past a square pillar that had a gaudy potted palm near it.

"In the throat!" husked Larry.

Todd turned quickly and saw the clerk clutch at his neck. His mouth was open and he was trying to scream. Something had paralyzed his throat muscles, and he fell forward clutching at the edge of the counter as he shoved the brown paper package toward Todd.

"Book—page—," he choked.

That was all. His body gave one quivering jerk and slipped off the counter to the space behind with a cruel thud.

Todd grabbed the package, darted around the counter, and saw the body flat on its back. In the neck trembled a short four-inch dart, a black cigar-shaped missile that had snapped off a life in terrible silence. Todd winced as he watched the reflex action of the dart tremble and stop, drooping at a slight angle. The form gave another convulsive jerk and a foot kicked a rattan waste-paper basket over.

"A Malay blow dart!" whispered Todd. "Must be tipped with the famous Japanese five poisons known as *wu tu*. There's one you didn't think of."

"Knocked him deader than King Tut," commented Larry. "Who did it?"

"Don't ask me," Todd said, getting up off one knee.

Then someone put on a Luna Park fireworks display. There was a dull *thock*, and Todd was knocked senseless. Comets charged across a pale pink sky. Thirty-five flaming onions went up and formed a loud oath. A flock of giant salutes blew up somewhere near the lot and started a new display of crashing pyrotechnics.

When he came to, Todd found himself sprawled out across the floor near the feet of the dead office clerk. He made his eyes behave and tried to move a lump the size of a sand-bag from somewhere behind the back of his head.

The Leadbetter guy was on the other side of the counter bellowing for all the constabulary in Japan, and waving an automatic half the size of an anti-tank gun. Todd scrambled to his feet, tottered across the floor, and grabbed Larry about the waist and hung on.

"What happened?" he gasped. "Two big guys came out of nowhere behind you, and socked you with a hunk of wood. It sounded like a cracked gourd—your noggin, I mean. I tried to get at them, but one of the guys slipped a piece of yellow cord around my neck and almost cut my head off."

"Jap garrote!" said Todd. "You're lucky! You're supposed to be dead."

"Thanks! They got away with the package—the book. That's what they came for."

Todd rubbed the back of his head, and Larry fingered his collar while hotel men and two Jap policemen made some attempt to clear it all up.

"So sorry, gentlemen," a Jap plainclothes man said as they stood by and watched the clerk's body carried out. "You will not be annoyed further. Unfortunate. We shall investigate."

Larry and Todd said nothing but exchanged glances.

"Nice, eh?" Todd said finally. "They got the book, eh? Pieplate must have wanted us to have it, too. What the hell is all the Hallerton stuff about, anyway?"

"This business gets screwier every minute. Where's someone who knows something about this joint? I've got to have a drink," said Larry. "Hey, boy, come here!"

A toothy youth in a uniform jacket and black silk trousers came forward.

"Is there a bar here—where we can get something to eat, too?" Larry asked.

The boy bowed, half-smiled, and led them across the lobby to a doorway that was bordered in palms. There was a series of leather screens through which they passed and then a bar—a real bar with bottles and cigarettes and cigars. There were deep leather seats and comfortable wide tables. It was snug and warm and they sat down, still pondering the events of the past few minutes.

"Okay, boy, mix up something. Brandy-soda—make it two—double, before Mr. Hallerton blows in again," said Todd.

"Mister Hallerton very wet, sir," the boy said. "He no come here. Mr. Yoshida look for him, too. No come yet. Probably very wet."

"As you say in America," added Larry.

"No," the boy peered over from the other side of the bar, "not as you say in America. Mister Hallerton most likely very wet—in junk."

"Junk! Gets wet in junk? What sort of talk is that? What's he flying?" argued Leadbeater.

"Him no fly, sir. Him in junk—Mister Hallerton. Him missing now many long days."

"In junk?" probed Larry again. He was intrigued by this junk business.

"If that bird don't soon get those drinks around here, I'll be on a junk pile myself," said Todd wearily, rubbing the back of his head. "I'm going crazy! We've got to get that book back."

The boy brought the drinks around, and they ordered a breakfast to be brought into the bar. They gulped the first drink and ordered another, for the first real pangs of hunger and the weariness of fatigue were beginning to take their toll.

A pungent breakfast of ham and eggs was brought in along with a generous pot of steaming coffee, and they fell to without a word.

3

WHY HAD THEY BEEN so courteously treated by the customs man? It was obvious that they had been expected, for he had been waiting for them at the airport. Why had he failed to mention any of the escapades they had experienced and the battles they had had with the Mitsubishis and Nakajimas of the Japanese government? Why had Sturgis Sands ordered a book, Hallerton's book, all the way from Osaka, the famous Japanese naval base?

''We've walked into a beaut,'' muttered Todd, breaking a slab of buttered toast. ''They're setting the shop out for us for something, you can depend on that.''

''I'm worried about that girl,'' Leadbeater mumbled into his coffee. He looked worried, too. His neck still ached.

''I'm not,'' Bancroft stated with decision. ''That girl is somewhere about. She didn't get it in that plane. As a matter of fact, I'm not sure now she was in that one.''

''Don't be goofy! Of course she was in that Koken. She called from that plane, didn't she?''

''We have no concrete evidence that she did. Except—'' added Todd with a mournful mug, ''except that she stopped speaking the instant those Nakajimas started firing at her.''

They continued with their meal and washed it down with plenty of hot coffee, still pondering on their strange situation. Then signing the chit for the meal and the drinks, they had the boy show them to their room on the third floor. They were weary and the drag up the two flights of stairs about finished them. They threw themselves across the beds with complete relief. The boy opened the windows, placed their bags on the bag-stands at the foot of each bed, and quietly left the room.

''Hallerton—Hallerton,'' said Todd, kicking off his shoes. ''Isn't there a writer named Hallerton—some nut who goes all over the world doing screwy things to get material for travel books?''

''Junk! I mean aboard a junk—a Chinese junk.'' Larry was gnawing on his thumbnail, deep in reflection of his own. ''Sure. He's a writer. Had an elephant once. Went over the Alps with it like Bismarck or Lady Godiva. He writes books!''

Todd placed his hands about his throbbing temples and closed his eyes.

''What a memory for details,'' he moaned.

''He was crossing the Pacific to go over Fujiyama in a Chinese junk,'' added Larry.

''That's it! He wrote a book called *Twentieth Century Vagabond*, a best seller. His name is Reynal Hallerton. The guy must be missing.''

''It's a gag—he ain't, I'll bet,'' Leadbeater argued.

''Pieplate tried to get a book of his to us. The poor mug downstairs tried to get the message to us—a message written somehow in the book on a certain page.''

''But we get conked and someone swipes the book. We're where we started, only you got a sock on the noggin and I almost choke to death.''

''He's missing. We've been tipped off, only we muffed the play.''

''Yoshida got the book somehow, Todd.''

''The move smells of Yoshida,'' agreed Bancroft. ''Let's get some sleep. We're both dead on our feet. We can't think or act like this.''

And in spite of their despair, their fears, their frustrations, they both curled up on their beds and were sound asleep in a few minutes.

Larry was awake first. He stared at his wrist watch and noted that it was about 2:30 in the afternoon. He decided to get a bath somehow and went prowling around the corridor in his dressing gown and finally found the elusive bathroom he was looking for.

He returned to their room and aroused Todd. Bancroft sat up and pondered with sleepy eyes.

''Hello—what's that?''

The even *room-room-room* of aero engines sounded somewhere outside. Larry ran to the window and peered out.

''What is it? One of the Jap Douglasses?'' Bancroft repeated.

''No. A Savoia-Marchetti flying boat. Carrying Japanese Navy markings. Wait a minute. I guess this one is an amphibian of some kind. Yeah, she's turning over the city now. I can see the wheel gear down for a ground landing.''

''That's a new one on me. I never heard of that job before. Must be a special for the Japs.''

''Well, that's what it is, all right, Something like our new Grummans. What is that doing way up here?''

''I don't care,'' snapped Todd suddenly. ''I'm worried about that book.''

"Maybe you can get a boy to go out and get one."

Todd growled, pulled on his clothes, combed his hair, and went downstairs. He hurried across the lobby to the desk when he suddenly spotted Kato Yoshida sitting in earnest conversation with a woman whose back was toward him.

Yoshida had a yellow-jacketed book in his hand.

Todd made a bee-line across the floor to the side of the Jap Secret Service man.

"That doesn't happen to be my book, does it, Yoshida?" he snapped.

Yoshida looked startled for a minute, stared at the book in his hand and back at Todd. Then he recovered.

"Why, Mr. Bancroft! What are you doing here in Sapporo—here in Japan?"

Todd was taken aback at that for an instant. He saw that the book in Yoshida's hand was a copy of *Twentieth Century Vagabond*, by Reynal Hallerton.

"I'm still working for the U.S. Meterological Survey, Yoshida, and I won't stand this sort of thing. That's my book."

Then he turned and glanced at the woman. It was Madam Olinka Ivanovna, the woman spy whom he had last seen apparently dead on the floor of the hotel Moderne lobby in Vladivostok.

"Hi, Madam Ivanona," he said bluntly. "Nice trick you pulled back there in Vladivostok, eh? The old red ink game to make it appear you had been hit. You'll be wanted for murder if you ever go back."

"I, wanted for murder, Mr. Bancroft?" her voice had a tingling, dulcet sound. "You accuse me of murder? What about you?"

"I beg of you, Miss Ivan Ivanovna," broke in the Jap. "Please remember that Mr. Bancroft is a respected member of the U.S. Meteorological Survey."

"Never mind the gagging, Yoshida. What about my book?"

"Your book, Mr. Bancroft? This? I have been reading it for several days. I bought it in Vladivostok just before we left."

He handed it over and inside was stamped a trade-mark of a noted Russian merchant in Vladivostok.

"We are all very interested in the fate of Mr. Hallerton. Very unfortunate, his being missing like this. A most interesting young man," Yoshida went on in his oily tônes. "Have you lost a book, Mr. Bancroft?" Bancroft?"

"Look here, Yoshida," snapped Todd. "What happened to that bird?"

"You mean to say you don't know, Mr. Bancroft?" said Yoshida.

"I thought the whole world knew about the loss of Mr. Hallerton. He has been sought for some time now."

"He was crossing the Pacific in a Chinese junk?"

"Yes. Last heard from near—well, about one thousand miles west of Midway Island."

"Where were you going to say he was near, Yoshida?" asked Todd with a taunting gleam in his eye. "You almost tripped up on that one."

"My dear Mr. Bancroft!" replied the Japanese Secret Service man with a pained glance. "You do me an injustice. You know that I have been carrying out routine missions in Vladivostok."

"You mean you were *trying* to carry out your missions, Yoshida. Now why did you so suddenly hurry to Sapporo? Why are you so interested in a popular writer of travel stories?"

Yoshida did not answer. He gave Olinka Ivanovna a glance and then turned to stare at a group of American news-reel men who were noisily entering the hotel lobby. They were dragging cases, boxes of film, coils of heavy cable, and all the impedimenta of their trade.

Yoshida frowned. "You see," he said, turning to Bancroft, "there is much interest in your Mr. Hallerton. These news-reel crews have been working on the case from here"

"From here? And you said he was last heard from a thousand miles west of Midway Island. That's about eight or nine hundred miles away from Sapporo, even at a rough guess."

Yoshida stiffened as he glanced over Todd's shoulder. Bancroft turned instinctively and saw that a young Japanese Naval Aviation officer was approaching. To his surprise the young officer came up to him, stiffened to attention, and spoke.

"Mr. Bancroft of the United States Meteorological Survey?"

"Yes, what do *you* want?" answered Todd with a scowl.

"The compliments of Commander Yano, Imperial Japanese Navy, sir. A message for you, sir."

"A message for me? What's this, Yoshida? Another gag?"

He slipped his fingernail under the flap of the flimsy tissue envelope and withdrew a sheet of paper. It was a regulation Japanese Navy "signals" form and to his somewhat incredulous eye came the message in scrawled pencil.

> Read Page 343, third paragraph, Hallerton book under Ivanovna.
> Must get him out.Be at airport in an hour.
>
> Pieplate

Todd crumpled the message quickly and crammed it into his pocket. Then he turned to explain to the Japanese lieutenant that there was no answer, but the message carrier was nowhere in sight.

"Where did *he* go?" he asked, puzzled.

"What's wrong, Mr. Bancroft?" asked Yoshida in reply. "The lieutenant? He hurried out through the side door."

"Nothing's wrong. I have an invitation to dinner at the Naval Aviation mess this evening. What's the gag?"

Yoshida did not answer, and Todd Bancroft glanced down at Olinka Ivanovna who still sat in the same stiff position. Then he got an idea.

"Here, boy," he called. "Bring us three drinks. What will you have, Yoshida? And you, Miss Ivanovna? I feel lucky."

The boy took the orders, a Benedictine for the woman, a whiskey san-tan for Yoshida, and a shell of imported German beer for Todd.

"Do you know Commander Yano?" asked the still puzzled Yoshida.

"Never heard of him in my life," said Todd truthfully.

"He's in charge of Naval Aviation in this area. He probably wants to talk to you about Mr. Hallerton."

"Hallerton again, eh? He seems like an interesting guy all of a sudden. Too bad you can't find him, eh?"

"Do *you* expect to find him, Mr. Bancroft?" the girl said in a strange, throaty tone. She added a smile that might have been put on by a Bronx Zoo adder.

"I do now," answered Todd quietly.

The Jap bit his lip, twisted around to allow the waiter through with the drinks, but made no comment. Todd first signed the chit for the drinks, passed the san-tan over to Yoshida, and then gingerly raised the small cordial glass of Benedictine and moved toward the girl with it.

"The nectar of the gods, they say, Miss Ivanovna. I admire your taste in liqueurs."

The young woman smiled faintly, raised her hand to take the glass, and then something slipped. The small glass somehow twisted in Todd's fingers and it flipped across the space between his hand and the outstretched fingers of the girl. The gleaming liquid splashed and spilled down the front of Miss Ivanovna's dress. Instinctively she arose to her feet and in the same instant Bancroft stepped half a pace to one side and made a quick gesture. His hand came away from the seat of the big club chair with another copy of Hallerton's *Twentieth Century Vagabond*.

"Thanks!" he smiled, glancing quickly at the inside of the cover.

"Sorry to have to do that, but you *were* sitting on my property all the time."

"You beast!" was all Miss Ivanovna could say.

Todd simply picked up his beer, drank it down in a long comfortable gulp, bowed to the enraged people before him, and threw a dollar down on the waiter's tray.

"I'll be seein' you, Yoshida," he grinned and hurried away.

4

BANCROFT RACED UP the stairs and explained in a few short sentences what had happened and flaunted the book in Larry's amazed mug.

"Well, what does page three-forty-three say?" demanded Leadbeater, rubbing his head briskly with a large coarse towel.

Todd flipped the pages till he came to the page and paragraph mentioned. He read:

> I have seen many strange and interesting things in my travels. Man is the strangest of all. As I wander the world's highways, skyways, and seaways, I never fail to find some new evidence of man's inherent treachery to man. I have seen men at war and men preparing for war. I have seen their well laid plans, and I fully expect to see more—particularly in the Pacific. One of these days I am going to satisfy myself on one point concerning the little yellow man in the Pacific, for I am a man of peace and from now on my work in this world will be to betray those who plan for war.

"There it is," beamed Bancroft. "You see what happened?

"No. Do you?"

"Just about. This fellow Hallerton had an idea in his mind when he started this trip across the Pacific. He used a Chinese junk because it suited his purpose in several ways. He could move almost anywhere in the Pacific without being conspicuous. The craft, they say, is very seaworthy. He crossed, somehow, and headed for something he had been suspicious of for some time. Now what has happened?"

"He's missing."

"Maybe, but if so, why are the Japs all so anxious to find him?"

"Because he has found out something."

"Right! Now the question is, what has he found and where is he now to tell us what he has discovered?" demanded Todd. "Here! You're bathed and dressed. You pop downstairs and avoid Yoshida somehow and get in conversation with those news-reel men. Get hold of a picture of Hallerton's junk, if possible."

"Wait a minute!" said Larry like the popping of a cork. "What about that message? I mean the guy who brought it?"

"I don't know. He was just a Jap officer, a navy aviation bird of some sort."

"And he said the message was from the commander of the area?"

"Sounds woozy, doesn't it?" said Todd reflectively.

"Sounds like Pieplate to me."

They both raised their eyes until their glances met.

"I wonder!" said Todd finally. "She was saying something about this guy Hallerton—just before."

"And now she signs a paper that picks out a certain passage in his book. Why, you dope!" exclaimed Leadbeater. "I'll bet that was Pieplate, herself, all the time!"

Todd considered that for a minute, said nothing, but was convinced that Larry was right.

"Maybe, I don't know," he finally admitted. "I really didn't look at the guy. I was watching Yoshida, making sure he didn't read any part of the message."

"Well, I'll go downstairs and try to get a line on this Chinese junk of Hallerton's. You get a bath and we'll rush out to the airport."

Larry ducked out, and Todd hid the book under the dresser and went out to get his bath. He made it quickly and was soon back and climbing into some clean garments. He left his laundry to be picked up by the hotel staff, arranged the rest of his stuff to make it appear that they were there for some time, but was careful to place all code books and papers where he felt they would not be found.

Larry was back in a few minutes, excited and flustered.

"Come on," he said. "Here's an out. The news-reel guys are going out to the airport. We can ride with them. Yoshida won't give us a tumble."

"Swell! What are they going to do?"

'They are making another effort to contact freighters in this section to see if any of them have picked this bird Hallerton up anywhere."

"I get it. Okay, I'm ready."

They left their room with a last glance around and locked the door. Downstairs they found the American news-reel crew under the command of one Pete Donovan, a bulgy, red-faced gent with a cigar as big as half a whiffletree stuck in one side of his face. He was fat, but he moved with the ease and grace of a swordsman. He studied Todd for several seconds after they were introduced and said quietly:

"You work with Blaisdell, don't you?"

Todd gave an almost imperceptible nod, and the fat news-reel man nodded toward Larry.

"Believe it or not, he's one of the anointed, too," smiled Bancroft.

"Bong!" burst out Donovan, which was his way of expressing satisfaction. "You guys got the inside on this yet?"

"No. We didn't know a thing about it until we arrived a short time ago. Have the Jappos got him?"

"No, not yet, but they're planning to pick him up somewhere. They got a Savoia-Marchetti out at the airport—and they ain't got it there for nothing. What are you flying?"

"A Seversky Convoy fighter—on wheels."

"Ugh! That's bad. I guess you need floats. Can you get any out here?"

"Down at Osaka. That's miles away—below Tokyo."

"I know it. We're stuck, too, if they land on the water anywhere. We got an Electra."

They went outside and clambered into a truck Donovan had hired to transport their gear to the airport. Nothing more was said about Hallerton or the possibility of finding him. Donovan simply sat on a pile of coiled cable and blew vast clouds of blue smoke at the Japanese afternoon sunshine. Todd and Larry squatted on a huge camera case and pondered.

They reached the airport with a few minutes to spare, according to the time set in the message delivered at the hotel. Todd and Larry sauntered off and sought their own ship in the hangar, making certain that servicing orders had been properly carried out.

"Hey, pipe this," whispered Larry, leaning over from his cockpit. "A note on the radio set. Pieplate, I guess."

The small sheet of paper gave a wave-length number and added:

> Tune in at 3:30—your clock time.

They both glanced at the clock on the instrument board. It showed 3:29. Larry went on checking to cast off suspicion, but Todd dropped in his seat, held one of the ear phones to his ear and snapped the switch. He sat there apparently checking the set, but his eyes were watching the hand on the clock crawl down to the "6" at the bottom of the dial. Then before he realized it there was a crackle in his ear phone and he caught the words:

"Thought you would never make it. Wander over to the Savoia-Marchetti and be ready for anything. Same guy."

Todd had just time to answer, "Be right over, Pieplate. What's the idea?" But there was no answer.

"Come on," he said to Larry. "Act dumb now, but move fast if we have to."

Sauntering out, they spotted the Savoia-Marchetti amphibian staked out at a point a short distance beyond the row of hangars. There was a Jap marine on guard just under the high nose. About the plane the news-reel men were putting on a swell show of feverish activity that held the sentry spellbound. They were busy setting up portable microphones and cameras. Donovan gave them a knowing glance as the Secret Service pair sidled around the hangar and approached the amphibian from the blind portion of the tail.

Donovan's voice was raised again and again. He set his stage beautifully and then moved the sentry over to a new position, clear of the wheels and the wing tips. He muttered something to him and took new sights on the plane and then on the sentry.

Todd and Larry missed most of this as they eased their way around to the cabin entrance of the Italian plane and slipped unseen into the fuselage.

They got a shock at first for all they could see was the shapeless back of a Japanese flying officer crawling up the narrow companionway to the control hatch. Todd followed quickly and made a grab for the officer's arms as Larry closed and bolted the cabin door.

"Take it easy, cave man," a voice said from over the shoulder of the Jap officer. Then there was a billowing of honey-colored hair from under a dislodged cap, and Sturgis Sands grinned into Todd's amazed mug.

"Sturgis!" he gasped.

"Pieplate!" added Larry from the depths of the cabin.

"Take it easy and lie low," the girl ordered. "We've got to get this thing off before they spot you. Stay there and watch Donovan."

"Gosh!" gurgled Leadbeater. "Did you see how she was made up? I was fooled until her hair came down."

The rest of his startled observations were drowned out with the bellow of two motors that were suddenly opened up. They crowded close to the bulkhead separating the control compartment from the main cabin and watched through a small window the antics of Donovan.

First he yelled and pointed wildly at the motors. Then he pulled the little Jap marine away and ran toward the ropes that were holding the wing tips steady. He slashed at them with a jack-knife that had seen service in someone's navy and had a blade big enough to sever a hawser. In ten seconds after Sturgis had opened the engines they were free and rolling wildly right out to the center of the field.

Todd watched carefully from the small port. The little Jap marine was running around in circles shooting into the air. Donovan was trying to make him stand still, risking being skewered with the bayonet in his effort to carry out the pantomime of taking a news-reel picture.

Sturgis turned the bouncing ship into the wind and yelled, "Okay. Come and get it."

She slipped out of the pilot's seat and allowed Todd to take her place. Larry stayed at the foot of the companionway, and the girl plunked over into the co-pilot's seat with a happy laugh.

"You got a lot of explaining to do, lady," said Todd with a serious grimace. "Where're we going now?"

"Head almost due north for Uruppu Jima!" the girl answered.

5

TODD GAVE HER a look and then turned his attention to getting the new Savoia-Marchetti off. She was slow at first, but as she gained speed, he was able to lift her clear, climb slowly, and head for the sea on his left.

He drew down the switch that retracted the wheels, set his engines for normal cruising, and then turned to the girl.

"What was that again?" he asked.

"Head due north for Uruppu Jima," she replied.

"Quit gagging. Where're we going?"

"Good heavens!" the girl responded. "Can't you ever get away from the New England shore? You're in Japan now. Uruppu Jima is a small island along the Kuriles and it's about four hundred and eighty miles from here. Now get going. Here's a chart—it's as plain as day."

She drew a Japanese Admiralty chart out of the jacket pocket of the uniform she was wearing. Todd glanced at it and saw that Uruppu Jima actually was one of the series of the Kuriles curving out from the north shore of Hokkaido toward the Peninsula of Kamchatka. There were several such names with the suffix "Jima" which he figured must mean "island" in Japanese.

"Where did you get that makeup?" he then demanded, satisfied that the girl knew what she was talking about.

"I borrowed it from the locker of one of those Nakajima planes you shot down. I didn't have to take it off a body. The poor man must have been carrying an extra outfit with him and it certainly came in handy, because when I got out of that rice paddy I was a muddy mess."

"We didn't see you jump. We only heard you cut off when you were talking to us about Hallerton," explained Todd. "Figured you were done."

"I thought I was, too. I had to make it fast and I got clear, but to play safe I pulled a delayed drop for fear they would follow me down if they saw my 'chute open too soon. I was using a black one and I guess they didn't see it since I think I opened it well under one thousand feet. Too low for comfort. I had only just stopped swinging when I hit in the paddy."

"Nearer five hundred then," added Todd. "You certainly took a long chance."

"Then the first Nakajima fell with a wing off, not twenty yards from me. I wallowed over to it, to get papers—if any, and a map to see what they were heading for. They had a point off Uruppu Jima marked with a red circle. So I got the first tip on what was up. I found the locker and the suit of clothes and decided to check on it."

"And you think this guy Hallerton is up there?" Todd interrupted the girl again.

"No doubt of it now. He has probably been there for some time. He contacted one of our seal patrol boats by radio, but he had made up a code of his own and it had to be relayed on to Washington so that it could be broken down. It was a tough one based on his book, but they eventually broke it and discovered that he had found something and that he had better be picked up at once."

"Then why wasn't a sealer sent in after him?"

"The code was too tough to figure that much or else he had failed to include his position. I found out about this Uruppu Jima angle when you shot down the Nakajimas. They were on their way up there, or else they were to escort this Savoia-Marchetti late this afternoon. They were waiting for more escort planes, figuring they might run into trouble."

"Probably some smart Jap picked up his code, too, and deciphered it," suggested Todd.

"No doubt now. That's why they are so interested in getting hold of him first. He has found out something here in the Pacific that should be attended to. They probably know he has, for it is obvious now that his junk has been identified in or near some prohibited area."

Sturgis sat back with a relieved smile. There was a new color in her yellowed cheeks now and a certain fire in her eye. She was happy and she brought out a vanity case from somewhere and began removing the remains of the makeup that had transformed her from a Mid-west beauty to a smug, bland Jap.

"It was really fun while it lasted," she said, smiling across the cockpit.

"Being shot down?" asked Todd dryly.

"No, playing at Japanese soldiers. It's queer what a uniform will do to the man who has to salute the braid on your sleeve, but I'd rather be what we are—members of an army that wears no insignia or braid."

"You're right there, Sturgis," agreed Todd, staring ahead into the mystery of the north. "If you don't get caught."

Three hours later they were circling the northern tip of Uruppu Jima. The island was about one hundred miles in length, and, like the rest of the Kuriles group, abounded in volcanic cones and stretches of wild conifers. It was practically uninhabited except for a few wandering groups of Ainu tribesmen shoved into these vast wastes by illegal seal fishers, some wilder aborigines, and the authority of Nippon which was gradually creeping north out of Etorofu Jima, the largest and most southerly of the group.

Smoke seeped out of lava crevices and crawled through the parched vegetation. Steam from boiling wells threw hazy plumes across the rocky valley. Stubby patches of *Shikotanchiku*, a strange species of bamboo having brown spots on the cane, bravely tried to add a warmer tint to the picture.

By flying low, they were able to discover that much of the wild country was carpeted with heavy ferns and a tangle of flowering vine that promised slow footing. The shore was an even worse tangle of seaweed netting that indicated that practically no coastal commerce of any kind had been attempted.

"Coney Island on a warm Sunday," said Todd, peering down.

Larry peered over his shoulder and added, "I can smell the hot dogs and pop corn. What'll you have, Pieplate?"

"Will you two get serious? Where's the junk?"

"Don't *you* know? This is supposed to be a personally conducted tour."

"Well, he's likely to make for a bay or sheltered spot of some sort. We'd better fly low over the whole coastline until we find the junk."

"Here's a picture of it," said Larry, offering a newspaper clipping of a typical high-sterned vessel, broad of beam and carrying the usual lug sails made of bamboo matting.

"Reminds me of Lipton's 'Shamrock'," said Todd.

They were skirting the coast now in the lowering daylight. Ten minutes later they came upon a natural harbor that formed the base of a volcanic mountain, gray and parched, that carried a plume of yellow smoke at its forepeak.

"There's the junk!" yelled Larry. "Look, down there in that narrow opening off to the right of that bay."

The girl gave it a glance, turned back into the main cabin, and grabbed an Aldis signal lamp from a bracket on the wall.

"Circle as low as you can while I give him the tip-off," she said, moving across to a window that could be opened. Then as the big Savoia-Marchetti circled the bay, she pointed the lamp down toward the little bay and began to send a series of signal flashes by means of the trigger switch.

In a few minutes they got an answer. A fire was lighted at the end of a small jetty built of stones, and they could see a small, compactly built man in shorts, white canvas shoes, a blue-and-white striped basque shirt, and with a shock of blond hair, waving to them with a strip of white cloth.

"Okay! Steady everything for a landing," barked Todd, "but be ready for anything!"

He checked the wheels and saw that they were up, set the flaps and prop blades for a slow glide in. He curled out to lose more height and brought the ship around so that she would land directly down the main channel.

The man on the jetty continued to wave and watch them anxiously as they came in. He paced up and down and glanced back from the amphibian to his junk as the big plane settled and began to move carefully up the channel.

He bellowed advice as they brought the plane up to the side of the junk, and Larry slipped under the instrument board and into the marine locker where he opened a hatch and threw the man a line.

"You Hallerton?" yelled Leadbeater as the man drew the ship up and planted canvas-covered buffers over the side to snub her.

"I certainly am, and am I glad to see you chaps! You Bancroft and Leadbeater?" he asked with a clipped university intonation.

"I'm Leadbeater. Bancroft is at the controls and Miss Sands is aft. She signaled you."

"Splendid! Come aboard. How soon can you get away again?"

Larry laughed at that. "Glad to see you, here's your hat sort of thing, ah? We can get going any minute. How about *you* coming aboard?"

"No, you probably need to stretch your legs and get a drink."

Larry was over in three moves at that suggestion. Todd helped Miss Sands out and followed. They introduced themselves all around and made themselves comfortable with a bottle of brandy and soda from a charged metal bottle.

"All the comforts of home," beamed Larry, sticking his nose into a cold beaker.

They drank up, set their glasses down, and in three distinct voices asked:

"Well, what about it?"

Hallerton glanced around anxiously, took another pull from his glass, and set it down on a hatchway.

"There are three of you here," he opened up with a serious face. "I look all right, don't I? I mean, I'm acting normal? I don't *seem* crazy, do I?"

"You sound perfectly normal to us," encouraged Todd Bancroft, "what's up?"

"The brandy is swell," added Larry.

"Go on, Mr. Hallerton," said Sturgis. "We may be wasting time."

"All right. You'll say I'm crazy when I tell you. For several hours after I saw it, I was not sure myself. That's the worst of working alone on a show like this. You get talking to yourself and you answer yourself and after a while you begin to wonder. But I actually saw all this."

"Let's have it. The brandy will help us take the shock," suggested Todd.

Hallerton sat staring at them for several seconds. He acted as though he were trying to make a great decision. Then he suddenly blurted out:

"Ever hear of the L Z One-thirty-one?"

They were all silent for a minute wondering what would come next. The L Z 131!

"I have seen the L Z One-thirty-one not far from here, anchored to a mother ship with a regulation airship tower." He might have been opening a lecture.

"Wait a minute," Bancroft interrupted, getting to his feet. "Haven't you made a mistake? I know that the L Z One-thirty-one was built at

Friedrichshafen. She was finished after the disaster that destroyed the *Hindenburg* at Lakehurst. They could not get helium from the United States, so they stopped work on the L Z One-thirty-one after the keel had been laid. That dirigible was never finished.''

''That's what I thought, said Hallerton with a weary smile. ''I know about the *Hindenburg*. I made a trip to Friedrichshafen on her. I saw them completing the L Z One-thirty-one, later called the *Graf Zeppelin* in honor of the older ship of that name. I also saw the keel and several rings of the L Z One-thirty-one with Japanese insignia on her envelope, tied up to a mother ship.''

''You *looked* all right when we came aboard,'' offered Larry, glancing around for the brandy bottle.

''I don't blame you,'' said Hallerton, shoving the bottle over, ''but I saw her—the L Z One-thirty-one being loaded for a raid.''

''A raid on what?'' Miss Sands said quickly leaning forward.

''I can show you their map,'' said Hallerton with decision. ''Here, look at this!''

He drew out a German nautical chart of the western Pacific upon which was marked in graphic detail a course from a point only a few miles east of Uruppu Jima that followed a Great Circle route across to the Aleutians, then skirting the southwest tip of Alaska, and down clear along the British Columbian coastline to Seattle. Several important cities along the west coast of the United States were marked with red circles and alongside these circles were dates.

''Where did you get this?'' asked Todd.

''You won't believe me, but I found it aboard the mother ship. She's called *Kamoi*. She used to be a United States-owned tanker and at one time was listed as an aircraft tender. She's an airship tender now.''

They all stared up from the chart to the face of this amazing little man.

''You were aboard?''

''Absolutely. I almost ran into it in a fog. They didn't see me at all and I just drifted by on the Kuro Siwo current which is prevalent in these waters. So I dropped anchor a few yards off, slipped into the water, and went up their anchor chain, through the hawsehole and into the ship. The whole crew was busy loading the airship through the anchoring mast. The rest was hectic, but I got away with it and returned to my junk just in time to have the fog lift momentarily so that they spotted me.''

"You got away?"

"Yes, I raised my anchor and drifted into another bank of fog. They were helpless with the airship at their mast. They tried to find me, but Providence, or the fog, was good and I managed to get in here where—well, where I have been ever since!"

"No wonder the whole world—and the Japs are looking for you," beamed Todd. "This certainly looks like they're planning a raid on the United States and in particular on all cities that have important aircraft plants. Notice how they have marked Seattle, San Diego, Santa Monica, and Burbank to bop off Boeing, Consolidated, Lockheed, and Douglas?"

"Well, what are we waiting for?" demanded Larry, getting up and putting down his glass.

6

HALLERTON MADE MORE explanations, but they were satisfied now that he had seen something that was almost unbelievable.

"You see," he explained, "had I mentioned the L Z One-thirty-one in my message, I would have been ignored, but she's out there. I can plot you a course to her. Of course, Washington thinks that airship was never finished, but there she is, and if she gets away with this raid, they'll have a devil of a time proving what airship it was, who owned it, and who was responsible. The markings will mean nothing because Japan will deny ever having built such a ship. Germany probably has a lot of old junk lying around Friedrichshafen to show that the L Z One-thirty-one was never actually built. They'd never find out what blew up what."

"Let's get going," said Todd. "According to this chart, they are due to set out early in the morning and figure to get somewhere near Seattle about sixty hours later. We'll get off in time to hit them soon after dark. How far out did you say she lay?"

"Less than fifty miles. Got anything to use?" asked Hallerton.

"Machine guns, that's all. Still, a few bursts in the right place will do the work. You any ideas?"

"None as good as yours, I suppose. I'd like to go along, of course, if you can use me."

"Anyone who can pull the stunt you pulled getting this chart should be made to go along. I'll bet you'll have some more bright ideas."

"You mean getting the chart? I'm afraid I do things that way. The idea occurred to me, and I had little chance of ignoring it. I had anchored the junk and was climbing up the anchor chain before I asked myself why I was doing it. What I did after that was only done to justify my initial gesture."

"You can explain all that as we go," said Sturgis. "In the meantime we had better be getting away. It's getting dark now and we don't want to let them get too big a lead, should they get started."

They took turns enjoying the comparative luxury of Hallerton's quarters and conveniences aboard the junk and Hallerton was told the story of their adventures thus far. He was amazed at their experience in getting away with the Savoia-Marchetti.

"And I think I have had some adventures," he remarked as Sturgis Sands came up the teak companionway from the cabin below. Her hair was tucked under a Basque beret and she looked very refreshed.

"I've borrowed a pair of your tennis shorts, a clean shirt, and that lovely chain-stitch sweater," she said, smiling at Hallerton. "I was beginning to feel clammy in that Jap uniform. I hope you don't mind."

They made the junk snug and climbed aboard the amphibian. By throttling both motors in turn, Todd was able to turn the ship in the narrow channel and head her out into the open. Once in the clear he looked around, saw that Larry and Hallerton were busy setting out the stage for the next move, and then thumped her off a roller and put her into the air.

"What are we going to do after—after this mess?" the girl said to Todd from the co-pilot's seat.

"Turn back for Sapporo in triumph and arrive with the missing adventurer. That's all we can do."

"What about Yoshida and the Japs?"

"What about them? They can't charge us with destroying an airship that apparently is not yet built. They will have to keep their mouths shut and try to get us on some other gag."

"Such as stealing a government plane?" the girl suggested.

Todd grinned at her.

"We'll get away with that. We can say we got a quick call which we picked up on the Seversky Convoy fighter set and made the most of the fact that the amphibian was at the airport. After all," smiled Todd, "they were all so solicitous about Hallerton's welfare. They will have to continue their enthusiasm to save face."

"You know all the answers, don't you?"

"I have to do something on this junket. Got a pile of opposition aboard. You swipe Savoias and turn up in a Jap uniform. Hallerton swipes a secret chart right from under the noses of the Japs. The Leadbeater guy nails Nakajimas and Kawasakis by the dozens. I've got to do something, so I think up the answers.

"Yeah?" came a voice from the companionway. "Well, think up one for those guys up ahead!"

It was Larry, and as usual he had spotted the opposition first. A beautiful wide V-formation of Japanese Navy 96s sitting over a long, silver, cigar-shaped dirigible that was turning slowly to get its nose around into the northeast.

"Good gosh!" gasped Bancroft. "We're sunk against that lot!"

"You see," murmured Hallerton. "I told you. There she is, and there's the *Kamoi*, the airship tender, a mile or so ahead. See her mooring mast mounted on the aft platform?"

"I see too much," muttered Todd. His eyes were mere gun-turret slits now. "They're certainly taking no chances, are they? Look at all that stuff!"

"Well, hurry up!" taunted the girl. "She'll be well under way soon and may drop a lot of ballast and get altitude fast!"

"Okay! Get to those guns, you guys. You take care of the Mitsubishis. I'm going to sit on top of that gas bag until I think of something to do. You keep those Jappos off!"

True to his word and while Miss Sands sat tense watching with unbelieving eyes, Todd slammed the Savoia-Marchetti with the Jap markings on her wings, straight through the narrow angle of the V formed by the navy fighters. He shoved through so close his wide wing tips almost brushed those of the two escort planes lined up behind the leader. He continued on through as the guns behind him opened with their first rattle of revenge.

The Savoia-Marchetti was through before the startled Japs could make a move to stop her. Todd, his face grim and tense, turned and looked at the girl. She was gripping the arms of the cockpit seat, staring ahead with honest fear in her eyes.

"Don't worry, Pieplate," he said out of the corner of his mouth. "You're going to blast that baby to Hades. You, I said."

She turned and stared at him and saw that his right hand was pointing at a small steel spade-grip handle set in the upper right-hand corner of the instrument bank. Under the handle was a small steel tag with two words in Italian riveted below it. She read them and gasped.

"Right!" he clipped tersely. "The port wing jettison gear. When I say 'Pull,' you pull, Pieplate. You'll see some real fireworks then."

"We won't get back!" she almost screamed.

"We'll get back to Hallerton's island. We'll go back to Sapporo in the junk—in style. Get it?"

She nodded, but with indecision.

"Come on, make it fast now. We've got to time this right."

The Savoia-Marchetti nosed down toward the high fin of the big airship. Behind them Larry and Hallerton were blazing away at the covey of fighters that was slamming down at them. Todd glanced at the girl quickly, got a reassuring smile in response and then nosed down lower until it seemed that they must dive through the top of the gas bag. Then he yelled.

"Pull!"

Miss Sands pulled with both hands. There was a strange metallic retching sound somewhere, and the amphibian jerked as the load of fuel was dumped all along the top of the gas bag. Todd kept the bow of the amphibian's hull well down close to the upper girder and skimmed along the top of the big airship.

All around them fanged enemy slugs and tracer. That was what Todd had banked on.

"Come on, pour it to us," he bellowed, peering back through the upper hatch. "Pour it to—"

The amphibian leaped under a violent blast of concussion. She almost went over on her back, and Todd fought to hold her out of a stall. They were suddenly in the blistering limelight of a scarlet giant spot. A garish aerial bombshell built into the dural girders of an airship had blasted itself against the night sky.

"What—what happened?" Sturgis gasped, pulling herself back into the seat.

"You did that, sister," Todd replied grimly, fighting the amphibian out of the widespread storm of fire and dural. "You and your little jettison gear. We dumped half of our fuel on top of her. Most of it ran down and was ignited by the exhausts from the motors. The cells of hydrogen did the rest. Lovely, eh?"

They somehow cleared the storm and got far enough away to see the butt end of this cigar of catastrophe begin its final plunge into oblivion. They could see the tangle of blackened dural framework being eaten away by the hungry flames. Giant sections of bulkhead slithered across the sky, and puny black objects, all arms and legs, went fluttering out into the blackness below.

"Whew!" ejaculated Todd, wiping his brow. "We'd have never done that with machine-gun fire."

They darted away into the heavy darkness of night that was intensified by the still flaming airship, and evaded the frantic Jap pilots who knew they had "lost face" and would make no further effort to head them off.

"Who did that?" bellowed Larry through the companionway.

"Little Pieplate and her atomizer," grinned Todd. "We dumped fuel."

"And now?" asked Hallerton.

"We return to the junk. There is still a little left in that bottle of yours!"

"Back to the junk?" beamed Larry.

"Back to where we belong," said Bancroft, laughing. "We've got to get rid of this boiler, and then we'll return in state with the missing adventurer, sublimely ignorant of current events, and with nothing more on our minds but to kill the fatted calf—to which banquet, ladies and gentlemen, we shall be most pleased to invite one Kato Yoshida—who, I am quite sure, will be speechless!"

"Cheers!" boomed Leadbeater. "We'll sell him a book, eh, Hallerton?"